# THE GATHERING STORM!

A low growl of thunder rolled hollowly across the lawn, accompanied by a more defined crackle of lightning within the roiling clouds. The brief flare picked out two more figures in battledress uniform as they hurried out onto the grass from the shadows of the building, eyes turned skyward under uniform berets.

"Oi! Archie! D'ye see that?" one of them yelled. "Where did all these clouds come from?"

Before Archie could venture a response, an eye-searing bolt of bright-white lightning ripped the sky above the castle roof, accompanied by a deafening crack of thunder. The lightning bolt struck the north turret of the great square tower with the force of a mortar round, hurling stones and roof slates up and outward in a blazing fountain of destruction. . . .

*THE ADEPT SERIES*
*by Katherine Kurtz and Deborah Turner Harris*

THE ADEPT
THE LODGE OF THE LYNX
THE TEMPLAR TREASURE

# THE ADEPT

## BOOK TWO: THE LODGE OF THE LYNX

by

# KATHERINE KURTZ

and

# DEBORAH TURNER HARRIS

ACE BOOKS, NEW YORK

This book is an Ace original edition,
and has never been previously published.

THE LODGE OF THE LYNX

An Ace Book / published by arrangement with
Bill Fawcett & Associates

PRINTING HISTORY
Ace edition / June 1992

ISBN: 0-441-00344-3

Ace Books are published by the Berkley Publishing Group,
200 Madison Avenue, New York, New York 10016.
The name "ACE" and the "A" logo
are trademarks belonging to Charter Communications, Inc.

PRINTED IN THE UNITED STATES OF AMERICA

10  9  8  7

For
Our Aunts and Uncles:
Stephen and Janie Carter
and in loving memory of
Gretchen and Marshall Fisher

# ACKNOWLEDGMENTS

Grateful thanks are due to the following, for their assistance in rendering this novel:

Sgt. Graham Brown, PC Alan Jeffries, and PC Ian Richardson, Lothian and Borders Police, Edinburgh, for background on Scottish Police procedures;

Dr. Richard Oram, for continuing to provide a wealth of scholarly information on matters of Scottish history and archaeology;

Mr. Kenneth Fraser, for his on-going help in the St. Andrews University Library;

Mrs. Edith Rendle, for her advice on Scots law and Scottish legal procedure;

Dr. Ernan J. Gallagher, for general medical advice, and Dr. A.V.M. Davidson, for her advice on Scottish medical facilities and practice;

Scott MacMillan, for his expertise on weapons, police procedures, and interesting motor vehicles;

Peter Morwood, for military advice, especially on the SAS;

Bob Harris, for general aid, comfort, and research assistance;

And once again, to the St. Andrews branch of the Scottish Tourist Information Bureau, especially Rhona McKay, for their tireless efforts in running down local information not to be found in the guidebooks.

# PROLOGUE

Abrooding stillness lay upon the chill night air. High above the tower's conical roof, the old man could feel the energy beginning to gather—a faint electrical prickle that stirred the hackles at the back of the neck and crawled on the tiny hairs of bare arms like invisible insects. At first it seemed little more than a tense, ongoing flicker in the silence, skittish as a flight of hunting bats. Then the pulses gathered strength, growing more potent with each passing moment. Before long, the energy was beating about the roof slates like some huge, winged predator struggling to break free from the restraint of its jesses—held only by the strength of will of the one who had summoned it.

Even to undertake such a summoning was both difficult and dangerous. To direct the power thus summoned required exquisite control, acquired only through long years of study and unspeakable sacrifice. The merest wavering of will, the slightest distraction, might release the tight-leashed energy prematurely, to rebound with disastrous consequences upon the very tower where the summoner sat surrounded by his chosen Twelve. But the venerable Head-Master who ruled the tower was one well-accustomed to taking calculated risks.

He had chosen both the venue and his acolytes with care. The chamber from which they worked occupied the entire topmost floor of the tower—a massive, twelve-sided structure that dominated the castellated manor house of which it was a part. Bleak and remote among the cataracts and crags of Scotland's Cairngorm Mountains, the house had been built in Victorian times upon the foundations of an Iron Age *broch*, with the tower and even parts of the house incorporating undressed stones from the earlier structure.

Nowhere were these primitive origins more apparent than in the topmost tower chamber, whose thick, nearly windowless walls had been plastered starkly white, the ceiling above divided like a wheel by converging beams of black oak. Though the house and

*1*

the floors below were wired for electricity, gaslight remained this room's sole source of illumination. Gas jets hissed behind shades of crimson glass in brass sconces at the room's four quarters, dispersing the fitful yellowish glow and casting only soft, vague shadows before the twelve white-robed figures seated cross-legged around the room's perimeter.

No shadows at all intruded upon the center of the room, with its mound of scarlet cushions. From there the white-clad Master directed the Work, palms upturned upon splayed knees, hairless head bowed, eyes closed in a gaunt, wizened face that resembled a mummified skull.

Before him on a mat of black ram skin lay a stacked heap of parchment, the pages yellow and brittle with age. And weighting the stack of parchments, its arc as wide as the span of a man's spread hand, was the object of the old man's concentration—a Celtic torc wrought of black meteoric iron. Its crafting was of the same distant age as the *broch*, with geometric knots and flowing zoomorphs cunningly inlaid with fluid traceries of silver. Smoky cairngorms smouldered baleful as serpents' eyes among the interlocking shapes and whorls.

Focusing upon its ancient energies, the old man extended his hands over the torc like a man warming his hands at a fire, feeling its potential danger prickling beneath his hands, only barely contained by the dark hallowing he had imposed upon it. Even with his eyes closed, he could sense its potent magnetic influence acting upon the elemental energies building outside the tower, straining to be away.

And soon would *be* away. The moment was nearly at hand. Hardening his intent for the ultimate exercise of his will, the old man lifted the torc in palsied hands and slipped it around his scrawny neck. The kiss of the cold metal against his throat plunged him even deeper into trance as he felt the ancient energies mesh with his own, and he flung back his head and raised blue-veined arms in a gesture both of invocation and command. Only then did he at last allow the image to form in his mind of the distant object of his intention.

Some forty miles away, the royal castle of Balmoral lay quiet under a clear, frosty sprinkling of November stars. With the Queen and Royal Family back in London for the winter, the Scots Guards in charge of grounds security went about their appointed late-night rounds with the relaxed efficiency of men who had no reason to expect any serious trouble but were nonetheless prepared for it—in battledress and black berets for night patrol, and armed with the latest Enfield "Bull Pup" rifles.

Corporal Archie Buchannan had just completed his hourly circuit of the south lawn and was headed for his post by the south door, shifting the weight of his rifle on its shoulder sling, when a flicker of movement in the sky overhead made him glance up. He stopped short in his tracks, his brow furrowing sharply in surprise and astonishment.

A dense bank of black cloud was sweeping down on the castle out of the west, moving faster than any storm Archie had ever seen before. Its curdled vapors writhed and boiled like pitch in a cauldron, stirred by erratic pulses of sheet-lightning, so that within the span of only a few heartbeats, the clouds had blotted out half the stars in the sky.

"What the de'il?" Archie murmured under his breath.

A low growl of thunder rolled hollowly across the lawn, accompanied by a more defined crackle of lightning within the roiling clouds. The brief flare picked out two more figures in battledress uniform as they hurried out onto the grass from the shadows of the building, eyes turned skyward under uniform berets.

"Oi! Archie! D'ye see that?" one of them yelled. "Where did all these clouds come from?"

Before Archie could venture a response, an eye-searing bolt of bright-white lightning ripped the sky above the castle roof, accompanied by a deafening crack of thunder. The lightning bolt struck the north turret of the great square tower with the force of a mortar round, hurling stones and roof slates up and outward in a blazing fountain of destruction.

The concussion flung Archie to the ground. As he frantically scrambled for cover underneath the nearest hedge, trying to protect his head from the debris already beginning to rain down, he could only think that it must have been a bomb, regardless of what his own senses told him. Above the ringing in his ears, he started to hear the intermittent clangor of security alarms going off. As the patter of falling debris subsided, an attendant clamor of shouts began to rise from other parts of the castle grounds, along with the thud of booted feet approaching.

Cautiously Archie raised his head to look around, squinting against the sudden glare of security lights fitfully coming on all around the castle and grounds.

"Archie? Are ye all right, man?" said a voice close beside him, as a hand roughly grasped his shoulder.

"Aye, just let me catch my breath," Archie muttered, rolling over to see the smudged faces of two of his colleagues, both looking slightly wild-eyed and dishevelled.

"Jesus, what happened?" demanded the one who had shaken him, as his larger partner shifted his grip on his rifle and looked around uneasily. "It sounded like a bloody bomb!"

Archie shook his head and let the other man help him sit up, testing gingerly for injuries beyond the bruises he knew were inevitable. Ears still ringing, he pulled himself stiffly to his feet, then gaped as he gazed across the lawn in the direction of the baronial tower.

Where the north turret had stood but minutes earlier, the bomb—or lightning strike—had left only a burning stump of charred masonry.

Forty miles away, on the other side of the mountains, the old man in white exhaled with a long-drawn sigh of satisfaction and savored his moment of triumph. Outside confirmation would have to wait until morning, when the news services undoubtedly would be full of it, but he had no doubt that his aim had been successful.

Slowly he reached to his throat, removing the ancient torc with both hands and carefully laying it back atop the stack of parchments before him. Then he let his arms sink to his sides, bowing his head in deep obeisance as he acknowledged the Power that had delivered the lightning into his hands. His twelve acolytes bowed with him, their shadows blurring together as they touched their brows to the floor.

But it was only outwardly a gesture of humility. A silence born of dark exultation reigned in the room as the acolytes straightened and then bent again, this time in homage to *him*.

Smiling primly, the old man acknowledged their deference with a nod and a hand gesture and dismissed them, waiting until they all had gone before lying back in his cushions to exult in private, and plan the further exercise of his art. . . .

# CHAPTER ONE

THE silvery jingle of snaffles rang clear as sleigh bells in the frosty air of a fine November morning as two men on horseback approached the crest of the wooded hill overlooking Strathmourne House. Sir Adam Sinclair's grey thoroughbred pricked his ears and snorted softly at the scent of the stables below and would have quickened his pace to a trot, had his rider not applied legs and reins with gentle firmness.

"Easy, Khalid. Walk," Adam said.

The big gelding crested and tried a few tentative, prancing steps in *piaffe*, all but floating just above the ground, then settled back to a resigned, sedate walk, as if there had never been any difference of opinion between horse and rider. The second rider, a younger man with gilt-bronze hair and gold-rimmed spectacles, chuckled aloud at the sheer artistry of the partnership.

"Ah, the master's touch," he remarked with a grin. "He really *is* an exceptionally fine animal, Adam. You must let me capture the pair of you on canvas one of these days—perhaps something along the lines of that study of your father and *his* grey hunter in your drawing room." He cocked his head appraisingly at the older man.

"What about it? Shall I do you an equestrian portrait for Christmas?"

The question elicited a companionable chuckle and a pleased smile from Adam.

"Do you think your painting hand is up to the strain? If so, there's nothing I'd like better!"

Peregrine Lovat lifted his gloved right hand from the reins of his own mount, a blood-bay mare with a silken mouth and a coquettish disposition, and flexed the leather-clad fingers so that Adam could see them.

"Oh, not to worry on *that* account," he said cheerfully. "My hand's virtually good as new, thanks to your exacting supervision of the repair job. As a matter of fact, I've been back at my easel for nearly a week now, and haven't had more than an occasional twinge.''

"All the same, I wouldn't overdo," Adam cautioned. "It was a nasty laceration that might have ended your painting career once and for all. I'd hate to think you might yet jeopardize it through impatience."

Peregrine set his hand back on the reins, all at once very conscious of the protective bandage under the glove that he continued to wear when engaged in strenuous or dirty activities. The circumstances of the injury itself still gave him cause to cringe, whenever he thought about it too long. Sword cuts were not exactly common in this day and age. But in fact, it was precisely the sharpness of his recollection that had prompted him to take up his paints and brushes so quickly, as soon as the sutures were out and he felt able to hold a brush properly again. He bit at his lip thoughtfully, trying to find words to explain his recent sense of compulsion.

"It isn't really impatience," he told Adam. "Perhaps I pushed myself a little, but—well, this may sound a bit odd, but the fact of the matter is, I didn't think I dared delay it. The—ah—studies I've been doing are all connected with what happened at Loch Ness."

Adam gave him a sharp look from under his velvet riding cap. The two had met little more than a month ago, but that initial, brief social acquaintance, sparked by professional concern, had led to an esoteric partnership that was as welcome as it had been unexpected. Without Peregrine's unique and hitherto unsuspected talents, employed both at Loch Ness and in the days leading up to it, the outcome might have been far less satisfactory. The young artist might not yet understand a great deal about that part of his talent that went beyond the mere artistic, but he was learning every day—and obviously had been busier than Adam expected.

"I haven't yet dared to try that self-portrait you suggested," Peregrine said, guessing the possible direction of his mentor's speculations. "Somehow, it's seemed more important, for now, to make a pictorial record of everything I could remember about that night at Loch Ness. My recall of it seems to be somehow linked to this cut on my hand—almost as if the wound itself is the very thing that ties me into that part of the affair. Right after it happened," he continued, "all my mental impressions were crystal-clear, right down to the smallest details. But since my hand's started to heal, those impressions have begun to fade. I can still recover them, but it takes much more effort."

Adam now was watching him closely, as their horses picked their way down the last of the sloping trail.

"That's an interesting speculation," he said. "What makes you so sure that it isn't simply the passage of time?"

Peregrine grimaced and gave a snort. "Well, maybe *you* could get at the memories by using hypnosis or something, but the only way *I* seem to be able to do it is by first concentrating my attention on the cut on my hand. And since that's healing, I thought I'd better push on with the paintings before I maybe lost the recall."

A smile lit Adam's dark eyes. "You're learning more quickly than I thought. I think I'd like to have a look at what you've done."

"Somehow I thought you might," Peregrine said, with an easy grin that would not have been possible for the tight-wound young man of a mere month before. "I brought them along in the back of my car this morning. I thought they might make for interesting conversation over breakfast."

The ring of steel-shod hooves on the cobbles of the stable yard summoned John, the ex-Household Cavalry trooper who looked after Adam's horses. With a grin and a wave that was almost a salute, he came to take the reins as Adam and Peregrine dismounted.

"Did you and Mr. Lovat have a good ride, sir?" he asked, as Adam ran up his stirrups on their leathers and loosened Khalid's girth.

"Yes, splendid," Adam replied. "We had a good, long canter along the ridge in the upper field, and Mr. Lovat even tried a few easy jumps—successfully, I might add. At this rate, we'll have him legged up enough to hunt by Christmas."

Peregrine, tending his own mount, rolled his eyes in good-natured self-deprecation.

"In this case, I'm afraid that *successful* is a very relative term, but I did manage not to fall off!"

Adam chuckled as the horses were led on into the barn, and Peregrine fell in beside him as they walked briskly on through the garden adjacent to the back of the house and headed for the back door. There Peregrine diverted briefly to collect a portfolio from the back of a green Morris Minor Traveller. When he joined Adam in the mudroom, hanging his riding helmet on a hook beside Adam's, the older man had already exchanged his boots for velvet slippers crested with the Sinclair phoenix and was drying his hands on a monogrammed towel.

"I'll take those on into the morning room while you wash up,"

Adam said, relieving Peregrine of the portfolio. "Humphrey's left a second pair of slippers there by the bootjack. If we track mud on Mrs. G.'s clean floors, she may not speak to any of us for days."

Grinning, Peregrine peeled off his riding gloves and applied the bootjack to his own muddy boots, then thrust stockinged feet into the indicated slippers. After ducking into the adjoining washroom to douse his face and hands and run a comb through his hair, he followed the way his host had gone, along the service corridor and on into the gold-damasked morning room.

Humphrey, Adam's butler of more than twenty years' service, had set up for breakfast in the sunshine of the room's wide bow window. As always, the table was an immaculate array of crisp Irish linen, fine china and crystal, and antique silver. Adam was sipping fresh-squeezed orange juice from a Waterford goblet while he glanced at the front page headlines of the morning paper. Humphrey was pouring his master's first cup of tea. Both men looked up as Peregrine entered, Adam raising his glass in salute and Humphrey poising the silver teapot over the cup set before Peregrine's place.

"Good morning, Mr. Lovat. May I pour you a cup of tea?"

"Yes, thank you, Humphrey. Good morning."

"Sir Adam tells me that you've moved the last of your boxes into the gate lodge," the butler went on. "I trust that the new accommodations are proving satisfactory?"

Peregrine grinned as he pulled out the Queen Anne chair and sat, shaking out his napkin with a flourish. It was barely two weeks since he had accepted Adam's invitation to come and live in the vacant rear gate lodge, and already he was finding it a decided improvement over the cramped studio loft he had occupied in Edinburgh.

"More than satisfactory, Humphrey," he said happily. "You know, I thought I'd miss the hustle and bustle of the city. Oddly enough, though, I find myself settling quite contentedly into the life of a country gentleman. There really *is* more room to breathe."

This expansive remark gave Adam cause for private amusement, for he knew that literal breathing space was not at all what Peregrine had in mind. If the truth were strictly to be told, he suspected that Peregrine's new-found sense of liberty was due as much to a change in outlook as it was to a change in environment. As a psychiatrist, Adam was not unfamiliar with the general phenomenon, but Peregrine's case had presented factors Adam encountered all too seldom. Though reserved and withdrawn at

*8*

their initial meeting, brooding like a hawk in captivity, Peregrine gradually had been given the opportunity to try his wings. Even now, though Peregrine himself was not altogether aware of it, the young artist was in the process of joining the Hunt in earnest, like the falcon-breed for which he was named. And if Adam Sinclair was reading the signs aright, the process was rapidly nearing completion.

"Have a scone, Peregrine," he murmured with a smile, as Humphrey offered the younger man a linen-nested basket. "And you ought to know that Mrs. Gilchrist brought these by fresh this morning, especially for 'that nice young Mr. Lovat.' Apparently she's taken quite a fancy to you."

Peregrine had started to take just one scone, but now he plucked a second out of the basket before Humphrey could offer it across to Adam.

"I'd better have two, then, hadn't I?" He grinned wickedly. "After all, I shouldn't want Mrs. G. to think I wasn't properly appreciative. Good housekeepers are worth their weight in fresh scones!"

"Aye, and you won't find a better one in the entire county," Adam agreed. "She accomplishes more for me in three half-days a week than most folk could manage working at it full-time. I don't know what Humphrey and I would do without her. If she's offered to do for you, down at the lodge, don't let her get away, whatever happens!"

"Oh, I shan't!"

As breakfast conversation ranged on from appreciation of domestic staff to their morning's ride and the clouds now glowering to the north, the scones slowly disappeared, washed down with cups of tea. Humphrey, eyeing the portfolio Adam had set casually just inside the door, brought in a folding rosewood card-table from the adjoining parlor and set it up beside the breakfast table while they ate.

"Suppose we have a look at what you've brought now, shall we?" Adam said, when Humphrey had retired to the kitchen and they were about finished with breakfast.

Peregrine, after popping the last bite of his last scone into his mouth, wiped his fingers hastily on his napkin and shifted his chair around to the rosewood table to unzip his portfolio, delving deep inside to draw out several sheets of watercolor paper, cut to varying sizes.

"My hand was still a bit stiff for pencil work when I started these, and oils take too long to dry," he explained, as he handed one across to Adam. "I managed to get a fair amount of detail, though, even with the watercolors. Besides, I've always felt that watercolors were the best medium for capturing the feel of rotten weather."

The first painting showed three figures crouched in the driving rain in Urquhart Castle's car park, eerily backlit with a wash of luminescent green. The figures meant to be Peregrine and Adam himself were little more than vague suggestions of form, glimpsed from behind, but the third, brandishing a long, metal-cased police torch, quite clearly was Detective Chief Inspector Noel McLeod, Adam's professional and esoteric colleague of many years' standing. Rain spattered the inspector's wire-rimmed aviator glasses and streamed off his short-clipped grey moustache as he turned slightly to glance back at them, and both he and Adam wore the dark green waxed jackets peculiar to country pursuits all over Britain. Peregrine sported his familiar navy duffel coat.

"Yes, indeed," Adam murmured, smiling as he turned the painting face-down and read the caption Peregrine had penciled lightly on the back: *Master Huntsmen and rank amateur.* The smile died as Peregrine handed him the second painting.

It had the same greenish luminance as the first one, but the perspective had shifted down to the rain-lashed shore of Loch Ness. Marching across the center of a night landscape, silhouetted by lightning flashes, was a procession of four dark-robed and hooded men. The two in the middle were struggling to carry a small but heavy chest of archaic design. The one bringing up the rear bore what appeared to be a framed picture above his head, ducking beneath it like a shield.

The fourth man, masked across the eyes like an executioner, was brandishing a sword as he led the odd procession. Light glinted from a heavy, silvery medallion around his throat and a ring on his right hand, but the very light made it impossible to see the items in detail. Above and around them all, whirling like a swarm of angry hornets, hung a hungry cloud of green-glowing spheres. The spheres in the foreground each contained the spectral impression of a winged homunculus with gaping jaws and razor-sharp teeth.

On the back of this painting Peregrine had scribbled, *The fury of the Sidhe.*

"Whoever would have believed that anything so tiny could be so deadly?" the artist said, surveying his own work with a wondering shake of his head. "The next one's even more fanciful, if you don't believe in monsters."

He passed Adam a third sheet of watercolor paper. This painting, a much darker night scene, showed two men cowering in the stern of a sleek, high-powered speedboat as it tossed about on a stormy sweep of black water. The speedboat was overshadowed by a huge serpentine form rearing out of the waves off the starboard bow. Reptilian eyes glittered green in a basilisk head, as the creature gathered its coils to strike and dive. . . .

Anyone else viewing the picture might have taken it for the cover illustration from some modern horror novel; but Adam knew better. He had witnessed the event with his own eyes from the beach below Urquhart Castle, overlooking Loch Ness—but Peregrine's painting showed far more detail than anyone could have seen from the shore.

For Peregrine Lovat had the gift of seeing more than other people. It was part of what made him such a gifted portrait artist—this ability to see more about his sitters than mere physical appearance—and it was what had driven him to seek Adam's help. In learning to accept his talent for the gift it was, he was coming to understand what Adam already knew—that the truth sometimes went beyond empirical evidence and what would be admissible in a court of law.

Being privy to the truth could be dangerous, of course. Peregrine's last two paintings bore testimony to that fact. The first framed the upper body of the hooded man with the sword, the blade now discernible as an ornate Italian rapier. The detail of the sword-hand and the rapier hilt was good, the blade just striking the blow that had left Peregrine wounded, but the red-stoned ring on the sword-hand was not clearly visible.

"Here's a better detail of the leader's ring and medallion," Peregrine said, handing Adam the last painting. "I had to think about this for a long time, but I finally got a clear look at what was on them."

It might have been artwork submitted for a jeweller's commission, so finely was it done. The opaque red gemstone set into the golden bezel of the ring had been skillfully cut to show the snarling mask of a big cat with the tufted ears and side-whiskers of a lynx. The disk of the medallion, sharply delineated in shades of black and grey, bore the same design. Adam's long mouth thinned at the sight of the device, for it stirred memories that were far from pleasant.

"You've seen one of these before, haven't you?" Peregrine observed quietly, noting the narrowing of the other's dark eyes.

"Aye," Adam said quietly. "As a matter of fact, the ring

you've depicted was recovered at Loch Ness. McLeod showed it to me, after we got back from having your hand sutured."

Peregrine gaped, glancing at the painting again, then returned his attention to Adam.

"What does it mean, then?"

Adam pulled a tight smile that had no mirth in it. At Loch Ness, he and McLeod had guessed the truth, but they had kept the knowledge to themselves. However, if Peregrine was to join the Hunt, he had to know something of what they were up against.

"You've seen the rings that Noel and I wear when we're working. Many Black Lodges do the same. This is the Sign of the Lynx." He tapped the illustration of the Lynx ring with a well-manicured forefinger. "Let's just say that the Lodge of the Lynx is an old enemy."

Peregrine's hazel eyes widened, but he said nothing. After a moment, Adam continued.

"We last encountered them about fifteen years ago. At that time, their leader was a man named Tudor-Jones. We lost three members of our own Hunting Party before we succeeded in bringing the Lodge of the Lynx to its reckoning. At the time, I dared to hope we'd gotten most of the ringleaders."

Peregrine blanched slightly. "*Gotten*?" he murmured.

His tone roused Adam from his abstracted recollection, and the older man smiled briefly at his young colleague's discomfiture.

"I'm sorry. Perhaps it would be more accurate to say that we—*arrested* them. You'll perhaps remember that conversation we had in the car, the morning after the incident at Loch Ness, in which I said that Noel and I were something like an occult police force? Well, the analogy holds true on several levels. Like our more mundane colleagues, we're committed to upholding the Law—in this case, the Law of the Inner Planes. The members of organizations like the Lodge of the Lynx, like any other criminal organization, want what they're not entitled to, and will stop at nothing to get it. It's our job to apprehend such people and bring them to justice before they can wreak harm on the world at large.

"Which is not to say that there haven't been fatalities on both sides," he continued soberly. "As it happens, in the case of Tudor-Jones and his followers, most of those who were most heavily involved in the work of the Lynx are dead. But that was certainly through no intention of ours. We're enforcers, not executioners. Our job then—as now—was to stop them from committing serious violations against the Law of the Inner Planes. When we're obliged to use force, we try to utilize only that force

*12*

already employed by the opposition—optimally, to turn it back against those who summoned it—but even then, only as a matter of necessity.''

He might have said more, but at that moment there was a brief rap at the door, followed by the precipitous entry of Humphrey carrying a small, tabletop TV.

"I beg your pardon, sir, for barging in like this," he said over his shoulder as he made hurriedly for the nearest electrical outlet, "but one of the headlines on the morning news may interest you. The actual report should be up any second now."

He set the TV on one of the mahogany side tables, plugged it in, and switched it on. Almost immediately, the jagged silhouette of grey turrets against a greyer sky filled the screen, to the accompaniment of a cultivated BBC voice-over.

''. . . Grampian Police are investigating a mysterious explosion that took place early this morning within the grounds of Balmoral Castle," the voice said, as the camera tilted down to a wet-looking expanse of formal garden and well-manicured lawn. "The explosion, which severely damaged the baronial tower of the castle, occurred shortly after midnight. No one was injured. Chief Constable William McNab declined to comment on the probable cause of the explosion, asserting that the facts will only be known following detailed examination of the wreckage. A police forensics team from Aberdeen and another team from the army are presently sifting through the debris in search of clues.''

The steadicam panned to the damaged tower of the castle, showing a blackened stump of blasted masonry where the north turret ought to have been. Several figures in military and police uniforms were picking through the rubble that littered the grass around the base of the building. The camera pulled back to focus on the figure of a cold-looking newscaster in rain slicker and tweed cap, standing in the foreground with microphone in hand.

"A spokesman from Buckingham Palace has confirmed that no member of the Royal Family was in residence at Balmoral at the time of the incident," the newscaster reported gravely. "The authorities are looking into the possibility of a gas explosion, but it is understood that they have not yet ruled out the possibility of a terrorist bomb. To add to the mystery, there have been several unconfirmed reports by local witnesses claiming to have seen a freak bolt of lightning strike the roof of the castle. There has been no official statement as yet on behalf of the police or of the regiment currently in charge of castle security. So until the authorities are prepared to come forward with an explanation, the cause of the explosion seems destined to remain a mystery. This is Alan Cafferty, BBC News, Balmoral Castle.''

The story concluded with a final close-up of the ruined turret, smoke still rising in thin wisps from the blackened stones. As coverage shifted back to London for the business news, Adam signed for Humphrey to switch off the set and take it away, and glanced aside at the wide-eyed Peregrine.

''Mystery, indeed,'' he murmured. ''I wonder . . .''

Reaching behind him, he snagged the telephone and punched out the numbers that would give him the residence of Detective Chief Inspector Noel McLeod, veteran of many such unsolved ''mysteries.'' The line picked up on the third ring.

''Edinburgh 7978,'' rumbled a familiar bass voice at the other end of the line.

Adam's expression eased slightly. ''Noel? Adam here. I don't suppose you were listening to the news just now?''

''The bit on Balmoral? Aye, that I was,'' said McLeod. ''I was in the middle of shaving when Jane called me out to see it.''

Adam found himself smiling at the mental image of McLeod hurrying into the sitting room with the shaving foam still on his chin.

''I don't suppose you know any more about it than I do, then,'' he said. ''What did you think?''

''My first thought was to be thankful it's outside my jurisdiction,'' McLeod replied. ''It was only the bit about the lightning strike that gave me second thoughts.''

''Hmmm. Me, too,'' Adam said. ''At the very least, I wonder who the unnamed witnesses are. It seems strange that anyone should attribute the damage to a freak lightning strike, unless that was precisely what they thought they saw. It could be that there's nothing more to it than some odd trick of the weather, but I don't know that I'm prepared to make that assumption.''

''Aye.'' McLeod's brusque reply made it clear that he was digesting what Adam had just said—and not said. ''Well, I don't suppose it would do any harm to have a wee look over the ground, once the press have backed off the case—if only to set our minds at ease.''

''My thinking, precisely,'' said Adam. ''If you can arrange the time off, perhaps we could drive up to Balmoral some time early next week.''

''No problem there,'' said McLeod. ''I'll ring you once I've had a chance to set it up. Were you maybe thinking to bring along young Lovat?''

"If he wants to come," said Adam, with an inquiring glance toward Peregrine, who had been listening avidly to Adam's half of the conversation and now nodded vehemently. "As a matter of fact," Adam went on, grinning, "he's here with me now. We've been out for a ride. I'm being given to understand that a team of wild horses couldn't keep him from coming along."

McLeod chuckled.

"In the meantime," Adam continued, "I don't see any reason why you shouldn't be left to enjoy the weekend in peace. Give my love to Jane, and I'll look to hear from you in a few days."

With that assurance, he rang off. No sooner had he set down the receiver, however, than the instrument gave out with another trill of summons. Surprised, Adam answered it himself.

"Strathmourne, Sinclair here."

"Adam? Good Lord, you've answered your own phone!" said a man's musical tenor, as familiar in Adam's ears as McLeod's gravelly bass. "Oh, capital! I was afraid I might have missed you. It's Christopher here. Seen the news broadcast this morning?"

"If you're referring to that incident up at Balmoral, I've just been on the phone about it with Noel," Adam said.

"Ah, then it struck you as odd, too," the other replied, with jaunty good humor. "Well, we can talk about it further when we meet up. You *are* still coming?"

"Of course. I was planning to leave as soon as I'd finished breakfast and gotten cleaned up," Adam said. "I gather there's been no change since we last spoke?"

"No, not that I know of."

"In that case, we'll carry on as planned. By the way," Adam added, "I happen to have someone with me at the moment who might be useful to have along. His name is Peregrine Lovat."

"The artist chap?"

"That's right. Would you mind if I were to bring him?"

"Mind? Good Lord, no!"

"In that case, I'll see if *he* minds."

He turned to Peregrine, who was manfully struggling to mask his curiosity.

"Well, what about it?" said Adam. "Have you got any plans for this morning?"

"Actually, I was going to spend a fascinating morning unpacking cartons of books," Peregrine said drily, the hazel eyes eager behind the gold-rimmed spectacles. "But if this is an invitation, the books can wait!"

15

Adam chuckled. "He says he thinks he can break away," he told his caller. "We'll meet you at the rectory as planned."

"Splendid! See you then."

As Adam returned the receiver to its cradle, Peregrine sat forward eagerly.

"So. What have I let myself in for?"

"Oh, nothing *very* serious," Adam said. "The gentleman on the phone just now was Father Christopher Houston, an Episcopal priest and a very good friend of mine. A former parishioner of his has been complaining about her new flat being haunted. He's asked me down to have a look at the place."

At Adam's use of the word *haunted,* a dubious expression crossed Peregrine's open face.

"Now, there's no need to look like that," Adam said. "I don't for a minute believe that the flat is really *haunted,* in the gothic sense of the word. Christopher has already been out once to visit the premises, and he doesn't think it calls for anything like a formal exorcism. On the other hand, the young woman who lives there has been having nightmares ever since she moved in. Whether the cause is psychic or psychiatric remains to be determined."

"Which is where you come in," said Peregrine.

"Which is where I come in," Adam agreed. "We'll approach the situation with open minds. The young lady in question may simply be undergoing some passing stress. Or there may actually *be* something unwholesome in the atmosphere of the place. Either way, we shan't let the matter rest unresolved."

"So, where do *I* come in?" Peregrine asked.

"Well, when Christopher and I first discussed the case," Adam continued casually, "I mentioned you as someone possessed of unusual artistic insight. Christopher was very interested to hear about your gifts, and expressed a strong desire to see some of your work. It occurred to me that this might provide an opportunity not only for me to introduce you to someone I value as a friend, but also for you to exercise your talents to good purpose."

"You want me to draw what's in the flat?"

Adam nodded. "Assuming that there's anything to draw."

Both men knew they were not talking about furniture or decor.

"Fair enough." Peregrine grinned. "Just tell me when you want me ready to go."

"Well, Christopher lives in Kinross," said Adam. "He's expecting us round about ten."

Peregrine glanced first at his watch and then at his clothes.

"Good God, Adam, you keep the tightest schedule of anybody I know! Have I got time to take a shower and change?"

"If you're quick about it," Adam said with a chuckle. "*I* intend to."

Peregrine tossed off the last of his tea and began hurriedly bundling his watercolor studies back into his portfolio.

"I don't know how you do it!" he muttered. "What's the uniform of the day, for meeting vicars and exploring haunted flats?"

"Oh, casual—but do wear a tie," Adam replied, as the young artist made for the door. "I'll collect you at the lodge in half an hour," he called laughingly to Peregrine's back. "And don't forget to bring your sketchbox!"

# CHAPTER TWO

THE rhythmic thump of helicopter rotors reverberated across the granite summits of the Cairngorms, little muffled by the dusting of snow on the peaks. A trio of white-tailed deer started up from their browsing and took to their heels, bolting off across the frost-burned heather and bracken as a sleek private chopper swooped over the top of a ridge and skimmed along the floor of the valley below. At the far end of the valley, at the edge of a bleak escarpment, the glancing rays of the morning sun picked out the bluish roof slates and Gothic-arched windows of a Victorian manor house, poised breathlessly above a rushing cataract of white water.

The chopper followed the contour of the river as it made for the house, its shadow ghosting along the valley floor. It surged upward just before the cataract, circling once around the great central tower before settling like a wasp on the grass of the walled forecourt.

The pilot cut the rotors and got out of the chopper, rangy and economic of movement, barely ducking under the decelerating sweep of the blades as he came around to open the door for his passenger. He wore the brown leather flying jacket and scruffy peaked cap affected by military pilots half a century before, but sunlight flashed briefly off thoroughly modern mirrored sunglasses.

The man who alighted from the passenger seat was pale and slender by comparison, with silky fair hair going thin at the top and brushed back at the sides. By his dress, he might have been anything from a successful barrister to a university professor. The well-cut topcoat suggested the former, thought it *might* have been within the budget of a very senior university lecturer; the suit beneath it spoke more of Saville Row than the halls of academia.

In fact, Francis Raeburn dabbled in both areas of enterprise— and had made his fortune in neither. When pressed as to the source of his not inconsiderable wealth, it was his wont merely to smile and look inscrutable, murmuring vaguely about prudent investments, an indulgent bank manager, and the hint of family money.

The light grey eyes were even more inscrutable than usual as he stood motionless on the lawn, silently contemplating the Gothic grandeur of the house. Behind him, the pilot stretched back into the cockpit to retrieve an expensive leather document case, which he handed over to his employer with a deferential nod.

"Anything else, Mr. Raeburn?"

The man called Raeburn shook his head distractedly and tucked the case under his arm, his attention now focused on the upper reaches of the tower.

"Not for now, Mr. Barclay. Consider yourself at liberty for the next hour or so, but don't wander too far. In fact, you might head down to the kitchen and see if Cook can provide something for that insatiable sweet tooth of yours."

At his glance and bemused half-smile, the pilot grinned and sketched his employer an appreciative salute.

"Yes, *sir*, Mr. Raeburn!"

As the man leaned back into the chopper to make certain everything was properly switched off, Raeburn set off briskly across the lawn toward the house. The front door opened as he approached, a man in what looked like a white monk's robe greeting him with a nod that was almost a bow. Without speaking, the man ushered him respectfully through the entrance lobby and into a long corridor panelled in oak. Off the corridor to the left, an interior door gave access to a small cloakroom, where another open-fronted robe of white wool was hanging next to a full-length mirror.

Raeburn shrugged himself out of his topcoat and suit-jacket, handing them into the care of the waiting acolyte before sitting briefly on a small stool to remove his shoes and socks. He donned the white robe over his shirt and trousers, retrieved his document case, then allowed the acolyte to lead him back out into the main corridor.

A steep turnpike stair at the far end took them up to a circular landing with doors on two sides. The acolyte knocked at the south door, waited for a word of acknowledgement from within, then admitted Raeburn to the opulent confines of a Victorian library.

The south wall of the library was dominated by a great bay window, its upper panels worked in stained glass and grey-patterned grisaille. Sunlight spilling in from outside laid jewel-like splashes of color on the floor across a rich array of Oriental rugs. Where the walls were not lined with bookshelves, a patterned paper of crimson and gold echoed drapes of a heavy, antique damask swagged to either side of the bay.

At the center of the room, silhouetted dark against the bright window, stood a broad mahogany library table, its scrolled legs decorated in ornamental boulle-work. Seated at the head of the table, in the deep velvet comfort of a heavily-padded wing-back armchair, was the old man Raeburn had come to see.

"Head-Master," Raeburn murmured, inclining his head briefly but never taking his eyes from the other man's.

After a moment's penetrating scrutiny, the old man lifted a gnarled finger and beckoned the newcomer nearer, indicating the chair at his right hand.

"Sit down," he rasped, in a voice that was thin and rough with age. "Sit down and let me hear your report."

Raeburn lowered himself into the chair, pausing only to settle the folds of his robe and lean the document case against the chair leg to one side.

"You will not welcome what I have to say," he warned. "Our worst fears concerning Geddes and the others stand confirmed. All of them are dead, and the treasures lost."

When the other's stern expression did not change, Raeburn went on.

"Barclay, you will recall, was in the van on the further side of the loch that night, waiting to receive Michael Scot's gold, along with his book of spells. From all the evidence I've since been able to piece together, it now seems certain that the storm of lights he reported seeing can only have been a Hosting of the Sidhe. I must conclude that *they* were responsible for the loss of those concerned."

The old man gave a contemptuous snort. "It would appear, then, that Geddes fatally overestimated the virtue of the Fairy Flag of the MacLeods."

"Perhaps," said Raeburn, "but I think not. If the Flag failed to protect our men, I would guess that it was because of a change in the Flag's status. Our agent in the Edinburgh constabulary tells me that the Fairy Flag—*minus its frame*—was handed back to the Chief of the MacLeods at Urquhart Castle by another member of the Edinburgh police force, an Inspector Noel McLeod. This means that the frame and glass containing the Flag must somehow have gotten damaged before Geddes and the others could make good their escape. And once the Flag was no longer encased, it became a danger rather than a protection."

"Explain."

"There is a legend," Raeburn went on, "that if anyone not of the Clan MacLeod should lay hands on the Flag, that individual will suffer instant immolation. The police are saying there may have been a bomb, but I suspect that, in fact, the legend is true. The glass and frame somehow got broken—perhaps through the agency of this Inspector McLeod—but our man forgot the legend, in his panic. He tried to take it up again and, not being a MacLeod, paid the ultimate price. And once it was clear that to touch the Flag was certain death, the survivors had no choice but to take their chances among the Faerie Host—who tore them to shreds."

The Head-Master pondered this conjecture in silence for a long moment, then fixed the younger man with a sharp eye. "You're sure that Geddes was among the victims?" he said.

"Oh, yes," said Raeburn. "I'm quite sure."

He slipped a graceful hand into his trouser pocket and drew out a handsome gold ring set with a blood-red carnelian, mate to one he wore on his own right hand. When he held it up for the other man to see, the sunlight flashed on the device incised in the face of the gemstone: the snarling head of a stylized lynx.

"This was Geddes' ring," he informed the Master curtly. "It was still encircling a severed finger when the busy Inspector McLeod booked it into evidence, along with other shreds of human flesh and bits of clothing, pieces of the boat, and the Hepburn Sword. Our Edinburgh police agent was able to check the print taken from the severed finger against the set of Geddes' prints on record in our own membership files. The match was conclusive."

The Head-Master reached out a bony, blue-veined hand. When Raeburn laid the ring in the open palm, the old man curled his fingers tightly over it and closed his eyes. For a long moment he sat motionless, as if lost in deep thought. Then he opened his eyes with a grim nod of confirmation.

"Yes, this is Geddes' ring," he said. "With regard to the fingerprint, I trust that the police will not be able to repeat your comparison of prints and identify him?"

"Impossible," Raeburn said with cool certainty. "Geddes had no police record. We're quite safe there."

"What about his medallion?"

"It wasn't recovered," said Raeburn. "It must have been lost in the loch."

"And the others?"

Raeburn inclined his head. "Barclay claims that two members of the party started to make an escape in the boat. They even had

21

the chest aboard. He caught a glimpse of the boat heading away from the beach below the castle, but it apparently hit something in the water. Barclay didn't want to tell me at first what he thought he saw, but I gather that it was—what one might expect, stirred up by magic from the depths of Loch Ness. In any case, the boat broke up and sank, and the men themselves must have drowned; no bodies have been recovered. That would account for all of our operatives.''

The Head-Master's expression was veiled. ''Where does that leave us?''

Raeburn shrugged. ''The police have put forward a rather muddled official theory concerning explosives gone wrong, with possible terrorist associations. As to the boat, they're postulating the presence of a submerged log. Far-fetched as these explanations may seem, no one has ventured any others, at least officially. At this remove, and with no one to raise the hue and cry over our missing men, no one is likely to. After all, who would guess the truth?''

''Your Inspector McLeod?'' the Head-Master suggested.

Raeburn's fair face registered a flicker of dislike. ''Possibly. I haven't forgotten about him. Right now, he's doing us a service by diverting attention away from the supernatural elements in the incident, but his motives in doing so are far from clear. He will bear watching.''

''I should think so.'' The old man's hooded eyes held a dark gleam of malice. ''He has been far too closely involved for my liking—first at Melrose, then at Dunvegan, and finally at Urquhart. And always with the same two men in attendance—Sinclair and that young artist.''

Raeburn elevated a flaxen eyebrow. ''It *could* be argued that McLeod's presence has been largely coincidental. He apparently *is* the accepted police authority on matters that smack of the occult, and Melrose is certainly within his jurisdiction. As for Dunvegan—it might be judged sufficient that the inspector bears the clan name, and probably had the authority of his Chief. Urquhart, however, is another matter, and our man in Edinburgh has his orders to keep McLeod under surveillance.''

''And Sinclair?''

''His true role is also open to conjecture. I've had some inquiries made, and it seems that he's a fairly eminent psychiatric physician who occasionally gets called in by the police as a consultant. It would be worth some trouble to learn whether his interest in the occult is limited to professional curiosity.''

"What about the artist?"

Raeburn nodded. "In a way, he strikes me as possibly the most dangerous of the three, precisely because he's so different from McLeod and Sinclair. His name is Peregrine Lovat, and apart from the fact that he seems to be Sinclair's protege, he's the one whose presence is most difficult to explain. Were he twice the age he is, I might suspect him of being the leader of a Hunting Party. As it is, he's little more than a boy."

"Is he a *pretty* boy?" the Master asked, with a contemptuous curl of his lip. "If the answer is yes, then perhaps you need look no further for reasons why Sinclair is his patron."

Raeburn snorted. "That might explain some of it, but I don't think it's the case. The titled Dr. Sinclair has a tiresomely consistent reputation for prowess where women are concerned. I think we must look elsewhere for the Lovat connection. I intend to do so."

"Lovat is not worth your personal attention," the Head-Master said. "If you want him watched, put someone else on him— someone you can easily spare. If our plans are to proceed on schedule, you have far more important things to do."

"I wonder." A slight frown pleated the smooth skin between Raeburn's blond eyebrows. "What if the presence of these three men was *not* coincidental? If, in fact, they *are* adepts of some kind—then they could represent a very real threat. They'll have seen the sigil on Geddes' ring. If they knew enough to recognize—"

The old man snorted. "If they knew enough to recognize it, we would know by now. Still, if it pleases you, keep them under surveillance. If they become a further nuisance, we shall deal with that when it occurs."

"But, if they were responsible for our losses at Urquhart—"

"Our losses at Urquhart are ultimately of little consequence," the Head-Master said dismissively. "What have we really lost? The gold? Unfortunate, perhaps, but we have other means of generating wealth. The book of spells? Who can say for certain that the spells it contained were as potent as tradition claims? Let us bear in mind that even the bumbling Geddes was able to entrap the spirit of Michael Scot and force it to do his bidding. Could he have done that, I wonder, if Scot had truly possessed all the knowledge and power that legend attributes to him?

"As for Geddes and his men," he continued scornfully, "must we regret the loss of those who fail to accomplish what they set out to do? No, the Lodge of the Lynx has no room for failures. We are stronger without them. Let it be as if they had never been!"

Clutching the carnelian ring in one claw-like hand, he heaved himself shakily out of his chair and moved over to a plain oak side table set into an alcove to the left of the window bay. On top of the table stood a small portable furnace, along with an assortment of tools and moulds for making models from lead.

The Head-Master switched the furnace on. While it was heating up, he locked the band of the ring in the jaws of a table vise, then picked up a small jeweller's hammer. A swift, sharp tap to the stone reduced it to half a dozen shards, like crystallized blood, which he swept into his cupped hand and placed in a mortar. A few seconds under an electric pestle rendered the shards into a fine, scarlet powder, which he poured into a plastic vial and capped. The setting he removed from the vise and dropped into a tiny crucible, which he then set inside the furnace.

Raeburn watched the procedure from his seat at the table, half coming to his feet as the Master rejoined him and deftly catching the plastic vial which the Master tossed in his direction.

"So much for Geddes," he remarked, as the old man seated himself again. "Where do we go from here?"

"Where we have always intended to go," the Head-Master said testily. "The end remains unaltered. We shall simply resort to other means."

Raeburn's head lifted with a slight jerk. "You mean the Soulis torc?"

"And why not?"

He opened a drawer in the end of the table and produced an oblong box of polished ashwood, which he pushed across the table towards Raeburn. After a sidelong and almost incredulous glance at his superior, the blond man thumbed the latch on the front of the box and carefully lifted the lid. Inside, cushioned on scarlet silk, lay a heavy necklet of meteoric iron worked in Pictish designs. Raeburn's pale eyes widened in awed recognition.

"Impressive, isn't it?" murmured the Master. "Its Druidical makers were masters of their craft. The elemental powers with which the torc is imbued are as potent as any spell Michael Scot ever devised—and it is already in our keeping. Haven't I urged from the very beginning that we should reawaken its slumbering energies and make use of them according to our own purposes?"

"You have," Raeburn acknowledged. "But after a lapse of so many centuries . . . the risks—"

"Are well within acceptable limits," said the Master. "And you are wrong in thinking that the torc has not been used for many

24

centuries. How could I possibly vouch for its potency, if I had not already personally put it to the test?''

Raeburn looked up sharply at this disclosure. ''The Balmoral incident? I *did* wonder. Who was your subject, then?''

''No one of consequence,'' said the Master, with chilly indifference. ''An underling with ideas above his station. Next time, however, we shall want someone more eminent. I hope you have found him for me.''

Raeburn had resumed his air of silken composure. ''Have I ever disappointed you?'' he asked, reaching for the document case on the floor beside his chair.

As the Head-Master looked on, Raeburn opened the case and took out a black-and-white photograph, which he tendered to his superior. The old man glanced briefly at the photo before turning it over to read the typed bio taped to the back of the print. When he had finished reading, he took a second, longer look at the photograph before placing it face-up in the open lid of the box containing the torc.

''Excellent,'' he murmured. ''A most appropriate choice. Will you require any assistance?''

''It would, perhaps, be helpful,'' Raeburn said. ''My own men know what is expected of them, and are prepared to assume their roles when the time comes. But this undertaking will require much more than simply putting a few rounds through the head of a no longer useful pawn. If I could count on some extra backup, I would be that much more confident of success.''

The Head-Master's wrinkled lips framed a cold smile.

''Of course. Choose whichever six you wish.''

# CHAPTER THREE

T HE rectory for St. Paul's Scottish Episcopal Church, Kinross, was a rambling Victorian cottage adjacent to the church, set well back from the street amid an exuberant riot of rose bushes. As Adam eased the blue Range Rover into the gravelled driveway in front of the house, avoiding a miniature pink bicycle with training wheels, Peregrine glanced ruefully at the sky, which had clouded considerably since their pleasant ride of earlier in the morning.

"I don't think there's anything quite so fickle as Scottish weather," he said. "It's a good thing we started when we did. We'll be lucky if it doesn't bucket before lunch time."

As Adam cut the engine, an active, upright figure in a clergyman's collar and trenchcoat emerged from behind a yellow-painted door, a small briefcase clutched in one hand. He gave them a jaunty wave and bounded down off the trellised porch to meet them as they got out of the car.

"Good morning again, Adam! So glad you could make it. Is this Mr. Lovat, then?"

"The same," Adam said. "Peregrine, allow me to introduce you formally to Father Christopher Houston, a friend of long standing."

Peregrine studied his new acquaintance over a firm handshake. Seen at close range, Christopher Houston was lean and loose-jointed, with a wide, good-natured mouth and a flyaway shock of fine brown hair that made him look artlessly dishevelled, like a schoolboy newly come from the playing fields. He wore his black clerical suit with casual ease, but the brown eyes above the long, straight nose were disconcertingly shrewd.

Peregrine summoned what he hoped was an appropriate air of respect and said sincerely, "I'm very pleased to make your acquaintance, sir."

"No, Adam's the 'sir.' I'm just Christopher," the priest said amiably.

"What my husband means is that there's no need to be so

formal,'' said an amused female voice from behind Christopher's shoulder. ''The fact that he wears a collar is absolutely no reason to stand on ceremony—particularly since you've come to us in Adam's company.''

Taken slightly aback, Peregrine shifted his gaze and found himself looking into a fine pair of blue-grey eyes. The face that went with the eyes was attractive rather than pretty, with a smooth, wide brow and an agreeably determined chin. She had two little girls with her, the elder about five years old, and the other a toddler of two or so. All three were dressed to go out, in coats and hats.

''My wife, Victoria, and my daughters, Ashley and Alexandra,'' Christopher explained fondly. ''Vicky, did you happen to catch the introductions just now?''

''I did,'' she said. Her smile afforded him a glimpse of lurking dimples. ''Welcome to Rosemount, Peregrine. I've been an admirer of your work for quite some time—though I had no idea you were so young. You should be at least twenty years older, to paint the way you do!''

Adam chuckled and set his hand under the elbow of a blushing Peregrine, edging him back toward the car and casting a summoning glance in Christopher's direction.

''He's an old soul, Victoria,'' he said casually, ''but you're going to have to wait until we get back to discuss that further. Besides that, you and the girls look like you're on your way out as well.''

Victoria cast an indulgent glance in her daughters' direction. The girls were gazing up at Peregrine in wide-eyed curiosity. The friendly innocence of their regard dispelled his own initial stiffness. Feeling all at once at home, he smiled down at them, and had the satisfaction of seeing them smile shyly back.

''We're only going as far as my mother's,'' Victoria said, ''if, that is, the girls will stop flirting with Peregrine. But the three of you *are* going to be coming back here for lunch, aren't you?'' Christopher nodded yes. ''Oh, good. We'll see you later, then. Come on, girls. Grandma was expecting us for ten, and we're already late.''

''We'll be late too, if we don't get going,'' Christopher said.

''We're only waiting for you,'' Adam replied with a laugh. ''Come on, man, get into the car.''

Peregrine repaired to the back seat, deciding that he liked the Houstons. Christopher handed back his briefcase, and Peregrine stashed it on the floor beside his sketchbox while Adam started the car. But as everyone buckled up and Adam and Christopher briefly discussed the best route to take, Peregrine found himself momentarily far more curious about the Houstons than whatever might lie in store for them in Edinburgh.

Of one thing only was he certain yet, concerning the two. He had the distinct feeling that there was far more to both of them than met the eye. Though the brief conversation in front of the rectory had dealt only in friendly commonplaces, Adam's manner had been unusually open, suggesting that he felt no need to be on his guard where the two were concerned. And that seemingly casual remark of his, about Peregrine being an old soul. . . .

Curious to test his intuition, at least about Christopher, Peregrine took a deep breath and sat back in his seat, letting his eyelids droop until the physical images before him softened to a blur of color and motion. Turning his attention to the back of Christopher's head, he took another deep, slow breath and prepared to let his deeper sight take over. . . .

Before he could capture his first impression, Adam's mellow voice intruded on his reverie.

"So, my friend," he said, addressing the priest, "before we meet this young lady of yours, is there anything more you think I ought to know about her?"

Peregrine snapped out of near-trance to discover that Christopher Houston was frowning thoughtfully into the windscreen.

"Rather think I've already told you everything of substance," he said. "Helena Pringle's a sensible lass, not at all the sort to give way to flights of fancy. That's what made me prick up my ears when she first phoned me up to say there was something wrong about the flat."

"Has she actually claimed to see anything like a physical manifestation?" Adam asked.

"No, thank God. But since I visited her there, she's had more of the nightmares—nasty enough to make her afraid to go to sleep. I know I told you before that I didn't think there was any need for a formal exorcism, but you ought to know that I did bring along a few things, just in case."

He gestured toward his briefcase in the back as he spoke, but his use of the word *exorcism* had already given Peregrine an unpleasant jolt. He looked up sharply and found himself meeting Adam's amused gaze in the rearview mirror.

"Don't worry," Adam said. "I know I told you we didn't think it was serious, but Christopher likes to be prepared, as do I. Whatever else we're going to do today, I doubt very seriously that we'll be casting out demons by bell, book, and candle. Just keep your eyes open, and be ready to draw anything that comes strongly to mind. . . ."

Nicholson Street was an area inhabited largely by students from Edinburgh University. Helena Pringle's flat was located on the second floor of a large, mid-terraced house across from a row of small shops. Christopher led the way up two flights of stairs and knocked briskly on the door at the left-hand side of the landing. Almost at once a girl's soft voice called hesitantly from the other side of the door.

"Father Houston?"

"At your service, m'dear," Christopher said jauntily. "Brought along some reinforcements as well. If we're to do a proper investigation, I thought we might as well make a thorough job of it."

Helena Pringle opened the door. In person she was plump and fair, with a fresh complexion and lustrous ginger-blond hair. She made an effort to smile as she ushered them through into the sitting room, but Adam was quick to note the shadows of sleeplessness underscoring her wide blue eyes.

"This is Dr. Adam Sinclair," Christopher said, performing the introductions. "He's a psychiatrist—specializes in hypnotherapy. And this is Mr. Lovat. Between us all, we should be able to sort this thing out."

Helena glanced uneasily from Christopher to Adam, standing tall against the light from the sitting room windows. She was nervously twisting her hands together.

"A psychiatrist?" she murmured. "Does that mean I'm mentally ill?"

"Not in the least," Adam said with a reassuring smile. "But from what Christopher has said, I understand that you've been having some exceptionally disturbing dreams. It occurred to both of us that it might be useful to look more closely at those dreams, to see if we can find out what's causing them. With your permission, I thought I might try hypnosis to help you recall details that you might have overlooked."

"You want to hypnotise me?" she whispered apprehensively.

"I assure you, it won't be anything like what happens in the more lurid late-night horror films," he said, trying to reassure her enough to elicit a smile. "I've never yet bitten a patient on the neck."

At her startled look, he smiled gently and continued. "Seriously, the procedure is perfectly safe, and quite clinical. You will always remain in control. My own function is merely that of guide. Christopher will be here the entire time. He can even hold your hand, if you like.''

Despite an obvious effort not to, Helena did allow a brief, self-conscious smile to flicker on her lips.

''I—I see,'' she murmured. ''I suppose I'm being silly, to be so frightened.'' Her blue eyes shifted uncertainly to Peregrine, hovering uncomfortably in the background. ''Are you a psychiatrist, too?'' she asked.

''No, I—''

''Mr. Lovat is an artist,'' Adam interposed easily. ''He's assisted me before. He has a gift for translating psychic impressions into concrete images. And there's nothing at all silly about being frightened. But once you understand what's frightening you, I think you'll find that you aren't frightened anymore. Again with your permission, I should like Mr. Lovat to make sketches as you narrate the events in your dreams.''

''Father Houston?'' Helena turned appealingly to Christopher, who gave her an encouraging pat on the shoulder.

''Wouldn't have brought them, if I didn't think they could help,'' he told her firmly. ''Think you might be willing to give it a try?''

Helena swallowed hard, then gave an affirmative nod. ''All right,'' she said tremulously. She squared her shoulders and transferred her attention to Adam. ''I've never been hypnotised before, Dr. Sinclair. What do you want me to do?''

Adam had already made a survey of the room. It was cosily furnished, its old-fashioned cast-iron fireplace tastefully altered to accommodate a modern gas fire. The glow from the grating reflected warmly off the flowered print upholstery of an over-stuffed three-piece suite arranged around the hearth. The assortment of small ornaments in the room included half a dozen small crystal prisms strung up across the right-hand window on transparent strands of nylon thread.

''First of all,'' he said, ''I suggest we all make ourselves comfortable. May I call you Helena?''

''Yes, of course.''

''Thank you. Then perhaps you'd care to take a seat in that armchair to the right of the fireplace, Helena, and I'll ask for the loan of one of these lovely prisms in the window. Yes, this should do very nicely.''

Watching as Adam set the stage for the work he was about to do, Peregrine was reminded of his own initial experience with hypnosis. Like Helena Pringle, he had been bedeviled by fears and spectres—until Adam had helped him discern the gift beneath his fears. He hoped that Helena's case would end as happily as his own.

Carrying the prism by its nylon thread, Adam brought it back from the windowframe and hung it temporarily over a candlestick on the mantel, so that it dangled over the edge and could catch the light.

"Now, we'll just draw the inner curtains to filter out some of the light," he said, heading back to the windows. "You'll find it much easier to relax with the lighting a bit more subdued."

Helena watched him closely, her manner stiff with shrinking uneasiness, and Christopher moved closer on the adjacent settee.

"There, there," he murmured. "Nothing to be afraid of, I promise you. Here—hold my hand, if it will make you feel better."

He reached out and took one of Helena's small, tense hands firmly between his own. When her fingers tightened on his, he moved closer yet, so that they were almost touching knee to knee.

Peregrine, meanwhile, had selected a straight-backed chair between the windows, where he knew the light would be best for sketching. It would also put him outside Helena's peripheral vision, and therefore less likely to distract her. He sat down and was just arranging his sketchbook and pencils when something about Christopher's apparently casual double handclasp with Helena struck him as being somehow significant.

He took a closer look. Then his gaze focused sharply on the priest's right hand. The ring had not been there before—Peregrine was certain he would have noticed. The gold-set sapphire was square-cut rather than oval like those Adam and McLeod sometimes wore, and somewhat smaller, but Peregrine suddenly had no doubt that the ring served the same purpose.

*Good God, he's one of them!* Peregrine thought, hardly knowing whether to be scandalized or impressed by his discovery, though somehow it did not really surprise him. *He's doing the same sort of thing Adam does—helping him, starting to guide that girl safely into a hypnotic trance, so she won't be afraid. And it isn't the first time they've worked together this way!*

The priest had brought two fingers to rest lightly over the pulse point in Helena's wrist, and was speaking to her in a voice too low for Peregrine to make out the words, but his expression was serenely distant, almost as if he were listening to faraway music.

Even as enlightenment settled into acceptance in Peregrine's mind, a greyish film seemed to pass in front of his eyes. It was like looking through some sort of heavy, semi-transparent veil, like a shower curtain. Six weeks earlier, such a clouding of his vision would have terrified him—and *had* terrified him. Now, thanks to Adam, he knew what it meant, and what he had to do.

Blinking once, he leaned back in his chair, letting his eyelids droop behind his spectacles and bidding his vision focus through and beyond Helena. During the succession of slow, deep breaths that followed, the veil before his eyes began to take on the character of a ghostly overlay of images. Disregarding for the moment all concrete aspects of the room, he set himself to capture on paper the visual resonances of past events. . . .

The light in the room was subdued now, filtered through the sheer inner curtains Adam had drawn. Peripherally aware that Peregrine had begun to sketch, Adam returned to the fireplace and cast an inquiring look in Christopher's direction. The priest gave him a slight nod, and Helena also glanced up at him, looking far less anxious than she had before.

Taking his cue with a smoothness born of long practice, Adam reclaimed the prism from the mantel candlestick and sank down in the chair opposite his subject. Holding it by its transparent thread, he extended his hand so that the prism hung slightly above Helena's eye-level. Its multiple facets caught the glow off the gas fire, fracturing the flickering amber light into rainbow glints of red, yellow, and green. The sparkling play of colors drew Helena's gaze like a magnet.

"Now, this is your own crystal, Helena, so you know that there's nothing particularly mysterious or frightening about it," Adam said quietly, moving the thread of prism slightly between his fingers so that it twirled slightly. "It's simply a focus, so that you can turn all your attention to one, single point. This is the way we distract your conscious mind, so that gradually your unconscious mind, where dreams come from, can rise closer to the surface, and recall things in greater detail that you need to see.

"So I want you to focus all your attention on this crystal. Watch it turn and sparkle, watch how it catches the light. Let the crystal be the only thing in your vision, and listen only to my voice, as all the background sounds outside recede and you focus completely on the crystal and what I am saying."

Adam watched the movement of her eyes, locked already on the subtle flashing of the crystal, and shifted to more specific instructions in a low, conversational tone.

"That's just fine, Helena. Just drift and let yourself relax. You're quite safe and comfortable. Christopher is right here beside you. . . .

"You haven't been getting your rest of late, have you? You must be very tired. So tired. . . . I imagine there's nothing you'd like better right now than a little bit of sleep. Why don't you let yourself go? Just relax, and let your eyelids droop . . . that's right. You're feeling warm and safe and drowsy . . . very, very drowsy. . . ."

By degrees the tension went out of Helena's face and neck. Her eyes closed, and her breathing settled into a slow, regular rhythm. Adam lowered the pendulum and eased back in his chair, continuing to speak reassuringly of sleep and greater relaxation. When he was satisfied that his subject had achieved a sufficient level of trance, his suggestions began to shift more specifically to their needs.

"You're doing very well, Helena. Just fine, in fact. You're a very good subject. You can hear me quite clearly, can't you?"

"Yes." The girl's response was a mere whisper.

"Very good," Adam said in the same gentle but confident tone. "Now, in one sense, you're awake—fully aware of your present surroundings. But in another sense, you're like someone sitting in a cinema, waiting to see a film. The film is a recording of the dream you had the night before last. In a moment I'd like to start the film running. Are you willing to watch the film and tell me what you see?"

"Yes." The affirmative came after only a slight hesitation.

"Excellent," Adam said with soft approval. "I'm going to start counting backwards from five now, just like you sometimes see on the screen before the actual picture begins. When I reach the number one, that will be the sign for *your* film to begin, and you'll begin to describe everything you see on the screen. Five . . . four . . . three . . . two . . . *one*."

Helena's eyelids trembled, watching the inner memory unfold, and after a moment she drew a deep breath, eyes remaining closed.

"It's this room, but different. There's frost on the windows. The carpet is dull red, instead of blue, and the chairs have bare wooden arms. The people have all gone away, but they've left their shadows behind. The shadows are drifting in and out like ghosts—"

She broke off abruptly, a look of consternation furrowing her brow.

"It's only a film," Adam reminded her quietly. "You can turn it off anytime you want, but there's nothing you see there that can do you any harm. Christopher and I are right here. You're not afraid, are you?"

"A—a little," she murmured.

"Then here, take my hand too," he said, enfolding her free hand in his two, as Christopher had done with the first. "Now, you're perfectly safe, with both of us here. So when you're ready, I'd like you to go back to the film and continue telling me what you see. Will you do that for us?"

At her timid nod, he patted her hand reassuringly.

"There's a brave girl. Now, you mentioned something about shadows. Can you tell me what it is about these shadows that you find so frightening?"

Helena bit her lip. "They're—so dark—like cutouts made from black cellophane. And they won't keep to the walls. They keep coming out into the middle of the room. I can hear them whispering. They're cruel. They want to break the things they can't have—"

This time the break in her voice was a small gasp of fear.

"That's enough for now," Adam said, glancing back at Peregrine, who was still sketching busily. "You needn't be afraid. It's time to turn off the film. When the lights come on, it will be as if you've moved into a different room—someplace where you feel safe and secure. What room would you like that to be?"

"My old room at home, in my parents' house."

"That's where it will be, then," Adam said confidently. "The lights are now on. What do you see?"

Helena was smiling again, relaxed. "My bed, with the quilt my grandmother made for me. All my dolls are lined up along the footboard."

"That sounds like a wonderful, cozy place, Helena," Adam said approvingly. "Why don't you go lie down on the bed and have a little nap? Nothing will disturb you, and you'll remember nothing of what you might hear. In a little while, I'll give you a touch on the forehead and call you by name. At that point you will wake up feeling refreshed."

Helena sighed and sank back in her chair with a small wriggle, like a child nestling under the blankets. Satisfied that she was comfortable, Adam disengaged his hands from hers and straightened up, shifting his attention to Christopher with a look of inquiry. The priest likewise released the hand he had been holding and shook his head.

"Whispering black shadows," he muttered. "Sounds to me like

there really is something darkening the atmosphere of this place. Wonder what it could be."

"So do I," Adam agreed, in a thoughtful undertone. "I doubt we can glean much more from Helena, though, at least at any practical level. If I thought it involved her directly, I could probably get at it with more aggressive techniques—drug support, and such—but I don't think it's warranted, in this case. My suspicion is that she's simply been picking up resonances of things that took place here in the flat long before she moved in—and what she's picked up suggests several intriguing possibilities. Fortunately, we have other resources at our disposal besides her dreams."

He cast a pointed glance in the direction of the windows. Peregrine was still sketching, his pencil darting back and forth across the page in front of him with swift, unerring precision. From the expression on the young artist's face, Adam could tell that he was temporarily oblivious to the present scene, his attention focused wholly on the task of isolating and capturing a significant image of the past.

Christopher elevated an eyebrow, clearly impressed.

"He sees what took place?" he said, almost incredulously. "And he's learned all this in only a month?"

Adam nodded. "Less, actually. I suspected, from our first meeting, that he had the makings of a Huntsman. At Melrose, I became convinced of it. You see now, don't you, why I was so keen that you and Victoria should have a chance to meet him for yourselves?"

"Indeed," Christopher acknowledged with a fleeting grin. "I can hardly wait to see what's going down on that bit of paper."

Even as he spoke, Peregrine made a few more decisive flourishes with his pencil, then leaned back in his chair. With his next breath, his hazel eyes snapped back into normal focus. He gave himself a slight shake before glancing down at the page in front of him.

"Adam!" he exclaimed. "Come and take a look at this!"

Adam rose swiftly to answer the summons, Christopher following after a glance to reassure himself that their subject still slept. Peregrine handed over what he had drawn, and Adam turned it to the light, his dark eyes intent as he looked it over. Christopher edged closer and peered over his shoulder.

The sketch showed Helena's sitting room as seen from Peregrine's perspective, but with some features altered—notably the chairs and the settee, which were far more severe than the present furnishings.

35

Other elements in the room included a Christmas tree in the window bay and a large oriental screen shielding the room's other window. Of greatest interest, however, were the two human figures sketched in the foreground.

The most prominent of them was an intense young man with longish, dark, straight hair. Dark-robed like a monk, with a hooded cowl pushed back on his shoulders, he was kneeling upright on the carpet, offering up his crossed wrists to a somewhat older man, also robed, who was reaching out as though to bind them with a cord that Peregrine had labeled as being red.

The binding was being supervised by a third robed man who watched from the background, a short distance away. Though his features were little more than an impressionistic blur, it could be seen that he wore a medallion on a chain about his neck.

"Look there," Peregrine said, using his pencil as a pointer. "Where have you seen a medallion like that before?"

# CHAPTER FOUR

THE arrested expression on Adam's face was answer enough for Peregrine, but Christopher obviously was missing something. Somewhat bemused, he glanced from Adam to Peregrine and back again.

"Afraid you've lost me, chaps," he said to Adam. "Where *have* you seen a medallion like that?"

"In far too many places of late," Adam said thinly, "if Peregrine intends what I think he does, by this sketch." At the artist's tight-lipped nod, he went on. "Most recently, in a series of paintings he showed me just this morning. I regret to inform you that the Lodge of the Lynx appears to be active again."

Christopher breathed out softly through pursed lips. "Angels and ministers of grace defend us! I'd wondered, with everything else that's been going on. But who would have thought we'd stumble across their tracks *here*, in a student flat in Edinburgh?"

Adam set his jaw in grim disapproval. "They have to recruit new members from somewhere. Where better, than from the ranks of the young and impressionable?"

Peregrine had been following this exchange so closely that it only belatedly occurred to him that Christopher had spoken as a man with knowledge—and why. He blinked and took a closer look at the clergyman. Gone, for the moment, was the air of a cheerful schoolboy. All at once Christopher Houston looked deadly serious, no more to be trifled with than Adam or McLeod. As Peregrine recalled his earlier conjecture, he glanced furtively at the ring the priest still wore.

"I see you've arrived at the proper conclusion," his mentor said with a slight smile, as he handed back the sketch. "I was wondering how long it would take you to figure it out. Yes, Christopher and his good lady are members of the same enforcement group as Noel and myself. They've assisted in the Hunt on many past occasions."

"But never in anything where the Lodge of the Lynx had a

hand," Christopher put in, a little distractedly. "Before my time, you see. I rather hoped our predecessors had put a stop to their doings, once and for all." An uncharacteristic grimace momentarily distorted the schoolboy face. "Appears we were overly optimistic."

Peregrine blinked once behind his wire-rimmed spectacles, then returned his attention to the sketch in his hand, now consciously comparing what he had drawn with what the room now held. Silently commending the young artist for his swift grasp of priorities, Adam turned his attention briefly to a glance around the room.

"Well, I wonder how long it's been since the flat was last furnished in the style shown in our drawing."

Christopher's brows knit, also returning to practicalities.

"Seem to recall Helena saying something about it having been refurbished before she moved in," he said breezily, returning to the clipped phrasing of his usual repartee. "I'll have a word with Mrs. Beaton before we leave—that's the landlady. She ought to be able to tell us when the work was done—and also who some of the previous tenants have been."

"In the meantime," Adam said, "the flat itself remains a problem." He took the sketch again and glanced at it distractedly. "The fact that Peregrine sketched this particular scene, which seems to be a ritual binding of some sort, suggests that this was the high point of the rite, if you can call it that—which ought to reassure everybody that the chap with the tied hands wasn't done to death right here in the flat. If he *had* been, I'm sure Peregrine would have seen and sketched *that*. Death, as he's learned, leaves a different kind of residue."

As Peregrine nodded his emphatic agreement, Christopher took the sketch and studied it more closely.

"We can rule out a simple ghost, then, as I suspected from the beginning. Would you say that it was an initiation, then?"

Adam nodded. "That would be my guess, though it's impossible to know for certain, at this remove. Negative enough, in its own way, if the Lodge of the Lynx was behind it, but not as heavy-duty as it might have been. Still, it's nasty enough to bother our Helena after close to a year, if the Christmas tree is an accurate indication of time. Whatever the cause, the effect now needs to be dealt with. What do you recommend, Christopher?"

Since their very first meeting, Peregrine had come to take Adam's leadership for granted. He was momentarily surprised to hear Adam asking Christopher for advice, until he reminded himself that one of the most valuable gifts of command was the ability to exercise a discerning trust in the competence of others. Christopher deliberated a moment before replying.

"Earlier, I'd have said the place just needed a spiritual airing out—a general benediction to lighten the atmosphere. Now, knowing the Lodge of the Lynx is involved, I'd say we do need something more like an exorcism.

"Not the formal rite of the Church, though—poor Helena would probably find that as frightening as a disembodied spirit. No, I'd rather try something a trifle more subtle—something Helena herself can take part in. It's important that she have faith in what we're doing, and that's best achieved through sharing in the work."

The ceremony he went on to propose was both graceful and straightforward, containing nothing overt to suggest that it was anything more than a simple house blessing and dedication. When Christopher had finished, Adam nodded his approval.

"I think that will answer the purpose very well," he told the priest. "Let's wake our young lady and acquaint her with what you have in mind."

Helena roused easily in response to Adam's prearranged cues, Christopher once more holding her hand.

"Hullo, m'dear," the priest said, smiling and lifting the back of her hand lightly to his lips. "Nice to have you back with us again. How do you feel?"

"I—I do feel better," she acknowledged, with a tremulous smile. Then a small shadow of anxiety crossed her face. "Did you—were you able to find out anything?"

Adam smiled and sat back casually in his chair, toying with the crystal he had taken up before waking her.

"Indeed, we did. And you were a most cooperative and useful subject. After reviewing the evidence, I think we may safely say that these nightmares of yours owe their origin to influences outside your own psyche."

Helena blinked at him owlishly, as though she hardly dared believe him.

"Then, it wasn't just me!"

"Not at all," Adam said. "Not unless you count having more than your share of womanly intuition—and that has nothing to do with *causing* such things, just perceiving them."

At Helena's puzzled look, he went on.

"It's a fact that physical objects—even whole houses—can and do act as psychometric receptors, storing up emotional resonances from past events," Adam explained. "Anyone who happens to be sensitive to such things can be adversely affected—as seems to have been the case with you."

Seeing that Helena was still looking a bit bewildered, Christopher gave her hand a sympathetic squeeze and smiled.

"What Dr. Sinclair means is that there must have been a lot of bad feelings connected with some of the people who used to live in this flat, Helena. Bad vibes, if you like—a bit like a nasty smell. Once it gets into the woodwork, it tends to hang about till you give the place a good clean-out.

"So that's just what we're going to do," he went on decisively, echoing Helena's hopeful nod. "We're going to give this place a metaphysical house-cleaning. Only we'll use spiritual fortitude instead of ammonia solution."

Helena giggled in spite of herself.

"That's the ticket, m'dear," said Christopher. "Now, I know you have both a Bible and a prayer book. Thought you probably wouldn't mind giving me the loan of them, so I didn't bother to bring mine. Could you fetch them for me, while I get my other things? That would be splendid."

He opened his briefcase and lifted out a clerical stole of green silk, along with a small plastic bottle of what Peregrine assumed must be holy water. Helena brought the required books from the bookshelf and sat down beside him as Christopher laid the stole around his neck and began leafing through her small, leather-bound copy of the Scriptures. While the girl's attention was focused on her pastor, listening to his murmured instructions on the passages to read, placing the colored ribbon markers, Adam drew Peregrine into a corner of the room by the door.

"Stand here and watch," his mentor told him. "You're the one who can *see* what we're after. I want you to be certain we get it all."

"But, how—"

"Just watch," Adam insisted, shaking his head to belay any further argument. "You'll know, when we're done."

They both were out of Helena's line of vision. Even so, Adam was careful to shield what he withdrew from his coat pocket, so that even Peregrine caught only a fleeting glimpse of it.

Adam called it his toothstone—dark and oblong, curved like a wolf's fang, all but hidden in the cradle of his palm—but it was, in fact, a piece of lodestone, spiritually as well as magnetically polarized for drawing off malevolent psychic energy. Peregrine had seen it used once before at Melrose Abbey, to dispel the residue of dark intent left by those who had summoned the spirit of Michael Scot back to his grave.

Even though he was not afraid, Peregrine felt his heart thudding in his chest as Adam turned full toward him, the dark eyes already taking on an otherworldly depth, the toothstone closed in his hand between them. The older man bowed his head briefly over his closed fist, touching it to his lips, then raised hooded eyes to Peregrine's, suddenly far more than Dr. Adam Sinclair, psychiatrist, or Sir Adam Sinclair, Baronet.

To Peregrine, he seemed inches taller as he drew a deep breath and used the top of the toothstone to sign first himself and then Peregrine with a symbol of personal warding. Peregrine fancied he could feel the path of the toothstone in the air before him, and imagined himself drawing the symbol about him like a protective mantle as Adam smiled faintly, nodded, then began making what appeared to be a casual, clockwise circuit of the room, ritually sealing it off so that the evil was trapped and could not escape.

Christopher, meanwhile, had invited Helena to join with him in a moment's quiet meditation, kneeling with her in the space contained before the fireplace, defined by the chairs and settee. The furniture also provided additional screening for what Adam was doing, should Helena look up—though in response to Christopher's gentle instructions, she had bowed her head into her hands, eyes closed.

Once Adam had finished his circuit of containment, briefly disappearing into the short corridor off the sitting room to deal with any residuals in bedroom and bath, he returned to his starting point by the door and took the toothstone between the thumb and first two fingers of his right hand. His hand steady as a surgeon's, he then began going over the sitting room walls with a sweeping motion, back and forth just a few inches from the surface. Peregrine looked on in silence as all around him the ghosts of past events were sucked away like so much dust into a vacuum cleaner.

What remained behind was a kind of emptiness. The evil was gone, but the vacancy left behind was not a comfortable one. It was a dullness that made the surrounding air seem stale in his mouth. Even as Peregrine looked instinctively toward Adam in search of an explanation, Christopher broke the silence.

"I think we may begin now," said the priest, getting to his feet. He took a step backwards and made the sign of the cross over the still-kneeling Helena, intoning as he did so, "In the name of the Father, and of the Son, and of the Holy Spirit, let us pray. Our Father . . ."

There followed a succession of readings from Scripture, interspersed with other prayers, some of them read by Helena herself, beseeching divine intervention to keep evil at bay and restore peace to the house. As Peregrine listened, only partly comprehending, he felt the flat emptiness of the room begin to give way to a new freshness of life. It was almost as if the room were like a cup. Adam had emptied the cup, had gotten rid of the poison and cleansed it, and now Christopher was refilling it with a lightness that eased the heart and mind like sparkling wine.

Except that Christopher was merely the vehicle—the steward at the feast, not the Master. The real Authority lay above and beyond him, even while It invested him with Its power. As Christopher moved on to asperse the corners of the room with holy water, Peregrine was forced to acknowledge that he understood what the priest was doing even less than he understood what he had seen Adam do.

Religion was a mystery to him. As a child he had learned the forms of Christian worship, but the substance had always eluded him. Eventually he had come to the conclusion that there was no substance. Lately, though, he wasn't so sure.

He was still puzzling over what it was that he seemed to be missing when Christopher brought the apparently simple service to a close. Helena was smiling, all her earlier anxieties clearly laid to rest, now that the oppressive atmosphere in the flat had been lifted. Christopher waved aside her thanks with airy good humor.

"All in the line of duty, m'dear," he told her cheerily. "Must be off now, but I'll be sure to stop in early next week to see how you're getting on. And don't hesitate to call me if anything at all still bothers you."

They said their farewells on the doorstep before heading downstairs to the basement flat occupied by the landlady. Mrs. Beaton, a motherly widow, greeted Christopher with a pleasure that was tinged with relief.

"I'm that glad to see ye, Father Houston," she said broadly. "I've been worried about our poor lamb all this last fortnight, but now ye've been in to see her, she'll perhaps be easier in her mind."

She proved quite ready to answer Christopher's questions regarding the flat and its previous occupants. When at last Adam and his companions took leave of her, they had a short list of names, along with the fact that Helena's flat had been redecorated only a few months earlier. Outside, the weather had turned wet and gusty. They beat a path back to the car under a stinging splatter of cold rain.

"I suppose it was only a matter of time," Christopher said resignedly, futilely brushing rain from the shoulders of his trenchcoat when they had reached the shelter of the car.

Adam glanced over the scrap of paper they had obtained from Mrs. Beaton, then tucked it carefully away in the breast pocket of his coat.

"I'll pass the names on to Noel," he said. "He'll know how to track down whatever additional information may be available. How are we doing for time, Christopher?"

The priest glanced at his wristwatch. "Not too badly. Vicky will be hoping we're back by one, but she knows better than to plan anything for lunch that won't hold for an hour or so. Why?"

"Oh, I had a note from Randall yesterday, saying that he'd managed to find a book for me that I've been after for some time," Adam said, turning the key in the ignition. "Would you mind if we made a slight detour to his shop, to pick it up?"

"Might as well, since we're here," said Christopher. "Don't fancy your chances of getting parked, though—not in this weather and on a Saturday."

"We can but hope," said Adam, and eased the blue Range Rover deftly into traffic.

The bookshop in question lay at the upper end of a stepped close opening off the Royal Mile. The street itself was ablaze with headlamps as cars and lorries ploughed doggedly through the worsening rain. After two passes, Adam gave up looking for a parking place and pulled up at the curb in what was formally designated as a loading zone.

"This will have to do," he said ruefully, glancing up and down the street for signs of a traffic warden. "I shan't be long. Christopher, could I prevail upon you to stay behind and keep an eye out for the 'yellow peril'? I doubt very much that even the most punctilious traffic warden would award a ticket to a man of the cloth."

"Benefit of clergy, eh?" Christopher cocked a sly grin at his seat-mate, then made a show of adjusting the neck of his trenchcoat so that his collar was more clearly visible.

"Very well, heathen that you are! I'll stay here and keep dry, and hope I shan't be obliged to move the car."

"In that eventuality, I do hope you'll come back for us," Adam said with a smile. "Come on, Peregrine. This place might interest you."

The Parnassus Bookshop was warm and still inside, an Aladdin's cave of library shelves crammed full with volumes of every size, shape, and binding. The air had a pleasant, powdery smell that reminded Peregrine of the manuscript collections housed in the Oxford University libraries.

Almost at once, his eye was drawn to a complete set of the collected fairy tales of Andrew Lang, their gold-embossed covers proclaiming them to be first editions. As he paused to admire them, a slim girl with a long mop of dark curly hair popped out from behind the counter at the back of the shop and came forward with a smile.

"May I help you, sir?" she began, then her face lit up with pleased recognition. "Oh, it's you, Adam! How lovely to see you. Papa didn't tell me you'd be calling in today. Is that a friend you've brought with you?"

She tilted her head in Peregrine's direction, her dark eyes bright as a wren's.

"Miranda, if you flirt with that rascal instead of me, I shall be inconsolable!" Adam informed her with a chuckle. "However, I *will* admit both to having brought him and to him being a friend—a uniquely talented one, as it happens. His name is Peregrine Lovat, and he's a portrait artist."

"A portrait artist?" Miranda was intrigued. "Have you ever painted anyone famous, Mr. Lovat?"

Peregrine flushed at the question, but found himself already caught up in the good-natured banter.

"Well, I once did a sketch of the Queen Mother," he told her with a wry grin. "It was only from someone else's photograph, though, so I don't really think it counts."

"Don't let him get away with false modesty, Miranda," Adam said easily. "He hasn't painted any of the Royals—yet—but he's had some very distinguished clients. Peregrine, this is Miranda Stewart, my friend Randall's daughter."

Peregrine had already taken note of the piquant face and the way she had draped a silk paisley shawl, Romany-fashion, about her slender shoulders, and now he cocked his head at her in new reflection.

"I'm very pleased to meet you, Miss Stewart, though I should tell you that the most famous faces are not necessarily the most interesting ones."

Miranda gave him a tip-tilt glance from under long, dark eyelashes.

"Now I'm not sure which I'd rather be—famous or interesting. Would you paint my portrait either way?"

"With pleasure," Peregrine said, and added recklessly, "Anyway, I don't see why you shouldn't be both."

Miranda laughed, and Adam, not without regrets, took the opportunity to intervene.

"Much as I would like to continue this merry exchange, I have Christopher waiting in a loading zone outside, and I need to have a word with your father, if I may. Is he in?"

"He's in the stockroom," Miranda said. "If you'll excuse me a moment, I'll nip back and tell him you're here."

She was gone in a gypsy whirl of dark skirts, vanishing through a door at the back of the shop. When she returned a few minutes later, she was accompanied by a slight, elderly man in spectacles. When he caught sight of his two visitors, he hurried forward.

"Adam!" he exclaimed. "What a delightful surprise on an otherwise gloomy Saturday morning!"

"You'll spoil me with such greetings, Randall," Adam said with a chuckle. "Perhaps I should have telephoned, but I must confess, this is a slightly impromptu visit."

"It matters not a whit," said the elderly bookseller. "You know you're always a welcome visitor."

His mild blue gaze turned to Peregrine. "And who is this?" he inquired. "I don't believe we've met."

"This is Mr. Peregrine Lovat," Adam said, beckoning Peregrine forward. "Peregrine, my very dear friend, Randall Stewart."

Peregrine surveyed Miranda's father as they exchanged handshakes. Lightly-built like his daughter, Randall Stewart had silvery hair and the finely-chiseled face of an aging scholar. The gentle, old-world courtesy in his manner was suggestive of more courtly times.

"Peregrine Lovat," the old man mused. "That name is not unfamiliar to me—ah, I have it! You're the portrait artist, aren't you? The one whose works were so favorably reviewed in *The Scotsman*."

Peregrine had the grace to blush. "The critics have been very generous, sir."

"And *you* are too modest," Randall replied. "I myself saw an exhibition of your work in the National Gallery. The critics' praise was well-merited, and I'm happy to have met you in person."

Before Peregrine could summon a suitable reply, the old man turned back to Adam.

"Forgive me, but I was almost forgetting. You've come about

45

the Bartholomaeus, haven't you? It's locked up in my desk. Come upstairs and I'll get it for you—you, too, Mr. Lovat. Miranda will look after the shop while we chat, won't you, my dear?''

They followed him up two flights of stairs to a large garret room at the top of the building. In addition to the heavy oaken desk by the windows, there were two comfortably well-worn armchairs drawn up on either side of a gas fire, as well as a sink and sideboard built into a nook in one corner.

''My home away from home,'' Randall explained to Peregrine with a smile. ''Adam, would you and your young friend care for some tea?''

''I'm afraid we really haven't a great deal of time,'' Adam said apologetically. ''I've left Christopher minding the car, with instructions to invoke benefit of clergy if a traffic warden gets stroppy, and Victoria will be holding lunch for us. Besides that, we appear to have caught you in the middle of some work.''

He gestured toward the desk, which was dominated by an ancient manual typewriter. A sheet of typing paper half-covered in print stuck up above the platen.

''It's nothing that can't wait a few minutes,'' Randall said with a faint smile. ''A letter to the editor of the *Sunday Times*. It won't make this week's edition anyway.''

''*Another* letter?'' Adam quirked an eyebrow. ''I admire your diligence, Randall. Your piece in last week's *Times* was quite an elegant apologia for the institution of Freemasonry.''

The bookseller looked pleased. ''Why, thank you. That's high praise, coming from someone who is not a member of the Craft—though I know you're sympathetic to the work.'' Then his face sobered. ''I must confess, I'm not a little worried about the recent attacks that have been made on our fraternal order. Just the other night, vandals broke into the Freemason's Hall in George Street and did damage to several of the rooms. And there have been other incidents. . . .''

His voice trailed off and he shook his head. ''I don't know what the world is coming to. Granted, the public have not always understood the nature of our institution. Our detractors mistrust what they regard as our secrecy. But it's only through secrecy that we can guarantee that the knowledge entrusted to us will not be abused by men of self-seeking ambition. And so we must continue to guard our rites, hoping at the same time that our works themselves will stand as proof of our benign intentions.''

Adam was nodding. ''To quote from a more modern rendering of the passage from St. Matthew, *Be careful not to parade your good deeds before men to attract their notice, for by doing this you will lose all reward from your Father in heaven.* You make a very able advocate, Randall. I'll be watching for your letter in next Sunday's editorial section.''

"In that case," said Randall, "I shall make a point of getting it finished. Now, let me show you the Bartholomaeus."

Beckoning Adam to accompany him, he crossed over to the desk and unlocked the lowest drawer on the left-hand side. Peregrine followed, peering over Adam's shoulder as the elderly bookseller lifted out a stout volume bound in tooled leather.

"This is merely a Victorian facsimile of the 1495 edition by Wynken de Worde," Randall explained, "but I think you'll find that it faithfully mirrors the original."

Adam opened to the title page, then lifted the book in his hands so that Peregrine could read it: *De Proprietatibus Rerum.*

"Concerning the Properties of Things," he said aloud, automatically translating the Latin. As Adam continued to leaf through it, Peregrine realized that the book itself was written not in Latin, but in Middle English.

"It's a late medieval encyclopedia," Adam said, answering the unasked question. "It was compiled in Latin by Bartholomaeus Anglicus—Bartholomew the Englishman—and later translated by one John of Trevisa. It's a repository of a wealth of knowledge, as it was understood by the readers of the day, and therefore of considerable interest to anyone interested in the evolution of ideas."

He smiled over at Randall Stewart as he closed the book, cradling it against his chest with pleased possessiveness.

"Thank you for finding this for me, Randall. I know it was no easy task, and I hope you'll not undervalue your own efforts in setting the price. Don't give me any numbers now!" he warned, holding up a hand and shaking his head emphatically. "I insist that you come up to Strathmourne in the next week or so, and we'll discuss it over drinks."

"I'd like that," Randall said, smiling. "As it happens, I've got to make a trip up to Stirling tomorrow to do an estate appraisal. It's supposed to be a large collection, so it may take me several days. Why don't I give you a ring when I'm finished? If it turns out that you're planning to be in, I'll make a slight detour on my way back home."

"That should mesh nicely with my plans," Adam said. "I'll look forward to your call."

Downstairs, Adam and Peregrine tarried long enough for

Miranda to wrap up the book, then bade her and Randall a cordial good-bye. Back outside amid the rainy bustle of the Royal Mile, the Range Rover had disappeared. Mildly dismayed, Peregrine turned up his collar and cast a searching glance over the moving lines of traffic. Just then, the hoot of a familiar car-horn caught Adam's attention.

"There's Christopher now," he said, pointing. "Run for it, before we both get utterly drenched!"

They arrived back at the rectory closer to two o'clock than to one. Victoria met them at the door and hustled them into the shelter of the hall.

"Lord, it's turned perishing cold, hasn't it?" Christopher observed, as the three of them shook themselves out of their dripping coats. "Sorry we're late, Vicky. If this keeps up, I think we'll see snow before dark."

"Never mind," said Victoria. "The kettle's on the boil, and so is the soup. Come along through to the dining room and I'll start serving up."

Shortly thereafter, the four of them sat down to steaming bowls of Scotch broth, with omelettes and hot buttered toast to follow. In the course of the meal, Christopher and Adam related what had occurred at the flat. At length, prompted by Adam, Peregrine brought out the sketch he had made on the premises. Victoria studied it gravely for a long, thoughtful moment before handing it back. He noticed, hardly even surprised now, that the center stone in her engagement ring was a sapphire.

"I suspect we should count ourselves lucky to have stumbled across what might turn out to be an important lead," she observed. "Do you think there's any chance that Noel will be able to find the young man in the picture?"

"If he can't, no one can," Adam said. "The youth himself is probably no more than a novice. But it's just barely possible that he might be able to tell us something useful concerning the older man in the background."

"The man with the medallion?" Christopher paused to give his long nose a rub. "Are you thinking this fellow might have been mixed up with the events at Loch Ness?"

Adam frowned. "I wouldn't want to rule out the possibility."

Victoria gave her head a thoughtful shake. "Whatever was in Michael Scot's spellbook, they wanted it badly enough to risk lives for it. What do you suppose they're up to?"

"I only wish we knew," Adam said. "Whatever it may be, they obviously intend to stop at nothing to achieve it."

"What about the wee lassie?" asked Christopher. "Scot's current persona—what's the name, Talbot?"

"Gillian Talbot," Adam said with a nod. "It's still too soon to tell. When I saw her in the hospital, she was in a bad way—her entire personality disrupted, *at every level*. I was able to leave one of my cards with the mother, but so far there's been no follow-up. If I don't hear anything by the end of next week, I'll give some thought to finding a way to renew the contact."

"Couldn't you just telephone?" Victoria asked.

Adam grimaced. "That could be a bit awkward, explaining my interest. Besides, there may well be a better way. I've got to go down to London toward the end of the month; Mother's coming over for the holidays. If her schedule permits, I may arrange to call in at the hospital again. We'll just have to see."

A fresh gust of wind rattled the windows at his back. Christopher squinted down at his watch and clucked his tongue.

"Lawks, is that really the time? Sorry, Adam, but I'm going to have to think about leaving. I've got a christening in half an hour."

"We've got to be going as well," Adam said, with a glance that included Peregrine. "Thank you, Victoria, for an excellent lunch. I hope I can count on seeing both of you tomorrow night?"

"Wouldn't think of missing it, old fellow, even if there's a blizzard," Christopher said with a grin. "To paraphrase what the postmen say where your mother comes from, *Neither rain, nor snow, nor sleet, nor hail shall stay these dinner guests from their appointed feast. . . .*"

# CHAPTER FIVE

THE thickly forested hills to the north of Blairgowrie were blanketed with newly-fallen snow. Thinking back over his twenty-seven years' service as a gamekeeper, Jimmy McArdle could recall only a handful of times when there had been snow on the ground so early in the season, with the first of December still nearly a fortnight away. It would bring the deer down early this year. He must see about having extra bales of hay set out at the usual places—and keep an even closer watch than usual for the poachers, who would be drawn by the deer's easier accessibility.

Pausing briefly on the whitened footpath, Jimmy inhaled deeply of the clean tang of pine resin and turned his face to the dark sweep of starlight overhead, then eased the weight of his rifle to his shoulder and put his eye to the scope to sight in briefly on the splendor of Sirius, flashing red and green and white like a beacon. With no moon, even with the snow but newly fallen, the night was tailor-made for poachers. His breath made a filmy plume of steam against the far-flung scattering of winter stars as he lowered his weapon and drank in the sounds of the night, savoring the stillness and the solitude.

Jimmy loved these woods, and he loved these rugged hills, especially in winter. But now that the weather was clearing, the cold was beginning to bite deep. In another few years he would be too old to do this. Lately, he noticed that he seemed to mind the cold more.

Aware of an aching touch of frost in his bones, Jimmy set down the red-filtered woodsman's torch he always carried but rarely used and delved beneath his parka for the hip-flask of brandy that was a welcome anodyne to creeping winter chills. Fingers clumsy in their heavy gloves, he unscrewed the cap and lifted the flask to his lips. Even as the brandy hit his tongue, the stillness of the surrounding woods was broken by a muffled noise that sounded not unlike a cry.

The noise came from uphill, somewhere off to his right. It had not sounded like a deer. Instantly suspicious, Jimmy cocked his head to listen, gradually picking up a more muted scuffle of movement among the trees beyond. An unpaved forestry access road skirted the

*50*

other side of the hill, but it was a private one, and no one should be using it at this hour, much less without Jimmy's knowledge.

Hastily stowing his flask away, Jimmy shifted his rifle into the crook of his arm and picked up his torch. He had been told not to tangle with poachers personally, for there had been some nasty incidents in the Highlands of late, and even a few killings, but if he could get close enough without being seen, he might at least get a better look at tonight's culprits through the rifle's scope.

The snow underfoot was ankle-deep and powdery. Scuffling through it rather than on it, so as not to give himself away, Jimmy began to work his way toward the origin of the sound, taking advantage of the cover of the snow-laden trees. He was halfway up the slope when a low, sing-song wail rang out through the surrounding woods, bringing him abruptly to a standstill. As the echoes died away, a thin chorus of whispering began.

Sibilant in the dark, the whispers rose and fell with the eerie cadence of a chant. The sound of it made Jimmy's flesh creep. For a moment he stood rooted to the spot, unable to bring himself to move. Then he took a firmer grip on his rifle and forced himself to push on.

A dim red glow began to show through the trees ahead. Creeping forward almost against his will, Jimmy arrived at the hill crest and found himself gazing down into a hollow dell turned suddenly strange, though he had known it all his life. About a dozen figures in hooded white robes stood ranged in a circle around a central clearing. Alone at the center, on the flat grey stone that often had served as a picnic site in Jimmy's youth, stood another white-robed figure, cowled head thrown back and arms raised, facing another kneeling figure at the edge of the stone, whose bowed grey head was bare.

Sullen pockets of fire burned red at each of the four quarters of the circle, sending up heavy spirals of evil-looking black smoke. The moving flicker of the flames cast eerie shadows on the kneeling man. Looking more closely, Jimmy realized that his hands were bound behind his back.

Even as Jimmy stared in mesmerized horror, the chanting abruptly ceased.

The old man had offered no resistance as his captors dragged him uphill through the new-fallen snow, nor could offer any. His captors had seen to that. From the moment they had seized him—from behind, with a chloroform-soaked pad clamped over mouth and nose—their mastery had been complete. He did not even know how long they had been holding him, for they had never allowed him to recover fully from the effects of the chloroform. A succession of injections kept him drifting in and out of consciousness. He remembered being shaken awake enough to use the toilet once or twice, and a meal of sorts a few hours before—a stale, oatmealy sort of scone and a glass of harsh red wine—but little else.

Shortly after the meal there had been another injection, just before they bundled him into the back of a large, closed car; and then a long ride lying on the floor, loosely covered by a tartan rug. Despite his efforts to stay awake and try to see where they were taking him, he had nodded off most of the time, his fleeting dreams peopled by nightmares.

He had roused as they hauled him out of the car, groggy and half-sick, his head throbbing from the drugs and the fear. They were parked beneath some trees—a bewildering maze of tangled evergreens, the scent of them sharp and pungent on the frosty night air. He had no idea where he was or what they intended. All he knew was that his life was in mortal danger, and he was powerless to put up a fight.

Once they left the car—he thought there was a second one, parked close behind it—the only illumination came from the electric torches of the two men going ahead and behind to light the way for the rest of the party. The old man guessed there might be as many as a dozen of them, but he could not be sure. They moved too quickly, and all were dressed alike, anonymous in long white robes like the vestments of some strange priesthood, cowled hoods pulled low over their faces. He had never seen his kidnappers clearly—and his keepers had worn Balaclava helmets—so he had yet to see the faces of any of his captors. That gave him some hope that they might eventually release him, for he certainly could not identify any of them.

What began to worry him most was that they had put one of the white robes on him, too. They must have done it during the long car ride, while he faded in and out of drugged sleep. He was bundled in an overcoat over the robe just now, his bare feet jammed into rubber Wellington boots several sizes too large, but he could sense that they had left him wearing nothing underneath the robe. Even drug-blurred logic told him that this did not bode well for whatever future he might have, even if he *hadn't* seen their faces.

They had taken away his glasses, and his eyes wouldn't focus properly anyway because of the drugs, but peering blearily ahead, he could see that they were approaching the crown of a hill. The iron hands at his elbows propelled him forward, up and over the crest, to descend toward a tree-ringed dell. Open to the sky from above, the clearing was blanketed in white except for a flat grey

52

stone in the center, nearly the size of a car. The air was icy, silent as a tomb, and his ghostly escorts spoke not a word.

Fear gripped him like a vise, and he cried out once as he tried to balk. His keepers did not seem to care, and easily overcame his feeble struggles, shoving him bodily between the trees and into the center of the clearing. There rough fingers stripped off the overcoat and forced his bare, half-frozen hands behind his back, securing them with a length of thin cord while others pulled off the boots, first one and then the other. The icy shock of the snow beneath bare feet elicited a gasp, and the cord bit cruelly into his wrists. He bit back a sob of pain and bewilderment as they forced him to his knees in the snow, just at the edge of the huge, smooth stone, and stood over him to make sure he remained there.

The snow was numbing his legs from the knees down, soaking through the thin robe, chilling his blood, threatening to numb what little sense he still had left to him. Dull-eyed, increasingly sluggish, he watched his captors trace a wide ring of ashes on the whitened ground around the clearing.

Flames flared red and golden in the darkness as small fires were set to burning at the four quarters of the circle, each tended by one of the white-robed men. At a signal from another, who seemed to be their leader, each of the four cast a handful of powder upon his fire. The powder flared up like gunpowder, then gave off dark, noxious tendrils of smoke that snaked slowly upward in serpentine spirals.

The smell of the smoke was sickly-sweet, heavy as opium, biting at the nostrils. The old man shivered, dread supplanting cold, for his captors' likely intentions suddenly acquired new menace. As his two keepers stood back from him a little, and their leader stepped imperiously onto the flat stone, the old man made a final, valiant attempt to get to his feet; but frozen legs refused to respond.

The effort nearly made him overbalance and fall over, and he teetered precariously on numb knees until one of his keepers leaned forward to steady him for a moment. As the man drew back again, the leader raised both arms above his head and began to recite a deep-throated invocation, in a language full of trills and liquid vowels, teasing at the edge of familiarity but not quite recognizable.

The other members of the circle joined in, their voices low and full of menace in the freezing night. The invocation yielded to a guttural chant, harsh as stone on stone. The odorous smoke from the firepits was thick in the old man's nostrils. Paralyzed in mind and body, he wavered on the edge of fainting.

The chant rose to a sudden, sharp crescendo, then ceased. The leader crossed his arms on his chest and bowed low from the waist, then pulled something dark and metallic from underneath his robe and came to kneel gracefully before the old man, offering the object on both extended palms for the old man's inspection.

It was a torc of blackened metal, overlaid in silver with primitive designs and set with tawny gems. The old man stared at it in blank incomprehension, cringing then as hands seized his upper arms from either side and more hands clasped his head, one cupping over his nose and mouth so that a sharp whiff of ammonia suddenly cleared his head and all at once he knew *exactly* what was about to happen.

Another moved in the darkness then, swooping down on the old man from behind. Pain exploded at the back of his skull, but heightened consciousness lingered a few heartbeats longer—just until the breath suddenly caught in his throat and hot fire seared below his right ear.

And the trembling Jimmy, watching by now through the scope on his rifle, stifled a horrified gasp as metal flashed and bright blood suddenly spurted from the old man's neck, gushing in great, steaming jets onto the object that the other kneeling man held in his outstretched hands. The old man's body convulsed, mouth agape in a rictus of silent agony, back arching against the restraint of his captors, but none showed him any mercy.

Within seconds, his blood had drenched his robe, his nearest captors, and the snow around him, dark crimson in the firelight, his struggles gradually diminishing, strength draining away with his blood. No more able to move than the victim still held upright by his unrelenting captors, Jimmy continued to stare in horror as blood overflowed the suppliant's cupped hands and ran down his arms, streaming from the dark, metallic object that he finally raised in triumph as his minions at last allowed the old man's lifeless body to crumple on the blood-drenched snow.

The stark heartlessness of it finally broke the spell and released Jimmy from his frozen horror. Outraged now, as well as appalled, he made a fumbling attempt to chamber a bullet. To his dismay, the mechanism jammed with a crunch in his quaking hands.

The sound carried almost like a gunshot. Down in the hollow, the white-robed figures stiffened, hidden faces turning to scan the surrounding trees. At a curt gesture from their leader, three of the hooded figures broke away from the circle and began heading in Jimmy's direction, fanning out as they came.

Terrified, Jimmy dropped flat and began wriggling backwards as swiftly as stealth would allow, dragging his rifle with him, praying they would not spot him. And when he reached the game trail below, he sprang upright and took to his heels like a man running for his life.

# CHAPTER SIX

THE BBC's Late Night Sunday Movie ended shortly after 2 A.M.
It had been the 1940 black-and-white classic, "The Sea
Hawk," starring Errol Flynn, Claude Rains, and a host of others.
Detective Chief Inspector Noel McLeod, of the Lothian and
Borders Police, Edinburgh Branch, waited until all the final credits
had finished rolling, immersing himself in the heroic Korngold
score, then thumbed the off button on the remote control with the
nostalgic reflection that the old movies still were some of the best.

Beside him on the couch, both his wife and the family cat had
fallen asleep. He smiled to recall how earlier in the evening, Jane
had loyally volunteered to stay up and keep him company, only to
doze off during one of the romantic interludes between a sea battle
and a sword fight. The large grey tabby on her lap tended to doze
whenever a lap was available.

McLeod, by contrast, felt wide awake, his mind oddly restless.
During the course of the evening he had sought distraction from
one or the other of his several hobbies, first intending to paint the
most recent of several decoy ducks—of which there were dozens
perched on the boxed cornices above the sitting room windows,
which at least relieved Jane of the chore of dusting them on any
regular basis—then moving on to the less demanding art of
origami, the Oriental pastime of decorative paper-folding.

He had learned the rudiments of origami technique from a
Japanese police colleague, met when they were both participants
at the FBI-sponsored National Academy in Quantico, Virginia.
Since then, McLeod had gone on to become a skilled practitioner
of the art. But tonight, even the challenging intricacies of origami
had failed to command his attention. The coffee table was littered
with thin, brightly-colored bits of rice paper he had been forced to
abandon only half-finished as his distraction got the better of him.
Something had been preying on his mind since teatime, without
his being able to put a name to it. He was just debating whether to
step out for a breath of air when the telephone rang.

Jane roused at the sound, disturbing the cat, who mewed in protest. McLeod stretched across her to snatch up the receiver in mid-ring, wondering what police crisis was about to make itself his headache at this hour.

"Edinburgh 7978, McLeod here," he said gruffly.

"Inspector McLeod?" The male voice at the other end of the line was wide-awake, despite the lateness of the hour, tending to confirm McLeod's suspicion that this was an official call. He didn't recognize the speaker, though.

"Aye," he growled. "Who's this I'm speaking to?"

"This is Sergeant Callum Kirkpatrick, calling from Blairgowrie Police Station," the voice said crisply. "You may not remember me, Inspector, but I also hail from Huntingtower Lodge, in Perth. We met briefly last year at a meeting of the general council. I'm sorry to disturb you at this hour, Brother McLeod, but we think we may have a bit of a problem up here, and we're needing someone of your experience to advise us on how to proceed."

Memory jogged by Kirkpatrick's succinct recap of their meeting, McLeod now remembered being introduced to a police sergeant of that name from Huntingtower—a nice enough chap, as he recalled: well-read and very professional, an aficionado of American cowboy films and a crack shot, both with pistol and rifle, on Tayside's Police Olympic team.

What sent a shiver of premonition through his nerve-ends was Kirkpatrick's appeal as a fellow-Freemason as well as a fellow-police officer. Having himself been a Mason nearly all his adult life, McLeod knew well that Kirkpatrick would not invoke the fraternal bond without good cause.

"No apologies necessary, Brother Kirkpatrick," he said, shifting into professional mode. "Just tell me what's happened."

There was a pause from the other end of the line, as if Kirkpatrick were not entirely certain how to begin. Then he spoke in a rush.

"We've got a man up here at the station, name of McArdle—works as a gamekeeper on the Baltierny estate. He swears—an' this is going to sound daft—but he swears he's witnessed some kind of human sacrifice up in the middle of Baltierny Forest. Black magic, he says."

Kirkpatrick's voice paused almost apologetically, and McLeod made himself draw a deep breath and let it out slowly.

"That *is* a pretty spectacular claim," he said noncommittally, wondering if this was what had had him on edge all evening. "Have you checked out his story?"

"Not yet." Kirkpatrick sounded uncomfortable over the admission. "The area's awfully rugged, so it really isn't practical until first light. I ought to say here that I'd usually consider McArdle a reliable witness. He's worked for Lord Baltierny for more than forty years, and been head gamekeeper for twenty. He's well-respected in the town.

"When McArdle first came in, though, he was smelling strongly of spirits," Kirkpatrick went on. "The desk officer was new to Blairgowrie, and didn't know McArdle. He thought it was probably just the drink talking, and advised him to go home and sleep it off. But McArdle wouldnae have it—kept insisting he'd seen what he'd seen, and only took a wee drink afterwards to steady his nerves, before coming in to make a report. He got so agitated that the desk officer eventually agreed to give him a breath test."

"And?" McLeod prompted, when the voice did not immediately continue.

"Well, he didn't even register; stone cold sober, according to the breathalyzer."

"I see," McLeod murmured.

"That's when the desk man called me in," Kirkpatrick went on. "He told me over the phone what was being claimed, and by whom, and I had McArdle repeat it twice when I got there." He sighed.

"Inspector, I've known Jimmy McArdle for nearly ten years, and I don't think he's lying. But if he *does* have the right of it—if there *was* a black magic killing somewhere out there in his bailiwick—we're certainly not equipped to deal with it, here in Blairgowrie. Burglars are more our speed, an' rowdies in pubs, an' even poachers, but not murderers—and especially not black-magic loonies. I remembered someone telling me that you were the one who generally handles cases like this on behalf of Lothian and Borders. So it seemed like a good idea to ring you up rather than risk mishandling the case."

"I can appreciate that, Sergeant," said McLeod, "but before I go handing out advice, I could do with a bit more information. What made your man so certain that what he saw was some kind of occult ritual?"

"He says the perpetrators were all wearing white robes with hoods pulled down over their faces. He claims to have heard them muttering some kind of chant over the victim before they struck him down," Kirkpatrick said, then added dubiously, "I suppose it could all be some kind of a hoax—a university lark or something."

"Aye, perhaps," McLeod said, "but I don't think we dare make that assumption. Your witness sounds solid. Maybe I ought to drive up to Blairgowrie myself."

"I was hoping you'd say that," Kirkpatrick said frankly, "and I'd be mighty grateful if you would. I hate to call you out on a night like this, but—how soon could you get here?"

"I'll try to be off within the next half hour," McLeod said. "How are the roads?"

"There's been a good four or five inches of snow since about eight last night, but the main roads are all passable. We've got four-wheel drive vehicles, once you get here, to go up to the site. Is there anything we ought to be doing in the meantime, till you arrive?"

McLeod scowled abstractedly. "Just try not to let the press get wind of this, until we know what we're dealing with," he said. "I don't suppose you have anyone up there with homicide training?"

"Afraid not, Inspector."

"Well, no matter. We'll deal with that when and if it proves necessary. If your witness has his facts right," he continued grimly, "there won't be any need to hurry where the victim is concerned. And the perpetrators themselves will be long gone."

He thought a moment longer. "There's someone I'd like to bring with me, if he's available—a psychiatrist friend of mine, with a great deal of experience in dealing with cases like this. In fact, he's the man I call when *I* need an expert. I've worked with him many times, and value his opinion."

"If you think he can help," said Kirkpatrick, "you'll get no objections from me."

"I've got to get in touch with him first—but that's my problem, not yours," said McLeod. "Either way, God willing, I should be joining you in Blairgowrie in about three hours' time. See you then."

With that he rang off and turned to his wife. Jane was sitting quietly on the couch, absently stroking the cat. She arched a reddish eyebrow, with an expression of long-suffering resignation.

"Don't tell me," she said. "You have to go out. Shall I make you a flask of coffee, then?"

"Aye," McLeod said ruefully, "I suppose you'd better." He leaned across to give her shoulders a fond squeeze, and added broadly, "Och, you're a braw wee trooper, Janie, my lass. I promise to make it up to you when I get home."

"That you will, Noel McLeod," she agreed with some astringency. But her dark eyes were twinkling. McLeod held her a moment longer, before releasing her with an effort. As she rose and made off towards the kitchen, the cat following expectantly at her heels, he picked up the telephone again and dialled the number for Strathmourne House.

58

                                        * * *

While Inspector Noel McLeod was on the phone discussing the
possibility of an occult-related homicide, Adam Sinclair was hosting
a formal dinner for several dozen of his fellow patrons of the *Societas
Musica Escotia*, a social organization dedicated to the appreciation
and support of the musical arts in Scotland. It was a black tie affair,
with most of the men attired in Highland dress, or at least tartan
waistcoats, and all the women decked out in formal gowns, many of
them also sporting colorful tartan sashes and other accessories. In the
course of the long, full evening, the guests had partaken of an
excellent dinner featuring such Scottish culinary delicacies as
poached wild salmon, roast pheasant in oatmeal, and *Creme Auld
Alliance*, a sweet, heady blend of heather honey, whisky, and cream.

   Now they were being shepherded into the drawing room by the
Society's president for coffee and musical entertainment, the latter
supplied, as was customary, by volunteers from among their own
ranks. One end of the bow-fronted room had been set aside as an
impromptu stage, and several of the guests busied themselves with
final arrangements there as the rest filed in and began taking seats
in the audience area, Adam among them.

   While the last few stragglers were still getting settled, Lady
Janet Fraser leaned forward in her seat and laid a slim, jewelled
hand affectionately on Adam's shoulder.

   "My dear Adam, you really do throw the most excellent dinner
parties!" she murmured. "True hospitality must surely count as a
form of art, don't you agree, Caroline?"

   The question was addressed to the sylph-like blonde woman
seated at Adam's side. Lady Caroline Campbell responded with a
flutter of long, delicately tinted lashes.

   "Indeed," she said with a roguish look in Adam's direction, "I
can't think how you manage it. It must be very difficult with no
one but Humphrey to help you with the arrangements."

   The calculated coquetry of the remark caused Adam to wince
inwardly. After an evening spent in Lady Caroline's company,
he was heartily wishing that Janet had not been so determined to
provide him with a partner, lovely though Lady Caroline certainly
was. She had skin like fine porcelain and the figure of a ballerina, and
the emeralds clasped around her milky throat were just a shade paler
than the couturier gown of bottle-green velvet—and probably cost
enough to re-roof the entire east wing of Strathmourne House.

   For all her physical beauty, however, there was a slight note of
shrillness and even desperation to her laughter that told him she was
forcing it for his benefit—and not simply out of a desire to please. It

                                        *59*

was a reaction he encountered all too often. He could hardly fail to be aware that he was considered a prime catch on the marriage market.

Not that he blamed Janet. She had tried. She and her husband Matthew were old and treasured friends from his childhood, ideally matched in their interests and affections; and having achieved such fulfillment in her own marriage, one of the burning ambitions of Janet Fraser's life was to help Adam find a similarly suitable bride.

But he was beginning to weary of playing Lady Caroline's game of verbal cat and mouse. Even as he made a polite rejoinder to her most recent sally, he gave inner thanks for the music which shortly would be putting an end to conversation.

The northwest corner of the drawing room was dominated by the presence of a harpsichord that had belonged to Adam's grandmother. It was a lovely instrument, the honey-colored wood of the sound-box overlaid in traceries of fine gold leaf. Several straight-backed chairs had been arranged in a semicircle in the space to the right of the harpsichord, each with its accompanying music stand. On the floor in the background, still shrouded by its green velvet cover, stood a Celtic harp.

A shadow fell across Adam's shoulder. He glanced aside to find Peregrine Lovat crouching down beside him. The young artist pulled a wry face and balanced himself with one hand against the back of Adam's chair.

"Lord, Adam, I haven't played in public since I was at school," he groaned, easing the silk bow-tie above his elegant wing-collar. "I don't know why I let Julia talk me into this!"

Adam smiled at Peregrine's discomfiture, his gaze sweeping the room to light on a slender girlish figure in a white satin evening gown, with tartan bows at the shoulders and tartan ribbons wound through her piled tresses of rose-gold hair. Peregrine had met Julia Barrett little more than a month ago, and since then, their relationship had blossomed—yet another change from the stiff, repressed young man Adam remembered from their first encounter.

"Just keep reminding yourself that this is a music appreciation society, not a convocation of critics," he said bracingly. "Now, relax and remember you're among friends."

Peregrine rolled his eyes, but he went up onto the stage and sat down at the harpsichord, settling the pleats of his kilt with an unconscious nonchalance that would not have been possible two months before. A moment later Julia joined him, accompanied by her uncle, Sir Alfred Barrett, a sturdy, distinguished figure in dinner clothes rather than a kilt, with twinkling blue eyes above a flourishing silver moustache.

"Friends and colleagues," Sir Alfred began, with mock formality, "as the senior member of our trio, I have been elected to inform you all that for our part of the program we will be performing selections from the musical notebooks of Anna Magdalena Bach. Before we begin, I would like to assure you that we will make every effort to conform to the notes on the pages before us."

This droll assurance elicited a chuckle from the room at large. With a humorous salute to his friends in the audience, Sir Alfred took his seat in a chair opposite the harpsichord and gathered up his own chosen instrument: an Italian-made cello from the studio of a pupil of Stradivarius. Julia, with an oblique smile at Peregrine, remained standing at the front of the improvised stage, with only a music stand before her on which she unfolded a black-bound book of sheet music. An expectant hush settled over the company as the members of the trio poised themselves to begin.

The three songs they had chosen were among some of Adam's favorites. The precise music-box chime of the harpsichord and the mellow notes of the cello supplied a delicate counterpoint to Julia's lilting soprano, a voice as light and pure as a young boy's. There was no faltering on the part of any member of the trio. When they had finished, their performance drew an enthusiastic round of applause.

"Right, Janet," said Sir Matthew Fraser, as the acclaim died down and the performers began to shift properties on stage. "Looks like it's you and Caroline now."

He and Adam stood up as the ladies rose, music in hands, and prepared to make their way forward. Caroline cast a pretty frown toward the stage, where Peregrine was helping Julia shift the harp into position.

"I do hope that child has some experience as an accompanist," she remarked—as much out of envy as concern, the psychiatrist in Adam suspected. "If she fails to follow the voice lead properly, it will quite spoil the effect."

"Have no fear!" Janet laughed. "I've heard Julia play, and I assure you, I have every confidence in her ability."

From glancing at the music in Janet's and Caroline's laps, Adam knew that the two women had decided on a series of duets based on the poems of Robert Burns. But though he had a great personal fondness for the works of the great Scottish bard, he found the first song something of a disappointment. Janet, who had few illusions about the modest extent of her talents, performed quite creditably, her genuine enjoyment of the music itself lending a sparkle to her delivery.

Caroline, on the other hand, seemed determined to attack the notes, pursuing the soprano line with more aggression than style. Recalling the lyrical sweetness of Julia Barrett's clear voice, Adam grimaced at the comparison. He was just girding himself mentally to sit through the rest of the selections when he felt a light, respectful touch on his sleeve.

"Pardon the intrusion, sir," murmured Humphrey, "but you have a telephone call. It's Inspector McLeod."

Adam slipped out of the drawing room as unobtrusively as he could, wondering what could have prompted McLeod to call so late. It was well past two. Once outside, he made his way along the hall toward the library and sat down at the desk to wait for Humphrey to transfer the call. At the signal, he picked up the receiver.

"Hullo, Noel, I'm here. What's going on?"

"I'm not entirely sure," said McLeod's gravelly bass. "Sorry to drag you away from your guests, but I've just had a damned peculiar call from a police sergeant up in Blairgowrie, name of Kirkpatrick. One of the local gamekeepers turned up at the station a few hours ago, claiming to have witnessed some kind of ritual killing, somewhere up in the woods north of the Baltierny estate."

Adam listened with growing interest as McLeod went on to supply what further details were available.

"Anyway, I told Sergeant Kirkpatrick that I'd drive up to Blairgowrie and lend a hand if I could," McLeod concluded. "I was going to ask you to come along, but I didn't realize you had guests. It's odd enough that I thought you should know, but it may turn out to be nothing but a wild goose chase."

"Oh, don't worry about the interruption," Adam said. "In fact, on several counts, I'm very glad you called. The way things have been going recently, we can't afford to dismiss anything at face value. I haven't had a chance yet to tell you about the odd thing Christopher and I uncovered yesterday in Edinburgh. It looks like a pretty cold clue right now, but it would appear that our Lynx chappies were busy around this time last year."

"Indeed?" McLeod said. "Maybe you *should* come up to Blairgowrie with me, then. You could tell me about yesterday on the way."

An outbreak of polite applause from the direction of the drawing room reminded Adam of Lady Caroline and her predatory affectations. Whatever might turn out to lie behind the gamekeeper's story, all at once the prospect of a night drive to Blairgowrie seemed like the promise of a breath of fresh air.

"As a matter of fact, that sounds like a splendid idea," he said firmly. "My guests should be going home soon anyway. How soon can you get here?"

"Thirty to forty minutes—assuming that the roads aren't too bad north of the bridge."

"Fine," said Adam. "That gives me ample time to get changed. We can take the Range Rover. Come round by the garage, and Humphrey will let you in."

With this assurance, he rang off. He relayed the necessary instructions to Humphrey over the house phone, then returned to the drawing room. Julia, Janet, and Lady Caroline were just taking their bows when he stepped through the door. Adam moved forward smoothly to meet them as they left the improvised stage.

"My abject apologies for being obliged to miss the end of your performance, ladies," he told them. Then, turning toward the rest of the company, he cleared his throat and called out, "Might I have your attention, please?"

Pitched clear and low, his voice penetrated the furthest corners of the room. As heads swung in his direction, he spread his hands before him in a graceful gesture of regret.

"I'm sorry to interrupt this lovely recital, ladies and gentlemen, but I'm afraid something has come up that requires my professional attention. You're all welcome to stay as long as you like. Indeed, I hope you'll feel free to continue in my absence. At the same time, however, I must ask you to excuse me."

A murmur of disappointment greeted this announcement. As he made them a sketchy bow and retired toward the doorway, he succeeded in catching Peregrine's eye from across the crowded room. The artist acknowledged the summons with a small nod and bent his head to speak a word of explanation in Julia's ear. A moment later, he joined Adam outside in the hall, his hazel eyes wide with unspoken curiosity.

"I've just had a call from Noel McLeod," Adam said, coming right to the point. "The Blairgowrie police have had a report from a gamekeeper who says he saw a human sacrifice out in the woods. Noel and I are driving up to Blairgowrie to check the story. It occurred to me that perhaps you might like to come along."

"A human sacrifice!" Peregrine murmured. "Good Lord, of course I'll come, if you think I might be of some use."

"At this point, it's too soon to tell," Adam replied. "Noel himself allowed that this could be a wild goose chase. But if it isn't—if the gamekeeper's story checks out—your particular talents could come in very handy. I ought to warn you now, though, that the evidence will be anything but pretty."

He paused expectantly, and Peregrine squared his shoulders determinedly.

"If you're trying to leave me a graceful way out, I appreciate it," the artist said quietly. "However, you've given me the impression that I'm capable of some rather unique contributions to what you and Inspector McLeod do—and squeamishness is hardly a good excuse for trying to evade responsibility. That doesn't mean I may not faint or throw up, if there's a lot of blood—you'll have to bear with me, on that—but any physical failing on my part won't be for want of giving things my best effort."

It was a statement he never would have made six weeks earlier.

"Good man," Adam said warmly. "I hope we won't have to put your intestinal fortitude to the test. In any case, I'll be glad to have your company. Now." He drew himself up to his full height, his mind moving on to the practicalities of what lay ahead. "Noel's driving up from Edinburgh, and expects to be here within the next forty minutes. That gives us both time to change into more suitable clothes—and make peace with our respective companions of the evening."

Peregrine pulled a rueful grimace. "I wasn't thinking of Julia just now," he admitted. "I'll go have a word with her at once, and arrange with Sir Alfred to see her home. . . ."

A harried half hour later, Peregrine was in the hallway of the gate lodge, tugging on heavy boots, when he heard the sound of a car pulling up outside. Shrugging on his navy duffel coat over a heavy sweater, he snatched up his sketchbox and darted outside to find Adam's blue Range Rover idling at the gateposts. The blunt profile of the man in the passenger seat belonged unmistakably to Noel McLeod, wire-rimmed aviator glasses reflecting in the outside light, moustache bristling.

Peregrine slammed the gate lodge door behind him and bounded down off the steps to scramble into the back seat on the passenger side. Adam's medical bag was on the floor behind the driver's seat, along with a nylon zip-bag that had POLICE stenciled on both sides. McLeod turned to greet him with a shrewd glint in his eye.

"Welcome to the party, Mr. Lovat. Did you and your wee lassie part friends?"

"More or less," Peregrine said, stashing his sketchbox on the seat above the other bags. "She was disappointed, of course, but I explained that I'd been doing some forensic drawing for Adam, and that he'd asked me to come along tonight. She seemed not to mind too much."

"That's more than can be said for some women," said McLeod, as they pulled away from the gate lodge. "If you ever get the chance to marry your Miss Barrett, I'd advise you to take it."

# CHAPTER SEVEN

T HOUGH traffic had melted the snow on the road, the
pavement still was slick as Adam piloted the Range Rover
northward along the M90 toward Perth. The occasional lorry
rumbled past in the southbound lanes, glaring headlamps thrusting
cones of light into the darkness, but few vehicles were headed
north.

Snow began to fall again in light, wet flurries about the time
they reached the junction with the A93 to Blairgowrie, rapidly
degenerating into sleet. Through the steady swish and clap of the
laboring windscreen-wipers, McLeod scowled ahead into the
darkness.

"God, what a foul night," he muttered. "If this keeps up, we're
going to find ourselves wading in slush, when we head out to the
scene."

"You'd better hope your witness is a good enough woodsman
to be able to *find* the scene again," Adam said. "Otherwise, this
could turn into a game of blind man's bluff."

"Aye, not to mention what it will do to any evidence," McLeod
agreed.

After that no one said anything for a while. At Adam's
suggestion, Peregrine settled back to try to catch some sleep,
McLeod also dozing in the passenger seat. Adam's head was clear,
largely unaffected by the modest amount of wine he had taken in
the course of the evening's festivities. But at the same time, he
reflected ruefully that, had he known he was to be called out on an
errand such as this, he would have chosen to fast rather than
partake of a five-course meal. His deeper senses felt sluggish
in contrast to his body's feeling of comfortable well-being, though
he reckoned he would be largely restored by the time it became
really important, out at the crime scene.

The dashboard chronometer read 4:53 when he slowed coming
into the outskirts of Blairgowrie. The change of speed roused

McLeod from his cat-nap, and he pulled himself upright in his seat and stifled a yawn as he began looking for landmarks.

"The turn is just before we get to the town square," he told Adam, pointing. "It's called Leslie Street, and it'll be a sharp right. There it is." They made the turn. "Now, watch for another very narrow turning to the right—that's it, right into Ericht Lane. The station's just ahead and to the left."

Peregrine, too, stirred as they made the final turn, knuckling sleep from his eyes and settling his glasses back on his nose as he peered out to the left. Blairgowrie Police Station was a two-story Edwardian building of red brick, the front steps lit by two round lamps that imitated old gaslights. The car park, largely empty, lay on the opposite side of the lane, to their right.

Adam pulled into a gap between a white police vehicle and a mud-spattered yellow jeep, its undercarriage mired with sticks and sodden leaves. All of them gave the jeep a long look as he cut the ignition.

"Do you suppose that could be the gamekeeper's car?" Peregrine wondered aloud.

"If so, it looks like it's had a rough ride," McLeod said. "Let's go meet the man, and see what he has to say for himself."

The three got out of the Range Rover and trudged across the snow-encrusted lane and up the icy steps. The station door was locked. Stamping his feet to shake loose the snow, McLeod reached over and thumbed the bell.

"These smaller, outlying stations aren't usually manned between pub closing and about six," he explained over his shoulder. "There're patrol cars out on the streets, of course, but—ah!"

A clank and a thud preceded the heavy door swinging inward. The man on the other side was tall and thin, with a spiky head of reddish hair above a prominent Highland nose. The epaulets on his uniform coat bore the three chevrons of a police sergeant. When he saw McLeod, his big-boned face brightened in obvious relief.

"Inspector McLeod," he said. "Welcome to Blairgowrie. Glad to see you could make it in spite of the weather."

"We've been out in worse," said McLeod, with a significance that was not lost on Peregrine, as Kirkpatrick stood aside to admit them. "Adam, Peregrine, this is Sergeant Callum Kirkpatrick. Sergeant, this is Dr. Sinclair, the consultant I told you about over the phone, and this is his associate, Mr. Lovat. He's something of a forensic artist."

Kirkpatrick shook hands all around with the newcomers.

"I have to say, I'm hoping I've called you out for nothing,

gentlemen," he said, with a dubious shake of his head. "If what my man says is true, I dinnae look forward to the next few hours."

"Where *is* your man?" McLeod asked. "McArdle? Was that his name?"

"Aye, he's down in the lock-up," Kirkpatrick said. "We weren't holding anybody, and he was looking pretty knackered, so I told him he could bed down on a bunk in one of the cells till you got here. Want to look over his statement before I take you down?"

McLeod glanced aside at Adam, who shook his head minutely.

"Let's talk to Mr. McArdle first," the inspector said. "We'll see if he tells us anything different from what he told you."

Kirkpatrick gave a quick nod of agreement. "You're the expert here, Inspector. Whatever you think best. Just follow me."

Without further preamble, he ushered them out of the lobby and along an adjoining corridor to a flight of stairs leading down to the basement level. At the bottom of the stairs, a security door gave access to the station's modest holding facility, but the door was standing open. A sturdy young constable in uniform was sitting at a desk to the right of the door, idly thumbing through a computer magazine. At the sight of Kirkpatrick, he shunted the magazine aside and stood up, his blue eyes frankly curious as he glanced beyond his superior at McLeod and his companions.

"This is PC Forsythe, who's kindly agreed to do a spot of extra duty in order to help out," Kirkpatrick explained. Shifting his gaze to his young subordinate, he inquired, "How's McArdle?"

"Havin' a bit of a kip, last I looked, Sergeant."

"Well, go give him a shake, and tell him the authorities from Edinburgh have arrived," said Kirkpatrick. "We'll be along in a minute, once these gentlemen have had a chance to shed their coats. And Davie—"

"Aye, sir?"

"See if you can get that poxy vending machine in the dispensary to kick out enough cups of coffee to go around."

"Aye, sir. I'll do my best."

The basement level was well-heated. Adam was not sorry to shed the weight of his sheepskin coat. He and his companions left their outdoor garments hanging in the adjacent property closet before following Kirkpatrick through another doorway into a short cell corridor. PC Forsythe met them coming in, and jerked a thumb toward the door of the first cell.

"He's awake now, sir, and just as stroppy as before," he told his superior. "I'll see about that coffee now."

McArdle was sitting on the edge of the bunk in his stocking feet. He was a sturdy, balding man in his early fifties, with a snub nose and fierce brown eyes above a bushy brown beard. His manner, as Kirkpatrick performed the necessary introductions, was not exactly cordial. Upon learning that Adam was a physician, he pulled a glowering look and said flatly, "I dinnae have any need of a doctor. Nor does that puir man lyin' out there in the snow!—not that anyone believes me."

"No one *wants* to believe you," McLeod said sternly, "because it's horrible, if it's true. But if the good sergeant didn't have cause to believe you, he wouldn't have called *me*. And if I didn't believe the both of you—even though I've never even seen *you* before!—don't think for a minute that wild horses could have dragged me up here on a night like this. Dr. Sinclair even left his dinner guests so he could come along."

Somewhat subdued by McLeod's gruff declaration, McArdle glanced sullenly at his feet.

"I suppose he's a psychiatrist or something," he muttered.

Adam chuckled and took the straight-backed chair that Kirkpatrick handed in to him from the corridor outside, setting it deliberately in front of McArdle. Peregrine had stationed himself unobtrusively just outside the door but in full view, and McLeod was glowering near the door, playing the heavy to Adam's more open and friendly manner.

"Why, Mr. McArdle, you've guessed my deep, dark secret," Adam said lightly. "Actually, Inspector McLeod calls me in as a technical consultant in cases involving the occult, and the psychology of people who commit crimes involving the occult. Actually, I deal with suspects and victims far more than witnesses—though I *have* had some success helping witnesses recall more precisely what they've seen. I think that's more along the lines of what he had in mind for you and me."

McArdle unbent slightly. "Then ye dinnae think I'm out o' my heid?"

"Far from it," Adam said. He sat easily in the chair, noting with approval that Kirkpatrick had quietly slipped from the room to leave them alone with the witness. "On the contrary, it sounds like you've had the misfortune to stumble upon something very dangerous—and you can probably remember even more than what you've already told the sergeant. I'd like to help you do that."

As he spoke, he casually slipped a silver pocket watch out of the pocket of his trousers and gave it a cursory glance, releasing it then, so that it swung gently back and forth, seemingly idly, at the length of its chain. As intended, the gamekeeper's gaze was drawn to it. Continuing to let the watch swing, pendulum-fashion, from his fingertips, Adam carried on in a conversational tone, gradually letting his volume drop as his unwitting subject slipped gradually under his influence.

"Now, your experience earlier this evening must have given you quite a shock, Mr. McArdle. It would have shocked anyone. I know you've been up most of the night. Tired as you must be, though, the important thing right now is for you to try to relax."

McArdle's gaze had been tracking the rhythmical swing of the watch at the end of its chain, but now he blinked and drew breath to speak, probably suspicious that he knew why Adam was doing it. Smiling slightly, Adam merely slipped the watch casually back into his pocket, never breaking the flow of the patter that was really accomplishing what was needed.

"So I want you just to take a few deep breaths and lean back against the wall, if you will," Adam went on. "When you breathe out, try to let the breath all the way out." He drew out the word *all*, so that the very cadence of the word helped to underline the instruction.

"That's right. You'll find that the deep breathing will help you to relax. And God knows, you need that, after what you've been through tonight, don't you?"

"Aye," the man whispered.

"Take another deep breath, if you will—that's right—and let it out slowly. . . . Now another. . . . And another. . . . Are you feeling more comfortable now?" McArdle nodded. "Good.

"Now, I want you to cast your mind back to what you saw in the forest. You'll find you can remember everything clearly—but nothing that you remember will cause you distress. It will be like looking at pictures in a book. Tell me about it whenever you feel ready."

The gamekeeper nodded his balding head, his gnarled hands resting loosely in his lap, his breathing easy.

"I suppose Callum told ye that I'm head gamekeeper fer Lord Baltierny," he said quietly.

"He did," Adam replied. "And that you're one of the best around."

"Well, I like to think so." McArdle paused to draw another deep breath. "Anyway, tonight I was walking the north woods on the Baltierny estate, just as I've done for nigh on forty years, when I heard some scuffling off in the distance, an' a hoarse sort o' cry—something between a cough and a croak."

"A deer, perhaps?"

McArdle shook his head. "Never heard a deer sound like that," he said flatly. "Poachers, now—that was my first thought. There's a logging road up behind where the sound came from, but no one's meant to be up there without permission, an' certainly not at that hour."

"About what time do you think that was?" Adam asked.

"Long about eleven, I reckon. I had my rifle with me, so I headed up the hill in the direction of the noise, to see what I could see. It was pretty dark up there, with nae moon an' all, but I'm used to workin' by starlight on nights like that. An' somehow I had the feeling I oughtn't to use my torch. A man as spends as much time in the woods as I do develops pretty good instincts, after so many years—an' I was glad I paid attention tonight."

"Why was that?"

"They would've seen me!" McArdle replied. "Lucky fer me, they had fires goin', so they couldnae see very well in th' dark. But I'm gettin' ahead o' myself. I hadn't yet gotten to the top o' the hill when the chanting started up."

"Chanting?" Adam's tone was merely conversational.

"I dinnae know what else to call it," said the gamekeeper. "It was eerie—sort o' whispery-like. I couldnae make out what they was saying, but the sound of it made the hair stand up on my heid—"

He broke off abruptly, his respiration quickening, his eyes now focused on something only he could see.

"Don't let the memory disturb you," Adam murmured softly, with a glance across at McLeod, who was leaning against the wall and listening avidly. "I think I know the kind of thing you're trying to describe. You're not in any danger now. Just take a deep breath and let out the tension along with the breath."

When the gamekeeper had relaxed a little, Adam said, "Let's see if we can go on now. You heard chanting. It was only natural for you to be afraid. Did you run away?"

McArdle's face stiffened in remembered indignation. "That I did not!—not then, at any rate. Whoever they were, carryin' on like that, they were on His Lordship's property without leave. By then, I was pretty sure they weren't poachers—they'd hae scared away all the game for miles!—but it was my duty to see what they were about."

"So you went to take a closer look?"

"Aye. I made my way to the top o' the hill, quiet as I could. There was firelight showin' through the trees, down in a hollow about a hundred yards below me. I didnae want anyone to spot me—that chanting had scared me plenty—so I kept under cover and edged close enough to take a look through the scope on my rifle. I dinnae ken what I expected to see, but it certainly wasnae the likes o' what was going on.''

Again he stopped short, and Adam glanced briefly at McLeod and Peregrine. The inspector looked grim, the blue eyes dark behind his aviator lenses, and Peregrine's face, above the bulky knit of his Arran sweater, was several shades paler.

''What did you see?'' Adam urged.

McArdle shivered slightly. ''There must've been about a dozen of 'em,'' he muttered, ''all muffled up in long white robes with hoods, almost like they was monks or something. One was standin' in the middle with his arms in the air, an' the rest was marchin' round in a circle—widdershins, ye ken?''

''I know the term. Go on.''

''Well, then they stopped all of a sudden, an' I noticed there was this other mannie, inside the circle by this big, flat rock. He wasnae standing, though; that's why I didnae see him at first. He was crouched down like he was sick or something—only, then I saw his hands was tied behind him. That's when I *really* knew it was somethin' queer goin' on!''

''What happened then?'' Adam said. His voice was almost a whisper.

''The one standin' in the middle went over to the one with his hands tied, an' he kneeled down too. He had somethin' in his hands—maybe a bowl or somethin', I couldnae see—an' he held it out to t'other man. But then one o' t'other men in the circle gave a sort o' howl and rushed forward. I think he coshed the one mannie in the heid. An' then metal flashed—a wee knife o' some kind, I think—an' there was blood spurtin' everywhere!''

McArdle paused to swallow. The sound was startling in the taut silence.

''The man wi' the tied hands kicked an' struggled, but they wouldnae even let him fall over,'' McArdle whispered. ''His— blood just kept pourin' all over the thing that t'other man had in his hands—frae his neck, I think. When they finally let him fall, I—*know* he was dead.''

Adam had not taken his eyes from his subject for some time now.

''What did you do then?'' he said in a neutral voice.

The gamekeeper's face worked, and he gave his head a shake. ''I—I didnae tell the sergeant before, but it was nae branch breakin' that made me light out o' there. I was outraged at what they'd done, and I wouldhae shot at 'em, if I could. But my rifle jammed when I tried to chamber a round—made a noise like a bloody cannon going off! I didnae stop to see if those geezers in the hoods heard it. I just took to my heels. I didnae stop till I got back to my jeep!''

He was breathing hard by the time he came to the end of his narrative, and Adam leaned across to lay a hand lightly on his shoulder.

"Steady, Jimmy," he murmured soothingly. "You're in no danger now. Just sit back and catch your breath. Close your eyes, if you want. You deserve a rest. You have nothing more to worry about just now."

The gamekeeper subsided, even when Adam took his hand away, but his expression still was troubled.

"They killed that man right before my eyes," he mumbled. "I should hae done something sooner—"

"There was nothing you could have done," Adam said firmly. "I want you to remember that, and believe it. By the time you realized what was happening, the deed was done. You did well to get away and inform the police."

"But they didnae believe me—"

"They believed you enough to send for Inspector McLeod and me," Adam replied firmly. "As I told you before, it was a case of not *wanting* to believe that such a thing could happen here in Blairgowrie. It was nothing to do with you, personally. And no one blames you for what happened."

Seeing that his assertion had had the desired calming effect, Adam shifted back to his earlier line of questioning.

"Now. Can you remember where you saw this killing take place?" he asked.

McArdle nodded.

"Do you think you could lead us there?"

"Aye." The man's voice carried the strong ring of confidence.

"Good," said Adam. "Then that's just what we'll do, as soon as it comes light. You'll lead us to the hill you spoke of, and we'll see what we can find. Until then," he continued, "I'd like you to close your eyes and try to get some rest." He reinforced the suggestion with one firm hand on McArdle's shoulder, the other one passing lightly over eyes already closing in relieved response.

"Lie back and go to sleep," he said, easing him back, with McLeod's help, to lie placidly on the bunk. "Relax and sleep deep, with no disturbing dreams, and awake when I call you by name, feeling rested and refreshed.''

A moment longer his hand remained over the reclining man's eyes, making sure his subject was truly and deeply asleep. Then he straightened and glanced up at McLeod, motioning for him to step outside the cell with Peregrine.

''Well, I'm afraid I'm convinced,'' he said quietly.

McLeod nodded grimly. ''So am I.''

''But, how can you be sure he didn't make it up?'' Peregrine asked, hushed.

Adam raised a patient eyebrow. ''For one thing, the man's no occultist. He wouldn't have had the knowledge necessary to invent a story like that, even assuming he had the inclination to do so. As it is, you saw how agitated he became, when he was describing the murder itself. It was almost enough to snap him out of trance.

''And I have no doubt that he was in a trance, and that he was telling the truth—at least as he perceived it. He even told us about wanting to shoot the perpetrators, and being stopped because the rifle jammed—which it sounds like he didn't even tell Kirkpatrick.''

''But, a human sacrifice, Adam—'' Peregrine's face was pale. ''If that really is what he saw, what does it mean?''

''It means, laddie, that someone or other has set some very dangerous plans in motion,'' McLeod said darkly. ''And we'd better do our level best to find out who they are and what their objectives may be, before any of us gets much older.''

He stole another glance at the snoring McArdle and shook his head. ''I suppose I'd better pass the word to Kirkpatrick. Wherever this investigation may lead before we're through, it begins here in Kirkpatrick's jurisdiction, and he'd better be the one to organize the official expedition of inquiry.''

# CHAPTER EIGHT

SOME of Scotland's prime ski areas lie north of Blairgowrie—the Spittal of Glenshee, then Devil's Elbow, halfway to Braemar, famous for its summer Highland games—but the two vehicles that left from Blairgowrie Police Station shortly after 7 A.M. would not be going that far. Kirkpatrick led the way in the white police Land Rover, with Jimmy McArdle directing from the passenger seat and two additional police officers sitting in the back, hand-picked by Kirkpatrick from the ranks of the men on the morning shift. Adam's blue Range Rover followed close behind, his two passengers silent in the pre-dawn darkness, each alone with his own thoughts.

This early, the snowy landscape north of Blairgowrie was patched with heavy pockets of ground fog. With luck, they would be heading off-road just about at first light. It was heavy going now, though, and Adam had to concentrate all his attention on the road ahead. For the first fifteen miles of the drive to Baltierny, there were moments when he completely lost sight of Kirkpatrick's Land Rover, forging out in front of them like a hound leading the hunt.

The simile had an ominous ring, to Adam's way of thinking. They had not yet identified their quarry, but after hearing the gamekeeper's story firsthand, he did not doubt that they were on the trail of something dark and deadly. He did not want to let himself jump to the premature assumption that the Lodge of the Lynx was behind it, but the possibility was not illogical, given recent evidence of a Lynx resurgence. Or perhaps he was becoming paranoid.

"I hope this bloody fog lifts before we get where we're going," McLeod grumbled, craning forward to keep track of the twin red taillights bobbing along ahead of them. "If it doesn't, I'll be surprised if McArdle can even find the Baltierny turn-off—let alone a body in the woods."

But by the time they reached the junction with a "B" road and turned right, the mists had begun to lift, showing fugitive glimpses of clear sky overhead. The road offered a dismal ribbon of soft grey slush—happily, free of ice—but the evergreens flanking it carried heavy festoons of white, and snow still covered the ground on the open spaces and drifted deep in the hollows.

The "B" road was a single lane, with turn-outs every quarter mile, but they carried on without meeting anyone for another seven or eight miles until they came to an unpaved track branching off into the woods on their left. A hundred yards or so beyond, both vehicles pulled up before a chain-link gate set between the end-posts of a barbed wire fence, with a mud-clogged cattle-grid set into the ground before it.

The gate was secured by a padlocked length of heavy chain. Hunched deep in the warmth of his parka and blowing on his fingers to keep them warm, McArdle scrambled out of the police Land Rover to open the padlock with a key from the ring on his belt. He hauled the gate aside to let the two vehicles through, then made a move to secure it again, but McLeod stuck his head out the window as they passed through.

"Better just leave it, Mr. McArdle. If we have to call for additional personnel, I want the way left open so they can get in."

McArdle scowled slightly, but did as he was told. Once he was back in the Land Rover, the two parties set off again. The forest track was narrow and winding, little more than an ongoing pair of muddy ruts cutting through the trees, though the base was solid. They went past several opportunities to turn off, proceeding for nearly two miles before the police vehicle slowed and then pulled to the right into a muddy turn-out just about long enough for two cars. High ground rose to either side, and as Adam pulled in close behind the police Rover, he caught sight of a footpath snaking off up the slope to their right, little more than a game trail.

The two vehicles disgorged their occupants, who spent the next five minutes pulling on snow boots and donning heavy coats and hats and gloves. As they gathered at the foot of the path, Peregrine noticed that one of the constables had a camera slung over one shoulder, and all three of the Blairgowrie officers were packing pistols.

McLeod had armed himself as well. Peregrine had watched him pull the familiar Browning Hi-Power out of the zipper bag behind the seat, slap a magazine into the butt, and tuck the weapon into the waistband of his trousers before zipping up his black anorak. Adam, he guessed, carried more esoteric protection inside his sheepskin coat. Peregrine himself was armed with his sketchbox.

"You're quite sure this is the place, Jimmy?" Kirkpatrick said.

The gamekeeper bristled slightly. "Just you remember that I've been patrolling these woods for more years than you've been alive, Callum Kirkpatrick!" he said. "It's the right place, just you wait an' see. The dell I told you about is round the back o' this rise. Just follow me, and watch yer step."

The lower levels of the path were wet and slushy. All around them, the woods were sibilant with the moist drip and trickle of melting snow. The sound rasped at Peregrine's nerves as he struggled after Adam and McLeod up the miry trail, with his sketchbox banging against his side. A cold knot of dread began tightening somewhere in the center of his chest, but he forced himself to press on in tight-lipped silence.

Had he known it, his feelings of foreboding were shared in full measure by Adam. That inner tension continued to grow with every step. This was by no means the first time that he and McLeod had been obliged to confront the aftermath of a death by violence, but rarely had he experienced so sharp a premonition that this crime was to prove personally significant.

As the party advanced over the crest of the hill, the sun broke through the wintry haze of lifting fog. Below them, on the north face of the hill, stood a rough circle of oak trees, their leafless branches creaking stiffly in the lightly moving air, and in the center—

McLeod stopped short in his tracks with a muttered imprecation. Kirkpatrick swore softly under his breath. Adam went very still. In the middle of the circle of trees, sprawled face-down on a bier of melting snow, lay the limp, greyish figure of a man. Even at this distance, a dark stain of red could be seen surrounding the upper half of the body.

"All right, Sergeant," McLeod said quietly, when he had drawn a deep breath. "This is your jurisdiction, so you call the shots, but I do believe we're going to need a Serious Crime Team."

"Aye. That, and an ambulance," Kirkpatrick agreed soberly. "Mr. Heriot!"

"Sir?" The constable with the camera moved a step closer.

"Leave the camera with me, then get back to the car and radio back to base," said Kirkpatrick. "Tell 'em what we've found, tell 'em what we need, and get somebody to ring Perth for a police pathologist and the other necessary personnel."

"Aye, sir."

Heriot handed over the camera, then withdrew smartly. McLeod watched him go with some misgivings.

"Pity there isn't any way to scramble the call," he remarked, "but I suppose the nearest telephone is—what, an hour or so away?"

At Kirkpatrick's confirming nod, McLeod sighed.

"Well, it can't be helped, I suppose. Still, we'll be lucky if we don't have half the press in Scotland down on us by noon. Before that happens, however, I suggest we go in carefully and take a closer look, get some preliminary photos, just in case there are any clues that will be lost as the snow melts."

"Right, Inspector. Mr. Jamison?" Kirkpatrick glanced at the other waiting constable. "I'll ask you to work your way around the clearing to the left. Watch for footprints, and keep clear if you find any. Also, McArdle said there's a logging road on the other side of the hill—which may be how the perpetrators got in and out, since they didn't come through that locked gate. See what you can find *there*, especially tire tracks."

The young constable nodded and headed off in the direction his superior had indicated, and Kirkpatrick turned back to his Edinburgh counterpart.

"Anything else you can think of, Inspector?" he asked.

McLeod shook his head. "Let's have a closer look."

At Kirkpatrick's gesture of invitation, McLeod carefully moved out across the untrampled ground toward the edge of the trees. Kirkpatrick followed, taking pains to tread in McLeod's footprints, and Adam followed directly behind him. Peregrine shadowed Adam, himself shadowed by McArdle, reluctant to go any closer yet drawn by something he could not name. Even from the edge of the clearing, the scene was as disturbing as Adam had warned him it might be.

The dead man was lying face-down, his white-clad body resting partway on a smooth, flat rock that was iced over with spilt blood. He appeared to be naked under the thin, blood-stained white robe he wore. His feet and legs showed bare below the robe's mud-bedraggled hem, and his hands had been bound tightly behind his back with a fine crimson cord. His head was very bloody, the grey hair matted stiff over an ominous depression in the back of the skull.

"I *told* 'em, so I did," McArdle muttered hoarsely to Peregrine. "They thought I was making it up—as if anybody would make up something like this!"

Peregrine wasn't listening. They had reached the ring of ancient oaks now, Sergeant Kirkpatrick snapping an occasional photograph, and as Peregrine gazed down at the fading circle in the snow, traced out with dirty-grey remnants of ash, a black sense of violence struck out at him with the sudden, unforeseen force of a physical blow.

All at once he found himself breathing in the charnel stench of spilt blood, mixed with the sickly sweet reek of incense that somehow was not quite—right. In the same instant, he caught a residual backlash of terror, resonating outward from the dead presence of the victim.

Suddenly the clearing was full of ghosts—a gathering of semi-transparent images superimposed over the solid forms of McLeod and Kirkpatrick. Transfixed with horror, Peregrine counted a baker's dozen of robed figures treading their death march in the snow around the fallen figure in their midst. And as he looked on, knowledge of the dead man's identity struck him like a fist in the pit of his stomach.

The revelation was so abrupt and so painful that he gasped aloud and staggered backwards, clutching blindly at the nearest branch to keep from falling. Alerted by the gasp, Adam glanced back to see the young artist staggering against the trunk of one of the palisade oaks, his face nearly as white as the snow, his hazel eyes dilated behind his glasses.

Adam made a brisk lunge to his side and caught him before he could fall.

"Steady on, I've got you," he said in a low voice, gripping the younger man's shoulders with strong hands and searching his eyes. "I can see that it isn't just the blood. Take a deep breath and relax, and tell me what you're seeing. Mr. McArdle, can you give him a little privacy, please?"

As McArdle moved off, murmuring uneasily under his breath, Peregrine gulped air and shut his eyes tight, trying to obey. For a moment he neither moved nor spoke. Then he managed a deep breath and exhaled with a shudder, making a visible effort to pull himself together.

"I'm sorry, Adam," he muttered in a constricted undervoice. "I've just realized who it is, lying dead there in the clearing. It's your friend—the old fellow from the bookshop."

"*Randall*?" Adam mouthed the name more than he said it, his senses reeling at the disclosure. He shot a swift, involuntary glance over his shoulder, at the unwitting McLeod still approaching the frozen body, then felt the young artist sway slightly against the strength of his support.

"Easy!" he murmured, returning his attention to Peregrine. "You aren't going to faint on me, are you?"

Peregrine gave a negative shake of the head and drew himself up. "Don't worry about me," he said thickly. "I'll be all right in a few seconds." He gave Adam a queasy look and added, "I could be wrong, Adam. I hope so."

Adam made himself draw a careful breath and let it out. Unfortunately, he had no doubt that Peregrine was telling the truth.

"I know you do," he said softly, "but you can't help what you see. Whatever has happened, the blames belongs to those who committed the crime. Now wait here. I'd better warn Noel."

Peregrine's face was still blanched with shock, but he managed a careful nod. Steeling himself, Adam released him and moved off to overtake McLeod and Kirkpatrick down in the hollow. The two policemen were crouching on either side of the body, McLeod on the left and Kirkpatrick on the right, heads bent intently as they made note of the obvious wounds and the sergeant took more photos. From McLeod's air of professional detachment, Adam could tell that he had not yet recognized the dead man.

As Adam drew nearer, he could see for himself the bloody abrasions on the back of the head, indicating that the dead man had been struck more than once from behind. The sheer volume of blood, however, was owing to a deep gash in the jugular area below the right ear.

Wordlessly Adam knelt across from McLeod, checking the body for vital signs, as a matter of formal medical convention. He shifted his weight, then carefully lifted and turned the head just enough to get a clear view of the dead man's profile.

A single fleeting glance was enough to confirm the truth of Peregrine's visionary revelation. Adam closed his eyes for a brief instant, forcing a host of hard questions to the back of his mind as he braced himself to deliver the necessary pronouncement.

"Dear God, I know this man," he murmured, choosing his words for Kirkpatrick's benefit, as well as to prepare McLeod. "So do you, Noel."

He reinforced the warning with a look. McLeod's blue gaze sharpened in surprised acknowledgment. He leaned forward, peering down at the half-averted face cradled between Adam's supporting hands, then sat back on his haunches with a heavy jolt.

"Jesus," he croaked. "It's Randall!"

Kirkpatrick's mouth opened as if to speak, but then he took a look at McLeod's face and abruptly subsided. Gently Adam lowered Randall's head to the ground and gingerly reached inside the breast of his coat for a handkerchief to wipe the traces of blood from his fingertips. After a moment's stunned silence, McLeod picked himself jerkily up off the ground and eased himself back onto the edge of the flat stone, pulling off his glasses with one hand and knuckling his forehead in grey-faced bewilderment.

"Sorry," he muttered gruffly. "Just give me a minute to catch my breath."

Adam clasped him briefly by the shoulder, then rose and beckoned to Kirkpatrick to join him a few feet away.

"I suppose one of us had better give you a formal identification," he said bleakly, leaving McLeod to his grief for a few minutes. "The victim's name is Randall Stewart. He is—was—an antiquarian bookseller in Edinburgh."

"Edinburgh?" said Kirkpatrick. "Christ, what's he doing up here?"

"I don't know," Adam said flatly, "though I can't imagine it was his choice." His voice sounded leaden in his own ears. "Randall was a widower. There's one daughter. Her name's Miranda. They lived together in a house in Mayfield. . . ."

Shaking his head, Kirkpatrick somberly noted down the information Adam dictated concerning Randall Stewart's full name, address, occupation, and family. He stared down at his notebook for a moment, blowing on stiff fingers to warm them, then gave a small exclamation of discovery and glanced back at the body.

"Randall Stewart—I've just been thinking the name sounded familiar. He was a Masonic historian, wasn't he?"

"That's correct," Adam replied. "He'd been doing a series of articles on the Craft lately, for several different newspapers. You might have seen a rather controversial letter of his recently, in the *Times*. He'd made it a crusade to defend Freemasonry as an institution—"

His voice broke off abruptly.

"You're not thinking that he might have been murdered on account of his Masonic writings?" Kirkpatrick said.

"Frankly, I don't know what to think at this stage," Adam replied. "In his personal life, Randall Stewart was quiet and scholarly—not the sort of man who generally makes enemies. But he was also a man of principle. It isn't inconceivable that he might have drawn hostile attention to himself through his writing."

"Aye," Kirkpatrick agreed, "but it does seem drastic." He cocked his head at Adam. "I don't suppose you're one of his Lodge brothers, are you, Dr. Sinclair?—or Inspector McLeod's?"

Adam managed a dour smile, for he did share a Lodge with both McLeod and Randall, though not a Masonic one.

"No, I'm not a member of the Craft, Sergeant, though I

certainly honor and respect it. My father and grandfather both were Master Masons.''

"Ah, well then, you're at least aware that controversies have always surrounded our Brotherhood. Unfortunately, we've had a few notable scandals in recent years—accusations of corruption and the like. But that's the dirty work of a few isolated individuals. It has nothing to do with the real intentions of the whole organization.''

"Which is precisely the point that Randall was trying to make with his articles and his letters to the papers,'' Adam said. He sighed. "All organizations, including the organized churches, are human institutions, even if inspired by God. And so long as humans form and run them, some few will be tempted to misuse the privileges of selective membership.''

A stir of movement from the opposite side of the clearing signalled the return of Constable Jamison from his reconnaissance tour of the area.

"I couldnae find anything of use, Sergeant,'' he called down from the edge of the trees. "There *is* a road down yonder, but it's worse'n a pig's mud-wallow, an' the snow's meltin' everything down tae mush. Cars were down there, all right, but there's naught of a clear tire tread or footprint.''

Kirkpatrick rolled his eyes in gloomy resignation.

"All right, then,'' he called back to his young subordinate. "Go on back tae the car an' get yourself thawed out—an' send up Mr. Heriot to relieve me. We'll stand by in shifts, until the SCI lads get here.''

He waved the younger man on with a sweep of his hand, then turned back to Adam, flexing his shoulders as if to shrug off the damp chill of their surroundings. McLeod was on his feet again, and looking somewhat recovered.

"You gentlemen might as well head back too,'' Kirkpatrick said. "It'll be several hours before reinforcements can get here. Take McArdle and your Mr. Lovat with you. We've got coffee in the Land Rover. Have Mr. Jamison give you some. I'll join you in a few minutes.''

The comment was directed mainly at McLeod. The inspector roused himself with an effort, looking every one of his fifty-two years.

"That reminds me of something else that needs doing,'' he said grimly. "Where *is* Mr. Lovat?''

"Right here!'' called a light voice.

They turned to see Peregrine still standing beside one of the encircling oak trees, but with sketch pad and pencil already in his hands. McArdle was watching curiously from several feet away. The young artist still looked more than a little white about the mouth, but his expression was one of dogged resolution—and exasperation that the gamekeeper was hovering so close.

"I figured you'd want my services eventually," he said, with a fair show of bravado, "so I thought I'd get a start before my hands got too numb to draw. I'll need another fifteen or twenty minutes, but you needn't wait on my account."

"You're sure?" Adam asked.

Peregrine shrugged and returned to his sketching, though Adam noticed that he still shied away from looking too directly at Randall Stewart's body.

"Yes, go on. The sergeant will be here for a while, and then PC Heriot. I'll be along when I've finished."

# CHAPTER NINE

MCARDLE forged on ahead alone, glad enough to be quit of the spectacle in the ring of oaks now that he was vindicated, and no doubt eager to regain the relative warmth of a car. Adam and a still shattered McLeod followed more slowly, Adam casting a last, thoughtful glance back at Peregrine before they topped the rise of the hilltop and started down, losing the artist from further view.

That Peregrine had already begun his sketching, obviously intending to open himself voluntarily to the visions that had nearly floored him when he first came upon the scene, was the one heartening event in a morning blighted by tragedy. Badly as Adam wanted the information Peregrine might be able to supply, he had not been prepared to ask that of him. Peregrine's earlier impressions had been devastating, far more powerful and overwhelming than anything he had yet experienced since coming under Adam's tutelage; and past experience had shown that the young artist would not willingly refuse anything that he thought Adam might require.

But apparently Peregrine had already decided to bear the strain of any further psychic recall, and felt confident enough to brave it alone. It spoke much of his personal courage, as well as his growing commitment to the cause Adam and his colleagues served. From that, at least, Adam took comfort.

In the meantime, with McArdle ranging farther and farther ahead, circumstances at last permitted a few words in private with McLeod. Weighing up all the questions that were clamoring in his own mind, Adam gave the inspector a sidelong glance. McLeod caught his look and scowled, his brow as black as a thundercloud.

"Even in my darkest dreams, I never would have imagined this," he muttered, "that one of our own Hunting Lodge should have been butchered like a sheep, and none of us any the wiser until it was all over!"

He set his teeth almost savagely in his lower lip and shook his head. "It's true I was uneasy all yesterday evening—but I never once suspected the cause. Not even when Kirkpatrick phoned."

"That's no fault of yours," Adam said. "Christopher and Victoria were with me up at the house, and none of us had any intimations of trouble."

"That's what I don't understand," McLeod said. "Randall was one of us—a trained occultist. He had the resources to put out an astral distress call. Why didn't he?"

"I suspect he was heavily drugged," Adam said. "That would have prevented it. His murderers probably would have kept him unconscious as long as it was practical to do so. From the gamekeeper's testimony and the physical evidence, it's clear that Randall's death was intended as a ritual sacrifice. That being the case, the killers wouldn't have taken any chances that something might go awry."

"The bloody *bastards*!" McLeod spat out the word as if it tasted of bile. When he turned to Adam, his blue eyes were smouldering.

"Who the hell were they, Adam? Even if Randall was too drugged to cry for help, a killing like that should have generated some shock waves of its own. Why didn't we sense *that*?"

"I don't know," Adam said bleakly. "It's possible that the killers themselves were unskilled personnel, simply acting out a prescribed sequence of motions without actually raising any power. It's equally possible that they knew *precisely* what they were doing, and were competent enough to shield their work while it was in progress. We can't know at this point. There simply isn't enough evidence to go on."

"But why *Randall*?" McLeod persisted.

"That's what I've been asking myself ever since we found him," Adam said grimly. "So far, I haven't found a satisfactory answer. But this much I'm sure of: Randall was *not* chosen at random. On the contrary, he was carefully selected by someone who went to a lot of trouble to lure him away from the protection of his family and friends."

"Lure him away?" McLeod stopped and stared. "Are you saying you have a theory about all this?"

"A theory, yes," Adam said, "though it's only now occurred to me. I was with Randall on Saturday—I'd taken Peregrine round so that Randall could meet him. Just before we left, Randall mentioned that he was planning to go across to Stirling on the Sunday to do an estate appraisal on a collection of rare books.

Now it makes me wonder if the whole thing could have been the setup for a kidnapping.''

"Well, at least that's *some* kind of lead,'' McLeod said bitterly. "We certainly haven't got a bloody lot else to go on. I'll put a couple of my men on it as soon as I get back to Edinburgh. God knows poor Randall wasn't much for keeping written records, though,'' he added with a dour shake of his head. "But maybe Miranda will remember the name and the address of the supposed collector—assuming that the shock of this whole sorry affair doesn't prove too much for her.''

"Which reminds me that someone ought to go to her, before she hears the news from strangers,'' Adam said. "Christopher or Victoria would be ideal, if I can reach them. I don't suppose you brought along that rather handy cellular phone?''

"Aye. But the Houstons might not be able to get there in time, if they have to drive down from Kinross,'' McLeod said. "Let me send Jane. I've got to call her anyway. Once she hears what's happened, she'll know what to do.''

Constable Heriot passed them just before they arrived back at the cars, heading back up to the crime scene, and they found Jamison huddled in the driver's seat of the Land Rover, talking earnestly to someone over the radio and making notes. McArdle was sitting in the back seat nursing a Styrofoam cup of coffee, looking tired and morose.

"You go ahead and make your call,'' Adam murmured, waving McLeod on toward their own vehicle. "I'll see if I can get us some coffee. We drank all yours on the way up.''

McLeod gave a grunt and continued on to the car, simply collapsing onto the passenger seat for nearly a full minute before bestirring himself enough to pull the portable phone from his zipper bag behind the seat. Jane answered almost immediately, but he kept his conversation brief and purposefully vague; times like this made him all too aware that a portable phone did not constitute a secure line.

Jane wept when he told her there had been an accident, and that Randall Stewart was dead, but promised to go immediately to be with Miranda. McLeod, in turn, promised to give her more details when he got home, though he warned her that he might be quite late. If Jane remembered his side of the original conversation with Kirkpatrick, she might put two and two together and guess something of what had happened, but he knew he could trust her not to alarm Miranda needlessly. Best that someone else tell her how her father had died—though he wished desperately that no one had to tell her at all.

Afterwards, suddenly weary almost beyond telling, he revved up the engine so he could run the heater for a few minutes—the Range Rover's leather seats were like ice—then leaned back over the front seat to return the phone and his pistol to the zipper bag. Gradually, by holding his hands directly over two heater vents, he began to regain a little feeling in his fingers—though not in his soul.

After a little while, Adam returned with two steaming Styrofoam cups and the news that the first reinforcements could be expected within the hour. As they sipped at what McLeod declared was the worst coffee he had ever tasted, Kirkpatrick returned, raising a hand to the two of them as he trudged past to his own vehicle, but Peregrine was not with him. When a full half hour had passed since leaving the scene of the murder, with still no sign of Peregrine, both Adam and McLeod began to worry.

"He's been out there a long time," McLeod said, irritation masking his concern as he glanced at his watch. "You don't suppose our young Mr. Lovat has taken on more than he can handle, do you?"

Adam grimaced. "If he isn't back in another five minutes, I'll go and check. I *thought* he was up to it—but maybe not."

Just then, Peregrine himself emerged from the trees at the foot of the path, looking pale and drained, but also triumphant. He was stumbling from fatigue, his sketchbox dragging at his arm as if it were weighted down with bricks, but he waved them back when McLeod's car door opened, slogging doggedly across the remaining snow to wrench open the back door of the Range Rover and practically tumble inside. After slamming the door closed, he hugged the sketchbox to his chest and seemed to collapse back against the seat, closing his eyes briefly.

"I think the first drawings will satisfy any forensic curiosity, Inspector," he said huskily. "Then there are a couple more. . . ."

His voice trailed away, and he seemed about to nod off from exhaustion. After an alarmed glance at McLeod, Adam whipped off one glove and delved inside his sheepskin coat for the small silver flask he usually carried with him on outdoor excursions. He unstoppered it with a deft twist and proffered it to Peregrine with a gesture that brooked no refusal.

"Here. Take a good, stiff swig," he ordered.

Meekly Peregrine accepted the flask and raised it to his lips in

86

shaking hands. The first swallow made him gasp, but it also brought a measure of color back to his white face.

"Now take another," Adam said. "That's right. Feeling any better?"

Peregrine nodded rather breathlessly and handed the flask back to Adam.

"I'll be all right," he said in a little stronger voice. "I've stowed all the sketches away in my box. The ones that are for your eyes only are on the bottom. I wasn't sure whether I'd have to run a gamut of curious policemen. And I thought you'd never get McArdle out of there."

Adam returned the flask to his pocket and reached to take the sketchbox from Peregrine. As the artist sat forward to watch, elbows propped on the backs of both front seats, Adam opened the sketchbox on the console between him and McLeod and lifted out the drawings one by one.

The first few sketches were the proper forensic studies Peregrine had promised, reproducing the murder scene from several angles with the clinical exactitude of photographs. Adam's long mouth tightened as he glanced over them in passing, but when he came to the last two sketches, his dark eyes widened in shock and dismay.

The first of these showed Randall on his knees, pinioned from behind in the midst of several white-robed men whose faces were hidden within deep, cowled hoods. One of them knelt before Randall with head bowed, his back to the sketch's vantage point, holding something out to him that was shielded behind the man's body—probably the bowl or whatever McArdle had seen. More of the white-robed men formed a circle around them, just inside where the ring of ash had delineated the working area, but all the faces except Randall's were heavily obscured as if by a thick black fog, in malevolent contrast to the crisp detail of the rest of the picture.

Such shielding by itself was enough to confirm that Randall's slayers had been accomplished black adepts. But what drew Adam's gaze like a magnet, even more than the look of dawning horror on Randall's face, was the suggestion that each of the robed men wore a medallion around his neck and a ring on his hand—both items trademarks of the Lodge of the Lynx.

Peregrine's remaining drawing confirmed Adam's suspicions, and also brought home the full horror of the killing as even the previous one had not. Peregrine was getting *too* good at this. The look of mortal anguish that he had captured on Randall's face was something Adam hoped never to see or even imagine again.

It was a closer study of Randall and his actual slayer, just before the death-blow, the ringed hand of the latter clenched purposefully about the handle of what proved, on closer scrutiny, to be a surgeon's scalpel, poised beside Randall's right ear. The man's left hand—and others' hands—wrenched the victim's head back brutally to expose the throat. The angle was wrong to see what was on the medallion around the killer's neck, but the ring on his third finger showed the intaglio image of a lynx head.

Beside him, McLeod made a noise at the back of his throat like the warning growl of a bull mastiff.

"So," he managed to mutter. "The Lodge of the Lynx rears its ugly head again. "I suppose this is their idea of revenge for what happened at Urquhart Castle."

"I wonder," Adam said slowly. With difficulty, he forced his gaze away from the look on Randall's face, back to the hand holding the scalpel.

"What's to wonder at?" McLeod's roughened voice held a note of incredulity. "It's their calling card, plain and simple."

"Yes, but revenge can hardly have been the motive," Adam replied, wrenching himself back to a more detached perspective—as if that were possible, after this. "Randall wasn't involved—even indirectly—in any of the events that eventually took the three of us into that confrontation by Loch Ness. Without that association, there's simply no reason why the Lodge of the Lynx should have connected him with us."

"But, our names were in most of the newspaper accounts— mine, at least," McLeod said. "If the Lodge of the Lynx started looking into our backgrounds, someone might well have found out that Randall was a close acquaintance of ours—"

"In which case, it's even more unlikely that they would have murdered him by way of retribution," Adam said sharply. "Think, Noel. If our opposite numbers now know enough about us to guess how and why we came to interfere in their affairs, why should they bother with Randall at all, when *we* are more obvious targets? Besides, if they were merely interested in taking a life for a life, there are far easier and more mundane ways of killing off an adversary than going to the trouble of setting up a ritual murder.

"But they *did* set up a ritual murder—which means that the ritual itself was the important thing. Had they guessed for an instant that Randall was one of us," he concluded, "they never would have touched him, for fear of alerting the rest of us. That makes me believe that they didn't know."

"And Randall—God rest his soul—wasn't about to do anything that would give himself away—or us," McLeod said somberly, "even if it cost him his life."

"Even if he had any choice in the matter," Adam amended. "I'll bet you money, marbles, or chalk that the post mortem will show a high concentration of mind-altering drugs in his system. If the gods were kind, he was never really aware of what was happening to him."

His shudder, as he covered the last sketch with the previous one, suggested that he did not believe that. Peregrine certainly did not. As he, too, shivered, hugging his arms across his chest against a chill that had nothing to do with the cold, Peregrine thought he had all too clear an idea of what had happened to Randall Stewart.

"As for who, specifically, was responsible," Adam went on more strongly, gesturing toward the sketch that now lay on the top, "the fact that Peregrine wasn't able to see anything but blurs for the faces in the circle strongly suggests that there was at least one adept present with powers that might well rival the best we ourselves could muster. Whoever that individual may be, he's sufficiently master of his craft to cloak his work even from the eyes of those who know what to look for."

Assailed by sudden doubt, Peregrine blinked and glanced at the two older men.

"Maybe it was *me*," he whispered bleakly. "Maybe I *didn't* know what to look for."

"Oh, you knew what to look for," Adam said, collecting the rest of the drawings and returning them all to the box. "You couldn't have drawn these last two, if you hadn't known *exactly* what you were about." He tapped the lid of the box for emphasis. "No, we're dealing with professionals here. And I *do not like* their profession!"

This bald statement produced the stunned silence that Adam had intended. Only after several taut seconds did McLeod clear his throat.

"All right. We're somewhat agreed on the generalities of the *who*—and the *how* is all too clear. What I still want to know is *why*? Why Randall?"

Adam sighed and shook his head, gazing out sightlessly at the virgin snow beyond his window, trying not to see Randall's face.

"I wish I could answer that," he said quietly. "If we discount the revenge motive, it follows that he must have been chosen because there was something else about him that made him a suitable victim for—whatever his murderers intended to do. If we only knew more about that intent—beyond the mere performance of a ritual murder or sacrifice—we might be in a position to guess why Randall should have been targeted. As it is—"

When he did not finish his sentence, Peregrine glanced from Adam to McLeod and back again in some uneasiness.

"So, where do we go from here?"

"Dear God, I wish I knew," Adam said, visibly pulling himself back to practicalities. "The fact that the murder weapon was a scalpel might suggest the involvement of someone in the medical profession. But that's all it is—a suggestion. Literally anyone can buy a scalpel. Without any more information to go on, we might as well be looking for the proverbial needle in a field full of haystacks."

Never before had Peregrine heard him so impatient with himself. After another uncomfortable silence, McLeod sighed heavily and folded his arms across his chest.

"Well, I suppose it could be worse," he muttered. "There's still the post mortem to come, and the forensic reports. Any one of those could turn us up a lead."

Adam lifted his head. His dark eyes held a sharp glint that Peregrine was at a loss to interpret. But before the older man could speak, there was a tap at McLeod's window. As he thumbed the electric window control to lower it a crack, PC Jamison bent to speak to him.

"Beg pardon, Inspector, but the SCI team are on their way in," he said. "They've just passed the gate, and advise that they've been picked up and tailed by some media people. Sergeant Kirkpatrick thought you ought tae know, sir."

McLeod drew a deep breath and squared his shoulders with the belligerent air of a wrestler about to grapple with an opponent known to be particularly difficult and prone to dirty tricks.

"Thanks for the warning, Mr. Jamison," he said with a nod. "Tell the sergeant not to worry himself. If he'll deal with the SCI team, I'll see what can be done to hold the press at bay."

When Jamison had sketched him a salute and withdrawn, McLeod grimaced and zipped up his jacket before starting to pull on his gloves.

"Well, time for all of us to start acting like professionals again. This is the sort of case the press love. Kirkpatrick's men will know to keep their mouths shut, but I think I'll have a word with that gamekeeper. The news hounds could have a field day, if they get him talking."

As he got out of the car, slamming the door purposefully, Peregrine took off his glasses and gave the lenses a rub with his handkerchief. He glanced at Adam thoughtfully before putting them on again, trying to assume the professionalism McLeod had called for.

"How long does it usually take to get back the reports Inspector McLeod mentioned?"

Adam shrugged, glancing distractedly in the rearview mirror for sign of the expected police and press.

"Three or four days to a week, depending on how many other cases are awaiting the attention of the police pathologist. We'll do all we can to speed the process, of course, but—ah, here's our reinforcements."

As the first of the police vehicles pulled in close behind them, Peregrine turned to gaze out the back window at them, then returned his attention thoughtfully to Adam, who was pulling on his gloves and preparing to get out of the car.

"Adam, I know this is maybe a bit off the track," he ventured, "but you did mention it last night. We're not that far from Balmoral. Do you think we still ought to go take a look at that tower that got damaged by lightning—once we're finished here?"

Adam sighed and nodded. "Probably we should. But frankly, I don't think any of us is in any fit state to make the extra trip. That errand can be deferred for another few days. Right now, it's more important that I get home. There's Miranda to comfort—possibly in the professional capacity Noel so rightly reminded us of—and there are other people I need to get in touch with—mutual associates who have to be told what's happened."

"Like the Houstons?" Peregrine asked.

"Among others," Adam said grimly. "Even if Randall hadn't been the victim, all of this confirms that the Lodge of the Lynx is definitely on the move again. And if they *have* tumbled to the fact that we're onto them, and knew that Randall was one of us, then it's important for everyone to be on their guard. In either case, I have no doubt we're seeing only the beginning of what may turn out to be a very dangerous affair."

# CHAPTER TEN

IT was mid-afternoon before McLeod judged that they were at last free to leave Baltierny. He and Adam trekked back up to the murder site with Kirkpatrick when the ambulance finally arrived at mid-afternoon to take the body away, but Peregrine elected to remain in the car, having seen as much of mayhem as he thought he could stomach for one day. Up at the site, Adam and McLeod took over from the attendants to bring down the stretcher bearing all that mortally remained of Randall Stewart, zipped in a black plastic body bag.

Back at the ambulance, they gave him into the attendants' keeping. Following standard procedures, the body would be transported to the morgue at the Perth Royal Infirmary, where the post mortem and other forensic examinations would be carried out. Adam judged that it was likely to be at least a week before the body could be released to the family for burial. As the attendants slid the stretcher through the open back doors of the ambulance, he searched his memory for a few private words of farewell, drawing on the imagery of the Gael, so beloved of the man so cruelly slain:

> The compassing of the great God be upon you,
>     Randall, my friend—
>         the peace of God,
>         the peace of Christ,
>         the peace of Spirit.
> May Michael shield you in the shade of his wing,
> to bring you swiftly home to the court of the Chief of Chiefs,
> to shield you home unto the Three of surpassing love. . . .

No one spoke much on the way back to Strathmourne. Adam and McLeod seemed to have withdrawn into private worlds of their own grief, and Peregrine sat huddled in a weary heap in the back seat, conscious of a dispiriting sense of isolation. Not having known Randall Stewart well himself, he could only speculate about what

Adam and McLeod might be thinking as they headed home through the gloom of a dreary November twilight. After a while his own exhaustion got the better of him, and he drifted into uneasy sleep.

He roused some time later, jarred awake as the Range Rover pulled up at what he soon realized was the rear gate to Strathmourne. Adam let him out at the gate lodge with an abruptness that would have seemed almost like a dismissal, had not Peregrine recognized the grieving preoccupation that lay behind the brevity. Painfully conscious of his own inability to help, he watched despondently until the car's taillights had disappeared into the darkness.

His forlorn demeanor was not lost on McLeod, who glanced across appraisingly at Adam as they pulled away.

"I'm not sure he understands as much as you think he does about all of this, Adam," he said quietly. "And if you really do have it in mind to bring him into the Hunt, it isn't going to help to leave him guessing."

"Don't you think I know that?" Adam's normally mellow voice held a harsh note of fatigue. "With Randall gone, we need Peregrine more than ever—and I know this was tough on him today. But explanations are going to have to wait for a better time. Right now, I have more pressing responsibilities to attend to."

"I could stay and lend a hand—if you'd allow yourself the indulgence," McLeod said.

Adam shook his head. "Thank you, but no. You have your work to do as well, and you're going to need your rest if you're to do it effectively. As Master of the Hunt, it's up to me to contact the other members of the Hunting Lodge and acquaint them with the tragedy that has occurred. If I can't offer them answers, at least I must offer them whatever comfort I can. . . ."

Back at the gate lodge, Peregrine paused in its tiny vestibule to shrug himself out of his outer clothes before trudging through to the kitchen. He went through the motions of putting the kettle on to boil, then collapsed in the nearest available chair trying not to think, finally bending to unlace his boots with fingers that trembled with fatigue.

Earlier that day, he had come close to cursing the faculty of vision that had made him the involuntary witness to a brutal murder. A part of him still cringed at the memory of what lay in his sketchbox—left in Adam's car, he suddenly realized, though the morning would be soon enough to retrieve it.

But as disturbing and even sickening as the experience had been, his revulsion had since been tempered by the reflection that his skills still had given them information they might not otherwise have obtained concerning the circumstances of Randall Stewart's death. Looking back over his actions and behavior, he scolded himself mentally for nearly letting his squeamishness get the better of him. He only hoped he hadn't done anything to shake Adam's faith in his commitment—for he realized that, for good or ill, he *was* committed. He just wished that he could think of something constructive to do.

Eventually, too tired to continue trying to puzzle it out, he turned off the kettle without bothering to make tea and collapsed into bed. Most blessedly, he did not dream.

He awoke an hour later than usual the next morning, feeling reasonably well-rested and a little distanced from it all. Shaking off the lingering stiffness of fatigue, he managed to shower, shave, and dress without quite engaging his brain, only really starting to wake up as he ducked out onto the front porch to collect his morning edition of *The Independent*. When he flicked it open, the main headline brought back all the horror of the previous day in a rush, and proclaimed an angle on Randall Stewart's death that had never even occurred to him.

*Satanic Slaying on Scottish Hunting Estate* the front page screamed, in bold black letters a full inch high. And in smaller type, but no less black: *A Masonic Murder?*

Taken completely aback, Peregrine blinked at the lurid headlines, then dropped his eyes to skim hastily over the article below. The accompanying photograph showed only a long shot of the circle of trees, with police lines stretched across the snow and anoraked police officers moving behind it, but the author of the piece had taken ghoulish relish in painting a more lurid verbal picture of the murder scene. The article was rendered even more sensationalist by its dark suggestions that Randall Stewart's death demonstrated a clear connection between Freemasonry and the practice of black magic.

What he read was enough to send Peregrine darting back indoors for his coat and his car keys. His Morris Minor was parked in the garage at the rear of the gate lodge, where he had left it Sunday night, and he backed out swiftly and sent the little car shooting up the drive in a spray of water and gravel. A few minutes later he screeched to a halt at the door to the west wing and bailed out, tucking the offending newspaper under his arm. His agitated tug at the bellpull produced a grave and somewhat surprised looking Humphrey.

"I don't suppose he's expecting me," Peregrine said rather breathlessly, "but do you think I might have a word with Sir Adam?"

Adam was standing at the bay window of the breakfast room

when he heard the sound of footsteps approaching along the corridor outside. The quick, impetuous tread proclaimed his caller's identity at once. Before Peregrine could even knock, Adam turned away from the window and called softly, "Come in, Peregrine."

The doorknob turned with a rattle, and the young artist all but tumbled into the room, brandishing a furled newspaper in one hand.

"Good morning," Adam said drily, a mirthless smile plucking at the corners of his long mouth. "I gather that *The Independent* shares the same, rather fanciful Masonic slant on the Baltierny murder as both *The Times* and *The Scotsman*."

This arid observation brought Peregrine up short. He took a deep breath and nodded mutely, his gaze flickering sideways to the two other newspapers spread out on the dining table amid the Spartan remains of a largely uneaten breakfast.

"I was just about to send Humphrey down to the village to see what the other dailies had to offer," Adam continued, "but it looks as if we can safely concur that all the major journals are in agreement over the motives underlying Randall Stewart's death."

Peregrine found his tongue, his tone indignant.

"Adam, how can they get away with this kind of cheap sensationalism? I mean, just because the Masons choose to practice their rites in private, that's no reason to assume they're dabbling in Satanism. There's no proof whatsoever to support these allegations. It's all a bag of moonshine!!"

"You know that, and so do I," Adam said with a shrug. "But restraint doesn't sell newspapers."

Peregrine scowled and tossed his paper on top of one of Adam's. "Isn't there anything you can do to set the record straight?"

"Not in the short term," Adam replied. "In the long run, I hope we'll be fortunate enough to catch up with the real conspirators behind this."

He kept his tone cool and level, but inside his mind and soul were still in turmoil after the shared pain of the previous long night. Wrenching his thoughts away from the remembrance of it, he took a closer look at Peregrine's pale, intense face and asked, "Have you had anything to eat yet this morning?"

The young artist shook his head.

"In that case," Adam said, sitting down and reaching for the phone, "allow me to have Humphrey bring you up some more toast and a fresh pot of tea. You can be eating while I telephone Noel to see if there've been any further developments since we parted company last night."

For an instant Peregrine was tempted to protest, but Adam was already issuing the necessary instructions to Humphrey. As he shifted to an outside line and set about tracking down McLeod, Peregrine slid into his customary seat opposite Adam and settled back to wait, as an afterthought snagging a slice of toast from the silver rack in the center of the table.

As Adam had hoped, McLeod was in his office at police headquarters. The inspector picked up almost immediately, after leaving Adam on hold for only a few seconds.

"Oh, aye, I've seen the bloody papers," he growled, in response to Adam's inquiry. "If you haven't caught any of the television coverage this morning, it's well nigh as bad—except they're talking about governmental corruption and conspiracy instead of black magic. Which is to say that none of 'em knows anything at all. Not that I'm sure we're that much the wiser, as matters stand at the moment."

"Then there's been no progress?"

"None whatsoever—unless you count going round in circles. To make matters worse, I've bee ordered up to Perth for the day to liaise with their investigators. They've set up a press interview for five o'clock this afternoon. I just hope to God we've turned up something useful by then. Otherwise, the media are going to go on feeding the rumor-mill."

He sighed gustily. "In the meantime, I'm sending a couple of men over to Randall's bookshop to see if they can turn up anything useful there. I wish I thought they'd be likely to find Randall's appointment diary lying around on a countertop somewhere, but I'd be willing to bet Randall had it with him in his car—wherever *that* is just now. We're looking for it, but we'll just have to wait and see."

"Have you had any chance to talk with Miranda yet?" Adam asked.

"No, she's still more or less in shock. Jane brought her home to our house last night, after a couple of jackals from one of the tabloids showed up on the doorstep at Mayfield Terrace. She knew by then that there'd been no accident, that her father'd been murdered—the police came by to make official notification, late in the afternoon—but neither she nor Jane had any of the details. The poor lass was *really* distraught after that, so Jane called in our family physician to give her a sedative. She was still sleeping when I left this morning. I didn't have the heart to wake her."

"So Miranda is still at your house?" Adam asked, mentally applauding McLeod's redoubtable wife.

"Aye. Her aunt's coming down from Aberdeen on the train this afternoon to fetch Miranda away with her till the funeral—

whenever that is. In the meantime, it seemed a good idea to keep her safely out of harm's way. And at least if she's asleep, she can't grieve.''

Adam glanced at his wristwatch. The dial read twenty past eight, a tacit reminder that he himself had had fewer than five hours' sleep since arriving back at Strathmourne the previous evening. As Humphrey entered with fresh tea and toast for Peregrine, Adam flexed his aching shoulders and tried to put his weariness out of mind, for there remained much to be done.

"Very well. I've got rounds at the hospital starting at ten—and I missed them yesterday, so I can't skip today—but once I've finished there, perhaps it would be a good idea for me to drive round to your house and see Miranda myself."

"I know that's going to involve spreading yourself pretty thin," McLeod said frankly, "but I think a visit from you would help more than just about anything, right now."

"Let's consider it settled then," Adam said. "If you speak to Jane before I do, tell her I'll phone before I leave Jordanburn, to let her know I'm on my way."

"Right you are," said McLeod. "Good God, would you believe I've got in-coming calls waiting on two different lines? They're probably all press hounds, too. I'd better ring off, but I'll try to get back to you later this afternoon."

"Right you are. Thanks, Noel."

As the connection went dead, Adam replaced the telephone receiver distractedly and turned back to Peregrine, who had listened wide-eyed to Adam's half of the conversation.

"Well, duty is calling from Edinburgh, I'm afraid," he said with a grimace. "I'm going to have to leave you to your own devices just now, while I get ready to leave."

Hastily Peregrine swallowed his mouthful of toast and washed it down with a swig of tea.

"Would you like me to come with you?" he inquired huskily.

"Not today," Adam said, with the ghostly flicker of a smile. "I seem to recall you're supposed to be working on a portrait of Edinburgh's former provost."

"It could wait—"

"No, it can't," Adam said firmly. "Whatever else happens, I'm still a psychiatrist with patients to attend to, and you're still an artist with commissions to fulfill. Don't worry," he added drily. "When I need you—and I assure you, I shall again, as soon as some of the immediate dust has settled—you'll hear about it soon enough."

This reassurance left Peregrine sufficiently relieved that he was able to settle down and do proper justice to Humphrey's tea and toast, readily accepting the offer of a proper cooked breakfast when the butler came in to inquire, after Adam had headed upstairs to change. As he tucked into a bowl of steaming porridge, rich with honey and cream, the aroma of bacon sizzling in the kitchen reminded him just how long it had been since the stale sandwiches of the afternoon before.

He had wolfed down the porridge and was halfway through a plateful of bacon and scrambled eggs when Adam poked his head in to say good-bye before heading out to his car. The sight of Peregrine devouring his meal with such obvious relish elicited a smile and a "thumbs-up" sign from the Master of Strathmourne, and a further sense of well-being on the part of Peregrine.

As Adam's footsteps receded, Peregrine decided that when he had finished—perhaps another egg and a couple more rashers—he probably *would* be ready to tackle the former Provost of Edinburgh again. Actually, the portrait was going rather well.

Outside, since the Range Rover was still covered in mud from its run to Baltierny, Adam slid behind the wheel of a more dashing member of his stable of motorcars—a sleek, dark blue Jaguar XJS. The roads were slick with rain, but inbound traffic was relatively light. He arrived at the hospital in good time to carry out his routine rounds, covering up his own preoccupation with a proficiency born of long practice. Fortunately, all his regular patients were in stable condition, there were few new admissions, and his covey of student doctors managed to restrain their curiosity about the day before. One of the tabloid correspondents had recognized Adam at the crime scene, and mentioned him by name in the accompanying story.

By a little past noon Adam was finished, free to pass on to the matters that had been standing paramount in his mind all morning. He caught a quick lunch, because he knew he had to eat, put in the promised call to Jane McLeod, then delayed only long enough to sign out before hailing a taxi to drive him out to the McLeod's comfortable house in Ormidale Terrace.

Jane opened the door before he had the chance to knock. With a swift glance after the departing cab, she drew Adam inside and closed the door firmly behind him. The click of the automatic snib-lock sounded loud in the vestibule as Adam bent to give his red-headed hostess a fond kiss on the cheek.

"So, have you been repelling journalists again?" he asked.

"Thank God, no," Jane said, with a militant sparkle in her eyes. "Fortunately they don't seem to have rumbled us so far. But I must confess you gave me a bit of a turn just now, when you arrived in a Black Maria. I was expecting you to be driving one of your own cars.''

Adam paused in the act of shrugging off his topcoat. ''I'm sorry,'' he said. ''I thought it might be as well to keep things inconspicuous. Did you take me for an agent of the press?''

''Something like that,'' said Jane. ''But never mind. Here, let me take that for you and I'll hang it up.''

Together they moved through from the vestibule into the front hall. ''How's Miranda?'' Adam asked.

Jane made a waggling motion with one hand. ''As well as can be expected, I suppose. I got her to eat some soup a little while ago, but she's still awfully shaky. It didn't help,'' she added with a grimace, ''that she got up and wandered downstairs around mid-morning. I didn't hear her until she'd already gone through into the sitting room, and by then it was too late. Noel had thrown away today's newspaper before he left for work, but I hadn't had a chance to empty the bin.''

''So she at least saw the headlines,'' Adam said grimly.

''I know we couldn't have kept it from her indefinitely,'' Jane said with a sigh, ''but I would have liked the chance to prepare her a little. Now that you're here, perhaps you'll be able to ease her mind.''

''I shall certainly try to do that,'' Adam replied. ''Where is she just now?''

''Upstairs in the spare bedroom,'' Jane said. ''Come along and I'll show you in.''

Miranda Stewart was sitting up in a big, old-fashioned brass bed, the lacy coverlet pulled up under her chin. She started slightly at Adam's entrance, then relaxed when she saw who it was. With her white face and big, dark-shadowed eyes, she looked more like a chilled linnet than Peregrine's gypsy dancer. Adam sat down in the bedside chair and took her small nervous hands in his own strong, sure clasp.

''Hello, Miranda,'' he said gently. ''I can't tell you how sorry I am about your father. He will be sorely missed. He was as good and upright a man as it has ever been my privilege to know.''

Miranda's pale face twitched slightly. ''That's not what the papers are saying.''

''No,'' Adam agreed steadily. ''But what the papers say is an irrelevance to anyone who knew your father personally. Don't do yourself any further injury by dwelling on slanders written in ignorance. Reflect instead on the assurance that, where your father's life and reputation are concerned, there are at least as many other people out there committed to restoring the balance of truth.''

"But none of this makes any sense at all," Miranda said in a small, tight voice. "Why would anyone go to such lengths to kill my father, when he never knowingly hurt anyone in his entire life?''

"At this point we can only guess," Adam said, "but that situation is bound to change, as the evidence accumulates. At the moment, the police would like to find out as much as possible about the circumstances surrounding your father's trip to Stirling. Can you remember if he mentioned the name of the person who contacted him about doing the appraisal in the first place?''

Miranda sighed and shook her head. "I don't think he ever said. But—''

"But what?" Adam prompted.

"I—*think*," Miranda said uncertainly, "that it was someone he'd met before.''

"A friend, you mean?" Adam cocked his head to one side.

"No-o-o." Miranda frowned as she thought. "Just an acquaintance," she decided, though she still sounded somewhat unsure.

"What makes you say that?" Adam asked quietly.

"The way Papa spoke on the telephone." Encouraged by Adam's attentive silence, she went on. "We were together in the shop on Thursday afternoon. About an hour before closing time, the telephone rang. I was up on the ladder doing some stock-taking, so Papa answered it. After he'd identified himself, he said, *Oh yes, of course I remember*.''

Her brow furrowed as she tried to recapture the exact words. "Then he said, *Indeed, it was—a very good conference*—or something very like that. I remember thinking that it had to be one of Papa's business colleagues on the line. I just wish now that I'd bothered to ask him who it was—''

As her voice quavered and broke, and tears welled in the dark eyes, Adam pressed her hand in comfort and gave her an encouraging smile.

"You have no reason to blame yourself," he said firmly. "On the contrary, this is a very valuable piece of information you've just given me.''

"It is?''

"Indeed," Adam said. "Don't you see how it gives the police a solid lead to investigate? Inspector McLeod is going to be very proud of you. . . .''

Adam left Miranda in a considerably brighter frame of mind than he had found her. Downstairs in the sitting room, he found Jane serving tea to a slender, sweet-faced woman whose resemblance to Randall Stewart was so marked that Adam knew at once she must be Miranda's aunt, even before Jane performed the necessary introductions.

Miriam MacLellan accepted his condolences with stoical composure and expressed a touching gratitude for his concern over her niece. After offering his professional recommendations over Miranda's future peace of mind, Adam asked Jane to call him a taxi, satisfied that Randall's daughter would be in good hands. Jane accompanied him to the door when the taxi arrived.

"Thank you again for coming," she said in a low voice.

"It was my pleasure," Adam said. "Incidentally, when do you next expect to hear from Noel?"

"I wish I knew," she said bleakly. "I doubt he'll be home much before midnight." Then she took a second look at Adam's face and her eyes widened. "Have you some news for him, then?"

Adam managed a thin smile. "Miranda believes that her father was called out to Stirling by someone connected professionally with the booksellers trade. If Noel should happen to call, tell him it might be worthwhile getting one of his men to go through the telephone directory and compile a list of antiquarian book dealers in the area. . . ."

The taxi deposited Adam in the car park of Jordanburn Hospital, where he retrieved the Jaguar and headed wearily for home. The frosty November twilight had closed in as he guided the powerful machine up the final approach to Strathmourne. He put the Jaguar safely into its garage, then walked briskly around to the front door and let himself in. His butler arrived to greet him just as he was divesting himself of topcoat and scarf.

"Hullo, Humphrey," Adam said. "Have there been any messages?"

"Just one, sir," Humphrey said, reaching out to relieve Adam of the coat. "Your mother telephoned around half past three to confirm that she'll be arriving in London next Tuesday as planned, but on a different flight. The new flight number is British Airways 311, and the new ETA is 9:14 A.M."

"Oh, right. Very good," Adam said, automatically making a mental note of the changes. "Was there anything else?"

"Yes, sir," Humphrey went on. "Lady Sinclair instructed me to tell you that she fully expects this to be a *working visit*."

Humphrey's careful emphasis on the last two words told Adam that his trusted butler was repeating the message, tone for tone, exactly as it had been imparted to him—which perhaps meant that Philippa Sinclair was already aware that there was trouble afoot.

That his mother should be forewarned came as no surprise to Adam. He had inherited far more from her than their shared blood kinship. For Philippa's talents, like Adam's own, were exceptional, both professionally and esoterically. Herself an initiate in the higher Mysteries, it was she who had guided her son toward the spiritual awakening that had roused the sleeping powers of his mind and soul. At seventy-five, she had largely retired from active esoteric work—though she still maintained a thriving psychiatric practice in her native New Hampshire—but should the Hunting Lodge now come under direct threat, Adam knew that his mother's presence would add weight to their defenses. At the same time, however, he had no illusions concerning the possible risks.

And right now their worst liability was ignorance. Even as he responded to Humphrey's inquiries concerning tea, his mind continued to be preoccupied with the many questions surrounding Randall Stewart's death. His lack of knowledge made him feel like a falcon hooded and caged. Somewhere out of his sight, his lawful prey was running free—and he and his were thus far powerless to join in the hunt.

The mellow peal of a clock chime broke in upon his thoughts— the grandfather clock in the upstairs landing, striking the half hour. A glance at the pocket watch in his waistcoat confirmed the time as half past five.

"On second thought, Humphrey, I'll have that tea in the front parlor," he said, catching the butler just on the verge of returning to the kitchen. "I want to catch the Scottish news at 5:45."

Randall's murder was the lead item mentioned in the headline summary at the start of the program. Sitting forward, Adam forgot all about the cup of tea at his elbow.

"Investigation continues today into the death of Edinburgh Freemason Randall Stewart," the on-screen presenter announced soberly. "Stewart, whose battered body was recovered yesterday from a forested hill on the Baltierny estate, north of Blairgowrie, is believed to have been the victim of a bizarre ritual slaying. The murder was discovered by a local gamekeeper while making his routine rounds on Sunday night. So far the incident has been accompanied by wide speculation, but the police have yet to come forward with any theories regarding the possible identity of the killers or their motive. We take you now to Perth, where our correspondent, George Gourlay, has been covering the first official press briefing on the murder."

The scene switched from the BBC newsroom to the front entrance of the Perthshire police station. A grim looking McLeod, flanked by two uniformed officers, was standing on the rain-slick steps surrounded by journalists.

"No, I cannot comment further on the actual cause of death," he told his questioners patiently. "We expect the usual forensic reports and results of the post mortem in a few days. Until those reports come in, I will not be in a position to make an official statement."

A sleek young man pressed forward with the officious air of one determined not to be put off, shoving a microphone in McLeod's face.

"Inspector McLeod, I believe you've come up from Edinburgh, haven't you?" the young man said. "Yet the murder took place in Perthshire's jurisdiction—quite far north, in fact. How did you come to be involved in this case?"

McLeod's air of weary patience became slightly wary, as if he sensed a hidden trap.

"At the time the initial complaint was lodged, Sergeant Callum Kirkpatrick of Blairgowrie called me in to assist with the investigation."

"Any ideas as to why he called you, rather than notifying a superior officer from Perth?"

"The case was presented as a possible ritual murder," McLeod said shortly. "Sergeant Kirkpatrick was aware that I had had experience dealing with similar cases on behalf of the Lothian and Borders Police."

"So you and Sergeant Kirkpatrick were acquainted with one another prior to this incident?" The sleek young man seemed to be enjoying himself. "In fact," he added, ostentatiously consulting the notes on his clipboard, "isn't it true that you and he—in common with Randall Stewart—are members of the fraternal order of Freemasons?"

*So that's where this line of inquiry is heading!* thought Adam.

"I fail to see what possible bearing—"

"Please answer the question, Inspector. It's a matter of public record, isn't it? Are you and Sergeant Kirkpatrick and the victim all brother Freemasons?"

"Yes, we are," McLeod agreed through gritted teeth—and waited for the inescapable *coup de grace*, which was not long in coming.

"I find this very interesting, Inspector," said the young man, twirling his pen. "One Masonic policeman goes outside his jurisdiction to call in another Masonic policeman, in order to investigate the violent death of yet a third member of the Masonic fraternity. Would you care to comment on this curious coincidence?"

McLeod drew himself up, his blue eyes blazing, though the control was steely-cold.

"If you want evidence of some kind of cover-up conspiracy, you're going to have to look elsewhere. First of all, neither Sergeant Kirkpatrick nor I were certain that a man had in fact been killed until we went out to the site of the reported incident—and only then did we discover the victim's identity. Since then, both Sergeant Kirkpatrick and I have done—and will continue to do—everything we can, consistent with our sworn duty as officers of the law, to apprehend the parties responsible. If I thought it would do any good, I would invite the members of the press to exercise a similar degree of professionalism."

With this parting shot, he strode forward so forcefully that his questioner was obliged to leap back out of his way. The cameras followed him down to his waiting car as the eager reporter briefly recapped what had just been said and signed off.

As the scene cut back to the newsroom and an item on further demonstrations against the Poll Tax, Adam punched the "off" button on the TV remote and sank back in his chair, tight-lipped, staring sightlessly at the blank screen for a long moment while he struggled to master the seething frustration that once again gnawed at the edges of his control.

It was bad enough that a good man had died horribly, at the hands of evil men; it was even worse that the circumstances of his death should be the cause for casting doubt on the benevolent institution he had supported loyally all his adult life. It now occurred to Adam to wonder if the whole untidy spate of conspiracy theories was somehow being deliberately engineered as a smoke screen to mask the real purpose behind the killing—though he was forced to admit that this notion, like all the others, had no solid basis in fact. Not for the first time, he wished that Randall could have found some means to communicate with the Hunting Lodge before his enemies silenced him.

But Randall had not, and no amount of wishful thinking could change that. Yet the longer innuendo was allowed to breed unchecked, the greater the risk that the truth would become obscured beyond retrieval, even if justice prevailed in the end. The physical body that had housed the noble mind and spirit of Randall Stewart was now an empty shell; but spirit itself was an enduring reality, accessible on its own ground according to the Laws of the Inner Planes. Perhaps—just *perhaps*—there was something Adam could do to shift the odds back just a little on the side of ultimate justice.

He reached for the in-house telephone and rang Humphrey in the kitchen.

"I'm sorry to tell you this at such short notice," he said, "but I'm afraid I shan't be taking dinner tonight. I'd be obliged if you'd kindle a fire in the library. I have work to do tonight, and I must ask you to make sure that I am not disturbed—*by anyone.*"

# CHAPTER ELEVEN

A hot shower and a fresh change of clothes went a long way toward restoring the energies Adam knew he was going to need for the night's work to come. He took his time dressing, schooling himself to serenity and a centered determination as he pulled on a favorite dressing gown of quilted blue velvet over grey flannel slacks and a crisply laundered white shirt. Crested slippers made his footsteps silent as he glided purposefully down the main stair to the library.

In his master's absence, Humphrey had kindled a healthy log fire on the hearth and switched on the matched pair of brass lamps flanking the mantelpiece to create a fireside island of warmth and light. Another lamp glowed on the drinks cabinet in the corner of the room, providing further unobtrusive background illumination. With a grateful thought for Humphrey, who served him so well, Adam closed the door quietly behind him and turned the key in the lock.

Not that the gesture was necessary on Humphrey's account, of course. Given the instructions Adam had issued, the intrepid butler would never dream of intruding without direct summons. Physical intrusion was the least of Adam's concerns, though that must always be a factor.

Still facing the door, he delved deep into the right-hand pocket of his dressing gown and drew out his *skean dubh*. The little knife resembled a Highland dirk in miniature, the black leather sheath mounted with silver interlace at throat and tip, the black grip carved with an intricate basket-weave design and studded with tiny silver tacks at the intersections. From the tip of the sheath to the clear blue gemstone set into the pommel, nearly the size of a pigeon's egg, the *skean dubh* measured a mere seven inches; infinitely useful for carrying concealed in pocket or sleeve or tucked in the top of kilt hose—which, indeed, was how Adam sometimes wore it. To the uninitiated, it might seem little more than a pretty piece of Highland affectation—or perhaps an expensive toy—but in Adam's hands, this particular *skean dubh* represented a weapon of no inconsiderable potency.

And a tool of manifold purposes. Wrapping his hands around hilt and sheath, and breathing an almost voiceless invocation, Adam drew the two apart and raised the weapon to touch his lips lightly to the flat of the blade, at the same time repocketing the sheath. Subtle power tingled along his right hand and arm as he directed the tip of the blade to trace a invisible pentagram in the air before the door, sweeping down from the center of the lintel, back up to the left-hand side, across and down, back to the center top, finally directing his focus to the centerpoint, sealing his intent on the sigil thus inscribed.

Once the pattern was completed, he kissed the blade again, brought it to his left breast in salute as he bowed his head briefly in homage to the Source of whatever power he commanded, then moved to the fireplace to seal it in the same way—for a chimney represented just as vulnerable a physical access to a room as any door or window.

Last to be sealed was the big bay window in the west wall. Humphrey had earlier drawn the drapes so that they formed a rich brocaded backdrop to the handsome mahogany work desk and chair. When Adam had made his final salute, he sheathed the *skean dubh* and put it back into his pocket as he turned left to scan up a handsome Gothic bookcase.

Perched high on one of the shelves was an elegant, fist-sized paperweight of Caithness glass, from a limited edition entitled "Saltare." Its clear depths held a diaphanous spiral swirl of white and gold, like some exotic bell-flower frozen in ice, already soothing and drawing him as he reached for it. His hands caressed the cool, silken weight of it as he took it down and carried it back to the fireside end of the room.

His favorite armchair was drawn up in its accustomed place to the left of the fireplace. After shifting it slightly closer to the fire's warmth, he set the paperweight on a small rosewood table and moved that into position in front of the chair before switching off the lamps flanking the fireplace and sitting down.

He took his time getting comfortable, adjusting his position so that, sitting erect but relaxed, he could see the moving flames reflected through the sphere's convex curves, like a scryer's crystal ball. Focusing his attention on the heart of the globe, he lifted his palms in a gesture of supplication and drew a deep centering breath, slowly releasing it on the scarce-breathed syllables of a centuries-old hymn to the Most High.

> *Praise be to Thee,*
> *Author of Lights.*
> *Daystar of heaven,*
> *Be Thou my guide and guard. . . .*

The prayer of petition was simultaneously an offering of self to the service of the Divine, renewal of an unreserved dedication he had made countless times before in the course of many lives. At the culmination of his prayer, he brought his hands together, palm to palm, touching his fingertips to his lips in reverent acknowledgment of the Presence Which he served. Then, drawing another deep breath, he set his hands lightly on his thighs and bent all his attention to the fire-lit globe, which now became a focal point for entry into trance.

*"As Above, so Below,"* he whispered. *"As Without, so Within. . . ."*

The globe magnified the fiery glow from the hearth. The starry spindrift pattern took heat and color from the flames. As Adam continued to gaze deep into the heart of the glass, the spiral image trembled before him in his mind's eye and made mere physical vision superfluous.

He drew another slow, centering breath and let his eyes close. Into the depths of his being came a sudden tinkling chime, like the distant shattering of glass; and all at once he was drawn out of himself and into the clear nighttime of the Inner Planes, looking down from above on a morning-glory nebula of stars.

Only here the stars were not fixed but in motion, caught up in the shimmering revolutions of a cosmic dance. Adam let himself be drawn into the midst of that dance on a luminous skein of silver—the silver cord of his own lifeline, glistening like spider-silk as it stretched away from him into the shining whirl of suns and planets. Like a castaway mariner feeling his way along an anchor-rope, he followed the slender silver line down, downward, deeper into trance, into the heart of the astral spiral.

The transition to the Inner Places was a quick, icy shock that left him more than usually disoriented before his senses stabilized. But when he had regained his equilibrium, he found himself standing at the head of a shining path, gazing up at two immense doors supported between towering pillars of fire and cloud, light and dark. His astral form seemed to wear a robe of flowing white, the feet left bare in reverence to the holiness of the ground on which he stood. He drew a deep breath as he turned his gaze upward, for the sight never failed to make his heart almost miss a beat. He had ventured many a journey here in the past, but the awe that touched him was ever fresh and new.

Hands crossed reverently on his breast, Adam approached the threshold and pronounced the Word of an Adeptus Major. At this utterance, the great doors parted smoothly to admit him. Beyond the portal stretched the chambered vastness of the Hall of Akashic Records, the imperishable chronicles of all creation, past, present, and to come. Its vaults were as infinite as the mind of the Absolute, and only some of them accessible to those still bound to mortal flesh. But if permitted, Adam now proposed to find and enter that vault containing the life-records of the soul he had known as Randall Stewart.

*Randall Stewart.* The name itself became a pole star and Adam the compass needle, drawn unerringly along the curving reaches of a softly glowing labyrinth. Its corridors stretched before him with a pearly luminescence, each branching different yet the same. A profound silence reigned over all—still, but not static—yet as he skimmed along the winding courses, Adam was aware of a growing dynamism investing the very air he breathed, drawing him ever onward.

An arched doorway loomed ahead. From the magnetic draw on his senses, Adam had no doubt that he was approaching the place he sought. In spite of this certainty—or perhaps because of it—he advanced with measured circumspection, as one preparing to enter into a sanctuary; for such it was—a chamber of immortal record, where all the many lifetimes of the soul of Randall Stewart were recorded, bound together like chapters in a book.

Because Adam envisioned the Record in these terms, it was in the form of a book that Randall's chronicle of lives appeared to Adam's inner sight as he passed over the threshold. The thick volume rested upon a raised lectern of white marble, its binding rich with gem and enamelwork, as befitted the wealth of its contents.

As Adam reverently approached the lectern, the still, pregnant atmosphere within the chamber was quickened by a sudden, whirling gust of moving air. It lifted the cover of the Book like a movement of unseen hands. Simultaneously, the room was filled with a sense of presence—recognizably Randall's, but resonant with overtones and undertones that Adam had not encountered before in the living man.

Adam stood his ground, mentally framing all the questions he had come to ask. As if in response, the leaves of the Book began to turn, riffling swiftly past lifetimes of centuries gone by before falling open to the account of Randall Stewart's last days. The reading came not in words, but in a string of powerful impressions.

*Confusion . . . weakness . . . a rising tide of fear. Dark sleep . . . white snow . . . Awareness . . . breathless terror . . . a blinding blow . . . the agonizing slash of a flashing blade . . . and the crimson outpouring of the life's blood. . . .* But Adam had guessed all of that.

Suddenly, from out of the dark moil of sensation and emotion, a new image surfaced, hazy but discernible. Though the image lacked focus, it seemed to be that of a heavy, ancient-looking necklet fashioned in black metal.

A torc? Yes, the solidity of the shape suggested as much. Adam judged it to be perhaps a hand-span wide, overlaid with paler interlaced tracery that he could not quite make out. Its very nature suggested Celtic or Pictish origins.

What required no conjecture was the incontrovertible recognition, by both Adam and the essence that was Randall, that the torc was an object of power. The woven shapes twined across the malevolent blackness seemed to shift and change, as though they bound a dark, elemental life of their own. Blood—Randall Stewart's blood—had activated the torc's latent powers. Now enlivened, it was ready—waiting—to be used.

The soul Adam had known as Randall could not put a name to the owner of the torc, or to any of his murderers. Nor had he any idea why he had been chosen as a sacrificial victim. The Record remained silent on these points, for Randall simply had not known.

Another approach, then. Shifting the focus of his inquiry, Adam requested the identity of the individual who had invited Randall to Stirling—of whom Miranda had guessed a prior acquaintance with her father.

But though letters began to form on the page in front of Adam, the page suddenly was obscured by a wave of shadow, before the writing became at all legible. Like a flood of spilled ink, it blotted out the lettering so completely that Adam could make nothing of it.

Its source, he realized, was not in the Chamber of Records itself—for that was inviolate—but imposed upon Randall's own memory. The shadow effect was further proof of interference from a black adept with no little power at his disposal. Clearly, someone had no intention of letting the name be known.

Which suggested, along with the evidence Peregrine had gathered at the murder site, that if the black adept and Randall's mysterious summoner were not one and the same person, both were closely affiliated with the Lodge of the Lynx. The connection was too close to be mere coincidence.

So. If the culprit or culprits were managing to cover their tracks on the astral, perhaps more mundane investigations might yield the key that would help run the Lodge of the Lynx to earth. If Jane McLeod had managed to convey Adam's message to her husband, that Miranda thought her father's caller might have been a fellow antiquarian or bookseller, then the police were even now compiling a list of relevant names from the telephone directory. Randall's diary was another potential source of valuable information—if it could be found.

Meanwhile, there was also the newly discovered involvement of the mysterious torc—perhaps the object the gamekeeper had seen and described as possibly a bowl. On reflection, Adam became convinced that the nature of the torc's powers was bound up in the designs that he had been unable to visualize clearly enough to read. He wished he had known of the torc's existence while they were still at the murder site, so he could have tried to direct Peregrine's focus for a closer look. Even now, it might be done; but so long as the young artist remained on the fringes of the Hunt, there were limits to how far Adam dared ask him to extend the application of his gifts.

This realization crystalized his desire to see Peregrine brought into full communion with the Hunting Lodge as soon as that might be accomplished, for he had no doubt of the strength of Peregrine's commitment. But the authority to confirm the young artist in such a vocation was vested in hands other than his own. Briefly Adam paused to acknowledge the primacy of those to whom he himself answered on the Inner Planes. And before he had formed any conscious intent, that acknowledgment translated itself, unbidden, into a wordless request for an audience.

His heart missed its next beat, almost as if time itself were suspended for an instant. Then all at once the Chamber of Records was suffused by a sudden, racing shimmer of light. Fleet as quicksilver, the light brought with it a keen sense of imminent presence. Recognizing that presence, Adam bowed his head and opened his hands in a gesture of grateful receptivity.

The Master manifested not in human form, but as a radiant pillar of light, so bright that it obscured the dimensions of the chamber. The brightness wavered for an instant before Adam's dazzled vision, then surged forward to enfold him in a scintillating column of white fire. A voice, sparkling and chill as a spring freshet, spoke to him mind-to-mind.

*111*

*A hungry predator is stalking the fold, Master of the Hunt. What is it that holds you back from the Chase?*

There was a light sting in the question, almost as if the Master were testing him.

*The loss of a Huntsman*, Adam replied, *and a trail obscured by darkness.*

*To catch a creature of the night, the Lodge needs must sometimes hunt by darkness*, the Master said.

*This is true*, Adam acknowledged. *But it is also true that the darkness itself is as much our enemy as any human adversary. The Huntsmen who remain are keenly willing. But we are not at full strength.*

Scarcely breathing, he waited for the Master's response. It came veiled, designedly inscrutable. Wordlessly Adam understood that he was being left to explain himself in an atmosphere of strict neutrality, neither hindered nor encouraged by anything outside his own powers of discernment and judgment. Cleaving fast to his convictions, he steeled himself to frame his request.

*Not so long ago, Master, a certain fledgling hawk was entrusted to my care. He was a hunting hawk, with rare gifts of vision and far sight, but his wings had been damaged by rough handling, and it was granted that I should render healing and instruction. Though I undertook the task gladly, I hardly dared to hope for rapid progress.*

*But the fledgling welcomed the healing, and in doing so, has exceeded all expectations. His wings are all but re-pinioned. Though he remains earthbound, his visionary gifts are manifest, and his yearning to fly grows stronger with each passing day, as his true nature asserts itself. I have tested him repeatedly, as he now begins to test himself, and I stand convinced of his vocation. I therefore request permission to bring him past the threshold of initiation, that he may be admitted to the ranks of the Hunting Lodge.*

There was a timeless pause during which Adam could feel the beating of his own heart like an apprehensive fluttering of caged wings.

*Permission cannot be granted at this time*, came the piercing-clear voice of the Master in his soul. *The fledgling is not yet free to pledge his loyalty to the Hunt. First a duty must be performed on behalf of another.*

This was wholly unexpected. Adam was taken aback. After some slight hesitation he asked, *Is it permitted that I know the identity of this other?*

*It is permitted*, the Master responded coolly. *It is he who was Michael Scot, but now in the Outer life answers to the name of Gillian Talbot.*

Michael Scot—or Gillian Talbot, as she now was. On the face of it, this second disclosure was even more startling than the first. But as Adam cast his mind back over the events of October, he realized that he might have anticipated something like this. At Melrose, the spirit of Michael Scot had made a point of selecting Peregrine as the medium through which to communicate the location of his treasure and his spellbook—and apparently far more than that.

At the time, Adam had assumed that Peregrine was merely the passive recipient of given information, chosen for convenience. Now, all at once, it seemed that Scot's choice had been anything but merely convenient, and Peregrine's participation anything but passive. However untutored Peregrine might be in his present incarnation, his immortal soul was that of an initiate. At some level deeper than consciousness, Scot must have solicited the aid of his fellow adept; and Peregrine, for his part, must have accepted that charge. No one understood better than Adam the inviolable nature of such a solemn bond. Whether or not Peregrine was yet able to realize the nature of his mission in conscious terms—or to act upon it—was another matter.

*I discern the nature of the tie which may link the two of them*, Adam told the Master gravely. *But Peregrine Lovat is only just awakening to his potential. May I know what is to be required of him, if the pledge is to be fulfilled?*

*The artist must be also the craftsman. Broken images must be restored. The temple of lights must be rebuilt.*

The Masters of the Inner Planes rarely spoke in plain terms. With them, a simple utterance was merely the key to something vastly more complex, requiring time and thought to unravel. Even as Adam paused to ponder this enigmatic revelation, the Master spoke again.

*Beware, Master of the Hunt, for the Predators grow stronger. Not only sheep but Hunters do they seek. One Huntsman slain already, and another will they stalk. Take heed one is not lost before he is truly found.*

The lightning change in tone was accompanied by an upsurge of radiance too bright to look upon. Dazzled, Adam flung up a hand to shield his eyes, hanging for a heartbeat between vision and blindness.

When he could see again, he was alone in the Chamber of

Records. With his next breath, the walls of the Chamber dissolved around him. An instant later, he found himself rocketing upward through a pearly sea. He surfaced like a diver suddenly come up for air, gasping slightly at the faint psychic jar that signalled the soul's reunion with the body. For a moment he sat motionless, to allow his physical senses time to come back into contact with his surroundings. Then, with a slight shiver, he opened his eyes.

The fire on the hearth had died back to a few dull, glowing embers. A glance at the carriage clock on a side table told him that nearly two hours had passed since he had entered into his trance. Now that he was awake, his body felt chilled and cramped, as it always did after a long foray onto the Inner Planes. He rose stiffly to unlock the door, dutifully retraced his wardings to dispel them, then rang for Humphrey to bring him sandwiches and hot cocoa and collapsed back into his chair to think over the results of his night's work.

Already details of the experience were fading, sinking back into the uncharted seas below the level of consciousness. Two facts, however, remained indelibly clear in his waking mind.

The first was the revelation regarding the involvement of the mysterious torc in Randall's slaying—and the probable adeptship of the one who had lured him to his death and would continue to stalk the Hunt.

The second was that the future of Peregrine Lovat as a member of the Hunting Lodge was somehow contingent on the fate of Gillian Talbot.

# CHAPTER TWELVE

HIS sleep that night was dreamless—which probably was a good indication that his unconscious was busily processing the possible significance of the Master's disclosures. He awoke punctually at eight, feeling more refreshed and clear-headed than he had since the night of Randall Stewart's death. By half past, he was sitting down to breakfast in the morning room, already dressed for rounds in a dark three-piece suit. He had just picked up the morning's edition of *The Scotsman*, and Humphrey was pouring his tea, when the telephone rang.

Humphrey set the teapot on its trivet and walked unhurriedly to answer the summons, frowning slightly at the prospect of his master being disturbed before a proper breakfast.

"Strathmourne House. Oh, it's you, Inspector." His expression had lightened as he quirked an inquiring eyebrow in Adam's direction. "One moment, if you please, sir."

"Inspector McLeod?" Adam said, laying aside his paper and holding out a hand. "I'll take it, of course."

With a slight bow, Humphrey nodded and ferried the telephone across to the breakfast table, handing the receiver to Adam.

"Here I am, Noel. What's happened?"

"No new catastrophe, so you can relax on that account," McLeod's deep voice rumbled from the other end of the line. "One of our mobile units just called in a report. They've found Randall's missing car."

"Where?"

"In a pond, about a mile east of Boghall," McLeod said. "A farmer was out rounding up stray sheep, and noticed something metallic sticking up out of the water that hadn't been there earlier in the week. When it turned out to be the back bumper of an abandoned vehicle, he called the police. The car's still underwater at the moment, but we have a tentative ID based on the rear number plate. I'm just heading out to join the police recovery team, on the off chance that there may be something left inside the car by way of a clue—hold on a minute."

In the background, someone was asking McLeod a question, to which the inspector replied testily, "Well, fine. Go run it through the computer and see what you come up with. How should I know? Use your imagination!"

A moment later, he came back on the line. "Sorry about the interruption. This place is like Picadilly Circus this morning! By the way, thanks for relaying that bit of information you were able to pick up from Miranda. I've put young Cochrane on it. I've got him ferreting out the names of everyone in the Stirling area who has a documented interest in antiquarian books, either as a dealer or collector. Once we have that list, I intend to pay a few visits and ask a lot of questions."

There was another intrusive buzz from the background. .

"They aren't going to let me alone," McLeod said, with a sigh of exasperation. "I'd better get out of here, before someone presents me with an iron-clad administrative reason for staying. What's your schedule like for today?"

"Not too bad," said Adam. "I have a ten o'clock lecture at the hospital, with rounds to follow, but I should be back by mid-afternoon. If not, Humphrey will always know where I'm to be reached."

"I'll track you down, never fear—hopefully with good news. Talk to you later."

After breakfast, which he was allowed to finish without further interruption, Adam packed his lecture notes into his monogrammed leather briefcase and set off for Edinburgh. His lecture went well—his students asked far more intelligent questions than usual—and the morning passed reasonably quickly. He was home in time for a belated lunch in the library. He had just finished a second cup of tea when the telephone rang. He set his lunch tray aside in order to answer the summons.

"It's Inspector McLeod telephoning from Boghall, sir," said Humphrey's voice.

"Ah. I'd hoped it might be. Put it right through, please."

"Yes, sir."

As soon as a click on the line confirmed the transfer, Adam said, "That you, Noel?"

"Aye, but the news is disappointing, so don't get your hopes up. Randall's car is a write-off." Adam could hear the dejection in McLeod's voice. "Whoever arranged to dispose of it took the precaution of setting fire to the interior. Forensics are still going over the outside, but frankly I don't think they're going to find anything much. Looks like it's back to the drawing board."

Back to the drawing board. . . . The image gave Adam sudden pause for thought.

"That reminds me," he said. "What about that list of names I passed along to you regarding previous tenants of that 'haunted' flat?"

"Haunted flat?" McLeod sounded blank.

"The place now being rented by one of Christopher's parishioners," said Adam. "Peregrine and I told you about it on the way up to Blairgowrie."

"Bloody hell, I'd forgotten all about that!" McLeod exclaimed. "What the devil did I do with your note? It must be in my other jacket."

"I'm not saying there's necessarily any connection," Adam said, choosing his words with care, "but we can't afford to overlook even a tenuous lead right now."

"Aye," McLeod agreed. "I'll swing by home and collect it on my way back, and get a man right on it. Back to you later. Thanks, Adam."

The line disconnected. As Adam cradled the receiver, he found himself gloomily reflecting how little they still knew about the individuals who had murdered Randall Stewart, or even the specifics of his death.

*Somewhere there has to be a key to all this*, he told himself firmly. *Maybe even in the means of the death itself. . . .*

Even as the thought crossed his mind, a new possibility occurred to him. Following a sudden impulse, he slid open the upper right-hand drawer of the desk and brought out his personal directory. A quick skim through the entries produced the number he was looking for.

"Hello, Royal Infirmary?" he said, when a pleasant voice answered with the lilt of the Western Islands. "This is Dr. Adam Sinclair. Can you tell me if Dr. David diCapua is there this afternoon?"

Less than an hour later, Adam was easing his blue Jaguar into a space in the car park of the Perth Royal Infirmary. He had enjoyed the brief run up from Strathmourne, even though the light drizzle had forced him to leave the soft top up. He turned up his collar against the mist as he dashed for the shelter of the nearest entrance.

The vast medical complex that was Perth's Royal Infirmary encompassed a sprawl of modern extensions grafted onto the original grey stone facility. The forensics section was attached to the pathology department—a sanitized, relatively new annex on the north side of the hospital. Following the appropriate arrows posted at intervals on the walls, Adam made his way along a zigzag course of stairways and corridors, eventually coming to a set of double doors marked *Pathology Department*, and below that, *Medical Staff Only*.

Adam pushed open the doors and entered. The corridor beyond was floored with green carpet tiles; the walls bore paint of that pallid shade of mustard which seemed to be the institutional norm for hospitals all over Scotland. The air in this part of the building was several degrees colder than it had been elsewhere. The pungent smell of industrial-strength disinfectants seemed almost thick enough to manifest itself as a visible presence.

No stranger to hospital odors, Adam set off down the hall toward the T-junction at the far end. Just before he reached it, a skinny young lab assistant in a baggy green coverall whisked around the corner from the opposite direction, carrying a tray of tagged specimen jars. Startled, she only just avoided colliding with Adam—who was ready to rescue the tray if disaster seemed imminent—but he disarmed her with a smile as she checked and eyed him somewhat warily.

"Hello, I'm Dr. Sinclair from Edinburgh, here to have a word with Dr. diCapua. He's expecting me. Can you tell me where to find him?"

The woman's manner thawed perceptibly in the face of Adam's particular blend of authority and charm.

"Sorry, Doctor, I believe he's just finishing a post mortem," she said, a little self-consciously. She indicated the left-hand branch of the corridor with a jerk of her sharp little chin and added, "The autopsy theatre is down there—the second doorway on your right."

"Thank you very much," Adam said, and moved on past her in the direction she had pointed out to him. A dozen brisk strides brought him to the threshold of the door in question. The upper half was fitted with a small plate glass window, and through it he glimpsed the averted back of a wiry, active-looking man that he recognized, even from behind, as David diCapua.

The name was not a Scottish one, of course. DiCapua's father had been an Italian army captain who was captured in Sicily during the Second World War and subsequently shipped to Scotland for internment in a POW camp. When the war ended, a number of these Italian POW's had elected to remain in Scotland rather than return to their devastated and impoverished homeland—a fact which accounted for the widespread incidence of Italian surnames throughout Perthshire, Tayside, and Fife.

DiCapua himself was short and spare, with straight dark hair and a clean-shaven profile that recalled the faces stamped on Roman coins. Adam was accustomed to seeing diCapua in dinner clothes of uncommonly fine cut, for the more usual venue of their meetings, perhaps half a dozen times each year, took place in the context of the Scottish National Opera, of which both men were avid patrons. Somehow, however, the dapper little forensics expert managed to look almost equally dashing in the green scrub suit and Wellington boots that were regulation attire for his present occupation.

At the moment, diCapua was hunched over the partly draped figure of a male cadaver, working away with the scholarly precision of a Swiss watchmaker, clearly oblivious to his cheerless surroundings. When Adam rapped at the glass, however, he straightened up and looked around, flashing a welcoming smile at the sight of Adam's face at the window and waving his visitor inside with a flourish of one surgically-gloved hand.

Adam opened the door and stepped into an atmosphere reeking of formalin.

"Adam, how nice to see you!" the pathologist exclaimed. "I wasn't expecting a reunion before next month's *La Traviata*!" The profile might proclaim him a son of Rome, but the accent was pure Scots.

"Hello, David."

DiCapua stripped off his right-hand glove and switched off the Dictaphone into which he had been speaking, before reaching out to trade handshakes with his visitor.

"Now then," he said genially, "tell me what brings you up to the wilds of Perth."

"I've come," Adam said, "to ask a professional favor."

"Ah." DiCapua nodded sagely. "Needless to say, I shall be happy to oblige in any way I can. Let me guess. It has something to do with the Randall Stewart post mortem."

Adam nodded. "You've guessed correctly. With your permission, I'd like an advance look at the autopsy report."

"Ah." DiCapua sounded suddenly thoughtful. "Well, the official report won't be ready to go out until tomorrow morning—I still have a summation to do, tying in the lab results—but I believe the transcripts are done of what I dictated."

"I don't necessarily need to see a finished report," Adam said. "Frankly, I'd be just as well-satisfied to see the transcript and lab results."

DiCapua gave him a measured look, then shrugged. "I don't see any reason why not, especially," he added, "since your signature was on the death certificate." He glanced back at his cadaver. "I've got about another ten minutes' work to do here. Why don't you go upstairs to the staff lounge and wait for me there? I'll bring you the file as soon as I've had a chance to clean up."

Adam went up to the lounge to find it empty except for a pair of interns brangling over the projected treatment for an orthopaedic patient. As soon as they caught sight of Adam, they rather sheepishly broke off their argument and took themselves off. The coffee out of the vending machine was something both Humphrey and Mrs. Gilchrist would have condemned as "strong enough for a mouse to walk on." After a single taste, he set his cup aside and summoned the patience to await his colleague's arrival.

Twenty minutes later, diCapua pushed his way through the lounge's swinging door and made his way across to the table where Adam was sitting. He had shed his green scrubs and Wellies in favor of an elegantly cut grey suit and a glossy pair of Italian-made leather shoes. His burgundy silk tie had a discreet pattern of tiny gold paisleys. As the pathologist sat down across from him, Adam privately paid tribute to the minor miracle of personal grooming by which diCapua managed to avoid bringing with him any residual whiff of the dissecting theatre.

"Here you are," said diCapua, handing over a manila folder. "It doesn't make pleasant reading—but I don't suppose that will come as any great surprise to you."

Set down in black and white, the cold medical facts surrounding Randall Stewart's murder allowed a degree of clinical detachment, for which Adam was grateful. The victim had been struck three times in the back of the head, with cranial fractures resulting from two of the three blows. DiCapua speculated that the probable implement might have been a hammer.

As Adam himself had observed at the crime scene, the victim's right jugular vein had been opened with almost surgical precision, swiftly emptying the body of blood.

However, it was diCapua's considered professional opinion that neither the head blows nor the wound had been the direct cause of death. To Adam's surprise, Randall Stewart had also been garroted.

Frowning, he read on with even keener interest. The ligature had not been apparent at the scene of the crime because it had been drawn so tightly into the wrinkles of the victim's neck. It had been inflicted by means of two strands of catgut—possibly a violin or guitar string—knotted three times. The garrote had snapped the victim's cervical vertebrae and severed the spinal cord at the same time that it closed off his airway. DiCapua postulated that the jugular incision had been made while the victim was dying from the twin effects of strangulation and a broken neck, leaving time for the laboring action of the dying heart to pump a massive quantity of blood from the failing body.

The three blows to the head, the garroting, the letting of blood—added to what their eyewitness had reported, it all confirmed the probability of a grisly ritual pattern. Queasy and heartsick, Adam forced himself to keep reading, searching for some fragment of information that might provide the clue to help him identify the specific origin of the ritual—for only when he knew that could he hope to guess its underlying purpose, and perhaps determine why Randall, in particular, had been chosen to die.

Additional details came to his attention without yielding the vital clue he was hoping for. DiCapua had noted the presence of incidental bruises here and there, along with evidence of preliminary frostbite affecting the hands and feet. A series of needle marks on the victim's arms, along with a high concentration of barbiturates in the blood, indicated that he had been kept heavily drugged throughout his captivity. There were also traces of drugs to be found in the contents of the stomach, to indicate that Randall had been given yet another dose of sedatives along with his last meal.

His last meal. . . .

Here Adam sat up with a slight start, his dark eyes narrowed in sudden, intense interest. Randall's last meal had consisted of red wine and some kind of scone or bannock made from oatmeal. The bannock had been scorched, and the wine had been laced with—mistletoe?

Burnt oat bannock, and wine laced with mistletoe. . . . The combination, coupled with the injuries inflicted, rang a note of familiarity just at the edge of conscious memory. He sought it, but the effort pushed it back beyond immediate recall. He would have to go after it more rigorously, later on. He had seen this pattern before!

Filing the information for later consideration, Adam returned the pathologist's notes to the manila folder and mutely tendered it back across the tabletop to its owner. DiCapua accepted it and arched an inquiring eyebrow.

"Well?" he said, when Adam volunteered no comment. "Does any of this make sense to you?"

"Nothing coherent, at the moment," Adam said truthfully. "Given time, I may be able to come up with a theory or two—but right now I'm as lost for an explanation as you are."

"I was afraid you'd say that." DiCapua pulled a wry face, then eyed Adam speculatively and said, "Forgive me if I seem to be prying, but what exactly *is* your interest in this case? For the life of me, I can't help wondering how you, of all people, happened to be the first qualified physician to arrive at the scene of a murder that took place in Blairgowrie."

Adam smiled briefly. "No mystery there. Noel McLeod had gotten called in for police expertise, and he called *me*. He wanted professional backup from someone experienced in dealing with the psychology of the bizarre. As you know, I do consultation for the police from time to time."

"Well, bizarre is certainly the word for it!" diCapua agreed with a snort. "In all the fifteen years I've been involved in forensic medicine, I've never encountered anything quite like this. Whoever did it must have been real loonies—but I guess that's why you're involved, isn't it?"

As Adam shrugged, diCapua sighed and went on. "Well, I'm glad it's you and not me who has to take it on from here. CID in Perth will be getting their official copies of the autopsy report tomorrow, and I'm sending a courtesy copy to your Inspector McLeod. I wish I felt confident that it would be very helpful. Where do you begin looking for someone who would do something like this?"

"Under rocks, perhaps; I don't know," Adam replied, though he had some better ideas than that, at least. He shook his head and sighed. "Just as an aside, when do you think the body will be released? As if this weren't a small enough world, I knew the victim. His daughter will want to see her father buried as quickly as possible."

"Ouch! That's a tough one!" diCapua said, shaking his head. "The Procurator Fiscal may well want to retain the body for as long as it takes to track down the perpetrators and make an arrest."

"Which means it could be weeks, even months."

"Well, the courts have to protect the bad guys, too, Adam," diCapua said airily. "As you know, anyone formally charged with murder has the right to commission his own forensics examination of the victim's remains—one of those delightful oddities of Scottish law."

"Yes," Adam murmured darkly. "And sometimes the law, to quote Dickens, is an ass!" He gave diCapua a bleak smile. "But griping about the problems of the law isn't going to get Randall Stewart buried any faster, is it? Besides that," he added, eyeing the clock beside the coffee machine, "I'd better be on my way, or I'll make you late for whatever plans you may have for the rest of the day. Give my love to Catriona—and thanks very much for your help. If I have any thoughts between now and tomorrow that might prove useful to you, I'll be sure to give you a call."

# CHAPTER THIRTEEN

ADAM had not managed to solidify anything by the time he arrived back at Strathmourne; nor did enlightenment come over the simple supper Mrs. Gilchrist urged upon him. He took it on a tray in the library, visually scanning the bookshelves from a distance while he ate, racking his brain for some clue as to where he had seen the reference that had sparked a glimmer of familiarity as he read diCapua's report. When he had finished eating, he asked Humphrey to bring him coffee and set about a more active evening of research.

Adam's library was a working scholar's haven as well as a repository for rare and valuable bibliotheca. His father and grandfather both had been notable collectors, and had accumulated a quite respectable selection of titles. Adam was a collector too, but the library under his custody had assumed more eclectic proportions, reflecting the encyclopaedic scope of his personal interests. It still housed its share of rare folios and first editions and even unbound manuscripts hand-lettered on vellum—for Adam rarely sold off anything—but now modern texts sheathed in glossy dust jackets and even paperbacks nestled companionably beside antique volumes in tooled leather bindings.

Adam had a vague idea what he was looking for, but it took him the better part of an hour to locate it. After pausing repeatedly to pull out likely volumes and then replace them, he came upon a recent title in archaeology that suddenly arrested his interest.

He had never quiet gotten around to reading it, but he vaguely recalled skimming through an excerpt in the *Sunday Times* a few years back—something about a body being found by a peat cutter in Lindow Moss, near Manchester, at first thought to be a recent murder victim—except that ''Lindow Man'' had turned out to be the victim of a sacrificial slaying more than 2000 years before. Already dipping into the prologue, he carried the book back to his favorite armchair by the fireside, switched on the lamp, and settled down for an in-depth read.

He spent the next hour immersed in the book, pausing excitedly now and again to scribble a note or insert a place marker. When he at last looked up, the last page read, the clock was striking ten o'clock.

Breathing a heavy sigh, he closed the book and set it aside, absently flexing his shoulders as he mentally summed up the import of all he had just read. Then, after a moment's further reflection, he got up and went over to the desk to telephone McLeod at home. It was McLeod himself who answered.

"I've been doing some research," Adam said, when greetings had been exchanged. "I think I've hit on something that may have some bearing on Randall's death—nothing about the perpetrators, but perhaps a framework for the killing itself. Do you think you could find time to drop by my office at the hospital tomorrow afternoon—sometime after lunch, perhaps?"

Jordanburn Psychiatric Hospital, now a part of the Royal Edinburgh Hospital complex, lies in the midst of Edinburgh's fashionable Morningside district, within sight of Blackford Hill. The following day, Adam returned from lunching with two of his students in the hospital canteen to find McLeod solidly ensconced in the spare chair in his office. On the desktop blotter was an origami swan made from hospital notepaper.

"Hello! I didn't expect you quite so early," Adam said, smiling at the swan as he moved around behind his desk and sat. "I hope you weren't waiting long."

"Well, I had to do *something* to pass the time," McLeod said of the swan, a shade defensively, "but no, I haven't been here long." He rocked back in his chair and cocked his head in Adam's direction. "It's a good thing, too, because my curiosity might have killed me, just sitting here. What have you found out?"

Adam gave the swan a gentle prod with one forefinger before leaning back in his chair. "First let me ask you this: Have you seen the autopsy report on Randall Stewart?"

"Aye," McLeod said grimly. "A courier brought it in a little after eleven this morning."

"Did you read it?"

"Aye."

"And what did you make of it?"

McLeod's jaw tightened. "Bloody awful way for anybody to die. Especially a friend."

"I agree," Adam said quietly, "but that wasn't what I meant."

This statement earned him a sharp look from McLeod. "All right. What *did* you mean?"

"I drove up to the Royal Infirmary in Perth yesterday afternoon," Adam said. "The chief pathologist is an acquaintance of mine, and let me have an advance look at his findings. As the clinical facts began to emerge—as distinct from the emotional atmosphere of what we saw at the murder site—it struck me at once that certain features of the killing ritual sounded vaguely familiar: the presence of mistletoe in the wine and the murderers' use of the garrote. Since then, I've been able to match things up."

As he spoke, he slid open the left-hand drawer of his desk and took out a hardback book with a mostly red dust-jacket.

"Have a look at this," he said, passing the book across the desk.

Wordlessly McLeod took the book, pausing to adjust the set of his gold-framed aviator glasses so that he could read the title on the cover: *The Life and Death of a Druid Prince: the Story of an Archaeological Sensation.* Adam was leaning forward, the glint in his dark eyes like storm-light on a winter loch.

"Either they know this book or they're working from the same tradition, Noel," he said softly. "They did him just like Lindow Man. Look through it. I've marked the pertinent passages and made marginal notes."

As McLeod flipped agitatedly through the book, skimming swiftly over the passages that Adam had flagged and highlighted, Adam reiterated what the inspector was reading.

"I doubt it would have been possible to duplicate Lindow Man's sacrifice much more closely," he said. "Lindow Man's last meal was a burnt oak bannock and wine laced with mistletoe; so was Randall's. Lindow Man was struck three times in the head to stun him, he was garroted, and he was bled via a jugular incision on the right side; so was Randall. Lindow Man was then deposited face-down in a pool of water; Randall wasn't, but he was left face-down in the snow—only a minor variation.

"Both deaths fit the classic profile for a triple-sacrifice to the three principal Celtic gods," Adam went on. "These authors claim a Druidic framework. Taranis was the Celtic Thor or Thunderer; Esus, the lord and master, was roughly equivalent to Odin, the All-Father; and Teutates was the overall god of the people or tribe—and each had a specific manner in which sacrifices were to be rendered.

"The three blows to the head made it a sacrifice to Taranis, recalling the might of his thunderbolts and magic hammer—and you'll recall that the report postulates that a hammer might have dealt the head injuries. The burnt bannock also connects with Taranis' fire aspect. Esus preferred victims who were hanged from a tree—shades of Odin, there—or stabbed to death, or both; and garroting equates with hanging. Teutates was associated with sacrifices in water. That's the one that's most tenuous, but Lindow Man's water connection was hardly any better; both men were already dead by the time they went into the water—or snow.''

McLeod had stopped even trying to read as Adam spoke, only listening with increasing horror. When Adam finally wound down, the inspector was slowly shaking his head, his expression slightly stunned.

"My God, those bastards really did their homework, didn't they?'' he murmured. "But why?'' He scowled. "This book puts Lindow Man's sacrifice in a specific historical context—and there's certainly no historical parallel to call for such a sacrifice in this day and age. I mean, why should the Lodge of the Lynx go to such lengths to execute a modern-day Freemason according to an ancient Druidic ritual?''

"That worried me, too,'' Adam admitted, "but I think I've come up with what is at least a plausible theory.''

"Which is?''

"Well, some historians postulate a historical connection between the Druids and Freemasonry, claiming a degree of continuity between the two traditions. If we assume that those historians have the right of it—that the Masons are latter-day heirs to the mysteries of the Druids—that would help explain why a Master Mason might have been chosen as an appropriate sacrificial victim.''

"*I've* never run into that theory, and I'm a Master Mason,'' McLeod said, and tapped the book before him. "Besides, these folks claim the victim was a prince.''

"Ah, but in some ceremonial contexts, royalty is not so much a matter of bloodline as it is a matter of the individual's having been ordained or consecrated according to the appropriate mysteries,'' Adam said. "It could be argued that the various degrees of high-level Masonic initiation fulfill that function. As to the underlying purpose—''

He broke off briefly, choosing his words, then went on. "I haven't mentioned this before now because I didn't feel free to discuss it over the telephone, but the night before last I made a foray onto the Inner Planes. I had intended to consult the Akashic Records, hoping for some revelation concerning the identity of Randall's killers. What I got instead was a vision involving some kind of artifact—which I think is what our eye-witness saw but couldn't describe—and an unexpected interview with the Master about Peregrine. But more of that later.''

"Aye, what about this artifact?'' McLeod said.

"Well, I couldn't see it clearly,'' Adam went on, "but it

seemed to be a torc of some kind—which would support our theory of a Druidic link. I got an impression of Pictish design and workmanship, but we know that Pictish art forms filtered down to the Druids—and the Pictish religious framework was far more bloodthirsty than even that which the Druids practiced. If such an artifact has fallen into the hands of someone belonging to the Lodge of the Lynx, then Randall's death may have been orchestrated as a means of reawakening that artifact's potency—whatever that potency may be—by means of blood sacrifice. *That's* what I think Randall's killing was all about.''

''God, poor Randall!'' McLeod whispered, shaking his head and pushing his glasses up onto his forehead to massage the bridge of his nose. ''Do you think they succeeded?''

Adam shrugged, his face very grim. ''If they did, I expect it won't be long before they attempt to exercise their new-found power—knowing the Lodge of the Lynx. If they failed, undoubtedly they'll attempt another sacrifice before long. Either way, someone is going to suffer—unless we stop them.''

McLeod grunted. ''That's a bit of a tall order, considering that we haven't one shred of solid evidence that the Lodge of the Lynx is behind this. Oh, you and I know, in a general sort of way, but there's nothing I can hang anything on in any legal sense. And we haven't a clue as to the identity of any of their members.''

''I know.'' Adam was unable to keep the edge of frustration out of his voice. ''I wish there was some way we could lure our opposite numbers out into the open. Fighting an unknown enemy is always more difficult.''

After a long moment's pause, McLeod cocked his head at Adam.

''I've got a suggestion,'' he said. ''But I doubt you're going to like it.''

''Tell me anyway.''

''Maybe it's time,'' said McLeod, ''that we offered our friends some bait.''

He accompanied this statement with an arch glance, which immediately produced a sour grimace from Adam.

''I hope you're not seriously proposing that I should let you *deliberately* betray yourself to the Lynx, are you?''

McLeod shrugged heartily. ''Have you got any better ideas?''

''The answer is no!''

''That's what I thought you'd say,'' McLeod went on. ''Here's what I have in mind. Donald has finished compiling that list of book dealers and antiquarians in the Stirling area. I'd say there's a fair chance that one of them is a Lynx, or at least has a Lynx connection. Suppose that, when I go out to conduct my interviews, I do a little psychic sleuthing, deliberately let my defenses slip a bit? If there *is* anybody out there with ties to the Lodge of the Lynx, he won't overlook an intrusion like that. If and when he makes a countermove, we'll have found the lead we've been looking for.''

"Provided the whole thing doesn't blow up in our faces," Adam said thinly. "What you're suggesting is far too risky. We've already lost Randall. We can't afford to lose anyone else."

"We can't afford to sit on our hands, either," said McLeod. "You just said yourself that the Lynx will certainly strike again. At least if we draw their fire, we'll stand a chance of diverting them from those less able to defend themselves."

"You can't be sure of that," Adam said. Seeing the stubborn jut to McLeod's jaw, he added, "Believe me, Noel, I'm every bit as anxious for results as you are—but it's too early in the game yet to play our hand openly. By all means, carry out your inquiries—but for God's sake, don't lower your defenses, even for an instant. That's an order!"

McLeod sighed heavily, then gave a nod, conceding defeat. "All right. We'll play it your way for now." He picked up the little origami swan and turned it in his fingers. "Returning to the subject of those less able to defend themselves, you mentioned Mr. Lovat a little earlier. I hope the Master isn't having second thoughts."

"No, quite the contrary. If anything, he's pushing for faster progress—or at least I think he is. Sometimes it's hard to make sense of his somewhat oracular pronouncements, though."

Briefly he outlined the gist of his audience with the Master, and the growing certainty that Peregrine's further advancement some-how hinged on a successful resolution of the Gillian Talbot case.

"He said, *The artist must be also the craftsman. Broken images must be restored. The temple of lights must be rebuilt.* I take that to mean that Peregrine is somehow to be involved in restoring the Talbot girl to wholeness. I plan to try contacting her parents next week, when I go down to London to collect Philippa. I'm not sure how I'll engineer it all, to get the two of them together in a setting where we can work uninterrupted, but I don't suppose I would have been told to do it if it weren't possible. Of course, 'possible' does not always equate with 'easy.'''

"Almost *never* does, where the Master's instructions are concerned," McLeod rumbled. "But as we keep saying, we knew the job was dangerous. . . ." He sighed, glanced at his watch, then sat forward explosively. "Jesus, I've got a press conference in half an hour! I'll be in touch, Adam. Ring me if you come up with anything else."

The next day brought no new counsel, and only one piece of news that could be construed as good. After lengthy consultation with the police, the Procurator Fiscal finally agreed that Randall Stewart's body could be released to his family for burial. McLeod passed the word to Adam, and Adam and Christopher assisted Randall's family in making the necessary arrangements. Because of the wide variety and number of Randall's friends and acquaintances, Christopher contrived to secure St. Mary's Episcopal Cathedral for the following Tuesday, rather than the much smaller parish church he had attended nearer home. Six of Randall's Masonic Brethren were deputized to act as pall bearers, and members of his Lodge also made arrangements for their own commemoration of their slain brother, at a Lodge of Sorrow on the Friday evening.

"Later in the month, the Brethren will also be organizing a party to go down to Melrose Abbey for the annual Mason's Walk," McLeod told Adam, when they had exchanged final decisions about the funeral. "That's St. John's Eve, the day after Boxing Day. Jane and I will definitely be going down, and you're welcome to tag along."

"I'll do that," Adam said. "It's the sort of commemoration Randall would have liked."

Once Adam's part in the planning was accomplished, however, he determined not to waste any more time or energy brooding over their lack of progress in finding Randall's killers. Rigorous self-examination left him convinced that he had not overlooked anything of material value to the case, so he turned his thoughts instead to the more accessible if no less perplexing mystery of Peregrine Lovat and his ongoing part in all of this. That Peregrine was a key figure in the overall strategy against the Lynx, Adam had no doubt; but first Peregrine must prove his worthiness on a cosmic scale by doing whatever he was intended to do regarding Gillian Talbot—or Michael Scot. Perhaps it was *Scot* who was the key. Perhaps that was why the Master had linked Peregrine's admission to the Hunting Lodge with success in restoring the scattered psyche that was both Michael Scot and Gillian Talbot—and a host of others, Adam had no doubt.

Very well. He had made plans to contact Gillian's parents next week, if they did not contact him first. Meanwhile, there were things Adam could do to further pave the way for Peregrine's eventual entry into the Hunting Lodge. As yet, Peregrine had met only three of Adam's esoteric colleagues. It was time he made the acquaintance of a fourth.

# CHAPTER FOURTEEN

"I think you'll like Lady Julian," Adam told Peregrine, as they motored south on Saturday morning under a chilly and changeable November sky. "I've known her since I was a lad of about twelve. She's like a favorite aunt. Her late husband was a businessman, mainly engaged in trade in India and the Far East, and they amassed an incredible collection of Orientalia over the years. A lot of it's gone to museums now, but Julian's kept some of the best pieces for herself. She and Michael were actually friends of my parents first, and she and my mother were and still are close. She's also one of the most talented jewelry designers I know—which is why I've had her do the repair on my ring. You'll love her place—and her work."

"She sounds delightful," Peregrine said.

What he did not say, because Adam had not brought it up, was his suspicion that Lady Julian might be rather more than an old family friend who happened to dabble in jewelry—just as he *knew* the ring in question was no ordinary piece of jewelry. It perhaps had saved more than just his hand from serious injury, that awe-ful night at Urquhart Castle, and he doubted that Adam would ever have let it out of his possession except under a bond of unshakeable trust—which made it more than likely that there was more to Lady Julian than Adam was letting on.

They continued to chat of inconsequentials as Adam threaded the Range Rover through the elegant environs of New Town, finally entering a quiet crescent tucked well away from the bustle of Queen's Street. Midway along a row of Edwardian townhouses, he pulled in at the curb and they got out, Adam pointing out one of the flats on the other side of the street. Behind a wrought iron gate painted the pale green of verdigris, cut stone steps led up to a door of vivid vermilion, guarded by a pair of fierce granite Fu dogs.

Peregrine bent briefly for a closer look at one of them as Adam rang the doorbell, also admiring an unusual boot-scrape set into the stone beside the door, cast in the shape of a Chinese dragon. The door was opened a moment later by Lady Julian's live-in companion, a stout, practical-looking woman in her mid-fifties, with apple-cheeks and a twinkle in her eye.

"Good morning, Mrs. Fyvie," Adam said with a smile. "I believe Lady Julian's expecting me—and this is Mr. Lovat."

Mrs. Fyvie beamed at them both and stepped back from the door, bidding them enter.

"Indeed she is, Sir Adam! Do come in, both of you, and let me take your things."

Still beaming, she ushered them through a tiny, tiled vestibule and into a broad hallway papered in pale green damask with a raised pattern of lotus flowers. Two lofty cabinets of fine Chinese lacquer-work faced one another across the width of the carpeted floor, and an almost life-sized Kwan-Yin gazed serenely down the corridor at them from beneath a gilded medieval baldachin. As the two men divested themselves of coats and scarves, a fluffy Himalayan cat sauntered out from behind the large potted fern in the corner and made a move to twine itself around Peregrine's legs. Mrs. Fyvie clucked her tongue and shooed it away as she hung up their coats.

"Here now, off you go, before you get the young gentleman's cuffs all covered in fur," she told the cat reprovingly, though she was smiling as she turned back to face the visitors. "Lady Julian's in the sun parlor, if you'd care to follow me, please."

The sun parlor was a spacious, south-facing chamber at the back of the house. A bowed set of French windows afforded an unobstructed view of a sheltered rock garden with an ornamental fishpond set down in the midst of it, though the garden itself was looking somewhat subdued in the thin November daylight.

The room, by contrast, was a riot of colors, textures, and shapes, flung together to create an effect of fairy-tale opulence. Oriental rugs in rich shades of emerald, ruby, and gold covered all but the edges of a fine parquet floor. The walls were hung with subtly figured yellow silk as background for a delectation of fans, embroideries, and pale watercolors that, to Peregrine's trained eye, bore the unmistakable stylistic features of the Edo Period. By contrast, he thought the festoons of transparent silk swagged across the top of the window and down the sides in lieu of drapes might be saris, with their rich edgings of metallic gold embroidery.

Every shelf and tabletop displayed its selection of curios and objets d'art—pieces of antique cloisonné, intricate carvings in ivory, soapstone, and jade, fragile vessels of thin, translucent porcelain, lacquer-work inlaid with gems and mother-of-pearl, all sweetened with the faint, spicy fragrance of sandalwood and cinnamon. Gazing round him in growing delight, Peregrine felt almost as if he had stepped out of the workaday world into an enchanted palace in an Oriental fable.

The presiding genius of the fable, Lady Julian herself, was sitting ensconced in an old-fashioned wicker wheelchair at the center of this room, a slight, twisted little figure with an Indian shawl draped over her head and another across her lap. At the sight of her visitors, her thin, ivorine face brightened in a welcoming smile.

"Hello, Adam, my dear!" she exclaimed, and lifted both hands to him in a musical chime of bangles and bracelets. "I'm so pleased that you could come, to brighten such a grey, dreary day. *And,*" she added with a twinkle, "I see you've finally consented to bring along your Mr. Lovat."

"Didn't I say that I would?" Adam said with a laugh. He lifted one of her beringed hands to his lips with an air of affectionate gallantry, then beckoned his companion closer. "Peregrine, allow me to present you to Lady Julian Brodie."

Smiling shyly, Peregrine stepped forward and found himself under friendly scrutiny by a pair of bright black eyes, sage and candid as a child's. Liberated from his usual reservations, for there was that in her expression which invited him to return that regard, he gazed back at her and found himself looking deeper than he had consciously intended.

Lady Julian, he estimated, was somewhere between sixty and seventy years of age, but he could see, as if in overlay, the girl she once had been—a dainty, doll-like creature with raven hair and laughing black eyes. She had retained, he saw, the fair transparency of skin and the fine, winged arch of her eyebrows, but some of the laughter had been lost along the way, diminished by pain and a tragedy he could only guess at. As he bowed over the hand she offered, Peregrine found himself comparing her to a Chinese willow, at once delicate and gnarled.

"Lady Julian," he murmured.

Lady Julian smiled wistfully, as if somehow aware of his mental analogy, and the overlaying image dissolved with a shimmer. Then her face brightened again, as abruptly as a beam of sunlight breaking through a cloud.

"Mr. Lovat," she said, "I've been looking forward to meeting you ever since Adam first mentioned he'd made your acquaintance. I fear I've not yet had the opportunity to see any of your work, but I gather from the reviews I've seen that we can expect great things from you in the artistic sector.''

Peregrine had the good grace to blush. "If you're referring to that article in *The Scotsman* last month, I'm afraid Mr. McCallum was being overly generous—though I certainly appreciate the compliments, both his and yours.''

"I wasn't thinking of Mr. McCallum," Lady Julian said serenely. "I was thinking of something Adam said to me when he was last here. And there's no need to blush. I have every confidence in Adam's critical instincts.''

She gave Peregrine's hand a confiding pat, then turned to Adam. "He's charming, Adam. But I was about to ask Grace to bring us some refreshments. Will you have tea or coffee?''

"Tea, if you don't mind," Adam said. "And if I might put in a request, I don't imagine Peregrine has ever tasted anything quite like that excellent green tea you get sent to you from Kwang-chow.''

"I imagine Grace can manage that," she replied.

The tea Adam had recommended turned out to be the color of palest jade, and savored subtly of jasmine. It was accompanied by fragile biscuits glazed with honey and sesame seeds and an exotic assortment of sweetmeats flavored with anise, ginger, and orange flowers. Talk ranged amiably over a variety of subjects, from the growing acceptance of acupuncture in Western medicine to the provenance of a bronze Buddha overseeing the room from a corner shelf to the technical refinements of Japanese brushwork. Peregrine became so caught up in the latter topic of conversation that he forgot all about the reason he and Adam were here, until Grace Fyvie arrived to collect the tea tray, and Lady Julian herself returned briskly to business.

"You've been admirably patient, Adam, my dear," she said, "but I know you must be eager to have your ring back again. Give me half a moment and I'll fetch it for you.''

Before either of the two men could offer to assist her, she had spun her chair around and was propelling herself over to the sumptuously-inlaid writing desk on one side of the room. When she returned, her lap contained a small, brass-inlaid wooden box with a Chinese dragon coiled rampant about a large moonstone set into the lid.

She brought her chair to a standstill and opened the box. Gold and blue gleamed through her fingers as she plucked out a handsome gold ring set with an oval sapphire, which she handed across to Adam with a small, graceful flourish. He took it from her with a smile that broadened as he lifted the ring to the light for token inspection.

"Ah, Julian, you've made a masterful job of it," he told her warmly. "If I didn't know better, I never would have guessed it had ever been damaged."

"The stone, fortunately, was unscathed," said Lady Julian, as Adam put on the ring. "And it took some doing, but I managed not to have to recast the entire setting. However, do try to be more careful in the future."

At the mild note of censure in her tone, Peregrine squirmed uncomfortably, for it was he who had been the cause of the ring's damage, not Adam.

"Please don't be cross with Adam, Lady Julian," he said ruefully. "I don't suppose Adam will have told you this, but it's my fault the ring was damaged in the first place."

Lady Julian regarded him with a degree of amusement he found difficult to fathom. "Oh, he told me," she said. "That's why he and I thought that in the future it might be advisable for you to have this."

She reached into the box again. Peregrine blinked—and found himself gazing down at a second ring. The stone was a large, emerald-cut sapphire about the size of Adam's, held deep in a plain gold bezel, but the wide band sported a bold tracery of Chinese dragons. Though the physical design was quite different from Adam's ring, its psychic "presence" was very similar. Peregrine shrank from taking it, his hazel eyes wide with stunned surprise.

"Surely this isn't for me," he managed to say.

"On the contrary," Adam said, "it *is* for you. And yes, it's a gift—but a gift that carries with it certain responsibilities."

He emphasized this statement with a look, the significance of which was not lost on Peregrine. As Lady Julian continued wordlessly to hold out the ring, Peregrine summoned the boldness to reach and take it.

"It's beautiful," he breathed, turning it clumsily in his fingers. "I—thank you."

"Aren't you going to try it on?" Adam asked, quietly amused.

"Oh," said Peregrine. "Oh yes, of course."

He slipped the ring onto the third finger of his right hand. The fit, he discovered, was perfect.

"That's amazing!" he exclaimed, and turned to stare at Lady Julian. "You made this, didn't you? And how on earth did you manage to get the size right?"

"Oh, I didn't make this one, my dear," she said drily. "The stone is new, but the setting is—very old. As for the size, I had Adam's expert guidance."

"But, how did *you* know?" Peregrine asked Adam.

Adam snorted in genuine amusement. "Really, Peregrine. You'd think there was some magic to it. I took the liberty of making a guess while I was cleaning up that hand wound you took at Urquhart Castle. I—ah—believe you were doing your best to look everywhere *except* at your hand just about then—for which I don't suppose one can blame you."

Peregrine shuddered, but he also grinned a little shamefacedly. "I suppose I *was* a trifle preoccupied," he admitted. "But so would you have been, if you'd been worrying whether you'd ever paint again." He glanced at the ring. "You were certainly thinking ahead, though. There appears to be no end to your craft!"

"I sincerely hope not," said Lady Julian.

Her tone was grave enough to give Peregrine pause for thought. Wondering what she could have meant, he gazed down again at the ring on his hand. The fit *was* perfect, but the ring seemed all at once strangely heavy for its size, and he slipped it off for a closer look. The dragons on either side had their tails intertwined at the bottom of the band, and tendrils from their scales and fins extended up and around the bezel in fine tracery.

"This ring," he said hesitantly. "Does it have any . . . any . . ."

"Any powers?" said Adam. "None inherent to its physical makeup. Whatever powers may come to be vested in it in the future will be up to you."

"And how do I do that?"

"As I told you once before," Adam replied, "it isn't a matter of *doing*, so much as a matter of *becoming*—and you're doing that very well already. But if you're asking me for some kind of direction—Julian?"

Lady Julian nodded sagely. "I suspected he might want something more specific," she said. "If Peregrine is willing, I'm quite prepared to do a reading."

Peregrine looked from Julian to Adam and back again. "What kind of reading are you talking about?" he asked. "Some kind of fortune-telling?"

Lady Julian laughed indulgently, and for just an instant Peregrine could see in her the girl who once had been.

"I suppose the uninitiated would call it that," she said. "I propose we should consult the *I Ching*."

"The *I Ching*?"

"The name translates roughly as the 'Book of Changes,'"
Adam said. "The legendary Chinese Emperor Fu-hsi is said to
have invented it around the third millennium B.C. It serves as a
book of sacred scripture for some people, but philosophical
niceties aside, it's one of the most ancient and useful methods
available for divination—or sortilege, as it's sometimes called.
The questioner consults the oracle by tossing coins or yarrow
sticks. The patterns made when they fall yield hexagrams,
so-called because the coins or sticks are cast six times. Interpre-
tations of the hexagrams are set out in the Book of Changes."

Lady Julian corroborated this explanation with a nod and picked
up where Adam had left off.

"The *I Ching* is unique as an oracle, because it does not advise
us that something in particular is going to happen. Rather, it
directs the questioner's attention to alternatives that are condi-
tional upon the choices that he has at his disposal." She smiled at
Peregrine and added, "I learned the art of interpreting the *I Ching*
while my husband and I were resident in Hong Kong. Will you
trust me to guide you through a reading?"

Her eyes met Peregrine's. In that brief moment of contact, he
sensed that she had no secrets that she would not be prepared to
share with him, should the need arise. That confidence was
contagious.

"Of course," he said. "Tell me what you want me to do."

Lady Julian smiled. "First, let me introduce you to the coins."
She slipped a hand beneath the paisley shawl covering her lap and
took out a small drawstring bag made of heavy, undyed silk. "In
theory any coins will do, but I prefer these."

Unloosing the strings, she tipped the bag and shook out three
circular gold disks the size of ten-pence pieces, each with a square
aperture cut through the center. Looking more closely as Julian
turned them in her hand, Peregrine saw that each disk had one side
plain and the other side patterned. The characters on the patterned
side were Chinese.

"These coins were struck during the reign of the last Manchu
emperor," Lady Julian said, caressing one between thumb and
forefinger. "For many years now, I have treasured them for this
purpose. They have been faithful friends."

The coins chimed softly as she handed them to Peregrine.

"Cup the coins between your hands while you formulate the
question you wish to ask," she said. "The more specific the
question, the better. The other thing you must do is address

yourself to the divining spirit of the *I Ching*, bearing in mind that the same spirit simultaneously resides within you. When you feel yourself sufficiently at one with the oracle—'centered,' Adam would term it—cast the coins six times on the table before you. I shall note the patterns and give you the message at the end."

Peregrine nodded his understanding. Setting aside his ring, he pressed the bright gold coins between his palms as he had been instructed, then leaned back and closed his eyes, schooling himself to discipline his breathing as Adam had taught him to do. A sense of composure stole over him, quieting his conscious awareness so that his inner faculties could come to the fore. As he continued to breathe deeply, centered and serene, a question took shape, *How may I serve my friends?*

He gave himself time to consider other possible questions, but every variation continued to reiterate the same basic concern. Obviously this was the question he was intended to ask.

The matter of invocation was more delicate, for he was uncertain whether to conceive of the "spirit" Lady Julian had spoken of as personal or animistic. He tried looking at the notion from several different perspectives, but eventually he cast all debate aside and merely offered up his willingness to be guided.

*Here I am,* he told the oracle. *Show me what I am meant to do.*

He opened his eyes and nodded his readiness to cast the coins. Adam moved a tiny side table closer, and he and Julian leaned forward to watch as Peregrine made six successive casts, Julian taking note of each combination of patterned and smooth sides on a scrip of rice paper. When he had finished, she held out the paper so that he could see what she had drawn—a hexagram of lines, some solid, others broken.

Then she sat back in her chair, her black eyes abstracted as she considered the results. At last she spoke with slow deliberation, pointing out individual aspects of the hexagram as she did so.

"Your answer lies in the sky above—*Chi'en*—and in the marsh below—*Tui*. These signs, taken together, signify *Lu*, which denotes 'treading carefully.' This greater sign points to danger on the road to achieving some desired end. The Book of Changes says, *The subject treads upon the tail of a tiger. The superior man discriminates between high and low, and gives settlement to the aims of the people.*"

She paused. Her attention narrowed and sharpened. After a moment she resumed.

"You have a task to perform, at risk to yourself. Discrimination and settlement—these are the key to a successful outcome. To discriminate is to perceive distinctions in the midst of confusion. To give settlement is to act in the capacity of a judge, awarding redress where there has been wrongdoing.''

She paused again, as if casting about her for further inspiration. As Peregrine watched expectantly, her face stiffened into an ivory mask.

''I can see no more,'' she muttered. ''The rest will become clear when the moment of judgement is upon you. But be warned. There is more to be feared here than the tiger.''

''The Lodge of the Lynx?'' Peregrine blurted, before he could stop it. Lady Julian flinched at the name.

''They are the companions of Shadow, and respect no law, either of man or of Nature,'' she whispered. ''There is nothing they will not dare for the sake of power—''

She shuddered and fell silent with her eyes clenched shut. Looking closer, Peregrine was shocked to see a sudden, telltale silvering of tears on her cheeks. His gaze flew to Adam.

Without speaking, the older man leaned over and gently clasped Lady Julian's nearer arm. She covered his hand with hers and drew a deep breath. A moment later she opened her eyes and, seeing the look on Peregrine's face, managed a strained smile.

''I'm sorry, my dear,'' she said softly. ''Some wounds never quite heal.''

''Julian lost her husband in our last campaign against the Lodge of the Lynx,'' Adam said, by way of explanation.

''And part of me died too,'' she added, glancing past Peregrine to something only she could see. ''That was nearly fifteen years ago. I always told myself it was the price that Michael paid to seal our victory. But now they've killed Randall, and the fighting is set to begin again—''

She turned her gaze back on Peregrine. ''When Adam asked me to make you a ring, we both thought you would be a valuable addition to the Lodge, if still untrained. Now it seems you find us already embattled, with a breach in our ranks. For your own safety, perhaps it would be better for you to withdraw now, while you can.''

Peregrine's jaw tightened, and very deliberately he picked up the ring again and closed it in his fist.

''I won't withdraw, Lady Julian. Six weeks ago, I was almost ripe for suicide, because I couldn't control the gifts I'd been given. But for Adam's help and counseling, I would probably now be either dead or locked up in a mental institution. If I said I wasn't frightened, I'd be lying through my teeth. But the fear counts for less than the chance to do something really worthwhile with my life. I'd like to think I've already made at least some minor contributions."

Lady Julian's lips quivered, as if she would have liked to remonstrate further, but Adam intervened.

"Peregrine knows his own mind, Julian," he told her firmly. "He's aware of the dangers—and he *has* made some contributions that are far from minor. Time and the Powers that Be will decide the rest."

A subdued silence followed, broken by the soft chime of a clock tolling the hour. Adam glanced reflexively down at his watch and sighed, and Peregrine took advantage of the distraction to slip the dragon ring into his pocket.

"I'm afraid we'll have to be off, my dear," Adam said, as if nothing untoward had happened. "I've a man coming up to Strathmourne this afternoon to discuss the cost of reroofing Templemor Tower. One thing more before we go, however—have you made arrangements to attend Randall's funeral?"

Lady Julian shook her head. "No. I know it's Tuesday, but I'm afraid I've been too grieved to give the matter any practical thought."

"Then don't worry yourself about it now," Adam said. "I'll send Humphrey round to collect you at about half past ten. Maybe afterwards, we can talk again."

When they had taken their good-byes of her and were heading down the front steps to the car, Peregrine pressed his hand over the slight bulge of the ring in his pocket, not speaking until they were outside the front gate.

"I'm not going to wear the ring until you think I'm ready, Adam," he said, as they crossed the street toward the parked Range Rover, "but I want to know more about it. She made a point of saying only the stone was new. Who owned the ring itself, before me?"

Adam cast him a wry smile across the roof of the Range Rover as he unlocked the doors. "You don't miss much, do you?" he said. "I should think you would have guessed. The ring belonged to Sir Michael Brodie, her husband."

# CHAPTER FIFTEEN

THE house called "Nether Leckie" was situated on a gentle ridge of high ground, tucked away behind a partial screen of trees that yielded in turn to a well-tended lawn. It was a substantial residence of cut stone, built as a country retreat by a successful Victorian industrialist from Stirling, who had made his fortune supplying steel for Scottish bridgeworks. Kippen, the nearest village, lay some twelve miles to the west of Stirling, which made Nether Leckie secluded enough to be private, but near enough to the city to guarantee ready access to the amenities. It was a home that its present owner, Francis Raeburn, had for some years found admirably suited to his needs.

On the Monday afternoon following Peregrine's introduction to Lady Julian Brodie, Raeburn had retreated to the privacy of his library at Nether Leckie to examine his latest acquisition, just arrived by post: an anonymous thirteenth-century manuscript entitled *De lapidibus.* Prior to the German Occupation of Paris in 1940, the manuscript had been included among the holdings of the *Bibliotheque Nationale de Paris*, and still bore its penciled cataloging notations. Raeburn's source had not volunteered how the manuscript came into his hands, and Raeburn had not asked. He had good reason to believe that it had been written by a scholar-scribe in the employ of the Knights Templar.

Unwrapping the manuscript in the seclusion of his library, Raeburn reflected that he was probably one of only a few people living who could appreciate it as much for its content as for its value as a medieval artifact. It was an exceptionally valuable find, the fruit of a long search, and he savored the possession of it now like a man tasting a fine wine.

He stroked the pages lovingly, fingertips sensitive to the accumulated patina of centuries. Behind him, the afternoon sun was slanting brightly through the windows, glancing off the panes of the breakfront bookcases to turn all the glass to mirrors, reflecting back a stunning view of the Gargunnock Hills. Oblivious to the wintry glare, Raeburn feasted his eyes on the manuscript's illuminated borders, noting the elegance of the scribal hand, the neatness of the Latin abbreviations, and the marginalia, some of which was itself worthy of much note.

He was still gloating dreamily over the satisfactions of ownership, occasionally examining some fine point of artistry with a magnifying glass, when he was disturbed by a knock at the door. The entrance of Rajan, his Indian houseboy, produced a look of displeasure on Raeburn's blond face.

"I seem to recall giving instructions that I was not to be disturbed," he said coldly.

The turbanned head bobbed in almost cringing apology.

"I am very sorry, Mr. Raeburn, but two policemen are waiting in the hall. They say they desire to have a word with you. I have already verified their credentials. The senior of the two gives his name as Detective Chief Inspector McLeod—"

"McLeod?" Raeburn's annoyance yielded abruptly to interest, tempered—though he did not show it—with a measure of suspicion. Casually he closed the volume in front of him, saying as he did so, "One could wish that these gentlemen of the law would have seen fit to arrange an appointment. Still, whatever the reason for this unannounced visit, we may as well get it over as quickly as possible. I'll see them in here. Go ahead and show them up."

Rajan bowed himself out. In the ensuing brief interim, Raeburn returned the manuscript to its protective wrapping and secreted it away in the upper right-hand compartment of the desk. As he closed the drawer, the muffled sound of footsteps approached along the corridor. A deferential knock at the door heralded the return of Rajan, followed by two men in overcoats and suits.

"These are the gentlemen, Mr. Raeburn," the houseboy announced, hurriedly retreating to the hallway then, to leave Raeburn alone with his two unwanted visitors.

"Good afternoon, Mr. Raeburn," said the older of the two, stepping forward to display his ID. "I'm Detective Chief Inspector McLeod, Lothian and Borders Police, and this is my associate, PC Cochrane. With your permission, we'd like to ask you a few questions."

Raeburn took advantage of the other man's short introductory speech to let his first impressions sink in. The sturdy young constable was of negligible consequence—a fresh-faced youngster in his mid- to late-twenties, hardly more than a boy. Inspector McLeod, on the other hand, was not unknown to Raeburn, at least by repute, and definitely warranted further consideration. Broad-shouldered and burly, he looked to be exceptionally fit for his age, which Raeburn guessed to be somewhere around fifty. The blue eyes that glinted from behind the gold-rimmed aviator spectacles were uncommonly shrewd.

But that was not all. Without being able to put a name to it, Raeburn sensed the faint, indefinable presence of something more. His curiosity growing, he rose from his chair and offered the older policeman his hand, in what his own associates would have regarded as an almost-unheard-of gesture of familiarity.

"Francis Raeburn," he said with a cool smile. "I haven't the faintest notion why you should want to question me about anything, but if you consider it necessary, I certainly have no objections about cooperating."

The inspector's hand was hard and capable, the fingers knotty and strong. Raeburn briefly tightened his grip, simultaneously seizing the chance to extend his deeper faculties of perception. To his surprise and consternation, he detected the faint but distinct impression of an invisible ring on the third finger on McLeod's right hand, though a swift visual survey, as their hands parted, revealed that the inspector was wearing no physical ring. A gold wedding band glinted on the other hand, below an unremarkable wristwatch, but his only other visible jewelry was a gold tie pin.

Now even more curious, Raeburn sat down again, gesturing toward two chairs on the opposite side of the desk. "Please sit down," he said casually, "and tell me how I may be of service."

The two policemen took the chairs indicated. Without further preamble, McLeod reached into the breast of his overcoat and brought out a photograph, tendering it across the desktop to Raeburn.

"For starters, I'd like you to take a look at the individual in this photo, and tell me if you recognize him."

Raeburn accepted the photo. The image was that of a slight, elderly man with silvery hair and the faintly abstracted air of a scholar, recognizably the same individual whose photograph and dossier Raeburn had presented to the Head-Master hardly a fortnight ago. He made a show of peering at the present image with some uncertainty, gradually allowing a slight frown to furrow his brow.

"The face does look familiar," he told McLeod. "I can't recall a name offhand, but I've certainly seen him somewhere before. . . ."

He paused elaborately, as if searching his memory, then gave an exclamation of minor triumph. "I've got it now! It was in Edinburgh—some kind of shop. Antiques?" He looked hopefully at McLeod.

"Try books," the inspector said grimly.

"A bookshop?" Raeburn considered further, then feigned an air of enlightenment. "Of course!" he exclaimed. "Now I understand what this is all about. This is the bookstore owner— that Freemason fellow who was murdered so spectacularly—what was it, last week? What *was* his name now? Stanley? No, Stewart! Randall Stewart! That's right, isn't it?"

"Aye," McLeod said dourly. "That's right." He drew a deep breath. "We're trying to account for Mr. Stewart's movements on the Sunday prior to his death, Mr. Raeburn. According to his daughter, he left Edinburgh around nine o'clock that morning, supposedly bound for Stirling where, by arrangement, he was to have carried out an appraisal on a consignment of rare books. No one seems to know what happened to him after that, but since Stirling was his intended destination, we're interviewing anyone in the Stirling area who might possibly have seen him.

"Your name figures prominently in the sales records of several local book dealers," he continued. "Judging from your expenditures, you're a fairly keen collector of rare books—which were Randall Stewart's stock in trade. We thought it might be worth asking to see if he might have made contact with you during the week prior to his death."

He flashed Raeburn a swift look over the rims of his glasses, and Raeburn countered the look calmly.

"I'm afraid he didn't. Actually, I never even met the man." He reached across the desk to return the photograph. "While it's true that I occasionally make an independent purchase, I generally prefer to rely on the acquisition skills of my regular dealers—one or two of whom you have obviously already met. You must appreciate, gentlemen, that the rare book trade is rather territorial in that respect. If your Mr. Stewart contacted anyone, I suspect it would have been one of my suppliers—not me personally."

"We'll bear that in mind," McLeod said drily. He shifted his weight solidly in his chair and said, "Let's move on to another point—the question of the collection Randall Stewart was coming to look at. Do you recall hearing anything about a collection of rare books to be sold off? Perhaps an estate sale?"

Raeburn shook his head blandly. "Again, Inspector, I'm afraid the answer is no. But then, as I've said, I'm a collector, not a dealer. The people you really should be talking to are those who make a living in the trade.''

''Oh, we're doing that,'' said McLeod, ''never fear.''

The constable, Cochrane, had been taking notes. He paused and glanced over at his superior. McLeod again leveled his blue gaze at Raeburn.

''Just one more thing for the record, Mr. Raeburn. Could you please tell me where you were and what you were doing on the night of Sunday, November eighteenth?''

Raeburn permitted himself a small grimace, as if he considered the question slightly impertinent. Then he leaned back in his chair and pursed his lips thoughtfully.

''November eighteenth. . . . Let's see, that's the weekend before the one just past. That weekend I was in Glasgow, visiting a friend. And yes,'' he added with an ironic smile, ''I have several witnesses who can corroborate that.''

''That's fine, Mr. Raeburn,'' said McLeod. ''Perhaps you'd be good enough to give us the name and address of the friend in question?''

''If you really think it's important,'' Raeburn said with a shrug, ''though I hope you'll be discreet, as it's a lady involved.'' He directed his attention to young Cochrane and said, ''That's Ms. Angela Fitzgerald, number twenty-three, Queen's Terrace.''

As he spoke, he shot a covert glance at McLeod. The inspector appeared resigned enough, apparently satisfied with Raeburn's answer, but there was a darkling flicker behind his blue eyes that betrayed more than a suggestion of personal frustration. For no reason that Raeburn could immediately fathom, it suddenly occurred to him that McLeod might well be one of Randall Stewart's Masonic Lodge brothers. A closer look at the inspector's tie pin confirmed what he must have noticed unconsciously before—a tiny square and compass discreetly embossed on the decorative lozenge.

*So, the inspector is a Freemason*, Raeburn thought. *And is he anything else, I wonder?*

His troublesome involvement in the Urquhart disaster would certainly suggest it—though even Masonic training could account for at least some of what had been reported of him. Perhaps the impression Raeburn had gotten of an invisible ring was from a Masonic ring that, for some reason, he did not wear on duty.

The young constable, Cochrane, had been dutifully writing down the name and address Raeburn had given, and now handed his notebook to McLeod for verification. So while McLeod's attention was momentarily distracted, Raeburn bent his gaze once more on the inspector's right hand and narrowed his eyes. In that brief psychic blurring of his outward senses, he got a faint visual impression of the ring McLeod wasn't actually wearing at the moment—a gold band set with a deep blue sapphire—and this time as well, the throbbing pulse of tight-leashed power kept contained and channeled by control of which the ring was a symbol.

The discovery was enough to make Raeburn withdraw instantly behind the bulwarks of his own inner defenses, feigning to rub at something in his eye as cover for his consternation.

*That* was no mere Masonic ring!—though it had elements in common with Masonic resonances. It bespoke high-level initiation in some powerful esoteric tradition. It could even be the badge of membership in one of the detested Hunting Lodges—which would account for a lot of hitherto unexplained happenings, especially at Urquhart. Whatever it was, this McLeod was *not* the mere policeman he appeared to be.

Maintaining an urbanity that he was far from feeling, Raeburn turned his gaze back to McLeod. His investigation had occurred in a breath of an instant, and McLeod was just now looking up from the notebook he handed back to his associate, apparently satisfied for now.

"So, Inspector, is there anything else you'd like to ask me?" Raeburn said neutrally.

"Not at this time," McLeod replied, standing. "Thank you very much for your time, Mr. Raeburn. You'll be right here, will you, in case we find we need any further information?"

Raeburn chuckled genially as he reached for the bellpull to summon Rajan.

"Don't worry, Inspector. I haven't made any plans to leave the country. Good luck with your investigation. My houseboy will see you out."

Once the two policemen had departed, Raeburn sat silent for several minutes, pondering the import of his discoveries. The arrival of a Huntsman on his doorstep raised a host of difficult questions—if, indeed, that was what McLeod was. To begin with, there was the matter of McLeod's actual status within his Lodge—for that would partially determine how he must be dealt with. Upon consideration, Raeburn doubted that McLeod was actually a Master of the Hunt—but that didn't mean he wasn't a potentially formidable opponent. The residual from the ring was proof enough of that.

A more pertinent question concerned McLeod's particular abilities. Of all the things he might have been—empath or telepath, clairvoyant or psychometrist, medium or diviner—the first three seemed unlikely in view of the fact that he had not appeared to notice that he was being assessed psychically. At the same time, however, Raeburn could not be absolutely sure that he had not betrayed himself by some sign that McLeod, upon further reflection, might recognize.

In any event, the presence of someone like McLeod on the police force was like a time bomb waiting to go off. If the bomb went off too soon, it could seriously imperil a host of carefully laid plans. Removing McLeod would be risky, admittedly—but not nearly so risky as leaving him at liberty.

The desktop telephone stood within easy reach of his hand. Raeburn toyed with several of the items on his desk while he took account of all the foreseeable variables, then came to a decision. Picking up the receiver, he dialled the Edinburgh branch of the Lothian and Borders Police. Three rings later he had an answer.

"Good afternoon," Raeburn said. "I should like to leave a message for Inspector Napier. When he comes in, please ask him to call his uncle. . . ."

The call was returned within an hour. Raeburn took it in the library, where he had gone back to the perusal of his new treasure.

"This is Napier," said a hard tenor voice on the other end of the line. "What's going on?"

"Quite a bit, as it happens," Raeburn said blandly. "Where are you calling from?"

"A public phone box, of course. Where did you think I'd be calling from?"

Raeburn disregarded the question. "We have a problem," he stated.

"So I gathered. What's wrong?"

"McLeod's been here. Have you any idea why?"

Silence. Then: "I should think it was routine."

"I do hope so," Raeburn replied. "He *said* he was interviewing people associated with the rare book trade, trying to sniff out anyone who might have seen Randall Stewart in Stirling on the fatal Sunday. I'm inclined to believe that's all it was, but something else leads me to believe that he is, indeed, a member of the opposition. In fact," he amended, "I'm virtually certain of it."

Napier swore briefly but fluently, then said, "Do you think he suspects anything about you?"

"I can't say for certain," Raeburn said with brutal candor. "But he must not be allowed to become a problem. Not at this stage of the game. Do you understand?"

There was a pause from the other end of the line. Then: "I understand. What do you want me to do? Arrange a hit?"

"Too gaudy," Raeburn said shortly. "It needs to be something less overt."

Another pause. "What do you suggest then?"

"I want you to obtain a few necessary items," Raeburn said, making pencilled notations on a scratch pad. "Something with his signature on it—an original, not a copy—and ah, yes. How about a Styrofoam cup that McLeod has used? Those should be reasonably available and sufficient. Bring them to me here tomorrow night, and we'll discuss the plan in greater detail."

# CHAPTER SIXTEEN

RANDALL Stewart's funeral took place the following morning within the Gothic grandeur of St. Mary's Episcopal Cathedral, in the heart of Edinburgh. For Peregrine, this funeral was not nearly as difficult as another he had attended with Adam barely a month before, but it carried its own stark tragedy, for both of them were all too aware of the brutality of Randall's passing, having seen its aftermath firsthand.

Unlike Lady Laura Kintoul, whose long and happy life had wound gently to a close, with ample time for preparation and good-byes, Randall had been thrust untimely into death, his last conscious awareness that of terror and of pain. Peregrine had only met Randall the one time, that Saturday morning in the bookshop, but he knew what the old man had meant to Adam—and that healing would be long in coming for all those who had known and loved Randall. Finding his killers and bringing them to justice would help—and thwarting whatever black purpose they had hoped to accomplish by their unholy sacrifice—but it would not bring Randall back, or fill the empty places in the lives of those left behind.

Saddened by the utter waste of it all, Peregrine let his gaze wander unobtrusively around the church as he waited for the service to begin. He made a point not to dwell on the flower-banked catafalque awaiting the arrival of Randall's coffin. The organist was playing a Pachelbel fantasia in G minor as a prelude, and Peregrine let a part of his mind follow and enjoy the music while another part noted faces he knew.

The cathedral was crowded. Humphrey had returned a short time earlier with Lady Julian, parking her wheelchair at the end of the row where Adam and Peregrine himself sat, afterwards withdrawing quietly to the side aisle to pay his own private respects. Lady Julian wore a shawl of dark paisley over her silvery hair, and buried her face in her gnarled old hands as she made her silent devotions.

McLeod had arrived at about the same time, escorting a quietly attractive redhead in dark blue who Peregrine decided must be the ever-patient and long-suffering Jane. Heads bowed, they were sitting toward the back, just ahead of the formal ranks of Randall's brother Freemasons, though McLeod was not wearing Lodge regalia.

The organ prelude ended, and the Stewart family came in through a side door and sat in the front row. Victoria Houston was among them, sitting close beside Miranda and holding her hand. Peregrine had seen Christopher back at the main doors when he and Adam came in, awaiting the arrival of the body with two more clergymen, a cross-bearer, and two small boys holding processional torches. Miranda seemed to be holding up bravely, displaying at least the semblance of a measure of composure, but Peregrine was sorry to see her so subdued, and had to wonder whether she would ever again be quite the merry gypsy dancer he remembered from their first meeting.

"Let not your heart be troubled," Father Christopher Houston said from the back of the church, reading from the Gospel of St. John as the crucifer and torch-bearers began processing in for the service to begin. They were followed by the Masonic pall bearers in aprons and gauntlets and blue collars, carrying a coffin draped with the blue-and-white flag of Saint Andrew and crowned with a single wreath of red roses. The three clergymen came behind.

"Ye believe in God, believe also in me," Christopher continued. "In my Father's house are many mansions. If it were not so, I would have told you. I go to prepare a place for you."

*Many mansions. . . .* As Peregrine glanced aside at Adam's austere profile, rising with the rest of the congregation as the procession came near, he wondered if there really was a place for him among those who made up Adam's working fellowship. And how could he even presume to be able to fill the void left by Randall's death? He lost himself for the rest of the service beseeching God for guidance, praying His blessing on Randall and those who had loved him, and asking that he himself might prove worthy to take up a part of that Work Randall had left unfinished, and which Adam continued to serve.

Adam himself played no active role in this funeral service, and used the time to pay his own, personal tribute. Though Randall Stewart had been a close and deeply valued friend, it was a friendship that neither Adam nor Randall had ever widely advertised in the eyes of the world, for the Hunting Lodge, like the Freemasons, had good reason to regard secrecy as a condition of safety. As the dean of the cathedral read the closing prayer, Adam found himself praying that he and the remaining members of the Hunt would be able to preserve that safety throughout the trials that lay ahead.

"O Father of all, we pray to Thee for those we love but see no longer," the dean prayed. "Grant them Thy peace; let light perpetual shine upon them; and in Thy loving wisdom and almighty power work in them the good purpose of Thy perfect will; through Jesus Christ our Lord. Amen."

A benediction followed. The cathedral bells began to toll as the procession formed up to leave. At the wishes of the family, the body was to be privately cremated later that evening, but for now, Randall's six Masonic brethren shouldered his coffin once again to carry it out between two lines of their brethren standing at attention.

Adam let himself be drawn along with the slow exodus of mourners following behind the family and the coffin, Peregrine right behind him—in no hurry, for he suspected that the cause of the growing congestion in the cathedral porch was a deterioration of the weather. Craning to see over the heads of those in front of him, he could see umbrellas going up on the steps beyond, and sheets of rain gusting along Palmerston Place.

With a surreptitious glance at his pocket watch, Adam turned to gaze back along the nave, hoping that Humphrey had not left yet—for the plan had been for him to take Lady Julian home and then meet them at the wake to follow at Randall's bookshop. But Humphrey must have already whisked Lady Julian through a convenient rear exit, for he was nowhere to be seen.

"Do you want me to see if I can catch him before he leaves?" Peregrine asked.

"It's worth a try," Adam replied. "I'll go on and wait in the porch—and snag a taxi, if I see one."

As Peregrine retreated down the aisle, Adam returned his attention to the crowd ahead—and immediately noticed a tall, fit-looking man in a military greatcoat, slightly older than himself, working his way along the side aisle, another man in uniform preceding him. The older man noticed Adam at about the same time, and sent his companion on ahead as he raised a hand to Adam in greeting.

Smiling, Adam changed course, easing between two rows of chairs toward the shelter of a side chapel. The red tabs of a general officer showed at the throat of the uniform glimpsed above the collar of the older man's greatcoat, and heavy bullion traced the bill of the cap tucked under the man's arm.

"Hello, Gordon," Adam said cordially, offering his hand. "I wasn't sure I'd see you here."

The older man smiled beneath a steel-grey military moustache as they exchanged handshakes, steel-grey hair framing steel-grey eyes. "I could say the same of you, Adam. But you knew Randall from the book world as well, didn't you?"

"Aye, a legacy from my father," Adam said. "He was one of Randall's regular patrons, and passed the association on to me when I was old enough to appreciate it."

"Your father did you a great service," Gordon said. "Randall Stewart—God rest his soul—was a man of rare principle. Did you know he'd served with my regiment in the Second War?" Adam shook his head. "That was before my time, of course, but I'm told he was a good soldier; I *know* he was a good human being." He sighed. "There are all too few like him these days, of *any* generation. His loss would have been grievous under any circumstances—though we all have to go sometime—but losing a brother like this—"

He shook his head and sighed reminiscently, fingering the signet ring on his right hand. Light glinted off a Masonic symbol etched in the face of the dark stone, drawing the flicker of Adam's glance, and the general's expression was somewhat wistful as he raised the hand slightly to also look at it.

"One of these days, I really do hope you'll ask me the right questions about this, Adam," he said. "You're surrounded by Freemasons, in almost everything you do—McLeod and his crew, me—and there's the tradition of your father and grandfather, both of them Masons of the highest degree."

The look that accompanied this statement conveyed a friendly challenge, but also resignation, for he and Adam had had this conversation many times before.

"I'm flattered that you keep exploring the question, Gordon," Adam said with a chuckle, "but you tell me where I'd find the time. Given all the responsibilities already incumbent upon me, I've always felt that I'd be doing your Order a grave injustice if I were to join with less than full commitment."

Gordon gave him a rueful grin. "You demand more of yourself, I think, than we would ever expect of you. But if you should ever change your mind, don't hesitate to let me know." He glanced toward the doors. "Well, I expect my driver will have brought the car around by now—beastly weather, isn't it? Can I give you a lift anywhere, or is Humphrey taking care of you?''

"Actually," Adam said, "I'm afraid I foolishly arranged for Humphrey to take Lady Julian home before I realized it would be bucketing when we came out. Peregrine and I were going to take a taxi to the wake, and Humphrey's to meet us there, but it *would* make life easier if you could drop us at the bookstore. You don't mind meeting Peregrine under these circumstances, do you?"

Gordon smiled and shook his head. "I thought that might be who he was, sitting with you during the service. Here he comes now."

"And he obviously didn't manage to catch Humphrey," Adam said, noting Peregrine's expression of resignation. "I'm sure he'll be pleased he doesn't have to drown after all. Peregrine, come and let me introduce you to Sir Gordon," he said, beckoning Peregrine to join them. "Gordon, this is one of my associates, Mr. Peregrine Lovat. Peregrine, General Sir Gordon Scott-Brown."

"How do you do, Mr. Lovat," Sir Gordon said, shaking Peregrine's hand.

"Honored to meet you, sir," Peregrine murmured.

"Gordon's going to give us a lift to the bookshop," Adam said breezily, already urging the artist toward the doors.

They were clambering into the blue Ford Granada almost before Peregrine realized what had happened. As they sped along Princes Street and then south across the bridge that passed over Waverley Station, Peregrine sat back wide-eyed and silent while Adam and the general exchanged innocuous comments about the weather and Adam directed the driver toward Randall's bookshop. They were there in ten minutes, and Peregrine paused to watch the car pull away as Adam stamped water from his shoes and prepared to go inside.

"Adam, was that *the* Gordon Scott-Brown?" he asked.

"So far as I know, there's only one," Adam said.

Peregrine's eyes widened, and he whistled low under his breath. "But, he's the top general in Scotland, the General Officer Commanding. I've seen his portrait in the regimental museum in the castle."

"Well, he *is* governor of the castle, and that *is* his regiment," Adam said, as if that explained it all. "That's why he was able to give us a lift, on his way back to work."

Peregrine had begun to grow accustomed to the fact that Adam knew a wide variety of very important people, who seemed to turn up when needed, but something about this particular coincidence struck him as a little unusual, even for Adam. The utterly offhand nature of Adam's reply seemed to discourage any more serious inquiry just now, but Peregrine found himself wondering, after they went inside, whether Sir Gordon, too, was more than he seemed on the surface.

They met up with McLeod after they went inside, though Jane was no longer with him. After paying their respects to the family, Adam sought him out and drew him aside for a brief update on his ongoing investigation. The inspector was in a dour frame of mind.

"Donald and I must've interviewed more than a dozen people yesterday," he muttered, "but for all the useful information we've gotten out of it, we might as well have saved ourselves the trouble. I wish to God somebody would get the media off our backs. It's bad enough that we're not getting anywhere on this case without my having to share that fact daily with a dozen gentlemen of the press."

He paused to bite savagely into a sandwich. "If I were twenty years younger," he declared with a glower, "I'd quit this job and become an accountant. As it is, I'm beginning to think I ought to retire and keep bees!"

Adam knew better than to take such a statement seriously, but he shared the underlying frustration in full measure.

They parted shortly, McLeod to return to his investigations, Peregrine to spend a few hours working on his portrait commission of the former Provost of Edinburgh, and Adam to finalize arrangements with the young locum who would be covering his patients for the two days he expected to be in London. On the way home, because it was growing late, Adam had Humphrey stop at a fish and chips shop, where Peregrine dashed in for paper-wrapped portions for the three of them. He and Adam spread this elegant fare on the burled walnut picnic trays that folded down from the backs of the seats; and Adam briefed both Peregrine and Humphrey on his expected timetable for the London trip.

He was booked on a midday shuttle the next day, and on Wednesday morning set out for the airport with Humphrey and a single carry-on bag, intending to stop at Jordanburn only long enough to make his regularly scheduled hospital rounds. Unfortunately, one of his more volatile patients had chosen this particular morning to edge into a near-suicidal depression. In the end, it was nearly three o'clock before Adam was able to get away.

Fortunately, Humphrey had not been idle while his master dealt with the unexpected medical crisis. The next flight to London-Heathrow was set to depart at three forty-five, and Humphrey had contrived to change Adam's reservation and get him a seat on it. The doughty manservant even managed to get him to the airport in time to make the flight—though the status of Philippa Sinclair's flight, also inbound to London, was yet unknown.

It was dark by the time Adam landed at Heathrow, with a frosty haze hovering over the runways. Once inside the terminal, he headed immediately for the nearest Arrivals monitor, for the delay had now made it a near-run thing to meet Philippa's flight. Fortunately, a rapid scan of the flight numbers revealed that Philippa's flight had been delayed by half an hour—which, given the weather, was hardly unexpected.

Taking advantage of the reprieve, Adam shifted his carry-on onto his shoulder and strolled off to the airport cafe nearest the International Arrivals Hall, where he ordered a large cup of tea and settled down at one of the tables to wait. The large panel windows running along the opposite wall gave back bland reflections of the cafe's interior. Outside, the darkness was dotted with pale blurs of moving lights as planes landed and took off in a rumble of distant thunder.

Moving lights . . . fields of darkness. Almost before he was aware of it, Adam's thoughts were drawn yet again to the memory of his recent venture into the Inner Planes, and the cryptic utterances of the Master regarding the work that lay in store for Peregrine Lovat.

*Broken images must be restored . . . The temple of lights must be rebuilt. . . .*

As Adam mused, he found himself trying to reconcile those remarks with Lady Julian's reading of the *I Ching*. "To discriminate," Julian had said, "is to perceive distinctions in the midst of confusion. To give settlement is to act in the capacity of a judge, awarding redress where there has been wrongdoing."

Broken images. Confusion. Adam entertained no doubts that both the oracles were pointing to the disruption of all the underlying personalities of Gillian Talbot. The image of the temple to be rebuilt was almost certainly a metaphorical reference to the totality of the individual—but how to rebuild such a ruin?

He saw suddenly in his mind's eye an image of another ruin of a more physical nature—Templemor Tower, now in the process of restoration—and he tried to relate it to the Talbot case.

*How do you restore a ruin?* he asked himself. *It's obvious, in a physical structure like a tower house. You work from the ground up. . . .*

He was still ruminating on the possible implications of this insight when his reverie was abruptly interrupted by a loud crackle from the airport's public address system, followed by a squawky announcement that British Airways Flight 214 from Boston had just landed.

Adam took the time to finish his tea, knowing that she would be held up by the necessary formalities of going through Immigration and then through baggage claim and Customs. After about twenty minutes, he shouldered his bag again and made a brief foray into one of the concourse flower shops, where he bought a delicate spray of hothouse orchids. By the time he had ensconced himself near the Meeting Point in the Arrivals Hall, with a view through the doors that opened periodically to disgorge new arrivals, the first of the arriving Boston passengers had begun to spill into the waiting area, where friends and family stood poised to greet them.

Somewhat impatiently, Adam scanned the incoming throng. A moment later he caught sight of her—a slender, platinum-haired figure in a scarlet coat and hat, moving determinedly toward the hall at the center of a small whirl of airport employees.

In her youth, Philippa Sinclair had been a beauty. At seventy-five, she was still a strikingly handsome woman, polished and immaculately groomed, with an imperiously sculptured face and flashing dark eyes. A smart young man in British Airways livery was leaning in toward her, making small, conciliatory gestures with his hands, while behind them, a middle-aged man in a foreman's coverall appeared to be having words with a pair of uniformed baggage handlers, one of whom was pushing a baggage cart laden with Philippa's luggage. Philippa herself seemed regally oblivious to the curious glances they were attracting from the other people in the hall. Even at a distance, Adam could see the calm, purposeful set of her chin.

Smiling, for it was so like Philippa to wind up making a grand entrance, he moved smoothly forward and waved a hand to attract her attention. As soon as she spotted him, her formidable calm dissolved in a smile of dazzling warmth. Veering off on a sharp tangent, she sailed gracefully forward to meet him, leaving her escort to scurry after her with unbecoming haste. As they met, Adam gathered his mother into a long-armed embrace and saluted her with a kiss, then presented her with the orchids.

"Good Lord, Philippa," he murmured good-naturedly, "can't you go *anywhere* without creating a stir?"

His mother's response to this question was a small, ironic moue. After delightedly inhaling the flowers' perfume, she rose on tiptoe to plant an answering kiss on her son's bronzed cheek, settling then on his arm to glance back at her entourage.

"Somebody appears to have mislaid one of my cases between Boston and London," she said astringently, in an accent mixed of Yankee and Highland antecedents. "Inquiries are in progress, but so far no one seems to know where it's got to. I'm relying on Mr. Martin here to get it all sorted out."

The look that she directed at Mr. Martin was surgically penetrating. Endlessly compassionate with the truly unfortunate, Philippa had no patience whatsoever when it came to matters of petty incompetence. The airport official squirmed guiltily and cast Adam a silent appeal for mercy.

"We *are* working on it, Lady Sinclair," he said. "I'm frightfully sorry about the inconvenience. I'm sure the bag will turn up very soon. If it missed the flight in Boston, it will be on the next one. If you'll just give me the name of your hotel, I'll have it sent along just as soon as it arrives."

"Thank you, I'd appreciate that," Philippa said crisply, and threw an inquiring glance at her son.

"We'll be staying at the Caledonian Club until Friday," Adam said, handing the man a business card from a monogrammed case. "If it should take longer than that to resolve this, the steward at the club will advise you of my home address in Scotland. I trust that won't be a problem."

"Not at all, Sir Adam. Thank you very much. Sorry again, Lady Sinclair."

Philippa favored the man with her frostiest nod of acknowledgement and sailed off in the direction of the exit, Adam and a porter with the baggage trolley following in her wake.

They engaged a taxi from the rank in front of the terminal building. Adam gave the driver their destination and oversaw getting all the cases into the boot, then sank back in his seat to regard his mother with quizzical affection as they pulled away from the curb.

"I hope," he said, "that there wasn't anything irreplaceable in that lost bag of yours. If it turns up in Paris unclaimed, it'll probably be destroyed as a suspected terrorist bomb."

Philippa nodded abstractedly. "Yes, dear, I know." She settled herself against the upholstery like a bird settling its plumage and said more briskly, "No, there's nothing vital in it: just an uninteresting assortment of personal fripperies I can easily do without. If I seemed a bit severe with that young man back there, it was because he initially tried to fob me off. If there's one thing

I cannot abide, it's someone who's too lazy to do the job for which he's been hired!''

She broke off with a laugh and shook her head at her own vehemence. ''What a terrible old woman I've become since you were last over! We need to see more of each other. If I thought for a moment that anyone at the clinic could do the job half as well as I can, I'd retire to a cottage on the Isle of Arran and spend my declining years cultivating petunias!''

Adam thought of McLeod and chuckled. ''No, you wouldn't. You're as badly addicted to the work as I am. Which reminds me, how *are* things at the clinic?''

Philippa's shoulders rose and fell in an elegant shrug. ''Busy. Busier than ever, in fact. We're getting increasing numbers of referrals from hospitals outside of our own district. Probably a tribute to our reputation for achieving results, but it's meant a heavy increase in case loads for the staff. I've taken on three new consultants in as many months. Two of them are competent analysts, but the third shows real promise. I shall be interested to see where his talents lead him in the months to come.''

She paused to take a long look at her son's face. ''What about you? How are things on the home front?''

''If you mean how are things at the hospital,'' he said, ''we're getting on more or less as usual, though some of the recent changes in the National Health Service have generated a devilish amount of extra paperwork. As far as everything else is concerned . . .'' He lowered his voice. ''How much have you heard so far about Randall's death?''

''Enough to convince me that the affair is likely to prove more than the police can safely handle—other than your Inspector McLeod, of course.'' Philippa's chiselled face went very still, and she spared a fleeting glance for the averted back of the taxi driver before adding, ''That's one of the things I want to talk with you about, later on. Till then, suffice it to say that I'm deeply sorry you should have lost such a friend in such a way.''

The Caledonian Club was where Adam habitually stayed on his visits to London. Upon their arrival, he and Philippa left the porter to see to their luggage while they went on through to the reception area. The clerk at the desk recognized Adam at once, and bobbed up from his seat with a welcoming grin.

''Good evening, Sir Adam.''

''Good evening, Tom,'' Adam said. ''This is my mother, Lady

Philippa Sinclair. I believe my man booked adjoining rooms for us?"

"That's right, Sir Adam. I took the call myself. If you'd care to sign the register, I'll get the keys." Over his shoulder, he added, "There's also a message for you, sir. It came in about twenty minutes ago."

He tendered Adam a folded message slip, along with two sets of room keys, and Adam unfolded the paper and tilted it toward the light.

*For Sir Adam—Hold for arrival,* the block printing read. *Important news. Respectfully request you call home without delay. Humphrey.*

Wordlessly Adam passed the note to Philippa, who arched her eyebrows and muttered, "I suspect you'd better call him."

"If it's urgent, sir," put in Tom, "you're welcome to make your call from here."

"Thank you," said Adam, reaching for the phone.

"Just dial nine first to get an outside line, sir," Tom said.

As soon as he heard the dial tone, Adam punched out the code and telephone number for Strathmourne. Humphrey answered on the second ring.

"Hello, Humphrey," Adam said. "I've just collected Philippa and gotten the message you left at the club. What's up?"

"There's a lady trying to get in touch with you, sir, on behalf of her daughter," said Humphrey, his usual telephone formality not quite masking his excitement. "She gave her name as Mrs. Iris Talbot."

Gillian Talbot's mother!

"I see," he said neutrally, reining in his own feelings. "I gather she was phoning from London?"

"She was, sir. I have her number right here, if you'd care to make a note of it."

Adam was already reaching for a pen on the counter.

"Right you are, Humphrey. Go ahead."

He jotted down the number on the back of the hotel message slip, reading back the digits to Humphrey to double-check. When he had hung up, he turned to Philippa. Before he could offer an explanation, she raised a forestalling hand.

"I can see this is going to get involved, and I, for one, am perishing for a cup of tea. Why don't I see the luggage up to our rooms and meet you in the lounge when you're finished?"

"Better yet," he replied, flagging the attention of the porter, who was just rolling in the trolley with their luggage, "I'll call from my room, and you can have tea sent up."

He thought about Iris Talbot as he and Philippa followed the porter into the lift and headed for the rooms, blessing whatever had made her choose tonight to try to call him—though making the call at all suggested a further deterioration in Gillian's condition. Still, the timing could hardly be better. Once he had gained the privacy of his room, he paused only long enough to shed his topcoat before dialling the London number Humphrey had given him. A man's voice answered on the third ring, sounding worried.

"Good evening," Adam said. "This is Dr. Adam Sinclair, from Jordanburn Hospital in Edinburgh. I've received a message asking that I get in touch with Mrs. Iris Talbot—"

"Dr. Sinclair?" the other voice broke in before Adam could say more. "Oh, thank God, we've been hoping you'd call! I'm George Talbot. Iris is my wife. We—it's about our daughter Gillian."

"Of course. I remember the case quite well," Adam interposed smoothly. "How can I help you, Mr. Talbot?"

"It isn't for me—it's for Gillian," Talbot replied. "When you spoke to my wife last month, you told her—that is, you gave her to understand that if—if our daughter's condition didn't improve, we might refer her to you for treatment."

"I take it that Gillian's condition has *not* improved, then," Adam said.

"No, it hasn't. In fact, she's worse, if anything. The doctors at Charing Cross have tried everything they can think of, but nothing's working. She's just slipping farther and farther away. We had a word with Dr. Ogilvy—that's Gillian's attending physician—and she agreed that we should seek your professional assistance. I know this may be asking a great deal, but would you—do you think you might be able to see her?"

"Of course I'll see her," Adam said reassuringly. "As it happens, I'm in London at the moment on some personal business. Why don't I arrange to meet you and Mrs. Talbot some time tomorrow at the hospital? It would be helpful if Dr. Ogilvy could be there as well. What time does she normally make rounds?"

"She generally stops in around ten," said Gillian's father. "But if you think that's too early—"

"Ten o'clock will be fine," Adam said. "And if I may, I should like to bring another medical colleague of mine."

159

# CHAPTER SEVENTEEN

ADAM went into the adjoining room to find his mother ensconced in a tartan-upholstered armchair, shoes kicked off and stockinged feet tucked up under her like a girl, sipping tea from a delicate porcelain cup. Her smile lit up the room as she set the cup aside and leaned forward to pour him one.

"Well?" she said. "What *was* all that about?"

Adam slid into the chair opposite and accepted the cup and saucer that Philippa held out to him, setting it down to add milk and sugar.

"You remember I rang you a few weeks ago about that Gillian Talbot girl, and all the business with Michael Scot?" he said, giving the tea a stir.

"Of course."

"Well, the parents have finally made contact," Adam went on. "They want to put their daughter under my care."

Philippa raised a knowing eyebrow, all illusion of girlish abandon giving way to the focused attention of a professional—on several levels.

"From what you told me, I'm surprised it's taken them this long."

Adam sipped at his tea. "Better late than never," he said. "I just hope the situation can still be salvaged."

"Yes, there is that." Philippa gave a small, eloquent shudder and hugged her arms as if against a sudden chill.

"Poor soul, past and present! I certainly hope that when this present frame of mine is eight centuries dead, no miscreant will find reason to want to haul *me* back to the remains!" After a pause, she added, "How are you going to explain things to the parents?"

"If they press me for a concrete diagnosis," Adam said, with a gesture of his cup, "I suppose I'll define the problem as a *personality disorder*—which is accurate enough, as far as it goes." He shrugged. "Beyond that, I'm going to urge them to let me transfer Gillian to Edinburgh. I'm given to understand that my new fledgling is to be involved in the resolution, and I can't very well bring him down here to do the work—especially since we're not yet sure what the work will be. Besides that, I have other things demanding my attention in Edinburgh as well.''

"That's certainly true," she replied. "Well, I shouldn't think you'll get much opposition from the parents. I would gather they're already convinced that you represent their daughter's last hope for recovery." She paused and added thoughtfully, "I wonder if the Lodge of the Lynx knows anything about Gillian's existence."

Adam set down his empty cup and shrugged. "Difficult to say. One would think her existence must have been known to the team who originally carried out the Melrose summoning. They certainly must have known they'd hauled Scot out of a present incarnation. And if even one member of that team should have survived the faerie massacre at Urquhart, he or she would be in a position to pass that knowledge on to other operatives within the organization. For what it's worth."

"And what *is* it worth?" Philippa asked.

Adam grimaced. "I wish I knew. As she is at the moment, Gillian is of no consequence to them, either as a present threat or a future asset. But that situation might change overnight, if our enemies should come to suspect there was any likelihood that she might be healed. After all, at least one of her underlying personae—that of Michael Scot—has knowledge that the Lynx wanted. If they thought *we* might get it—and hence, gain some clue to what they're trying to do—that alone would be sufficient cause for them to try to destroy her, rather than risk her passing that knowledge on to us."

"In other words," Philippa said succinctly, "the less anyone else knows about this affair, the better."

Adam nodded. "I'm not even entirely happy about transferring her to Edinburgh—though it's necessary, if I'm to have sufficient access to do her or us any good. It puts her into closer physical proximity to whatever the Lynx are planning—and could make her more vulnerable."

"What about putting her in a private clinic?" Philippa asked. "You'd have better security, and better privacy for getting on with what needs to be done."

"This is Britain, not America," Adam reminded her. "I have to work within a system that's sometimes very rigid. Unfortunately, so long as she's a public patient, there are limits to how far I dare deviate from standard procedures. It's going to raise enough eyebrows, just getting her transferred up to Scotland. Once she's there, I'll need to keep a very low profile while we figure out what to do with her."

"In that case," Philippa said, "it seems to me that it wouldn't be a bad idea for some member of the Hunting Lodge to take responsibility for safeguarding this child while you do that." As she leveled a meaningful look in her son's direction, Adam smiled.

"Am I to understand that you're volunteering?"

"Why not?"

"Why not, indeed?" Adam grinned over at his mother in mingled affection and respect. "Any scion of the Lynx who sees *you* as easy prey is going to be in for quite a shock!"

"I do like to think that I've not lost my edge," she said, with a droll smile that transformed into a yawn as she indulged in a stretch. "Dear me, I assure you it isn't the company. It's been a long day, though, and I do need my beauty sleep."

"Good Lord, yes! You must be frightfully jet-lagged," Adam replied, preparing to rise. "You shouldn't have let me go on so." He glanced at his watch. "I—ah—don't want to put any pressure on you, but I wonder if you might like to come along with me to the hospital in the morning and meet our patient. I've arranged to be there at ten. The Talbots have already welcomed the suggestion that I might bring along a colleague, but that decision is entirely up to you."

"As if I would ever let myself be caught lolling idly about in my bed when the game is afoot!" Philippa's dark eyes had taken on a militant sparkle that belied her silver hair. "If I'm going to act as watch-dog, there's no time to begin like the present. Once we get back to Scotland, we may find ourselves under fire, and I for one would like to feel we've left nothing to chance."

Adam and Philippa, had they known it, were not the only ones to be laying long-range plans this November night. One hundred fifty miles north of the Scottish border, amid the snow-covered crags of the Cairngorm Mountains, twelve white-robed senior acolytes of the Lodge of the Lynx sat cross-legged in the topmost tower of their frowning castle retreat, their leader in their midst, there to await the coming of a visitor.

Above the wintry shrilling of the wind, the Head-Master was the first to hear the approaching chuff of helicopter rotors. Roused from his meditations, he lifted his hairless head and directed a piercing look across the circle at the acolyte nearest the door.

The woman nodded her acknowledgement and rose silently, signalling her withdrawal from the circle with a ritual gesture and then bowing herself out of the room. When she returned a short time later, she had Raeburn with her, barefoot and clothed like all the others in a loose white robe like a monk's habit. She was also carrying something wrapped in a swath of scarlet silk, which she bore reverently to the Head-Master and set into his hands before returning to her place. Palms pressed together at breast level before him, the newcomer advanced to the center of the chamber to make a deep obeisance.

"Head-Master," he said.

The Master eyed him up and down, his face sallow as parchment in the yellow glow of the surrounding gas lamps.

"Lynx-Master," he replied, his voice dry and cold. "Allow me to bid you welcome on this memorable occasion—though you are somewhat later than expected."

The faint note of censure sent a crackle through the air in the room, like a flicker of static electricity. Raeburn inclined his sleek blond head and said smoothly, "Forgive me, Head-Master. I am not yet privileged to control the Scottish weather."

The statement was neutral, a simple statement of fact, but it caused a slight ripple among the watching acolytes.

Not so the Master, who merely inclined his head.

"Now that you are here, you will render your report."

"Certainly, Head-Master," Raeburn said with a bow.

He squared his shoulders, conscious of the envy lurking behind the watchful eyes of some of the acolytes present, several of whom had personal reasons for resenting his successes. Recent developments dictated that he would have to tread carefully if he hoped to maintain his ascendancy.

"We are all aware of our objectives in this present campaign," he said silkily, folding his hands quietly in the full sleeves of his robe. "That being the case, I see no reason to reiterate them here. Suffice it to say that the next target has been designated, along with the time and the place for his execution. Before this week is out, another pillar of the Temple will have fallen, and we shall have gained another measure of power to give substance to the designs of our Patron."

All the while he was speaking, his pale blue eyes did not stray from the Master's writhen features. Nevertheless, he was keenly aware of what lay on the floor between them: a thick sheaf of yellow parchments cradled on a mat of black ram skin—and on top of the parchments, the scarlet-wrapped bundle of the torc Raeburn had just surrendered. He could almost taste its shadowy potency, pulsing like subsonic rumblings of thunder—power sealed with blood, and soon to be enhanced with the letting of more blood. The craving to have it back in his possession was like the compulsion of a drug.

Half-intoxicated, he recalled himself with an effort, reminding himself that he had not yet finished his report.

"In short," he went on, "our plans are progressing according to schedule. There is, however, one complication."

The Head-Master's face stiffened. "Explain."

Raeburn met the old man's hard gaze unflinchingly. "First, allow me to reassure you that the matter is being dealt with," he said. "It concerns a certain police inspector from Edinburgh. You will recall that we had a conversation about him not so very long ago."

The old man's sunken eyes took on a malevolent, reptilian gleam as he moistened withered lips with a flick of his tongue.

"Inspector McLeod," he hissed.

"The same," Raeburn agreed. "He did me the dubious honor of calling at my home two days ago. During the course of our conversation—which, by the way, seems to have been purely routine, as police matters go—I took the liberty of applying certain . . . tests. I am now in a position to confirm what we previously only suspected: that Inspector McLeod almost certainly is a member of a Hunting Lodge."

This bald announcement provoked a stir among the assembled acolytes, though no one ventured to speak. The Head-Master quelled the rustling with a piercing glare before returning his attention to Raeburn.

"You say you tested him. I hope you were not so foolish as to betray yourself in the exchange."

"No." Raeburn took pains to sound confident. "The inspector has considerable strength, but relatively little sensibility. Difficult to overcome, but easy to outmaneuver. That being the case—" he paused to smile thinly "—I have already devised what promises to be an effective means of putting him out of action—for good."

Seeing that he had the attention of all present, he went on to explain. When he had finished, the Head-Master favored him with a calculating look.

"You do appear to have the situation well enough in hand," he acknowledged coldly, "at least so far as McLeod himself is concerned. But he is not the only one to come to our attention from that direction. What of the troublesome Adam Sinclair? If you are correct about McLeod, then Sinclair is almost certainly a Hunts-man as well—possibly even their leader. What's to prevent him from intervening on McLeod's behalf?"

Raeburn's smile was cold like his eyes. "I've done my homework, Head-Master. Sinclair has gone to London for a few days. Even if McLeod should prove strong enough to withstand the initial shock of the assault, he won't be able to sustain a defense for more than a few hours without outside assistance. Not even a man of Sinclair's resources could hope to overcome the distance factor within the allotted time.''

"What of other Huntsmen nearer at hand, who might be able to interfere?''

"Obviously, we cannot rule out that possibility," Raeburn conceded. "But thus far, Sinclair is the only one we know of to evince the necessary talent and training. There may be others—but in order to intervene, they will have to show themselves. And if they show themselves, we will henceforth have them in our sights.''

The old man bared yellow teeth in a death's-head smile. "Satisfactory. You persuade me that you are worthy of the mission about to be entrusted to you. Are you prepared to be presented to our Patron?''

"I am," Raeburn said strongly, damping down a flutter of anticipation.

"Then, let us call upon our Patron to bear witness.''

Raising his hands palm outward in an imperious gesture of command, the Head-Master cast his cold gaze around the room. At once the assembled acolytes shifted onto their knees, then bent in unison to prostrate themselves, foreheads to the floor. As the Head-Master got slowly to his feet, Raeburn dropped to his knees before him, his face aglow with expectation. Standing over him, hands raised now toward the vaulted ceiling, the old man began to chant in a voice as hoarse as a crow's.

Slowly the air in the chamber came to life with darkling energy. Still chanting, the Head-Master gravely unwrapped the torc and presented it to the four quarters of the circle, beginning in the north and turning widdershins. His blood racing, Raeburn bent low and touched his forehead reverently to the parchment heaped upon the ram skin. The scent of centuries of secrets was in his nostrils as he straightened once again, gaze fixed on the Head-Master. All around him the other acolytes lifted up guttural voices to join in their leader's prayer of supplication.

The chant reached its crescendo. With a hoarse shout, the Head-Master drew himself upright, elevating the torc above Raeburn's head like a crown.

"Come, thou dread, invited guest!" he intoned. "Taranis the Thunderer, we beseech thee to hear us!''

Something rustled among the parchments on the ram skin. The top few leaves lifted and separated, as if stirred by a breath of moving air, then settled back with a susurrant sigh. Heart pounding, Raeburn threw back his head, his pale eyes alight with inner fire, swaying a little on his knees as the Head-Master circled round to stand behind him with the torc still poised above his head.

"Descend among us, dread lord," the old man urged in a rasping whisper. "Descend and look with favor upon these thy servants. I give thee one who desires communion with the Storm. Examine him, I charge thee, and if he be found acceptable in thy sight, let him be received into the fellowship of those who command the Lightning!"

So saying, he bent to slip the torc about Raeburn's neck from behind. Raeburn caught his breath and reared back, his face blanching white in the guttering gaslight. In the same instant, a sudden, heavy rumbling broke out deep underground.

Like the pulse of an underground earthquake, it shuddered its way up from the base of the tower to boom like a thunderclap, tumbling several of the acolytes onto their sides. The Head-Master kept his balance, feet splayed wide, and flung his arms wide as if to offer an embrace.

"Welcome, Taranis!" he crowed. "Hail, mighty Thunderer! Enlighten your servants with a sign of your pleasure!"

A breathless stillness suddenly filled the chamber, as if the air in the chamber had suddenly been withdrawn. In the next instant, a savage flash of blue light surged upward from the sheaf of parchment at Raeburn's knees, leaping in a hungry arc from the manuscript to the torc about his throat. He choked out a cry, half pain and half ecstasy, his body stiffening in the rigor of power almost too potent for the vessel.

For an instant, the only sound in the room was the raw crackle of energy, paralyzing all volition. Then, just as abruptly, the blue flare flickered and winked out.

Raeburn sagged forward on his hands, drawing breath in a deep, gasping gulp. Then he slowly straightened to sit back on his haunches, his hands stealing upwards to touch the torc, his expression one of mingled wonder and exultation.

"The bearer has been accepted!" The Head-Master proclaimed. "All praise to the Thunderer!"

Raeburn was rapidly recovering himself. Pale eyes bright with triumph, he wordlessly offered his hands to the Head-Master. The old man brought his own hands to rest on the younger man's upturned palms in a gesture of bestowal.

"The builders make bold to raise up a Temple to the Light," the Head-Master whispered. "Into your hands do I now deliver them. Destroy the builders, and the Temple itself will fall. In the absence of the Light, so shall the Darkness flourish. . . ."

Thursday morning dawned cold and grey. Adam and Philippa breakfasted Continental-style on hot chocolate and fresh croissants before setting out in a taxi for their morning appointment at Charing Cross Hospital. Philippa had changed her scarlet of the night before for a tailored ensemble in royal blue, stylish but professional looking; Adam wore the ubiquitous three-piece suit of his profession.

Outside the Caledonian Club, the inner London smell of Thames water and diesel fumes was sharpened by an icy touch of frost. As their cab skirted Hyde Park and then headed down Kensington High Street toward Hammersmith, just behind the worst of morning commuter traffic, Adam found himself looking forward to the impending meeting with an eagerness that was overcast with worry.

Like the streets outside, the lobby of Charing Cross Hospital was bustling with activity. Taking Philippa's arm, Adam ushered her past the central reception desk and onto the escalator, the two of them blending easily with the flow of consultants on their way to rounds and nurses and technicians going about their business. They alighted on the first floor and moved with the flow of people heading into the West Wing, toward the Pediatric Ward, making their way unchallenged up the hall to the nurses' station.

The ward had undergone some needed redecoration since Adam's previous visit, a month before. The nurses' station, like the adjoining corridors, had been done over in circus scenes picked out in cheery primary colors. As Adam and Philippa approached the desk, a spritely, dark-haired ward sister in a pastel-blue maternity uniform looked up from the stack of charts in front of her. She gave them a swift, all-encompassing glance and the beginnings of a smile as Adam produced his card from a breast pocket and laid it on the counter before her. He had already stolen a look at her name tag.

"Good morning, Mrs. Reynolds," he said pleasantly. "We've come to see Gillian Talbot. I believe Dr. Ogilvy is expecting us."

Philippa wordlessly placed her own card on the desk next to Adam's. The ward nurse picked up both cards, her rosy face registering a mixture of surprise and respect as she took stock of the Sinclairs' professional qualifications.

"It's a privilege to have you with us, Sir Adam—and you as well, Dr. Sinclair," she said as she handed back the cards. "We were told to expect you—but we didn't realize you'd be *two* doctors with the same name."

Adam chuckled. "Actually I don't believe I mentioned a second name when I spoke with Mr. Talbot last night—only that I intended to bring along a professional colleague—which my mother certainly is. But I assure you, this isn't the first time that the family tie within the profession has given rise to some confusion. Are the Talbots here yet? And Dr. Ogilvy?"

"Dr. Ogilvy should be along any minute, Sir Adam," the nurse replied. "She's just finishing rounds. And Mr. and Mrs. Talbot came in about a quarter hour ago. If you'd like to join them, they're waiting in their daughter's room, just down the hall."

"Actually," Philippa said, "I think we'd like to have a look at Gillian's chart first, if you don't mind—along with her case file, if you have that handy."

"Yes, Doctor, I have that right here," the nurse said, dragging out a manila folder from behind the desk. "And here's her chart as well."

With a word of thanks, Adam took the folder and opened the flap. There was a small handwritten note pinned to the topmost sheet of the enclosed sheaf of reports. The message, scrawled in the notoriously bad penmanship of most physicians, read, *Dr. Sinclair: Thought it might streamline matters if you were to find this waiting for you. Hope it proves helpful.* The signature, barely decipherable, was *H. Ogilvy.*

This voluntary gesture of cooperation spoke well of Gillian's attending physician. Relieved to discover he was not going to have to waste time soothing the ruffled sensibilities of a fellow consultant, Adam got down to the business of leafing through the file, Philippa glancing over the chart and then reading over his shoulder. It required only a cursory perusal to determine that Gillian's condition had deteriorated drastically since his last visit to London.

"From bad to worse, I'm afraid," he said grimly to Philippa. "Thank you, Mrs. Reynolds. I believe we'll go take a look at the patient now, and meet the Talbots."

Gillian had been moved out of the ward into a private room. Her parents were sitting in chairs on the far side of the bed, holding hands and gazing longingly at their daughter. When Adam and Philippa entered from the hall, both Talbots sprang to their feet with a nervous alacrity undoubtedly born of the stress of Gillian's mysterious illness.

"Dr. Sinclair! Oh, thank you so much for coming!" Iris Talbot exclaimed, clinging fearfully to her husband's arm. "This is George, Gillian's father. I believe you've already spoken on the telephone."

Iris Talbot was much as Adam remembered her from their previous meeting: a comely blonde woman in her late thirties, except that her prettiness was dulled now by additional weeks of sleeplessness and anxiety. Her husband was a sturdily built man in studious horn-rimmed spectacles, who might have been described as "comfortable" if he hadn't been looking so worn.

"Of course. A pleasure to meet you in person, Mr. Talbot," Adam said, extending a hand. "This is my mother, Dr. Philippa Sinclair, who's taught me a great deal of what I know. We hope that between us we'll be able to get to the bottom of whatever has caused your daughter's malady."

"So do I, Doctor!" George Talbot said fervently. His handshake was firm, but his brown eyes were deeply troubled as his attention strayed back to his daughter's unmoving form. "It's been so difficult, watching her just fade away—"

He stopped abruptly, before his voice could crack. Following George Talbot's gaze, Adam could well understand his distress. Though Gillian had already been ill when he himself last saw her a month ago, she still had been a fair, rosy child, gifted with the robust look of a tomboy.

Now, stretched supine in the starched hospital bed, she looked frail and desiccated, her round face blanched to a waxy pallor, the spray of freckles stark against the pale skin. The crown of golden curls was flattened now, the eyes closed behind blue-shadowed lids. A nasal feeding tube was taped into place along one sunken cheek, and a wrist-cuff loosely immobilized one wasted arm, from which an I.V. tube snaked upward to a drip-support frame beside the bed— ominous proof that Gillian was no longer even able to feed herself.

"If only *somebody* could reach her," Iris Talbot said helplessly. "George and I have tried our best. We come every day, but—"

Her small gesture of defeat made it clear that both parents were appalled at their apparent failure to communicate with their only child, but Philippa's brisk voice cut across their pained silence like an astringent breath of fresh air.

"If it's any comfort, I don't believe love is the answer here," she said crisply. "If it were, the problem would have been solved long before now. You mustn't blame yourselves."

The Talbots exchanged glances, as if slightly startled by Philippa's plain-speaking.

"I concur absolutely," Adam said. "Whatever is amiss with your daughter, you may be quite sure that neither of you is to blame that she hasn't responded so far. I assume that Dr. Ogilvy has discussed with you in detail the complications involved in the treatment of autistic behavior?"

"Indeed she has—insofar as clinical definitions can be said to

*169*

apply in this particular case," said a practical contralto voice from behind him. "And that's all the more reason for all concerned to welcome some input from specialists of your caliber."

Adam and Philippa both turned. Standing in the doorway was a tall, stoutly-built woman in her late forties, with brown hair liberally streaked with silver. Shrewd grey eyes favored Adam and Philippa with a smile of friendly irony.

"The Doctors Sinclair, I presume?" she said. "How do you do? I'm Helen Ogilvy."

Adam and Philippa spent the better part of the next half hour sifting through the medical particulars of the case with Dr. Ogilvy and conducting a brief neurological examination. From Adam's point of view, the conference was more for the benefit of Gillian's parents than it was for Gillian herself. He and Philippa already understood the true nature of Gillian's illness all too well, but it was important that they should win the confidence of Gillian's family and attending physician.

When they had run through all the questions Adam could think of to ask for the moment, he left Philippa to carry on talking with the Talbots while he stepped aside for a private word with Dr. Ogilvy.

"I greatly appreciate your cooperation," he told her with a smile. "I'm sure we've both had dealings in the past with other consultants who were far from helpful."

Dr. Ogilvy shrugged and smiled companionably. "This is a big inner city hospital, Dr. Sinclair. The psychiatric cases we commonly see on a daily basis are those related to drugs, alcoholism, and acute stress-related neuroses. Most of the disturbed children who come our way have every reason to be disturbed. They come from broken homes, deprived backgrounds, families with histories of violence or substance abuse—or all of the above. Autistic children are a rarity—*not* my area of specialization at all. And Gillian doesn't fit any of the rest of the profile either."

She sighed. "I've already got all the cases I can handle of the types I'm familiar with. Since I don't honestly see any way I can help Gillian, I'm only too happy to hand her into the care of someone with a fighting chance to get positive results."

Adam smiled at her directness. "Thank you for the vote of confidence. I promise I'll do everything I can to merit it."

"You're entirely too modest, Doctor," Dr. Ogilvy said. "Your reputation goes before you, even here in London." She glanced back into the room at the Talbots, still deep in conversation with Philippa, then continued bluntly, "To be frank, when Mrs. Talbot told me she'd been in contact with you early on in this case, I wondered why she and her husband hadn't elected to retain your services in the first place. I'm a qualified and seasoned professional, but I'm not ashamed to admit I'm out of my depth on this one.''

Adam shrugged. ''No mystery there. When I first saw Gillian, it seemed clear that everything that could be done was being done—and close to home, where family and friends could visit on a regular basis. There was always the chance that contact with the familiar might snap her out of it. But since that hasn't happened, it's time to rethink our strategy.''

''Does that mean you're thinking of removing her to another hospital?''

''Only, I assure you, for my personal convenience,'' Adam said. ''My practice is in Edinburgh; I can't work with her here. If Mr. and Mrs. Talbot are amenable, I intend to recommend that she be transferred to Jordanburn.'' He smiled. ''Here in London, you probably know it as the Royal Edinburgh Hospital. The name was changed a few years back, but old habits die hard with those of us who trained there. In any case, both I and my mother—who also has considerable experience in dealing with cases like Gillian's— will be able to give her a measure of concentrated care that wouldn't be feasible otherwise.''

The Talbots, when Adam broached the subject to them, evinced some signs of uncertainty. After hearing Adam out, they begged a moment alone to discuss the matter. Adam, Philippa, and Dr. Ogilvy stepped out of the room to leave them their privacy. When the Talbots joined them a few moments later, George Talbot was looking pale but resolved.

''We've been thinking over all that you've said, Dr. Sinclair, and we've decided we *would* like you to take Gillian's case. We'll— mortgage our house, if need be. What's important is that our daughter should have every chance to recover and lead a normal life.''

Enlightenment dawned on Adam. ''Are you worried about expenses, Mr. Talbot? Please rest easy on that account. I'll see that the hospital charges are limited to what's covered by National Health. And my mother and I offer our own professional services gratis, *pro bonum*. Let's just say that your daughter's case poses an interesting challenge.''

Both the Talbots looked astonished and visibly relieved.

''That's uncommonly generous of you, Dr. Sinclair,'' said George Talbot. ''We—I hardly know what to say—''

''Except to thank you from the bottom of our hearts!'' said his wife, crying and laughing at the same time. "I almost feel we might have something to hope for after all."

Philippa and Adam traded glances. The Talbots' faith was touching—and worrying. For their own part, the Sinclairs knew that the battle for Gillian's survival was only just beginning. There was still so much that could go wrong.

# CHAPTER EIGHTEEN

THAT same Thursday morning, Inspector McLeod paid only a brief visit to police headquarters in Edinburgh before heading off to Perth for another stint of press liaison on the Randall Stewart slaying. He departed before the arrival of the morning post, and therefore missed being spotted by one of his police colleagues who had a vested interest in keeping track of his movements.

Detective Inspector Charles Napier was a heavyset man in his middle forties, with thick, dark hair and bristling eyebrows that gave him the frowning look of a Rottweiler. He had a reputation for being taciturn, but on this occasion he seemed less reserved than usual as he strolled among the desks in the outer office, pausing now and again to pass a remark to a subordinate. In this leisurely manner, he contrived to be in the vicinity of McLeod's office cubicle just as the mail clerk arrived, pushing a tiered wire cart laden with stacks of mail bundled together with rubber bands.

"Good morning, Miss Desmond," he said with gruff pleasantry. "Anything there for me?"

"Aye, sir." As she flipped through the top stacks to pull out a tidy bundle of letters, Napier was able to confirm that the manila inter-office envelope he had pushed through the slot of the mail room earlier today had, indeed, found its way into the stack for McLeod.

"Here you are, Inspector," the clerk said, handing over his bundle.

"Thank you. That's fine."

While shuffling through what she handed him, Napier lingered long enough to see the mail clerk duck into McLeod's office to leave the augmented bundle of mail on the desktop. Then, satisfied that the trap had been successfully set, he went off to his own cubicle to await further developments.

But McLeod did not return to his office that day. Though Napier made a point of sticking close to his office, ostensibly to catch up on back paperwork, lunchtime and then the afternoon wore on without McLeod's putting in an appearance. By half past five, Napier was forced to conclude that his victim was not going to show up.

He did not look forward to the phone call he now must make. Finally setting his reports aside, he locked up his office, signed out for the day, and headed downstairs. Just inside the lobby, he dropped a coin in a public phone box and punched a number. The voice that answered was humbly respectful, with an accent that suggested the northwest region of Pakistan.

"This is Charles Napier," he informed the speaker curtly. "If my uncle is free, I would like a word with him."

A moment later, Raeburn's voice came on the line.

"Well?"

"Everything's in place, just as you ordered," Napier said. "Unfortunately, it looks as if the desired event is going to have to keep till tomorrow. He didn't come back to the office today."

There was a slight pause, pregnant with displeasure. "Very well," said Raeburn coldly. "Just remember the price of failure."

The next morning, McLeod trudged in to work feeling as if he could have done with a holiday, more than ready for a weekend off. The previous day's series of meetings and discussions in Perth had yielded no new insights into the murder of Randall Stewart. His jaundiced outlook was not brightened by the knowledge that the work load from all his other cases was beginning to mount up in the face of enforced neglect. This reflection was hideously confirmed when he opened the door to his own office to find the top of his desk nearly buried under tidy stacks of file folders, computer print-outs, mail, memos, and reports.

McLeod glowered at the clutter from the threshold. At the same moment, a smartly uniformed PC Cochrane shouldered his way into the general office through the door that led to and from Police Records and came over to greet him.

"Morning, Inspector," he said cheerfully. "How did things go with the Procurator Fiscal?"

"They didn't," McLeod grumbled. He cocked an eye at his subordinate and asked, "What about the MacIntosh burglary? The superintendent collared me on the way in. Any progress there?"

"A bit. Some of the stuff turned up in a pawnshop in Carlisle. The Carlisle police are going to get back in touch with us once they've had a chance to run down the lead the pawnbroker was able to give them." Cochrane added, "I've also finished typing up my notes from the interviews we did in Stirling. They're on my desk, if you want to look them over.''

''Not right now, thanks,'' said McLeod. ''Let me at least get some of this other rubbish cleared away first.''

Cochrane peered in at the mounds of paperwork and pulled a sympathetic grin. ''Aye, sir, I see what you mean.''

''And that's only the surface,'' McLeod informed him with a glimmer of returning humor. ''Now if you really want to make yourself useful, you could try finding me a cup of coffee.''

Chuckling, Cochrane went off to comply. Left alone, McLeod pushed his door shut, then rolled his chair back from several pieces of mail that had spilled off the desk and sat down. Where to start? Sighing, he picked up the fallen mail and tossed it on the desk, moved the sheaf of computer printouts to a side chair, and set the stack of file folders on top of that. Then he set about opening the mail.

The first batch yielded the usual collection of odds and ends: over-sized catalogues from a German gun-manufacturing company and an American firm that specialized in holsters and other leather goods; a flyer announcing an in-service course that had already taken place; a letter requesting an officer to attend a local Neighborhood Watch meeting; and two complaints from self-styled concerned citizens taking exception to his most recent statements to the press over Randall Stewart's involvement with Freemasonry.

He pitched the in-service flyer and dead envelopes into the wastebasket, marked the Neighborhood Watch request for redirection to Community Relations and tossed it in his out-basket, and bunged the rest into his in-basket for later attention. He paused to read more closely an interdepartmental update on police procedure for dealing with drug-related arrests, wondering where Cochrane was with his coffee, then reached for the next item on the stack.

It was a large manila inter-office envelope with McLeod's name and office number typed on a white self-stick label and ''Personal'' stamped in red beside it. Mildly curious, he picked it up and turned it over in his hands, reaching for a paper-knife when the flap proved to be stuck down tight. When he had slit it open, he parted the two sides with his fingers to peer inside, then up-ended the envelope to spill its contents onto the desk in front of him.

To his surprise, what fell out was a shiny gold origami figure of some kind of animal, about six inches long. He grinned, for it appeared that another of his department colleagues was ribbing him again—for his own prowess at origami was well-known throughout the building. The corkboard on the wall beside his head sported a colorful if rather tattered collection of other people's attempts alongside some of McLeod's better examples.

Chuckling, and wondering who could have provided this latest addition to his display, McLeod picked it up.

He knew instantly that he had made a mistake. The moment his fingers closed on the paper, a savage jolt of energy leapt up his arm. Searing as a lightning strike, the charge raced through his nervous system, paralyzing him from head to foot. Transfixed with shock, he reeled back in his chair, the origami figure dropping from nerveless fingers.

Ending physical contact did not end the assault. The material world around McLeod receded into a nightmare blur. As if in a dream, he found himself plummeting backward through phantom fog banks crackling with fire. The falling sensation ended with another blazing jolt. He fought to regain conscious control of his faculties, but the only physical image to penetrate the blanketing psychic fog was that of the origami sculpture now lying on the floor between his feet, which he now saw clearly was made in the likeness of a lynx.

With a venomous buzz like the amplified hiss of a cobra, the origami shape seemed to ignite in a billowing plume of sickly yellow smoke. As McLeod cringed away from it, struggling to ward off the attack, the smoke thickened and spread, resolving into a rearing feline shape with tufted cheeks and burning crimson eyes. The lynx spat at him in mingled hunger and contempt, baring fangs that dripped saliva like slow poison. Before he could summon the strength to move or cry out, the creature sprang at him, overwhelming him in a miasma like a gas-cloud.

Choke-fire filled his eyes and lungs, like an attack of tear gas only much, much worse. The intensity of the pain broke his paralysis. Racked with nausea, he groped blindly through the swirling mists for the inner pocket of his jacket. A heartbeat later, his quaking fingers located it, clawing inside for the one thing that might save him in his present extremity.

Warm and solid, his Huntsman's ring came to his hand. By then the pain had become a constricting crown of thorns, squeezing ever more tightly about his head until he was sure his skull would eventually burst. His breath came in labored gasps as he worked the ring onto his third finger, and he drew on everything it symbolized as he focused his dwindling reserves of strength to push back the lynx's killing force.

For an awful moment, he thought he might be too late to save himself. Then, as the seconds ticked away, he realized that the pressure on his skull had stabilized. It cost him to renew his own counter-imperative, but he felt the tight circle of pain give way a stubborn fraction. Yes, it was showing signs of loosening. If he could just—

An urgent voice penetrated the surrounding fog.

"Inspector? Inspector McLeod, are you all right?"

The words seemed to resonate and boom. The tide-wash of psychic reverberations threatened for a moment to plunge McLeod back into chaos. Importunate hands clutched at his shoulders, demanding his response.

Fixing the whole of his attention on the presence beyond the hands, McLeod forced his eyes open and found himself gazing fuzzily up into the face of Donald Cochrane. He blinked and realized that he was no longer wearing his spectacles.

"Donald—" he managed to gasp.

"I think I'd better call an ambulance," Cochrane said, reaching across him for one of the phones.

"*No!*" McLeod's hand grasped hard at the constable's sleeve. A part of him was somewhat astonished to find that he was still in his chair, if slumped rather precariously.

"Be all right," he managed to rasp, struggling to make his vocal cords work. "No fuss!" Seeing Cochrane hesitate, he added more forcefully, "This is—*not medical*, Donald! *No outside interference!*"

He tried to punctuate the directive with a shake of his head. The attempted movement very nearly caused him to pass out. Choking back a mouthful of bile, he repeated, "Be . . . all right in a minute. Shut the blinds. *Please*, Donald!"

To his infinite relief, Cochrane did as he was told. By the time the young constable turned back to him, McLeod had had time to get his bearings. By some miracle, the door to his office was all but closed. The origami lynx was lying intact a few feet from his chair. The fire evidently had been only a visionary manifestation of the triggering reaction.

"Close the door," he whispered, gesturing jerkily toward it and steeling himself against another wave of nausea as Cochrane obeyed. "D'ye see that?" he grated, indicating the lynx with a shaky forefinger. "Silk handkerchief . . . here in m' jacket pocket." He gestured toward it vaguely but could not seem to muster enough coordination to pull it out. "Wrap it around that an' pick it up—but don't touch. . . . For th' sake o' the Widow's Son. . . ."

Wide-eyed, Cochrane came to him and pulled out the handkerchief. He knew nothing of McLeod's esoteric connections other than Freemasonry, but his training with McLeod in the same Masonic Lodge had forged a bond of trust that could not lightly refuse an entreaty invoking that shared brotherhood. Bending cautiously over the lynx, he shielded his hand in several layers of silk before very tentatively plucking it from the floor.

"What the hell is this thing?" he whispered, casting a suspicious glance over it and then holding it at arm's length again. "It just looks like—one of your origami figures."

"Wrap it up and put it in the desk drawer," McLeod rasped. "Can't explain right now." He could feel the pain pulsing behind his eyeballs, and he propped his brow on his fists while he tried to think. The effects of the attack were still with him, circulating throughout his mind and body like a virus just waiting to break out again with renewed virulence.

*I can't fight this off on my own,* he thought dizzily. *Thank God it was Donald who found me, but he can't deal with this. I've got to get help from somewhere else.*

Adam was due back from London just after noon, but that was no help now. McLeod swallowed hard and thought again, even though the effort sent red-hot needles of pain shooting through his brain. It seemed to be getting worse, not better. A Styrofoam cup materialized in front of him, and with it, his spectacles.

"You dropped your glasses," Cochrane said worriedly. "Would some coffee help? Are you sure I can't get you a doctor?"

McLeod waved the cup away and mumbled, "No, on both counts." He drew a deep breath and said more distinctly, "Personal address file. Get Christopher Houston."

Keeping a close watch on his ashen-faced superior, Cochrane found the number, picked up one of the phones, and dialed. The number rang and rang at the other end, but with no answer.

"There doesn't seem to be anyone at home," Cochrane said. "You look bloody awful. I really think you ought to let me call a doctor."

The room seemed to be in danger of receding again. McLeod swallowed carefully and took a fragile grip on himself.

"Try to find Peregrine Lovat," he muttered through set teeth.

"Ring Humphrey at Strathmourne—the number's under Sinclair. Humphrey'll know where he's to be found."

John Edward Muir, former Lord Provost of Edinburgh, had a face that in another age might have belonged to a border chieftain. Standing back from the easel to survey his work with a critical eye, Peregrine was satisfied that he was doing full justice to the bold, enterprising spirit that he sensed dwelling beneath the former provost's apparently sober exterior. He glanced thoughtfully back at his subject, who was sitting patiently in his full ceremonial robes a few yards away.

"Excuse me, sir, but could I ask you to lift your head a little?"

The live sitting was taking place in the Muirs' own drawing room in the exclusive Edinburgh district of Ravelston Dykes. The provost did as he was requested and said with a gruff twinkle, "How much longer before I'm fully immortalised on canvas?"

"This ought to be the last time you'll actually have to sit for me," Peregrine said, his attention on his brush strokes as he added a few subtle touches of madder brown to the angle of the portrait's jaw. He finished the adjustment, approved it with a grin, and relaxed.

"There we are, sir. You can stand up a moment and stretch now, if you like."

The drawing room door opened, and the provost's wife stepped into the room looking slightly bewildered.

"I'm sorry to interrupt the sitting, Mr. Lovat," she said, "but I have a PC Cochrane on the phone asking to speak to you."

Puzzled, for he could not recall ever meeting a police constable called Cochrane, Peregrine set aside his brushes and palette and wiped his fingers on a clean paint rag as he followed Mrs. Muir into the hall and picked up the telephone she indicated. Perhaps Cochrane was one of Inspector McLeod's men. But why should McLeod want to call Peregrine here?

"This is Peregrine Lovat," he said.

"Yes, Mr. Lovat. PC Donald Cochrane," said the voice on the other end of the line. "I'm calling on behalf of Inspector Noel McLeod. He's instructed me to request that you come immediately to his office at police headquarters on a matter of utmost urgency."

It wasn't like McLeod to overstate a case. And why had the inspector not phoned himself? A warning light went on at the back of Peregrine's mind.

"What's the trouble?" he asked. "Can you tell me what this is about?"

"It's—a bit difficult to explain over the phone, sir," said the voice. "It would be better if you could come down here right away and see for yourself."

Curiouser and curiouser. *Why hadn't McLeod phoned in person?* The mental alarms began to sound in earnest. *Could something have happened to Adam?*

"Very well," Peregrine said. "Tell the inspector I'll be leaving at once and will join him as soon as I can."

After tendering a hasty apology to the Muirs, he packed up his painting things as quickly as possible and carried them down to his car. A quick glance at his Edinburgh street guide before heading out confirmed that police headquarters was in Fettes Avenue, as he had thought, less than two miles away. He found himself fantasizing all kinds of disasters as he pulled away from the curb, whipping the little Morris Minor in and out of traffic with an impetuosity that earned him more than one indignant glare from more sedate motorists.

He was there in less than ten minutes. Narrowly avoiding a brush with a glazier's van, he wheeled into the police station parking lot to find every space filled. With a muttered imprecation and a prayer to whatever god warded off traffic wardens, he left the Morris standing by the curb on a double yellow line and made a beeline for the front entrance.

It was the first time he'd ever been inside McLeod's working domain. A desk officer looked up attentively as he came through the glass doors and, when Peregrine had identified himself and his business, picked up the phone and called upstairs. Hardly a minute later, a strapping, sandy-haired young man in uniform, who looked to be about the same age as Peregrine, came out of a door beyond the desk and raised a beckoning hand.

"Mr. Lovat?" he said. "Come with me, please."

"What's happened?" Peregrine murmured, as they headed up a rear stairwell.

Cochrane shook his head. "Not here, please, Mr. Lovat. He's going to have to explain it himself—if he can. Try not to look too anxious as we go through the outer office."

He said nothing else as they reached the top of the stairs and turned down a windowed corridor that skirted the back of the building, leading Peregrine on through a big open-plan general office to a numbered row of doors at the far end. McLeod's nameplate was on the door numbered 5B, and the insistent ring of a telephone came faintly from inside.

Cochrane gave the door a brief rap before opening it and ushering Peregrine in, heading immediately for the phone—for McLeod clearly was oblivious to it and to their arrival, slumped over the desk with his head awkwardly pillowed on his right arm. As Peregrine closed the door behind them, appalled, Cochrane leaned across to snare the ringing phone.

"Inspector McLeod's desk," he said a little breathlessly. "No, I'm afraid he's in a meeting. This is PC Cochrane, his assistant. May I help you?"

As Cochrane dealt with the caller, Peregrine came a little closer to peer cautiously at McLeod. The inspector's face was the color of putty, etched with lines of pain, his body taut. As soon as Cochrane had hung up, Peregrine turned on him.

"What happened?" he demanded in a low voice. "What's wrong with him?"

"I don't honestly know," the young constable said softly. "And he wouldn't let me call a doctor. Whatever happened seems to have something to do with this." He pulled open the left-hand desk drawer. "We're not to touch it except with the silk. He was very adamant about that."

Mystified, Peregrine gingerly lifted a corner of the handkerchief and peeled it back to reveal an origami animal made from gold paper. A closer look established that the animal was a lynx.

A cold qualm of revulsion knotted his stomach. Making sure not to touch the gold paper, Peregrine hastily replaced the wrappings and closed the drawer before returning his attention to McLeod.

"Inspector," he called softly, setting his hand on one shoulder. "Noel, it's me, Peregrine. You asked me to come, and I'm here. Please, can you tell me what you want me to do?"

There was no response from McLeod. His concern mounting, Peregrine glanced back at Cochrane, hovering anxiously nearer the door.

"How long has he been like this?"

"I found him about half an hour ago," Cochrane murmured. "It couldn't have happened more than five or ten minutes before that, because he'd sent me for coffee. He was able to talk at first, but it's been ten or fifteen minutes since I last heard anything out of him—shortly before I reached you on the phone." Seeing Peregrine's expression, he added, "He had me try to call a Father Christopher Houston first. When there was no answer there, he had me call Sir Adam Sinclair's man Humphrey to find out where

181

you were. I begged him to let me call a doctor, but he wouldn't hear of it. He made me promise not to call for help until you got here."

*Why me?* Peregrine wondered to himself, returning his attention to McLeod. There was only one answer that he could think of: McLeod evidently had reason to believe that Peregrine might be able to help where conventional medicine was sure to fail. It was a daunting thought. He glanced at McLeod again and fought down a strong pang of fear and self-doubt.

*God, I hope you're right, McLeod,* he reflected grimly. *I've got to think! What would Adam do, if he were here?*

He made an effort to compose his thoughts, searching through his recent memories for images of Adam at work. Among them inexplicably surfaced a seemingly unrelated image of Michael Brodie's ring. Since receiving it from Lady Julian, Peregrine had emulated Adam in carrying it with him always, protected in a small snap-pouch of Chinese silk. It was in his trouser pocket now, and the impulsion to put it on was suddenly very strong.

The very idea seemed presumptuous, especially since he was not yet a member of the Hunting Lodge and had not been given Adam's official leave to wear the ring as a badge of membership. At the same time, however, he was conscious of a growing conviction that he was going to need the ring as a focus if he was to have any hope at all of assisting McLeod in his present straits. A glance at McLeod's right hand confirmed that he was wearing *his* ring. Perhaps Peregrine could use his own to somehow link with McLeod's, drawing on the other man's expertise for guidance in what to do.

Biting at his lip, he slid his hand into his pocket and closed the pouch and ring in his fist, bringing them out and pressing the fist to his lips as he reached for whatever vestiges of Sir Michael Brodie remained with the ring.

*Forgive me, Sir Michael, if this doesn't meet with your approval,* he told Lady Julian's husband, *but the inspector needs help, and I don't know what else to do.*

Keeping his back to Cochrane, he quickly unsnapped the pouch and took out the ring, tucking the pouch back into his blazer pocket and slipping the ring onto the third finger of his right hand. He half expected a punishing stab of power. Instead, a comforting sense of gentle warmth seemed to radiate along his hand. Encouraged, he turned to Cochrane.

"I'll see what I can do to improve matters," he told his counterpart. "Can you make sure we're not disturbed?"

Nodding, Cochrane came over to unplug the cords from both phones.

"Just for the moment, I'm going to disable these, so callers will just think he's out," he explained. "I had to field several calls while I was waiting for you to get here, but I don't like lying. This is safer, if we don't want to arouse suspicion."

Peregrine could not fault the logic of that. Moving the files and computer print-outs off the spare office chair, he dragged it around to the inspector's left side and sat down, leaving Cochrane to take up guard duty by the door. Mentally rehearsing all that Adam had taught him since their first meeting, he concentrated first on settling into a semi-trance state, regulating his breathing until he succeeded in bringing all his faculties into harmonious balance with one another.

A sense of deep calm came gradually upon him. He had a feeling that McLeod should be balanced as well—or at least as much as was possible in his present state—and after a moment, grounded in his own calm, he reached out with his ring hand and lightly touched his fingertips to McLeod's forehead, emulating the hypnotic cue he had seen Adam use on both of them in the past.

"Relax, Noel," he murmured. "Go deep asleep."

To his relieved surprise, McLeod drew a deep, shuddering breath, like a diver about to plunge into a well, and let it out in a heavy sigh. Instinctively Peregrine matched breathing with his subject, summoning all the mental voice he could manage.

"Noel, it's Peregrine," he called softly, shifting his hand to clasp McLeod's wrist, feeling the pulse beneath his fingertips. "If you can hear me, try to help me help you. Show me what's afflicting you."

The response came not in words, but in a shift of image. All at once Peregrine experienced the now-familiar blurring of his vision. When his inner Sight keyed in, he could see as if in overlay a spiky mass of grey tendrils wrapped round about McLeod's head and neck like a helmet of thorns.

Peregrine grimaced, horrified. The tendrils were not inert. He could see a throbbing pulse running throughout the interlacing branches, in irregular counterpoint to McLeod's own heartbeat. They were so tightly bound together that the very idea of untangling them seemed ludicrous. As he wavered, wondering what to do, a new light seemed to kindle just behind his eyes. In that brief instant of illumination, he shifted focus to the ring on his hand and felt a sudden rush of power to his fingertips.

The power seemed to be coming from a part of his being he

183

hadn't even known existed. In response, the ring itself seemed to come to life, the stone glowing in his inner vision with a pure blue radiance—very much the way the stone in the pommel of Adam's *skean dubh* had glowed that night at Urquhart, when he used it·to ward off the Faerie Host.

As the light continued to brighten, Peregrine took his hand away from McLeod's wrist and reached instinctively toward the stricken man's head. He could See the power surrounding his ring hand like an aura now, nearly a handspan out in all directions, and he reached out boldly to pluck at the nearest thorny tendril writhing around McLeod.

It sizzled and separated at his touch, giving off a noxious spurt of grey smoke. Encouraged, Peregrine pulled away a whole handful. The whippy grey briars adhered to his fingers and wrist, nettling his skin like mild acid, but they seemed to do no real damage. Setting his teeth against the prickling discomfort, he shook them loose above the wastebasket and saw them shrivel away in bursts of dirty flame. Smiling in grim satisfaction, he went after another handful.

By the time he had finished clearing the tendrils away, McLeod was beginning to breathe more easily, but the malevolent energy that had created the tendrils was still hovering around him. Instinctively Peregrine knew that its source was the desk drawer and what it contained; and until the lynx charm could be neutralized, McLeod would remain under threat.

He opened the drawer and pulled back the handkerchief covering it, wondering whether the ring would work on the charm as it had on the tendrils. He made a tentative pass over it with his ring hand, but a heat like the equivalent of a psychic blast furnace roared up at him, causing him to jerk his hand hastily away.

"Leave that!" a hoarse voice grated almost at his ear, as a hand shoved the drawer shut. "That's for Adam to deal with."

Peregrine started up to discover that McLeod had raised his head and was peering over at him through eyes that were bloodshot but fully aware. Cochrane, too, had roused at the sound of the inspector's voice, standing slightly away from the door.

"Sir!" he exclaimed, though he kept his voice down. "Thank God you've come round! What the hell is going on?"

McLeod winced visibly, like a man with a bad hangover.

"Ask me again when my head stops pounding like a bass drum," he muttered. He swayed slightly where he sat and pressed the heels of his hands to his temples.

"Is there anything else I can do for you?" Cochrane said uneasily.

McLeod's gaze returned to the desk drawer he had just closed.

"Aye," he rasped. "You can take that thing and stow it away in the office safe until Adam Sinclair has a chance to take a look at it. Then you can maybe see if you can find me a couple of aspirin and a glass of water. And not a word of this to anybody!"

Peregrine managed to catch Cochrane's eye. "Don't worry, I'll stay with him."

With a nod, Cochrane gingerly wrapped up the lynx charm again, stuffed it into an envelope and sealed it, scribbling McLeod's name on the outside, and stepped out of the office, closing the door behind him. Left alone with McLeod, Peregrine said heavily, "Am I wrong, or was somebody out to kill you?"

McLeod had his eyes closed again. Without opening them, he said, "You're not wrong. Whoever sent the little lynx meant business. Call it the equivalent of a psychic letter-bomb."

Peregrine grimaced, a part of him quite amazed that he accepted this explanation without question, another part already thinking what to do next.

"Adam's supposed to be coming in on the lunchtime flight from Heathrow. That's—" he glanced down at his watch— "about thirty minutes from now. Do you want me to go meet him and bring him here?"

"No. If whoever set this saw you come in here, you might well be followed back out," McLeod said. "It'll be less conspicuous if Donald goes. Just give him Adam's flight details, and leave it to him to do the rest."

# CHAPTER NINETEEN

FOR Adam, in London, arranging a bed for Gillian Talbot at Jordanburn had been the easy part. Arranging transport was slightly more complicated, given the guidelines laid down by the National Health Board, which stipulated that non-emergency transfers required a week's notice. After filling out the required ambulance request form, Adam telephoned the Ambulance Service itself to inquire about the possibility of setting up an earlier date of transfer. By dint of patience and persuasion, he succeeded at last in securing the necessary vehicle and staff for the following Monday.

"Actually, a four-day delay is probably no bad thing," Philippa remarked, as she and Adam made their way by taxi to Heathrow at mid-morning on Friday. "The last thing we want at this point is for anyone to connect Gillian with us before we've had time to set up a few basic defenses. This way, if anyone in Edinburgh *should* be watching your movements, there won't be much for him to see."

Their flight left London on schedule and touched down at Edinburgh-Turnhouse shortly before one o'clock. Earlier that morning before leaving the Caledonian Club, Adam had put in a call to Humphrey, leaving instructions to meet them at the airport with the Bentley, in honor of his mother's arrival. Therefore he was not surprised, as he and Philippa came out the jetway, to spot Humphrey's familiar figure among the cluster of people waiting in the arrivals area. Only belatedly did he realize that the dour, sandy-haired constable standing next to Humphrey was part of the welcoming committee.

"Interesting," Philippa said, also making the connection. "Either I've unwittingly violated some obscure immigration law, or—"

"Or something's happened," Adam said. "That's Noel's assistant. Let's go."

With Adam in the lead, mother and son wove their way

hurriedly through the other passengers emerging in the arrivals area. By then Humphrey and the young policeman had spotted them in turn and were converging toward them with every appearance of haste.

"Mr. Cochrane," Adam said, as Humphrey exchanged a worried nod of greeting with Philippa. "Should your presence give me cause for concern?"

After a slightly uncertain glance at Philippa, Cochrane turned his full attention on Adam and just missed a salute.

"I don't want to alarm you, sir, but Inspector McLeod's met with a—a sort of an accident. He and a Mr. Peregrine Lovat said I should come and fetch you."

Dropping his voice, he related how McLeod had suffered an alarming collapse after receiving an origami figure in the mail.

"Seeing as how you weren't available at the time, sir, he had me call Mr. Lovat," Cochrane continued. "Mr. Lovat was able to make the inspector a bit easier, but he's still in a good bit of distress. Both he and Mr. Lovat asked me to tell you that they urgently need your help. My car's out front. I could take you to the station direct from here, if you think you might be able to manage it."

For Adam, the shock of hearing that McLeod had come under what obviously was some form of psychic attack was tempered in some degree by the surprising revelation that Peregrine had been directly involved in McLeod's defense. However, the crowded environs of an airport concourse were not the place for soliciting further information on that account. His gaze flickered sideways to connect with his mother's.

"Don't hesitate on my account," Philippa said. "Humphrey and I are old hands at sorting out things like luggage. Shall we simply meet you at home or arrange to join you somewhere?"

"I don't know how long this is likely to take," Adam said honestly, "so you'd better go on home to Strathmourne and wait for me there. I'll telephone you later and let you know how things are faring. Humphrey, did you happen to bring my medical bag?"

"Yes, sir. It's in the boot of the Bentley."

"Good," said Adam. "Is the Bentley out front?"

"In the limo bay, sir. Shall I go fetch the bag for you?"

"If you would, please."

"My car's right behind it, sir," Cochrane said. "This way."

As soon as they were clear of the airport, Cochrane switched on his blue lights and siren and applied his foot to the accelerator. The loud bray of the siren made conversation difficult, but by dint of careful questioning, Adam was able to piece together a reasonably good idea of McLeod's condition. While Cochrane went on to tell him what had happened following Peregrine's arrival on the scene, Adam opened his medical bag on the floor in front of him and loaded a hypo from it, keeping what he did well below windowsill level so he would not alarm civilians.

"This will ease the nausea you've described and help him to relax," he said, at Cochrane's questioning look, as he slipped the plastic sleeve back over the needle and pocketed the syringe with a disposable alcohol swab. "Sometimes it's used in treating migraines." When his hand came out of his pocket, he had slid on his sapphire ring.

A few blocks short of the station, Cochrane switched off the lights and siren, coasting into the station parking lot without fanfare. As they rolled to a halt in one of the spaces reserved for police use, Adam caught a glimpse of a familiar green Morris Minor with wooden sides standing at the curb in front of the building, parked on a double yellow line. A white piece of paper was flapping in the wind under one windshield wiper. As Adam pulled a wry face, Cochrane caught the look and grinned.

"Oh, that's not a real citation, sir," he said with smug pride. "Or rather, it's a real one, but it's blank. I had a word with the traffic warden before I left for the airport. I'll collect it before Mr. Lovat leaves, so I can give it back."

"Sharp thinking, Mr. Cochrane," Adam exclaimed, wedging his medical bag partway under the seat. "Mr. Lovat owes you a favor."

"Well, he would if it had been at all difficult, sir," Cochrane said with a droll smile. "Fortunately, the traffic warden in question happens to be my fiancée."

They entered the building by way of a side door and rode up to McLeod's office level in one of the service lifts. "The inspector said it would be a good idea not to come through the main lobby," Cochrane explained as they stepped out of the lift into an empty corridor. "This way now, sir."

They reached McLeod's office without encountering anyone else head-on. Even so, Adam had the uncomfortable feeling that he was being watched. Aware that there wasn't much he could do about that, he kept his back to the general office while Cochrane knocked at the door. An instant later, it was opened by Peregrine, looking pale but militant behind his spectacles. As soon as he caught sight of Adam, his face cleared.

"Thank God!" he exclaimed in a fervent undertone, standing aside so that they could enter.

McLeod was leaning back in his chair with a wet paper towel pressed across his eyes, hair rumpled and tie askew. As the newcomers entered, he took the paper towel away and put on his glasses, giving Adam a ghastly grin.

"Welcome back," he said huskily. "I would've come to you, instead of making you come to me, but right now my legs are about as trusty as a pair of rubber bands."

"So I'm told," Adam said, coming to reach for McLeod's wrist to check his pulse. "By all accounts, you're lucky to be here at all. Where's the item that's caused all the trouble?"

Upon learning that the origami animal had been stowed away in the office safe, Adam sent Cochrane off to fetch it. McLeod's pulse was steady enough, but noticeably quicker than usual, and his face was taut with pain.

"I don't suppose you need me to tell you that this was the work of the Lynx," McLeod said, as Adam pulled the extra chair closer and sat down.

"No, the method itself bears their signature."

As he removed McLeod's spectacles and set them aside so he could look at the bloodshot eyes, McLeod drew a labored breath.

"After that conversation we had on Monday, I can guess what you must be thinking," he said, as Adam covered first one of his eyes, then the other, and reached into a breast pocket for a pen-light. "But I swear I haven't consciously done anything to give myself away."

"I know you better than that," Adam said with the flicker of a smile. "Now relax and let me finish looking you over."

He shone the narrow beam briefly into each of McLeod's eyes, and McLeod flinched and turned away with a mutter.

"Sorry," Adam murmured. "I've brought some medication with me that should take the edge off the pain, but first I need to ask you one or two questions. First of all, has anyone actively handled that origami charm but you?"

"No." McLeod sounded positive.

"That's good," said Adam. "I'm going to want to take it apart to see what's inside. I'll need something to use as forceps that won't conduct—wood or plastic."

"How about a couple of pencils?" Peregrine offered.

"No, the graphite could be a conductor. Has he got any plastic cutlery in his desk drawer, I wonder?"

McLeod shook his head before Peregrine could look, though his face increasingly was showing signs of pain only barely held in check.

"How about toothpicks?" Adam asked. "Noel, have you got any toothpicks?"

"No, but maybe something better," McLeod said, setting his teeth against his pain. "How about a set of chopsticks?"

"Chopsticks? Ideal. Where are they?"

"Had a Chinese take-away for lunch on Wednesday," McLeod explained, gesturing toward his pencil jar. "They put in two sets of chopsticks. The spare set's in there."

Reaching over to the pencil jar, Adam slid the chopsticks out of their paper wrapper. They were made of wood, with tapering tips.

"Yes, these ought to do nicely," he decided. "When Mr. Cochrane returns with the specimen, we'll perform the required vivisection. Peregrine, let's get his jacket off now, and roll up a sleeve so I can give him a hypo."

As Peregrine helped him off with his coat and unbuttoned the cuff of one shirtsleeve, McLeod eyed the syringe Adam took from his coat pocket.

"What is it?" he murmured.

"Something to relax you and help with the nausea," Adam said, pushing up the sleeve and briskly swabbing a spot at the back of the bicep. "You should get some relief almost immediately."

"It won't knock me out, will it?" McLeod muttered, hardly noticing as the needle went in.

Adam shook his head and gave him the injection. "No, I'll do that," he said. "This is going to work best if you'll let me put you to sleep for a little while."

"That's fine," McLeod said around a yawn, already starting to relax under the influence of the drug. "Be careful, though, if you're going to mess with that lynx thing. Whoosh, that's good stuff!"

Adam smiled and slipped the spent syringe back in his pocket, then laid his fingers along McLeod's pulse again, his free hand pressing briefly across McLeod's forehead. "You just let me do the worrying now, my friend. Time to take a good, deep breath and go to sleep. That's right. . . . Let go of the pain. Now lean forward and pillow your head on your arm."

When he had gotten McLeod settled, Adam turned at last to give Peregrine his full attention.

"Well, then. Cochrane's given me a partial account of what you've been doing here," he said gravely, "but obviously he hadn't a clue what was really going on. Fortunately, Noel's been laying some groundwork with him for some time. Farther down the line, he might be a likely recruit. Before he gets back, though, perhaps you ought to tell me *your* side of things, in your own words. Incidentally, you did very well; you bought Noel some valuable time.''

Without knowing why, Peregrine found himself flushing like a guilty schoolboy under the impact of Adam's penetrating gaze. The praise was heady, but Peregrine's own uncertainty blunted its edge.

''I'm not sure I can explain it clearly,'' he said. ''I tried to think what you would have done. . . .''

Somewhat haltingly, he described focusing his inner Sight to discern what was afflicting McLeod—the dirty grey tendrils like a crown of thorns—and how he had pulled off the tendrils with his hands and watched them shrivel and dissipate.

''I have to confess something else, though,'' he added, when he had finished his brief narrative. ''I—ended up making use of Michael Brodie's ring.''

He hung his head guiltily, and Adam asked, ''Why should that trouble you?''

He was watching Peregrine's face very closely. Without meeting Adam's eyes, the young artist said in a small voice, ''I told you I wouldn't wear it without your permission.''

''So you did,'' Adam agreed. ''But that was *your* rule, not mine.''

Peregrine's hazel eyes flashed him a startled glance.

''True virtue,'' Adam said gently, ''is not a matter of making rules and then sticking to them at all cost. On the contrary, it's a matter of weighing up a situation and judging the issues correctly. Remember the directive of the *I Ching: The superior man discriminates between high and low.* In this instance, you acted rightly in setting aside a lesser good in favor of a greater one.''

Peregrine's troubled brow cleared. ''Then you're not disappointed in me?''

''Disappointed?'' If the young artist hadn't been looking so solemn, Adam might have been tempted to laugh out loud. ''Hardly that,'' he assured Peregrine with a smile. ''Surprised, perhaps—but then, you've been almost a continual source of surprise to Noel and me ever since Melrose. And I mean that to be taken as a compliment.''

Seeing that Peregrine was now smiling weakly as well, he added, ''Is there anything else you feel I ought to know?''

''I don't think so—no, wait!'' said Peregrine. ''There is one other thing. After Cochrane left to fetch you, while I was waiting, I did a few sketches. They're impressions of images, rather than proper pictures, but they stuck in my mind till I got them down. Maybe you can make something of them.''

He reached into the inside pocket of his blazer and produced a folded sheaf of papers which, when opened, proved to be a series of drawings made on departmental letterhead stationery. An outsider would have dismissed the sketches as the fanciful work of a surrealist, but to Adam's initiated eye, they represented a symbolic view of the danger hanging over McLeod.

The first drawing appeared to be a still life compounded of two Styrofoam cups, several sheets of paper, a scalpel, and a crow-quill pen. The second showed four bleeding thumbs extended over a bowl. The third showed the figure of a man hemmed in by a circle of burning briars. Taken together, like cards drawn from some strange Tarot deck, they pointed the way to an otherwise hidden truth.

''They don't seem to make much sense, do they?'' Peregrine remarked.

''On the contrary,'' Adam said thoughtfully, handing the sketches back, ''they tell me a great deal.''

He might have said more, but a knock at the door heralded Cochrane's return with the envelope containing the origami lynx.

''Sorry it took me so long, sir,'' he said, ''but there were a couple of other people hanging about, and I didn't want to appear too eager.''

''Very wise,'' Adam said with a nod, as Cochrane handed him the envelope. He clasped it briefly between his hands, his eyes taking on that faraway look so familiar to Peregrine, then took one of the chopsticks and slid it under the flap to unseal it. While Peregrine and Cochrane looked on, he used both chopsticks to carefully pull the folded handkerchief out onto the desk blotter and lift away the top layers to expose what lay inside.

The paper lynx glinted gold as Adam prodded it with the chopsticks. He had never seen a lynx done in origami before. It was cunningly made, the work of someone with skills to match or even exceed McLeod's own. The body had a thickness that suggested something enclosed within.

Dropping the lynx back into its nest of silk, Adam sketched a warding sign in the air above it with his ring hand, then reached again to the pencil jar and pulled out a plastic ruler. Using that to hold the lynx steady, and keeping his own defenses closely around it, he reached in delicately with the chopsticks and began carefully unpicking the ornate creases, wielding the chopsticks with the precision of a surgeon.

Slowly the paper unfolded. It was gilt on only one side, but the paper itself was also a gold color. Gradually Adam exposed four long, narrow strips of what looked like white Styrofoam and a scrap of white paper with curious russet markings. There were markings on the un-gilt side of the paper as well, but Adam used the chopsticks to pick up one of the Styrofoam strips first, lifting it carefully for closer inspection.

"These would appear to be pieces of the rim of a Styrofoam coffee cup," he reported. "Used, no doubt, by Noel some time in the last few days, and later salvaged from his office bin for the purpose we have already observed."

"What about that bit of paper?" Peregrine asked in a hushed voice, as Adam put the strip back with the others. "Is that writing on it? Some sort of cuneiform or something? And what's it written in? It almost looks like blood!"

Grimly Adam picked up the scrap of paper in his chopsticks.

"What's written here and on the paper the lynx was actually made of would be the formal fixation of the charm itself," he said thinly, "and blood is, indeed, the favored medium for activating a dark charm like this. As to the writing on the other side . . ."

He turned the scrap to disclose a black-inked signature within a typed signature block.

"That's McLeod's signature!" Peregrine gasped.

"It is, indeed," said Adam. "The third link for tying the focus of this charm to him."

Cochrane was peering intently over Adam's shoulder, frowning at the scrap of paper.

"I don't like this, sir," he said with a troubled scowl. "That's been torn from some piece of official correspondence—something that originated right here in the department."

Adam nodded. Coupled with the rest of the evidence, Cochrane's observation pointed to the likely presence of an agent of the Lynx operating within the police department itself.

"I was hoping not to have to consider that possibility," he told Cochrane. "If you should come up with any more specific connections, I'd be obliged if you could let me know."

"I'll do that, sir."

Adam allowed the charmed strip to curl back momentarily while he reached for two sheets of plain letter paper from the reserves in the middle drawer. Using the chopsticks and one end of the silk handkerchief to shield his fingers, he paper-clipped the origami paper foil-side down to one of the sheets, securing the scrap of paper across the corner with the cuneiform writing uppermost, then laid the other sheet atop it and stuck the "sandwich" thus formed into the first report folder he could pull from McLeod's desk.

"I'm not sure how well that will copy, Mr. Cochrane, but I'd like to have a photocopy for closer study," he said, handing the folder to the constable. "Would you mind taking care of that for me? Be sure you don't touch it."

"No problem, sir," Cochrane said, "though it may take me a little while to find a copy machine that's not in use. I gather you don't want anyone else looking at this."

"You gather correctly," Adam replied. "Take as long as is necessary. It will be worth the wait."

Once Cochrane had departed to dispatch this latest errand, Adam turned back to McLeod and set his hand lightly on the inspector's wrist. McLeod appeared to be asleep, but the telltale flicker of movement beneath his closed eyelids signalled that he was, in fact, still in trance, a part of him fully conscious of his surroundings.

"Noel, I hope to get you out of here in a little while," he said quietly. "Before we attempt to move you, though, I'm going to put a little more protection on you. Is that all right?"

Without opening his eyes, McLeod murmured, "Aye."

"Good man. Deep asleep, then."

Closing his eyes, Adam drew a deep breath to trigger his own trance-state, sinking easily to a useful working depth. The shift in perception brought a momentary distancing of his outer senses; but with his next breath he was able to open the eyes of his mind to the psychic residue of what had happened here in the last few hours. The image that came to him was that of McLeod standing weakly within a ring of thorns, just at the limits of his armspan.

Shadows played over the thorns like black flames. With a murmured invocation to the Light, Adam moved out of himself to stand with McLeod in the circle. Power welled up like a fountain within him. Focusing that power in his right hand, he sketched a sign of warding in the air.

The movement of his hand left a shimmering tracer. Hissing, the shadows curled back from the symbol he had drawn. His concentration deepening, Adam circled to his right, pausing at each of the remaining quarters to repeat the warding sign. The drain on his energy was palpable. By the time he finished sealing off the circle, he was beginning to tremble with exertion.

But the circle, once drawn, held firm. Satisfied that McLeod was defended for the moment against further injury, Adam retreated to the center of the circle, making the origin his point of withdrawal. His shift in consciousness was accompanied by a familiar twinge of vertigo. When the dizziness eased, he opened his eyes.

McLeod had not moved, but his breathing had eased somewhat, though his face still was the color of wax. Peregrine was standing by, his expression more than a little anxious. Seeing that Adam had roused himself, he asked in an undertone, "Is he going to be all right now?"

"He won't be completely all right until the charm itself is disposed of," said Adam. "But that is *not* something I intend to attempt here."

He sat there quietly, giving further reinforcement to McLeod's defenses, until Cochrane returned with the requested photocopy. Carefully pulling the paper clips with silk-shielded fingers, Adam freed the foil-backed paper and signature scrap, and used the chopsticks to drop them back into a nest made by the handkerchief. The Styrofoam strips followed, so that Adam could fold it all into a more compact mass, surrounded by the silk, and stuff everything into another envelope, which he sealed. The copy he folded and slipped into his breast pocket, along with the envelope. The lining of his suit jacket was silk, and would further shield him from what he carried.

"Time to get him out of here," Adam said to his two young assistants, glancing at his pocket watch. "It must be near enough quitting time. Hopefully there will be enough people coming and going in the next quarter hour that we'll be able to slip out without anyone taking much notice of our movements."

Peregrine reached for his coat and scarf. Adam, meanwhile, addressed McLeod across the threshold of hypnotic trance.

"Are you with me, Noel? Nod if you can hear me. All right, that's fine. Now listen," he continued with soft urgency. "In a moment or two we're going to be leaving the building. When I tell you to, you will rouse to full awareness, remembering everything that has happened, but showing no outward distress. I know you're still experiencing considerable discomfort, but you will resist giving way to that discomfort for as long as it takes us to get you safely to your car. If anyone should inquire, you'll say that you think you're coming down with the flu. . . ."

They got McLeod's jacket and then his overcoat on him. Cochrane accompanied them out of the office, pulling the office door shut and locking up with a nonchalance that Adam commended on their way down the back stairs. Thanks to Adam's post-hypnotic suggestion, McLeod made it out to the car park without his legs buckling under him, though several of his colleagues gave him odd looks. While Cochrane went off to retrieve Adam's medical bag from the front of the police car and Peregrine's "citation" from the Morris Minor, Adam and Peregrine located McLeod's black BMW in its assigned space and used the inspector's keys to open the doors. With Adam's help, McLeod climbed into the passenger seat and laid his head against the headrest with a sigh.

Cochrane rejoined them a moment later. After handing over Adam's black bag, he leaned in at the car window to take a last anxious look at his superior.

"Much as I hate to say this, sir," he said, in an attempt to sound casual, "you don't look as if you're going to be in any fit state to attend St. Andrew's Day observances at the Lodge tonight."

"Much as I hate to admit it, I think you're probably right," McLeod agreed ruefully. "I wonder if you'd be good enough to convey my apologies?"

"Be glad to, sir," said Cochrane. "Any other last orders before I take myself off?"

"Aye. Sometime in the next twenty-four hours, go out and have yourself a pint," said McLeod. "You've more than earned it."

# CHAPTER TWENTY

A DAM drove McLeod home in the BMW, Peregrine following in his own car. Jane McLeod was momentarily alarmed to see Adam escorting her husband up the path, and a second car pulling in behind the BMW, but McLeod himself disarmed her concern with the excuse Adam had suggested back at the station.

"Looks like this year's flu virus has finally caught up with me," he announced with a queasy grin. "Adam assures me I'm going to live, but right now, the prospect is not entirely attractive."

"This husband of yours," Adam said with a wry grimace, "is not the most cooperative of patients—though I don't suppose I need to tell you that. If you can keep him in bed for a day or two, though, he should start feeling better."

"Och, that'll be the trick," Jane said with some asperity, taking McLeod's other arm and helping Adam get him inside. "The man's impossible sometimes. But you're going straight to bed, Noel McLeod, and if anyone from the department should happen to phone, I shall tell them you've gotten fed up with city life and have run away to sea!"

"He can have aspirin if the headache gets too intolerable," Adam said, "but otherwise, I think sleep is likely to prove the best medicine of all. I'll ring you in the morning and see how he's getting on."

After seeing McLeod settled comfortably and telephoning Strathmourne to alert Humphrey and Philippa, Adam joined Peregrine in the Morris Minor. Rush hour traffic was in full force as they eased along the approach to the Forth Road Bridge and home, and for the next several miles, Peregrine was too preoccupied with his driving to voice any of the numerous questions that were buzzing about like bluebottles in the back of his brain. Once clear of the city's environs, however, he could no longer keep his thoughts to himself.

"Adam," he ventured, "from what little I've heard so far

concerning the Lodge of the Lynx, it seems they make every effort to keep their doings a secret. And yet this attack on the inspector is plainly their work. Why do you suppose they were so careless as to leave their calling card?''

Adam stirred in his seat, as if rousing from some private reverie. ''I don't think it was carelessness so much as arrogance,'' he said grimly. ''The attack on Noel was intended to be fatal. If it had succeeded, the physical evidence would have been consistent with death by heart failure or stroke. No one who didn't know what to look for would have suspected a thing.''

''But what about the charm itself?'' Peregrine protested. ''It was a lynx, for God's sake! Surely whoever made it must have realized it might well be found.''

''Yes, but who would have thought anything of it?'' Adam said. ''For that matter, how many people even know the Lodge of the Lynx exists, or would believe it? Very few, I can tell you. But just about everyone in the department knows McLeod does origami. He's got dozens of examples right there in his office. Whatever way you look at it, the risks were minimal.

''Picture it for yourself,'' he continued, gazing off at the tail-lights ahead. ''Someone enters McLeod's office to find him slumped dead over his desk. There's an immediate alarm that brings everyone within earshot rushing to the scene to see what might have happened. While all attention is focused on the victim, who's going to notice yet another origami figure? And something like that could disappear very easily after the body was taken away. That may have been their plan, in fact.''

Peregrine nodded. He *could* envision the scene quite clearly.

''Most fortunately for us,'' Adam went on, ''and even more fortunately for Noel, the opposition seem to have underestimated Noel's ability to defend himself. He is, as you have observed for yourself, a man of uncommon willpower and fortitude. That kind of toughness is something the opposition didn't reckon on. I would guess that's probably what saved him—or at least gave him the strength to hold out long enough for reinforcements to arrive.''

Peregrine shivered slightly. ''I had no idea it was anywhere near as critical as that,'' he muttered. ''Probably just as well that I never suspected.''

Adam smiled. ''You came through with flying colors. Lady Julian knew well what she was about when she presented you with Michael's ring.''

Peregrine had the grace to blush at the praise. After a moment's silence, he said curiously, ''What do you suppose prompted this sudden attack? I mean, why *now*? If they'd been onto McLeod since Urquhart, wouldn't they have done something sooner than this? And if they were onto *him*, wouldn't they be onto us as well? Will we be next?''

"Not necessarily, on all counts," Adam said. "Sometimes it's advisable simply to leave well enough alone. But the fact that they don't appear to have had an accurate idea of Noel's strength leads me to suspect that perhaps they haven't been watching him for very long—which means that, at least until they realize he's survived, they may not have any strong opinions about us either.

"My guess is that something may have happened in the last week to convince them it might be safer to eliminate him than to leave him alone. When he's feeling better, and I've dealt with *this*—" he patted the breast of his suit jacket "—we'll review all his activities since Randall Stewart's death, and see if we can identify any potential hot-spots. . . ."

It was nearly seven o'clock when they turned in at the gates to Strathmourne. By then, Peregrine was feeling the weight of an aching weariness.

"God, I'm tired!" he muttered, as he pulled up at the side door of the manor house. "The first thing I'm going to do when I get back to the lodge is take a hot shower! And dinner would be a bowl of cornflakes, if I didn't know Mrs. Gilchrist had left me some stovies and oatcakes!"

Adam grinned. Stovies—a savory hash of corned beef, onions, and potatoes—was almost as much a feature of the Scottish national diet as haggis, and a favorite dish with more than one of Adam's baronial acquaintances. No one made it better than the redoubtable Mrs. Gilchrist, whose maternal concern for Peregrine's welfare not infrequently prompted her to provide him with offerings from her kitchen.

"I'm glad you mentioned dinner," Adam said, retrieving his medical bag from behind the seat. "That puts me in mind of something I meant to ask you earlier this afternoon. Have you made any plans for tomorrow evening? If not, perhaps you'd care to come up to the house round about seven for drinks and dinner. Nothing particularly formal—just a chance for you and Philippa to get acquainted."

"Thanks, I'd enjoy that," Peregrine replied. "See you then, if not before."

Dinner arrangements having been made, Adam bade the artist good-night and alighted from the car. Humphrey was on hand to greet him as he entered the house, and relieved him of his coat and bag.

"It's good to have you home, sir," Humphrey said. "I hope all is well with Inspector McLeod."

"Well enough for the moment," Adam said, "but there's still quite a bit of work to be done. Is Mother in the library?"

"She is, sir. And she instructed me not to proceed with dinner until she'd heard more from you."

Adam nodded. "I'd better confer with her, then. I'm afraid dinner may be scrubbed entirely."

Concern showed through Humphrey's usual imperturbability. "As serious as that, sir?"

"As serious as that."

"I see, sir." Humphrey paused briefly, then inquired, "Would a spot of tea be in order in the meantime, then?"

Adam allowed himself a grateful sigh and nodded. "An excellent suggestion," he said, "but don't bring it up right away. We'll ring when we're ready."

He repaired to the library to find Philippa ensconced before the fire with a book balanced across her lap, relaxed but elegant in a red cowl-necked sweater and a kilted hostess skirt of red Sinclair tartan. From the book's binding, Adam recognized it as a first edition, in German, of Carl Gustav Jung's *Aion*. In her youth, Philippa had been a student of Jung's.

"I see you're consulting with an old friend," Adam said lightly.

Philippa's smile was like a flicker of distant lightning. "Once a pupil, always a pupil," she observed. "And I hate to waste time, as you know. With Gillian Talbot arriving on Monday, I thought it might be appropriate to pay a mental visit to the lecture hall for a review of the phenomenology of Self."

She reached for her bookmark, a thin fillet of fine gold, and inserted it at her place before setting the book aside.

"You look more tired than distraught," she observed, searching her son's face with keen, dark eyes. "Is the crisis satisfactorily resolved, then?"

With a long sigh, Adam sank down in the armchair opposite hers and opened a long, casket-shaped box on the chair-side table, hammered brass over a carcass of fragrant sandalwood. The inside was lined with sea-blue silk, and into it Adam put the envelope containing McLeod's silk handkerchief and its dangerous contents.

"Thanks to Peregrine's brilliant holding action and McLeod's own resilience, I was able to contain the worst of the storm damage," he informed his mother with a grimace. "However, the situation is far from settled yet." He closed the box.

"Indeed?" Philippa arched an eyebrow curved like a blackbird's wing. "In that case, perhaps you'd better fill me in on all the details."

In as few words as possible, Adam related all that had happened since they parted company at the airport, presenting her with the copy he had made of the writing from inside the charm. Philippa offered no comment during the course of his recital, but by the time he had finished, her elegant, angular face had gone hard, like the mask of a sphinx.

"The writing is runic, not cuneiform," she said, handing back the copy, "probably northern European. The spell itself could be La Tène, relating back to that torc you've described. I'll do some further research to narrow it down more specifically, but in the meantime, the charm itself must be destroyed to remove the threat from McLeod." She gazed on the box at Adam's elbow with cold calculation. "Neutralizing it won't be easy, though—especially after what you've already been through today. Do you mean to deal with it tonight?"

Adam leaned his head against the back of his chair and rubbed at his eyes with a weary hand.

"It has to be done tonight," he said. "And if you're thinking to do it yourself, don't. If only because of my close ties with Noel, I'm the best qualified. But I'd welcome your assistance."

"Why else do you suppose I've been keeping poor Humphrey on tenterhooks regarding dinner?" Philippa said with a grim smile. "I devoutly hope he didn't have anything special planned for this evening! Much as I dislike having to cancel a meal at short notice, I'm afraid that in this instance it can't be helped. If we're to deal properly with *that*," she gestured toward the casket-shaped box, "we're going to need all our faculties about us."

Adam acknowledged the point with a sober nod. Fasting was a desirable part of the preparations for any major work of the kind he and Philippa were contemplating, for the physiological process of digestion diverted blood from the brain, dulling mental functions that needed to be razor sharp. More critical still, in esoteric terms, was the grounding effect of taking in food, interfering with the elevation of the psyche to the higher planes. Indeed, eating was *recommended* after a psychic working of any depth at all, to ground the operator back onto reality.

"I've already alerted Humphrey to the possibility that dinner might not happen," Adam said. "In any case, I believe Mrs.

Gilchrist said something about leaving a hot pot of some kind that could stand by in case of balky airline schedules. I'm sure it will keep, whatever it is. And Humphrey understands the need for abstinence as well as you or I, when it comes to the Work. Whatever culinary plans we may have overset, he'll not begrudge any effort lost where the welfare of the Hunting Lodge is at stake.''

After a cup of tea apiece, they retired to their respective rooms to shower and spend some time apart in preparation. When Adam came back downstairs an hour later, he was wearing a quilted blue dressing gown over grey slacks and a clean white shirt, and crested slippers on his feet—his preferred attire for formal Work. Philippa sported a caftan-type robe of a deep, mauvey-pink. As they descended narrow steps into the sweet, musty dimness of the wine cellar, Philippa bore before them an antique oil lamp in the shape of a papyrus leaf, augmenting the electric light with a yellowish glow and a whisper of lemon verbena. Behind her, Adam carried the long metal casket containing the debris of the origami lynx.

When they reached the bottom of the stairs, Adam led the way past shadowy racks of vintage wines to the far end of the barrel-vaulted chamber. Here, a recessed doorway echoed the curve of the vaulting, the projecting arch surmounted by the heraldic crest of the Sinclairs—a phoenix taking flight out of a nest of fire. The door itself was patterned in oblong panels of variegated wood, each panel about the size of a man's hand and decorated with its own design in marquetry inlay.

Handing the casket momentarily into Philippa's keeping, Adam ducked under the archway to set his right hand to a tulip-wood panel at the top center of the door. The panel yielded under the pressure of his fingers, then hinged upward, spring-loaded, to reveal a shallow recess. The adjacent panel on the left was made from maple, and shifted smoothly at Adam's touch into the slot prepared for it, like a movable segment from a Chinese puzzle box.

The sequential adjustment of several other panels uncovered a hidden compartment containing a polished brass key. Taking it out, Adam shifted more of the panels in a seemingly random pattern until at last the center panel slid aside to disclose the lock for which the key had been designed.

Adam turned the key in the lock and reclaimed the metal weight of the casket from Philippa, lingering to close and secure the door while she proceeded through a short vestibule passage to open another arched door. Beyond lay another vaulted chamber of a size similar to the wine cellar, its white-washed walls gently illuminated by the glow of an ever-burning lamp suspended by bronze chains from a boss at the center of the ceiling. Directly beneath the lamp stood a square, waist-high altar in the form of a double cube, centered on a large, fringed kelim rug and shrouded to the floor under the drape of a deep blue altar cloth. To the right of the altar and facing it was a high-backed armchair made from golden oak, its seat and oval-shaped back upholstered in blue velvet of the same shade as the altar cloth.

A narrow doorway in the right-hand wall of the passage gave access to a small sacristy chamber. Philippa had already gone inside with her lamp, but Adam proceeded to the temple threshold first to pay his respects, already beginning to focus his intentions for the work ahead. When he joined her a few minutes later, Philippa had put aside her caftan for a sapphire blue soutane and was operating a small, bronze-handled hand-pump to fill a creamware porcelain ewer with water.

Setting aside the casket, Adam stripped off his quilted robe and donned a soutane like hers, buttoning it close at the throat like a priest's cassock and closing a cincture of the same deep sapphire around his waist. He was already wearing the sapphire signet ring that was both the emblem and the tool of his calling as an Adeptus Major, and now he laid around his neck the Qabalistic stole of High Adeptship, black on the right side and white on the left, with a tiny red Maltese cross appliquéd over the joining of the two colors, recalling the *Beauceant* banner of his Templar heritage. On other nights, for other workings, he might have crossed the white side over the black and secured the ends under his cincture, symbolizing Mercy restraining Might, the Priest-King offering self in sacrifice to Deity; but tonight he let the ends hang free, for he was to be the instrument of that Deity, standing as the Middle Pillar between Might and Mercy to mete out a restoration of the Balance set awry by the dark working of the Lodge of the Lynx.

Clasping his hands before him, with the sapphire of his ring pressed lightly to his lips, he offered as a prayer the motto adopted by the Templars when they had numbered only nine Poor Knights in the Holy Land.

*Not to us, Lord, not unto us, but unto Thee be the Glory!*

When he turned back to Philippa, she was waiting with the creamware ewer and a matching basin, a pristine linen towel laid across one forearm. He came to her and let her pour water over his hands, inhaling the fragrance of attar of roses, then dried his hands on the towel and offered her the same service.

Her ring flashed in the lamplight, sapphire and gold fashioned like a scarab, the ancient Egyptian symbol of eternal life. Adam's father had bought it for her shortly before their marriage, not knowing then or ever that she was called to additional service besides that of physician, wife, and eventual mother. The pectoral hanging on her breast had been a later acquisition, but of far greater antiquity, bought at auction to celebrate Adam's birth— blue faience and enamel depicting a Horus hawk clutching a solar disk between two ostrich plumes, wrought in Egypt in the XXIst Dynasty. Sir Iain Sinclair was never to know that the soul looking out through the wise eyes of his infant son and heir had treasured the ornament as a sign of royal priesthood.

Adam drew himself back from the memory as Philippa laid aside the towel, himself tipping the basin over a piscina set into the wall, returning the water to the earth whence it came. While she carried several other items into the temple, he retrieved his *skean dubh* from the pocket of his dressing gown, tucking it temporarily into the front of his cincture.

She returned and they were ready. Lighting a new beeswax taper from the little papyrus lamp, Philippa led them in, Adam following with the metal casket. This time he halted just inside the doorway, leaving Philippa to kindle the beeswax candles that stood in mirror-backed sconces on each of the temple's four walls, making the responses in his mind as Philippa saluted each of the quarters and invoked their protection. The eastern wall bore a painted fresco of the Tree of Life, with the eastern candle set in the place of Kether, the Crown. Just before that wall stood a more conventional Christian altar, though they would not use that tonight. The glow of the candles picked out points of silver from the ceiling overhead, where the vault had been overlaid with a mosaic of stars.

She finished her circuit and extinguished her taper, laying it in a little niche to the right of the doorway before advancing between the center altar and the chair. Facing east, and bowing low in reverent acknowledgement of the Divinity she and Adam both served, she addressed herself to that Presence in the words of the Psalmist of Israel:

"The day is Thine, and the night is Thine; Thou hast prepared the light and the sun."

A light breath of air stirred through the chamber, quickening the candleflames so that they flickered and danced with brighter intensity. Rising up from her obeisance, Philippa turned then to her left to gaze at Adam, hands upraised to the level of her shoulders and palms turned upward.

"The Lord is in His holy temple," she announced. "Draw near with faith and reverence, that our work may find favor in His sight."

Thus invited, Adam approached the altar, passing to the east of it, opposite Philippa, to sink to one knee in a deep genuflection that mirrored the attitude of a knight swearing fealty to his liege lord, the casket on his knee. As he rose, Philippa folded the blue cloth back from the altar to remove it, revealing a white one of fine damask linen beneath.

She finished folding the cloth and slipped it onto one of two specially constructed shelves built into the base of the chair, then shook out a much smaller square of linen cloth, just the size of the altar top, which she spread over the white damask. Two small silver bowls followed, containing salt and clear water. These she set to one side of the altar where, after bowing briefly over her clasped hands, she pointed the first and second fingers of her right hand at the vessel containing the salt.

"I exorcise thee, creature of salt, by the living God, by the holy God, by the omnipotent God, that thou mayest be purified in the Name of Adonai, Who is Lord of Angels and of men."

She traced a cross over it, followed by an encompassing circle, then lifted the bowl to eye level between her two hands.

"Creature of earth, adore thy Creator. Thus be thou consecrated to the service of the Light, that thou mayest turn away the Darkness and bring purification to everything that feels thy holy touch. Amen."

After placing the bowl of salt to the right of the cloth, she bowed low to the altar, then pointed her first two fingers at the bowl of water.

"I exorcise thee, creature of water, by the living God, by the holy God, by the omnipotent God, that thou mayest be purified in the Name of Elohim Sabaoth, Who is Lord of Angels and of men."

Again the circled cross, before raising the vessel of water as she had raised the salt.

"Creature of water, adore thy Creator, and thereby be consecrated to the service of the Light, by that Name Which is above every name, before Which every knee should bend and every tongue give praise. Amen."

When she had set the bowl of water to the left, she bowed again to the altar, then used her ring-hand to trace first a cross, then a pentagram, and finally an ankh in the air above the linen square. To Adam's heightened senses, the figures seemed to hang on the air in afterimage as he set the casket in their midst.

He drew the *skean dubh* from his waist as he circled around to the left to take his place before his chair, Philippa moving in harmony so that she ended up standing directly opposite. Conscious of her strength ready to augment his own, he unsheathed the *skean dubh* and set sheath and blade to left and right of the casket before opening its lid.

The envelope made a creamy contrast against the casket's lining of sea-blue silk. Plucking it out, Adam tore the end across and carefully pulled the contents out by the edge of McLeod's handkerchief, letting all of it settle into the casket. A further careful prodding with his *skean dubh* lifted away the folds of silk to expose to the light of the hanging altar lamp what was left of the origami lynx, along with the curled slip of paper bearing McLeod's signature and the ragged strips of Styrofoam.

A crackling surge of unseen energies attended his action, centered on the casket, resistance already rising in response to his intent. Well aware of the sudden tension building there, Adam laid his blade across the width of the casket and spread his left hand above it, inhaling a deep lungful of air and focusing an invocation for protection and guidance. As he opened himself to the Divine Will, invoking the Middle Pillar, all apprehension fled before a wondrous sense of abiding calm.

Anchored in this calm, he slipped effortlessly from prayer into deeper trance, the sharpening of his perceptions bringing ever-clearer vision of the sheer malignancy surrounding the contents of the casket. The evil it exuded was like the stench of brimstone. Keeping it at bay with his left hand, he laid the *skean dubh* aside and took up the little bowl of consecrated salt, invoking the authority of the One in Whose Name it had been blessed. He uttered that Name under his breath as he dashed the salt over the contents of the casket.

With a corrosive sizzle like a spatter of hot grease, the paper that had formed the lynx began to curl in upon itself. Black burn marks peppered the golden paper, spreading from fold to fold. A sudden, lurid flare burst forth, along with a puff of dirty smoke. As it mantled and spread, Adam suddenly found himself looking through a window in the smoke.

A large room lay beyond, furnished like a Victorian library, with four mist-shrouded figures gathered around a table at the center of the room. By the light of a branched candelabrum, one of the four was drawing a scalpel across his left thumb, letting the blood drip into a small glass jar already partially filled. At least one of the others had already made his bloody offering, and pressed a ball of cotton between left thumb and fingers. Other paraphernalia on the table declared this the session which had created the lynx charm. A crow-quill pen lay to one side, and a flash of gold at the leader's elbow seemed to be the very piece of foil-backed paper used to fashion the origami lynx.

His gaze sharply narrowing, Adam attempted to catch a closer glimpse of the leader's face. Before he could do so, a dark shape with outstretched arms reared up before him, a sullenly glimmering torc about its neck and lightning bolts in both hands. In reflex, Adam's hand moved in a warding gesture. The image vanished in a blaze of white light.

He heard Philippa give a little gasp. For a moment, he could see nothing but the after-image. When his sight readjusted itself, nothing remained of the contents of the casket but a stinking smear of glowing ash and melted Styrofoam. Even the inside of the casket itself was gone, the silk lining burned cleanly away and the wood beneath it charred back nearly to the metal.

To complete the purification, Adam took the vessel of consecrated water and poured it along the length of the casket. Steam boiled up, far more of it than warranted by either the size of the fire or the amount of water. The stench of blood and brimstone dissipated swiftly, giving way to a faint fresh fragrance like the scent of clean snow. When it cleared away, in a last small puff of white steam, the casket was empty and dry, a shell of beaten metal.

Breathing a thankful sigh, Adam bent forward slightly to survey what was left, spreading his palms over the casket to verify that the work was complete, then sank to his knees in relief mixed with weariness, leaning his forehead gratefully against the edge of the altar as he offered up wordless thanks for the intercession of the Light.

Half an hour later, after returning the temple to order and divesting themselves of their ritual attire, Adam and Philippa had returned to the library for a belated and much-needed supper of hot stew, crusty French bread, and cocoa. Huddling close to the fireside, for she was still feeling the chill that invariably followed in the wake of a difficult working, Philippa studied her son's face for several minutes, trying to fathom his reaction to the events they had just witnessed. When he did not seem inclined to speak, she set her mug of chocolate aside and laid a tapering, blue-veined hand on his knee.

"You don't appear to be deriving much satisfaction from the night's work," she said quietly.

Adam shifted his gaze from his mug to the flames on the hearth. "I'd be better pleased if we were any the wiser for it," he said. "We've neutralized the immediate threat to Noel, but that doesn't alter the fact that the security of the Hunting Lodge has been breached. They'll try again, and they'll expand their net once they figure out that I'm involved—and Peregrine. The situation was already difficult enough without our being hampered by our enemies knowing much more about us than we do about them."

This bleak statement drew a grimace from Philippa. "Weren't you able to learn *anything* about those who took part in the making of that charm?"

"Little beyond what Peregrine's sketches had already hinted," Adam said. "There were four of them, who apparently all contributed to the blood used to letter out the charm, but I couldn't get a look at their faces. And right at the end, there was something else there to make sure that I couldn't—something non-human. I couldn't get a look at *it*, either—and I'm not entirely sure I would have wanted to—but the torc was there again. And lightning bolts." He shook his head, controlling a shudder.

"It's the same story, whichever way we turn. No names, no faces, just a lengthening account of crimes, each one more brutal and audacious than the last—and now, a hint of having tapped into something very dark and very powerful, perhaps an elemental of some sort. Whatever they're out to achieve, it's something very big. And if we don't get a break pretty soon, they may just carry it off—and us with it."

He lapsed into troubled silence. Thoughtful, Philippa refilled her cup from the chocolate urn and sipped at it daintily while she considered.

"I'll grant you that time is not exactly on our side," she acknowledged after a moment. "But don't let your frustration blind you to the fact that today's attack on Noel McLeod was in some measure a mistake. The fact that he survived, when by rights he ought to be dead, may be precisely the loose end we need to unravel the rest of the mystery."

"I hope you're right," said Adam, half-smiling now. "If there *are* any loose ends out there, I certainly hope they lead somewhere."

# CHAPTER TWENTY-ONE

THE next evening, after sleeping until well past noon and accomplishing very little in what remained of the day, Peregrine drove up from the gate lodge to keep his dinner engagement with Adam and Adam's mother. Humphrey was already waiting to admit him as he dashed up to the front door through flurrying snow.

"Good evening, Mr. Lovat."

"'Lo, Humphrey. What a night!" Peregrine exclaimed, stamping snow from his shoes in the entry lobby and shedding hat and scarf while Humphrey waited to divest him of his topcoat.

"Indeed, sir. 'Scarce fit for man nor beast,' as the saying goes."

Peregrine's spectacles were splattered with snow-water, which yielded to a quick polish with his handkerchief. Tucking it back into the breast pocket of his suit jacket, he replaced his glasses and gave his hair a swift brush through with his fingers.

"Right, Humphrey. Where to now?"

"Sir Adam and her ladyship are taking drinks in the Rose Room, sir," said the butler. "This way, if you please."

Eager if a little apprehensive, Peregrine followed Humphrey up the stairs and across the first floor landing, stealing a glance in one of the mirrors to assure himself his tie was straight. He liked the Rose Room, with its delicate tea-rose wallpaper and roseleaf draperies and delicate Louis XIV furniture. To his artist's eye it recalled gentler times, when the elegant little parlor had served as a Victorian lady's morning room and writing chamber. Adam seldom made use of it on his own behalf, but Peregrine could appreciate why he might have chosen to open it up on this occasion—and why it must have been a favorite of Philippa Sinclair when she was still mistress of this house. Smaller than the library and more intimate than either of the two formal reception rooms downstairs, the Rose Room offered a cozy and gracious environment for making introductions and quiet conversation.

Following Humphrey across the first floor landing toward the

Rose Room door, Peregrine gave his shirt-cuffs a last minute twitch, then drew a fortifying breath as Humphrey delivered a discreet knock and announced his arrival.

"Ah, Peregrine, there you are!" Adam said. He set a cut-crystal tumbler on the mantel and started forward in welcome. "Come in and meet my mother."

Behind Adam, a fire was blazing on the hearth beneath a fine mantelpiece of pink Carrara marble. Sitting before the fire in an open-arm chair upholstered in rose velvet was a slender, silver-haired woman with a spine like a ramrod and eyes that put Peregrine in mind of the goddesses painted on the walls of Egyptian tombs. A single glance at her face was enough to convince him that, had there been a hundred other people present, he would nevertheless have been able to single her out as Adam's mother.

For the resemblance between them was as strong as it was striking. Mother and son shared the same elegant height, the same strong, finely-sculptured features. More striking still was their kindred air of vibrant intensity. Drawn to look more closely in spite of himself, Peregrine had this impression reinforced by the ghostly rippling of images he was coming to associate with the presence of those who shared Adam's mysterious vocation. He was awed but hardly surprised to discover that Adam had more in common with his mother than physical appearances.

Still digesting the import of this fleeting but significant discovery, he realized belatedly that he was being introduced and started forward, bowing over the slender hand that Philippa Sinclair extended to him.

"How do you do, Lady Sinclair?" he said. "Ever since Adam told me you were coming, I've been looking forward to making your acquaintance."

His obvious respect drew a smile from Philippa.

"And I'm very pleased to meet *you*, Mr. Lovat," she said warmly. "Adam has shown me some of your work. In this age of the computer-generated image, it's a rare experience to encounter an artist with a gift for *true* portraiture."

Her voice was a low, clear contralto, its colonial accent subtly modulated by inflectional resonances from several other languages, and the slight stress she laid on the word *true* was unmistakable.

"You're very kind, Lady Sinclair," Peregrine said. "But in fact, I'm indebted to Adam for providing a working demonstration that there's far more to some people than meets the naked eye."

He accompanied this statement with a look that was both

significant and admiring, and Philippa's lips curved upward in a smile of genuine amusement.

"Touché!" she laughed. "That's what I get for needling you with compliments. Now that we all know who and what we're dealing with, perhaps Adam will be good enough to pour you a drink. And you must call me Philippa. I'd like to think that one of these days, Adam will see fit to bestow the title of 'Lady Sinclair' on another mistress of Strathmourne."

Adam rolled his eyes good-naturedly, and Peregrine found himself smiling along with Philippa as she steered him toward a chair opposite her own.

As he sipped appreciatively at a glass of Adam's favorite MacAllan, Peregrine continued to be impressed at the unstudied force of Philippa's personality. In spite of her age, she had a quicksilver quality about her that refused to be pinned down to easy definitions. He caught himself wondering if she had ever crossed swords with the Lodge of the Lynx, and decided that if she had, she was more than capable of defending herself.

After half an hour's easy conversation, dinner was served in modest state in the dining room, on a Regency table set with crested Sevres china, antique silver flatware, and Edinburgh crystal. The first course was a soup made from fresh mussels, cider, and cream, with poached turbot in Granville sauce to follow. While they lingered over it, enjoying the company as well as the meal, Peregrine inquired after McLeod and learned that the inspector was resting at home in reasonable comfort.

"I rang him this morning," Adam said. "The official story is that he's come down with a nasty case of flu and has been advised to take some time off to recuperate. In real terms, that probably means he'll be back at work Tuesday or Wednesday—sooner, if he gets his way. Young Cochrane's minding the store in the meantime. And at least we don't anticipate any permanent side effects."

"Well, that's a relief," Peregrine said. "When you next speak with him, give him my regards."

Following this exchange, Philippa deftly turned the conversation in the direction of the arts, professing an avid interest in the school of American realism. Peregrine was surprised and delighted to discover that she was very knowledgeable on the subject, and found himself drawn into an animated discourse on the relative merits of various American realists from Winslow Homer to John Sloan.

"The term *realism* is more apt than most critics realize," Philippa said with a touch of irony, over the fresh fruit terrine Mrs. Gilchrist had laid on for dessert. "As far as the critics are concerned, an artist is a realist if he paints scenes from daily life, rather than painting scenes from the realm of allegorical imagination. But there's far more to it than that. Artists like Whistler and John Singer Sargent make you look beyond the faces of their subjects to something interior—something more real, if you like, than shows up on a photographic print. It's something the eye of the camera can't catch—only the eye of the truly gifted artist.''

"Speaking of which,'' Adam said with a pointed glance at Peregrine, "have you finished that portrait of the provost?''

"Almost,'' Peregrine said with a smile, touching a napkin to his lips. "It would've been done yesterday, only I had to go and rescue Noel. I've already rescheduled the final sitting for Monday. Of course it won't be ready for delivery until it's properly dried and varnished, but I think even the provost is pleased with the results; I know his wife is. So I flatter myself we can consider this commission successfully completed.''

He bent his head over his terrine again, and thus missed seeing the glances his host and hostess exchanged across the table.

"In that case,'' said Adam, "I have in mind to offer another commission for your consideration.''

Peregrine looked up with an arrested expression on his face, his spoon halfway to his mouth. Meeting Adam's gaze, he said, "Why do I have this sudden feeling that you don't mean that in the conventional sense?''

Philippa smiled and darted one of her flashing looks at Adam. "You may as well come clean, my dear,'' she advised. "You've already lost the element of surprise.''

"So I observe,'' Adam said drily. "I trust, then, that you'll recall the name Gillian Talbot?''

Peregrine put his spoon down, sneaking a guarded glance at Philippa. "Of course,'' he said quietly.

"You needn't feel shy about speaking freely,'' Adam said. "Philippa knows all about the business at Melrose. Anyway,'' he continued, setting his napkin aside, "last week while I was in London, the Talbots finally got in touch with me and requested my professional intervention on Gillian's behalf. Philippa and I went to meet them at the hospital the next day. The upshot of that meeting is that Gillian is being transferred up to Jordanburn. She and her mother will be arriving on Monday.''

Peregrine nodded, still carefully noncommittal.

"I know you were hoping something like that might be arranged. But what does this have to do with me?''

"I have in mind something in the nature of an experiment,'' Adam said. "Once Gillian is comfortably settled in, I'd like you to come visit her in the hospital to make some sketches. I have a suspicion they may prove more than a little illuminating when we approach the problem of rebuilding her personality. At the very least, they may reveal the role that you yourself have been designated to play."

"*Me*?" Peregrine blanched slightly. "But I don't know anything about—"

"You may not think you know," Philippa interjected, "but I think Michael Scot made it clear, at Melrose, that *he* found your talents useful. Adam believes—and I agree with him—that the choice was not random. Quite the contrary. We think that Scot singled you out as someone who might be able to help him in the future—*his* future."

Peregrine looked from Philippa to Adam and back again. "I don't know," he said doubtfully. "What's her mother going to say about this? I'm not even a doctor."

Adam smiled. "I'm sure we can come up with a plausible explanation."

While Peregrine was sitting down to dinner with his host and hostess at Strathmourne, a far less amicable meeting was taking place in the library of a large country house twelve miles to the west of Stirling. Those present by demand included Charles Napier, a senior police inspector from Edinburgh, Dr. Preston Wemyss, an eminent physician, and Angela Fitzgerald, a prominent Glasgow society columnist. None of them had been offered refreshments. All of them were decidedly ill at ease under the cold, disparaging gaze of their host. Francis Raeburn, himself fresh from an earlier meeting with *his* superior, was in no mood to spare anyone.

"I don't suppose I need dwell on the fact that Noel McLeod is still alive, when by rights he should be dead," he informed his subordinates with biting sarcasm. "Our failure to neutralize him has created complications that I, for one, could well have done without. Henceforth, we can afford no further errors. I require the assurance of all of you that there will be none."

He fixed his gaze on each of his three subordinates in turn. Napier, his heavy face sullen under lowering brows, gave a wrestler's hunch to his shoulders and spoke for the rest.

"How were we supposed to know he'd prove so resistant to the charm?" he demanded resentfully. "Besides, *you* were the one who decided the form of the attack."

"And I relied upon you to evaluate the victim," Raeburn snapped. "*You* ought to have known. It was your particular business to know. None of you are novices at this game. You knew what tests to apply—''

''Really, Francis, it *was* a calculated risk,'' the lone female of their number protested. ''If you wanted a guarantee, you should have given us more time to make a full assessment of the victim.''

''How much time would you have considered adequate?'' Raeburn retorted. ''A week? A fortnight? A month? Until the Hunting Lodge arrived in force on our very doorstep? Leisure is not a luxury we can afford in this business. Or have you perhaps forgotten that our Head-Master is even less patient than I am?''

''If the Head-Master is that keen for results, perhaps he ought to consider taking a more direct role in this affair!'' Angela Fitzgerald primmed her hard, painted mouth as she plucked an imaginary fleck of fluff from the sleeve of her grey silk blouse. ''This McLeod didn't just *happen* to survive, you know. He had help from some of his cohorts.''

''Aye, that damned artist, Lovat,'' Napier grumbled. ''Who would have thought that effete puppy could possibly have had the knowledge to intervene? And I let him walk right into McLeod's office with Cochrane—who also will bear watching, after this. He can't have been totally oblivious to what was going on.''

''Could *he* have been the one to rescue McLeod, rather than Lovat?'' Wemyss asked, speaking for the first time.

Napier shook his head. ''If he'd had the ability, he wouldn't have needed to bring in Lovat and Sinclair. And the fact that he brought in both of them tends to confirm that it's Sinclair who leads them. If he or Lovat gets in my way again—''

''Don't make threats you may not be able to carry out,'' Angela said. ''We don't yet know their full strength. What we do know now, however, that we didn't know before,'' she went on, turning back to Raeburn, ''is that we're almost certainly up against a Hunting Lodge. McLeod may still be alive, but the exercise wasn't a total loss. We did manage to flush out two of his allies.''

Raeburn glowered at her sullenly.

''Is that intended as a piece of consolation, or is it merely an excuse?''

Wemyss, a thin, dark man with the hungry eyes of a weasel, had taken a handsome gold-plated pen from his pocket and was twirling it nervously between his fingers.

''For God's sake, what's done is done!'' he said petulantly. ''I don't see that recriminations are likely to improve our situation at this point.''

''I agree,'' Angela said. Levelling her piercing blue gaze at

Raeburn, she added waspishly, "Since the three of us apparently are so incompetent, perhaps Francis would care to suggest what we ought to do now."

Raeburn curled his lip, all but sneering.

"Lead you by the hand? Is that really what you'd like? Very well, I suppose *somebody* has to."

He leaned forward in his chair and laced his fingers together before him on the desktop, surveying them coldly.

"The only recourse now is to make sure there are no more failures. The next time we strike, it will have to be hard. You complain that I didn't give you time enough to gather the facts on McLeod? Very well, I'm giving you that time now. I want information—complete dossiers, not just on McLeod, but on Sinclair, Lovat, and anyone else who seems intimately connected with them. I want to know who they see, who they talk to, how they spend their time. And I want all of you ready to act when I give the word."

"You make it sound as if we've been idle all this time," the doctor said pettishly. "Let me remind you that I've already got people keeping an eye both on Sinclair's residence and the hospital where he works."

"Then might I suggest," said Raeburn, "that it's time these employees of yours began to earn their pay?"

Wemyss opened his mouth as if to utter an indignant protest, then subsided as he caught Raeburn's eye.

"All right," Napier said, with a glance at his two colleagues. "We all need to step things up a bit. But what about the event scheduled for next Friday?"

"It will go ahead as planned," Raeburn said.

Angela Fitzgerald scowled at him. "Don't you think that's perhaps just a bit risky? Our opposite numbers are sure to come running to investigate."

"Then let them," Raeburn said with a shrug. "Any evidence left behind should be sufficiently baffling to keep them busy for quite some time while we pursue our own objectives elsewhere. In fact, the more distractions we can offer our pious friends, the better. By the time they finish sifting through the evidence, our plans will be that much nearer completion.

"Who knows?" he added with a thin smile. "If we can count on them to put in an appearance every time we strike, we may be able to use their very predictability to our own advantage."

# CHAPTER TWENTY-TWO

IT was approaching teatime late on Monday afternoon when a London ambulance pulled up outside the entrance to the Royal Edinburgh Hospital, more commonly known among the local population as Jordanburn. As its driver and his partner headed around the back to open the doors, a pair of hospital porters and a motherly-looking nurse in uniform came out to meet it.

The patient lying pale and motionless on the stretcher that the five of them drew out was a young girl of perhaps eleven or twelve, with a tangle of I.V. tubing emerging from underneath the navy blue blanket buckled over her inert form. Disembarking close behind her came a worn-looking blonde woman in her mid-thirties, whose anxious demeanor made it obvious to all but the most casual of observers that she must be the child's mother.

One far from casual observer was a hospital cleaning woman making her way across the hospital car park, headed toward the bus stop on the main road. Sandy-haired and bespectacled, of indeterminate middle years, she wore a nondescript tweed coat over her cleaner's coverall and carried a capacious handbag clutched close to her body under one arm. The activity at the ambulance entrance would have provoked no undue interest had she not been startled to see the regular hospital staff joined by a consultant physician in a crisp white lab coat—a tall, aristocratic-looking man with dark hair going silver at the temples, the very man whose photo resided in the woman's handbag, and whose activities she had been ordered to observe.

Her interest piqued—for senior consultants of the standing of Dr. Adam Sinclair did not ordinarily meet patients at the ambulance entrance—she checked in her stride and delved into her coat pocket for a cigarette, going through the motions of lighting up while she strained to catch the drift of the conversation. The porters prepared to take their patient inside as the nurse conferred quietly with the driver of the ambulance and documents changed hands, but Sinclair's voice carried musically across the frosty dusk as he came forward to greet the blonde woman.

"Good evening, Mrs. Talbot," he said warmly. "You've had a long journey, haven't you? I hope it wasn't too wearing."

The blonde woman glanced anxiously beyond him at the child on the gurney before summoning a brave smile.

"Not too bad, thank you, Dr. Sinclair. But I'm glad to have finally arrived."

"Well, Gillian's bed is all ready and waiting for her," Sinclair continued, steering the patient's mother toward the disappearing gurney. "Come along in out of the cold, and we'll see about getting you a nice cup of tea."

The woman in the cleaner's coverall loitered long enough to see Sinclair and the woman disappear through the swinging doors before carrying on up the path in the direction of the bus stop. Once out of sight of the ambulance entrance, she rummaged in her handbag and dragged out a tattered pocket-sized notebook with a pencil thrust through the spiral binding at the top, flicking it open to note down this most recent development in the day-to-day chronicle she had been sent to compile on the professional activities of Dr. Adam Sinclair.

At noon the following day, Francis Raeburn received a calling card announcing a visit from Dr. Preston Wemyss. Dispatching his houseboy with instructions to fetch his caller up to the library, Raeburn seated himself behind his desk. Wemyss arrived looking harassed and slightly dyspeptic, an aged black leather briefcase clutched fast in one gloved hand. Raeburn dismissed the houseboy with a gesture and eyed his subordinate up and down.

"You're commendably prompt," he observed. "What have you got for me?"

Wemyss turned to make sure that the houseboy had departed before sinking into the chair Raeburn indicated.

"I hope you aren't expecting miracles," he said sourly.

Raeburn's thin mouth registered a twitch of impatience, but he declined to respond. Nervous, Wemyss shifted the briefcase onto his knees and plucked off his gloves before flicking through the numbers on the combination lock and thumbing the twin brass catches. The latches snapped up, and Wemyss lifted out an accordion file folder, which he offered across the desk to his superior.

"If I'd wanted to read through all that myself, I would have said so," Raeburn said coldly. "Give me a summary of what you consider important."

Wemyss' dark, close-set eyes showed a passing flare of

resentment. Flicking a monogrammed linen handkerchief from his pocket, he pressed it briefly to his lips, then took back the folder.

"As far as I can tell," he informed Raeburn sullenly, "there are only two developments worth mentioning. The first is that Adam Sinclair and his mother—who arrived Friday, as you know—had lunch yesterday with a medical colleague, Sir Matthew Fraser, and Fraser's wife Janet. Fraser's a surgeon. The connection appears to be purely social, but I have someone checking further into their backgrounds, just to be sure. The other development is that Sinclair has taken on a new patient."

At Wemyss' slight scowl, Raeburn cocked him a shrewd glance.

"Are you implying that this is something out of the ordinary?"

"I'm not sure." Wemyss' frown deepened. "The patient in question is a twelve-year-old girl name of Gillian Rose Talbot. Sinclair doesn't usually treat children. What also strikes me as odd is that she's not from this district. My informant was able to steal a glimpse of her records this morning and discovered that she comes from London."

"London? That does seem to be reaching a bit far afield," Raeburn agreed. "What's wrong with this child?"

"Coma. That's another odd thing," Wemyss said. "The case notes indicate no obvious trauma, and she appears to have had no prior history of psychiatric disorder. She was originally admitted to Charing Cross Hospital on the morning of the twenty-eighth of October, conscious but out of touch with her surroundings. Her condition has deteriorated since the—"

"Stop a minute!" Raeburn said sharply. "The *twenty-eighth* of October, you say?"

"That's right."

"Let me see those records," Raeburn ordered. "Pull them from the file."

Wemyss shot a puzzled glance at his superior, but did not delay in producing the required pages. As he handed them across, Raeburn plucked them unceremoniously from his hand and skimmed quickly through them.

"Very interesting," he murmured, when he had read through them a second time. "You may have stumbled across something of genuine value."

"Really? I wish you'd explain it to me, then," Wemyss said peevishly.

Raeburn, however, gave his attention back to the notes without vouchsafing any disclosures. Though he would not have expected Wemyss to recognize the significance of the date involved, it had already registered in his own mind that the child Gillian Talbot had been admitted to hospital with a mysterious psychiatric ailment mere hours after the soul of the wizard Michael Scot had been conjured back to its moldering remains in Melrose Abbey. It might, of course, be pure coincidence. But then again . . .

He restacked the pages and handed them back to his subordinate.

"This child interests me—if only because she appears to interest Sinclair," he informed Wemyss. "See if your obliging contact at Jordanburn can contrive to bring you something physically connected with her—perhaps some hair combings or fingernail parings. A blood sample would be best of all. Something, at any rate, that Barclay might be able to use as a focus for doing an astral search. I want to look into this child's background—see what kind of personal history she has."

"What do you expect to find?" Wemyss asked, genuinely puzzled.

"I'm not sure," Raeburn said thoughtfully, though he did, indeed, have a fair idea. "I'll tell you more if and when the need arises. For now, just get that sample for me—no later than tomorrow night."

While Raeburn was still pondering the enigma of Gillian Talbot, Philippa Sinclair was in Edinburgh having lunch with Lady Julian Brodie in the serene, informal opulence of Lady Julian's New Town flat. They dined Cantonese-style on three treasure soup, green jade scallops, and crystalized fruit in syrup of ginger. Picking daintily at her food with a handsome set of lacquered chopsticks, Philippa cocked a droll eyebrow at her lifelong friend.

"Why is it that Chinese menus always read like an inventory from somebody's jewelry box?" she said. "If I didn't know better, I'd think I was supposed to wear all this, not eat it."

"Pippa, you never change!" Julian said with a laugh, black eyes twinkling like marcasites.

"On the contrary, neither of us is getting any younger," Philippa replied. "Fortunately, we don't need to look too far afield in search of fresh talent. Adam is bidding fair to become quite an able recruiting officer. Speaking of which," she added, "what do you make of my son's latest prospect?"

"The Lovat boy?" Julian's expression was fond. "He's quite charming, besides showing a great deal of promise. He reminds me not a little of Michael, you know."

"Yes, I thought so too," Philippa agreed. She paused briefly before asking, "Is that why you gave him Michael's ring?"

"Partly." A trace of sadness marred her air of composure, and she tilted her chin to gaze up at her taller companion.

"The Bible speaks of heirs according to the flesh and heirs according to the spirit," she went on. "You were lucky enough that Adam is to you both one and the same. Michael and I never had a child, but when I met young Peregrine—I felt suddenly as if I were in the presence of someone akin to us, if not by blood, then by the spirit that is in him. I gave him Michael's ring in recognition of that kinship. And I have no doubts concerning my action."

"Nor have I, now," Philippa said, with a wry flicker of a smile. "I hope you don't think I had any reservations."

"Not at all," Julian said. "You were right to speak what was in your mind. Something *is* worrying you, though. Do you want to talk about it?"

Philippa shrugged. "I only wish it were something I could put my finger on. It's nothing to do with Peregrine or any of the rest of our people. Incidentally, he and Adam are going to start an experiment tomorrow, with the Talbot girl."

"Oh?"

Philippa shook her head musingly. "The boy's talent is really quite unique—this ability to lock in on resonances from the past. If the mother agrees, Adam's going to have him sit and sketch young Gillian, see if he can isolate aspects of her personality that can be used in the reintegration process later on."

"Is that possible?" Julian asked, raising an eyebrow.

"Well, that's the theory—though I grant you, it's several steps beyond what *I* was taught, back when I was studying with Jung before the War. He used to encourage his patients to paint or sketch what they saw in their dreams and daydreams. Often he found that the resulting pictures were an effective aid to diagnosis, treatment, and cure of certain psychiatric disorders."

"I see," Julian said. "And Adam's going to have Peregrine try to produce such pictures?"

Philippa chuckled. "I know, I know, it sounds far-fetched, even to me—and I'm a psychiatrist. But if it works, we're halfway toward pinning down an approach for bringing all the shattered fragments of Gillian's personality back into focus—which, besides giving her another chance at a normal life, will hopefully give us access to Michael Scot again. From what Adam has told me, I'm increasingly convinced that Scot knows what this most recent resurgence of the Lodge of the Lynx is all about."

"Well, if he does, I hope that Adam can make the contact soon and find out," Julian said. "I'd hoped to be long gone before *they* had to be dealt with again!"

"So had I, my dear, so had I," Philippa replied, patting her friend's hand. "But since we *aren't* gone, isn't it fortunate for Adam and this younger generation of Huntsmen that we're still here to lend our hard-earned wisdom?"

Julian laughed at that, as did Philippa, but there was a brittle edge to their laughter that belied their outward lightheartedness and spoke of a deep concern for the situation now unfolding.

Philippa rode in to Jordanburn with Adam and Peregrine the next morning, heading on up to Gillian's room while the two men detoured to Adam's office. Peregrine had come armed with his sketchbox and a handful of unspoken misgivings nurtured over the past few days, and glanced sidelong at Adam as they stepped into the privacy of the lift and the doors closed.

"Adam," he ventured, "I have to tell you, I'm more than a little nervous about this assignment—as you may have gathered from my sparkling conversation on the way in this morning. What did you have to tell Mrs. Talbot, to get her to agree to this?"

"Nothing that wasn't the truth—as far as it went," Adam replied. "I told her that you're a professional colleague of mine and that we've worked together many times before. I gave her to believe that you're the psychiatric equivalent of a forensic artist, but that you sketch from psychic impressions that you pick up from a patient."

Behind his spectacles, Peregrine's hazel eyes rolled upward in disbelief, but since the lift doors were opening then to admit a pair of nurses, and this was the floor where Adam signalled they should disembark, he held his tongue until they were safely inside Adam's office with the door closed.

"Adam, you didn't *really* tell her that, did you?" he demanded, as his mentor nonchalantly stripped off topcoat and scarf and hung them in a closet behind his desk, donning a white lab coat.

"Why not? It's basically true. I did talk about art being a valuable tool of psychiatry—that pictures often can give one valuable insights into a patient's problems. Here, put this on," he added, handing Peregrine a lab coat like his own. "You'll look more like part of the medical team if you're wearing the uniform."

Still unconvinced, Peregrine put down his sketchbox and did as he was told. When he had hung up his coat beside Adam's and settled the lab coat over his blazer, he turned uneasily to look at Adam again.

"She isn't going to buy this."

"I've told you, she already has."

"I'll bet *that* took some powerful persuasion," Peregrine muttered.

Adam cocked his head, a flicker of some unreadable emotion registering briefly in his dark eyes.

"Your tone suggests that you think I might have used undue coercion to force Mrs. Talbot to agree. Is that what you meant to imply?"

Peregrine's eyes went round behind his spectacles. "Well, I—"

"Sit down, Peregrine," Adam said quietly. "I'm going to assume that your uncertainty springs from natural nervousness at having to perform in front of someone you've not met before. But in case there *is* any doubt, I want to tell you something about authority and responsibility."

Peregrine obeyed, suddenly feeling like an errant schoolboy.

"We need to get something straight, before our relationship goes any farther," Adam went on, sitting on the edge of the desk. "I'm not obliged to justify my actions to you, but I want you to understand what's at stake here. You and I both know that Gillian can't be cured unless the damage that was done can be set right. And we both know that *you* may well have something material to contribute to the cure we're seeking. If Iris Talbot shared the knowledge that we have, she would agree to your participation without question. But she doesn't have that knowledge, and we have neither the time nor the mandate to teach her. Do you agree?"

"Yes," Peregrine whispered.

"So, what then?" Adam went on. "Which is of greater value: Iris Talbot's freedom to choose—a choice made without knowledge—or Gillian's life—a life already deeply endangered?"

Peregrine lowered his eyes to stare at his intertwined fingers.

"Well, Gillian's life, obviously, but—"

"There is no *but*, in this instance," Adam said quietly. "Listen to me carefully. When one is vested with authority, sooner or later one finds oneself obliged to exercise it in ways that one would prefer *not* to do, in order to achieve some greater good. Yes, I resorted to some powerful persuasion to convince Iris Talbot to agree to this experiment. I didn't apply force, but I was prepared to do so; I played on her fears instead.

"This decision was not made lightly, because it *does* interfere with another's free will. If I were to take such action for motives of personal gain, I should be unworthy to wield such powers and authority as are vested in me, and would speedily be relieved of my authority by Powers higher than my own. By the same token, it would be equally unworthy of me *not* to use the faculties at my command, in situations that warrant it. Part of the discernment required of those called as we are called is that we recognize those distinctions and be willing to abide by the consequences. Do you understand?''

''I think so,'' Peregrine whispered.

''There's more,'' Adam went on. ''Every act of significance involves a certain element of risk. Sometimes you must even dare to compromise what you see as your own integrity for the sake of someone else's welfare. And then it becomes a matter of humility, not of pride. There is, believe me, no greater penance than being forced to sacrifice your own self-esteem. And no greater burden than to have to make that kind of judgement.''

Peregrine was looking at him more evenly now, his former apprehension transformed to enlightenment.

''That's what Lady Julian was trying to tell me,'' he murmured. *''The superior man discriminates between high and low.''*

''Precisely.'' Adam nodded in grim confirmation. ''You're beginning to see. God willing, you'll be able to act as well.''

Nodding, Peregrine squared his shoulders and picked up his sketchbox.

''I do see,'' he agreed, ''and I'm ready to *act* now—if you'll still have me as a part of the team. Please forgive me if I sounded like a first-class prat!''

Gillian had been assigned a private room. When Adam and Peregrine arrived, they found Philippa standing just inside the door, going over Gillian's chart with a nurse. Iris Talbot was there as well, arranging a large bouquet of flowers on the bedside utility cabinet with the air of someone determined to keep busy. She looked up somewhat apprehensively when Adam and Peregrine entered.

''Good morning, Mrs. Talbot,'' Adam said, his voice conveying an easy, comfortable professionalism. ''This is Mr. Lovat, the gentleman we spoke about yesterday. With your permission, he'll be spending some time with you and your daughter in the course of the next few days.''

Iris stepped out from behind the bed and came forward, shyly extending a slim, small-boned hand. ''How do you do, Mr. Lovat,'' she said a little nervously. ''You're somehow younger than I expected. I must confess, I don't pretend to understand what you're about to attempt.''

Clasping the hand she offered, Peregrine was at once struck by the air of long-term fatigue and the blue shadows under her eyes, and compassion lent him inspiration and a resolution he had not been aware of a moment before.

"I'll let you in on a little secret, Mrs. Talbot," he said conspiratorially, lowering his voice as he pulled her slightly closer. "I don't really understand it either. I'm simply thankful that sometimes it seems to work. I don't blame you for being bewildered by it all."

His boyish and slightly self-conscious grin as he released her hand utterly disarmed her apprehension, generating an unexpected smile that conveyed some of the charm that must have been hers before having to deal with Gillian's illness.

"Why, Mr. Lovat. Whatever artistic abilities you may have, you do seem to have a knack for putting people at their ease," she said. "I must thank you for agreeing to do this. Whatever assistance you're able to provide, I'll be ever so grateful. How do you plan to begin?"

Controlling a smile, Adam retreated to the doorway where he could pretend to look over Philippa's shoulder at Gillian's chart, as Peregrine set his sketchbox on a wheeled bedside table and opened its catches.

"I'll warm up by making a few preliminary sketches," the artist said. "After that—well, I'll just have to wait and see what, if anything, comes to me. Nothing may even happen this first time—though I don't expect that to be a problem."

"Well, I suppose I ought to tidy Gillian's hair, then," Iris said confidingly, moving toward the head of the bed. "I only wish you could have seen her when she was—herself. She used to be so lively and pretty—"

"She's still a very pretty girl," Peregrine assured her, laying out his supplies. "When all of this is over, perhaps you'll allow me to do a proper portrait of her. Portraiture's my real forte, as Sir Adam may have told you. Today's work is hardly going to be typical of what I usually do."

Crouching down beside the utility cabinet by Gillian's bed, Iris pulled out a floral-print overnight satchel and rummaged briefly through its contents.

"That's odd," she said. "I can't find Gillian's hairbrush."

"What's that?" Philippa said, ears pricking up as she glanced up from the chart.

"Gillian's hairbrush," Iris said, still looking. "I always keep it in the bag with her other things, but now I don't see it. No, it's not in here. Now what do you suppose I might have done with it?"

Clucking maternally to herself, she peered first inside the

cabinet, then under the bed. As Adam's eyes followed her from the doorway, he became aware all at once of a faint warning tingle at the back of his neck. A side glance at Philippa confirmed that she too had had her suspicions aroused by this apparently innocuous development.

"How very peculiar," Iris said, getting up from her knees with the beginnings of a frown on her face. "If I didn't know better, I'd think that hairbrush must have vanished into thin air. It certainly isn't the sort of thing anyone would steal."

"Maybe it slipped off the shelf into the wastebasket and got taken out by the cleaner by mistake," Philippa suggested. "If you'll pardon me, I'll check with Matron and see if I can find out anyting."

"Oh, it isn't worth making any fuss over," Iris protested mildly, though Philippa had already disappeared. "After all, it's only a hairbrush. If it doesn't turn up, I can always get another out of the shop downstairs."

"Well, we'll see what we can find out," Adam told her. "Meanwhile, I need to look in on some other of my patients. We'll check back with you in an hour or so, and see how you're getting on."

Down at the nurses' station, Philippa had already obtained basic information on the cleaner for the ward.

"Matron says her name is Mrs. Lewis—she couldn't remember the first name," she told Adam, as they headed for the lifts. "Apparently she's only been here a few weeks. I don't *think* I'm being paranoid, but I'm not sure I like the feel of this development."

"Neither do I," Adam said. "I believe I'll put in a call to the hospital maintenance supervisor and see what he can tell us about this Mrs. Lewis. We'll go back to my office."

The information he received did nothing to reassure either of them.

"Mrs. Marjory Lewis has been an employee of this hospital for approximately two weeks," Adam reported. "Her job application lists Edinburgh Royal Infirmary as her most recent place of previous employment. Interestingly enough, she went home sick about an hour ago. Care to speculate?"

Philippa snorted, her patrician face scowling at this revelation.

"How much would you like to bet that there isn't any Marjory Lewis listed among the former employees of ERI? Or if there is, it isn't the same woman as the one who's been working here."

"No bets," Adam said. "I wonder if Peregrine will make anything out of this. . . ."

After Adam and Philippa had gone, Peregrine took one of the two visitors' chairs in the room and positioned it at the foot of Gillian's bed, rolling the table with his supplies closer beside it. Gillian Talbot *was* still a pretty girl, but not the rosy-cheeked child he had first seen in the vision given him by Michael Scot a month before. It grieved him to see her the way she was now, lying there so quietly, scarcely breathing, her face lifeless and pale. Whatever her connections with the legendary past, he saw her now only as an innocent victim of present-day criminal ambition. That realization made him appreciate Adam's determination to do whatever was necessary to see her sound and whole again.

Reminded of his assignment, he sat down and balanced his sketchbook on one upraised knee, selecting a favorite pencil from his sketchbox.

*Now then*, he thought to himself, *let's see what we can see.*

Iris had pulled her chair over by the window, out of his line of sight. Even so, Peregrine was aware that she was watching him closely, half-afraid, half-expectant. He made a few trial passes over the paper to limber up his wrist and hand, then began to sketch the literal scene before him. As the lines began to flow more fluidly, very similar to that first sketch he had made of Gillian in another hospital bed, he cast his mind back to images of Melrose Abbey and the rack of dry bones that once had housed the living spirit of Michael Scot, imploring that same Scot to reveal what he wanted of Peregrine Lovat.

His vision blurred, as if someone had drawn a veil of fine silk across his eyes. Attuned to the now-familiar shift in his temporal perspective, he drew another deep breath and waited for his spirit-sight to key in. The fog before his eyes dissolved. He blinked, then found his focus on another level of perception.

His first reaction was surprise, for the scene before him was apparently unchanged. Gillian Talbot lay supine before him in her bed, her eyes closed, her breathing light and shallow. But something, Peregrine realized, was subtly different. He narrowed his eyes and took a closer look.

In the same instant, a ghostly flicker of movement diverted his attention to his left. Shifting his gaze, he found himself registering a dual image of the door, one solid, the other semi-transparent, like a photographic negative superimposed over a finished print. As Peregrine studied the double-image, the transparency shifted into motion like a filmstrip. Focusing on the active image, he saw the door swing open, admitting a sandy-haired, bespectacled woman in a cleaner's coverall.

She bustled in and looked around. A look of crafty satisfaction crossed her face. By the light, it was morning, but Mrs. Talbot had not yet arrived. Closing the door behind her, the woman hurried over to Gillian's bedside and began to poke around, obviously searching for something. Without shifting his gaze, Peregrine flipped to a fresh sheet of paper and began rapidly sketching his impression of her face.

The woman peered first into the bedside wastebasket, then opened the door to the bedside cabinet and rummaged about inside, emerging a moment later with a hairbrush clutched in one hand. Even as the object registered, she thrust the hairbrush out of sight under her coverall and, with a last furtive backwards glance, beat a hasty retreat from the room.

Peregrine was sketching furiously when he realized that the scene had shifted again. Gillian still lay motionless on the bed, but now a grey-haired man in a white coat like Peregrine himself wore was bending over her right arm with a hypodermic syringe. At first he feared that the man was injecting Gillian with some unknown drug, but—no, blood was slowly filling the syringe. The man must be a lab technician, drawing blood for further tests.

Before he could commit the image to paper, however, a suppressed shriek from Iris Talbot startled him out of his semi-trance and drew his gaze. He blinked sharply in a whirl of shifting images and saw that Gillian's mother was gaping at her daughter in open-mouthed astonishment and pointing. Shifting back in alarm, Peregrine found himself confronted by a pair of wide blue eyes.

Gillian was staring directly at him. The impact of her regard was like a physical blow. Before Peregrine could turn away, he was assailed by a sudden tidal wave of conflicting images. Like a cataract of broken glass, the images tumbled over him in a flood of splintered colors and shapes.

Peregrine gave a choked gasp and tried to look away. The tide held him fast, buffeting him with impressions so intense and so confusing that the force of it sent him reeling with vertigo. His pencil slipped from his fingers and onto the linoleum in a wooden clatter, and he only just managed to keep the sketch pad in his grasp. His determination not to drop it cut short a last surge of broken pictures, after which everything suddenly was still.

He closed his eyes and exhaled on a long, swooping breath, a little surprised that he was still in his chair. Still clinging blindly to the sketch pad, he willed his dizziness to subside. After a seeming eternity, he cautiously cracked an eye open and found Iris Talbot bending over him, her face pale and excited.

"Did you see it, Mr. Lovat? Did you?" she demanded, half-fearfully. "Gillian opened her eyes! You saw it, didn't you?"

Peregrine nodded, then wished he hadn't. Taking a grip on himself, he said, "Yes, I saw."

"That's the first voluntary movement she's made in weeks!" Iris continued, already on her way back to Gillian as a nurse poked her head through the doorway in response to the outburst. "She opened her eyes!" she told the nurse. "Call Dr. Sinclair and tell him, please! I was afraid I might have been imagining things, but Mr. Lovat saw it too!"

As the nurse glanced at Peregrine in question, he merely nodded. With a quirk of one eyebrow, the nurse withdrew to call and Iris took up one of her daughter's slack hands to stroke it. Peregrine stole a glance at Gillian, but the shadowed eyes were now closed, and she appeared to have slumped back into whatever strange coma held her in thrall.

"Mr. Lovat, do you think this could be a sign that she's starting to come out of this?" Iris asked tremulously.

"I really couldn't say," Peregrine replied. The memory of the chaos he had just experienced was strong enough to make his head swim, and he casually turned the first sketch back over the second and laid the sketch pad in his box. "I think we'd better wait for Sir Adam and Lady Sinclair, and see what they think."

Adam and Philippa, however, were equally circumspect in their response to Iris' account of the incident.

"It *is* an encouraging sign—as far as it goes," Philippa conceded, after checking Gillian's vital signs, "but don't be tempted to place too much significance on so slight an occurrence. While, in theory, it's quite possible for an autistic patient to undergo a sudden dramatic awakening, such instances are highly unusual. It's too early for you to think of getting your hopes up."

Iris twisted her fingers together. "I suppose you're right," she said reluctantly. "All the same, I can't help feeling more optimistic than I've felt for weeks."

She turned to Peregrine with a smile almost of awe. "A week ago, I think I would have resented it if my daughter had responded to anyone but my husband or myself. But I don't feel that way anymore. On the contrary, I'm just glad to think that it's possible for *someone* to reach her. I don't know what you did, Mr. Lovat, but I'm grateful all the same. You *will* be coming again, won't you? Please say that you will."

Peregrine met her gaze squarely, surprised at the strength of his own determination.

"I wouldn't back out now for anything," he assured her.

"Your feelings do you credit, Mrs. Talbot," Adam interposed

gently. "But please bear in mind that we're still a long way from finding a working miracle. . . ."

That was all he and Philippa were prepared to say in Iris' presence. Peregrine wisely bided his time until the three of them had gained the privacy of Adam's office before pressing his own questions.

"Was Mrs. Talbot right?" he asked. "Was Gillian responding specifically to me?"

"So it would appear," Adam said, with a fleeting smile for Peregrine's lingering astonishment. "We've already noted that Gillian's earlier persona, as Scot, singled you out at Melrose as the appropriate person with whom to communicate. Evidently, in spite of all the damage her indwelling soul has suffered, some form of recognition is still possible, at least where you're concerned. With luck, that may give us something concrete on which to build in the days to come."

He eyed Peregrine more closely. "Now, tell us what you saw."

Peregrine grimaced at the memory. "Nothing very coherent, I'm afraid. It was a bit like looking at a large-scale painting by Picasso—everything broken to bits and scrambled around. I had the feeling all the pieces were still there—but what a job to sort them all out and put them back together in all the right places!"

Adam decided to let that issue lie fallow for the moment. "You did say you made some drawings, didn't you?"

"Only a couple," Peregrine said, handing over his sketch pad. "Nothing that's very helpful where Gillian herself is concerned, I don't think—but I *can* tell you what happened to her hairbrush. Don't pay any mind to the first one. It was just a warm-up."

Opening the pad, Adam flipped past the first sketch with only a cursory glance, turning his closer attention to the second.

"This is very interesting," he murmured, studying the drawing of the cleaner. "Take a look at this, Philippa. Marjory Lewis, I'll warrant—if that's her real name."

As Peregrine looked on in question, Philippa eyed the drawing in her turn.

"Well, that puts a whole new twist on things, doesn't it? Apparently we're more closely monitored even than we feared."

"You mean that cleaning woman is some kind of agent for the Lodge of the Lynx?" Peregrine looked revolted at the notion. "But what could they possibly want with Gillian's hairbrush?"

"They've obviously gotten curious about her," Philippa said. "They want to know who she is—or was. Next to a blood sample, a sample of hair is the next best thing to use as a focus for anyone wishing to carry out certain kinds of psychic investigations—in this instance, probably an inquiry into Gillian's existential past.''

Peregrine went very still, remembering the other image he had not had time to draw.

"Adam," he said apprehensively, "did you order more blood tests on Gillian? Or did you, Lady Sinclair?''

The way mother and son exchanged cautious glances confirmed to Peregrine that they had not.

"There was a man in the room early this morning," Peregrine said steadily. "I saw him after the hairbrush images. He was drawing blood. If you look, I'm sure you'll find a fresh needle-mark on her right arm. I'd assumed it was routine—and then Mrs. Talbot started squawking about Gillian's eyes being open. But it wasn't routine, was it?''

Adam shook his head, then flipped Peregrine's sketchbook to a fresh page.

"Draw what you saw, Peregrine," he said, handing it back. "See if you can attach a face. . . .''

Peregrine blinked at the blank page, but his hand seemed oddly reluctant to move to the paper.

"I—don't think I can, Adam," he whispered. "There's something—''

"Close your eyes and go back to the memory," Adam commanded, setting one hand on Peregrine's shoulder and clasping the other lightly across his forehead. "Take a deep breath, the way I've taught you, and settle into that altered state in which you can work most effectively. Just draw what you see. Let it flow. . . .''

As Peregrine drew a deep breath, trying to do what Adam wanted, Adam dropped his hands and sat back. Peregrine's eyes opened and his hand moved dutifully to the sketch pad and began to draw; but though the vague suggestion of a white-coated man took shape, bending over a figure that was unmistakably Gillian, his pencil kept avoiding the man's face.

"Draw the face, Peregrine," Adam's whisper urged. But Peregrine could not seem to get a clear look at it, and had to shake his head perplexedly as he came up out of trance.

"I can't do it, Adam," he said. "I just can't see it properly. It's like there's a veil—''

"Or a shield," Philippa said, turning the sketch for a better angle. "Just offhand, I'd say Peregrine may have stumbled upon one of the full members of the Lodge of the Lynx—protecting his identity as he goes about his evil business.''

"And now they have blood as well as hair to make the connection with Gillian," Adam said. "If they're at all competent, by this time tomorrow they're going to know precisely who Gillian is—and more important, who she was.''

"They could do that, just with blood and hair?" Peregrine asked, wide-eyed.

Adam nodded. "Depending upon the skill of the particular individual making the inquiry—yes. *We* could. And given that they had the knowledge to re-animate Scot's body and force his soul back into it, I would have to say that they probably do have the resources—unless, of course, their expert in that area was one of the casualties at Loch Ness. But a gifted investigator can plumb as far back as his subject's original awakening.''

"Well, if they *can* make the connection between Gillian Talbot and Michael Scot," Peregrine said, "what do you suppose they might do?"

"It's useless to speculate," Philippa said, scowling in Adam's direction. "One thing is quite certain, though: we can't adequately protect her in her present hospital environment. If you want my recommendation, I say we should move her out to Strathmourne as soon as is humanly possible.''

Adam grimaced. "That thought has crossed my mind as well. The only question is, can we do it without causing a stir?"

"Causing a stir is the least of our worries," Philippa said practically. "We have twenty-four hours' grace at the most, I should say, before our enemies succeed in breaching the bounds of secrecy where Gillian is concerned. After that, the only way we can be sure she's safe would be for you and me to mount guard round the clock over her room—and I promise you, *that* would cause even more comment.''

Adam pulled a considering frown. "All too true, I'm afraid. However, I believe Peregrine may have given us the beginnings of a plausible excuse for moving Gillian out of hospital and into a home environment.''

"I have?" Peregrine looked from Adam to Philippa and back again.

"Indeed, you have," Philippa said, slowly nodding. "Now that we've had some inkling of response, one could argue that it might be worthwhile to see how she reacts to surroundings more like a home environment—namely, Strathmourne, where she can be closely supervised by both her attending physicians." She tilted an inquiring glance at her son. "Didn't you mention once that your Mrs. Gilchrist used to be a nurse before she retired?"

"I did," Adam said. "I gather you're suggesting she might be persuaded to do a stint of private duty care under a familiar roof.

The hard part will be getting the ambulance service to agree to make the transfer at short notice—but I'll see what I can do.

"In the meantime, we have Mrs. Talbot to persuade." He cast a pointed glance at Peregrine. "And for tonight," he went on, "I'd be very much obliged, Philippa, if you could do whatever you can to ward Gillian's room."

# CHAPTER TWENTY-THREE

THAT same night, in the cellar level of a house near Stirling called Nether Leckie, Francis Raeburn and a select handful of his subordinates gathered to pursue their interest in Gillian Talbot. Present were the three who had done Raeburn's bidding in preparing an origami lynx, hardly a week before—Napier, Fitzgerald, and Wemyss—and the wiry, dark-haired man named Barclay, whose assorted talents ran far beyond the piloting of helicopters. All five had donned the hooded black robes that were their working uniform, and each bore the silver medallion and carnelian-set ring that were the badges of full membership in the Lodge of the Lynx.

Their working place was warded and ready, with fire guttering in black iron cressets on three of the whitewashed walls. The fourth wall presented a dark, brooding fresco of a faceless, vaguely humanoid form shrouded in shadow and roiling clouds, with an aureole of lightning bolts set about the area where the head should be, picked out in hammered iron. Facing this wall, and a rack of candles set between it and him, the pilot Barclay sat quietly in a high-backed wooden armchair, head tilted back, eyes closed in trance.

At his right hand, a black iron brazier on a three-foot tripod sent a thin thread of incense smoke curling lazily upward. A small table beside it held other accoutrements necessary for this night's work: more incense, a shallow glass vessel like a petri dish, an egg-sized tangle of golden hair, and a 10 cc hypodermic syringe filled with dark blood. Raeburn himself presided over this array, with the hard-eyed Angela Fitzgerald to assist him. On the other side of Barclay, Napier had pushed back the pilot's left sleeve and was tightening a length of rubber tubing around his upper arm while Wemyss loaded another syringe from a small vial of opalescent pinkish fluid.

"You're aware that he won't be able to fly for twenty-four hours," Wemyss said, withdrawing the needle and handing off the vial to Napier, holding the syringe to the candlelight and expelling a few air bubbles.

"I don't *need* him to fly until Saturday," Raeburn murmured, watching as Wemyss tore open an alcohol swab and scrubbed over Barclay's bulging vein. "This 'flight' is far more important just now. If, as I suspect, our young Gillian Talbot is the current incarnation of Michael Scot, then this night's work may well point the way to recovering access to what was lost at Loch Ness. Barclay was present when the late lamented Geddes summoned Scot back to his body at Melrose; he will know if the perception is true. Please proceed."

Without further demur, Wemyss slipped the needle into Barclay's vein and loosed the tourniquet, slowly injecting about half the contents of the syringe and then pausing to peer under one of his subject's eyelids. Napier had shifted to steady Barclay by the shoulders, so was prepared when, after Wemyss had injected more of the drug, Barclay gave a shudder and a moan.

"He's nearly there," Wemyss muttered, as the eyelids fluttered open. "Barclay, can you hear me?"

"Yes."

The pupils were dilated, Barclay's gaze fixed and unfocused. Satisfied, Wemyss tightened his thumb minutely on the plunger, delivering a small additional dose of the drug. Then, pressing the alcohol swab over the injection site, he deftly withdrew the needle and folded his subject's arm up against his chest before stepping to one side.

"Whenever you're ready, Mr. Raeburn," he said.

Smiling, Raeburn moved forward, leaning both hands on the arms of Barclay's chair to gaze into the drugged eyes.

"Are you comfortable, Mr. Barclay?" he said softly.

Barclay's head gave a slight nod. "I'm doin' okay, Mr. Raeburn."

"Excellent."

Stepping back, Raeburn had Angela help him move the brazier in front of the chair, nearly touching Barclay's knees. Simultaneously, Napier and Wemyss each took a shoulder and urged Barclay to sit forward, splaying his knees so that the brazier could be moved even closer. As Raeburn scattered a pinch of incense on the glowing charcoal, Barclay began inhaling deeply of the fumes. It was the same incense, Raeburn knew, that had been used that night at Melrose; and Barclay's shudder, and the intent look on his face, indicated that he knew it too.

"Yessss," Raeburn hissed. "You know that scent, don't you? It's taking you back to that night at Melrose. Will yourself there now," Raeburn urged. "See the scene before you in the smoke. Focus on the presence that was called up that night. And now here's something to help you lock in on the target."

At his gesture, Angela Fitzgerald cast the ball of golden hair onto the brazier. As the stench of burning hair wafted upward, Barclay bent closer to inhale of it deeply, eyes vaguely focused through the smoke.

"Reach for it," Raeburn commanded. "Bring the two together and compare them. *Is* the Talbot girl Scot's current incarnation?"

"It's coming," Barclay breathed. "Close. . . . Very close. Can't—quite—get the focus, though. Help me."

Nodding to Wemyss and Napier, Raeburn took up the syringe of blood, expressing a coin-sized pool of dark crimson into each of Barclay's palms as his two keepers upturned them. The rest of the blood went into the shallow glass dish, which Angela had already set on the charcoal. The blood sizzled on the hot glass, individual droplets racing around the edges, and Barclay inhaled deeply of the stench, nodding as he rubbed his palms together to increase the contact.

"Yes," he said, eyes closed as he brought his bloody hands closer to his face to inhale of the blood itself. "Oh, yes, they're one and the same. But Scot's angry. His cooperation won't be easily gained. He's powerful, even unfocused by the condition of his present body. But he *can* be used. Force can be brought to bear. Yes . . . it's definitely Scot. Mustn't let the Hunting Lodge enlist his aid. Powerful enemy . . . but also a powerful slave. . . . Careful. . . ."

Gradually he wound down, finally slumping forward exhausted, head supported by bloody hands. When it was clear that no more information would be forthcoming, Raeburn withdrew the brazier and signalled Wemyss and Napier to draw their subject upright once more. Barclay was still conscious, but only barely so, and Raeburn glanced at Wemyss in question.

"Is he all right?"

"He will be, when he's slept," the physician replied, leaning forward briefly to check as Barclay's eyes rolled upward in their sockets and he went limp in their grasp. "Yes, he's finished for tonight. Shall I take him up to a bed and get him cleaned up?"

"Yes, go ahead," Raeburn agreed. "Mr. Napier will help you carry him. We'll meet in the library in half an hour to decide how to use this information. I don't think it's urgent that we move before Friday night—nothing is apt to interfere with *that*—but I do believe we'll want to devote some attention in future to Miss Gillian Talbot."

# CHAPTER TWENTY-FOUR

THE following day dawned grey and dismal, heralding sleet and snow that swept across the whole of Scotland that night and left the Highlands firmly ensconced in winter. In Edinburgh, workmen from Lothian Council were kept busy all Friday laying grit on the streets and salt on the sidewalks, while the road traffic grumbled along between aisles of slush and pedestrians struggled to keep upright as they slogged stoically along the icy pavements on their way to work or to their local shops.

Despite the adverse weather, the Brethren of Masonic Lodge No. 213 gathered that Friday night for their regularly scheduled meeting in the Lochend district of Edinburgh. The Master of the Lodge was one of the last to arrive, having been delayed by an old-fashioned black taxi that seemed bent on making every turn just ahead of him, and at a maddeningly slow pace, road conditions notwithstanding. So annoyed was he by the time he pulled up in his reserved space at the rear of the Lodge's private car park—later by ten minutes than he liked to be on Lodge night—that he jotted the taxi's number on the back of an old parking receipt before bracing himself for the dash through the cold and wet.

Pulling his regalia case from the seat beside him, he locked up the car and jogged gingerly across the icy tarmac, already unbuttoning his overcoat as he gained the back entrance. The Lodge Secretary met him just inside, with a slip of paper in his hand and a concerned expression on his whiskered face.

"Och, there you are!" the secretary said. "There's a man been tryin' to reach you for the last half hour an' more. Says he works for you—name o' Murray. Here's his number. He said to ring him as soon as you got here."

Rolling his eyes heavenward, the Master of Lodge No. 213 took the slip of paper and glanced at the number—unfamiliar—then headed on toward the cloakroom and men's toilets, the secretary at his heels.

"I dinnae have time for this, Robbie. I got stuck behind a bloody taxi. Did he say what it's about?"

"Only that it was urgent," Robbie replied.

The Master sighed, sweeping off his hat. "All right, all right! I'll call him from the pay phone while I get suited up. Tell 'em upstairs I'll be there to open Lodge in just a few minutes."

"Aye, Worshipful Master."

As the Lodge Secretary clattered up a back stair to do his bidding, the Master charged into the cloakroom and pegged his hat onto a hook, throwing down his case on a convenient chair. As he stripped off his topcoat, he wondered what possible emergency at the plant could have induced Murray to phone him here at Lodge.

Throwing open his case, he pulled out the white moire apron with its borders and symbols of sky-blue silk and tied it around his waist, adjusting the flap to indicate his rank as a Master Mason. Next came the broad silk collar with its pendant jewel, the badge of his office as Installed Master of this Lodge. When he had looped this over his head, adjusting it so that the jewel fell squarely on his breast, he pulled out the gauntlet cuffs and hefted them, glancing at the slip of paper with its telephone number, then delved into a trouser pocket and fished out a twenty-pence piece. Dropping it into the pay phone on the wall beside the coat hooks, he dialed the number, trapping the receiver between shoulder and ear while he pulled on the cuffs and waited for the connection.

The number rang at the other end. He glanced at his watch, adjusting the cuff on that wrist. As he did so, the cloakroom door opened behind him. Before he could turn around to tell them he would be right there, a strong arm collared him roughly from behind and clapped a thick pad of cloth over his mouth and nose, effectively smothering any outcry he might have made.

The chemical reek of of chloroform flooded his nostrils and stung at his eyes. Choking, even gagging, he tried to throw himself forward in an effort to shake off his assailant. He was not a small man, but his captor hauled him back easily and locked a choke hold across his throat, pressing the chloroform pad even closer against his face.

His vision began to swim and his knees buckled under him as the chloroform did its work. Seconds later, he was sagging bonelessly in his captor's arms, still vaguely conscious but no longer capable of shouting or struggling. His captor kept him from falling, removing the chloroform pad just long enough for an accomplice to slap a broad strip of tape across his mouth. While he was still reeling from this treatment, the first man twisted his gauntleted wrists behind his back and secured them with tape. At the same time, the second assailant came before him long enough to fling a dark hood over his head.

They seized him from both sides then, half-walking and half-dragging him out of the cloakroom, down the short corridor, and out into the frosty night, to be hustled unceremoniously onto the floor of a waiting vehicle—the very taxi that had occasioned such annoyance not minutes before, had he but known. From a sudden, sharp jab right through the front of his shirt spread a dull wave of lethargy. The forward lurch of the vehicle was the last thing he remembered before he passed out.

Three-quarters of a city mile away, on the south side of Edinburgh's Calton Hill, a hard-lipped woman sat alone in a parked car outside the snow-crusted gates of Old Calton Road Burial Ground. Ahead and behind her stretched a straggling row of other parked cars, here to patronize the dingy pub that occupied a storefront on the other side of Waterloo Place, a short stone's throw away. Farther up the hill, behind the pub, the winter sky was broken by the dark bulk of the Crown Office Buildings and the Nelson Monument. Nearer at hand, the lightly falling snow did little to muffle the rumble of diesel engines as a train forged along the tracks behind the cemetery on its way in to Waverley Station.

The streets in the area were deserted, the weather having driven most folk indoors. Inside the cemetery gates, however, within the high stone walls of the burial ground itself, nearly a dozen shadowy figures hovered in the snow-crusted shelter of a graffiti-scribbled tomb house, stamping their feet and blowing on their hands while they waited for a sign from their leader. Francis Raeburn was prowling wolfishly back and forth before a weather-worn grave marker fashioned in the shape of a man-sized obelisk. As he paused to glance at his wristwatch, the chimes of a nearby clock tower rang out the hour of eight.

As the echo of the last bell died away, headlights appeared at the Regent Road end of Waterloo Place, heralding the approach of a large, black taxi which crawled ponderously downhill toward the cemetery entrance. As the taxi flashed its lights, the woman waiting in the parked car smiled grimly to herself in the rearview mirror and gave an answering flash of headlights.

The signal was relayed by a man waiting just inside the cemetery gates. Instantly shifting into action, Raeburn stopped pacing and gestured to his subordinates. With one accord, they began shedding hats and coats to uncover the thin white robes they had been wearing underneath. While one of the group swiftly piled the discarded coats and hats on a tarpaulin behind the tomb-house, the rest made shrift to draw concealing white hoods up around their faces. As Raeburn followed suit, also pulling a scarf from around his neck, a fugitive beam from a street lamp half a block away picked up the dark, metallic sheen of the Soulis torc close around his throat.

The woman in the parked car started up her engine. As she pulled smoothly away from the curb, the taxi slid neatly into the space she had vacated and stopped, dousing its headlights. The two dark-clad men riding in the back seat stole a swift glance up and down the length of the street to ensure that their arrival had aroused no unwanted attention, then threw open the door nearest the curb and scrambled out, hauling a hooded form from under a tartan car rug on the taxi floor. They supported the man between them as they quickly hustled him from the shadow of the taxi to the shadow of the entry archway.

One of Raeburn's white-robed associates met them at the gate, all but invisible against the snow as he ushered them in and closed the gate smoothly behind them on hinges obviously well-oiled. Two more of Raeburn's acolytes joined them to help chivvy their prisoner uphill, all of them slipping and stumbling in the snow. Under Raeburn's silent direction, they positioned their hooded captive with his back against the marker shaped like an obelisk, lashing him in place with cords of scarlet silk. This done, the men from the taxi withdrew the way they had come, leaving Raeburn and his subordinates to proceed with the work they had come here to do.

Anonymous now, all but invisible in their white hooded robes, Raeburn's minions arrayed themselves in a circle around the man held captive to the grave marker, leaving vacant a place directly in front of the victim. Taking that place, Raeburn reached inside the breast of his robe and drew out a disk-shaped medallion bearing the likeness of a snarling lynx head, hung from a length of heavy silver chain—the only such device to be seen here tonight, though all wore the carnelian-set ring of their Order.

Pale eyes glinting within his hood, Raeburn paused a moment to finger the insignia, then reached forward to pull off the hood that kept their captive from seeing. As the lolling head lifted, its owner reviving a little at the rush of cold air, drugged brown eyes ranged uncomprehendingly over the surrounding circle of white-clad figures, feebly recoiling as Raeburn hung the medallion around his prisoner's neck.

With an impatient grimace, Raeburn nodded to one of his

subordinates and stepped back to his place at the head of the circle. Without a word, the white-robed man glided forward and removed the tape from the prisoner's mouth, then seemed to snap his fingers under the man's nose. As the prisoner's head jerked back in reflex, a sharp whiff of ammonia wafted across the frosty darkness, as quickly dissipating. Silent on the snow, the man melted back among his fellows, leaving the captive alone in their midst, more reasoned fear now beginning to light the brown eyes.

Raeburn lifted his hands, and an even heavier stillness seemed to settle in the ancient burying ground, somehow insulating the company from the whine and squeal of the diesel engines and air brakes in the railway yard not far away, swallowing up the other distant sounds of a city. Fat, lazy snowflakes drifted down on the freezing night air, one of them catching in the captive's eyelashes. When anticipation had tightened to the desired level, Raeburn at last threw back his head and, in a sibilant whisper, began to chant the harsh, dread invocation that would call forth the power entrusted him by their Head-Master.

The chant frayed the air like the sound of a file grating on stone. The captive Mason tested feebly at his bonds, real terror beginning to fuel his struggles. Raeburn's voice gathered in intensity but not volume, until he finally reared back, flinging both arms wide over his head in a gesture that embraced the sky.

"Come, mighty Taranis!" he rasped. "Come and be our guest this night!"

The air within the circle seemed suddenly to come alive. With a rending sensation in the sky above them, the air at once began to seethe with unholy activity. As the darkness thickened and churned, an eerie half-light flickered from cloud to cloud, beginning to stir an electrical tingling on faces and hands, like a mild shock or crawling insects.

"Come, thou Master of Lightnings!" Raeburn urged. "Come and receive our homage! Behold the offering that is set before thee, an oblation meet and ripe for burning!"

His voice resonated with thirsty expectation, and the thunder answered in a low, subsonic rumble as the gathering clouds heaved and surged. Glancing wildly around him, the captive Mason threw himself weakly against his bonds, managing an audible squeak now, but to no avail. In the same instant, with a sudden, rending crash, a bolt of lightning seared the night sky, striking like an adder's tongue for the lynx medallion hanging on the prisoner's breast.

The white-robed acolytes recoiled, hands raised to shield

light-bedazzled eyes, as the lightning sizzled and snapped in a sustained blue-white arc. Impaled by the blast of raw energy, the victim's stricken body jerked and thrashed like a broken marionette, bluish smoke wreathing his head and chest, reeking of charred cloth and burnt flesh.

Simultaneously, the power embraced Raeburn, seizing him in an almost sexual paroxysm. Face upturned toward the sky, he gave a hoarse cry of exultation and breathed deep of the stench of immolation. The victim convulsing in his silken bonds gave a last jerking spasm and then was still, but it was the reflex reaction of flesh long past pain. Errant energies played briefly about the dead man's lolling head a final few seconds before abruptly winking out.

New darkness descended, the heavier for following elemental fire, and for a long moment, Raeburn was left trembling on the blind edge of ecstasy, intoxicated by the lingering kiss of power. The resonance left behind by the lightning's force infused his lean body with a rapture he had hitherto only imagined. He clung to that rapture as long as he could, hands pressed urgently to the torc in an effort to prolong the moment, only opening his eyes when the last of the fire had faded from his veins and someone in the circle coughed.

The lifeless form of their victim was hanging limply from the marker stone, wisps of smoke curling up from the deep black scorch mark over his breast. Both the medallion and the jewel pendant from his collar were slagged, acrid smoke still curling upward from scorched silk and wool. The surrounding snow had been melted, leaving the ground bare and blackened. Cautiously, at Raeburn's gesture of permission, some of the other members of the group edged forward to examine the victim. In their deference, Raeburn also noted fear and respect not unmingled with envy; and he savored the satisfaction that awareness brought.

Off in the distance, the wail of a siren gradually grew louder, very likely an indication that the recent pyrotechnics above the burying ground had not gone unnoticed. At Raeburn's curt instruction, as he pulled on coat and hat and scarf, one of his associates stripped the slagged remains of the lynx pendant from the victim's body with a well-insulated hand while another began loosing the silken bonds that bound the body to the marker stone. When they had lowered it to the ground, the first man cut and removed the tape binding the corpse's wrists. These measures completed, Raeburn allowed himself to be escorted back to the waiting taxi by two of his minions, leaving the other members of the group to disperse as swiftly and silently as they had come. By the time the first police patrol car turned into Waterloo Place, the Old Calton Road Burial Ground was empty except for the sleeping dead of bygone days and the charred corpse of a man lately struck by lightning.

At Strathmourne, meanwhile, Adam and his associates remained yet unaware of this latest escalation in the campaign of the Lodge of the Lynx. Focused for the past two days on protecting Gillian Talbot, they had this afternoon secured her transfer to Strathmourne to begin a new phase of her treatment. Gillian was now settled in a cozy room in the east wing that once had served as a nursery parlor, her mother installed in another room across the hall.

This evening, to welcome Iris Talbot to Strathmourne and underline the relaxed, homelike atmosphere they hoped would provide a breakthrough in her daughter's condition, Philippa had arranged an informal dinner party that included not only Peregrine, for whom Mrs. Talbot had conceived an adoring fascination since noting his effect on Gillian, but also Christopher and Victoria Houston, who had driven up from Kinross to bolster the ranks. The redoubtable Mrs. Gilchrist had readily agreed to take up her former vocation as a nurse, to sit with Gillian while the rest of the household dined.

By the time the dinner party had chatted their way amiably through leek and Stilton soup, Chicken Wellington, and damson crumble, Iris Talbot was well on her way to being at ease in her new surroundings. Philippa was about to suggest they retire to the front parlor for coffee when the telephone rang.

"Humphrey will see to it," Adam said, with a smile for Iris Talbot, who had started at the noise. "Unless it's an emergency, I don't take calls during dinner." A buzzer sounded discreetly from the telephone across the room. "On the other hand, some calls do have to be dealt with. Why don't the rest of you carry on into the parlor, and I'll join you in a few minutes."

That assurance was not to be carried out, however, for the caller was a grim-voiced Noel McLeod.

"Brace yourself, Adam," the inspector said. "A man wearing Masonic regalia has just been found dead in the Old Calton Road Burial Ground, between the railroad tracks and Calton Hill. Get this—the man appears to have been *struck by lightning*. I'm just on my way there, and thought you might want to join me—you

242

and young Lovat, if he's available. Make sure he brings something to draw with, just in case.''

Just over an hour later, with Peregrine sitting anxiously beside him, Adam nosed the Range Rover into line behind half a dozen police vehicles parked along the north side of Waterloo Place, just across the street from the entrance to Old Calton Road Cemetery. Police barriers had been set up around the entrance itself, and an ambulance was waiting at the curb, flashing blue lights eerie in the slight snowfall that continued to come down.

"This looks not a little ominous," Adam said, as he and Peregrine got out of the car.

With a grunt of agreement, Peregrine tucked just a sketch pad under his arm and followed Adam dutifully across the street, squinting against the snow and belatedly pulling on fingerless gloves.

"We're here at the request of Inspector McLeod," Adam told the uniformed officer posted at the barrier, presenting his card. "Can you tell me where to find him?"

"Aye, sir." The officer half-turned and pointed to a concentration of floodlights up among the gravestones at the upper level of the burial ground. "He'll be somewhere up there. Just watch yourself, though—the ground's pretty mucky."

"Thank you," Adam said briskly.

Together he and Peregrine sidestepped the barrier and made their way through the gate. In passing, Adam noticed the heavy length of chain lying on the ground beside the gatepost, the accompanying padlock neatly snipped, probably with a set of bolt-cutters. Farther up the slope, the air was tainted with the acrid odor of burnt flesh.

"Dear Jesus!" Peregrine murmured, on a constricted note of revulsion.

He raised a gloved hand to cover his mouth and nose, all but gagging. In the same instant, Adam caught sight of McLeod's overcoated form among the figures moving in and out among the floodlights. As he waved an arm to draw the inspector's attention, McLeod looked down and saw them. His strong, well-defined face showed pale and grim in the acetylene glare as he came to meet them.

"You took long enough!" he muttered, though the comment came of nerves rather than any real annoyance, for he knew they had come as quickly as they could. "The medics and the police pathologist have been after me for the last half hour to let them remove the body, but I wanted you to see things as we found them. Limber up your sketching hand, Mr. Lovat.''

Beckoning them to follow, he led the way up through a web-work maze of yellow police tape onto a stretch of winter-dead turf between two grey stone tomb-houses. Rounding the corner of the right-hand edifice a step behind Adam, Peregrine jibbed slightly at the sight of a corpse sprawled in an ungainly heap on a patch of scorched and muddy earth a few yards away, but he managed not to break stride as he continued forward. As he cast his gaze over the body, a chilly sense of residual violence took him in the face like a slap from an open hand.

He caught his breath and flinched back. McLeod and Adam both looked around, but he made a mute gesture of disclaimer and focused his attention on the dead man. The victim looked to be about the same age as McLeod; a solid, workman-like individual wearing the charred remnants of a Masonic collar and a now-muddy apron over a dark suit. The cause of death was plain to be seen from the blackened ruin in the center of his chest, almost as if he had been struck by a mortar round.

Reaching into his coat pocket for a pencil, Peregrine flipped open his sketch pad with the other hand and took a couple of deep breaths, narrowing his eyes as he also sought to look beyond the immediate scene to the events that had preceded it. It was hard to sift out the violence, but as he reached toward a deeper level of perception, the scene before him came to life with the ghostly transparency that betokened the visionary nature of what he was witnessing.

He Saw now an assembly of figures robed and hooded in white, drawn up in a circle around the victim, reminiscent of Randall Stewart's slaying. The lynx medallions those had worn were conspicuously absent, but rings adorned each right hand, as they had that other night, and the faces were obscured by more than just the hoods. The one who seemed to be the leader wore about his neck a dark, heavy necklet that drew Peregrine like a magnet—though when he tried to focus on it, the details blurred.

Calling up reserves of concentration, Peregrine tried to picture it more clearly. It had about it an unmistakable aura of malignancy. He was able to capture a fleeting impression of fluid pictographs assembled in configurations of power. But before the impression could stabilize, a sudden backlash of pain seared white-hot behind his eyes, blotting out the vision.

The pain was so intense that he choked and doubled over, vaguely clawing at his face. Two strong pairs of hands came to his support to save him from falling, gradually easing him upright again as he recovered, but even thinking about the unknown neck adornment made him nauseated, pain stabbing again behind his eyes.

"Steady on," Adam's deep voice said in his ear. "Let go of whatever's causing this reaction. It isn't worth it."

Cool, firm fingers came to rest on his brow. At once the pain grew easier. Peregrine gulped air, only gradually daring to open his eyes again as the hand fell away.

"Adam, I think this lot were the same ones that killed Randall Stewart," he murmured cautiously, surprised to find pad and pencil still in his hands. "The leader had something around his neck—a—a necklet or—maybe a torc."

"Somehow I thought he might," Adam said quietly. "But that's all for now. Don't try to work on the image. The object itself is far too well-shielded. How are you doing?"

Peregrine nodded. The pain had subsided and he found he could see normally again.

"Better. You—don't want me to focus on the leader, then?" he asked.

"Not at that cost," Adam said. "Not now. Not here. Were you getting any other images before he shut you down?"

"Oh, yes," Peregrine replied. "All *kinds* of good details. . . ."

His voice trailed off as his gaze shifted again toward the figure slumped at the foot of the gravestone, his pencil already moving over the top sheet of his sketch pad. At the look of abstraction that crossed his face, Adam and McLeod moved off a few yards, satisfied that the young artist was once more in command of his faculties but ready to come to his rescue again if need be. With Peregrine's help, they might yet learn something useful from tonight's outrage. Beside Adam, McLeod squared his shoulders.

"Well, then. Another Mason killed under circumstances that can only be described as bizarre," he muttered. "Don't you know the papers are going to have a field day tomorrow."

Adam grimaced. He could just imagine the headlines. Aloud he said, "Did you know the man?"

"Only slightly," McLeod replied. "His name is—was—Ian MacPherson. Had his own joinery business in Lochend, where his Lodge is located." He indicated the dead man's apron and collar and pursed his lips in darkling speculation.

"I'd be willing to bet this is their regular Lodge night. My guess is that he must've been nabbed just before the meeting was about to start—maybe even on the Lodge premises themselves. I've sent

Donald over there to make inquiries. As one of their own, so to speak, he'll be more likely to get information than some—but only if there's something to tell.''

He paused and shook his head. "I don't know, Adam. Randall's death was bad enough—but this begins to get *really* spooky. If we don't get to the bottom of this mess pretty soon, we're likely to find ourselves with a public witch-hunt on our hands. And what's worse, the self-appointed witch-hunters will be looking in all the wrong places—with the Masonic Order itself at the top of the list.''

"All too true, I'm afraid," Adam agreed soberly. "What else can you tell me just now? *Was* MacPherson struck by lightning?''

McLeod scowled like a thundercloud. "So the evidence would suggest. First there's the localized shock-burn in the center of the chest. Then there's the fact that MacPherson's wristwatch stopped at 8:17—which pinpoints the time of death. The coins in his pockets were reduced to slag—another documented feature associated with victims of lightning strikes. I'm not a doctor, but it seems fairly convincing to me.''

Adam nodded grimly.

"This would be far easier to explain," McLeod continued, "if this were summer in the tropics. But electrical storm weather is pretty freakish for Scotland in winter. I wish I could pretend to believe that this whole thing was an elaborate crime perpetrated under studio conditions by someone who'd seen one too many horror films. As it is, we've got a couple of witnesses who claim they saw strange clouds massing over the graveyard only moments before the lightning strike took place.''

Adam's gaze sharpened. "Why does this suddenly sound like some of the stories that came out in conjunction with that incident up at Balmoral last month?''

McLeod blinked. "Do you think there might be a connection?''

"I don't know," Adam said, "but it's a theory worth looking into.''

He might have said more, but at that moment, Peregrine hurried back to join them, his face showing a mixture of revulsion and excitement.

"Look at this!" he said, and held out his sketch pad for their inspection.

Adam took the pad and tilted it toward the light. The drawing showed MacPherson lashed to the memorial stone at whose foot he now lay, wearing not only the apron and collar of the Master of a Lodge but also a circular medallion hanging round his neck by a long chain. The device on the face of the medallion was that of a snarling head of a lynx.

"The others weren't wearing them this time," Peregrine explained, as his mentors gazed at the drawing. "They wore rings, but no medallions. It isn't there now, of course," he added, indicating the Lynx medallion with a touch of one finger. "They—the men in white—must have removed it after the lightning strike took place. But why put it on him, unless—"

"Unless it was a factor in completing the ritual," Adam mused. "Yes, that would fit the pattern. The medallion acts like a homing beacon, drawing down the fire of whatever force our opposite numbers are trying to unleash on the material world."

"X marks the spot," said McLeod, with a tight show of teeth. "Otherwise known as the Judas touch."

"But why here?" Peregrine wondered, casting a glance around him.

"There, I think, is part of the answer," said Adam, and pointed.

Peregrine looked and saw that he was indicating the fire-scarred grave marker behind the body of the fallen man. Looking more closely, he saw that the stone bore a curious carved device: a circle with a triangle inside, with a left hand inside the triangle, palm out and fingers together, with an eye in the palm of the hand.

"Unless I totally miss my guess," said Adam, "that's an old Masonic symbol of protection. Am I right, Noel?"

Nodding, McLeod ran one hand over the worn carving. "It certainly looks like it to me."

"Furthermore," Adam said, "I'd be very surprised if this particular burial ground hasn't been used in the past for significant Masonic interments. That being the case, I suspect our enemies were using these premises not only to perform a sacrifice, but also to test the strength of their own offensive power."

Surveying the scene yet again, he set his hands on his hips and heaved a bleak sigh.

"I think we may take it as read that they accomplished what they came for," he continued. "Wherever the trail leads from here, there will be more deaths along the way unless we can move more quickly than they can. For that, we're going to need knowledge. Noel, how soon can you get me the transcripts of those interviews you and Cochrane took in Stirling?"

"How about tomorrow?" McLeod said. "Sunday, at the latest. I'll bring a copy up to the house myself, and I'll see to it that you get a copy of the forensics report on MacPherson as well, as soon as one becomes available."

# CHAPTER TWENTY-FIVE

BY dawn the next morning, aerial visibility over the Cairngorms had been reduced almost to nothing by thick, low-lying fog. Flying mostly on instruments, Raeburn's pilot Barclay muttered under his breath as he nursed the helicopter forward above a creamy blanket of white that looked substantial enough to walk on, avoiding the occasional snow-capped peak that extended above the level of the fog. Raeburn himself sat impassive in the seat beside Barclay as the copter chuffed along in a preternatural silence. The strengthening beep of a homing beacon announced their imminent arrival.

The pilot half held his breath as he started their descent. It was like sinking into a glass of melted cream. After a heart-stopping few seconds of utter blindness, they emerged in murky twilight above a blanket of snow that shrouded everything. Just ahead, landing lights beside the castellated manor house pointed the way to a safe landing just before it.

Minutes later, Raeburn was making a quick, frigid dash from the helicopter across the snowy lawn to the front door, head ducked instinctively under the slowing blades, his briefcase tucked under one arm. Once inside, silent, attentive servants helped him exchange his outer garments for one of the loose, white robes that passed for a uniform under this roof. Thus adorned, he let them escort him to the foot of the stairs that led up to the Head-Master's tower.

It cost Raeburn some effort to make the ascent. His pale, ascetic face showed unwonted lines of strain as he mounted the steps one at a time. His limbs were still shaky with fatigue brought on by his first assay in the use of the torc, but it was a weariness in which he revelled, welcome proof of his growing aptitude for power. He drew a fortifying breath as he knocked thrice on the door and then eased it open.

The Head-Master sat amid his cushions at one edge of his circle of acolytes. Before him on its mat of black ram skin lay the manuscript, with something atop it wrapped in scarlet silk. The atmosphere within the circular chamber was charged with expectancy, a dozen pairs of eyes glinting hungrily in the gaslight. The Head-Master's wizened face was inscrutable, his eyes like burning coals within their matrix of wrinkles.

Stepping just across the threshold, Raeburn pulled the door closed behind him and made the Head-Master a profound bow, head bending almost to the level of his knees. As he straightened, aware of all eyes upon him, he announced, "It is done, Head-Master. The Lord Taranis has been pleased to accept our oblation."

The note of jubilation in his voice echoed off the ancient stones. A sigh whispered around the circle, a murmur of greedy elation. Echoing the sigh, the Head-Master beckoned Raeburn to approach, nodding as the younger man knelt in token submission before him.

"Welcome, Son of the Tempest-Bringer," he said. "This day has the Thunderer truly begotten thee."

He reached across the manuscript to trace a runic symbol on Raeburn's brow with his thumb. His touch was cold and dry as snakeskin, and the younger man shivered slightly at the touch of chill authority.

"Let it be recorded in the Annals of Shadow that the death-agony of the temple-builder has been judged a worthy sacrifice," the Head-Master proclaimed, with harsh satisfaction. "May his lifeforce nourish the storm that soon will blast the Temple itself with immortal lightnings. And may the hour be soon in coming when the Thunderer himself shall enter into the world through the gateway of flesh prepared to receive him."

This invocation was greeted by an echoing murmur of assent from among the ranks of his acolytes. Raeburn alone was silent, his face hard and pale in the wan flicker of the gaslights. The Master elevated a hairless eyebrow.

"Son of the Thunderer," he said, "have you something more to say?"

"I do, Head-Master," Raeburn said. "Something which concerns all present. I have further news of the Hunting Party that is dogging our heels. And unless I much mistake the matter, it could jeopardize all our plans."

This announcement provoked another rustle of movement around the room. The Head-Master's wrinkled lips framed a scowl of displeasure.

"Explain."

Raeburn made his superior another slight bow, rocking back on his heels.

"All here are aware that our recent attempt to neutralize a member of the Hunt was frustrated through the intervention of one Sir Adam Sinclair of Strathmourne, whom we now have reason to believe is actually Master of the Hunt," he said. "What has yet to be told is that Sinclair apparently has managed to use what he and McLeod and Lovat observed at Melrose, following our re-animation of the wizard Michael Scot last month, to track down Scot's latter-day incarnation. Very soon, if he has not done so already, Sinclair undoubtedly will attempt to bridge the gap of centuries to get at the knowledge Scot holds in his keeping."

If he had intended to cause a sensation, he was not disappointed. The Head-Master stiffened and glared, his parchment face contorted in the malevolent grimace of a gargoyle.

"How was this allowed to occur?" he demanded. "Why was I not informed of this sooner?"

"The information could not be verified until several days ago," Raeburn said impassively. "Until Tuesday of this past week, none of us suspected, and it took several days to confirm."

"And who *is* Scot's current incarnation?" the Head-Master demanded.

"A child named Gillian Talbot," Raeburn said, to stirrings of consternation among the Master's disciples. "She is currently listed as a mental patient under Sinclair's medical supervision. She first came to notice on Monday, when one of this house's lesser operatives noted her arrival at the Edinburgh hospital where Sinclair has his practice. Since Sinclair ordinarily does not deal with children, my operative was curious. Careful inquiry revealed that the child had been transferred up from a hospital in London, where she had lain in a coma since the morning after our summoning of Scot.

"To facilitate our further investigation, samples were procured of the child's hair and blood, which were subsequently used as the physical link for launching an inquiry into her astral past. Our researches sufficed to confirm that Gillian Talbot is, indeed, the most recent aspect of Scot. Fortunately, as a result of the prolonged separation of Scot's soul from the body last month, she is not at the moment in what can be termed her right mind—but should Sinclair be able to bring her to her senses, there is no doubt that she possesses past knowledge that could damage us significantly in our present enterprise."

The acolyte to the Head-Master's right raised a hand, face all but invisible in the shadows of the white hood.

"Speak," he said harshly.

"Head-Master, it is known that much of Scot's knowledge was committed to his book of spells," said a woman's voice, her speech touched with an accent that might have been German. "That book is now at the bottom of Loch Ness. If it is beyond our reach, surely it is beyond Scot's own as well, especially if his soul now resides in the body of a child."

"Except that, as Master of the Hunt, Sinclair may have the resources to retrieve that information directly from Scot or even from the Records themselves," the Head-Master said acidly.

He set his hands carefully on splayed knees, rheumy eyes hot and hard as he raked them with his gaze.

"Bah, what do any of you know!" he muttered, his breath wheezing in his lungs. "The *Führer* did not know. He moved too soon, without truly mastering the wisdom of Taranis, and the power turned on him."

One trembling, taloned hand reached out to caress the top page of the manuscript.

"*I* have not made that mistake," he whispered, not really seeing any of them in that moment. "For half a century have I studied and sacrificed, in ways that you can hardly hope to comprehend, and I understand what *he* did not. *I* can call Taranis' wrath to rend the frail canopy that keeps back Darkness! When the way is opened—"

A smothered cough recalled him, and he shook his head slightly, returning his gaze to Raeburn, his face set like flint.

"Do not fail me, Son of the Thunderer! I do not intend to stand by and see everything lost now, when success is within reach. Arrange matters so that this child does not survive to become a tool in the hands of our enemies."

"Would that it were that simple, Head-Master," Raeburn said cautiously, sensing a precarious balance between sanity and madness. "Yesterday Sinclair removed both the child and her mother to the safety of his own house at Strathmourne. We don't know for certain what aroused his suspicion, but unfortunately this puts the girl beyond our reach. The defenses about the place are unbreachable—we've already tried and failed to penetrate them. Our only other recourse, since we cannot get in ourselves, is to induce Sinclair to come out."

"What good will that do?" a woman asked sullenly, a faint French accent coloring her voice. "If anything, would not Sinclair be likely to strengthen his personal defenses outside the protection of his own home?"

"I would not presume to test his psychic defenses in such a

situation," Raeburn said with a thin smile, regaining a little of his confidence. "But such defenses are of little use against more conventional assaults."

"An assassin's bullet?" said the man seated at the Head-Master's right.

"That is one of the options being considered," Raeburn agreed. "I assure you, the matter will be resolved in time to prevent his interference in our next operation."

"See that it is," the Head-Master growled. "Sinclair has become entirely too inconvenient. Meanwhile, you are to keep me informed of the plans and their progress. Is that clear?"

"Perfectly, Head-Master," Raeburn said with a bow. "You will not be disappointed."

"See that I am not. More than your life may depend upon it." He scanned the room again, both anger and madness still smouldering in the rheumy eyes, then breathed out with a sigh.

"But enough of this. Work remains to be done which requires the full concentration of all present. You have brought the torc?"

"Here, Head-Master," Raeburn said, setting his briefcase flat beside him and thumbing open the clasps.

"And the medallion?"

"Here as well."

He handed over what was left of the medallion first—a small, silk-wrapped bundle of scarlet that gave off the clink of shifting pieces of metal. Folding back the scarlet silk, the Head-Master laid his hand over the lightning-slagged remains of the medallion used at Calton Hill, then passed it with a nod to the hooded woman on his left.

"See that this is consigned to the furnace," he instructed.

"It will be done, Head-Master," the woman said, and tucked the medallion out of sight among the folds of her robe.

As she did so, Raeburn bent over his briefcase a second time and took out the torc, also swathed in heavy scarlet silk. With some reluctance, he laid this reverently across the Head-Master's outstretched palms, still insulated in its silken wrappings.

"Excellent," his superior breathed. "Let us begin."

He set the torc on the floor before him as the acolyte to his right took up the smaller scarlet-wrapped bundle that still lay atop the manuscript on its mat of ram skin. As he carefully unwrapped it, gaslight glinted yellow off another silver medallion marked with the device of the Lynx, a twin to the one Raeburn had used at Calton Hill. A guttural invocation whispered among the ranks of the other acolytes as the Head-Master took up the medallion by its chain and lifted it to eye level in two claw-like hands.

"All hail to Taranis, Bringer of Lightnings!" he said, his voice harsh and cracked as the caw of a raven. "To thee, Master of Storms, do we consecrate this medal, ore of the earth and work of the hands of thy servants. Let iron be wedded to silver, conjoined by elemental fire. Let silver be handmaid to the iron, receiver of the flame of heaven!"

So saying, he bowed slightly in his place, then laid the medallion slightly to one side. Unwrapping the Soulis torc, he took it up in both his hands, raised it in salute, and passed it three times over the medallion in a circling fashion, anti-clockwise. On the last pass, he dipped his hands so that the torc and the medallion came briefly into contact. The touch produced a sizzling crackle and a brief burst of sparks, but did not seem to affect the wielder of this darkling magic. When the flare faded, the air was tinged with the smell of ozone as the Head-Master extended spider-thin arms, now elevating the torc above Raeburn's head in a gesture of oblation.

"Praise be to Taranis, Author of Thunders!" he rasped. "To thee, Tempest-rider, do we once more consecrate this man to be thy servant, herald of thy name and bearer of thy charge. Deliver into his hands the fire from heaven, and he shall honor thee with holocausts to thy greater glory!"

As he briefly touched the torc to the bowed head, Raeburn twitched at the sudden prickle of energy that blossomed at the base of his skull. Like static electricity it rippled down his spine, sending branching tendrils of power flickering along his nerve-lanes all the way to his fingertips and toes. The sensation gave him a delectable thrill of pleasure, all the more titillating for being laced with pain. He drew a sharp breath as he stiffened slightly, then released it with a sigh as the acute instant of delight dissipated into a certainty of latent mastery.

His sense of his own power was accompanied by an aching compulsion to exercise it, the sweeter for being restrained. He hardly heard the Head-Master's concluding incantations, so preoccupied was he with contemplation of the coming divine ecstasy, his again when he loosed the potency now vested within him. He mastered himself only with difficulty, to discover that the Head-Master was making him a formal presentation of the torc.

"Praise be to Taranis," he breathed as he accepted the torc from the hands of his superior. "I accept this charge and pledge the execution of His will."

The skies cleared during the next few days, but the weather remained bitterly cold. After the shock of Friday night's assault at Calton Hill, which Adam now had no doubt was the work of the Lodge of the Lynx, he made a point of warning those members of his Lodge not already under suspicion to avoid making contact except in the event of an emergency. As a matter of precaution, both he and McLeod kept to their respective routines, leaving Philippa to mount guard over Strathmourne and its occupants and pursue Gillian Talbot's treatment by conventional medicine. Peregrine, likewise, remained within the boundaries of the estate, and spent the better part of each day at Gillian's bedside making sketches that he was reluctant to show to anyone except Adam.

Adam himself was aware of a brooding sense of foreboding in the air, but could find no focus to the threat. The promised interview notes materialized on Sunday afternoon, dutifully delivered by McLeod himself, but failed to shed any new light on the situation. McLeod paid a visit to Adam's office at Jordanburn on Tuesday, but his only news had to do with the previous tenants of the "haunted" flat now occupied by Christopher's former parishioner, Helena Pringle.

"Unfortunately, there's nothing here that's really encouraging," McLeod said dourly, shifting his weight in his chair. "Of the three people on the landlady's list, the first—John Lariston—was single at the time of his tenancy, but has since married and moved down to England, where he's now practicing dentistry. The Central Post Office was able to track him down through three subsequent residences to give us his current address in Sussex. His life there seems to be more or less an open book. I doubt he's the man we're after."

"I would tend to agree," Adam said. "Go on."

"Joseph MacKellar, our second man, is a bit more problematical," McLeod continued. "Mr. MacKellar is employed by the Bank of Scotland, and was transferred to a branch office in Paris two years ago. We're still trying to run down his address on the Continent. I'll let you know if and when we find anything. Again, he doesn't seem a likely candidate for what Peregrine picked up in the flat."

He paused to consult his notes before resuming.

"That leaves us the tenant just before Helena Pringle, name of Stephen Victor Geddes. We haven't had much luck on him, either. At the time of his occupancy, he was working as a part-time lecturer in biology at Edinburgh University, but he's since left his post without leaving any record of his taking up employment elsewhere. We're still waiting for Social Services to get around to running his name through their computer to see if he's gone on the dole. If he has, they'll be able to give us his current address. If not, we'll have to try some other tack.''

Adam nodded. ''I still think it's worth pursuing, if only because of that glimpse Peregrine got of a Lynx medallion involved in whatever went on there. I assume none of the three have a criminal record?''

''Not under those names,'' McLeod replied. ''And we have no reason to suspect they've used any others.''

''This may prove a blind alley then,'' Adam said. ''We won't drop it yet, though. In the meantime, I suggest we pursue the Balmoral angle and continue working on the slaying at Calton Hill, of course. No autopsy report yet, I gather, or you would've mentioned it.''

''I've been promised it tomorrow,'' McLeod replied. ''You don't really think that's going to make a difference, though, do you?''

Adam smiled grimly. ''One can always hope.''

That hope, at least, was ill-founded. McLeod rang back on Wednesday, the promised report having arrived, but it was becoming increasingly clear that the physical evidence surrounding the death of the Master Mason MacPherson was not going to lead them any closer to the perpetrators. Like Randall, he had been chloroformed and drugged by his captors, but there any similarity ended, beyond the fact that both were Freemasons. The burn mark on the victim's chest did suggest the presence of something round and metallic around his neck—something besides the Masonic jewel, whose more irregular outline also had been branded into the flesh by the intense heat—but no trace of any such object had been found at the scene.

''It may well have been the Lynx medallion Peregrine postulated,'' McLeod said, ''but if so, the perpetrators took it off the body before they made their escape. I'm inclined to agree that it was exactly what Peregrine saw, but we have no proof. And even if we did, it isn't anything we could use in the official investigation. I can't advance the opinion that MacPherson was hit by deliberately directed lightning.''

''That may be exactly what happened, though,'' Adam said, ''just as I'm beginning to wonder whether that's what happened up at Balmoral. Have you gotten back anything further on that?''

''Not yet,'' McLeod replied, ''but I hope to send Donald up

tomorrow to run down copies of the reports and photos. I'll get back to you when I have something further to report. How're things going with the Talbot girl?''

''Nothing yet,'' Adam said. ''Peregrine's producing some very interesting drawings, and we're continuing with conventional therapy in the meantime. I hope to be ready for a definite move within a week or so.''

''Sounds like we all just hang tight for a while, then,'' McLeod replied.

That same evening, Francis Raeburn summoned the pilot Barclay to his library in the house outside Stirling.

''Time is growing short,'' he said. ''Have you decided how to deal with Sinclair?''

Barclay allowed himself a predatory smile as he folded his lean form into the chair across from his superior.

''By this time tomorrow, he'll be dead—or at least badly enough injured that his death will be inevitable. Dr. Wemyss will see to that.''

''There'd better not be any slipups,'' Raeburn said. ''I want no interference on Friday. You're sure it will look like an accident?''

''Sinclair drives fast,'' Barclay said with a smug smile. ''And tires do blow at speed. It will look like an accident.''

Adam did not venture from the house on Thursday, being preoccupied with a series of tests Philippa wanted to run on Gillian. On Friday morning, as Adam prepared to leave for the hospital, an early call from McLeod set up a meeting later in the day to go over the photos and reports Cochrane had secured at Balmoral.

''I haven't had a chance to look at it yet myself,'' McLeod told him, ''but Donald came in this morning looking like the proverbial cat with the canary.''

''Sounds promising,'' Adam said, adjusting a cuff-link. ''How about if I meet you for a late lunch? Say, the Pimpernel at two?''

''Sounds good to me,'' McLeod said. ''Will you book or shall I?''

''Would you mind doing it?'' Adam said. ''I skipped rounds yesterday so Philippa and I could work with Gillian, so I've got to spend some time with my other patients today.''

''Will do,'' McLeod replied. ''The Pimpernel at two. See you.''

Adam was preoccupied as he got into the Range Rover and buckled up. At just past nine, the morning was hardly brighter than when it had dawned, made grey and dismal by a drifting mist that

256

could not quite seem to decide whether it wanted to be sleet or rain—less than optimum driving conditions, but the Range Rover was designed to cope with just such weather, and Adam was an excellent driver.

Once he had negotiated the icy drive and was on the secondary road, picking up speed, his driving settled into semi-automatic, for he had many things on his mind. As a consequence, he made no special note of the man on the motorcycle who fell in behind him to trail at a discreet distance, or the yellow Mercedes that also joined in as he merged smoothly onto the motorway and pushed the Rover up to a comfortable cruising speed of about 70 mph.

He was approaching the Forth Road Bridge when the man on the motorcycle made his move. Adam had the blue Range Rover in the number one lane, nearest the divider, and had made only idle note of the big Italian motorcycle coming up fast in his rearview mirror.

Before he could ease over to let the machine overtake him, it was nearly even with his left rear quarter-panel, so he stayed where he was, only casually aware of the machine easing forward along the Rover's left side. He did not see the sawed-off shotgun the rider casually pulled from under his leg and coat and pointed at the Range Rover's left front tire, or hear the blast as the rider pulled the trigger.

As the Rover's left front tire went with a bang, Adam was only peripherally aware of the motorcycle shooting on ahead and out of danger; all *too* aware that the Rover was spinning out of control as the wheel's rim bit into the asphalt.

He fought the wheel, but the car's right rear swung around to carom off the center divider with a sickening *bam!* That might have set him skidding straight again, except that the left front wheel continued to grind into the road. He could feel the car going over—braced himself as it went—praying that following traffic would be able to avoid piling into him.

In terrible slow motion, the car fell onto the driver's side and kept rolling, now on its roof, skidding now on the passenger side in a sickening screech of tortured metal, Adam braced against the steering wheel and hanging from his seat belt. The windscreen had crazed and partly buckled, but he could see the metal guard rails on the side of the motorway approaching with horrible speed. The impact flung him hard against his seat harness, wrenching his right shoulder and bouncing his head off something hard. Pain exploded from the point of impact, and his world momentarily went black.

# CHAPTER TWENTY-SIX

A DAM clawed his way desperately back to consciousness, surfacing in the eerie silence that often seems to follow trauma. He had a death-grip on the steering wheel and was hanging sideways from his seat harness, half-sitting on the side of the center console of the Rover, which was on its left side.

Somehow, through the first fog of pain that radiated from his head, his right shoulder, from nearly every part of his body, he knew that he had to get out. The smell of petrol made it imperative, and through the now-shattered windscreen, he could see smoke or steam escaping from under the Rover's bonnet. A cold blast of air from above his left shoulder drew his groggy gaze to a gaping opening where the sunroof had been, apparently popped out when the car rolled.

Forcing his left hand to uncurl from around the steering wheel, he pushed the switch for the emergency flashers, fumbled at the ignition switch until he could turn it off, then shifted his left knee to brace against the center console, only then groping along the side of the seat to thumb the seat belt release.

He groaned as the sudden shift of his weight left him half-kneeling on the side of the console, still braced against the steering wheel, and it was all he could do to extricate his legs the rest of the way from under the steering column and scramble to a standing position on the passenger door. As he thrust one trembling leg and then the other through the sunroof opening and crouched to shoulder through, gasping as bruised muscles protested, he found himself facing oncoming traffic, the first cars only now pulling up to render aid—which at least meant that he could not have been unconscious very long.

Wincing as he straightened, every muscle protesting, he staggered around to the front of the car to stare stupidly at the damage, raking hair out of his eyes with a shaking hand that came away bloody.

"Hey, are you all right?" a woman's voice called behind him.

A little dazedly he turned to see a fortyish-looking brunette in a bright red suit and Christmas bells on her lapel darting toward him on dangerously high-heeled shoes, her brightly-painted mouth agape with concern.

"God, you're lucky you weren't killed!" she said, eyeing the car. "You're bleeding. Can I take you to a doctor?"

He looked down blankly at the blood on his hand, a medically detached part of him warning that he probably had a concussion, possibly was going into shock, and definitely needed medical attention.

"Maybe I ought to wait for an ambulance," he heard himself saying. "I don't want to put you to any trouble."

"Don't be daft. It could take an hour for official transport to get here. Come on. I work right next to the Royal Infirmary. You can't get any better facility than that."

Some vague stirring at the back of his mind made him want to decline, but it *was* the best emergency facility around. Injured police officers were taken there, if they had a choice, and Adam knew several consultants on staff. Whatever his injuries, he would get the best of care.

Mumbling his thanks—he feared he *was* going into shock—he let her help him back to the yellow Mercedes idling behind the wreck of his own car, stifling a groan as he eased into the passenger seat. She moved the seat back to give him more leg room, then pulled the seat belt down to buckle him in and closed his door.

As she came around to the driver's side, he folded down the sun visor to peer into its mirror. His pupils appeared to be the same size, but the blood was coming from at least two lacerations that would require suturing, one on his forehead and another just into his hair. He dabbed at the wounds with a silk pocket square, but the movement sent sharp pain through his wrenched right shoulder. As his benefactress got into the car, he shifted his attention to checking his pulse. It was steady enough, but every muscle in his body was starting to ache as the adrenaline surge from the accident started to dissipate.

"You really totalled the car," she said, as she put the Mercedes into gear and pulled out into traffic. "Do you know what happened?"

"A tire blew," he said, leaning his head against the seat back and closing his eyes. "Listen, I really do appreciate this."

"Just think of me as the Christmas Samaritan," she said with a tight-lipped smile that he did not see. "Why don't you just lie back and relax? I'll have you at the hospital as quickly as I can."

He did try to relax, though he knew he should not let himself fall asleep—not if he was concussed. He spent a few minutes taking himself into a light trance, doing what he could to stabilize heart-rate and respiration, then let himself drift with the drone of the engine and the motion of the car, trying to reconstruct what had happened. Every second seemed clear, but there was something not quite right, something he could not put his finger on. He was still trying to puzzle it out when the car gently came to a halt and then the engine stopped.

They had pulled up outside a hospital emergency entrance, his rescuer already getting out of the car to go and summon help. Carefully, because it already was harder to move, Adam released his seat belt and opened the car door. He had managed to get both feet onto the pavement when a porter came barging up with a wheelchair.

"Now, you just stay where you are, sir, till I get this chair in close, okay? You're going to be just fine." The man's voice had a musical lilt, soft with the accents of Jamaica, and his hands were gentle but strong. "Right, sir. Just shift yourself around now— that's my man!"

Things moved quickly after that, especially once Adam identified himself as a physician. His benefactress disappeared sometime during the process of filling out necessary forms, without him ever learning her name, and almost before he realized, Adam found himself flat on his back in an examining room, stripped to his shorts and shivering under a blanket, a blood-pressure cuff constricting his left arm.

The doctor who came to examine him was an attractive, no-nonsense brunette whose accent suggested American or Canadian origins. The name tag on her green surgical scrubs read *Dr. X. Lockhart*. She seemed satisfied with his blood pressure and neurological signs, but poking and prodding at his physical discomforts had already suggested that he had several cracked ribs and possibly a cracked collarbone.

"I'm sending you over to X-ray before we take care of those lacerations, Dr. Sinclair," she said, as she began filling out the forms and the orderly, whose name was Sykes, assisted Adam in poking his arms through the sleeves of a hospital gown. "We'll have a look at the ribs and that shoulder, and I'm also ordering a skull series. I don't suspect any problem, but you *were* unconscious, even if only for a few seconds. Mr. Sykes will put a temporary dressing on those lacerations before he takes you over to X-ray, and I'll see you when you get back."

She had clipped the forms to Adam's chart and was gone before he could bestir himself to ask any questions. He did ask for another blanket after Sykes had applied his dressing, and had the orderly retrieve his ring from the pocket of his trousers before preparing to wheel him off to X-ray. Other items in his pockets were valuable but replaceable; the ring was not. He slipped it on his hand and turned the stone inward as Sykes gathered up the rest of his belongings and stashed them in a locker.

"I don't suppose I can make a phone call before we go to X-ray?" Adam asked, as Sykes adjusted the new blanket and then raised the side rails on the gurney.

"Afraid not, Doctor. The sooner we get to X-ray, the sooner you'll be done. How about if you call from there, after they've taken their pictures? We'll have a five- or ten-minute wait anyway, while they develop the film."

"Fair enough," Adam agreed. But he wanted to call as soon as possible, because he had a suspicion that the obviously competent Dr. Lockhart was going to keep him overnight for observation—which was entirely correct under the circumstances, but it did complicate matters considerably.

He settled back resignedly as the orderly wheeled him over to X-ray, too uncomfortable to banter much with the technicians, but doing his best to make their work as easy as possible. At least he was starting to be able to think a bit more clearly. Afterwards, as Sykes had promised, he was wheeled into a waiting area and a telephone receiver placed in his hand.

"What's the number, and I'll dial it for you, Doc," the orderly said.

"It's 311–3131," Adam said, putting the receiver to his ear.

The man dialed, then moved off a few feet as the number began to ring.

"Police headquarters," said a voice at the other end.

"Let me speak to Detective Chief Inspector Noel McLeod," Adam said. "This is Adam Sinclair calling."

After a short delay while the operator transferred the call, McLeod's bass voice echoed from the other end.

"What's up, Adam?"

"I'm afraid I'm going to have to cancel our luncheon date," Adam said shakily, choosing his words to produce minimum alarm. "I've—ah—bunged up the Rover—totalled it, in fact. I'm all right, but I'm at the Royal Infirmary, waiting for X-rays to come back."

"Good God, what happened?" McLeod demanded.

261

"Blew a tire at speed. Lost control and rolled it. It could happen to anybody. Thank God it was the Rover I was driving. Probably saved my life."

"I should say!" McLeod replied. "You mentioned X-rays—anything broken?"

"I dunno. My shoulder hurts like hell from the seat belt, which I suppose is to be expected, and I may have a bit of concussion. I lost consciousness for a few seconds. I expect they'll keep me overnight. Listen, could you call home and let them know what's happened? I don't want them charging down here, because there's nothing they can do, but I'd appreciate it if you'd pass the word."

"Glad to do it," McLeod agreed. "Do I need to chase down your car?"

Adam chuckled weakly. He had not even thought about the abandoned car.

"Good question. I'm afraid I just left it. A very kind woman in a Mercedes insisted on driving me to the hospital, so I have no idea what's happened to the remains. Lord, I didn't even get her name to thank her."

"I'll see what I can find out," McLeod said. "Where did it happen?"

"Southbound on the A90, just before the Forth Road Bridge. I'm afraid it was rather spectacular. Fortunately, I was able to avoid involving any other vehicles."

"You're babbling, you know," McLeod said gruffly. "Make sure they're keeping an eye on you. When I've made those calls, do you want me to come over?"

Adam blinked. He *was* babbling.

"I think that might be a good idea," he said. "I doubt they'll let you see me for an hour or two—I've got a couple of lacerations requiring suturing—but they should be through with me by one or two."

"You're sure you're okay?" McLeod said.

"Yeah," Adam replied, lifting his head slightly as the orderly went over to collect the bright orange envelope with the developed X-rays. "Gotta go now, Noel. My pictures are done, and my driver needs to take me back to Emergency. See you in a couple of hours."

He lay back wearily as the orderly took the receiver from him and cradled it, laying the big envelope on Adam's chest.

"Okay, let's go find Dr. Lockhart and show her your pictures," Sykes said cheerily, releasing the gurney's brake. "And no free previews!" he added, as Adam started to open the envelope.

Scowling, Adam let the envelope fall back on his chest. "Mr. Sykes, they're *my* X-rays. And I *am* a physician."

"Yessir, and a doctor who tries to diagnose himself has a fool for a patient," Sykes said smugly. "Besides, you can't see 'em proper without a light box. Just hang on till we get back to the examining room. If she isn't there yet, I'll even put 'em up for you."

"Fair enough," Adam said, lying back with a satisfied sigh.

Sykes just had time to switch on the light box and start slipping the X-rays under their clips when Dr. Lockhart came back in, carrying a tape-sealed bundle of surgical green. Adam had his head up to watch, but he lay back meekly as she shot him a disapproving glance and deposited her bundle on a stainless-steel table, wheeling it close beside his gurney before going back to look at the X-rays Sykes had finished putting up.

"You can prep Dr. Sinclair's lacerations now, Mr. Sykes," she said blandly. "And you, Doctor, can lie back and pretend you're the same as any other patient, and that you really do believe I know what I'm doing."

As Adam lay back, somehow guessing he was not going to win any concessions where Dr. Lockhart was concerned, she silently studied the X-rays. Adam studied the trim figure, the dark braid escaping from under her surgical cap, trying to get an angle on Dr. X. Lockhart.

After a moment, a rubber-gloved Sykes rolled over another of the stainless-steel tables, this one bedecked with a steel basin and disinfectant solutions, and put a towel under Adam's head before removing the temporary dressing. It hurt a little as Sykes began gently cleaning the wounds, but Adam kept his attention focused on Dr. Lockhart, who finally nodded and went over to the scrub sink to start washing her hands.

"Well, the news is basically good, Doctor," she said, dark eyes meeting his in the mirror as she scrubbed. "No apparent fractures to the skull, though I do want to admit you overnight."

Adam sighed resignedly. "I'm not surprised, under the circumstances. I suppose that if I were you, I'd admit me too."

"I'm glad you're not going to fight me on the point," she said. A ghost of a smile softened her look of severity. "You're lucky on the shoulder too. Unless you've injured it in the past, you do have what appears to be a hairline fracture of the clavicle, but it's nothing serious—other than seriously uncomfortable, of course. Ditto the cracked ribs. We'll put you in a sling, mainly to remind you not to over-use it, and I'll write you orders for mefenamic acid to knock down the inflammation and some of the pain. Other than that, I'm afraid you're just going to have to tough it out."

"Just keep reminding me how lucky I am," he said with a strained smile. Out of the corner of his eye, he could see the bloody swabs piling up on Sykes' table, and grimaced as the orderly took up a razor-blade to shave deftly around the laceration that went into his hair.

"Careful with that razor, Mr. Sykes," he said. "I pay my barber £25 a time to cut my hair exactly the way I like it. I'll give you the same to leave as little evidence of your work as possible."

"Just don't you worry, Dr. Sinclair," Sykes said, with a flash of white teeth. "You'll hardly even know I've been here. And Dr. Lockhart sews the neatest little stitches you've ever seen."

As Adam scowled up at him, trying to decide how serious he was, Dr. Lockhart came over, now gloved as well, to inspect Sykes' work. Beside her, a male nurse had come in to fold back the top layers of green surgical toweling that housed a suture kit, exposing the gleam of scissors and hemostats and needle-holders to the light of the big operating lamp that he now switched on overhead and brought to aim on Adam's head. In the glare of the light, Adam could just make out Dr. Lockhart as she snapped the top off a glass ampoule and began filling a syringe.

"I expect you've heard this before, Doctor, but in just a few seconds you're going to feel a little pinch," she said, setting the empty ampoule aside. "I assume you have no problem with .1% lignocaine?"

"None that I know of," Adam replied.

She was good. She came in from above his head, so that he never saw the needle—only her other hand, partially blocking his vision, just before she set to work. It was more a tingling than a pinch, after the initial needle-prick, but she infiltrated the edges of the first laceration without a wasted motion, finished almost before he realized she had begun. The one in his scalp took more doing, for the skin was tougher, but that one, too, quickly yielded to her skill. He could feel pressure, but no pain, as she started the actual suturing, and he closed his eyes against the glare of the overhead light.

"You needn't worry that I'll fall asleep on you, Doctor," he said, seeing the after-image of the light against his closed lids as she set the first suture. "I'm aware that I ought to stay awake for a few hours, until we're sure my brain wasn't bruised by all that banging around. Your light is brutal, though. Besides, you don't need me to supervise."

"I appreciate the vote of confidence," she said archly, continuing to work. "Talk to me, if you want. Tell me about your accident."

"Not much to tell," Adam said. "I blew a tire at speed, just north of the Forth Road Bridge. Fortunately, I was driving a Range Rover—totalled the car, but here I am."

"Happy Christmas," she said lightly. "Is your practice here in Edinburgh?"

"Aye, over at Jordanburn—or Royal Edinburgh Hospital, to your generation, I suppose. Jordanburn would be before your time."

She chuckled. "I'm not *that* young, Doctor," she said. "Besides that, I'm fond of ancient history. What's your specialty?"

He cracked an eye up at her again, venturing a faint smile. The efficient Dr. Lockhart had a tart sense of humor, besides being very attractive.

"Would you be put off if I told you I'm a psychiatrist?" he asked.

"Not at all. It beats the hours of *this* job. *Are* you a psychiatrist?"

Closing his eyes again, Adam controlled a chuckle. "I am. How about you? Surgical resident?"

"No, ER specialist. I'm here on a two-year contract to help set up trauma centers in the Edinburgh area. It's a notion that's just catching on, this side of the pond—and about time, too."

"Well, especially this morning, I have to agree," Adam said. "May I ask where you did your training?"

"Stanford and USC," she replied. "California's really on the cutting edge of this kind of technology. I started out in reconstructive surgery, after I finished my general surgical residency—which means you shouldn't have much scarring to show for this morning's misadventure. I found I missed working in the ER, though, so I switched to trauma management. There's a special exhilaration about working with patients who come in messed up and you fix them. Every day is different. And you can't beat it for people-watching."

Adam grimaced slightly as a stitch pulled, though it didn't really hurt; a part of him just thought it should.

"I prefer my people-watching under slightly less chaotic conditions," he said. "What does the 'X' stand for?"

She chuckled. "I was wondering how long it would take you to ask. Everyone does. Care to guess?"

"If I guess it in three, will you allow me to take you to dinner

265

some evening?'' he countered, cracking an eye open and squinting against the light. ''Assuming, of course, that I survive this.''

''Oh, you'll survive,'' she said blandly. ''But that's hardly a fair wager—unless Mr. Sykes told you, of course. Did you, Tony?''

The orderly's rich chuckle rumbled from Adam's other side.

''No, ma'am, I did not. But maybe Dr. Sinclair would let *you* pick the restaurant, if he doesn't guess.''

She laughed as she set another suture. ''That sounds fair to me. Dr. Sinclair, what do you think?''

Adam closed his eyes and smiled. ''Is it Xenia?''

''No.''

''Xanthe?''

''No, you're not even warm.''

''How about Xanthippe, the wife of Socrates?''

''Sorry, you owe me dinner. It's Ximena.''

''Ah, the wife of El Cid,'' Adam replied.

She laughed delightedly. ''Very good. That's precisely where my mother got the name. The film had just come out, a few months before I was born. It's actually spelled Chimene on my birth certificate, but I changed it to the 'X' spelling when I was an undergraduate—my gesture toward rebellion, I suppose. I liked the spelling even after I'd grown past that, though, so I've kept it. And it's a great conversation starter, as you've just aptly illustrated.''

''I can't argue with that,'' Adam murmured, looking up at her again. ''That makes your initials *X.L.* And you do, don't you?''

She was setting a last suture and cocked him a droll look.

''Why, Doctor, how kind of you to say so. I'll assume that you *may* still be in shock, but that's one of the nicer things a patient has ever said to me.''

Adam smiled. ''I'm trying to live down the old adage that physicians are notoriously poor patients.''

''Well, you're bidding fair to prove the adage wrong,'' she said, tossing her instruments onto the tray. ''That's it, you're done. Mr. Sykes, let's get a dressing on that.''

As Adam tentatively opened his eyes, squinting against the light, Dr. Lockhart was stripping off her gloves, tossing them inside-out on the instrument tray. She switched off the light, then retrieved Adam's chart and began writing up her notes.

''You're about to ask, so I'll tell you anyway,'' she said, not looking up. ''You have eight sutures in the first laceration and six in the scalp wound, in case you lost track of the count. I could've done it in less, but you didn't need a scar on your noble brow. Give it a few months, and you'll never know you were cut."

"Thank you very much," Adam said with a grin, suffering Sykes to apply a sterile pad smeared with antiseptic goo, which he then taped in place with strips of adhesive.

When that was accomplished, Sykes helped him sit up so that Dr. Lockhart could fit a sling to his right arm—an ungainly contraption of canvas and nylon straps. As he lay back, exhausted with the effort that sitting had cost him, a lab technician stuck his head into the room, glass tubes rattling in the wire rack he carried.

"Is this the patient for admission, Dr. Lockhart?" he asked.

"Yes, it is," she said. "Dr. Sinclair is being very cooperative— for a doctor—so I'm sure he won't object while you ply your vampire trade for a minute or two."

The prospect of blood being drawn made Adam flash on the clandestine visit someone had made to Gillian Talbot's bedside at Jordanburn.

"Actually, I *will* object," he said uneasily. "I don't think we need to run up additional expense for National Health with needless blood work. I'm only going to be here overnight."

"But those are hospital rules," the technician began.

"And I'm telling you it isn't necessary," Adam said, glancing at Dr. Lockhart. "I hope I don't have to threaten to walk out of here, to save the tax-payers unnecessary expense."

Chuckling, she waved the technician off. "Let him be, David. It isn't worth a fight. He's a psychiatrist. I don't think they like needles. And speaking of needles, Dr. Sinclair," she went on, making another notation on his chart, "what's the status on your tetanus immunization? When was the last time you had a booster?"

"I keep horses, Dr. Lockhart," he said, smiling. "I get a routine tetanus booster in January of years divisible by five. You've stuck me with as many needles as I intend to put up with for one day."

"Have it your way," she said with a shrug, though she smiled. "Mr. Sykes, you might as well take Dr. Sinclair up to his room."

As Sykes wheeled him out, Dr. Lockhart following as far as the charge desk, Adam failed to notice another staff consultant in scrub greens keenly watching his progress. It had not been part of Preston Wemyss' plan to get drafted for an emergency appendectomy this morning—not when he had already pulled so many strings to be on ER call to deal with this particular patient.

It was probably the fastest appendectomy Wemyss had ever performed—and done at no appreciably greater risk for the patient, who now was stable in recovery—but it had not been fast enough to get back down to Emergency before Angela brought in the injured Adam Sinclair. Also contrary to plan, Sinclair's injuries had been slight, and their nature such that the talented Dr. Lockhart had been a natural to take the case, especially since the patient was an eminent fellow physician; and once she had sent the patient off for X-rays, it was too late to try to intervene without arousing suspicion—which meant that Wemyss would have to resort to other means to accomplish his task.

Watching until the orderly had disappeared into the lift with Sinclair's gurney, Wemyss waited for Dr. Lockhart to disappear into the physicians' lounge, then casually walked over toward the treatment room that Sinclair had just vacated. When he was sure no one was watching, he ducked inside.

As he had hoped, Sykes had not lingered to tidy the room before taking Sinclair upstairs. Beside where the gurney had been, suturing debris still covered one of the stainless-steel tables, Sinclair's blood staining discarded gauze sponges and the surgeon's gloves. Smiling, Wemyss glided over to the table and stuffed several of the bloodier sponges into one of the inside-out gloves, which he then slipped into one of the pockets of his scrub pants. As he came out, he accosted one of the student nurses, directing her attention to the room.

"We need an orderly to prep this room right away, Miss Harper," he said. "Treatment rooms in the ER must always be cleared immediately a patient has left, so they'll be ready for the next emergency. See to it, please."

So saying, he headed off to his office to inspect his find. Foiled in his original intentions, he would explore alternative options for neutralizing the resilient Sinclair, or at least lowering his resistance to more esoteric attack; but one way or another, he was determined that Sinclair should not survive the night.

Adam, meanwhile, had settled into his cheerless room and was gazing at the ceiling. It was a double room, but he had no roommate. He was free to sit up if he wished, but his ribs and shoulder hurt less if he stayed nearly flat, and his head was starting to throb as the local anesthetic wore off, both from the lacerations and the thump he had taken. A nurse had brought him his initial dose of the medication prescribed by Dr. Lockhart, but the two yellow capsules were only beginning to take the edge off his discomfort. He knew he would be given something stronger if he asked, but he also knew that anything much stronger was likely to dull his edge for defending himself while he lay in these unprotected surroundings. Erecting the necessary wards around the room took far more effort than it should have done, for his head pounded when he tried to concentrate, but by the time McLeod stuck his head in the door, grinning as he saw the face he was looking for, the inspector could sense the potency of what Adam had wrought.

"You've been a busy lad, haven't you?" McLeod said, as he came in and dragged a metal chair nearer the head of the bed. "How're you doing? You look like something the cat dragged in."

"I *feel* like something the cat didn't want anymore," Adam replied with a grimace, pressing his slung arm against his chest to brace himself as he operated the mechanism that raised the head of his bed slightly. "Did you make those calls?"

"I did. Your mother was appalled, of course, but realized immediately that she must stay where she is to protect Gillian. I persuaded young Lovat that he was needed there for the same reason. And the others have also been informed. They'll all be working to send you healing energy over the next few days."

Adam allowed himself a relieved sigh. "You're a good man, Noel, and an indispensable Second. God, this was rotten timing! I didn't need to be laid up just now."

"Well, accidents happen," McLeod replied. "At least you weren't killed. Incidentally, your car's been towed to a police impound yard north of the Firth. Apparently you did a hell of a job on it. I've given the information to Humphrey, and he's checking on the insurance details, but it's pretty clear that you're going to be ordering up a new one."

Adam managed a wan grin. "Can't complain. It saved my life. Odd about the tire, though. I must've hit something."

"I hope so," McLeod said, suddenly very sober.

"What do you mean?" Adam cocked his head at McLeod. "Do you know something I don't?"

McLeod shook his head. "No, no, it's just that you yourself commented on the timing. And you *could* easily have been killed. Certain parties would have found that very convenient."

A shiver raised the fine hairs on Adam's forearms.

"I wish you hadn't said that," he murmured. "I'm already paranoid enough that I wouldn't let them do a routine blood work-up on me. I found myself remembering how someone got to Gillian. They could have killed her just as easily. I'm vulnerable here."

"Maybe you shouldn't stay here overnight, then," McLeod said. "Or I could put a guard on the door. . . ."

"Now we're *both* being paranoid," Adam said with a shake of his head. "The plain truth of the matter is that I've just suffered a serious car crash and ought to be under medical observation for twenty-four hours. I'm probably fine, but it really is easier on everybody if I stay overnight. It's pointless to burden Philippa. Besides, trauma assessment is a little outside her recent experience—probably about fifty years outside it. I'll be fine. As you obviously noticed when you came into the room, I've already put a fair amount of energy into warding it."

"I can't argue *that*. You think they'll let you out in the morning, then?"

"They should, unless Dr. Lockhart and I are both totally wrong. Incidentally, I'd appreciate it if you could arrange for Humphrey to collect me around eleven. As you can see, this room hasn't got a phone."

"Will do," McLeod agreed. "And since you've caved in to independent medical opinion and actually agreed to stay, I have to assume that you really are hurting, and that you're too knackered to bother with that Balmoral material this afternoon."

Adam closed his eyes briefly. "You assume correctly," he said. "Could you plan to bring it up to the house tomorrow afternoon, after I've got my wits about me better? It's about time we all touched bases together anyway. Peregrine ought to see it too."

"I'll set it up. Anything else I can do for you?"

"Not that I can think of."

"I'll let you get some rest, then." McLeod rose and tossed him a mock salute. "So long, then, boss. Get a good night's sleep, if you can find a comfortable position, and I'll see you tomorrow."

Adam had missed lunch by the time he was installed in his room, but after McLeod left, he succeeded in wheedling a snack of tea and sandwiches out of one of the nurses. He napped then, even though someone came to rouse him every hour to take his vital signs, until Dr. Lockhart came to check on him just before dinner. Even broken sleep seemed to have eased his aching head, other than a tenderness about his bandaged wounds, but nearly every other part of his body ached even worse. At his request, Dr. Lockhart increased the prescribed medication, then bade him a friendly good-night, with permission to sleep, and continued on about her rounds. After a light supper and two more of the yellow capsules, Adam let himself escape into proper sleep. He had been asleep for perhaps an hour when he had the dream.

270

At first he thought the man was Ian MacPherson, the Mason blasted by lightning the week before, but then he realized it was another Master Mason. In fact, there were lots of Master Masons, formally bedecked in blue-bordered aprons and sashes and collars, standing on the black and white checkerboard floor of a Masonic temple, working a ritual. Though Adam was not a Mason and had never witnessed a Masonic ritual firsthand, he knew it for what it was, because most workings of this sort tapped into a common pool of esoteric tradition, forms differing but alike in their focus toward the Light.

The dream unfolded. The man he had taken for MacPherson, who seemed to be the Master of this Lodge, was reading from a great book, several of his officers around him, perhaps thirty other men listening attentively to his words. Adam could not hear what the man said, but he sensed that it was sacred teaching—which followed, if Freemasonry truly tapped into the universal Mystery Schools.

Suddenly the Master faltered, he and then his officers and brethren starting to look uncertainly around the Lodge room, wide, frightened eyes apprehensively searching empty air, which suddenly was charged with static energy. In the split second before it happened, Adam knew what was coming and tried to warn them, but it was too late. With an ear-splitting crack, the ceiling exploded in fire and a shower of falling plaster and tangled roof beams and shattered slates, utterly blasting the roof away so that the room lay open to the sky! Clouds roiled and churned above the breached roof as lightning continued to pound at the building, ceasing abruptly then as a terrible silence descended, gradually broken by the moans and cries of the injured.

He was gasping as he came up out of it, heart pounding, and he had no doubt that he had tapped into something real and terrible—whether about to happen or already done, he had no idea. If it had already happened, there was little he could do; but if the dream had been a premonition, as his dreams sometimes were, it might be possible to convey a warning and avert some of the disaster.

He racked his brain for some clue as to *which* Masonic Hall it might have been—as if his limited knowledge of such things would enlighten him. But maybe McLeod would know. McLeod was a Master Mason. Maybe McLeod could help him track it down.

That hope lent him the strength to haul himself out of his bed and stagger over to the wardrobe, every muscle protesting. God, he couldn't believe how stiff he'd gotten just from a few hours' sleep! A part of him longed for a hot shower to ease the aches, but he knew that would have to wait.

Pulling a robe from the wardrobe, he thrust his left arm through its sleeve and drew the rest of the robe over his right shoulder and sling, then hobbled out to the nurses' station to look for a phone. The head nurse looked shocked.

"Dr. Sinclair! What are you doing out of bed? Go back this instant!"

"I have to make a phone call," Adam said. "It's important. Can I use this phone?"

He was already leaning over the counter to lift up one of the instruments from behind, setting it on the ledge and shifting the receiver to his right hand as he poised his left to dial.

"Is it nine for an outside line?" he asked.

"Yes, but—"

"Thank you."

He dialed 9, then McLeod's home number, but it rang busy for the next five minutes. It took him three tries to get through, as his keeper became more and more impatient and other staff congregated and wondered what to do about the eccentric Dr. Sinclair. It was McLeod's wife who finally answered.

"Jane, this is Adam," he said. "Is Noel there?"

"No, he isn't, Adam," she said. "He got a call-out just a little while ago, and he rang up your Mr. Lovat and left. You've just missed him."

"Damn!" Adam said softly. "Did he say where he was going?"

"I'm afraid not," Jane replied. "But it must have been north of here, because he asked Mr. Lovat to meet him—and Mr. Lovat lives up on your estate, doesn't he?"

"Yes," Adam whispered.

"Dear me. He said something about an explosion at a Masonic Lodge. Adam, do you think this is connected with that awful business last week? Is Noel in danger?"

"I don't know. Maybe," Adam murmured. "Jane, are you sure he didn't mention anything more specific?"

"I'm sorry, Adam, but you don't realize how little he talks about his work."

"No, I can appreciate that," Adam said quietly. He sighed. "When he comes home, Jane—or if he should ring you—tell him it's important that he get back to me as soon as possible. Have him call the twenty-four-hour number here at the hospital, whatever the hour. Have you got that?''

"Of course, Adam. Are you all right?"

"Yes, I'm fine. Just tell him. I've got to go now. Sorry to disturb you.''

He was shaking as he hung up the receiver, and the head nurse was staring at him. She drew herself up officiously as their eyes met.

"Dr. Sinclair, I really must insist that you go back to bed, or I'm going to have to call Dr. Lockhart. This is most irregular.''

"Sorry to have disturbed your routine, Matron,'' he said quietly. "It really was important. And if an Inspector McLeod should ring back later tonight, no matter what the hour, I want you to call me to the phone. I can't tell you how urgent this is. Would you make a note of that, please?''

Reluctantly she agreed. Adam watched her write it down, then suffered her to follow him back to his room, where she lingered to take his vital signs and make notations on his chart before returning to her station. When she had gone, he lay awake for several hours staring at the ceiling, casting back in memory for the dream, gradually coming to wonder whether his accident and the dream were in any way connected.

# CHAPTER TWENTY-SEVEN

IN Dunfermline, within that hour, Peregrine Lovat pulled up at a scene of chaos and confusion. Parts of Dunfermline's Masonic Hall still were burning, half a dozen fire engines knocking down the last of the flames while rescue workers sifted through the rubble for survivors. The school across the street had already become a temporary morgue for the dead, and yet another ambulance pulled away, blue lights flashing and siren wailing, as Peregrine slid the little Morris Minor into a space directly across from McLeod's familiar black BMW.

Eager but also a little nervous, for he had never gone on one of these assignments without Adam, Peregrine collected his sketch-box and piled out of the car, shading his eyes against the glare of acetylene work lights and rescue spots as he crossed the street and approached a uniformed officer manning the barricades.

"I've been asked to meet Detective Chief Inspector McLeod here," he said. "My name is Lovat."

"Right through there, Mr. Lovat," the officer said, pointing into the haze behind him. "Just mind the rescue workers."

"I'll do that. Thank you."

Peregrine ducked under the yellow tape the officer lifted and headed toward a familiar grey head and topcoat at the center of a small group of uniforms. McLeod's gruff voice filtered through to him above the surrounding din.

"I want statements in writing from anyone in the area who saw anything—*anything,* you understand?" the inspector was saying testily. "I don't care how outlandish it sounds. We'll sort out the sense from the gibberish back at the precinct."

The uniformed group broke up and dispersed. McLeod started to move away himself, then caught sight of Peregrine picking his way toward him across the litter-strewn ground.

"Finally!" the inspector muttered somewhat ungraciously, motioning him to hurry up. "What did you do, come by way of

Aberdeen? Come on, I want the two of us to take a look around inside.''

Peregrine knew better than to take offense at the older man's brusqueness. He had spent time enough now in the inspector's company to know that with McLeod irascibility was a sign of a troubled mind—and he had every reason to be deeply troubled now. Even from outside, Peregrine could sense the harsh, discordant residue of intentional violence emanating from the building's smoking interior.

It was a resonance he was learning to recognize and abhor, very like what he had sensed at Baltierny and Calton Hill. No need to ask McLeod for any confirmation concerning the agency responsible for the destruction he saw before him. The inspector's strong face bore something of the bruised, angry expression of a boxer pulling himself up after being downed by a foul blow—and the look of someone determined to settle the account with compound interest.

McLeod was first up a flight of stone steps to the doorway that had been the Lodge's front entrance. On the way in, they stood aside for a pair of rescue workers carrying a motionless black-bagged form between them, belted onto a stretcher. Both men were covered in dust and ashes, their faces filthy and haggard.

"God, MacKinnon, how many does that make?" McLeod said bitterly, his expression one of bleak disbelief.

The men shuffled to a halt, both of them clearly numbed by what they had seen.

"Eleven to hospital and seventeen for the morgue," the one in front said, with a dour shake of his head. "Nobody walked away from this one. The only good news is that we think that's everyone accounted for.''

He threw a pitying glance over his shoulder at the shrouded figure on the stretcher.

"This old gent must've been their Lodge Master. We found him under half a ton of rubble in the meeting room upstairs—he must have been standing right under a beam when the roof collapsed. Poor bastard probably never knew what hit him!''

He sighed and signalled his companion to move on. McLeod stood aside to let them pass, his grizzled head bowed low. Whether the inspector was thinking or praying, Peregrine couldn't be sure. A few seconds later, the older man gave himself a shake and squared his broad shoulders with a snap.

"Right, Mr. Lovat," he said heavily. "The medics, it seems, are all through. Now it's our turn.''

He led the way through the remains of the vestibule into what had once been a spacious entry-hall. The parquetry floor was a tangle of fallen plaster and charred lathes and timbers. Off to their right, a handsome staircase led up to a mezzanine now open to the sky. The whole place was saturated with the stench of burning. The magnitude of the destruction made Peregrine feel sick at heart. He could only guess at the effect it was having on McLeod, who had shared a fraternal bond with the men who had died here.

"We'll take it room by room," McLeod said. "And watch where you put your feet. I don't want you falling through a hole and landing in hospital like Adam. We're short-handed enough, as it is."

By "we," Peregrine suddenly realized, he meant the Hunting Lodge. This tacit indication of McLeod's acceptance was as heartening as it was unlooked for. Somewhat reassured, Peregrine shook off his sick dismay in a wave of fresh resolve.

"Are we looking for anything in particular," he asked quietly, "or are we just looking?"

McLeod leveled bright blue eyes at him through his aviator spectacles.

"You just *look*, laddie. And if you *see* anything, I want to know about it."

The doorway just beyond the stairs led into what had once been a formal reception room running the full length of that side of the building. Ducking under the door's burn-scarred lintel with McLeod, Peregrine found himself surveying a devastation of smashed glass and broken picture frames.

"This looks like some sort of gallery," he remarked softly.

"Aye." McLeod had stopped to right a life-sized, three-quarter length portrait of a silver-haired man with a handlebar moustache who wore the regalia of a Masonic Master. "This Lodge has had a long and distinguished history. Its members set this room aside for displaying their mementoes. . . ."

His voice trailed off. Coming over to stand at the inspector's side, Peregrine took a long look at the portrait. Despite smoke stains and singe-marks, he could see it had been sensitively done. The Past Master's face was strong and stern; the painted blue eyes that looked back at Peregrine seemed infinitely sad, as if the man himself were grieving for what had happened here. The sense of living presence was so strong that Peregrine couldn't believe it was just his imagination.

*We're here to help*, he found himself assuring the man in the portrait. *I just wish you knew what happened and could tell us about it.*

Beside him, McLeod gave a sudden, jerking shudder and groaned aloud. Startled, Peregrine looked to stare. The inspector was weaving on his feet, his blue eyes blank and unfocused behind his glasses. His mouth worked. For a few seconds, there was no sound. Then an unfamiliar voice whispered from his lips.

"An intruder broached the defenses," it rasped. "The vile servant of a viler master. The temple was profaned . . . marked with the sign of an ancient enemy. . . ."

The hoarse voice trailed off on a shuddering sigh. Peregrine gaped at McLeod, then realized what was happening. One of McLeod's particular esoteric gifts was his ability to act as a medium—as Peregrine himself had witnessed once before at Melrose, where McLeod had allowed the spirit of Michael Scot to speak through his physical body. Now, evidently, he had given permission for a past member of this Lodge to do the same.

Another shudder shook McLeod's powerful frame, causing him to stagger, and Peregrine caught him under one arm, uncertain what he should do.

"Cleanse the temple!" the voice urged on a rising note. "Find and remove the sign of desecration!"

The urgency of the plea seemed to demand a response. Heart pounding, Peregrine found his tongue.

"We will!" he promised. "Just tell me, please, where to look!"

But the speaker's further discourse was reduced to an inaudible mutter. Without warning, McLeod's head snapped back as if he had been given an upper cut to the jaw. Peregrine felt him stiffen; then he exhaled on a soft groan and buckled at the knees.

Peregrine tried to ease his collapse, scrambling to brace himself as McLeod sagged toward the floor. As both of them staggered to their knees, Peregrine's vision blurred. All at once, in his mind's eye, he saw the image of a heavy marble-topped table, like an altar. The sides of the table were decorated with panels carved in low relief.

Details of the central panel stood out in his mind—the image of a circle enclosing a star-symbol made from two interlocking triangles that he somehow knew to be the Seal of Solomon. The circle was flanked by columns on either side, each column surmounted by a globe that represented on one hand the map of the world and on the other the map of the heavens. Even as he tried to visualize the adjacent panels, McLeod gave a muzzy mutter and raised his head.

His blue eyes focused with a snap. As his free hand groped for support, he gulped air and let it out again with a *whuff.*

"God, I *hate* it when they do that!" he wheezed in a voice that was once again his own.

His face was drained of color, exactly as it had been at Melrose, after the spirit of Michael Scot had released him. Searching the other's eyes, Peregrine said, "Can you stand up? I'd suggest a sit-down, but the bloody floor's literally covered with glass. You haven't cut your hand, have you?"

Shaking his head, McLeod lifted his free hand from the floor and gingerly dusted glass and ash from it, using Peregrine's support then to stagger shakily to his feet. Still gripping Peregrine's arm for balance, he drew a succession of deep breaths that gradually grew easier, till his respiration came back to normal.

"Better?" Peregrine asked.

"Aye," McLeod said. He straightened up slowly and tested his balance before letting go of Peregrine's arm. "Aye, that's more like it." He let out another heavy sigh. "I shouldn't do that without preparation. But the need was urgent."

"Did those references to *the temple* make sense to you, then?" Peregrine asked.

"What did I say about the temple?" McLeod replied. "I don't always remember what comes out in these exercises."

His nonchalance was heartening. Dutifully Peregrine repeated what had been said, word for word, as nearly as he could recall it. Sighing again, McLeod nodded, assessing what Peregrine had told him.

"All right. I can't tell you yet *exactly* what it means, but he's given fairly clear instructions. In a sense, all work done in the Lodges is done in the Temple of the Inner Planes—but every Lodge also has its physical temple, usually on an upper floor of the building. That's where we need to go."

He flicked his gaze to the battered portrait still leaning against the wall. The inscription at the base of the sprung gilt frame identified the subject by name, *John Joseph Anderson,* along with the dates of his tenure as Master of the Lodge. Smiling grimly, McLeod gave the portrait a grave, understated salute.

"Thank you for your good counsel, Worshipful Master," he said softly. "Mr. Lovat and I will take it from here."

Despite damage to the carpeting and the banisters, the stairs themselves were still solid underfoot. The upper floor was strongly lit by acetylene lanterns as teams of firemen continued their task of securing the building, damping down exposed floorboards and clearing away still-smouldering debris. An icy wind was blowing down through the gaping black hole in the roof, with the occasional snowflake swirling in the lantern light.

"This way," McLeod said, pointing ahead to what remained of a doorway on the other side of the mezzanine.

The large room beyond, like the mezzanine itself, was lit up by torchlight. They had to duck low to get past a tangle of fallen beams. The floor here was dangerously weak in places, a checkerboard maze of fractured black and white tiles laid over wooden underflooring, interspersed with ragged gaps where the fire had eaten its way through to the rooms below.

The worst of the damage was at the eastern end of the room, perhaps the very center of the devastation. Here, open to the sky, large heaps of rubble and shattered roof beams made a veritable maze. A few picks and spades lay near a remaining lantern, to show where the rescue workers had been digging in their efforts to recover the body of the Lodge's Master. Two large slabs of scorched and sooty marble jutted at angles out of the mound of ashes and plaster like a pair of bookends knocked askew.

"That may be what we want," said McLeod, pointing to the concentration of debris. "Let's have a closer look."

Taking the lantern with them, the two men worked their way cautiously toward their goal. Seen at close range, the canted slabs proved to be two parts of a marble-topped table which had been split down the middle. The charred remains of the supporting wooden side panels showed a variety of what Peregrine took to be Masonic symbols, carved in low relief, including a Seal of Solomon.

"I had a glimpse of a table like this, while you were occupied with your Mr. Anderson," he murmured, touching the design of interlocking triangles. "This symbol, in particular. I'd guess that the *sign of desecration* he spoke of must be buried somewhere underneath all this."

"Aye, let's see if we can shift some more of this rubbish," McLeod agreed.

First with hands and then taking up the tools the rescue workers had not yet come back to retrieve, they set to work clearing away the larger pieces of debris from the base of the table. When there was nothing left but heaps of still-warm ash, they went more slowly, taking time to sift each spadeful of grey powder as they shoveled it aside. Peregrine was starting to wonder if they were going to be at it all night when his shovel turned over something that glinted a dull metallic grey in the light of their worklamp.

Without thinking, he reached down with his bare hand to pick it up and got a jolt like a brush with an electrified fence. He gave a yip and sat abruptly back on his haunches.

"Peregrine, what the—"

Peregrine pointed to the fragment of metal he had uncovered, almost too shaken to register that this was the first time McLeod had ever addressed him by his Christian name.

"That," he said. "It gave me a shock when I went to pick it up. I think it may be what we're looking for."

He flexed his fingers. The knuckles were still tingling unpleasantly. As he picked himself up, dusting ash off his seat and hands, McLeod crouched down to inspect the find more closely. The inspector's hand dipped into a coat pocket as he continued to study the item, and emerged wearing a familiar sapphire ring. The hand with the ring sketched a sequence of symbols over the item which seemed to enliven the very air around it—then dipped again into the coat to produce a handkerchief.

"Well, well, well," McLeod muttered, clucking his tongue as he carefully lifted the object in the handkerchief's insulating folds.

As he held it up to the light, Peregrine could see that it was the slagged and twisted remains of a silvery disk, perhaps two inches across. His eyes went wide behind his spectacles.

"Is that it?" he faltered. "Is that the *sign* we were told to look for?"

"You tell me," said McLeod. "Is it?"

Drawing a deep breath, Peregrine narrowed his eyes and shifted his focus. The ensuing blur resolved into the ghostly image of a snarling lynx head.

"Dear God, it's a Lynx medallion!" he whispered. "It's what I've been getting glimpses of, since this all began, except I've never really seen one at firsthand."

McLeod grinned wolfishly and wrapped the handkerchief more securely around it, then sketched another symbol over the bundle.

"Well, we've got one now," he told the artist, "and I'd say it confirms responsibility for this piece of work." He presented the bundle to Peregrine. "Adam's certainly going to want to see it. Since I don't know how soon I'll be free to get back with him in person, maybe you'd better take it and deliver it to him as soon as he gets home."

Nodding, Peregrine wrapped the bundle in another layer of his own handkerchief, then gingerly stuffed it away in an inside pocket of his duffel coat and got to his feet. McLeod threw a glance back over his shoulder, then spread both his hands palm-down over the area of the ruined altar. He held that posture for the space of several heartbeats, lips moving silently in what Peregrine assumed was a prayer. Then his right hand moved to sketch a banishing pentagram in the air.

Peregrine felt a slight tug at his senses, as if something sticky had just been pulled away from his skin. Then all at once, the atmosphere in their immediate area seemed to clear. Peregrine was reminded of that moment in Helena Pringle's flat, when Adam had united his efforts with those of Christopher Houston to rid the place of uncleanliness.

After another moment of introspective silence, McLeod squared his shoulders and sighed.

"There," he said quietly. "Now the Brethren can rest easy."

# CHAPTER TWENTY-EIGHT

EVERYTHING was quiet at Edinburgh Royal Infirmary, where Adam Sinclair lay restless in his hospital bed. His dream of earlier in the evening had left his nerves a-jangle. Ten o'clock had come and gone without bringing any word from McLeod. He knew he should try to get some rest, but between the aches in his body and the worry brewing in his mind, he found himself unable to settle down for more than a few minutes at a time. Dutifully he went through the familiar exercise of composing himself for sleep, usually fail-proof, only to wake up again with a start a few moments later, haunted by the vividness of the dream he feared increasingly had been a portent of whatever disaster McLeod now was dealing with.

A brief flurry of activity at around eleven marked the nurses' change of shift. By then, Adam had abandoned all pretense of trying to go to sleep. As the changeover bustle died away, the nighttime hush of the hospital floor became almost oppressive. After another quarter of an hour, unable to stand the suspense any longer, he struggled once more out of bed and dragged on his hospital-issue dressing gown, clutching it sketchily about him with his good hand as he hobbled lamely over to the door and peered out.

The dimly-lit corridor was empty. The nurses' station at the far end of the hall appeared to be unoccupied. He could hear lowered voices coming from the wardroom toilets; evidently some other patient had gotten up without leave and was about to be chivvied solicitously back to bed. Sighing inwardly over the sheepdog instinct that seemed to be an ingrained feature of all competently trained nurses, he eased out of his room as quietly as his sore muscles would allow and made for the door to the television lounge, determined to catch the late night news before he was discovered and sent back to his room.

At this hour he had the place entirely to himself. He left the overhead light switched off—no point in advertising his presence—and limped stiffly over to turn on the TV. As he was shuffling back to the nearest chair, the sound came on, cutting in with the late night credits and voice-over headlines for the local regional news. The first item on the agenda was a grim proclamation of disaster.

*"Seventeen die and more are injured as a mysterious explosion causes the collapse of a Masonic Lodge in Dunfermline."*

Adam's senses reeled as other, lesser headlines passed through his awareness as a blur. Eyes drawn to the brightening screen, he groped for the arm of the chair and lowered himself into it as the on-screen presenter went on to deliver a more detailed account of the facts:

"Seventeen men died tonight and at least eleven more were injured in a freak explosion which utterly destroyed the upper floor of a Masonic Lodge in Dunfermline and seriously damaged the rest of the premises. The incident, which is being investigated by the police, occurred shortly after eight o'clock. Eyewitnesses claim to have seen what has been described variously as a bolt of lightning or a ball of fire strike the roof of the Lodge. . . ."

The story continued, accompanied by camera footage taken at the scene. Adam grimaced at the sight of the roofless, smouldering building, its shattered windows gaping like blind eyes in the lurid glare of the emergency floodlights. There was no doubt in his mind that this was the event he had witnessed in his dream. Thinking back on the timing, he realized that the two events must have occurred simultaneously.

The camera cut away from the devastation to an earnest television journalist.

"Given the controversial nature of the eyewitness reports," she was saying, "the task of determining the cause of the explosion has already been complicated by public speculation. When we asked whether or not the police intend to treat the incident as suspicious, Detective Chief Inspector Noel McLeod had this to say."

Adam sat forward as McLeod's familiar face appeared on the screen, a streak of ash smudged across one cheekbone. He was looking drained and worn, and spoke curtly into the microphone, as if at least a part of his mind was preoccupied with matters far more important than satisfying the demands of the media.

"Yes, there is some evidence to suggest that the source of the explosion might have come from outside rather than inside the building," he told his interviewer, "but we have not yet ruled out more conventional explanations, such as a gas mains explosion."

"Could it have been a terrorist bomb, Inspector?" another reporter asked from off-camera.

McLeod's gaze turned wearily in the direction of the questioner. "We have no evidence at this time to support such a suggestion. Any speculation that anyone might make at this time must be purely conjectural. Quite frankly, we're still most concerned at this time with making certain that there are no more bodies buried under the rubble."

"When *do* you expect to have a statement on the cause, Inspector?" the first reporter asked.

"When we do, I assure you it will come through the appropriate channels and the media will be notified," McLeod said patiently. "I must emphasize that assessing the forensic evidence in a disaster of this magnitude will take time. I have no further statement at this time."

As he turned away and the camera switched back to the reporter for a quick recap, Adam reflected that this might almost have been a repeat of the Calton Hill incident, but on a much grander scale. The masters of the Lynx were escalating their operations at a frightening rate. He switched off the TV and stared blindly at the blank screen while he weighed up the import of this latest act of mayhem. He was not aware that anyone else had entered the room until suddenly the overhead light switched on and a female voice broke in upon his reverie in tones of mingled concern and exasperation.

"What *are* we going to do with you, Dr. Sinclair? It's nearly midnight, when all *good* patients are supposed to be in bed!"

Adam blinked himself out of the blackness of his thoughts and raised his eyes to meet those of a very attractive accuser. She was a nurse he hadn't seen before, a slight young redhead with a tip-tilted nose and more twinkle than frown in her grey eyes. Her name tag read *J. Brown, RN*. She folded her arms across her chest and cocked her head at him sympathetically.

"I have to say, you don't look as if you're much enjoying being up. If you're too uncomfortable to sleep, there's no point in being too polite to say so. You've got more medication on the way up, if you're needing some relief. Why don't you come on back to your room while I ring the pharmacy and see what's holding it up?"

Adam's wrenched and tired joints were aching like a bad tooth. Suddenly the thought of sleep seemed overwhelmingly attractive. But first he had one last task to fulfill.

"I'll come quietly," he told the nurse with a strained smile. "I believe the arrestee *is* entitled to one phone call, though."

"At this hour?"

"Please," Adam said. "It's very important."

The nurse took a second look at his face, then capitulated with an indulgent shake of her head, like a mother humoring a wayward child.

"All right, then," she told him. "But only a short one."

It seemed like a mile from the television lounge to the nurses' station. Leaning heavily on the counter, Adam repeated his performance of earlier in the evening in order to ring up McLeod's home telephone number. Jane answered almost at once.

"Hello, it's Adam again," he told her. "Look, I'm sorry to be phoning so late—"

"Not at all," said Jane. "I've been waiting up in case Noel should happen to call."

"Then he hasn't checked in yet?"

"No—which probably means he's still in the thick of things up at Dunfermline." She paused, then asked, "Have you seen the late night Scottish news?"

"Yes, that's why I'm ringing back. Naturally, I'm appalled, but if Noel's going to be in for a long night of it, I'm thinking it might be better for all concerned if we postpone our conversation till some time later tomorrow. He's obviously needed where he is. Better that the pair of us should get some sleep and come at the problem fresh."

"All right, I'll tell him, Adam."

As he was ringing off, the lift door adjoining the nurses' station opened with a whoosh to eject a spruce young man in a white lab coat marked *Pharmacy*. He was carrying a trayload of prescriptions packaged up in individual dispensing envelopes. He greeted the red-haired nurse with a jaunty wave and deposited the tray on the desk in front of her.

"There you are, Jeanne, my lass," he said cheerily. "All present and accounted for."

Jeanne cast an eye up at the clock above her head and clucked her tongue in mock disparagement.

"You weren't in any great hurry to get here, were you, Neil Redmond?" she observed. "Dr. Sinclair here was just about to write up a fresh set of orders for himself."

"Hey, don't blame me," Redmond said, with an apologetic look in Adam's direction. "I got waylaid by Dr. Wemyss. He barged into the office just as I was getting ready to bring these up to the floor."

"Dr. Wemyss? What's he doing here this late?"

"Must be on night call," the pharmacist said with a shrug. "He had a bee in his bonnet about somebody on the day shift misreading his orders for one of his patients—made me put the tray down and go back into the dispensary to check the records. If it hadn't been for that, I'd've been here ten minutes ago."

"All right, you're forgiven," the red-haired nurse said with a twinkle. She picked up the envelope with Adam's name attached and turned to him with a smile. "Come along, Dr. Sinclair. You've had your phone call—now it's time for your medicine."

Adam hardly glanced at the pair of yellow capsules the nurse tipped out of the envelope onto his hand. He swallowed them meekly and lay back with a long-drawn sigh to wait for the welcome painkiller to take effect, idly fingering his ring as he checked his wards for the last time. Very shortly, his eyelids began to droop. As his strung-out muscles began to relax at last, he allowed himself to drift into exhausted sleep.

For a long while his rest was deep and dreamless, a quiet voyage across calm, silent, featureless seas, blessedly tranquil. But after a time, the stillness began to resolve into sequences of imagery. Initially he viewed the passing scenes from outside, like pictures displayed in an art gallery. Then one of the pictures expanded to engulf him, and he found himself suddenly taking part in another extraordinarily vivid dream.

Only this time, the focus of the dream was entirely personal. He was lying on his back in his hospital bed, but the curtains surrounding the bed had been partially drawn, obscuring his view of the door and the room at large. The only illumination was the dim glimmer of a nightlight from the direction of the corridor. Suddenly he had the feeling that he was completely alone in this dream version of the hospital wing.

The sense of isolation sparked a vague sense of menace. Cautiously, he eased his dream-self up on one elbow to listen. After a moment his straining ears picked up furtive scuffles of movement somewhere in the region of the door. The sound conveyed the impression of some large, feral creature padding about in the dark.

Adam tensed at the sound and what it implied. Fortunately, his dream-self was not hampered by the injuries that impaired his physical body—though his thinking seemed more sluggish than usual for dreamtime activity. Moving very quietly, he drew himself into an upright sitting position. His ring was on his right hand, the stone turned inward, and he turned it under his thumb, seeing the flash-point of the stone as a clear blue beacon of more-than-light. The indistinct scuffling gave way to a stealthy scrabbling and sniffing, just on the other side of the curtains—which were the visual manifestation of the wards he had set, he suddenly realized. And whatever was approaching was working its way inexorably toward the place of Adam's concealment.

Something brushed against the curtain on the right of the bed. Instinctively, Adam flung up his hand and sketched a symbol of power in the air between himself and the unseen thing that was seeking to creep up on him. With the responsive quickening of the wards, the curtain went translucent. In the same heartbeat, the shadows at the bedside suddenly coalesced into a looming, bestial presence just the other side, all teeth, eyes, and darkness.

With a slavering hiss, it threw itself at the bed. The wards flared blue in the dark in a raw burst of sparks. For an instant, the creature hung silhouetted against the light of the energy grid as a huge, shambling cat-thing, fanged jaws gaping in menace. Then it uttered a piercing screech of pain and recoiled with a spring.

The backlash of opposing powers set the wards flickering. One of the boundary markers guttered and winked out. Outside the collapsing perimeter of power, the shadow wheeled and crouched for another spring. Adam knew what he *should* do, but his will seemed to be embedded in treacle. Before he could bring any new defenses to bear, the creature lunged again for his throat, *through* the breached wards!

The impact hurled him flat again, with enough force to drive the air from his lungs. As he gasped for breath, trying to fight it off, the shadow seemed to spread, crushing him under a smothering mass of darkness.

It was like being blanketed with a quilt weighted with lead, all suffocating weight and give. Groaning with the effort, Adam shifted its bulk with a massive effort and somehow managed to curl onto his side. The weight of darkness promptly redistributed, pressing in on him hungrily now from three sides instead of one.

The blood was pounding in his ears, his vision starting to blur, and he knew he did not have much time. He could feel his strength waning—and the evil fingering at the edges of his very soul, as the beast tested at his failing defenses. Seeking desperately beyond it for the source of the attack, he at last became dimly aware of a hostile human presence directing and controlling the dark beast from without.

The awareness gave him focus, so that, working his shoulders to and fro, he managed to bring his hands together long enough to execute a tight gesture of command. With the last air left in his lungs, he cried out the Word that was his to command in the world of the unseen.

The black pressure of the dream exploded into sudden, blazing radiance. The explosion stripped away the shadow and sent Adam hurtling backwards through gulfs of light so bright he had to close his eyes or risk being blinded. The dizzy sensation of freefall finally ended with a disorienting jolt that signalled his soul's return at last to his body. When he opened his eyes, gasping for breath, he saw around him once more the clean, bare confines of a hospital room.

His chest ached and his heart was racing. He made a move to lift himself on his elbows and moaned aloud as a fierce stab of pain shot down the right side of his body from his abused shoulder. He fell back dizzy and faint. He felt as bruised and breathless as if the struggle he had just survived had been physical rather than psychic.

He drew a deep breath to ground himself more solidly in the physical world, then painfully rolled onto his left side and levered himself to sit up without stressing his injured shoulder. Heart still pounding, he cast a groggy glance around the room at large, stiffening as he spotted an irregular patch of darkness underneath the bedside chair.

It was too dark and solid-looking to be a shadow. Trembling now with exhaustion, Adam sketched a banishing sign in the air and channeled the force of the gesture with a casting motion of his hand, gasping at the pain the movement cost him. But the shadow rippled and curled. Writhing like a worm on a griddle, it shriveled up and finally vanished in a puff of thin black smoke.

The psychic residue was like a chill whiff of carrion. Recoiling with a grimace of disgust, Adam gathered up the shreds of his remaining energy to reinstate the protective wards he had set earlier about the bed. By the time he was finished, he was close to passing out. Breathing hard, he lay back on his pillow and tried to clear his mind sufficiently to think. A part of him wanted desperately to go back to sleep, but he knew he didn't dare succumb. His thoughts were sluggish and oddly disjointed, as if he'd been drugged.

*This is not right,* he thought hazily. *Mefenamic acid shouldn't do this. The first two doses didn't affect me this way. Could Dr. Lockhart have changed my medication?*

*Surely not!* another part of him replied indignantly.

But the culprit had to be the medication he had taken just after midnight—not the expected painkiller and anti-inflammatory but a powerful sedative. The yellow capsules had looked the same as the ones he'd taken earlier, but he had not really paid that much attention.

A chill rippled up his spine as he realized he could easily be dead—from some other drug rather than the psychic attack facilitated by his vulnerable state. That he was not dead of a drug only pointed up the supreme arrogance of whomever was responsible for the attack—or perhaps their understandable reluctance to have his death seen as murder. Hence, the psychic attack. It also pointed to an agent of the Lynx in medical circles as well as in law enforcement. Now that Adam knew his danger, he did not intend to sleep again until he was back within the safe confines of Strathmourne.

Groaning at the pain, he rolled over and punched the nurses' call button. A few moments later, the door opened and the pretty red-haired nurse poked her head around the door frame.

"What can I do for you, Dr. Sinclair?" she said solicitously. "What's the matter? Can't you sleep?"

"What time is it?" he asked.

"Just five."

"Then there *is* something you can do for me," he said with an effort. "I'd like you to help me to a telephone. And as soon as I've spoken to my family and arranged transport, I intend to sign myself out."

Philippa Sinclair was already awake when she heard the telephone ring somewhere deep in the heart of the house. The sound carried with it the air of a summons. She slipped from her bed and reached for her quilted satin dressing gown. A moment later, the house-phone on her bedside table gave a tinkling chime. She sat back down on the edge of the bed and picked it up.

"Yes, Humphrey, what is it?" she asked calmly.

"It's Sir Adam, milady, ringing from hospital."

"Indeed?" she said. "Then you'd best put him on at once."

"Right away, milady."

There was a brief successions of clicks as Humphrey transferred the call, then Adam's familiar voice came on the line, shaky and roughened by stress and pain.

"Hello, Philippa. Sorry to ring so early. I expect I've woken you."

"No, I was already stirring," Philippa said. "What's wrong?"

"I—ah—don't think I ought to spend any more time in hospital than can possibly be helped," he said thinly. "I've asked Humphrey to come and collect me."

The words themselves were neutral enough, but the tone carried an ominous note.

"Adam, are you all right?" she asked.

"I am now," he replied. "Just send Humphrey. Not to worry."

"I see," she said. "Well, this early, there won't be much traffic. Do you want me to come as well?"

"No, I'll be all right. I'll see you in a couple of hours."

Humphrey arrived at the hospital shortly after six, bringing a complete change of clothes. By this time, with several cups of coffee in him, Adam had decided he was past the worst of the sedative's effects, but the effort of dressing, even with Humphrey's assistance, took far more out of him than he would have wished. After he had dealt with the necessary paperwork to check himself out, he raised no objection to being conveyed to the waiting Bentley in a wheelchair.

He allowed himself to breathe a little easier once he was tucked up in the back seat and they were on their way. But responding to Humphrey's worried inquiries about the accident set him to thinking again about that aspect of his last twenty-four hours—not the effect, but the cause.

"Humphrey, I don't mean to be rude, but I really am knackered," he said, trying to find a more comfortable position. "I'm going to try to catch a nap."

"Of course, sir."

But as Humphrey continued to drive them toward home and its greater safety, Adam cast his mind back again to the accident itself. Even McLeod had expressed concern from the start that it had been no accident at all—which Adam, still in shock, had dismissed with only passing consideration. Now Adam thought he knew how it might have been arranged, and by whom.

He remembered the motorcycle coming up fast along his left side—and shooting on ahead just about the time the tire blew. He doubted it could ever be proved, but he was willing to bet that what his tire had "hit" was probably a bullet, fired by that very motorcyclist whose luck in avoiding the accident had struck Adam even as he fought to keep control of the car.

And the timely arrival of his "good Samaritan"—that, too, must have been part of the setup, to make sure that if he survived the crash, he would end up in the right hospital for yet another of the "hit team" to make sure he did *not* survive that.

"I think you're probably right," Philippa said, when he had gone over everything again, over breakfast in the morning room. "I must say, it was all very cleverly planned. If you'd been one whit less skilled a driver, things might have turned out quite differently."

"If I'd been one whit more alert, the whole thing might not have happened at all," Adam said, scowling as he stirred at a cup of tea left-handed.

"And now you're being unreasonably hard on yourself," she replied. "If the 'hit' *was* set up as you've postulated, there wasn't a great deal you could have done to prevent it. And once you'd survived the crash itself, you handled things quite well, especially given that you were in a state of shock. You obviously sensed something was wrong from fairly early on, or you wouldn't have balked at having blood drawn."

"That doesn't appear to have made much difference," Adam said sourly, pushing his tea cup away. "They obviously managed to get something else to use for a physical link—probably the bloody sponges left over after my head was sutured. And no, I don't think Dr. Lockhart could have been in on it."

Philippa shrugged as if to say, *I wasn't even going to suggest it*, and Adam continued uneasily. "They also managed to tamper with my medication—which is *really* unsettling, not knowing what I took!"

Philippa smiled thinly. "We can probably find out, if that's what's bothering you. You're obviously past its peak effect, whatever it was, but there ought to be enough still in your system to show up in a drug profile. Would you like me to pull a sample and have Humphrey run it down to Jordanburn?"

He chuckled bitterly and propped his head on his left hand, gently fingering his bandage. "That mightn't be a bad idea—though my guess, from my reaction, is that it was only a sedative of some sort. Nothing I'd notice, as I drifted off to sleep—not after the day I'd had—but enough to take the edge off my resistance, especially if it was slow-acting, something that wouldn't peak until three or four hours after taking it. That's how *I* would've done it."

He yawned and sighed. "And if my attacker *had* succeeded, my death would have been put down to a cerebral hemorrhage or something of that sort—an extension of injuries sustained in the car crash. Under the circumstances, a little Valium or Librium in the system wouldn't even have raised an eyebrow.''

"I think I *would* like a drug profile on you, Adam," Philippa said, setting her napkin aside. "And I think I'd like to see you get to bed for some proper sleep. I also don't like the idea that the Lodge of the Lynx has samples of your blood. It makes me wonder what they may be holding in reserve—to try a second attack, if the first one failed."

"They can't get at me here, Philippa," he said quietly.

"I know that. But eventually, you're going to have to go out."

"That's true. But I do have obligations."

"I realize that, too," Philippa agreed, "but I don't want to see you taking any unnecessary risks either. Promise me that you'll lie low for the next few days—at least until you've had a chance to mend a little. With the best will in the world," she added practically, "you can't very well go chasing down malefactors with your arm in a sling and your ribs creaking every time you breathe."

"Not a very heroic image, is it?" Adam said, smiling as he flashed on Dr. Lockhart's "noble brow" comment. "I can't promise miracles, but I give you my word I won't do anything that smacks of bravado."

"That will have to do, I suppose." Philippa said with a sigh. "If you've quite finished with breakfast, you can begin your regimen of common sense by taking yourself off to bed. I'll be up in a few minutes to draw that blood sample."

# Chapter Twenty-nine

ADAM woke just before five that evening, aching in every muscle but with only a vestige of headache or mental cobwebs. He was still considering whether he had the energy to get up and go downstairs when Humphrey came in with supper on a tray.

"Ah, you're awake, sir!" Humphrey exclaimed. "Her ladyship said I wasn't to let you sleep past five. I'll go and tell her you're stirring."

Adam would hardly have called his efforts thus far to constitute "stirring," but while Humphrey was gone, he did manage a shaky trip to the bathroom, and had settled himself stiffly in an upholstered chair at the table by the window by the time Philippa came in.

"So, how are you feeling?" she asked, as she watched him begin investigating what was under the napkin covering his supper tray.

"Like a truck hit me," he replied with a grin. "You shouldn't have let me sleep so long."

"You needed it," she said crisply. "And I want you back to bed fairly quickly, as soon as you've had a chance to get some food in you."

She put a small amber plastic vial of yellow capsules beside his tray.

"That's what you were *meant* to be taking and what I'd still recommend," she said. "What you *got*, in the pills you took around midnight, was a dose of Valium roughly equivalent to pre-op medication for major surgery, but in a time-release form that would've hit you about four hours later. Anyway, the lab says that's *all* it was. You were very lucky, or your would-be assassin was being very cautious."

Glancing at the familiar pharmacy label on the vial, from Royal Edinburgh Hospital, Adam pried off the cap one-handed and dumped out two of the capsules, which he took with orange juice from his tray. "Supper" was actually scrambled eggs, grilled tomatoes, and mushrooms, with toast and scones to accompany. He glanced up at Philippa as he picked up his fork awkwardly in his left hand.

"So, catch me up on what else has been happening while I slept the day away," he said, tucking in.

"Well. Noel and Peregrine have both called and been by. They'll be back tomorrow, after Sunday brunch. They found *this* in the rubble down at Dunfermline last night."

From a pocket of her mauve cardigan she took a small bundle wrapped first in one of her silk scarves and then in two layers of handkerchief. Adam noticed she was wearing her scarab ring. As she peeled back the layers of wrappings, he put down his fork. Nestled in the folds of fabric was a blackened metal disk about two inches across.

"Don't try to touch it," she said, as he leaned closer to see it better. "It's contained now, of course, but there's still a great deal of residual energy. You can play with it tomorrow. I thought it was silver, at first, but it actually appears to be iron or steel sandwiched between two layers of silver. Noel and I checked it with a magnet, and it's definitely ferrous—which agrees with what Donald Cochrane found up at Balmoral."

"Did he find one of these up *there*?" Adam said.

"Well, what was left of one," Philippa replied. "What's important is that we now have a Lynx medallion in our possession—and a definite link between the Balmoral lightning strike and the two at Calton Hill and Dunfermline. I'd say that Balmoral was probably a trial run, to see if they really *could* control the lightning—which, obviously, they can. Eat your supper now, dear, before it gets cold."

As she wrapped up the remains of the medallion, Adam automatically resumed eating, though his mind was racing furiously over the implications. After a few minutes, Philippa switched on the portable TV to catch the evening news. International coverage was mostly devoted to the worsening situation in the Persian Gulf, but Scottish news devoted several minutes of air time to an update on what was being referred to as "the Dunfermline disaster."

There were several short interviews, ranging from the moderate to the extreme. A spokesman for the police in Dunfermline stated that since no chemical traces of explosives had been found in the wreckage, the incident was being treated as a natural disaster. A local environmentalist professed his belief that the accident had been caused by natural forces, but went further to suggest that perhaps it was time the country took stronger measures to clean up the environment before the natural world was thrown completely off balance.

The last interview was with an off-duty police inspector by the name of Napier, who was invited to comment on the apparent similarities between this incident and the one that had taken place at Calton Hill in Edinburgh a week before. His response, to Adam's way of thinking, was far more invidious than the others for being couched in terms that uninitiated people would consider reasonable.

"I can't say that I was ever much of a believer in divine retribution," Napier said with a sardonic curl of his lip, "but even I can't overlook the fact that these two recent lightning strikes both seem to have been directed specifically at members of the Order of Freemasonry. If I were a religious man, I'd be tempted to say they must have done something to earn the wrath of God. Maybe we ought to be asking ourselves what they've been up to, and start taking a serious look into their so-called secret affairs."

His statement was the final item on the news agenda. Adam's fatigue had shifted increasingly to indignation as he watched, and he was scowling as Philippa switched off the TV.

"So far as the Masons are concerned, that was just about as damning a statement as anyone could possibly have made," he said flatly, pushing his tray away.

Philippa nodded. "You'd almost think someone *wanted* to set a latter-day witch-hunt in motion. I wonder," she continued thoughtfully, "if Noel is in any way acquainted with this Napier fellow."

"I think I'll give him a call," Adam said. "Aside from checking in to reassure him that I'm all right, I think I'll ask him to see what he can dig up about the rather unpleasant Inspector Napier."

He spoke briefly with both McLeod and Peregrine before going back to bed. His sleep that night was dreamless, but it was not entirely easy. All through the night, he was aware of a feral presence prowling restlessly about the perimeters of the estate, repeatedly testing his defenses as it tried to find a way inside. But he had spoken no more than the truth to Philippa when he assured her that nothing could get at him here. Strathmourne was well-guarded against unwelcome astral intruders.

Sunday dawned frosty and bright. Adam awoke to the sound of distant church bells, physically even stiffer than the day before, but with his mental faculties largely restored. A long, hot shower did much to ease the aches; and dressing properly for Sunday brunch with Philippa and Mrs. Talbot, in grey flannels and a navy blazer instead of a dressing gown, further improved his spirits, even though it took a great deal of physical effort and he had to have help from Humphrey. His sling of canvas and nylon webbing did little to enhance the sartorial image, but its support considerably eased the strain on his injured shoulder, so he wore it. He looked in on Gillian after brunch, and spent half an hour sitting by her bedside while her mother read to her, thinking about the shattered soul trapped in the frail, wasting body and hoping that physical proximity might spark some new inspiration for her treatment.

Peregrine arrived just on two o'clock and McLeod shortly thereafter, the latter bringing with him the folder on the Balmoral incident. Humphrey showed the two into the library, where Adam had already ensconced himself in his favorite fireside chair, legs stretched out on a footstool. Philippa remained upstairs, to conduct one of her daily sessions of touch-therapy with Gillian.

"I gather Philippa's told you that Donald hit pay-dirt," McLeod said, opening the file on his lap and shuffling through several stapled documents, obviously looking for one in particular. "He's a cool one, though. Not a word about that whole origami episode, and nary a false step on this—though I know he must be bursting to ask me more about it. When the dust has settled, we'll want to think seriously about whether he ought to be enlightened a bit—and see how he reacts."

He found what he was looking for, turned back a page, and handed it across to Adam as Peregrine looked on silently.

"This is what's important," McLeod said. "Most of the rest of this is just the official reports—the eyewitness accounts of the incident, the forensics reports compiled by the bomb squad investigators, and the statements submitted by various insurance adjusters involved in assessing the overall damage to the building. There're photos, too, but they don't tell you much. I brought it all along so that you'd have the complete file at your disposal, if you want to read it later, but Donald hits it on the head, I think."

*I don't know if this is significant,* Donald had handwritten in his personal report to McLeod, *but when I was climbing around in the debris at the base of the tower, very near "ground zero," where the lightning must have hit, I noticed something metallic wedged between two of the stones at that corner. Part of it had melted and run down the lower stone. It looked like it might have been melted pewter or silver. I tried to pry out what was left with my penknife, but it was fused into the crack. I did notice, however, that whatever it was, was strongly magnetized. (It attracted my knife blade, which is NOT magnetized.) It occurred to me to wonder whether that might have been what attracted the lightning strike.*

"He couldn't get a sample?" Adam asked, looking up.

"No, he said it was practically welded to the stone—which is what one might expect, after being struck by lightning. Also, he had a couple of soldiers with him, showing him over the site, and he didn't want to have to answer any difficult questions."

"No, he was perfectly right," Adam agreed. "And Philippa tells me that the Dunfermline medallion also tests strongly magnetic."

McLeod nodded, but Peregrine had been looking increasingly troubled.

"Adam, this doesn't make sense. I can't argue with the evidence—but why Balmoral? It doesn't fit in with the pattern."

"No, the pattern comes later," Adam replied. "Philippa suggested last night—and I think she may be right—that the Balmoral strike was probably a trial run, to see if they could do it. Or maybe it was a demonstration of authority—a test of strength, if you like. When it succeeded, those responsible knew they were ready to proceed to their next objective."

"Aye, the systematic assassination of various Freemasons," McLeod said bitterly.

"Yes, but I can't help wondering whether there isn't some darker purpose beyond that," Adam replied. "If you merely want to kill people, you don't go to all the trouble and, no doubt, psychic expense to blast them with elemental lightning—though I'm sure that, in moments of exasperation, most people have been guilty of wishing lightning would strike an annoying adversary. Guns and bombs and such are far more efficient.

"However, the fact that our adversaries *are* going to such considerable trouble and expense places their ultimate motive far beyond a mere grudge against Freemasons. And it makes it all the more important to discover who they are and what their ultimate aim is, before it's too late. Fortunately, we now have one of their medallions—and that may be the break we've been looking for. Peregrine, do you have any further plans for this afternoon?"

Peregrine sat forward eagerly. "Not a thing. I'd cleared the decks, in case you needed me."

"Good. Then I need you to go out and get me some maps,"

Adam said. "I want ordnance survey maps—the biggest and most detailed you can find, covering the whole of Scotland."

Peregrine whistled low under his breath. "I know the ones you mean, but I'll probably have to go all the way into Edinburgh for a full set, especially on a Sunday."

"Then you'd better get started, before the shops close. Off you go, then."

Once the artist had departed, Adam sighed and shifted uncomfortably in his chair, returning his attention to McLeod.

"Now, what about this Inspector Napier, who seems so eager to cause trouble for your fellow Masons?"

McLeod snorted. "Good question. I don't know what's put a bee in that man's bonnet, but I made a point of catching the late news last night, after you'd called. The man's entitled to his opinion, of course, but people of his professional standing generally have the discretion to keep opinions like that to themselves."

"Aye, there are few things he could have said that would have been more damaging," Adam said. "Which makes one wonder if it wasn't a *deliberate* indiscretion, calculated to fuel the fire. What have you found out about him?"

McLeod shrugged. "Nothing particularly striking, I'm afraid. I stopped by the office this morning and pulled his file. His psychological profile paints him as a bit of a plodder. You know the type—someone who gets by on hard work rather than brilliance. But he has his share of ambition. His records show that he's spent his last ten years with the department plodding his way methodically up the ladder of advancement till we find him where he is today."

"So you'd say there's nothing unusual about him?"

"Nothing at all. In fact, he's so ordinary—on paper, anyway—that that, in itself, is almost an oddity. He's by all accounts a bit of a loner—not married, no close family ties. Not particularly popular with his subordinates, but no enemies to speak of. The worst anyone seems to be able to say of him is that he's a bit surly and keeps very much to himself."

"What about his service record?"

"There again, not much to tell. He does the job, and that's the sum of it. He's never been reprimanded, even for a minor infraction. However, he's never received any commendations, either."

McLeod paused and scowled. "Come to think of it, that's a bit strange for someone of his rank and seniority. Offhand, I can't

298

think of any other inspector I know who doesn't have at least one distinguished service citation to his credit. I wonder how our friend Napier could have reached this point in his career without doing anything outstanding, one way or the other.''

"Hmmm, yes. It's almost as if he's deliberately avoided drawing attention to himself, all the while he's been working to improve his professional standing,'' Adam said. "What do your instincts tell you?''

"My instincts tell me that there's more to the man than shows up in the files,'' McLeod said frankly. "Unless you need me here, I'm thinking I'll head out and do some more nosing around. We know the Lynx has got someone on the police force. I'm going to gamble that it's Napier.''

After McLeod had departed, Adam took advantage of the lull in activity to snatch a much-needed cat nap. He roused himself two hours later and was just sitting down to a cup of tea in the library when Peregrine arrived back at Strathmourne with the maps Adam had requested.

"Would you believe I had to visit two motorway service plazas and four different bookshops before I could put together a complete set?'' the artist exclaimed, brandishing the fruits of his labors. "I could *not* get the Orkneys, so we'll have to hope nothing nasty is happening there. Where do you want them?''

"Just toss them on the settee for now,'' Adam said with a smile. "Have you had anything to eat?''

"Nothing since lunch. Why?''

"Good, then you aren't *going* to have anything for another hour or two, because I've got a spot of work for you to do, and it's something best attempted on an empty stomach when you're first learning how. Fancy trying your hand at some pendulum dousing?''

"Me?''

The procedure was not unknown to Peregrine, for he had seen Adam use a form of pendulum dowsing at Dunvegan Castle, also in conjunction with maps, to determine the approximate location of the stolen Fairy Flag. His eyes widened slightly at the prospect of attempting something like that himself.

"I'm certainly willing to have a go,'' he said, "but I hope you're intending to talk me through.''

"I'm intending to do precisely that,'' Adam said. "We need to make some preparations first, though—principal of which is to free up more floor space than we've got here. Humphrey's gone to fetch that medallion from the house safe. As soon as he joins us, we'll see about transferring operations to the drawing room."

The drawing room seemed chilly after the cozy, familiar warmth of the library. Still moving stiffly, Adam steered himself to a Victorian chaise lounge set along one wall and directed Humphrey and Peregrine to clear floor space in the center of the room. As they began unfolding the maps and laying them out in their proper order and orientation, Adam thumbed open the silk-lined box Humphrey had brought him and gingerly took out the slagged remains of the Lynx pendant.

It lay quiescent in his palm, still bound by the restraints Philippa had placed upon it the day before to reinforce McLeod's initial binding, but he could sense, nevertheless, a lingering residue of the malignancy that had gone into its fashioning. With any luck at all—and if Adam had accurately assessed Peregrine's potential in this regard—the medallion should enable them to trace the fine psychic thread still binding the medallion to its makers.

Setting it temporarily aside, Adam delved into the box again for a pool of fine blue silk thread and called Peregrine over to break off a length as long as his own arm. Then, while Peregrine returned to his task with the maps, Adam used mostly his left hand to awkwardly wind one end of the thread securely around the Lynx medallion to create a free-swinging pendulum. He briefly tried wrapping the free end of the thread around his right index finger and testing the pendulum's swing, but the strain on his shoulder was too much, and certainly would not stand up to what he had in mind. No, Peregrine was about to win his own wings in *this* exercise.

He looked up to find Peregrine waiting expectantly before the chaise lounge, Humphrey attentive by the door. The carpet of maps was now complete, showing the whole of Scotland laid out in two dimensions, all its geological features and contours marked out in variegated patterns of greens and golds. Adam smiled to see that his two assistants had taken the initiative of joining the maps up with masking tape at the overlapping corners. Laying the pendulum back in its box, he dismissed Humphrey with a word of thanks and turned back to Peregrine.

"Pull up a chair and make yourself comfortable for a moment," he directed. "This is where things get technical."

"It was bound to happen sooner or later," Peregrine said, grinning as he went to fetch a balloon-backed chair from the opposite corner. Plumping it on the carpet opposite Adam's chaise lounge, he sat down and said wryly, "All right, let's hear the worst."

"Relax. You're ready for this," Adam said with a smile. "Now, a very quick lesson on pendulum theory. To put it as simply as possible, pendulum dousing works according to a principle best described as the law of correspondences. This law postulates that the world of symbols and the world of material objects exist in reciprocal relation to one another. In other words, what exists physically may be perceived symbolically by anyone with knowledge sufficient to the purpose.

"Take that map of Scotland you and Humphrey have just so painstakingly constructed," he said, gesturing with his left hand. "In one sense, it's only so much printed paper, but in another sense the map is a direct symbolic extension of the country it's meant to represent. What occupies space in the material world holds an equivalent place in the world of symbols—and for that reason, it's possible to locate the one in terms of the other. Are you following?"

Peregrine nodded. "My brain is buzzing a little, but yes, I think so."

"Very good. In that case, we'll move on to the next point—the pendulum itself. Anything, potentially, can be used as a pendulum, so long as it carries some charge of residual energy associated either with the person doing the dousing or with the object he's trying to find. In this case, we're going to be using what's left of that Lynx medallion you found at Dunfermline."

He gestured toward the medallion, with its length of silk trailing out of the satinwood box.

"Now, the theory behind the particular connection we're seeking: In order to perform the function for which it was designed—to act as a form of lightning rod—this medallion would have to have been magically bonded with the person who actually summons the lightning, probably via a power-object. I'm guessing the latter to be the torc you envisioned at Calton Hill. Where the torc is, there also is the person who is wielding it. By having you walk the map, using the pendulum to detect correspondences, I'm hopeful that we can discover the lightning wielder's location."

Peregrine glanced at the maps, pursing his lips, then back at the medallion.

"Okay. Any particular way I should pick it up?"

"You'll get the most sensitive contact if you hold the end of the thread between thumb and forefinger, just tightly enough not to drop it."

Cautious after the shock it had given him before, Peregrine gently grasped the end of the thread and lifted the medallion clear

301

of the box. As he looked at it, seeing it rotate slightly, he could start to sense an odd tingling, almost as if the medallion had a life of its own.

"I suggest you take off your shoes as well," Adam said. "That will help you make a physical connection with the surface of the map and what it represents. Then clear your mind and try to make yourself as passive as possible. We want the pendulum to be drawn toward 'home'."

Peregrine nodded and kicked off his brown leather loafers. The tingling pull from the pendulum became stronger. Standing up, he took three slow, deep breaths, grounding and centering himself as Adam had taught him to do. Letting himself be guided by the pendulum's now-insistent pull, he walked over to the southern edge of the maps.

As Adam watched from his vantage point on the chaise lounge, Peregrine set off slowly across the expanse of crackling paper. Treading delicately on his stocking feet, he kept to the center of the pictured land mass, edging slowly north and west.

"I can certainly feel a pull," he reported, without looking round. "It doesn't seem much interested in Edinburgh. It's tending more in the direction of Falkirk. . . . Yes, the pull seems to be getting stronger. A little more west . . . a little more north . . . toward Stirling, maybe. . . ."

The pendulum's movement seemed to be stabilizing as Peregrine moved closer to Stirling. He half-held his breath, waiting to see what would happen. But just as he thought it might be coming to rest, he felt a sudden, sharp tug and the pendulum began to vacillate, swinging erratically back and forth with no discernible consistency.

"Damn, I think I've lost it!" Peregrine muttered.

"Not to worry," Adam said quietly. "And don't try to force the issue. It's important to remain passive. Just stand still and wait. Close your eyes, if that will help. When the connection settles in again, don't try to anticipate or interpret—just go with what you feel."

Nodding his agreement, Peregrine closed his eyes and concentrated on bringing his breathing back under control. His excitement subsided, leaving him quiet and receptive once more. Gradually he nudged his attention back toward the pendulum. After a minute or two, he felt the tug at his fingertips again, even stronger than before.

This time the inclination seemed to be due north, with a slight westerly bias. Fixing his gaze on the banjo clock on the wall at the further end of the room, Peregrine put all speculation out of his mind concerning the pendulum's ultimate heading and allowed himself to be tugged along in its wake. After several minutes, the pull subsided, leaving the pendulum spinning round on its thread.

"But, there's nothing here!" Peregrine declared, as he crouched down to see what lay below. "There's nothing on this part of the map but mountains."

"All right," Adam said. "Come back to the edge of the map and try again."

Under Adam's direction, Peregrine repeated the process several times more, starting from different quarters of the compass. Each time, he experienced a slight but unmistakable diversion toward Stirling before the pendulum gravitated toward the same unsettled region of the Cairngorm Mountains.

"Very curious," Adam said, after the fifth assay. "If I'm reading this correctly, we seem to have located two separate concentrations of power. I'm particularly curious about that area in the Cairngorms. If the snow weren't so heavy over the Highlands just now, we might get Noel to see about arranging an aerial reconnaissance flight. As it is, I doubt there'd be much to see from the air. . . ."

As his voice trailed off thoughtfully, Peregrine cocked his head in question.

"What have you got in mind?"

"Perhaps a land excursion into the Scottish interior," Adam said, with a sidelong glance. "A four-wheel-drive vehicle ought to be able to handle the roads—though we'd have to see about renting a replacement vehicle for the Range Rover, and I'm afraid I'm in no fit condition to drive myself with my arm strapped up like this. But if you think you can handle it, we might make a go the next time there's a break in the weather and plan to spend a day or two up in that area."

"Sure, I'm game," Peregrine said. "In the meantime, though, why not try Stirling? It's a lot closer than the Cairngorms, and you don't need four-wheel drive to get there."

"I'm already giving that some thought," Adam replied. "For now, though, it's getting late, and I confess I'm feeling the need of a nap. Let's call it an afternoon, and I'll get back to you tomorrow."

# CHAPTER THIRTY

AFTER Peregrine had gone, Adam remained in the drawing room for some time, musing thoughtfully over the array of maps and the puzzle posed by the behavior of the pendulum, and eventually dozed off. At length a light knock on the door roused him from his reverie.

"There you are," Philippa said, poking her head around the doorframe. "Are you planning to camp out in here all evening? If you are, I think I ought to point out that you are not exactly in any fit state to spend a night on the tiles."

"You may very well have a point there," Adam acknowledged with a wan smile. As he sat up, he was all at once conscious of his various aches, and he grimaced as an ill-considered movement made his shoulder give a sharp twinge.

Philippa cast a knowing eye over the map-strewn floor and quirked an ironic eyebrow at her son. "Judging by the looks of this place, you've been rather busy," she observed drily.

"Oh, Peregrine did most of the work," Adam said. "I'll tell you all about it over dinner—or is Mrs. Talbot joining us?"

"No, she's ensconced in her room with a TV and supper on a tray. I think she's afraid of intruding on our hospitality—which, in this case, she would be. Shall we eat up in the Rose Room?"

They dined frugally on baked chicken and a green salad, with Adam eschewing wine in the interests of what he was planning for later on. Philippa was keen to hear about Peregrine's performance in the pendulum exercise, and nodded approvingly as Adam finished his account.

"The boy is really coming along, isn't he?" she remarked. "The decision is yours, of course, but it seems to me that he's ready—more than ready—to be presented as a candidate for initiation."

"I agree."

"The solstice is only a matter of days away," Philippa went on. "That would be an appropriate time."

"It would—and I'm thinking in those terms. Before then,

304

however, I'd like a whole lot better idea what is going on. So far, *they* are calling the shots. We don't even know for certain yet who *they* are—except, of course, that it's the Lodge of the Lynx. We've got to break that cycle, regain the upper hand.''

"I agree," Philippa said. "But keep in mind that you aren't operating at peak efficiency just now. Don't underestimate the toll this episode has taken on your strength.''

Adam snorted and shifted his arm in its sling.

"I'm aware of my limitations, and I'm not too proud to ask for help if I need it. On the other hand, if our enemies think they've rendered me *hors de combat*, they're sadly mistaken. I've been giving some further thought to Peregrine's suggestion that we concentrate at least some of our attention on Stirling. And I've come up with an idea.''

Briefly he explained his intention to Philippa.

"Sounds promising," she acknowledged. "It's certainly worth a try. Would you like some of that help you say you're not too proud to ask for?''

• Smiling, he shook his head. "Not for this one—but thanks for the offer. I'm still working out the details. Once we've had coffee, I'll take myself back down to the library and see what transpires.''

"All right," said Philippa, "but remember you're supposed to be convalescent, so don't sit up *too* late.''

After dinner, Adam shed his tie and exchanged shoes and blazer for slippers and dressing gown, then went down to the library. The box containing the Lynx medallion was already on his desk. From his desk drawer he drew a pad of foolscap and the manila envelope containing the transcripts from the Stirling interviews. He had already read though them several times without finding anything obviously worthy of note. This time, however, he had another plan in mind.

Settling himself more or less comfortably at his desk, Adam eased his right arm from its supporting sling and set to work, bracing his elbow on the arm of his chair and jotting down only the names and addresses of those who had been interviewed, disregarding the text. That completed, he returned the transcripts to their holding envelope and tossed it on the floor beside him, to leave his workspace clear.

Next, from the top drawer of the desk itself, he took out a stack of blank index cards, a calligraphy pen, and a bottle of India ink. The latter he opened, setting the cap aside and then laying his right hand flat on the desk before him, shifting his attention to and through the sapphire on his hand. For a long moment thereafter he sat very still, composing himself while he allowed his intentions to crystallize in the back of his mind. As his sense of purpose deepened, he turned his attention inward, concentrating on his breathing. When all was stilled and centered, he drew a slow, deep breath, then reached out and took up the pen.

It felt weightless in his hand. He paused to imagine its tip as a pinpoint of fluorescent light, illuminating the presence of unseen elements in a matrix of inert matter. Moving a blank card in front of him, he dipped the pen in the ink bottle and carefully traced out the name and address that appeared at the top of his list, all the while holding in balance the thought of a travelling beam of radiance piercing the darkness like a shaft from a miner's torch.

*Author of Lights*, he implored silently, *make visible that which is invisible. Make manifest those things which lie hidden.*

Slowly, carefully, he copied each of the names onto a separate card. He had twenty-nine when he was finished. He studied them while he waited for the ink to dry on the last few, letting the resonance of each name and place reverberate in his mind. When he was satisfied that they would not smear, he gathered the cards into a pack and shuffled them several times. Then he spread them face down on the desk in front of him, in five rows of six across, with one space blank at the lower right corner.

Next he took an Exacto knife from his desk catch-all and used it to pare a small sliver of silver from the Lynx medallion and attach it to a new length of thread. He closed his eyes for a moment, formulating an image of the pendulum as a compass needle attuned to the energy source he was trying to find. Then, holding the pendulum suspended over the assemblage of cards—with his left hand, for the right shoulder would not sustain the strain—he concentrated on sending the silver home to the person who had enlivened it.

Beginning at the top left-hand corner of the configuration, he set the pendulum in motion. To keep his sweep methodical, he deliberately traced horizontally between the rows of cards, looking for a deflection. On his first serpentine, going between the third and fourth rows, he experienced a subtle twitch toward a card in the fourth row down, third from the left. He got the deflection again as he came between the fourth and fifth rows.

Nodding softly to himself, he pulled a pencil from the center desk drawer and lifted the card enough to slide the pencil underneath it and make a mark on the hidden face. Laying the pencil aside, he scrambled the cards without looking at the one he had marked and set them out again, repeating the exercise and marking a card two rows down and two from the right. When he had repeated the exercise a third time and marked the card singled out by the pendulum, he laid the pendulum aside and picked up the card, weighing it briefly in his hand before turning it over. Three erratic pencil marks marred the front of the card, surrounding the name, *Francis Raeburn,* and beneath it the address: *Nether Leckie, By Stirling.*

Adam sat motionless for several minutes, his mouth set hard as he considered the import of this revelation. Simply zeroing in on the name proved nothing, but it was certainly a strong indication that this Raeburn was involved in some way. Three "hits" on the blind pendulum dousing went far beyond the possibility of coincidence.

And if Raeburn *was* the man directing the lightning—and responsible for the deaths of Randall Stewart, Ian MacPherson, and the Masons of Dunfermline—it was Adam's sworn duty to hunt him down and disarm him of his powers, and expose him to civil justice as well, if that could be done. But only the edges of the picture were starting to emerge, and Adam was well-aware of the pitfalls inherent in acting too soon on too little evidence.

Thoughtful, he picked up the phone and punched out McLeod's home number.

"Noel, sorry to disturb your Sunday again," he said, when McLeod himself answered, "but I've come up with a lead I think bears pursuing. I've been going over those interview notes from Stirling, in connection with that item you and Peregrine retrieved at Dunfermline. I think we need to make some very careful, discreet inquiries about a man called Francis Raeburn."

While Adam Sinclair was carrying out his experiments with maps and pendulum, Dr. Preston Wemyss was on his way to an interview to which he was not looking forward in the least. Huddled miserably in one of the back seats of Francis Raeburn's helicopter, he spent the entire hour and more of the flight northward rehearsing his defenses, while the snow-covered forests of Balmoral rolled away beneath them and the white peaks of the Cairngorms rose ahead. His head was still aching dully from the backlash of power he had caught more than twenty-four hours before, in his unsuccessful attempt to finish what Barclay had begun, and dread of what lay ahead made him almost sick to his stomach.

Neither Raeburn nor Barclay had spoken to him since they took off. Wemyss knew he was in disgrace. By the time they at last caught sight of the castellated manor house that was their destination, what little confidence he had started out with had mostly eroded to queasy despair. As Barclay brought them in low for a landing in the back courtyard—Wemyss was not even to be afforded the courtesy of entering the castle through the front door—Wemyss was all too aware that his explanations were more likely to sound like excuses.

The thought of facing up to the Head-Master's displeasure caused Wemyss to curse anew the combination of ill luck and random happenstance that had allowed Adam Sinclair to survive the attempt on his life. In retrospect, he was bitterly aware that Raeburn had done him no service in leaving it up to him to engineer the medical contingencies, should Sinclair survive the car crash. He glanced sullenly at the back of Raeburn's head, seeing now how he had been skillfully manipulated into a position where *he* would be obliged to take the blame in the event of failure. But that realization was unlikely to save him, if the Head-Master should choose to mete out punishment.

His heart was in his throat as he followed Raeburn and Barclay from the helicopter. The castle seemed even colder than usual, coming through the back service entrance. His stomach was churning with sick tension as he put off his shoes and pulled on the requisite white robe. As he set off to meet the Head-Master, nervously fingering the carnelian ring on his right hand, he wondered how much longer he would be allowed to wear it.

The barefoot climb up the spiral stair did nothing to diminish the chill of dread permeating his very bones. At the library landing, Raeburn left him to continue on alone. Eleven members of the Circle of Twelve were already in their places as Wemyss entered the tower room, uniformly anonymous in their white woollen robes, their faces overshadowed by their hoods so that expressions could not be seen. The whole situation looked and felt like a tribunal—which, Wemyss reflected sickly, was exactly what it was. He squared his shoulders, determined not to reveal himself as craven as he felt.

A moment later, there was a stir outside the door and the Head-Master himself entered the room, leaning heavily on the arm of his senior acolyte. The Head-Master's wizened face had never looked more skull-like than it did now, in the flickering glow of the gas-lamps. Withered lips compressed in a tight grimace of displeasure, he made his way unhurriedly to his place at the far edge of the circle and sank down amid the scarlet cushions placed to accommodate him. A deathly silence prevailed while he settled himself, broken only by the faint, stertorous wheeze of Wemyss' nervous breathing. The Head-Master allowed the silence to draw itself out a few heartbeats longer, then fixed his coal-black eyes with implacable steadiness on the thin, grey-haired man standing wretchedly at attention before him.

"Dr. Wemyss." The Head-Master's voice stirred through the

room like an icy draught. "This is an occasion I relish as little as you do. Your failure to carry out your assigned task forces me to mete out discipline appropriate to that failure. Are you aware what it may have cost us?"

Wemyss said nothing, sickly aware that there was nothing he could say.

"A week ago," the Master continued, "you were enlisted to assist in the task of removing a particular obstacle from our path—the man we now know to be the leader of a Hunting Lodge. It was a commission which reflected not only the vital necessity of the moment, but also our high estimation of your merits as a servant of the Lynx—and yet you failed us. I think, *Doctor*, that you owe us an explanation."

The words were delivered with spitting venom. Wemyss quailed in spite of himself.

"I—I took every precaution, Head-Master, I swear I did," he said falteringly. "The blood sample was sufficient. I arranged to switch the capsules in his prescription envelope for ones I had prepared for the purpose. In his already weakened condition, and with that much Valium in him—"

"*Valium*!" The Head-Master gave a snort of contempt. "If you were going to go to all that trouble, why didn't you fill the capsules with an appropriate amount of cyanide?"

"But that would have pointed obviously to a case of murder," Wemyss protested weakly. "I understood that we were to use only such methods of attack that would not be traceable under forensics investigation."

"Whatever methods you use," the Head-Master said brutally, "I expect you to make a success of the attempt. Outright murder at least would have gotten him off our hands. As it is, you have yet to account for why your psychic attack failed."

Wemyss flinched away from the Head-Master's glare. "Even drugged, he put up a fight. I nearly had him, nonetheless, but he—had a Word of Power that I wasn't expecting, that I couldn't countermand—"

"You incompetent fool!" The Head-Master's voice cracked like a whip. "Sinclair is Master of the Hunt. Don't you understand what that means? You had authorization to commandeer whatever assistance you required. And yet you thought to take him on by yourself. Why?"

Wemyss' lips worked, but no sound came out.

"Shall I tell you why?" the Head-Master shouted. "It's because you were too greedy—too eager to claim this kill for yourself! You were prepared to risk failure rather than share the credit with anyone else. Very well. Now that you have failed, I shall not ask anyone else to share the full penalty."

Wemyss' lean face blanched, and his clenching hands lifted involuntarily. "Mercy, Head-Master!" he whispered. "Have mercy I beg you!"

"*Mercy*?" The Head Master's black eyes were mocking. "Mercy is the vice of all those sentimental fools who really believe the Light will save them from the Dark. It was one of the first things you rejected when you joined our Order. Having failed me, how *dare* you beg me to be merciful?"

Wemyss' legs were quaking under him. With an abject moan, he sank to his knees and buried his face in his hands. There was a stony silence broken only by the sound of the doctor's sobbing breath. Then the Head-Master moved, gesturing curtly to the acolytes sitting on either side of the door.

"Take this worm out of my sight," he ordered in tones of withering contempt. "Let him be stripped of his tokens of rank and relegated to the grade of Menial until I have leisure to decide what to do with him."

The two acolytes rose from their places. Wemyss bit back a whimper as they laid rough hands on him and hustled him from the chamber. As silence descended on the room, the Head-Master allowed himself to be assisted to his feet. Face set hard in iron composure, he waved his assistants aside and made his own departure.

Francis Raeburn was waiting for him downstairs in the library. The Head-Master made his way unsteadily to his chair and sank down in it with a bitter air of spent rage.

"There must be no more failures," he muttered.

"There won't be," said Raeburn steadily. "Not unless the Thunderer himself declines to keep his bargain."

"He will keep it." The Head-Master rounded on the younger man, his withered hands spread claw-like on the table. "What else do you think keeps me fettered to this miserable frame? Not any love of life, but dedication to the service of our Dark Master. From him I shall look to receive fitting recompense when the hour of awakening arrives."

His glittering gaze fixed on Raeburn's fair face, and he sat back in his chair.

"You will not go back to Nether Leckie. After this latest setback, our enemies may be close enough on our trail to begin looking for you there. You will remain here, in seclusion, until time for our next assault in the name of the Thunderer."

# CHAPTER THIRTY-ONE

THE following morning, just before eleven o'clock, Peregrine went up to Strathmourne House to see how Adam was getting on. It was a grey, dreary Monday, and he found his mentor still at the breakfast table, not yet shaved or dressed. He accepted a cup of tea and an offer of scones from Humphrey, then settled down to eat and listen with some eagerness as Adam related what he had discovered the night before.

"Raeburn," Peregrine said around a mouthful of scone, gesturing with the rest of it. "I swear that name rings a bell. I'm not just thinking of Sir Henry Raeburn, the famous Scottish portrait artist, either," he hastened to add. "This is something else, much more recent—certainly since I met you."

His hazel eyes narrowed as he chewed on his bite of scone, thinking.

"Nope, I can't remember," he said finally. "It's knocking around somewhere in the back of my mind, but I can't quite seem to get a fix on it."

Adam had been watching the younger man's face as he considered. If Peregrine even half-remembered something about a man named Raeburn since this whole thing began, it might well be worth exploring further.

"Now you've got me curious," he said, folding his napkin left-handed and setting it aside, for he was still in his sling. "In light of our present situation, anybody by the name of Raeburn is worth giving some thought to. Finish up your scone, and let's see if we can't retrieve that memory."

Grinning, Peregrine popped the last bite of his third scone into his mouth and washed it down with a swallow of tea.

"*Voila!*" he said, dusting the crumbs from his fingertips. "I'm ready any time you are."

Smiling a little over the demands of a young man's appetite, Adam reached his left hand across the table to lightly touch Peregrine's forehead.

"Close your eyes and relax," he murmured, removing his hand as the hazel eyes closed at the post-hypnotic suggestion. "Take a deep breath, and as you let it out, feel yourself sinking to a good, comfortable working level of trance, as you do when you're trying to See. Take several breaths. That's right. . . ."

Peregrine relaxed visibly as Adam spoke, eyes closed behind his spectacles, his breathing becoming light and regular as his head nodded forward slightly.

"That's very good," Adam said quietly, sitting back. "Now cast your mind back to the month of October, to our first meeting, and slowly begin moving forward, one day at a time. Let the name Raeburn act as a magnet, and let your mind be drawn toward it like the needle of a compass."

Peregrine nodded his understanding. Adam could see the flicker of movement behind his closed lids as he responded to the direction. The seconds ticked away in silence broken only by the faint hiss of the gas fire on the breakfast room hearth. Then Peregrine caught his breath with a small shiver.

"I've got it," he breathed, head lifting but eyes remaining closed. "The British Museum. It was—Monday, October 29. I'd been looking at maps. Your friend there—Mr. Rowley—was speaking on the telephone to a colleague named Middleton. They were talking about someone called Raeburn."

His brow creased. "Something about a Highlands and Islands Conference. I got the impression something unpleasant had happened. Rowley said, *I'm sorry to hear that. Still, Raeburn was bound to be there, wasn't he? After all, he's got business interests in Inverness, as well as academic ones. . . .*"

His voice trailed off. Considering the date, Adam realized that the conversation would have coincided roughly with the theft of the Fairy Flag from Dunvegan Castle—and linking the name of Raeburn with Inverness, just at the north end of Loch Ness, surely was too much coincidence to be mere chance. Whether Peregrine's Raeburn and Francis Raeburn were one and the same remained to be seen. . . .

"That's very interesting," he said, returning his attention to the artist. "I don't suppose that a first name was mentioned?"

"No."

"All right, you've done very well," Adam told him. "I'm going to count backwards now, from three to one. When I reach one, I want you to return to normal waking consciousness, refreshed and relaxed, in full possession of the memory we've just called to mind. Three, two, one."

Peregrine, like Adam, was quick to appreciate the coincidences of time and place.

"It's *got* to be the same Raeburn, Adam!" he said excitedly.

"No, it doesn't *have* to be," Adam replied, getting carefully to his feet, "but I intend to find out whether it is. Come with me."

Five minutes later, he was sitting at his desk in the library, listening to a telephone ring at a London number. Peregrine had pulled a straight-backed chair closer and straddled it, leaning his hands and chin on the back as he watched and also waited. He could almost make out the words as someone picked up at the other end and Adam turned his attention to the conversation.

"Mr. Rowley, please. This is Sir Adam Sinclair calling."

As the call went on hold, Adam quirked a slightly roguish smile at Peregrine.

"One of the more useful things about a title is its power to get one past intermediaries more quickly," he murmured. "Hello, Peter? Yes, good to hear your voice, too. No, nothing special. I'm afraid Christmas has managed to sneak up on me this year. Somehow, it usually does.

"Listen, Peter. I need to pick your brain. I didn't make it to the Highlands and Islands Conference in October. Was there a chap there called Raeburn? Yes, Francis Raeburn—that's the one. Lives up by Stirling. You don't sound too pleased."

He listened avidly for several minutes, nodding occasionally and making noises of agreement, jotting a few notes on a pad of foolscap that Peregrine craned his neck to see, at last flicking his glance at Peregrine as he drew breath to speak.

"Oh, I agree. He sounds most disagreeable. Interesting credentials, though. Yes, I thought he might. It sounds like we'd be at cross-purposes, though. No, that's good to know.

"Listen, Peter, I've got to run. Thanks very much for the info. Yes, indeed. No, I'll buy *you* a drink the next time I'm in London. Right. Happy Christmas to you too, Peter."

Without even taking the receiver from his ear, Adam pressed the switch hook to end the connection and began dialling another number.

"Adam," Peregrine muttered under his breath, "what did he *say*?"

"In a minute," Adam murmured, holding a finger to his lips for silence as the number rang. "Yes, Detective Chief Inspector McLeod, please. Sir Adam Sinclair calling."

Peregrine sat forward on his chair, eyes alight, as the lines clicked and transferred.

"Good morning, indeed. Not bad, all things considered," Adam replied. "Listen, Noel, can you call me back from another phone? Right. I'm at home. Five minutes. I'll be waiting."

A predatory look had come into his eyes as he spoke, and he refused to be drawn out as they waited for McLeod to return the call. Adam had Humphrey bring in an extension phone and patch it into the one on Adam's desk, so that when the instrument rang and Adam had verified that it was McLeod, he had Peregrine pick it up.

"Yes, thanks for getting back so quickly," Adam said. "By the way, Peregrine's on the extension, so I don't have to tell this twice. Did your departure seem to arouse any undue attention?"

"Morning, Peregrine. No, I don't think so. Napier's off somewhere, but we don't know for sure that he's our mole. Right now, I'm suspicious of just about everybody. What's up?"

"Something else on our Francis Raeburn chap," Adam replied. "Peregrine remembered something that connects."

"Oh? What have you got?"

Briefly Adam related the memory Peregrine had retrieved of the conversation overheard.

"So I called Rowley to see if they could be one and the same—and they are. Apparently he made a rather vitriolic attack on someone's paper at the Highlands and Islands Conference. What's important, though, is that it places him in the area at the time the whole Dunvegan–Loch Ness caper went down. All circumstantial, granted, but at least it's a starting place."

"I'll say. Good work, Peregrine."

"Thanks," Peregrine murmured.

"I got an interesting academic precis, too," Adam went on. "According to Rowley, Raeburn took a First in Classics at Cambridge, started an M. Div. but didn't finish, has funded several archaeological digs, dabbles in local folklore. And I'd be willing to bet that he does more than dabble in certain other areas—though that may be difficult to prove in a court of law."

"Aye, sounds like I ought to have another word with him," McLeod said. "I'm thinking maybe I've got some more questions I'd like to ask him about the rare book trade. In fact, I think I'll go and ask them this afternoon."

"Be careful, Noel. If he *is* our man—"

"Och, aye, I'm not daft, Adam. I've got a healthy respect for anybody connected with putting that lynx letter bomb onto me. But even if he *is* our man, I doubt he'd dare to touch me in broad daylight—especially if I show up in a police car, with Donald to

*314*

back me up, and dragging a trail of red tape after me to show where I've been. I'll ring you from Stirling after I've seen him.''

After McLeod had rung off, Peregrine stayed a while longer, speculating eagerly about what the inspector might discover, but he left shortly before noon.

"There's a Christmas recital at Holyrood Palace this afternoon," he told his mentor. "Something to benefit the National Trust for Scotland. I promised Julia I'd take her—and after abandoning her that night we went up to Blairgowrie, I'd better not disappoint her today. The place should look splendid, all decked out for Christmas."

When Peregrine had gone, Adam looked in on Philippa, who was doing a therapy session with Gillian, spent a few minutes assuring Mrs. Talbot that he really was feeling better than he looked, then decided that perhaps a nap might do him more good than lunch. He had retired to his bedroom and was just drawing the drapes when he looked out across the expanse of lawn and saw a lovely Morgan sportscar nosing up the drive—bright yellow, with black wings and top.

Cautious, he stepped back from the window and watched through a gap in the drapes as the car pulled up in front of the house and stopped. The car was not familiar, and he was not expecting anyone. His surprise was complete, then, when the driver's door opened and a tall, willowy brunette got out. She was halfway up the steps before he realized why her identity had not registered immediately. Green surgical scrubs had not done justice to the lovely Dr. Ximena Lockhart.

Grinning like a schoolboy, he let the drapes fall into place and picked up the bedside phone, buzzing the intercom in the entry hall, since he knew Humphrey would be on his way to the door.

"Ah, good, I've caught you," Adam said, when Humphrey picked up. "I know who the lady is at the door, and I'll be right down. Show her into the library."

Humphrey's "Very good, sir," was as correct and neutral as always, but Adam thought he caught just a hint of amusement. He supposed he *had* sounded a bit eager—and, in fact, he was. Feeling much revitalized, he ducked into the bathroom to comb his hair, lamenting that he had not taken the time to shave before going down for breakfast. Then he decided, what the hell? He was supposed to be convalescing, after all. And designer-stubble was said to be in fashion these days.

Grinning at the face in the mirror, he smoothed the lapels of his dressing gown as best he could under his sling, then headed downstairs. Humphrey was just coming out of the library, and gave him a ghost of a smile as he nodded greeting.

"A Dr. Lockhart to see you, Sir Adam," he said formally.

"Yes, thank you, Humphrey," Adam said. "I'll call if I need you."

She was standing in front of the fireplace, gazing up at the painting of a hunting scene above the mantel. Her dark hair was loose on the shoulders of her long black coat, parted to one side and gently curling. Her turtleneck sweater and skirt were the color of rich cream. She turned as she heard the door open, dark eyes lit with intelligence, wit, and just a hint of challenge.

"So, there you are," she said, one eyebrow arching in faint disapproval, though she was also smiling slightly. "Who told you you could check out of the hospital without your attending physician's approval? What do you think you are, a doctor or something?"

He smiled and slipped his left hand into the pocket of his dressing gown, returning her gaze measure for measure.

"I apologize. Something urgent came up. Since I *am* a doctor, and since my mother, who is *also* a doctor, is here for the holidays, it seemed a not unreasonable thing to do. As you can see, I'm following doctor's orders." He slightly raised his right hand in its sling. "I also have been sleeping in the last few mornings—which is why I haven't yet shaved today. And when you pulled into my front drive, I was just about to have a midday nap. Swear to God!" He raised his left hand in affirmation of his oath.

"Humph!" She looked him up and down critically, then nodded faintly.

"Well, you look like you're doing reasonably well," she conceded. "You might have stuck around a while longer, though. It's a hell of a way to get out of taking a lady to dinner."

"Oh, I have no intention of reneging on our dinner date," Adam said, gesturing for her to be seated. "May I have Humphrey bring tea or coffee? It's a bit early for a drink—unless you'd care to stay for lunch."

She smiled and sat, shrugging out of her coat. "I'd love to, but I'm afraid I have to get back to the hospital. I needed to escape the pre-Christmas crazies in ER for a few hours, so I thought I'd zip up and see how you're doing. A cup of tea would be lovely, though. The Morgan is not exactly snug in this kind of weather."

Smiling, Adam went over to the desk phone and dialled the kitchen.

"Tea for two, please, Humphrey," he said, when the butler

316

picked up. When Humphrey had acknowledged, Adam hung up and came to sit opposite her.

"How do you like your Morgan?" he asked. "I've always been fond of them myself. I ran a Plus Eight when I was at university."

"*Did* you?"

"Oh, yes. It was a bit shabby, I'm afraid, as student vehicles often are, but what it lacked in comfort, it more than made up for in panache."

She grinned. "*Road and Track* says that misery is a Morgan in the rain. They don't even *talk* about a Morgan in the snow. It's cold, it's drafty, it rides like a coal cart—and I love it. But I'm also thinking seriously about getting something else for the winter, laying up that beast until the spring." She eyed him sidelong. "What do you drive now, when you aren't totalling Range Rovers?"

"Oh, I have several old bangers in my stable," he said with a droll smile. "I'd take you out and show you, but I'm not really shod for it." He raised one slippered foot in illustration. "Perhaps you'll come again to visit when I'm better recuperated."

"Is that a variation on 'Come up and see my etchings'?" she replied, fixing him with her direct gaze.

He found himself chuckling. Hers was a good, strong face, pertly attractive rather than classically beautiful, with a clear forthrightness he did not often detect in the women he usually met. He was spared having to answer by a discreet knock at the door, followed by the entry of Humphrey with the tea tray. He started to signal Humphrey to serve, not being certain whether presiding over a silver tea service was standard training for self-assured California physicians, but Ximena moved in gracefully as Humphrey set the tray on a rosewood side table, with every appearance of knowing exactly what she was about.

"I love fine old antiques that actually get used," she said, as she moved the Sevres cups and saucers closer. "Milk and sugar?"

"Please. Two sugars."

"The man says two—and two for the lady. You realize, of course, that we'll both turn into diabetics." As she poured the tea, she looked again at the lines of the teapot. "Yes, this is beautiful work. I'd guess Regency or shortly thereafter, *possibly* very early Victorian. There's a distinct Scottish flavor to it, though."

He nodded appreciatively as she handed over his cup and saucer. She had a good eye to go with the wit and obvious intelligence—and other parts were not too bad, either.

"George IV—1817," he said. "It was made for a great great

grandmother as a wedding present. Those are her arms engraved alongside the Sinclair arms.'' He gestured toward the shields as she picked up the creamer to look more closely. ''Where did you learn about silver tea services?''

''My Austrian grandmother,'' she said, replacing the creamer on the tray. ''Not *all* Yanks are uncivilized, you know.''

''My mother will be delighted to hear you say that,'' he said with a chuckle. ''She's an American and a true Yank—good New England stock. Another psychiatrist, as it happens.''

''Yes, you said she's a physician. Does she practice here?''

''No, no, she's just here for the holidays. She mostly moved back to the States, after my father died. She's got a clinic in New Hampshire. I did some of my training in the States.''

''Really? Where?''

Their conversation treated mostly of medical training while they finished their tea, but Adam found himself increasingly intrigued by the forthright Dr. Ximena Lockhart. When she looked at her watch half an hour later and pronounced it time to leave, he was genuinely sorry, even though his aching body told him his rest was overdue.

''It really has been enjoyable, Dr. Sinclair—a welcome break from the chaos of the ER at this time of year.''

''Then you'll have to come out again,'' he said, standing as she rose. ''And do call me Adam—please.''

She eyed him quizzically, then smiled. ''I'd like that—on both counts,'' she said bluntly. ''And even though you went AWOL on me, I'd like to remain your attending physician, at least until those sutures are out.'' She gestured toward the bandage on his head. ''Which reminds me that I wanted to take a look under the bandage, see how you're healing. May I?''

''You're the doctor,'' he said, sitting at her gesture.

Her touch was gentle as she lifted the tape far enough to peer underneath the dressing, and he was pleasantly aware of her closeness.

''Yes, indeed, you're healing very nicely,'' she said, as she peeled the dressing off the rest of the way. ''Has Mum been taking care of you?''

He smiled slightly, for while Philippa had surveyed the damage shortly after he got home, the daily change of dressing had been the work of the indomitable Humphrey.

''It's handy to have a physician in residence,'' he said simply.

She folded the bandage in half and tossed it on the tea tray with a smile.

"Well, between her work and mine, you should be ready for the sutures to come out in another few days. You can leave it uncovered from here on out. Why don't I drop by a day or two before Christmas, and I'll do the honors? Can't have you looking like Dr. Frankenstein's monster for the holidays."

"Do I look that bad now?" he teased.

"Well, you won't frighten small children," she said archly, "but aesthetically, black silk works better as underwear than as sutures." She probed gently around the wounds again. "I did do a rather good job, though. Is that tender?"

"Not very," he said bemusedly. "The shoulder is what's slowing me down the most. I'm still pretty stiff."

"Well, keep taking the mefenamic acid. You *are* still taking it, aren't you? You didn't take a prescription with you, what with ditching so quickly at the hospital."

He chuckled. "Don't worry. I had Mummy write me new orders, and I've been taking my medication like a good boy."

"Ve-ry *good*," she said, as if amazed to hear it. "I'll have to meet this mother of yours, who can make you follow doctor's orders. I've really got to run now, though. Thanks for the tea."

As she picked up her coat, he rose and helped her into it, one-handed though he was.

"You're very welcome. And thank *you* for stopping by. I appreciate the visit."

"My pleasure," she replied. "ER physicians don't often get to make house calls—and to such amazing houses. And I *will* make another one in about a week, to take out those sutures—unless you're determined to do it yourself."

"No, I think I'll let my attending physician do that," he said, smiling as he walked her to the door. "It will give her another excuse to attend."

"Will you show me your 'bangers' next time?" she quipped.

"Oh, yes. And possibly my etchings too," he returned.

She laughed delightedly and waved as she headed down the steps to her car. Adam did not accompany her, for the steps were icy and his slippers not up to such footing, but he stood in the open doorway until the yellow-and-black Morgan had disappeared down the drive before returning to the shelter of the house.

He retired for a much-needed nap after that, and woke around four, now ready to eat again. McLeod rang as he was finishing, but the news was sparse.

"Our bird seems to have flown the coop," he said, as Adam

strained to make out his voice over the background noise of heavy traffic. "We talked to his houseboy, but Raeburn allegedly is out of town on business—funny business, if you ask me. Anyway, Donald and I are going to do some follow-up when we get back to the office—see what else we can find out about his personal history."

"What have you got so far?" Adam asked.

"A bit more, from checking the Who's Whos and such. He's listed in official bio's as a business entrepreneur—which is a pretty broad classification. All his current CV's make much of him being a native Scot, born and bred in Scotland. I'm going to do some further checking. I should have something more solid sometime tomorrow."

It wasn't until mid-afternoon of the following day that McLeod called back. But as soon as Adam heard the inspector's voice, he knew McLeod had something to be excited about.

"Well, chalk up another good hunch," the inspector said. "I knew there was something hinky about him, besides just being an unpleasant fellow. I had a contact at St. Catherine's House in London do a search on both birth and marriage records. Our Mr. Raeburn was *not* born in Scotland, and only one of his parents was Scottish. He was born in London and subsequently raised by his maternal grandparents at their house in Stirling, Nether Leckie, where he now lives. Raeburn is actually his mother's name."

"Was she not married to his father, then?" Adam asked.

"Oh, she was married to him, all right. The birth was legitimate."

"You're about to drop the other shoe," Adam said. "Who was his father?"

"How about a Welshman, name of David Tudor-Jones?"

A large number of the remaining pieces in the puzzle suddenly came together with a snap. David Tudor-Jones had been Master of the Lodge of the Lynx in the time of Adam's predecessor, and was the man most directly responsible for the death of Sir Michael Brodie, Lady Julian's husband.

"Good God," Adam said flatly. "You do realize who we're talking about here?"

"Aye. It appears that Philippa isn't the only one to have passed on her knowledge and vocation to her offspring. I thought that line had been cut off at the root, years ago."

"So did I," Adam said.

He stared distractedly at the wall in front of him, seeing not the wallpaper pattern of lilies and wheat-sheaves but the image of

Randall Stewart lying dead in his own frozen blood, in a snowy wood north of Blairgowrie—and a much earlier memory, when he himself was still hardly more than a fledgling like Peregrine, mourning with an earlier configuration of the Hunting Lodge over the slain Michael Brodie.

"So where do we go from here?" McLeod asked, after a pregnant silence, broken only by the sound of the traffic in the background.

"We shift into Hunting mode," Adam said incisively. "I'm thinking of the pendulum work Peregrine did Sunday afternoon. I'm thinking that it might be profitable to check out that area in the Cairngorms that he kept coming back to. We now *know* why he kept indicating Stirling. Do you think you could get tomorrow off?"

"Impossible, on such short notice," McLeod replied. "I'm still tied up with the Dunfermline case. I *might* be able to get away on Thursday."

"That will have to do, then," Adam said. "I probably ought to check in at the hospital anyway. I haven't made rounds since *last* Wednesday. I definitely want you along, though, if there's even a chance that the Lynx have established a new lair up there."

"Are you sure you're up to all of this?" McLeod asked.

"I'll manage—and better with you along than without," he said. "I'll dragoon Peregrine into coming too. It'll be a warm-up for his initiation. Incidentally, we're aiming at Friday night, to put back the pieces for Gillian Talbot and hopefully to bring Peregrine officially into the Lodge. Can I count on you?"

"Wouldn't miss it," McLeod replied. "We'll plan on Thursday, then, for our foray north. The snow's been heavy. What do you want to do about a vehicle? Your Rover isn't going anywhere besides the scrap yard, and we'll want four-wheel drive, for that terrain."

"How about if you ferret out a suitable rental and bring it up Thursday morning to my place?" Adam suggested. "Will your credit card stand the deposit? I'll put it all on mine, when I return it. And Peregrine and I will drive you home Thursday night, when we get back."

"That's workable on all counts," McLeod agreed. "What time do you want me there Thursday morning?"

"Make it about six, and I'll have Humphrey lay on a hearty breakfast before we head out. That way, we can clear Perth before the morning traffic hits. Meanwhile, keep me informed if anything else turns up tomorrow, will you?"

He had Humphrey run a written message down to the gate lodge when McLeod had rung off, for he knew Peregrine was off on a sketching session for a new portrait commission and expected to be back late. Mrs. Talbot joined him and Philippa for dinner later that evening, but afterwards Adam drew his mother aside for a quick update on developments and plans before an early bed.

He was recovering every day, though. On Wednesday morning he actually managed to tie his tie without assistance for the first time since his accident, and was feeling almost his usual self as Humphrey drove him in to Jordanburn. He had exchanged the industrial-strength sling of canvas and nylon webbing for a more discreet black silk scarf supporting his wrist, since he still needed to keep the weight off his abused shoulder. However, this only lent a subtle dash to his usual dapper appearance, almost disappearing against his navy suit, as he made abbreviated rounds of all his hospital patients and held an impromptu seminar for his students.

After lunch, on impulse, he had Humphrey detour past the Royal Infirmary. A distinctive yellow-and-black Morgan caught his eye in the physicians' car park, so he directed Humphrey to pull up in one of the ambulance bays outside Emergency while he poked his head inside. The place was a bustle of activity, as such places tended to be, but though he did not immediately spot Ximena, he did recognize the orderly who had wheeled him around the previous Friday.

"Good afternoon, Mr. Sykes," he said, as the dapper Jamaican glanced up and gave him a grin.

"Hey, Dr. Sinclair! How're you doing? Dr. Lockhart was really miffed when you did your Houdini on us last week. You here to have your stitches out?"

"Not for a few more days," Adam allowed with a smile. "Do you know if she's available?"

"Hmmm, I think she's with a patient, but let me see how long she's gonna be."

He ducked his head into several treatment rooms, but he was shaking his head when he emerged from the last one a few minutes later.

"Man, she's got two more waiting for her after this one," Sykes said. "You might catch a few words with her while she's in transit, though, if you move fast. You here to let her take you up on her dinner prize?"

"Well, a gentleman never reneges on a promise to a lady," Adam replied, constraining a grin. "It doesn't look too promising for tonight, though, does it?"

"Hmmm, 'fraid not, Doc. Everybody tries to get extra time off at the holidays, and one of our consultants hasn't shown all week. Poor Dr. X has been working her pretty buns off, covering for everybody—ah, no disrespect, sir. She's one hell of a doctor."

"Yes, I'd noticed both qualities," he said with bland neutrality, though something in Sykes' remark about a missing consultant had piqued his interest. "Who's the consultant who hasn't shown? Maybe I know him."

"It's Dr. Wemyss. You might have met him the day you came in. But here's herself. Move fast, if you want to catch her!"

Sykes melted into the background as Ximena came out of the treatment room, looking for and then spotting Adam. She gave him a weary smile and extended her hand as she came toward him, glancing approvingly at his silk sling as she briefly squeezed his left hand.

"Hello, Adam. What a pleasant surprise in an otherwise ghastly day. What are you doing out and about?"

"I thought I'd better make some rounds," he said easily. "I hadn't seen most of my patients for a solid week—even worse than your missing man."

"Oh, you mean Dr. Wemyss," she said. "Sykes must have told you. Kind of an odd guy—good physician, but not very personable. We're beginning to worry, though. Nobody's seen him since Saturday. But how are *you*?"

He shrugged and smiled. "Definitely on the mend—and up to dinner tonight, if you are."

She grimaced, wrinkling her nose. "Oh, you *are* cruel. I haven't gotten lunch yet, and there's no way I'll be able to get away for dinner. Maybe one night later in the week, if Wemyss comes back or we get a locum in."

"Unfortunately, I'm engaged for the next two evenings," Adam said, feeling oddly disappointed, "but maybe at the weekend. Do you still intend to come out and remove my stitches?"

"Beg pardon, Dr. Lockhart, but we're ready for you now," a nurse called from another treatment room.

Rolling her eyes, Ximena waved a hand in the nurse's direction, looking frustrated.

"That's certainly my intention, but this place is crazy! I'll try to call you first. It may be at short notice."

"Fair enough," Adam said. "If you take a peek out to the ambulance bays before you run off, you'll get a free preview of that tour I promised of my motor house."

As he jogged his chin in that direction, she moved a few steps closer to the doors to look where he directed.

"An old Bentley. Nice," she murmured, glancing at him in approval. "Sir Adam Sinclair, you are *on*! Gotta go now, though. I'll call you. Bye."

So saying, she darted in quickly to peck him on the cheek, then was gone, leaving him with a last glimpse of the dark bob of her ponytail against the clean line of her green-clad back. He must have had a silly grin on his face, because the orderly Sykes gave him a droll, knowing nod as he bestirred himself to go back out into the cold.

He wanted to keep her image in his mind on the drive home, but he found himself thinking instead about the missing Dr. Wemyss, who had last been seen on Saturday. He had heard the name before.

It took him a while to remember where, casting back in trance, but by the time Humphrey was guiding the big Bentley down the last stretch of drive toward Strathmourne House, he had tracked the memory to a conversation overheard between his pretty red-headed nurse of Friday night and the pharmacist who had brought up the medication that proved to have been tampered with—something about being delayed because a Dr. Wemyss had insisted on some pharmacy records being checked.

That had to have been when the switch was made—and Wemyss' disappearance as of Saturday suggested that he might have been the one responsible for the astral lynx attack the night before, gone to ground after his failure to take Adam out. It was a sobering thought, but having a name to attach to his possible attacker was encouraging. Now, if they could make a connection between Wemyss and Raeburn. . . .

He rang McLeod when he got back to the house, to have him put Donald Cochrane on the trail of the name, but the inspector and Cochrane had already left for the day, probably to pick up the car for tomorrow's outing. So he rang the Royal Infirmary to get Wemyss' first name—Preston—then filed the information to tell McLeod about it in the morning, on their way north.

# CHAPTER THIRTY-TWO

HE told McLeod and Peregrine over breakfast the next morning, while they all shovelled down porridge, eggs and toast, nearly a dozen rashers of bacon among the three of them, and Mrs. Gilchrist's ubiquitous scones washed down with tea—fuel for their day in the cold and open. Philippa joined them for the briefing, but confined herself to her usual fare of grapefruit, tea, and toast. They reviewed their maps then, finalizing their route, and McLeod rang Donald Cochrane at home just before they left, to put him on the Preston Wemyss trail before they headed out.

"Find out whatever you can about him without arousing undue suspicion, Donald," McLeod told the younger officer. "It sounds like friends and colleagues might be on the verge of filing a missing persons report, which would certainly make our lives easier, but right now, we don't *know* that he's done anything wrong. It isn't against the law to disappear. I do want to know if you can make any connection with Raeburn, though."

"Will do, Inspector," Cochrane replied. "And good luck to you, sir."

"Thanks, Donald."

They were on the road just after seven. The white Toyota Land Cruiser McLeod had rented for the venture was not as luxurious or as comfortable as the Range Rover, but it ate up the miles with ease, coping with sometimes atrocious road conditions once they got past Perth. In hopes of avoiding the worst of the winter conditions, they edged more westerly out of Perth rather than heading on through Blairgowrie and Braemar, making reasonably good time through towns with such historic names as Pitlochry, Killiecrankie, and Blair Atholl and skirting the evergreen sweeps of the Forest of Atholl. Climbing on through the Grampians then, as the A9 curved back northward toward Kingussie and Aviemore, they wound more easterly again, skirting the dark fastness of the Forest of Glen More and heading ever nearer the area Peregrine had isolated in the Cairngorm Mountains.

It was approaching noon as they turned off what passed for a main road in this part of the Highlands and snaked along a road still paved, but treacherous with ice and pot-holes, looking for an even narrower turn-off that showed on their maps only as a pale brown line. It finally materialized on the blind side of a sharp bend in the road, and McLeod had to brake sharply and reverse for several yards before nosing the Toyota through a narrow slot between two freestone markers.

The single-track road beyond was rough and rutted, all but snowed over in many places, and the Toyota's four-wheel drive became essential rather than merely handy as they crept along it, anxiously peering ahead. Several times, McLeod glanced back at Peregrine as if to question whether they should proceed, but Peregrine always nodded yes.

After half an hour of this, they came at last to a corrugated iron gate posted with a sign that read, *Private—No Trespassing.* A rusty but sturdy-looking padlock locked it shut, and to either side, barbed-wire strands receded into snowy banks and increasing gloom. Behind them, their tire tracks showed black as licorice against the snow, already icing up, with noon past and an early dusk already starting to descend. At one o'clock in the northern Highlands, just a day short of mid-winter, they had perhaps another two hours of decent light before darkness began to close in, even if the weather did not. A light fall of new snow had already begun to dust their windscreen, and Adam leaned across to switch on the wipers.

"What do you think?" he said quietly, as the swish of the wipers joined with the low idle of the engine.

"I think," said McLeod, as Peregrine craned to peer between the seat backs, "that from here, if we go on, we go on foot. I also think that I should turn the car around before we set foot outside. I don't like the feel of this place."

"Neither do I," Adam said quietly. "Not that we expected anything different."

McLeod had to back up nearly twenty yards to a slightly wider place in the road to accomplish the necessary maneuver, and even then, it took him half a dozen to-and-fro's to get the car turned. As he switched off the ignition, the silence of the place settled around them like a cloak, close and heavy. None of them dared to speak or even breathe for several seconds, until finally Adam reached behind the seat for Peregrine to hand him his snow boots, and they all began preparing to brave the elements.

Peregrine kept his head down as he laced up his hiking boots, but he saw McLeod tuck the familiar Browning Hi-Power into his waistband, a couple of spare ammo clips going into the pockets of his black anorak. Adam had left his sling behind today, and had McLeod help him pull on his sheepskin coat when they had gotten out of the car. He had looped a tiny pair of Pentax binoculars over his head while still inside, and tucked them into the front of his coat before partially buttoning it and then drawing on a white knitted watch cap and fur-lined gloves. Peregrine suspected he was also carrying his *skean dubh*. Certainly he and McLeod both wore their rings under their gloves, as Peregrine carried his deep in a trouser pocket.

Other than that, Peregrine was armed with only his wits and a sketch pad and pencils. He had decided against bringing his entire sketchbox—just one more thing to carry if they had to beat a hasty retreat. But he had thought to bring gloves with liners this time, so he could sketch in the cold, and he had a nubbly Arran cap to keep his ears warm. McLeod had come similarly prepared for the cold, and to his other accoutrements added a Polaroid camera which he pulled from his utility bag behind the front seats. He, too, had binoculars hanging around his neck, larger than Adam's pair.

"It occurred to me that photos would be useful," he said, patting the camera as he pushed his door closed but did not slam or lock it. "It'll probably be too dark to get much, but it can't hurt to try. Now let's see how far we can get. And keep your voices down. Sound carries farther than you'd think."

Their first obstacle was the gate, but they did not even bother with that. Heading them about twenty yards farther along the fence to the left, where some of the fence posts had sagged, McLeod gingerly poised the car keys about two inches above the top strand of barbed-wire, then dropped them to straddle the wire—without apparent effect.

"Well, at least it isn't electrified," he murmured, retrieving the keys and then grasping the top strand with both gloved hands, while a booted foot pressed the others to the ground. "Of course, I may have set off other alarms—and I may be plain paranoid. Come on through, you two."

Bending stiffly, Adam folded himself to ease through the gap, helped Peregrine through, then caught the top strand for McLeod as he followed. Ahead, the snow-covered road stretched into ever-whitening dimness, heading gently upward and around to the right.

"I'll take the point," McLeod murmured, heading out purposefully. "You two stay alert."

He forged on ahead then, keeping to one side, the aviator glasses constantly scanning, and Peregrine fell in opposite Adam as they followed after. They carried on up the road in silence for perhaps half a mile, till it bridged the stone-arched span of a narrow, half-frozen stream. From somewhere farther up the valley, they could hear the gurgle of water running under the ice. As they continued to advance, climbing now, Peregrine became aware of a strange undercurrent of vibrations in the air, like the subsonic rumble of distant thunder. A glance at Adam confirmed that he was feeling it, too—or maybe it was the stress of the climb.

"Are you all right?" Peregrine whispered.

"Aye."

Adam tightened his lips and narrowed his gaze as he scanned the lay of the land ahead. He was breathing a little more heavily than usual under the stress of his body's lingering aches and pains, and he leaned into the angle of the slope and struggled his way up the sharp incline. McLeod was waiting for them at the top, crouched behind the remains of an ancient stone wall and training his binoculars on something still at some distance off to their left, perched at the side of a low waterfall above the stream. As Adam signalled Peregrine to keep his head down, he struggled his way across the remaining few feet to slip in beside the inspector, Peregrine coming to his other side. Silently McLeod pointed toward what could just be perceived as an artificial structure of some kind, apparently built of stone.

"What do you make of that?" he whispered. "Maybe a Lynx lair?"

Not answering, Adam pulled out his binoculars and tried to focus them on the distant building. Snow was still powdering down, but even allowing for that, the image coming in seemed strangely indistinct. He blew on the lenses to clear any dust and readjusted them for a second look, but McLeod snorted softly.

"You too, eh?" he whispered. "It's no use. The place is so heavily warded, I can't make out anything more than a general outline. It won't photograph properly, either. Look at these."

He pulled several Polaroid snaps out of his pocket, but though the surrounds of the structure were reasonably clear for the distance and conditions, the structure itself was too blurred to see much.

"Can't we get any nearer than this?" Peregrine asked.

"Not without risk of exposure," Adam said. Even as he spoke, he could feel the dark potency residing within those towering walls rasping away at his nerves like iron chains wearing against raw flesh. At close range, the effect would be devastating without more strength to counter it than could be mustered here at this present time. Even so, he was reluctant to give the order to withdraw before they had had a chance to form some clearer impression of just what it was up there.

"What do *you* see, Peregrine?" he asked softly, turning his glance to the artist. "Have a look through the glasses, and see if you can get them to focus."

He passed the smaller binoculars to Peregrine, who pulled off his spectacles and put the binoculars to his eyes. The physical focus wouldn't quite come, but he had the feeling that if he let his vision kick in, he might be able to see something more.

"Let me have a go with a pencil," he said, with more conviction than he felt. "After all, isn't that why I'm here?"

As Adam and McLeod exchanged uneasy looks, Peregrine squirmed himself around until he could get at the sketch pad inside his duffel coat, pulling off his outer gloves with his teeth and then stuffing them into a pocket. He was pulling a pencil out of an inside pocket when Adam laid a restraining hand on his shoulder.

"Hold for just a moment, Peregrine," he said, as McLeod circled behind them both to settle on Peregrine's left. "Give us a chance to put a little protection on you before you begin. This is something different from anything you've dealt with before."

Mystified, but trusting their judgment, Peregrine paused with pencil in hand and spectacles once more in place, bowing his head as hands came to rest on his shoulders from either side. He did not understand the words that Adam murmured, close by his right ear, but he could feel a warmth that was not physical gradually surrounding him. After a moment, he felt Adam's hand tighten on his shoulder, in signal that he and McLeod were done.

"All right, go for it—but be careful," Adam said softly.

Peregrine drew a deep breath and raised his gaze to the target ahead, narrowing his gaze. The objects near at hand receded into a hazy blur. He took several more deep breaths, like a pearl fisherman preparing for a dive, then took the plunge, cautiously extending himself to see through the cloud of ill-intent that separated him and his guardians from the stronghold of their enemies.

It was like wading into a polluted stream. He could almost feel the noxious film of psychic corruption clinging to his skin. Shivering in disgust, he made an effort of will to penetrate to the heart of the fog. There was a queasy ripple before his eyes, and all at once, for the twinkling of an eye, he had an unobstructed view of the castle and its outer environs.

In the same instant of awareness, the brooding presence within the house became aware of an intrusion and struck back with a blind blast of energy. The force of it was like a whiplash aimed at his eyes. Even as Peregrine made a gasping recoil, the force of it broke against the invisible wall that Adam and McLeod had erected. There was a sharp crackle, like invisible sparks, and a sudden yawning silence.

"That's it! We're out of here!" McLeod ordered, physically seizing him by the arm and starting to shuffle him down the slope as Adam scrambled to his feet and followed. "Try to keep your mind as blank as possible, and don't look back!"

Together they beat a hasty retreat back in the direction they had come, slogging through snow now somewhat deeper than before. By the time they regained the car, all of them were breathing hard and sweating inside their heavy winter gear, and Adam was whiter than the cap he swept off as he almost fell into the front passenger seat. As McLeod clambered into the driver's seat and cranked the ignition, Peregrine fumbled urgently for his seat belt in the back, anticipating another of the wild rides of which he knew the inspector was capable.

"Brace yourselves, everybody," McLeod said, as he hit the accelerator.

The Toyota leaped forward, slewing and fish-tailing until McLeod kicked in the four-wheel drive. Twilight was deepening, but he dared not turn on the headlights for fear of revealing their position, if they were being pursued. Adam had pulled off his gloves and was holding onto the grab bar with his left hand, eyes closed and head bowed against the back of his right. At first Peregrine thought he was just concentrating on catching his breath after their wild sprint, but then he realized that the odd position of Adam's right hand was so that he could press the stone of his ring against his forehead.

"Adam?" he dared to whisper, as the car continued to jounce and skid.

"Leave him be!" McLeod snapped, muttering as he had to brake for another curve.

"But, what's he doing?"

"Protecting us. Try to do the same."

"But, how—"

"I told you before—try to keep your mind a blank!"

The order brooked no further discussion or question. Suitably subdued, Peregrine sat back and tried to do as he was told, doing his best to hold the image in his mind of a blank canvas awaiting his brush. It was difficult, because he kept wanting to paint on it, and some of the images that came to mind were not pleasant—which probably was precisely why he was supposed to keep his mind a blank.

Somewhere about the time McLeod got the car back on pavement again and could pick up speed, Peregrine had about gotten the knack of it; and by the time they were merging back onto the A9 and speeding south again, he had almost started to doze off.

"We're all right now," Adam said suddenly, when they had passed the turn-off to Kingussie and Newtonmore and were speeding southward into the Grampians again. "Noel, I think it's safe to pull off at the next lay-by for a few minutes. Peregrine, you'll find some sandwiches and tea in that hamper behind the seat you're sitting in."

The sigh of relief from McLeod's direction suggested to Peregrine that perhaps their escape had not been as foregone a conclusion as first thought. He kept his eyes and ears open and his mouth shut as he manhandled the hamper forward and set it on the seat beside him, starting to rummage inside and see what Humphrey had packed for them. After a few more minutes, the desired lay-by came up and McLeod slowed and pulled the Toyota to a halt. The snow seemed to have stopped, and when McLeod had switched off the ignition, he pulled off his glasses and tossed them on the dash as he breathed an enormous sigh.

"Well, that was a near-run thing," he said. "Hand me a sandwich, would you, Peregrine? Breakfast gave out several hours ago, and I'm about to perish for want of food."

Wide-eyed, Peregrine put a sandwich in the hand that reached back over McLeod's shoulder, handing another forward to Adam. As the two started eating, Peregrine attacked his own, dying to hear more but determined not to ask. McLeod's hands were shaking as he ate, and when Peregrine noticed, he passed Adam one of the thermos flasks, saying, "You want to get some hot tea in him?"

Murmuring his thanks, Adam filled a cup and set it in McLeod's hands. When the inspector had downed half of it, sitting back then to lean his head against the rest and cradle the cup between his hands, eyes closed, Adam half-turned in his seat to glance at Peregrine.

"All right. Before I comment on what's just happened, suppose you tell me what you saw."

Peregrine shook his head. He'd been trying to decide just what he *had* seen for the last hour and more, the whole time they were coming down from the Cairngorms.

"I really don't know, Adam. It was powerful, but it wasn't like the stuff connected with the Lynx that I've always seen before. This was different—even more malevolent, if you can imagine that. I'm going to have to think about it. I couldn't even begin to try to draw it yet."

"Noel?" Adam said.

McLeod tossed back the rest of his tea and put his glasses back on, apparently somewhat recovered.

"He's right," he said. "There's something more at work here besides the Lynx—something big enough that *I* don't want to tangle with it until we have a whole lot better idea what we're up against. Oh, the Lynx is involved, but this—this is heavy-duty stuff. It may be where the human sacrifice angle is coming in. The Lynx were never particularly oriented that way before."

"I agree," Adam said. "I couldn't even begin to speculate. Well done, both of you." He glanced at the clock on the dash. "But we'd better get going, for now. Noel, would you like Peregrine to drive the rest of the way in? You look like you're pretty well knackered."

"What about it, Peregrine, old son?" McLeod replied, wearily tilting his head back in Peregrine's direction. "Think you can take this bus in from here?"

"Of course," Peregrine replied. The easy camaraderie reassured him that he really *was* a full-fledged member of the team. He changed places with McLeod and buckled up, adjusting the mirrors and seat angle to suit him, but the inspector was snoring softly before Peregrine even pulled back into traffic. Out of deference to McLeod's obvious need for sleep, Peregrine kept silent for the rest of the drive back. He wondered whether Adam was dozing as well, but every time he glanced aside where there was light enough to see, Adam was always gazing distractedly through the windscreen, arms folded on his chest.

They got to McLeod's house just after eight and dropped him off, but as they headed back across the Forth Road Bridge toward home, Adam bestirred himself to direct Peregrine toward a turn-off just on the other side, which led eventually to a scenic panorama looking back across the Firth. Snow had started falling again, and the distant lights of Edinburgh twinkled like diamonds strung along the black velvet of the distant shore.

"What is it?" Peregrine asked, when he had turned off the engine. "Why did you want to stop here?"

Sighing, Adam gazed out across the twinkling darkness, leaning his head against the seat back.

"It's Solstice Eve," he said quietly, "almost the turning of the year. I make it a habit to come up here every year about this time, to remind myself what it's all about, what it's all in aid of—what we do."

Frowning slightly, Peregrine looked out across the Firth.

"I don't think I understand."

"Don't you?" He drew a soft breath and let it out slowly. "Listen to the silence, Peregrine. *Feel* it. The whole world is in darkness, holding its breath in expectation. 'When all the world was in still silence and night was in the midst of her swift course, Thine almighty Word, O Lord, leaped down from heaven out of the Royal Throne. . . .'"

"Oh, you mean Christmas," Peregrine said.

Adam smiled. "Not exactly. Or only in part, I suppose would be a better answer. Out beyond the physical lights of that city we guard, there's the glow of a different kind of Light, like a vast umbrella of pure white energy that's part of a vaster canopy that covers the entire planet. Its source is in the hearts of men and women of good will who, especially at this time of year, are turning their thoughts and prayers toward the coming of the Light. They belong to many races and creeds, but all of them, in all their myriad ways, are reaching toward a closer communion with that Light, regardless of the external form their acknowledgement takes. There are some lines by T.S. Eliot that say it very well. I think he understood. He may even have been one of us. He said:

'O Light Invisible, we praise Thee!
Too bright for mortal vision. . . .
We thank Thee for the lights that we have kindled,
the light of altar and of sanctuary;
small lights of those who meditate at midnight
and lights directed through the coloured panes of windows
and light reflected from the polished stone,
the gilded carven wood, the coloured fresco.
Our gaze is submarine, our eyes look upward
and see the light that fractures through unquiet water.
We see the light but see not whence it comes.
O Light Invisible, we glorify Thee!'"

As his voice trailed off, Peregrine was staring at him avidly.

"I could paint that," he whispered. "I saw the entire canvas as you said it. What's the name of the poem?"

"It's called Choruses from 'The Rock,'" Adam replied. "What's most important, though, is that at this time of year, all over this planet, literally millions of human beings are preparing to acknowledge the return of the Light. The rebirth of the Sun is a far more ancient and potent symbol than the commercial observances you'll see taking place in a few days, on a day called Christmas—which is an arbitrary date anyway, since no one really knows when the man who was to become the Christ was born."

Peregrine smiled. "That sounds almost cynical, coming from a Christian. I thought you were devout."

"Oh, I am. And in this time and place, and in this life, I choose to frame my service to the Most High in the outward form of Christianity. It provides one of the more powerful sets of symbols for what's about to happen. How did Paulinus of Nola put it? Let's see if I can remember a decent translation. Ah, yes.

"'For it is after the solstice, when Christ born in the flesh with the new sun transformed the season of cold winter and, vouchsafing to mortal men a healing dawn, commanded the nights to decrease at His coming with advancing day.'

"There, you see?" He grinned. "The Solstice Story in a Christian context, and beautifully put, too. Seriously, though, it's important to realize and really *know* that allegiance to the Light goes far beyond any sectarian differences. Oh, organized religions certainly serve their purpose, sending up little psychic beacons of light—you can see some of them, if you turn your vision toward that end, hovering above church steeples and the like.

"But the overall umbrella of psychic goodwill is what's most important, regardless of how people choose to frame their support of it, regardless what form the outward observances take. In fact, I suppose you could say that's one of the important things that Masons and other quasi-esoteric organizations do: they generate a substantial portion of the general umbrella of white light that protects the psychic consciousness of the world from the shadows of evil, filling in the gaps left by organized religions."

Peregrine thought about that imagery for a moment, then nodded.

"Then, maybe the Lodge of the Lynx is trying to punch holes in that umbrella," he said. "Maybe that's what the lightning bolts are for, and they're killing Masons because Masons help keep the umbrella intact."

Startled, Adam glanced at Peregrine. He had never considered the problem in precisely those terms before, but perhaps it was an angle worth pursuing. God knew, whatever was lurking up in the Cairngorms had something larger in mind than simply picking off Freemasons.

"You know, you may well have something there," he said quietly. "I'll have to think more on that angle." He paused to cover a yawn. "In the meantime, I suppose we ought to get home and let Philippa know what's happened. Let's go, and I'll buy you a drink."

They ended up gorging on stacks of Humphrey's hot ham sandwiches first, though, while Philippa pumped them for information on the day's near misadventure. Peregrine was feeling replete and slightly drowsy as he settled back into one of the chairs in the library with two fingers of the MacAllan in a crystal tumbler.

"By the way, that's the last alcohol you're to have until I tell you otherwise," Adam said, settling back with his own drink. "And tomorrow, no food after midday."

At Peregrine's look of dismay, Philippa laughed and set aside her sherry.

"I'm afraid Adam's gone and made one of his leaps of logic, my dear," she told him, reaching across to pat his knee. "We've been tentatively planning this for over a week now—since before Adam's accident, actually—but obviously no one bothered to tell one of the principal participants. We're going to try to sort out Gillian tomorrow night—with your help, of course. Along with that, if you're still willing, we'd like to present you for formal initiation into our company. You've seen enough by now to know that ours is a dangerous vocation. But should you choose to join us, we pledge you our fullest friendship and support, even unto death."

"And beyond," Adam added quietly.

All thought of drowsiness fled, and Peregrine fought down a queer fluttering sensation in his midsection as he glanced at Adam. His mentor had a tiny smile on his lips, and obviously was expecting him to say something.

"I—can't think of anything I've ever wanted more than what you've just been generous enough to offer me," he said with an effort, returning his gaze to Philippa. "Of course I'm willing. I only hope I can prove worthy of your confidence. But whatever abilities I've been blessed with—I gladly offer them in your service.''

"Fine, that's settled then—though it isn't only *our* service,'' Philippa said with a smile, picking up her sherry again. "Welcome to our company, my dear.''

She stayed with them only a few more minutes, while they went over practical logistics for the next day, retiring then to leave the two men their privacy. No one knew better than Adam that the prospect of initiation was likely to prove as daunting as it was exhilarating for his fledgling hawk, so he was not surprised when his young protege tossed off the rest of his drink and, with a look of sheer determination bordering on panic, turned to face him squarely.

"Adam, you're probably going to think me an awful fool,'' he said with the air of one making a confession, "but it only now occurs to me that I haven't got the faintest idea how to prepare for this. I mean, isn't there something I ought to be doing? Something I ought to be studying, or something I should at least be thinking about?''

Adam's dark eyes held a grave twinkle. "As far as preparations are concerned, I think you've already served quite a successful apprenticeship. Beyond that, the fact that you're asking me these very questions means that you're already moving toward the right frame of mind. I can recommend nothing better than to continue as you're already doing—searching your own heart and conscience with the intention of offering up all that you are and may become to the service of the One who is also the true Light.''

"But, isn't an initiation a kind of test?'' Peregrine asked.

"Oh, you will, indeed, be tested, if that's what you mean,'' Adam said with a smile, "but not so much to prove your knowledge as to try the mettle of your spirit, the way precious ore is refined and strengthened by firing.''

"It's an ordeal, then,'' Peregrine said.

"Well, not in the sense of anguish and pain,'' Adam replied, "but it *will* be a trial. It shouldn't be beyond you, though, if I've judged your potential correctly—and I'm confident that I have.''

"I see,'' Peregrine said quietly. "Is it permitted to ask what form the trial will take?''

"Oh, you may certainly ask,'' Adam said with a smile, "but that decision is not entirely mine to make. We've spoken before of your affinity with the spirit that was Michael Scot and now resides in the person of young Gillian, and how all the facets of her former incarnations must be reintegrated for healing to take place. The task that has been ordained for you—the task by which you will prove yourself—is to assist in the restoration of the order of her soul.''

Peregrine's eyes widened slightly. "Adam, you know that there's nothing that would please me more, to be able to help her,'' he said, "but I can't even pretend that I know how.''

"You will when the time comes," Adam said. "Don't be afraid to rely on your own intuitions. The true rite of passage takes place on an interior level. Whatever form the internal imagery will take for you, I also cannot predict at this point, but this much I *can* promise you: that you will perceive all in symbols appropriate to you.

"Nor will you be alone. Noel and I will be with you to guide you, and there will be others of the fellowship present, either in body or in spirit, to support you with their own hopes and aspirations.''

"Well, that's a relief,'' Peregrine said with a small, nervous chuckle. "But there's still one other thing.''

"What's that?''

"I keep thinking about that day we went with Father Christopher to cleanse that flat in Edinburgh. I watched everything that you and he did between you, and I realize that you both meant it to be an act of worship. But I have to tell you that I don't understand it. I mean, I don't think I know *how* to worship. What I'm feeling, even at this moment, seems to demand that I express it in some formal way, but I—don't know what gestures to make, what words to say. Hearing you speak just now of initiation as a refinement of the soul, I realize that it's an incredibly momentous occasion, but—nothing in my past experience seems to suggest anything about how I ought to behave.''

"It isn't a matter of behaving," Adam said with a smile, "but rather, of becoming. Such external ritual as we do is certainly important to our work, but only as a common framework, insofar as it serves to call forth what is already present by grace in our souls. If you really want guidance, I suggest that you go back to the dream-work that you've used before to get you pointed in the right direction. And tomorrow, I suggest that you sleep in and then spend the day painting that T.S. Eliot poem. I'll give you a copy to take back to the lodge. I advise you to read it before you go to bed, and see what happens.''

# CHAPTER THIRTY-THREE

PEREGRINE brought his painting up to the house shortly before ten o'clock the following night. He had done it in watercolors, to echo the imagery of the poem, and he thought he had captured most of what he had tried to convey of the images that had come to him regarding the Light in its many manifestations.

Philippa admitted him and McLeod was already waiting in the library, though more subdued than was his usual wont, which perhaps reflected the solemnity of the night's undertaking. Shortly thereafter, Adam came in with Christopher and Victoria Houston, and all of them gathered around the painting propped on one of the library chairs. The mood was at once grave and expectant, as if all present were about to offer up a sacrifice—as perhaps, Peregrine reflected wonderingly, they all were.

"I believe Peregrine's painting speaks to all of us of what this night is all about," Adam finally said, his quiet voice embracing each of them with the warmth of both mentor and colleague. "With that in mind, both Christopher and I felt that, before beginning tonight's Work, it would be appropriate to first celebrate Evensong. So we'll adjourn temporarily to the chapel, where Christopher will lead us in our devotions. Shall we go?"

This was the first time Peregrine had ever heard Adam mention the presence of a private chapel on the premises. He was even more surprised to discover that they were going down into the wine cellar. Some of his puzzlement must have been evident, because Adam held him back at the foot of the stairs to explain.

"The chapel was a subterranean feature of the house that stood on this spot before Strathmourne was built," he said. "Because its very existence was secret, it came to be used as a priest's hole, to shelter priests on the run from the secular authorities. The Sinclairs have always found it expedient to keep that secret, except that when Mother became a Sinclair, she decided to expand its use. It's still a consecrated Christian chapel, and we'll use it as such tonight, but it's also a place where the Hunting Lodge sometimes gathers on the physical plane for Work requiring a more formal setting.'' He glanced beyond Peregrine at the door where the others had disappeared.

''They'll be about ready for us now—and you can relax. This is *just* Evensong. The real work tonight will take place up in Gillian's room—and in *there*.'' He tapped Peregrine lightly on the forehead, smiling as he did, then urged him on past the wine bins.

Beyond the door that stood ajar, McLeod was waiting in a narrow passageway. Candlelight streamed from a chamber beyond, and the smaller room off to the right, where Victoria and Philippa were tending a pair of oil lamps, proved to be a kind of vestry, where Christopher was pulling on a long white surplice over a sapphire-blue cassock. He gave Peregrine one of his quirky grins as he adjusted a flowing sleeve.

''I've brought us communion as well,'' he said. ''When we have the luxury of pre-planning, rather than reacting to crisis, it's our custom to receive together before setting out to do any work as a group, both to fortify us as individuals and to affirm the common union of our working bond. I know you don't belong to the church in which I'm ordained, but I hope you won't be shy about partaking with us.''

''Well, if you're sure it's all right,'' Peregrine murmured somewhat doubtfully, as Christopher added a blue stole to his adornment.

It was McLeod who responded, not with his usual bluff tone but almost a tenderness, as he laid an arm reassuringly around the younger man's shoulders.

''Laddie, don't you worry about anything except what's all right for *you*,'' he said quietly. ''What we serve is the same, whether we go to a kirk or a church or a chapel or an abbey on Sunday mornings. When this company meets around the Lord's Table, there're no such things as denominations.''

Philippa turned to smile at him over her shoulder, shielding the light of her lamp with a cupped hand.

''Noel's right, my dear,'' she said. ''Truth is unified, even if our perceptions of that Truth may differ slightly in perspective and in how we choose to express them.''

''But, don't all religions say that *they* have the truth?'' Peregrine asked.

Adam smiled. ''This is hardly the time for an in-depth discussion on *that* subject, but suffice it to say, for now, that the rites and practices of organized religion are all intended to honor the ultimate Truth, and such formal acknowledgements can be an extra source of strength for people in our line of work, engaged in the active service of that Truth. As you refine your own spiritual direction, you may well find that active participation in a particular religion serves to point the way more clearly.

"I offer that only as a suggestion at this time, without endorsing any particular path for *you*. In the meantime, however, I hope you'll feel comfortable receiving with us under the Episcopal form."

With that, the two women led the way into the chapel beyond, bearing their lamps. McLeod went next, Peregrine falling in awkwardly between him and Adam, Christopher bringing up the rear. Peregrine caught his breath as he passed under the vaulted ceiling, with its panoply of stars spangled above the altar. A strange thrill he only partly understood made him falter briefly in his tracks. The sensation was both mysterious and familiar—as if he had stumbled into some ancient, hallowed temple and found himself at home there.

The women put their lamps on the altar, augmenting the light of candles burning in wall sconces, moving then to either side as Christopher took a place between them. Peregrine ended up standing between McLeod and Adam, in a small semi-circle. Beyond Christopher, he caught a glimpse of a silver chalice and a small silver bowl.

But then Christopher was lifting his hands in a supplication that embraced them all, offering words that seemed eminently appropriate to the night's intentions, and hardly like a ritual at all.

"The night is far spent, and the day is at hand," he said, joy lifting his voice. "Let us therefore cast off the works of darkness, and let us put on the armor of light."

The litany that followed took the form of an extended prayer of praise and petition, with responses that were easy to follow. Taking his cue from his companions, Peregrine felt all his doubts and uncertainties melt away. Whatever he did not know now, that he needed to know, he would learn in the fullness of time. In the present moment, he was at peace.

His sense of peace deepened as Christopher came to each of them to give them the Host, Victoria following with the Cup. The mingled taste of bread and wine upon his tongue brought with it an abiding sense of fellowship and satisfaction. He bowed his head over folded hands when they had passed, lost in contemplation of that satisfaction, until Adam's calm voice recalled him to the moment.

"Peregrine," his mentor said quietly, obviously loathe to intrude, "we need your ring now."

Nodding wordlessly, Peregrine drew it forth from its place of safekeeping and handed it to Adam, who passed it on to Christopher. The priest accepted it most soberly, closing it briefly between his hands, then passed his ring hand over it in the sign of the cross. Holding it then in his cupped hands, he lifted it in offering and prayed aloud.

"Almighty God, Creator and Preserver of all mankind, renew Thy blessing upon this ring, tool and sign of commitment to Thy service, that he who is shortly to receive it shall receive likewise all grace and guidance to execute his duty in accordance with Thy will, so long as he shall live."

The prayer was attended by a reverent "Amen" from the rest of the gathering. Christopher handed the ring back to Adam with grave formality, but his brown eyes, as he turned to Peregrine, were alight, as if the moment was for him a personal occasion of gladness.

"Adam will keep the ring for now," he told the younger man. "When you receive it back, your right to wear it will have been affirmed by far higher than I."

Turning, then, to face the altar, he lifted his hands once more in the great antiphon for the day:

"O Day-Spring brightness of the Light Eternal and Sun of Justice, come and enlighten those who sit in darkness and the shadow of death."

The service concluded with a prayer that seemed to echo the aspirations of Peregrine's own heart as he bowed his head for Christopher's final blessing. As he moved with the others in silence to go back upstairs, now directing his focus toward the task ahead, all other considerations receded from his mind. Gillian's face was before him as he climbed the stairs, still carrying with him the peace he had attained by what he had just witnessed, and paramount in his mind now was the resolute desire to see Gillian restored to health and sanity.

They regrouped briefly in the library while they waited for Christopher to join them, *sans* vestments, and so that Peregrine could collect his sketchbox. Then all of them followed Adam upstairs to Gillian's room. Mrs. Gilchrist had been given the night off, and Iris Talbot was asleep in the room across the hall. Seeing Peregrine glance toward the door on the way in, Philippa whispered, "You needn't worry, she won't wake. She's earned her peace tonight, poor thing, and I've taken every decent precaution to ensure that she should keep it. We won't be interrupted.''

The curtains were standing open, admitting the pale silvery light of the moon from outside. Illumined by that ethereal glow and the light of half a dozen blue-lit votive candles set round the room, Gillian herself looked fragile as a dry leaf, frail to the point of breaking. Gazing down at the sunken, childish face as Philippa closed and locked the door, Peregrine suspected they were not acting a moment too soon.

Philippa raised the wards set earlier around the room and took up a sentinel post by the door, reaching up to trace a symbol over the lintel to seal it fast against all intrusion. Adam moved a bedside chair to the foot of the bed and directed Peregrine to sit down in it while Christopher and Victoria brought more chairs and took up posts opposite one another at the head of the bed. McLeod stood at Peregrine's left, leaving Adam free to choose his own station once the work was in progress. For now, he stood at Peregrine's right, facing him.

''All right, for what we're about to do, I need first to put you into trance,'' he said quietly. ''There's nothing in this that you haven't experienced before, except that I'm going to take you deeper than usual. Sit back now and relax. Pick a point on the ceiling, up above the bed, and fix all your attention there. Be guided by the sound of my voice.''

Peregrine did as he was bidden, leaning back in his seat until his shoulders were resting comfortably against the chair's upholstered back, looking up. He was breathing lightly, Adam saw, with no sign of stress or apprehension in his face, and Adam was pleased at this evidence of the younger man's trust.

''Clear your mind now. And I want you to imagine yourself gazing up at the sky at night. There are no clouds—just a multitude of stars. Can you see them?''

''Yes.'' Peregrine's hazel eyes had taken on a faraway look behind his spectacles.

''Good,'' Adam said quietly. ''I want you to choose a star out of all those myriad points, and make it the center of your attention. Have you found one?''

''Yes.'' Peregrine's assent was soft but clear.

''Excellent. Keep your eyes fixed on that star. Watch it as it flickers and flashes. Its light is descending toward you. Let it carry you down into the depths of your unconscious . . . now.''

While he was speaking, he reached out and lightly touched Peregrine's forehead just above the bridge of the nose. The artist's eyes closed and he gave a sigh, settling a little more heavily into his chair.

"That's right," Adam murmured. "Go deeper . . . and deeper still. . . ."

As he continued to reinforce his suggestions, Peregrine increasingly evidenced every sign of deep trance. Finally satisfied that his subject had attained the working level desirable for the task at hand, Adam glanced across at McLeod. The inspector nodded back and made a sign with his right hand above the younger man's fair head. Then he moved to take a light hold on Peregrine's left wrist, fingers grasped firmly over the pulse point.

Peregrine could feel the throb of his heartbeat pulsing under McLeod's fingers, and it seemed to him that the light of the star he had been following had expanded to envelop him in a transparent cone of protective luminance. Adam was present beside him, as was McLeod, both of them clothed now in flowing robes of sapphire blue. He himself was wearing a simple white robe, the robe of a postulant. As all this registered in the back of his mind, his mentor spoke, his voice resonating with more than its usual melodic authority.

"Let those who have been called to the service of the Light enter now into the Temple of the Master."

Through the soft glow of the light that shielded him, Peregrine found he could make out other human figures gathering around him. He saw that some of them were those he already knew as his companions, likewise clothed in flowing robes of deep sapphire blue. Lady Julian was there in the midst of them, no longer bound to her wheelchair in this other realm beyond physical restrictions, and there were others whom he did not recognize. Each of them wore a point of starlight on his or her hand in place of the rings that would have been present on the earthly plane.

They seemed to be standing on the porch of a vast classical temple of white marble. Beyond the gateway, Peregrine could make out a shimmering pillar of light. The light emanated a sense of living Presence, even more authoritative than Adam's. In wonder he gazed at it, glad of the company around him.

"Come," Adam said quietly from his side. "Come and be presented to the Master."

Awed but not afraid, Peregrine allowed himself to be shepherded forward up the steps leading to the temple gate, where Adam halted on the top-most step and inclined his head in respect.

*Master*, he said, addressing the Presence, *I come on behalf of the Hunting Lodge to present this man, Peregrine Justyn Lovat, as a candidate for initiation. The fledgling hawk has found his wings and stands ready to assist in seeking healing for the soul now incarnate as Gillian Talbot. When this has been accomplished, I ask that he be received as a Huntsman, that our numbers may be strengthened against the threat that now hangs over the land given into our charge.*

The Presence within the temple seemed to grow taller, its brightness more active. A voice spoke, lighter than Adam's and carrying a crystalline ring of gentle humor.

*Rest content, Master of the Hunt,* the Presence replied. *Thy petition on the latter point is known to us and to our Captain-General. But understand that it is the healing of the child Gillian that must precede all else. Thou hast judged aright that thy fledgling hath the necessary talents. It remains for thee to bring him before that One whose province it is to quicken the sleeping skills yet required. The just exercise of his gifts shall be the fledgling's rite of entry into full fellowship as an Initiate.*

Adam bowed his head again. *I understand. It will be done as you have instructed.*

The mandate was a powerful one. Only once before had Adam himself been called into that other Presence, to receive affirmation of his own healing vocation. Philippa had been his sponsor then; and recalling that long-ago time, he thought he now could understand something of the gladsome humility she must have felt on that occasion.

Drawing a steadying breath and shifting focus briefly to the earthly level, he reached down and took Peregrine physically by the right hand.

"Your star is rising," he told the younger man softly. "Rise up and follow it, not in body but in spirit. Its light is like a beacon, drawing you out of your body toward the heavenly plane. . . ."

Peregrine felt a sudden lightness in all his limbs, as if he had suddenly grown wings. Aware of the grip of Adam's hand on his, he became conscious of McLeod clasping his other hand. Between them, they were lifting him up, helping him, like the fledgling Adam had called him, to take to the air. The sense of flying overwhelmed him. Closing his eyes even to astral sight, he gave himself unreservedly into the hands of his guides, until all at once his feet grounded and he found he was standing upright.

Timorously he looked around him and discovered that the rest of the company had accompanied him on his soul's flight. Though all around him was starry night, he somehow knew that his physical and spiritual orientation was to the east. The company was assembled on a wide dais before a tall pair of burnished golden doors, each marked with a device which, in his heightened state, he somehow knew was the sigil of Air—a point-up equilateral triangle bisected by a transverse line.

McLeod released his grip on Peregrine's hand and sank to one knee; the rest of the gathering save Adam did the same. Transferring his handclasp to Peregrine's shoulder, Adam reached out to trace the symbol on the right-hand door with the first two fingers of his ring hand. The Word he then pronounced did not seem to Peregrine to register as any earthly language, but at its utterance the doors parted and swung slowly inward.

The space beyond was all pale light and moving air. As Adam guided Peregrine forward, leaving the others behind, the light and air took the visual form of diaphanous golden curtains billowing in a shimmering breeze. As they passed through the curtains, a fragrance like a breath of frankincense hung on the air. Beyond lay a vast, airy hall flooded with pale golden light and, in its center, a tall pillar of golden light which slowly resolved before Peregrine's dazzled eyes into a gauzy image vaguely human in form, with a suggestion of sweeping wings that filled all the hall with the vital winds of their beating.

Eyes that were like deep lakes of living gold bent down upon him from a face neither male nor female but supremely beautiful in its androgynous delicacy. Points of golden fire were twined like a diadem through the floating tresses of golden hair flowing back from a high, noble brow.

Peregrine felt the pressure of Adam's hand on his shoulder and sank obediently to his knees, vaguely aware that Adam had dropped back to kneel as well. Gazing up entranced into the golden eyes, the artist sensed rather than heard the invitation to open his heart and communicate his desire.

He found his response coming in images rather than words. Submissive to his questioner, he pictured Gillian Talbot in the mirror of his mind, together with the companion image of the withered corpse that had once housed the self-same spirit in another guise, and the more chaotic image of the shards that represented the dreadful damage done to the soul that once had encompassed both.

*If there is any gift within me by which this wrong can be righted*, he tried to say, *show me how to use that gift. I ask nothing for myself. But if I may be found worthy in some small way, I will gladly pledge whatever I may have to the unswerving service of the Light.*

The angelic fiery gaze seemed to burn its way into the depths of his soul. Powerless to turn away, even had he wanted to, Peregrine suddenly understood, as he had not comprehended before, what Adam had meant when he had spoken of the trial of the soul's mettle. There was anguish in the awareness of his own imperfections. But without that knowledge, no higher vision was possible.

Humbly he acknowledged the angel's authority to judge him, miserably bowing his head to signify his readiness to accept dismissal, if that was all of which he should be found worthy. But instead of being sent back, he found himself suddenly enfolded by a pair of dazzlingly bright wings, naught in his vision save light ineffable.

Towering over him in shimmering majesty, the angel seemed to bend to him, clasping his face lightly between two beautiful, tapering hands. He raised his face wonderingly to the glory, all resistance fled, and felt the bright brush of fiery lips grazing his eyelids, accompanied by a voice that was all melody.

*May thine eyes see the way of healing. . . .*

Potent as an electric shock, the angel's kiss set every fiber of Peregrine's being reverberating like a bell. The sensation, beyond pain in its intensity, tempered to a warm ecstatic thrill that enwrapped body, mind, and soul to their very depths. An incandescence that was an extension of the angel's own essence played over his eyelids, blinding him to everything else but its glory. His senses swooned before the onslaught of rapture unlike anything he had ever experienced in his present life.

For a timeless moment it seemed that he would lose consciousness. Reeling, physically and psychically dazed, he only gradually became aware of Adam and McLeod supporting him, still holding both his hands, anchoring him to the real world and his physical body, still sitting in its chair. He blinked his eyes and discovered that he now was seeing not an airy temple suspended in some distant, ethereal plane, but the comfortable confines of Gillian Talbot's bedroom. When he shifted his gaze to Gillian herself, however, he found that his faculty of vision had been expanded so that he could see not only her physical presence, but also her astral image.

That image, thin and stressed as her physical body, was wavering amid a sea of fragments, like a child cast away amid a rack of broken mirrors. The fragments were all in motion, whirling and tossing about in utter chaos. And yet, as he looked more closely, he began to see pieces that matched up with one another, like separate parts of different jigsaw puzzles. As he tightened his focus, he could start to see the patterns more clearly, able to envision not only colors but affinities of shape.

It *was* possible to sort those pieces out and put them back together! Of that much he was sure. All he needed was the right tools.

"Adam," he said aloud, "do you remember how I once described the effect of my vision as looking like a stack of transparencies?"

Adam cast a keen glance across at McLeod. "I remember," he said quietly.

"That's the key to putting things right with Gillian," Peregrine said. "The sketches I've been doing were for practice, to identify the masks of her former incarnations. If I can draw those onto some kind of transparencies, we can use them as matrices to sort out the shards of the different personalities. Then we superimpose them to reintegrate her spirit as a unity."

"I understand," Adam said, nodding.

"What have you got that I can use?" Peregrine asked, his hand tightening on Adam's. "Glass, maybe, or tracing paper—"

"I've got something better than that," Adam replied. "There's some clear acetate down in my desk, like you use for an overhead projector. Can you hang on, if I leave you to go and fetch them?"

Peregrine's response was a tight nod. "I can manage," he murmured breathlessly. "Just don't be too long, will you?"

"I won't," Adam promised. "Noel will stay with you. He'll help, if you need him."

Philippa was already moving to erase the sigil over the door. As soon as the way was clear, Adam ducked past her and raced downstairs to the library. A swift rummage through the appropriate drawer brought the acetates to hand. Slamming the drawer shut with a flourish, he snatched a handful of felt-tipped pens out of the desktop hold-all and beat a hasty retreat to the room upstairs.

For the next hour and more, Peregrine sat drawing feverishly, while the others gave silent, strong support. When at last he laid his pens aside, he had made seven portrait sketches, among them a likeness of Michael Scot and one of Gillian herself, each representing one of the soul's previous incarnations. Peregrine himself was pale and trembling with exhaustion when he had finished, his breath coming in shallow gasps.

"Easy," Adam said quietly. "You're doing brilliantly. Time for you to rest a bit now, while Noel and I shoulder some of the next part of the work."

Carefully he laid the seven sketches across the foot of the bed in two rows, three and four. Standing before them then, he and McLeod together shifted focus back to the astral plane and, from this perspective, began to sort through the sea of psychic shards, fitting the individual segments to the various portraits like children playing with a set of wooden puzzles, each having the outline of a finished picture as a guide to show how and where the pieces fitted in.

The number of free-floating shards steadily diminished as the individual portraits built up. All the while they were working, Peregrine had the impression of fine spider-silk strands being pulled like candy floss from Gillian's motionless body, joining it to the drawings themselves. The body was being vacated—but unlike that other time, when Gillian's soul had been wrenched from her body to reanimate Michael Scot at Melrose, all the facets of that soul now were anchored close-by, and soon would be restored. Philippa had come to monitor the body as they worked, and kept a close watch on the functions that kept it going while its owner was away.

At last all the shards were sorted and all the portraits complete. Each shimmered with a living energy, no longer a mere physical image of the personality it represented but a glyph of the mask worn by spirit during that incarnation. After pausing to draw breath, Adam turned back to Peregrine. The artist had regained some of his color while Adam and McLeod worked, and he looked up attentively at Adam's look of inquiry.

"All right," Adam said quietly. "What order?"

Frowning slightly in concentration, Peregrine rose and briefly studied the array of sketches before him, then began arranging them in a stack, ending with Gillian's own portrait on the top. As Adam moved back the chair in which Peregrine had been sitting, Peregrine laid the completed stack on the floor at the foot of the bed, then stood back.

Gravely Adam betook himself to stand at the foot of the bed facing Gillian, the stack of drawings at his feet, McLeod at his left and Peregrine at his right. Bowing his head briefly over hands pressed together in prayer, he gathered the force of his will to draw on his authority as a healer.

To Peregrine, watching him, Adam suddenly seemed to grow several inches taller. And as he raised both hands slightly to either side of his head, lifting his chin in determination, he took on that aspect of an earlier mask of *his* incarnations that Peregrine had seen and drawn once before—lappets of boldly striped linen framing a lean, hawk-visaged face crowned with the double crown of Upper and Lower Egypt, with the solar disk set between twin ostrich plumes—the adornment of an Egyptian Priest-King.

"*By the Sign of Osiris Arisen*," Adam intoned, in a voice not quite his own, sketching a sigil of authority in the air over the portraits. "*Let the many become one, that wholeness may be restored.*"

As he extended both palms over the stack of sketches, a deep violet light began to play over the surface of the top one. After a moment, the sketch itself seemed to melt into the light. As Peregrine watched, an indigo light washed over the surface of the second drawing, welling up then to merge with the violet as the second sketch dissolved in the wake of the first. The third sketch yielded a glow of shimmering blue, that was joined in turn with waves of color from the rest of the visible spectrum: green and yellow, orange and red.

Peregrine looked on in fascination as the sketches he had made melted away amid the corona of colors, each one adding several handspans to the mounting column of changing light. What finally remained was a brilliant, seven-foot column of purest silvery white, hovering slightly above the floor where the transparencies had been.

Adam's other visage had melted away with the column's completion, but he still was more than merely mortal. Bringing his palms together, he gave the column grave salute, then opened his hands toward the still form of the little girl lying supine on the bed behind it.

"The vessel of the body waits to receive you," he said quietly but with authority. "Be welcome in your own house."

He expected to see the pillar of light melt away into its companion tabernacle of flesh. Instead, to his surprise, it remained in place, shimmering and pulsing like a living prism—the essence of pure spirit requesting a human agent through which to communicate.

"Noel," Adam said softly, "I believe you're needed."

The inspector nodded and moved into place between the bed and the column of light, slipping off his aviator spectacles and pocketing them before giving salute.

"I am here," he told the Presence. "You are free to speak with my voice."

As he dropped his hands to his sides, bowing his head in receptivity, the pillar of light flowed forward and overshadowed him. He stiffened with a shudder as its essence suffused him. When he looked up, another intelligence looked out through

McLeod's blue eyes, and as the lips parted below the bristling moustache, the voice that came forth was the one Peregrine had heard at Melrose—the voice of Michael Scot.

"Thanks are owed to all within this room, but chiefly to you," he said, addressing himself to Adam and Peregrine, "not only for this great labor of healing undertaken on my behalf, but for keeping my gold and my book of spells from profanation at the hands of our common enemies. If there be aught I may offer in return for the great services ye have done me, ask now, and I will give it freely."

Adam thought only an instant, quite aware what he must ask, and that time was limited.

"We seek no reward for ourselves, brother, but only a focus for how we may carry out what we began in your behalf. We would have you share your knowledge of our common enemies. Do you know what they sought from your book of spells?"

"I do not," came the response, "but the magic that summoned me to Melrose was dark, indeed—alien magic—the same that brought about the physical death of the incarnation previous to this one, more than half a century ago. . . ."

The voice trailed off briefly, as if at a recollection of old pain. When it resumed, its tone was hard.

"The Lord of Shadows in that day was one called Hitler. His work did great damage to the canopy of Light. Had he succeeded in all his intentions, he would have called down all the fury of the darker elementals. . . ."

The reference to Hitler chilled Adam to the bone.

"Was it Hitler's magic that summoned you?" he asked.

"I know not," came the reply, "but I would swear by all I hold holy that the power to summon me was worked from a common source. And the Lord of Shadows had a book of spells. . . ."

"*Hitler* had a book of spells?" Adam asked, his mind racing now.

"He did," the voice of Scot acknowledged, "but I know not what became of it. More than this, I cannot tell thee. I wish thee good hunting, Master of the Hunt. But now, lest mine absence undo the good thou hast done here, I would beg leave to resume my present-day incarnation, to take up the life which, by thine intercessions, I now am free to continue."

"I would not cause you further pain," Adam said. "You have suffered all that anyone could ask. Go in peace, with the blessings of the Seven, to fulfill your appointed destiny. The body you inhabit shall be protected, until such time as you are strong enough to walk your path alone.''

With a nod, McLeod's body turned to lay hands on Gillian's feet. Prismatic light flowed out of him into Gillian. At the instant of severance, McLeod uttered a slight gasp and crumpled to his knees, catching himself on the foot of the bed. In that same instant, the child in the bed gave a sudden, convulsive shiver and opened her eyes.

Her wide, bewildered gaze swept the room and the sea of unfamiliar faces. She gave a small whimper of fright and recoiled against the pillows, too weak to do more than stare, and Victoria moved in to enfold her in her arms and comfort her while Christopher took one of her hands.

"There, now, Gillian, you needn't be frightened," Victoria said softly, rocking her like a baby, stroking the blonde curls. "I know this all looks a little strange, but you're quite, quite safe. You've been ill for rather a long time, but you're going to be just fine. You'll see your mummy in the morning. She'll be so happy to see you've woken up."

Philippa was already moving in to deal with the medical aspects of the situation, quickly assessing Gillian's vital signs and then taking advantage of the shield presented by Christopher's body to inject a light sedative into the girl's I.V. While Adam eased McLeod to a sitting position on the floor at the foot of the bed and snapped an ammonia capsule under his nose, Peregrine kneeling anxiously at his side, Gillian shivered and whimpered a little, clinging baby-like to Victoria's supporting arms.

"Mummy?" she whispered almost voicelessly, her pale lips framing the word.

"She's asleep in the next room," Victoria said soothingly. "But let's not wake her just now, shall we? She's been watching over you day and night since you fell ill, and she's very tired. Think of the wonderful surprise she'll have in the morning, when she wakes up and finds that you're getting better."

With the help of Adam and Peregrine, McLeod picked himself up, satisfied despite his own lingering unsteadiness when he saw that Gillian had come to her senses, if only for a brief time. Her blue eyes were already glazing under the influence of the sedative as she drifted into sleep, but this was a sleep that was controllable, unlike her previous state. Victoria continued to rock her and croon endearments until the little girl subsided against her shoulder. When they had settled the sleeping child back under her blankets,

Adam fished in his pocket and brought out the ring that was intended for Peregrine.

"I'm afraid your part isn't over quite yet," he told the artist, displaying the ring. "I think there can be no doubt you've proved worthy of this, but it's up to a much higher authority than I to give you the official affirmation that this physical ring represents. Are you up to one more foray onto the astral?"

Peregrine was looking more than a little dizzy, overwhelmed by what he had already seen and experienced that night. Even so he managed a nod. Smiling, Adam took the younger man's right hand in his left, feeling the faint scar as he isolated the ring finger.

"Noel, are you with me?" he asked softly over his shoulder.

McLeod closed ranks on Peregrine's left, signifying his readiness with a nod.

"All right," Adam said to Peregrine, "close your eyes once more, and prepare to go very, very deep."

As Peregrine obeyed, Adam gathered his own focus, also closing his eyes.

"Peregrine Justyn Lovat, be blessed now and forever in the service of the Light," he whispered. "Receive this ring in memory of one who wore it before you, and be joyful in that abiding fellowship of which you both are now a part."

With this instruction, he slipped the ring onto Peregrine's finger.

At once, the three of them were once more standing in spirit in the astral temple. Glancing down at himself, Peregrine saw that he, like his companions, was wearing a robe of deep sapphire blue. The orientation this time was to the south, where a crimson gateway stood waiting, its doors flung wide and its crimson curtains swagged back. The One who waited beyond wore the guise of a towering figure armored in red-gold light, with a diadem of scarlet flames bound across his brow. The pinions of his wings flickered like tongues of flame, adorned with fiery peacock's eyes, and his flaming sword rested with its point to the floor, the coppery quillons under his hands.

Christopher and Victoria joined them in the temple, coming forward to stand on either side as witnesses, followed closely by Philippa and Lady Julian. The others were there as well, whom Peregrine had yet to meet in the physical. Acknowledging their presence with a regal nod, the Being subjected Peregrine to a moment's close scrutiny, then flung back his head, so that his flowing coppery hair made a flaming nimbus all around his head and shoulders. As it had been in the presence of the other angel, Peregrine heard the musical voice in his head.

*Thou dost credit to thy mentor, who is Master of the Hunt,* the Being said. *He hath petitioned for thine admittance to the Hunting Lodge, and stands guarantor for thy devotion to this weighty vocation to which thou art called. One thing more remains to be asked of thee: Wilt thou pledge unreservedly thy fealty to the Most High, whereby thou shalt receive the accolade of His warriors and keepers of His peace?*

Peregrine's assent was unflinching. *I do pledge it.*

*Then as Captain-General of the Lord of Hosts, we do receive thee in His Name. Kneel.*

Trembling with emotion, Peregrine sank to both knees, Adam moving forward to take reverent charge of the flaming sword while the Master lightly clasped Peregrine's joined hands. An incandescent glow spread throughout Peregrine's fingers, concentrating about the ring that blazed on his right hand like a star.

*Let this ring be a sign that thy gifts are pledged to the service of the Lord of Hosts,* came the mighty voice in his mind. *Let all the works of thy hands and heart give glory to that Name Which is above all other names.*

So saying, the Master stepped back, hand outstretched to receive the sword once again into his keeping. Raising the fiery blade, he touched Peregrine lightly on either shoulder and then on the head. Each touch of the burning blade intensified the sensation of raw power coursing through Peregrine's veins.

The final touch sent him plunging over the edge, and he lost consciousness.

# CHAPTER THIRTY-FOUR

W HEN Peregrine came to his physical senses, he was flat on his back on the floor of Gillian's room. Adam was kneeling beside him, anxiously checking his pulse. McLeod was also on his knees, peering down at him with searching concern. As soon as he saw that the younger man's eyes were open, he uttered a gruff exclamation of relief.

"It's all right, he's coming round now," he announced to the Houstons and Philippa, hovering in the background.

Remembering the Archangel with the flaming sword, Peregrine blinked, unable to recall when he had last felt so drained and yet so at peace.

"Right," Adam murmured. "Let's get you up, then. Come on, Noel, give me a hand."

With his two mentors helping, Peregrine managed to get his legs under him and stand. He stole a glance at the ring on his finger as they steered him to the nearest chair. It seemed to him that the ring glowed with a new lustre, reflecting his joy, but it was a quality sensed rather than seen—an unstated pledge that what he had just experienced was real on a level which transcended all his previous understanding. As he closed his fist and brought the ring's stone to his lips in reverent thanksgiving, he realized that both Adam and McLeod had turned their gaze toward Christopher, who was standing expectantly beside Gillian's bed, hands clasped. He gave the priest his attention as well, easing quietly to his feet again.

"Lord," the priest said, lifting his hands in benediction, "now lettest Thou Thy servants depart in peace, according to Thy Word. And may the words of our mouths and the thoughts of our hearts be always acceptable in Thy sight."

Peregrine joined with the rest in voicing the responsive "Amen."

"This night's work by this Lodge is completed," Christopher continued. "Let us go forth joyfully to do the will of the One Who sends us."

"Amen, Selah, so be it," the others responded.

It was, Peregrine realized, a formal closing to their work, for with those words, the atmosphere changed and people began restoring the room to its normal order and preparing to leave. On impulse, Peregrine found himself moving to intercept Christopher, catching shyly at his sleeve.

"Father Christopher, may I speak with you a minute?" he said softly, though he did not shrink from the priest's gaze. "I—don't know how to ask you what I want to ask, but—would you give me your blessing before you go?"

The request earned him a gentle smile from Christopher, the usual banter put aside.

"You knew *exactly* how to ask," he said quietly, "and I'll give it with all my heart. Only remember that what you receive at my hands is the gift and blessing not of me but of the Light we serve."

As Christopher lifted his hands, Peregrine found himself sinking to his knees with head bowed over his folded hands. The priest's touch on his head was an earthly reflection of the benison he had received at the hands of what he could only imagine were angels, and he found his vision blurring with tears of joy and gratitude as Christopher spoke the words of blessing.

"May the blessing of Almighty God be upon your head and within your heart, and remain with you now and always." Christopher's hands lifted for the left one to drop to Peregrine's shoulder and the right one to trace a cross over his head. "In the Name of the Father, and of the Son, and of the Holy Spirit. Amen."

"Amen," Peregrine whispered, and did not bother to wipe away the tears from his eyes as he got to his feet.

After tea and sandwiches in the library, to finish grounding after their Work, the non-resident members of the Lodge took their leave of Adam and Philippa with fond good wishes—except for Peregrine, who accepted Philippa's suggestion that he spend the remainder of the night in his old guest room. When he had bade them good-night on the landing and retired, starry-eyed, to take some much-needed rest, Adam leaned down to plant an impulsive kiss on his mother's cheek.

"It's been rather a remarkable night, hasn't it?" he observed with a weary smile. "Now I have a little of an inkling what you went through, when you sponsored me all those years ago. Did I ever think to thank you?"

"The way you've turned out has been my reward," she said proudly. "It's all I ever asked, in all my prayers—to be for you the teacher you needed, to grow to your fullest potential. But as I recall, you *did* thank me, that long ago night. And now it's my turn to say thank *you*."

Smiling, he hugged her closer and kissed the top of her head.

"We did good work tonight, didn't we?" he murmured.

"We did, indeed," she agreed, with a look that spoke volumes. "And on that note, I suggest we both retire as well, to digest it all. I'll stay the night in Gillian's room. That child will probably be awake at dawn, and goodness knows how I'm going to explain to Iris."

Philippa's prediction proved accurate. Iris Talbot's delight was unbounded when she awoke the following morning to the news that her daughter had come to her senses in the early hours of the morning. Rushing across to Gillian's room, she found her just rousing, looking woefully frail, but with the gleam of intelligence restored to the blue eyes that for so long had been vacant and staring. Philippa had already been busy, removing the tubes that had sustained Gillian in the past weeks, and left mother and daughter alone to celebrate their reunion with tearful laughter and hugs while she headed downstairs for a much-needed cup of tea in the company of her son.

"Gillian's wide awake, and so is Iris," she informed Adam prosaically. "I've told Humphrey to give them half an hour, then go up and see what they want for breakfast. By then they should just about be ready for it."

Adam pulled a crooked smile. "One small battle won, at least," he observed. "But the war itself is still hanging in the balance."

"I haven't lost sight of that," Philippa said. "I suspected you were probably already considering our next gambit."

She sank down in the neighboring chair, her still-beautiful face sternly reminiscent. "Ever since I arrived, I've been aware of something in the air—a hint of something dark and dangerous that I thought I recognized, but couldn't quite put my finger on. We'd already agreed that it isn't just the Lodge of the Lynx."

Adam gave his mother an appraising look.

"Go on."

"I've been giving some thought to what Michael Scot said last night about Hitler being the Lord of Shadows, and him having a book of spells," she continued. "That's absolutely true. There's no doubt that Hitler was a black magician of the first order, with power enough at his disposal to carry out his wildest and most brutal aspirations. What ultimately stopped him was Hess. Hess was also a dabbler in the Black Arts, but even he couldn't abide what Hitler was doing, after a while. That's why he made that secret flight to Scotland in 1941."

Seeing Adam's look of bafflement, she went on.

"Didn't I ever tell you about that?"

"No."

"Good gracious. Well, it's ancient history now, but my uncle, Eric Rhodes, interviewed Hess several times after his capture. I didn't know about it at the time, because I was doing my internship then, but I saw some of the psychiatric transcripts, years later. Anyway, he was convinced that Hess was a raving nutter at first, but Dougie Hamilton's cousin always claimed that the real reason Hess flew to Scotland was not to have Dougie take him to meet the king, but to get Hitler's book of spells out of Germany; some manuscript he'd pillaged out of a monastery somewhere in northern Europe, but it was supposed to have had Celtic overtones—Druidic, maybe, or Pictish."

Adam stiffened, but she did not seem to notice.

"Anyway, word began to circulate in esoteric circles that the manuscript was in Scotland," she went on. "David Tudor-Jones got wind of it—the father, apparently, of our present adversary—and he tried to barter for it. But saner souls had decided it would be safer if it went to America, where Hitler was never likely to get his hands on it again. The Duke of Kent was supposed to take it as far as Iceland in a diplomatic pouch—he hadn't a clue what he was carrying, and everybody thought it would be safe with a Royal—but Tudor-Jones smuggled a bomb aboard his plane. Poor Georgie smacked into a mountain somewhere up in Caithness—Morven, I think it was, August of 1942. Anyway, the manuscript was lost, along with the most attractive and charming of the Royal Dukes."

She raised a wistful gaze to Adam, but he was connecting what she had said with a different thread of logic that led back to their present situation.

"Philippa, I don't think the manuscript was lost," he said in a voice of steely calm. "Tudor-Jones may have bombed the duke's plane, but he took the manuscript first. I think Francis Raeburn has it now—or Francis Tudor-Jones, as he should be called—and he's using it to carry out the present work. Or—no, they can't have had it all this time, or they would have used it before now. The Lodge of the Lynx have *never* had this kind of power at their disposal before. So someone *else* has to have had it until recently, someone closely associated with its wartime history. Someone—"

He stopped short, because an even more audacious thought had just occurred to him. "Good God, you don't suppose it could be Hess himself?"

Philippa stared incredulously at her son. "Don't be ridiculous, dear. Hess is dead. He died three or four years ago."

"*Did* he?"

"Well, of course."

"No, a man died in Spandau Prison who people *said* was Rudolf Hess; but a British surgeon who examined him in the late '70s claimed the man in Spandau *couldn't* have been Hess, based on the absence of scars from injuries known to have been sustained in the First World War. As I recall, two separate post mortems also failed to find the scars that had to be present in a man wounded as Hess had been. More recently, even Hess' son, Wolf Rütiger Hess, has tried to sue the Allied Powers who were responsible for his father's custody, claiming that the body returned to the family in 1987 was *not* his father's."

A deep frown furrowed Philippa's high forehead. "I do remember something about that, now that you mention it. The surgeon's name was Thomas, I believe. Hugh Thomas—another Welshman. And didn't David Irving write something shortly after Hess' death, about his movements between the time of the crash and the end of the war?"

Adam nodded. "Hess spent quite a lot of time in Wales after he was captured, while they tried to decide what to do with him. Incredible as it may seem, they used to allow him to go off on long walks alone—and it was during that time that Hess apparently underwent a radical personality change, except that I don't think it was Hess' personality that changed at all; it was the man himself. Hugh Thomas postulated a double.

"What if Tudor-Jones engineered the switch," he continued on a rising note, "then spirited the real Hess off to Scotland, along with the manuscript? What if *that's* who's holed up in that lair in the Cairngorms? It would certainly account for that impression that something's involved besides the Lynx—something incredibly powerful."

Philippa drew a long swooping breath. "Put like that, it does make a lunatic kind of sense, doesn't it? Still . . . ." She paused to bite her lip. "But surely Hess isn't still alive. Why, he'd be—goodness, nearly a hundred!"

"People do occasionally live that long," Adam said, a touch impatiently. "But even if I'm wrong, and the power behind all of this isn't Hess, we've still got the proven involvement of Tudor-Jones' son. Francis Raeburn is in this up to his eyeballs. And if his father *did* steal the manuscript, and if it's now in the hands of someone who knows how to use it—"

Mother and son gazed at each other in dismay.

"Hitler's book of spells," Philippa said flatly. "Dear God, what kind of power has that given them?"

"Well, power to call down lightning, at very least," Adam replied. "And however they're focusing that power, factoring in human sacrifices adds a dimension that's going to be very hard to counter cleanly. What was it that Scot said about Hitler? *Had he succeeded in all his intentions, he would have called down the fury of the darker elementals.*"

Philippa snorted. "It sounds like our opposite numbers are already doing *that*, albeit in a relatively modest way, compared to Hitler. But they're getting stronger, there's no doubt about that. And the toll of human life mounts with each new attack. The question is, why? What do they hope to gain, beyond mere chaos? Though perhaps that's enough, for now."

But their further speculation that morning suggested no new answers, and the busy lead-up toward Christmas permitted little time and energy to be spent in seeking out new leads. Over the next few days, Adam managed to pass on their suspicions to other members of the Hunting Lodge; but the spectre of a Hitlerian angle was a new perspective for most of them, and required a drastic shift of mental gears as they focused in on it. For the three of them who had brushed the edges of that brooding power firsthand, the prospect of taking it on without more information than they now had was repugnant to the point of almost paralyzing reluctance. Under the pretense of continuing to recuperate from his car crash, Adam was able to allocate several hours each day for delving into the vast resources of his library, but nothing emerged of note. They seemed to be at a stalemate, obliged to wait until the enemy should strike again—and even then, there was no assurance that guidance would be forthcoming in how to pursue the problem from that point.

Meanwhile, there were the practicalities of more ordinary life to deal with, and the very real complication of an increasingly mobile and vocal twelve-year-old under their roof. After a slow start on Saturday, as she eased into eating proper food again and starting to regain her physical strength, young Gillian bounced back to blooming good health with a resilience that was almost magical. By Sunday, she was strong enough to come downstairs for brunch, and that afternoon, her father flew up from London, after receiving the joyous phone call from his wife the previous day.

At Adam's invitation, the Talbot family settled in to spend a traditional Scottish Christmas at Strathmourne, for while Gillian was making astonishing progress, Philippa advised the parents that their daughter's prognosis would be far brighter if new psychological evaluations confirmed that the danger was past before allowing her to go home. Privately, she and Adam were reluctant to let Gillian out of their protection until she was less vulnerable, and were taking active measures to strengthen her own protection, under the guise of ongoing therapy. Meanwhile, just to know that she was safe under their roof was one burden eased in the face of their own present dilemmas.

They spent Monday morning putting up a tree in the drawing room, to Gillian's delight. That afternoon, after lunch and a nap, their rapidly recovering patient proclaimed her Christmas Eve wish to be introduced to Adam's horses. When Philippa saw no reason to object, the battle was lost. Gillian even badgered her mother into letting her put on outdoor clothes instead of a robe over her nightgown, for she intended to inspect Adam's stable as a proper lady should. Philippa declared her intention of retiring for a much-needed nap of her own.

As her adoring parents looked on in wonder, her father with a camera in hand, Adam put Gillian up on the gentle Khalid and led her around the yard several times, then swung up behind her and walked the big grey out of the stable yard to the front of the house, where the winter-dead lawn at least provided footing for a docile trot. Peregrine had come up from the gate lodge with his sketchbook after lunch, and followed the Talbots out to the front steps of the house to watch, pencil flying, as Adam put the horse into a gentle canter on the grassy verge that ran along the drive. The city-bred Gillian was thrilled.

They had gone perhaps a hundred yards along the drive and were turning to come back, Gillian breathless with excitement, when a yellow Morgan sportscar with black wings came nosing along the drive. Smiling, Adam pulled up and walked the horse over to the driver's side as Ximena recognized him and stopped. He brought his right hand to the bill of his riding cap in a casual salute as she rolled down her window.

"Afternoon, Dr. Lockhart," he said.

Mock disapproval raised her brows. "You're supposed to be convalescing."

"Oh, I am," Adam replied. "We both are. This is my very special friend, Miss Gillian Talbot, who specifically requested that she be taken for a ride this afternoon."

"Oh, I see," Ximena replied. "How do you do, Gillian?"

Gillian blushed and hid her face against Adam's hacking jacket.

"She's a little shy, I'm afraid. Go on up to the house, and we'll meet you there."

With an indulgent smile, Ximena put the car in gear and continued on. Gillian, once she was out of earshot, rolled grave

360

blue eyes up at Adam over her shoulder as he let Khalid walk on.

"Dr. Sinclair, is that your girlfriend?"

"Well, not yet," Adam replied. "But she might be. I only met her a week or two ago. She's a doctor. In fact, she's the one who patched up my head."

"Hmmm. She's pretty," Gillian allowed. "We'd better go fast, then. My mummy says that a gentleman should never keep a lady waiting."

"No, he shouldn't," Adam agreed, chuckling as he gathered the reins around her. "Besides that, you like to go fast, too, don't you? All right, then, my girl. Hold on and we'll go fast."

Even at the canter, Ximena was already getting out of the car by the time they pulled up at the end of the lawn. As Adam swung down, leaving Gillian in the saddle, Peregrine came to take Khalid.

"Your pretty lady doctor?" he murmured under his breath.

"Yes, indeed. Come to take my sutures out, I expect," Adam said blandly. "Do you mind taking Gillian and Khalid back to the yard?"

"Not at all," Peregrine said, grinning. "Come on, Gillian, and you can help me put this great, grey beast back in the barn, okay? And before we do that, your mum and dad can take some pictures of you sitting on him."

"Oh, that would be so kind, Mr. Lovat," Iris Talbot said, coming to stroke Khalid's neck as George moved in for a photo of that. "Gillian, did you remember to thank Dr. Sinclair?"

As they moved off, Adam removed his riding cap and tucked it under his arm, absently smoothing his hair and feeling to see that his protective Band-Aid was still in place over his sutures as he walked over to Ximena.

"One of my patients," he explained, jerking his chin toward the retreating party as his visitor closed her car door. "Actually, more my mother's patient, this last week or so—which has been handy, having a backup right here at home. Have you gotten your staff situation straightened out, or are you going to have to run off again?"

She sighed wearily as she followed him up the steps and into the house. Her hair was loose on her shoulders, but she was wearing surgical scrubs and a lab coat under the smart black coat of her last visit.

"Run, I'm afraid. I've got to be back on duty in less than two hours."

"Still short-handed, then?" he asked, ushering her into the library.

"Afraid so." She let him help her out of her coat. "I sure wish I knew what had happened to Dr. Wemyss. It's really rotten of him to ditch right at the holidays, and make everybody double up. We've got a locum from Thursday, though—if I live that long."

As she pulled a small green surgical pack from the pocket of her lab coat, obviously intent on business, Adam smiled and went over to the phone on his desk.

"Let me at least order up some tea, then," he said. "Sounds like you could use it."

"Fine, but tell your man to just serve it up in a mug, milk and two sugars," she said. "I love the silver, but I just don't have the time to fiddle this afternoon."

Adam gave the order, peeling off his Band-Aid as he did so, then came to sit where she had turned on a floor lamp at the end of the settee.

"I'm sorry to drag you out here for this," he said, extending his hands to hold the surgical pack as she began unfolding it. "You should have rung me. Philippa could have taken out the sutures—or I could have done it."

Picking up scissors and forceps, she gave him a grin.

"Are you kidding? And miss seeing the dashing Sir Adam Sinclair in tight riding breeches? Turn your head to the light, so I don't poke you."

Controlling a smile, Adam did as he was told, watching the knots of black silk mount up like a collection of small, hairy spiders on the green towel he held, until all fourteen were accounted for. After the first few, she moved his head forward to rest against her side, steadying it between her wrists as she continued working. She did not speak, nor did he, but he found the silence reassuring rather than awkward, and found himself relaxing under her touch.

"There, that's got them all," she said, pushing back his hair to inspect more closely. "You've healed very nicely. In a few months, you'll never know you got thumped."

He was just trying to decide whether to slip an arm around her waist when a discreet knock at the door heralded Humphrey's imminent arrival with their tea. He sighed as he sat back and Humphrey entered, holding up the towel to receive the forceps and scissors. She said nothing as she folded the towel back around the instruments to make a small packet again and slipped it back in her pocket, merely sitting down wearily across from him as Humphrey brought them each a mug of tea and then silently withdrew.

Lifting his mug in salute, Adam settled back in the settee, watching her. She looked more worn than last time he had seen her, but she seemed to revive a little as she sipped at the steaming tea.

"Ah, that's good," she murmured, leaning back gratefully in her chair, head against the headrest. "Other than to drive up here, I think this is the first I've been off my feet all day—and my day started at six."

Smiling, he pushed a footstool closer with one highly polished boot. She was wearing sensible white shoes like nurses wore, designed to give excellent support. On most women, Adam thought they tended to look clunky, but on Ximena they seemed to make a fashion statement in keeping with her profession.

"Put your feet up for a few minutes, then, and relax," he said quietly. "God knows, you've earned it."

"Yes, I have," she said, hooking the footstool closer and swinging her feet up onto it. "Mmmm, that's nice. I don't suppose you use hypnosis in your practice, do you?"

"As a matter of fact, I do. Why do you ask?"

"*Do* you?" she said, glancing at him with new interest as she took another sip of tea. "Is it true that ten or fifteen minutes under hypnosis is like several hours of normal sleep?"

"It *can* be, depending on the subject."

"Would I be a good subject?"

"I don't know. Would you like to find out?"

She glanced longingly at her watch, then shook her head regretfully. "Damn! I would *love* to, but I really have to get back." She sat forward and gulped another large swallow of tea, grimacing at the temperature.

"*God*, I'll be glad when we get this staff situation sorted out! I *am* taking off Thursday, though, *regardless* of who doesn't show up. I think I'll probably sleep the entire day." She cocked her head at him. "I don't suppose you'd like to pay off on that dinner Thursday night, would you?"

Pleasant anticipation immediately gave way to disappointment as he realized that Thursday was St. John's Eve.

"Ximena, I'm sorry," he said honestly. "There's nothing I'd like better, but I have to go down to Melrose Abbey that night—something called the Mason's Walk. I'm not a Freemason, but a dear friend of mine who was a very high-ranking one was killed last month. His Lodge and some of his other friends are going down to attend it in his memory. It's been taking place on that date for well over a hundred years now—maybe closer to *two* hundred—and I think Randall must have attended for probably the last fifty. It was something that meant a great deal to him."

"Randall?" she said. "Not Randall Stewart, that Mason who was killed in some ritual murder up north of here?"

Adam stiffened just slightly, as the thought suddenly streaked across his mind, previously always dismissed, that *she* could well be involved in all of this. After all, Wemyss apparently had been, and they both worked at the same hospital. But then he reminded himself that her recognition of the name could easily be chalked up to media coverage.

"Yes, I expect you read about it, or saw television coverage," he said a little cautiously. "Especially under the circumstances, you can see why I'm obliged to go."

"Gosh, yes," she murmured, shivering. "Adam, I'm so sorry. I mean—to have something like that happen to someone you know. . . . You found him, too, didn't you? Now I know why your name sounded familiar, when I first met you in the ER: I'd seen it in the papers."

"Yes, I—sometimes work as a police consultant," he admitted, gazing down at the tea mug cupped in his hands.

A silence fell between them for a moment, taut yet still companionable, and then she sat forward in her chair, shifting her feet back onto the floor.

"Adam, just tell me if I'm out of line, but if it wouldn't be too much of an intrusion, I'd be honored if you'd let me come along with you Thursday night."

Adam looked up sharply. "Why would you want to do that?"

She cupped strong, ringless fingers around her mug, staring at a point on the floor somewhere between them, looking a little uncomfortable.

"I could make some pert remark about enjoying the company, and that would certainly be true, because I find you incredibly attractive. But aside from that—well, my father and my grandfather and both my brothers are Masons, back in the States. In fact, when that story first broke, I clipped articles from the newspapers and set them back to Dad. I remember books by Randall Stewart being on our bookshelves when I was a teenager, and I know what the Brotherhood means to my family." She sighed and shook her head. "Anyway, if this is how his Masonic Brethren here in Scotland choose to honor him—well, I'd be proud to be a small part of it, just to witness it. I know I can't actually march, not being a Mason."

Slowly Adam allowed himself to smile, any doubts he might have had about her melting away.

"That makes two of us," he said softly. "But if you really want to come, and brave what undoubtedly will be a cold and dreary evening—and that's only the drive there and back!—then I'd be most grateful of the company." He quirked her a wry smile. "There's actually quite a decent restaurant in the hotel there in the town square. If you like, we can have dinner there, afterwards—and you can *still* pick the venue for a more properly festive one later on, to celebrate your name."

She smiled at that, the mood swinging back upward, as he had intended, then glanced at her watch again, shook her head, and swigged down the last of her tea.

"I *have* to go," she said, getting to her feet. "There'll probably be casualties stacked three deep in the corridors by the time I get back. Just *once* I'd like to see a Christmas Eve that really was a silent night, holy night. Do you go to church on Christmas Eve, here in Scotland?"

"Usually I do," he said, helping her on with her coat. "With Gillian and her family here this year, though, I suspect not. There's a lot going on. I always try to put a lighted candle in the window, though, even if I don't get to church. It's an old Celtic custom—a watch-light for Mary and Joseph, looking for a place to pass the night—and maybe a sign of the rebirth of the Light at this time of year. Do they do that where you come from?"

"No, but I like it," she said. "Maybe I'll put a candle in the window at the hospital."

"Shall I give you one to use?" he asked, smiling.

She cocked her head at him and grinned. "Would you?"

"Certainly." Moving over to the bookshelf beside his desk, he took down a votive candle in a blue glass cup and handed it to her.

"Happy Christmas," he said quietly.

"Happy Christmas," she replied, and resting her empty hand on his shoulder, leaned up to kiss him lightly on the mouth. He slipped his arm around her waist as he walked her to the door, neither of them saying anything, and she flashed him one of her forthright glances as they drew apart before emerging on the porch.

"So, what time shall I expect you Thursday?" she asked, as they went down to her car.

"Say, about four-thirty? I have to get the Talbots to the airport for a four o'clock flight back to London, so I'll be there as soon as I've seen them off. Where is *there*, by the way?"

"Blackett Place, Number fifteen," she said, sliding into the driver's seat and buckling up. "You'll see the car. What should *I* be watching for?"

"Well, not the Bentley, I'm afraid—not for a night run to Melrose in probably horrible weather. I've rented a nice, staid Toyota Land Cruiser until my new Range Rover comes in—boring white."

"Oh, drat!" she said. "You didn't show me the Bentley."

"I didn't show you my etchings, either," he said with a sly grin. "So I suppose you'll just have to make yet another house call."

"Hmmm, I suppose I will, at that," she said, grinning back as she turned the key in the ignition and the engine roared to life.

# CHAPTER THIRTY-FIVE

CHRISTMAS Day dawned mild but grey. Peregrine came up to the manor house for Christmas brunch in the drawing room and found Gillian ensconced amid a sea of presents beside the tree, examining a picture book on horses—the gift of Adam and Philippa. Her blue eyes brightened visibly at the sight of the artist—for whom, it was clear, she had conceived an adoring little-sister attachment—and she scrambled to her feet to fling both arms around him in greeting. She had taken to calling him "Hawk" in the three days of their formal acquaintance, and though she remembered nothing of her nearly two months in coma, she seemed to sense in some wordless way that he had had something to do with her emergence from shadow.

"Hullo, Uncle Hawk!" she cried, planting an enthusiastic kiss on his cheek. "Did Father Christmas bring you lots of presents?"

"Oh, he brought me everything *I* need," Peregrine said, glancing past her at Adam and grinning as he disengaged enough to set down the bag he had brought with him. "I believe he left a few things at my house by mistake, though." He reached into the bag to pull out a small, brightly-wrapped parcel with Gillian's name writ large on the gift tag.

"This is for you," he told the little girl with a smile. "Happy Christmas!"

It was a charm bracelet: a fine chain of pale gold, from which hung the tiny figure of a Christmas angel. Gillian gasped in delight and promptly presented her hand so that he could fasten it about her wrist.

"Thank you, Uncle Hawk! It's wonderful!"

"Mr. Lovat, it's lovely!" Mrs. Talbot agreed. "But surely you shouldn't have been so extravagant."

Peregrine met this accusation with a boyish shrug. "Maybe not," he conceded, "but it seemed appropriate somehow."

He had presents for the rest of the company as well: for the Talbots, a pencil sketch of Gillian, wide-eyed and full of life.

"It's a study for a proper portrait," he told them. "When it's done, I'll bring it down to you in London in person."

For Philippa, he had done a miniature portrait of Adam executed on ivory and set as a brooch, with Adam painted as a Victorian gentleman. She said only, "Thank you, Peregrine," but her eyes said all the rest as she bade him pin it at the throat of her lace-ruffled blouse.

Adam's gift came in the largest box—a bronze equestrian statuette, nearly a foot high. Adam whistled appreciatively as he took it from its nest of tissue and Styrofoam pellets, clearly delighted, then looked more closely and broke into a grin.

"Why, it's Khalid!" he exclaimed in surprise.

"That's right," Peregrine said. "Done from some of my sketches by a sculptor friend down in London. I commissioned it not long after Urquhart. I hope you like it."

"Like it?" Adam said. "It's magnificent! Thank you very much indeed."

"And I'm still going to do that equestrian study like the one of your father and *his* grey hunter that we talked about. I meant to have it finished for today, but somehow things kept coming up."

Adam chuckled and murmured, "Excuses, excuses!" as he handed Peregrine a gift from him and Philippa. It was a complete set of Chinese watercolor brushes in a case of fine lacquer, along with a bronze mortar and pestle for grinding down pigments. The artist's eyes lit with pleasure as he inspected all the bits and pieces.

"I'm glad you like it, my dear," Philippa said, smiling to see the expression on his face. "Julian was able to find it for us, through one of her late husband's antiquarian friends. I'm ordered to tell you that the Chinese characters on the case are all symbols of good fortune—which we hope you will enjoy all the days of your life."

Brunch was attended with champagne, after which Peregrine excused himself to move on to other celebrations.

"I'm invited down to Julia's uncle's for Christmas dinner," he told Adam, as they exchanged good-bye's at the door. "I was asked to stay over, and Julia's a little annoyed that I'm not, but I'm really keen to go on that Boxing Day hunt tomorrow, if the weather isn't too rotten. I wish you were up to it."

"Oh, I think I could probably manage," Adam replied, "but I expect I ought to take advantage of the time with everybody else out of the house to keep hitting the research. You have no idea how distracting it can be to have a twelve-year-old bouncing around the house—not that I begrudge her her newly regained health. Anyway, John will ride with you and see that you don't get into trouble. And I know Gillian and her parents are looking forward to following the hunt by car. That will be something else quite new to them.''

Peregrine grinned. "It's new to me, too—or at least it's a *re*-newal. God, I haven't hunted since I was at university.''

"Not on horseback, at any rate," Adam said, flashing him a mirthless smile.

Peregrine's mood yielded to sobriety, and he motioned for Adam to follow him down to the waiting Morris.

"I gather there's no progress?" he said.

"None worth recounting. I'm working on a theory, based partially on something Scot said the other night, but so far, I haven't got enough to go forward with any degree of confidence that we'd succeed. Unfortunately, we're in the position of having to wait until the opposition make their next move—not a strategy I'd ordinarily recommend; I prefer preemptive strikes, when I have a choice. But I won't risk the Hunting Lodge on what could become a suicide mission, if we move prematurely without adequate preparation.''

Shivering, Peregrine opened his car door and put his gift on the passenger seat.

"Well, I'm standing by, whenever you think we *are* prepared. And I'll certainly let you know if anything occurs to me.''

They parted on that note, Peregrine to attempt regaining a festal mood and Adam to play the congenial host. The next day, when Adam had seen off the day's hunters—Peregrine and the stableman mounted up and Philippa and the Talbots following in the Toyota, with Humphrey at the wheel—Adam retired to his books again. Around noon, the shrill of the front doorbell jarred him from his meditations. It was McLeod, bearing a bottle of the MacAllan. They opened it and shared a holiday libation, sitting in the bay of the library window with a vista out across the snow-powdered front lawn.

"I wish I had something in the way of news to go with this," McLeod said glumly, lifting his glass, "but our quarry seems to have gone to earth, and try as I will, I can't seem to pick up the scent. A missing persons report was finally filed on your boy Wemyss, but we've turned up zilch, so far. Interestingly enough, what little we *have* found out about him seems to point to the same kind of bland career we noted for the sinister Inspector Napier.''

"What's *he* been doing?" Adam asked. "I'd love to come up

with something to justify putting him into custody while we get this sorted out.''

"You and me both,'' McLeod growled. "It's hard to even look him in the eye, when we pass outside my office. But I haven't got a *thing* on him—not even enough to sic Internal Affairs on him.''

"More's the pity.''

They briefly reviewed the theory of the Hitler connection then, which only left both of them even more uneasy. Finally McLeod finished the last of his drink and stood, gathering up his scarf and overcoat from the settee.

"I suppose I'd better get back,'' he said gloomily. "Jane's got family coming over for dinner tonight, and I have to put in an appearance. Are you still planning to ride down to Melrose with us tomorrow night?''

"No, I meant to call you about that,'' Adam said, as they walked toward the door. "I'm bringing Dr. Lockhart—yes, my charming doctor who makes house calls—so we'll meet you there. How about a toddy at Burt's Hotel at about six?''

"That sounds delightful!'' McLeod agreed. "You and she can keep Jane company while the Masons walk. Is Peregrine coming?''

"No, he said something about plans with Julia, when I asked him.''

"Well, that's fine,'' McLeod replied. "He didn't really know Randall, after all. And I'm glad to see that he's spending some time with that lass of his. Do you think he's going to marry her?''

Adam shrugged and smiled. "He hasn't mentioned any long-range plans. I expect it's too soon to tell. He's certainly a different young man from what he was two months ago, though.''

"Aye, and you're largely the one responsible,'' McLeod agreed. "You've brought him along very nicely. And the other night—'' He smiled and gave a pleased nod. "Well, that was something special, indeed.''

"Now all we have to do is manage to keep him alive,'' Adam said, a touch of the cynic in his voice. "This isn't precisely the time I would have chosen to bring him in—but then, we aren't often given options on those kinds of things, are we?''

"No, but we usually manage to come out all right in the end.'' McLeod started to get into his car, then paused.

"You know, Adam, I don't know whether it's occurred to you or not, but this thing at Melrose tomorrow could spark the opposition's next move. I mean, there are going to be—oh, better than a hundred Masons all in one place, at a public event, with security almost impossible."

"Do you have a hunch?" Adam asked.

"No, it's just something that occurred to me. If I really thought something was going to happen, I wouldn't take Jane. But it might not be a bad idea to keep our eyes and ears open."

"I'll keep that in mind," Adam agreed.

He got no intimations of specific danger the rest of the day, though. He read in the library until the light began to fail, and had gotten up to turn on more lights when the Toyota pulled through the drive, heading for the garage to disgorge cold and hungry hunt followers. Shortly thereafter, Peregrine and John came trotting up the drive through lightly falling snow, Peregrine with a rosy-cheeked Gillian breathlessly astride behind him, holding tightly to his waist.

The next hour was a whirlwind of activity centered around putting up horses, shedding muddy Wellie boots, chivvying Gillian upstairs for a much-needed bath, and getting hot tea into the adults. Mrs. Gilchrist had done up a hearty stew for supper, and they ate it by Christmas tree light, sitting around the drawing room fireplace, while Peregrine and Gillian relived every minute of the day's hunt in enthusiastic detail, to the hilarity of the Talbots and the indulgent amusement of Philippa and Adam. By the time everyone retired for an early night of it, Adam was almost as weary as if he had gone on the hunt himself, and slid into dreamless sleep almost as soon as his head hit the pillow.

The Eve of Saint John promised to be even greyer than the day before, with a possible blizzard threatening to blow in by nightfall from the direction of Glasgow. Accordingly, Adam allowed ample time to get the Talbots to the airport. The parting from Strathmourne was both tearful and happy, for a recovered Gillian was going home. Peregrine came to see her off, bringing her a quick watercolor he had done of her sitting on Poppy, and even Philippa was a little misty-eyed as the Toyota pulled away from the front steps.

Adam got them to the airport in good time, saw them checked in, their flight apparently to depart on schedule, then bade them farewell and headed off to Blackett Place to pick up Ximena. Over a bulky Arran sweater and tan corduroy slacks, she was wearing sturdy snow-boots and a caramel-colored leather jacket with a sheepskin collar, an eminently suitable counterpart to his own cords and sheepskin coat. They exchanged a chaste kiss of greeting as she met him at the door, pausing for her to gather up a scarf, hat, and gloves before heading down to the Toyota.

"So, tell me more about the Mason's Walk," she said, as they headed south on the A7 after exchanging the expected pleasantries about progress at the hospital and Ximena's improved spirits after a proper stretch of sleep. Snow was blowing across the road in gusty swirls, but it was only enough to sift a light powder on top of the two or three inches already on the ground—enough to be atmospheric, but no inconvenience at all for the Toyota's four-wheel drive.

"Well, I've never been before," Adam replied, "but according to what I've been told, Masons from Lodges all over the Borders area attend. And of course, they'll be from even farther afield tonight. They gather at the Masonic Hall there in Melrose, make a torchlight procession three times round the Merkat Cross, then continue on to the abbey itself, where someone gives a patriotic address. Then a lone piper plays "Flowers of the Forest," in memory of all Scots who have died defending Scotland, and they process back to the Merkat Cross for a ceremonial dismissal, with the senior Lodge Master present taking the salute. That's it. It takes about an hour."

"It sounds lovely," she replied. "I wish my dad could be here to see it. Freemasonry's been getting some pretty bad press here lately, hasn't it—even before your friend was killed?"

"It has, indeed. My partner from the police department is a fairly active Mason, and he's been having to field a lot of the flak. You'll meet him and his wife tonight."

"Why would anyone want to attack the Masons, though?" she asked. "They only do good works. They certainly don't do any harm."

"Well, I'd certainly agree with that. One of the arguments put forward by their critics is that Freemasons use their Masonic connections to take unfair advantage in the workplace, giving jobs and promotions and contracts to other Masons in preference to non-Masons. That may be true in some cases, human nature being what it is, but the Masons I've known, who really live the Masonic ideal, say that the Masonic factor wouldn't enter into the equation unless all other qualifications were equal. And then, if you've got a choice between a non-Mason whom you don't know and a Mason who at least has pledged outward adherence to a certain moral code of excellence—well, I don't think it's unreasonable that a Mason would tend to get the nod over a non-Mason."

She snorted. "I've heard that argument in the States, too–

usually from someone who *wasn't* as qualified. They do a lot of good work, though, through their charities and such. For some of them, it's almost like an extension of their religion.''

"I'd tend to agree. In fact, I'd go so far as to say that in some respects, Freemasonry helps to fill in the gaps left by organized religion—contributing to that umbrella of good vibes, if you will, that's generated by men and women of good will all over the planet, that helps to keep evil from getting out of hand."

"Do you see evil as a tangible force, then?" she asked.

"It certainly can be," he replied, thinking of what he had sensed up in the Cairngorms. "In general, though, I think that what we perceive as evil in the world is more often indifference or preoccupation gotten out of hand. It isn't only the things we've done but the things we've left *undone,* as the General Confession puts it. I tend to believe that most people do want to do what's right."

He slowed as they made the transition onto the A6091, following the signs toward Melrose.

"But this is hardly the time to get into a philosophical discussion on the nature of evil. I'm hoping you'll enjoy this little taste of Scottish heritage, even if the reason for coming here is a little sad. Have you been to Melrose before?"

"No, I haven't had as much time as I'd like to explore the country. It's been mostly work since I got here last June."

"Well, you'll have to come down here again, when there's light to see," Adam replied, heading past the Waverly Castle Hotel and on toward the Merkat Square. "The Eildon Hills are one of the lovelier areas of the Borders—and of course, you've got the other Border abbeys all within less than twenty miles of here: Dryburgh, Jedburgh, and Kelso. They're all spectacular, in their own ways, but I have to admit to a special fondness for Melrose, myself."

The Merkat Square was more of a long triangle than a square, paved throughout, but with parking allocated in most of the center. The Merkat Cross was at the far end, at the center of a roundabout, but Adam stopped well short of the Cross to ease the Toyota into a parking space beside McLeod's familiar black BMW, just outside Burt's Hotel. Noel and Jane McLeod were already drinking in the downstairs bar, and McLeod raised a hand in pleased greeting as Adam and Ximena came in, stamping snow from their boots. McLeod wore the apron and collar of a Master Mason under his open overcoat, and Jane was clad in sensible tweeds.

"Well, there you are," McLeod said, signalling the barman.

"You've just got time for a hot toddy before we have to go out and brave the cold again. And you must be the intrepid Dr. Lockhart, who patched up our wayward friend here," he added, extending a hand to Ximena.

"Noel and Jane McLeod, Dr. Ximena Lockhart," Adam said, by way of introduction, exchanging a kiss with Jane. "And we've promised not to talk shop tonight. Ximena's just come off about five days on call, and through Christmas, and is only just catching her breath after a good sleep-in today."

"Good gracious," Jane said, shaking Ximena's hand. "You keep as awful hours as Noel does."

Their chatter kept to inconsequentials for the next twenty minutes, with McLeod forging off occasionally to greet another of his Masonic brothers and give an opinion about the order of march or help adjust a piece of regalia, and in between, advising his three companions on the best places from which to watch. Very shortly, though, he bade them adieu and went outside with the rest of the Masons who were vacating the bar.

After finishing their drinks, Adam, Ximena, and Jane went outside as well, pulling on hats and gloves and buttoning up coats as they repaired to a vantage point over near the Merkat Cross. A police car in the white-with-blue livery of Lothian and Borders Police was pulled up at the curb nearby to provide crowd control, but perhaps because of the weather, most of what crowd there was seemed to be participants in the event rather than observers, gathering by torchlight at the far end of the square, outside the Masonic Hall, while a pipe band started warming up.

Sharp on six-thirty, the procession began to move toward the Merkat Cross in a double line—a motley assortment of torch-bearing men from twenty to ninety-plus, in every variety of winter foul weather attire, most of them wearing their Masonic accoutrements over their outer clothing. A dark, handsome young man in a top hat and bearing a drawn sword led the procession—a Tyler, Ximena explained with an air of some authority—and marshals shepherded the company to either side with long white wands, as the pipe band played a jaunty marching air that Jane identified as "Merry Masons."

There were five or six pipers and a like number of drummers, all of them looking cold. The line of the marching Masons stretched the full length of the square before the front end began twining around the Merkat Cross in a clockwise direction, torches borne solemnly above their heads. McLeod was about halfway along the line, marching beside a very thoughtful looking Donald Cochrane.

A few of the men wore kilts, which Ximena thought looked very odd with a top hat, and many wore the traditional bowler hat often associated with formal Masonic attire. The variety of aprons and collars and other accutrements was astonishing, reflecting the traditions of literally dozens of Masonic Lodges, and the company formed a kaleidoscopic whirl of color and movement as they circled three times round the Merkat Cross, always in time to the pipes and the drums.

Jane grinned and took an arm each between Adam and Ximena as the Tyler began to lead the procession out of the circle around the Merkat Cross, heading straight for them and the street that led on to the abbey, a few blocks away.

"We'll scuttle on ahead to the abbey now," she said, "so we can get a good spot to watch. They won't be long, so we've got to hurry."

And as Adam and the two women strode briskly down Abbey Street, toward the lit-up abbey at the end, and the last of the Masons entered the street, following after, a man who had been watching from the shadows beside Burt's Hotel passed casually between a black BMW and a white Toyota Land Cruiser parked in front of the hotel, pausing with a hand on the latter as if to check something on his shoe, then deposited something silvery in the snow piled on top of the hood, just beyond the windscreen wipers. The chain he wound once around the base of the wiper itself, snaking the free end to fall through one of the narrow vent openings cut into that part of the hood. What was attached to the chain was not apt to slide off or be detected before it served its purpose.

A quick crouch to scoop up a double handful of snow, and the work was covered, the man on his way. He headed along another street that led toward the abbey, jogging once he was out of sight of the square, knowing he must inform his partner of the change of plans before it was too late. Deciding which of the two cars to choose had given him several minutes hard reflection, for either had its attractions, but he was confident his final choice represented a far finer target than the one previously selected.

He reached the wrought iron fence surrounding the abbey grounds just as the front end of the Masonic procession was disappearing into the abbey's south transept entrance, the rest strung all along the snow-shrouded burial ground to the abbey's south side. The pipe band was marking time just outside the gate, still playing, but the pipe major had followed on at the tail end of the procession, his pipes furled under his arm. The golden glow of the outside lights cast long, stark shadows behind the ancient tombstones, a slight snowfall shimmering in the illumination and touching the fair hair of a man in a handsome camel-colored overcoat standing to gaze near the caretaker's hut at the now-closed main entrance.

Inspector Charles Napier braced himself, drawing his own coat collar up closer around his neck, as he approached the younger man. Raeburn was going to be angry at first, but Napier was sure he would approve of the change of plans.

Raeburn turned at the sound of footsteps crunching on the new-fallen snow, his eyes widening in surprise and shock as he recognized the other man.

"What the hell are you doing out here?" he whispered. "Is the medallion set?"

"Oh, it's set," Napier said, blowing on his gloved hands to warm them, "but not in the abbey. Sinclair's here. I saw him get out of his car in the square. McLeod's here, too, as I suspected he might be, but Sinclair is the better target."

Raeburn looked as if he could not believe what he was hearing.

"You mean you took it upon yourself to change the target?"

Napier kept his gaze even and unwavering, though it was hard in the force of Raeburn's mounting anger.

"We can wipe out Masons any time. We may not get such a good crack at Sinclair for a long time. He should be a most acceptable offering. And without its Master, the Hunting Lodge will be out of our way for some time—long enough for the Head-Master's plans to come to fulfillment."

Raeburn looked as if he cheerfully would have liked to throttle Napier then and there.

"I very much hope we can pull this off, Mr. Napier," he said softly, between clenched teeth. "If anything goes wrong, we'll both have to face the Head-Master's wrath, but I intend to make it quite clear who was to blame."

"If you do what's required with that necklace," Napier gestured toward the torc peeping from beneath Raeburn's scarf, "I intend to claim the credit that's due for eliminating Sinclair. Come on. We need to stake out the car, so that we'll be ready when he's ready to leave."

Inside Melrose Abbey, the last strains of "Flowers of the Forest" died away amid the ruined walls, with snowflakes drifting down against the glare from the lights outside. The Masonic procession began to wind more informally out of the nave, out the south transept door and through the burying ground again, then out the gate and right this time, returning to the Merkat Square by a route that brought it out at the end nearest the Masonic Hall.

Adam and the women circled on ahead again to get the best vantage point, walking back part of the way through an alley short-cut with a young uniformed constable whom Adam recognized from his last visit to Melrose. They emerged from a side street in time to see the procession round the Merkat Cross one time, then march back toward the Masonic Hall, though the Tyler stopped before they reached it. Then the pairs of men drew apart to form an aisle down which the lead Tyler and two marshals with white wands came marching in lone procession, while the pipe band continued to play "Merry Masons" and the drums kept up a strong marching beat. Waiting at the end were the three senior Masters present, white-whiskered and top-hatted, the most senior of them leaning on the arms of his two juniors.

These the escort saluted and then led back up the aisle, as the Masons to either side doffed their hats and fell in behind, the line turning in on itself. It made a pretty picture by torchlight, with the skirling of the pipes and the beat of the drums behind. When the Masters reached the end, they passed under an arch made by the white staves of two more marshals and led on into the hall and the following procession gradually dispersed at that end of the square.

"Well, Randall would have liked that," Jane said, as they headed back across the square to wait for McLeod. "It was very nicely done, though the weather kept some away who otherwise would have come, I suspect. Still and all, a fitting tribute. Did you enjoy it, Ximena?"

"Indeed, I did," she replied. "I'm grateful that Adam allowed me to tag along. Are you and Noel joining us for some supper?"

"Thank you, my dear, but I'm going to take my husband home and unplug the phone," Jane said frankly. "This is the first night we've had to ourselves in weeks, and I intend to take full advantage. Adam, don't you even think about dumping some new crisis on his plate, or I shall never speak to you again!"

Adam chuckled and slipped an arm around Ximena. "I promise not to intrude on your planned night of wedded bliss. Does Noel know about this?"

"I think he might suspect," she said coyly.

"I see. Then I don't suppose you want to join us for a drink before you take off, or even a coffee?"

"Nope," Jane said flatly. "I have a bottle of champagne waiting in the refrigerator, and I don't want him falling asleep on me. Lovely to meet you, Ximena. I hope we'll see more of you in the future."

On that note, Jane headed off toward the cars, hailing her husband as he approached and diverting him toward the black BMW. McLeod raised a hand in farewell as he saw them passing a few cars down, giving a shrug as if to say that the situation was beyond his control, but he had a sheepish look on his face, and put up no argument as Jane bundled him into the passenger seat and then went around to drive. Adam was chuckling as he and Ximena went into the hotel to seek out the dining room.

"It must be rough, being married to a cop," she said, when they were seated.

"Oh, I think they've worked out something reasonably satisfactory," he replied. "They've been married for nearly thirty years. Ah, I see that venison is on the menu tonight. I heartily recommend it."

An hour later, they had tucked away a very creditable meal, washed down with a glass apiece of delightfully smooth Mondavi Cabernet that Ximena recommended. Adam was feeling pleasantly replete as they went out to the car. After seeing Ximena in, he pulled off his sheepskin coat and tossed it in the back seat before getting in on the driver's side. The Merkat Square was mostly deserted by now, most of the Masonic revellers having gone on about their business after the Walk.

"Well, that was quite an interesting experience," Ximena said, also shrugging out of her jacket before doing up her seat belt. "It's a pretty little town, too. I think I *would* like to come back here sometime to see it properly."

As Adam started the engine and pulled the Toyota carefully onto the road, heading back toward the Masonic Hall, he failed to notice the black Mercedes creeping along the square behind him.

"Spring's the best time," he said. "We'll have to pack a picnic one day when the weather's fine—whenever *that* is, in Scotland—and motor down here in your Morgan. Or we *could* take one of *my* bangers."

"All right, Adam Sinclair!" she said. "I'm tired of all this auto-innuendo! How many cars have you got, and what are they, that you refer to that gorgeous Bentley as a 'banger'?"

"Well, you know about the Range Rover that I *used* to have," he said, giving her a sidelong glance and a droll smile. "And my farm manager drives the Land Rover that belongs to the estate—

377

but it's rather industrial-strength. There are also assorted tractors and the like. Then there's the venerable old Humber Estate that Humphrey uses to do the marketing—''

''You're holding out on me,'' she said. ''You've got something else, special, that you've deliberately avoided mentioning. It has to be an open car of some sort. What is it?''

''Well—''

Suddenly a low, warning rumble of thunder intruded on his awareness, along with a sense of imminence that struck a chord of dread, harking back to mortal danger. A light snowfall was still coming down, lightly dusting the windscreen, and he squinted ahead and turned on the wipers as thunder growled again. Overhead, he was suddenly aware of dark clouds thickening where none had been a few minutes before. Far ahead of them, to the north, the sky came briefly alight with a febrile flicker of blue lightning.

In that instant he saw the flash of silver moving under the snow still piled on the hood of the car, as the windscreen wiper moved it but did not displace it. He tried a quick swerve to left and right to try to dislodge it, but it was stuck fast, the chain obviously hooked around something—and the sense of evil was growing.

''Ximena, bail out!'' Adam shouted, jabbing at the seat-belt releases but not hitting the brakes. ''Get out and as far as you can! There's a bomb!''

The word *bomb* galvanized her into action as no other word could have done. As he reached across her to wrench back her door handle, frantically watching the clouds boil above them, she was already hurling herself against it, catapulting out in a martial arts roll that carried her into the snow on the other side of the road. Adam was yanking his own door open, launching himself from the still-rolling car, as thunder cracked again and a searing bolt of lightning shot down out of the sky to encompass the vehicle in an annihilating blast of blue-white energy.

# CHAPTER THIRTY-SIX

A N explosion split the winter silence and rocked the ground, and the Toyota burst apart in a howl of ruptured steel. Tumbling into a ditch several yards beyond the shoulder of the road, Adam buried his head in his arms as sparks and glass rained down on the snow all around him. There was another secondary blast as the petrol tank went up. Then he could hear only the gusty roar of chemical flames and a ringing in his ears.

Shakily, Adam raised his head. Black smoke boiled up into the sky from the still-rolling carcass of the Toyota, illuminated from below by the garish light of burning petrol.

"Ximena!" he called hoarsely. "Ximena, are you all right?"

Instead of answering, a dark-haired figure in a now disreputable-looking Arran sweater heaved itself up out of the underbrush on the far side of the road and darted back across, as the car plowed into a snowbank up ahead and stopped rolling, still blazing.

"I'm okay," she said breathlessly, ducking down beside him. "What about you? God, was that really a bomb? Who'd want to put a bomb in your car?"

"Somebody who wants me dead," he said, wincing at a twinge of pain in one ankle as he pulled them both behind an ivy-covered tree trunk for cover. "And I think I'll let them think I am."

Off in the direction of the town, already there were sirens wailing. Urgently squinting against the glare of the burning car, he glanced up and down the road, trying to get his bearings. There had been no traffic ahead or behind them when the lightning struck, but cars were converging from both directions now. He guessed that they must be somewhere near the grounds of the Waverley Castle Hotel. With luck, they might be able to get a taxi there and get away before someone came to finish him off.

Up ahead, the Toyota was still burning savagely, the first few cars already stopping, their drivers leaping out to gather round, making tentative attempts to get closer, to see if anyone was inside. Grabbing Ximena's hand, crouching down, he began urging them into the darkness paralleling the road, heading them toward the gleam of lights back in the trees.

They made it to the hotel in about ten minutes time and managed to engage a taxi. The Toyota was still burning as their driver eased around it, heading for the alternative way out of Melrose, but emergency vehicles had arrived and were knocking down the flames with chemicals. Adam watched through the taxi's rear window until it had disappeared from sight, and as they came to the turn that would have put them on the A68, headed north back to Edinburgh, Adam had the driver turn south instead.

"There's an airport at Newcastle, isn't there?" he asked.

"Aye, sir." The driver glanced at him in the rearview mirror. "That'll be a pretty steep fare, though. Must be—hmmm, 60, 70 miles."

"Will £100 cover it?" Adam said.

"With or without a receipt?" the man replied.

"Without."

"That'll cover it, then."

"Then drive."

Beginning to shiver, then, from the cold and aftershock, he settled back with his arm around Ximena, both for comfort and for warmth, and tried to think as their driver sped them south along the snowy A68. Fortunately, she sensed enough of his mood—and the need not to say anything that the driver might overhear—to keep silent, though he knew she must be bursting with questions.

The opposition had tried again to kill him—not with premeditation this time, for they could not have known he planned to be in Melrose tonight, but they had made the attempt nonetheless. The scale of the attack suggested that it had, indeed, been intended originally as another strike against the Masons known to be gathering all in one place for their annual celebration of the Eve of Saint John, just as McLeod had postulated. Except that someone had changed plans at the last moment and tried to kill Adam instead.

Which meant that they were afraid of him. And if Adam could draw allies from among the others the opposition were trying to destroy— Yes, perhaps that was the answer.

By the time their driver pulled up in front of the airport at Newcastle-upon-Tyne it was after midnight, but Adam had formulated a plan of action. Leaving Ximena waiting in the taxi, he went inside to find the last flights departed for the day—Newcastle was not exactly Heathrow or even Edinburgh-Turnhouse—but he got a schedule for the next morning. When he came back to the taxi, after pulling money from an airport cash dispenser, he had the driver take them to the airport hotel and gave him an extra £20. The clerk at the counter at least pretended to believe his story of a car crash and all their luggage being lost and gave them the keys to a double room on the third floor. When they were safely in the room with the door locked, Ximena finally broke her silence, all dark eyes and taut question.

"I've heard of some intricate schemes to get a woman in bed, Adam Sinclair, but you really didn't have to go to all this trouble," she said, sinking down wearily in one of the chairs beside the little round table at the foot of the bed.

Opening the mini-bar in the passage to the bathroom, Adam pulled out a can of Coke. "Drink?" he asked.

"Anything soft and non-diet," she said. "Adam, what's going on?"

Pulling out a second Coke, he slammed the door and limped over to sit opposite her, not speaking until he had popped the top of his and taken a long pull.

"This has to do with my police work," he said truthfully, though he did not specify what *kind* of police. "I'm afraid I'm not at liberty to go into details." Which was also true. "I had no idea it would escalate the way it did tonight, or I wouldn't have let you come along. I'm sorry."

"Well, you couldn't have known," she said. "It isn't your fault. And no harm's done." She paused a beat. "Was it the I.R.A.?"

"No," he said flatly. "A different kind of terrorist. Listen, I have to make a couple of phone calls. Why don't you take a shower and get cleaned up, and I'll tell you more after I know more?"

"All right."

When the bathroom door had closed behind her and he heard the water running, he picked up the phone and dialled McLeod's number, on the off chance that Jane had not been scrupulous about unplugging the phone. It rang and rang with no answer, as expected. He called home next. Philippa had been asleep, but roused immediately at his news.

"So I want you to pretend to be the bereaved mother tomorrow," he said, when he had told her his plan. "I can't reach Noel at home to tell him what's happened, so in the morning, as soon as you decently can, I want you to go to him at his office, take him

*381*

aside, and let him know I'm safe. You can't telephone him there because of the police mole; the line may not be secure.

"If you *don't* manage to get through to him, he's going to find out about the car the hard way—either from the rental company, since the car was rented in his name, or from a routine police report coming across his desk with a report of a car bombing in Melrose—and he'll assume the obvious. It would be easier on *him* if he knew the truth before that happens. I don't know whether Peregrine was planning to return home tonight, but you ought to try to get word to him as well."

"I understand, dear," she said. "I'll take care of everything. What are you going to be doing in the meantime?"

"Making my way back to Edinburgh as quietly as I can, by means the opposition won't be likely to expect," he said. "I haven't worked out exact details yet, but I *can* tell you that I'll try to come into Waverley Station sometime tomorrow evening. I'll call someone with a line that's secure and tell him to call Noel with a message about what time his brother's Hogmanay party is going to start. Subtract two hours from that time, and that's when I'll be at Waverly. Have you got that?"

"Of course, dear. Anything else?"

"Not that I can think of, right now." He glanced at the bathroom door, where the sound of running water had stopped. "I've got to go now. I have a beautiful, intelligent, and thus far, very understanding woman about to come out of the bath who's going to want a lot of explanations."

"Oh, well don't kill the mood by explaining too much, dear," Philippa said archly.

"Yes, Mother. Talk to you later, Mother. And I do love you," he added, as he hung up.

Ximena came out a few minutes later, wrapped up in one of the hotel's monogrammed terry robes and with her hair twisted up in a towel. Adam thought he had never met a woman who appealed to him more, on all levels; and never had he felt so utterly disinclined to even get out of his chair.

"You look like you could use the shower next," she said, sitting opposite him again as she pulled the towel from her hair and began drying it. "Anything more you can tell me, now that you've had your phone call?"

"I'll have that shower first," he said, seizing the chance to avoid the inevitable yet a while longer and getting to his feet.

He stood under the hot water until his stiffening muscles began to unknot, letting the flow of the water clear his mind as well, and emerged a quarter hour later feeling almost human. He would have new bruises to show for the night's adventure, but other than a persistent twinge in his left ankle and a renewed soreness in his shoulder, he had come off remarkably well. Ximena was sitting up against the pillows on the bed, watching TV, but she hit the off button as the bathroom door opened, patting the bed beside her with a gesture that brooked no refusal.

"Okay, I've been thinking," she said, her forthright gaze disarming him as he sat down tentatively beside her. "You obviously don't want to talk about what happened tonight, and I probably don't want to hear about it, either. We both very nearly got killed tonight, though—and *that* was very scary.

"So I'd just like you to hold me while I get all the shakes out of my system and convince myself that this is something I can learn to live with, if I intend to spend much time with you. And then I want to make love with you—because the way you live, I'm afraid I may never get another chance."

Her composure slipped at that, and he found himself kissing away the tears she fought to keep back—bemused, flattered, and just a little incredulous that she should have come to care so much. Later, as he lay drifting on the contented tide between full consciousness and sleep, he found himself wondering where this all might lead—and determined, no matter what else might happen, that she should suffer no harm from the relationship.

He slept dreamlessly, when he finally did sleep, and awoke the next morning to the sound of Ximena in the shower again and the aroma of a cup of tea beside the bed. It was with great reluctance that he saw her off an hour later on the morning flight to Edinburgh.

"I'll call you, as soon as this is all resolved," he promised her, as they parted at the gate. "Meanwhile, you know nothing about any of this."

She obviously did not understand, but she apparently trusted him enough not to make a scene. When he had watched her plane take off, he went to a pay phone and dialled McLeod's office number. Since talking to Philippa the night before, he had figured out a way to give his second-in-command an advance warning—*if* McLeod picked up on the obscure hint Adam dared give over the police line.

"Inspector McLeod, please," he said, when the police operator picked up.

"McLeod here," the familiar voice said, a few seconds later.

"Don't react," Adam said, with as much weight as he could put into the order. "You're still Second."

With that he quietly hung up the receiver. Unless the line was being monitored continuously, no one else could have heard that—and if they had, they would not know what it meant. He hoped McLeod did. Relegating *that* problem to the back of his mind then, for worrying would serve no useful purpose, he set himself to scouring the morning papers while he waited for his flight to Glasgow, looking for any mention of the incident at Melrose the night before.

Meanwhile, McLeod had hung up his own phone in some confusion. The voice definitely had been Adam's, but the cryptic message—

"Morning, Inspector," Cochrane said, poking his head tentatively through the open office door. "Did you see anything of this car bomb and fire action last night, down on the road out of Melrose?"

McLeod looked up blankly. "What's that, Donald?"

"It's in the incident reports from overnight," Cochrane said, coming farther in to hand McLeod a sheaf of faxes. "Must've happened after *I* left. Melrose Police are saying it was quite a blaze. They don't know who the driver was, but it doesn't look like he got out. The anti-terrorist squad are bringing the carcass in for forensics."

Chilled, McLeod skimmed over the report, adjusting his aviator spectacles to stare in blank shock as he read the description of the white Toyota Land Cruiser.

"Jesus Christ, that's the car I rented for Adam!" he whispered.

Even as he said it, though, he knew what the cryptic phone call had meant. Adam had not perished in the bombed-out Toyota, but he wanted it to be thought that he had. Pulling off his glasses, McLeod buried his face in one hand to cover his relief, breathing a silent prayer of thanksgiving that Cochrane interpreted as the sudden shock of bereavement.

"That was *Sir Adam's* car?" the young constable ventured.

"Aye," McLeod whispered shakily, still not trusting himself to look up without betraying himself. "Give me a few minutes, will you, Donald? And see what else you can find out—where the car's been taken, and so on."

Twenty minutes later, after McLeod had concocted a cover story and steeled himself in private for the role he now must play, Cochrane knocked on the door and very apologetically reported on what he had found out. Tight-jawed, McLeod gathered up his hat and coat and headed out with the young constable, ostensibly to go to the impound yard where the car had been taken, but equally to get away from staring eyes. Word seemed to have spread during Donald's absence, and McLeod could feel the looks of sympathy and pity following him as they headed for the lifts. They were on their way out the main entrance of police headquarters when he saw the dark blue Bentley that had just pulled up to the curb, Humphrey emerging to open the back passenger door.

"Oh, God, it's Adam's mother," he murmured. "Donald, go bring the car up, would you?"

As the young constable headed off for the car park, obviously relieved to be spared the meeting about to take place, a black-clad Philippa got out. Beyond her, farther in the shadows of the back seat, McLeod could see an owlish-looking Peregrine Lovat, somberly attired in a dark suit. From their expressions, he could not tell if they knew that he knew—or even if *they* knew. Did they think Adam was really dead?

As he pondered how to approach this delicate question with prying eyes possibly all around them, Philippa opened her arms to his awkward embrace, burying her face against his shoulder as she murmured, "Don't you dare react, Noel McLeod, but he's alive and uninjured. He called me from Newcastle last night. Go ahead and pretend to cry before you choke."

McLeod's sheer relief made him do just that, and he retreated into the back seat of the Bentley with her and Peregrine for a few minutes to recover and tell them of *his* cryptic call, while Humphrey closed the door and stood grim sentinel outside.

"So he wants it kept quiet, and he wants you to see about those arrangements," Philippa told him, after she had explained Adam's plan. "Can you do it?"

"Aye, it will take some doing, but—aye, it can be done."

When they had worked out the last few details, McLeod got out of the car, Peregrine coming with him.

"We're going to have to keep up this charade, even in front of Donald," he told the artist, as they headed toward the police vehicle where Cochrane was waiting. "I trust him implicitly, and eventually he'll know anyway, but I think we're better off, until Adam's safely back, if as few people know as possible. That means we still have to go through the motions of inspecting the car. We'll try to keep up the official pretense of a bomb—which it was, in a way, if the Lynx zapped it with lightning."

The burnt-out hulk at the impound yard made it easier to

maintain the fiction of Adam's death, for surely no one could have survived that inferno. Intense heat had buckled the side panels, slagged the glass, and even twisted the heavy frame. The interior was totally gutted. The stench of scorched plastic and a heavier aroma of burned animal hide still clung to it, heavy and oppressive even after a night in the weather and a bath of chemical extinguishers to put the fire out—and proved to come not from human flesh but from the incinerated remains of a once-handsome sheepskin coat and a leather jacket, barely discernible in what remained of the back seat.

The outside of the car provided additional interesting evidence. Inspecting the twisted hood, McLeod found the fused remains of the Lynx medallion, so blackened and twisted that it proved impossible to remove and almost impossible to distinguish for what it was.

"You know," Cochrane said, prodding suspiciously at the slagged spot, "this looks a lot like what I found up at Balmoral. You don't suppose that lightning struck this car, too?"

"I don't know," McLeod said wearily. "I think I'll let the bomb squad carry on from here. I've no stomach for it. Let's go back to the office. I need to make some calls."

Adam, meanwhile, had landed in Glasgow and now set about lowering his profile before heading back to Edinburgh. He was feeling and looking fairly scruffy, still wearing the muddy cords and sweater of the night before, and cold as well, so he had a taxi take him to an army surplus store, where he purchased camouflage trousers, a black turtleneck submariner's sweater, and a khaki-green anorak of the type worn by Special Forces; his own snow-boots were still serviceable.

By the time he had added the severity of a black knitted watch cap to more than twenty-four hours' growth of beard, he looked nothing like the polished and sophisticated Sir Adam Sinclair that acquaintances—and enemies—would recognize instantly. He took his other clothes with him in a plastic carrier bag, hoping the touch of domesticity would make him appear less threatening. Even so, people tended to give him wide berth on the streets as he made his way to Glasgow Central Station to wait for his train to Edinburgh. He was way earlier than he needed to be for the train he planned to take, but he needed to make a cryptic telephone call.

Several hours later, Noel McLeod received his second cryptic phone call of the day from the man Adam had called earlier.

"Noel, old chap, glad I caught you," said a brisk, military voice at the other end of the line. "My brother wanted me to say that you're invited to dinner before his Hogmanay party Monday. If you'll turn up around eight, that would be splendid.''

"Yes, indeed. Thanks very much for telling me," McLeod replied, glancing at his watch—it was nearly six. "I wouldn't want to miss that."

"You're very welcome," said the voice. "Hope to see you soon."

As the caller rang off, McLeod hung up the receiver, heaved a heavy sigh, and lurched to his feet, reaching for his hat and coat. Peregrine and Cochrane also scrambled to their feet and gathered up their belongings, following him awkwardly out the door.

"Gentlemen, I think this has been one hell of a rotten day, and I think it's time to go home," McLeod said, for the benefit of whoever else might be listening. He pulled his office door shut heavily and locked it. "I don't know about you, but I, for one, am going to get very, very drunk."

It was only after the three of them had disappeared into the corridor that Charles Napier collected his hat and coat and hurried after them, rushing madly down the back stairs while his quarry took the lift. Watching McLeod suffer all day over the death of Sinclair was almost as satisfying as eliminating McLeod himself—which Napier also hoped to accomplish very soon. He watched from a nondescript blue Mazda as the three split outside the main doors, Lovat going with McLeod, and opted to follow them rather than Cochrane, who was believed to be a lightweight.

He followed the black BMW all the way to Waverley Station, waiting impatiently in a red zone down the street as Lovat got out and dashed inside, emerging a few minutes later with a tall, dark man in army surplus attire who moved very much like Adam Sinclair—except that Adam Sinclair was dead.

Or was he? The very thought put Napier in a panic, for if Sinclair was *not* dead, Napier was in serious trouble. Heart pounding, he managed to maneuver closer in the rush hour traffic to get a clear glimpse of the watch-capped man in the BMW's rear seat—just before McLeod made an unexpected right turn and darted off to disappear in traffic. Cursing, Napier pounded one fist against the steering wheel—there was no way he could get across traffic and follow.

For it *was* Sinclair! Of that much, Napier was sure. He had no idea how Sinclair had managed to escape the holocaust of the night before, but the *how* was not important now. The bitter reality was that he had done it! And whether or not Napier reported what he had just seen, when word eventually got back to the Head-Master, as it inevitably must, Napier was in trouble. No, far better to tell Raeburn now and try to salvage something from the situation. Maybe he could yet track down both Sinclair and McLeod tonight, and kill them—and Lovat as well!

Sweating inside his overcoat, Napier pulled up beside a telephone kiosk, put a blue flasher on the roof of his car, and got out, digging with trembling fingers in his coat pocket for his phone card and the special number Raeburn had given him the night before. He could feel the pulse pounding in his ears as he dialled, and he drew a shaky breath when the expected woman's voice answered and he identified himself and asked for Raeburn.

"Good evening, sir," he said, when Raeburn had acknowledged. "I—ah—have some rather unfortunate news to report."

And at the other end of the line, in a penthouse flat in one of the more fashionable parts of the city, Francis Raeburn listened to his subordinate with growing coldness.

"I see," he said, when Napier had finished. "And you're sure it was Sinclair?"

"I wish I weren't," Napier said bitterly.

"Quite so," Raeburn murmured, thinking furiously. "Very well. I'll take care of it. Are you calling from home?"

"No, sir, a pay phone near the station."

"Very well, then. Go home. Do nothing. Avoid further contact, in case he should be onto you. They've obviously put on this charade for our benefit. Have yourself a drink and put your feet up. I intend to have this all resolved by morning."

"Yes, sir. Thank you, Mr. Raeburn."

When Napier had hung up, Raeburn depressed the switch hook on the telephone, thought a moment, then lifted his hand to dial a number.

"This is Raeburn," he said to the gruff voice that answered. "Ask Mr. Scharf and Mr. Delaney to come up to the flat right away, would you? I have an assignment for them."


That night, in a small hotel off Minto Street that McLeod had used before as a safe-house for endangered witnesses, he and Peregrine listened while Adam reiterated what had happened the night before, gave them his evaluation, and outlined the plan that had taken on additional detail since calling Philippa.

"You're right," McLeod said, when Adam had finished, "and I think I know the right men to approach. We'll want to lay this before top-ranking police officers who are also Masons and apt to accept the esoteric element. I jotted down some names during the day, while we were waiting to hear from you, but I didn't want to make any further move until I'd talked to you, just to make sure

I'd understood correctly. We can sort this out in person in the morning, and get the wheels turning.''

They managed to get a few hours' sleep in what remained of the night, and next morning headed off to police headquarters, McLeod and Peregrine looking reasonably presentable, Adam looking like an undercover cop in his khaki-green anorak and watch cap. It was just past nine as they pulled into the car park, to be met by a uniformed officer who motioned McLeod to roll down his window.

''Might as well not even park, Inspector,'' he said, leaning down to look at McLeod. ''We've got a major incident underneath the Forth Bridge—police officer killed—very messy, from what I hear. They're saying it looks like a Masonic-style execution.''

McLeod's face went set and grim, and Adam leaned a little closer to hear better.

''Do we know who the victim was?'' McLeod asked.

''Rumor is, it's Charles Napier.''

With a grunt of acknowledgement, McLeod snapped the car into reverse and slewed the car around, gesturing for Adam to pull out a blue light from under the seat as he headed back out Fettes Avenue and into Comely Bank. Peregrine braced himself for another of McLeod's wild rides. Adam had the light in place and flashing by the time they careened through the roundabout and on along Craigleith Road, slowing as they approached the transition into Queensferry Road.

''Well, given what we've long suspected about Charles Napier, I can't say that I'm all choked up that it's him instead of some Mason,'' McLeod said at last, using the advantage of his flashing light to bull his way through the intersection. He punched the accelerator when he was clear, and the BMW fishtailed slightly and then straightened out as they sped westward. ''I wouldn't have wished this on him, though.''

''Do you think it *was* Masons who did it?'' Adam asked.

''Of course not. It will still look bad, though—a very convincing frame-up. If it follows the traditional pattern, the victim will have been staked out between the high and low tide lines, probably shortly before low tide last night. Beyond that, I can't predict how far the killers will have taken it.''

He spent the next ten minutes telling them in graphic detail about the penalties spelled out in the obligations that all Masons swore during the course of their various initiations, should they ever turn traitor to the Craft.

''Not that I think the penalties were ever meant to be invoked literally,'' he said, as he swung into the transition to the Edinburgh

Road, up and over the continuation of the road they had been on. "It's always been my contention that the penalties were largely verbal embellishments to underline the seriousness of the oaths. I'll grant you, though, that there've been notable examples of so-called Masonic executions. But they've usually been committed by non-Masons, specifically because the victim was a Mason and would have experienced the full horror of knowing what the symbolism meant."

He glanced worriedly at Peregrine in the rearview mirror. "This is apt to be pretty gory, son—quite possibly even worse than what we saw up by Blairgowrie. If it will help keep you from feeling too sorry for him, keep in mind that he's probably the one who set that lynx letter bomb and almost certainly the one who tried to kill Adam last night. You know, I almost thought I saw him at Melrose, Adam, but I dismissed it out of hand. I said, 'What would he have been doing at a Masonic affair?' "

"He was probably ordered to set a medallion, to call down a lightning strike on the abbey and kill all those Masons," Adam said, "only he decided I was a more valuable target. I suppose I should be flattered. . . ."

They could see the Forth Bridge ahead, this one the railroad bridge rather than the multi-lane one slightly farther to the west that carried vehicular traffic across the Firth of Forth. McLeod braked hard coming into the last curve before the road passed under it, slowing more as they caught sight of the dozens of mostly police vehicles gathered haphazardly just to the west side of it. Down on the beach immediately under the bridge, they could see dozens of men gathered apparently randomly along the shore, many wearing anoraks with POLICE stenciled across the back. McLeod swore softly under his breath as he nosed the BMW into a slot next to a much larger Ford Granada, also black.

"Chief superintendent's car, also a high-ranking Mason," he muttered, before the three of them got out. "He almost never goes out on a call. He was *not* on my short-list. This could get very sticky."

In tight-lipped silence McLeod led them past the police lines and down onto the beach directly under the bridge, where a tarpaulin covered all but one up-turned hand of what undoubtedly was the victim. Donald Cochrane was among those standing uneasily to one side, and seemed oddly to be giving a statement to a uniformed sergeant. As he saw McLeod approaching with Adam and Peregrine, doing a double-take as he recognized Adam, he extricated himself from the interview with some difficulty and came rushing over.

"Am I glad you're here!" he said under his breath. "And Sir Adam—"

"We'll explain later," Adam murmured. "What's going on here?"

Cochrane grimaced and turned desperate eyes to McLeod. "It's Inspector Napier, sir. Whoever did it copied all the classic penalties. But he wasn't even a Mason. He *hated* us—"

McLeod exhaled expressively, and Adam exchanged a warning glance with Peregrine.

"Well, at least it *wasn't* one of ours, this time," McLeod rumbled. "In a way, though, that's worse, because we're the ones who'll be blamed."

"We already are, sir," Cochrane murmured, glancing back at the sergeant waiting impatiently. "They've already been asking where I was last night, and why I wasn't at Lodge."

"Get back, then, lad, and keep them occupied for a bit while we catch a quick look at the victim," McLeod said, easing past Cochrane and heading toward the tarp.

Adam and Peregrine followed, Adam keenly scanning the men around them, aware that they were being watched with varying degrees of interest and hostility. Peregrine found the situation far more taut than any of the crime scenes he had visited hitherto with Adam and McLeod—perhaps because some of the men were looking at *him* as if they thought he might be a suspect.

The victim had not been moved, but a forensic crew were preparing to do so, since the tide was coming back in. As predicted, he had been staked out between the high and low water lines, ankles and wrists anchored to stakes driven into the sand. Peregrine hastily averted his eyes as he realized the man had been disemboweled. Adam walked over with McLeod to take a closer look at the victim's face and confirmed that the dead man was, indeed, Charles Napier.

It was hard to say which of the wounds had killed him. The gash in the lower abdomen showed a whitish tangle of entrails where his intestines had been dragged from the wound, nearly to his feet, and his throat had been slit ear to ear. The incredulous and anguished expression on his face suggested that he had known exactly what was happening to him for quite some time before he died, but the gaping mouth displayed only a stump of a tongue.

"Jesus," McLeod whispered, as he dropped the tarpaulin back over the man's face and turned away, white-faced.

Adam glanced quickly at Peregrine as the forensic team moved in with a stretcher and body bag and set about their work, but the artist, though whey-faced, was staring at the proceedings with rigid attention, perhaps seeing beyond the immediacy of the present scene, hopefully storing the images until he could get them on paper later on. Adam had already noticed some darkling looks being directed at McLeod's back from the definitely non-Masonic contingent gradually polarizing on the beach, and took McLeod's elbow, starting to draw him and Peregrine away from the immediate scene.

"This is going to be a difficult one to defuse," he murmured. "They're forming into two camps. I think we'd better scare up some of those open-minded Masonic superiors you mentioned last night."

"Too late, they've already found us," McLeod replied, glancing meaningfully beyond Adam at the distinguished-looking, grey-haired man coming toward him, surrounded by a phalanx of uniformed officers, a few of them conspicuously armed. "Whatever either of you do, don't offer anything unless asked and don't resist."

They stood their ground as the men approached. Their leader eyed both Adam and Peregrine as he came to a halt, his men surging in to surround them. He was wearing civilian clothes, but Adam guessed he might be the chief superintendent by whose car they had parked. When McLeod did not back down from his gaze, he gave McLeod a nod, pulling off a glove to flick it impatiently against his other hand.

"Detective Chief Inspector McLeod," he said quietly, grey eyes as cold as the wintry water of the Firth behind him. "*Brother* McLeod." There was a Masonic ring on the hand that flicked the glove. "I trust that you had no part of this."

"I should hope you'd have no doubts in that regard, sir," McLeod replied, not batting an eye.

"I should hope not, too," the other replied. "However, it has not escaped my notice that whenever anything has happened to one of our brethren lately, you always seem to be close at hand—and your friends as well. I'll ask you to come along quietly, but I'm perfectly willing to place you under arrest if you prefer."

"We'll come quietly, sir," McLeod said.

"A wise decision." The man shifted his gaze to Adam. "You're Sir Adam Sinclair, aren't you? Rumor had it yesterday that you were dead."

"I'm Sinclair," Adam admitted. "And obviously I'm not dead."

"No, and I can't help wondering whether there's a connection between the fact that you aren't and Napier is. And you're Lovat, the artist," he went on, shifting his attention to Peregrine.

Peregrine said nothing, only jerking his chin in agreement, hoping he did not look as owl-eyed as he felt.

"Very well," the man said, glancing aside to call up four men kitted out in the black attire of special weapons experts. "You'll go with these officers, and I'll get back to you in a few hours. Inspector Crawford, go with them, please."

Another, younger plain-clothes man fell in with them as the four officers escorted McLeod, Adam, and Peregrine to a closed police van parked up on the road. Half an hour later, they had been whisked through a rear entrance of police headquarters and down into the bowels of the building, where they were left in a locked room that, to Peregrine's way of thinking, all too closely resembled a cell.

"What's happening? What are they going to do with us?" Peregrine asked, when the clang of closing doors in the corridor outside had faded into silence.

As Adam held one finger to his lips and shook his head, McLeod pointed silently to tiny protuberances in the corners of the room and made it clear that they contained microphones.

"We just wait, laddie," the inspector said. "Don't worry. We're in good hands."

They settled in then to wait, taking turns catching cat-naps, for Adam made it clear that sleep might be at all too dear a premium once things started moving again. Peregrine toyed with the idea of sketching what he had seen down on the beach, but there had been a presence there that did not want to be drawn, very possibly Raeburn himself, and Peregrine gave it up after a while, until he could try it again in a setting less personally threatening. The man named Crawford brought them sandwiches and coffee around one and brought them out one at a time to use toilets down the hall, but he made it clear that he had been instructed not to talk to them.

Shortly after two, the chief superintendent came back in with another man of similar age, not a police officer, whom McLeod recognized as probably the top-ranking Freemason in Edinburgh and one of the senior Grand Officers for Scotland.

"Please don't get up, Mr. McLeod," he said, gesturing for them to stay seated as he and the chief superintendent came and pulled out chairs opposite the three. "I gather that you know who I am, but I'd prefer not to use names at this meeting. I shan't use police or Masonic titles, and you may refer to me as just 'sir.' Agreed?"

As the newcomers settled, "Sir" setting a portable tape recorder on the table between them, McLeod exchanged a glance with Adam, who nodded for him to go ahead.

"Agreed—'Sir.'"

"Thank you." The man switched on the recorder and sat back.

393

"Now. It has not escaped the notice of our mutual superiors that there have been some extremely strange goings-on over the last few weeks, centered around the deaths of a number of our Brethren. Interestingly enough, you and your two companions here always seem to be in the thick of it. This leads us to suspect that you know far more about these incidents than you have so far seen fit to share with anyone. Perhaps you would be so good as to elucidate."

McLeod shifted somewhat uneasily in his seat, bound by his fraternal oaths to render an account as ordered, but uncertain how much or how little to say, now that the moment had come. Adam had been expecting something like this, from the moment the chief superintendent first approached them at the bridge. Seeing that his Second was still weighing his words, Adam took it upon himself to intervene.

"Forgive me if I interpose at this point," he said, with a glance at McLeod, "but as the person most deeply accountable in this instance, perhaps I'm the one best qualified to clarify certain aspects of these incidents to which you refer. If we haven't come to you voluntarily before now, it's only because we were still in search of an explanation ourselves. I don't pretend for an instant that what I'm about to say will sound logical or even credible—but I hope you and those to whom you will report," he gestured toward the recorder, "will nonetheless bear with me."

So saying, he propped his elbows lightly on the arms of his chair and laced his fingers gracefully together. Peregrine noticed that he was wearing his ring, and it gleamed darkly against his black turtleneck sweater, underlining his authority, if only in Peregrine's eyes.

"Now. The press have been dancing around the suggestion of supernatural intervention—and Noel has been trying to steer them in other directions, because that's his job, on several levels. It isn't appropriate for me to go into detail, but those who have targeted your Order as their enemies have done so at least partially because of the nature of your esoteric work in maintaining the Temple— the true edifice your enemies are seeking to destroy.

"Oh, yes," he went on with a nod, seeing the startled glint in both men's eyes. "Though obviously I'm not acquainted with the intimate details of your sacred mysteries, not being a Mason myself, I am nonetheless aware of the *kind* of work you do. As it happens, my own colleagues and I are engaged in a similar line of work—not identical to yours, but certainly complementary to it. Which is how we first became aware of the danger that has been hanging over you and your brethren these last two months—a danger we have since been laboring to identify and counter.''

Seeing that he had the men's full attention now, he went on to brief them on the essentials of what he and his associates had been able to piece together concerning the activities of the Lodge of the Lynx, outlining his theory of how the charged medallions acted as homing devices to call down the lightning strikes. He omitted only his private speculations concerning the possible identity of the Head-Master apparently directing the Lynx and any mention of the Hunting Lodge itself. By the time he had finished his account, both his listeners were looking slightly shell-shocked.

"Sir" glanced at his colleagues, then at Adam.

"As you warned," he said, "all of this sounds incredible, but I don't feel myself competent to make a unilateral decision on behalf of the Brotherhood. If you'll excuse me, we'll get back to you as quickly as we can.''

So saying, he switched off the recorder and got to his feet, his colleagues hurrying to open the door, which closed with a clang behind them.

"Damned high-handed of them, if you ask me," Peregrine muttered. "You'd think we were criminals.''

"Relax, Peregrine," Adam replied. "This is all new to them. We've had weeks to get used to the idea gradually. I have no doubt, however, that when they take this information to *their* superiors," he gestured meaningfully toward the hidden microphones, "we'll gain a hearing by someone empowered to act upon it.''

On that note, they settled down to wait again. More sandwiches arrived at around seven, with another foray to the facilities, and at about eight, the chief superintendent reappeared.

"I'm instructed to request that the three of you come along with me, no questions asked. I'm also instructed to assure you, on the level, that no harm will come to you. There's someone who wishes to speak with you.''

The words were affably spoken, but the entire situation was beginning to get on Peregrine's nerves. He threw an uncertain glance in Adam's direction, but Adam's expression was studiously neutral. McLeod, however, seemed to catch some hint of his uneasiness.

"Not to worry, Mr. Lovat," he said over his shoulder, as he gathered up his coat and hat. "I promise you there's nothing worse in store for you than a cup of coffee and a bit of conversation.''

# CHAPTER THIRTY-SEVEN

TWENTY minutes later, the three of them found themselves sitting blindfolded in the back of a closed van, speeding along unknown roads. Peregrine was somewhat reassured by the presence of Adam and McLeod on either side of him, but he had no idea where they were going. He thought Crawford was driving; he knew that the four black-clad special weapons men were sitting across from them. He felt very helpless and not a little intimidated, even though the men had not been anything but courteous and coolly detached. He wanted to believe he was in no danger—and Adam and McLeod did not seem particularly concerned—but the situation made him nervous and uncomfortable all the same.

They drove for nearly two hours—which could have taken them anywhere over a very large area of Scotland or even into England. By the time the van slowed to a halt, Peregrine was practically squirming in his seat. It was a profound relief to hear the clang of the rear doors opening and feel the sudden, chill bite of outside air, even though he had no idea what came next.

They took Adam out first. Then strong hands were guiding Peregrine toward the back of the van, helping him down. He felt the shift of gravel underfoot, and breathed a sigh of relief as someone loosened his blindfold from behind and plucked it away. Blinking around in the sudden glare of headlights from another vehicle pulled up behind the van, he saw they were standing in front of stone steps leading up to what looked to be a substantial stone house.

He groped in his pocket for his glasses and slipped them on for a better look. The house appeared to be a Victorian or Edwardian game lodge, with dark conifers looming close at either side; he could smell the tang of pine along with the clean scent of new-fallen snow. From somewhere toward the rear of the house, the gurgle of running water suggested the presence of a small stream.

McLeod jumped down on the gravel beside them next, blindfold already pulled off, and gave Peregrine a thumbs-up sign of reassurance before putting his own glasses back on. Their escort officers slammed the van doors, then began shepherding them up the snow-dusted steps.

"Don't be alarmed by anything you see," Adam said aside to him, in an undertone. "I assure you, *I'm* not."

Inside, they were met by a militant-looking man in a butler's uniform, who inspected them dispassionately, exchanged a few low-spoken words with one of the escorts, then conducted the party as a group down a long corridor and through a set of double doors, into a large half-timbered room with the aspect and dimensions of a hunting hall.

The far wall was adorned with a number of fine stags' heads and other trophies of the hunt, but Peregrine was not disposed to admire any of them. As their escort walked them forward, his eyes were all for the dozen men who were sitting on the other side of a long table that ran the width of the floor in front of a great, grey stone hearth. All of them were wearing Masonic collars and aprons over their clothes, even the three or four in police uniforms, one of whom was of very high rank, indeed. The chief superintendent and Crawford sat at one end, the other Mason who had interviewed them earlier at the other. In the center, in a place of obvious dignity, sat a silver-haired man with keen blue eyes who wore the regalia of a Masonic Grand Master.

"Worshipful Master," said McLeod's chief superintendent, as the party halted, "may I present Brother Noel McLeod, Sir Adam Sinclair, and Mr. Peregrine Lovat."

"Thank you for coming, gentlemen," the Master said. "I believe I may have met Brother McLeod once at Grand Lodge. Sir Adam, I knew your father and grandfather well."

Adam inclined his head slightly in acknowledgement, saying nothing. At a sign from the Master, two of the subordinate members of the Edinburgh escort brought straight-backed chairs and set them behind Adam, McLeod, and Peregrine. All four of the men in black then retired smartly from the hall, leaving the three standing alone before this Masonic tribunal. The Master folded graceful hands on the table before him, but he did not invite them to sit.

"Gentlemen, I have listened to the recording of your earlier interview with two of my esteemed Brethren," he said. "Since you have come of your own free will, to render service, you are welcome among us. Before we may proceed, however, I must insist that nothing said here goes beyond these walls—not even the fact that this meeting is taking place. Brother McLeod is already bound by his obligations to keep silence, but I must have your assurance, Sir Adam, and yours, Mr. Lovat. Will you swear on the Volume of Sacred Law to abide by this condition?"

"I will," Adam said.

Peregrine gulped and found his voice. "So will I," he murmured.

At a sign from the Master, Crawford fetched a Bible from a stand at his end of the table and brought it around to present it to Adam and Peregrine in turn. When they had laid their hands upon it and repeated the required oath after him, the Master gestured for them to be seated, once again focusing his attention on Adam.

"Now, tell us more of the danger you perceive and the alliance you propose to deal with it," he said gravely.

Thus invited, Adam reiterated the basic information he had offered his earlier inquisitors, then proceeded to outline a basic strategy for how to proceed. When he had finished, the Master sat silent for a long moment, then glanced at McLeod.

"Do you concur with what Sir Adam has just told us?"

"I do, sir, in every respect," McLeod said. "He is a man of probity and honor, well-known to me. He has the tongue of good report."

"I see," said the Master. "As a Master Mason, what is your personal recommendation in this matter?"

"Worshipful Master, it's as clear to me as it must be to you that the sooner we join forces, the better our chances of overthrowing the designs of our common enemy," McLeod said bluntly. "Sir Adam is not a novice in the realm of esoteric work. He knows whereof he speaks. I would therefore urge that the Brotherhood ally itself with those he has at his command. And I would further recommend that he be given authority to direct our combined forces."

The Master raised an elegant grey eyebrow. "A strong endorsement, Brother McLeod. Are you aware what you're suggesting?"

"I am, Worshipful Master."

"I see." The Master shifted his gaze to Adam. "And you, Sir Adam—would you be prepared to do as Brother McLeod suggests, to command a joint venture, your people and mine?"

"If such an arrangement meets with your approval, sir, I am," Adam said.

Their eyes met. It seemed to Peregrine, watching, that each man was taking the full measure of the other. He was not surprised when, after long scrutiny, the Master withdrew his gaze first, apparently satisfied by what he had seen.

"I am inclined to accept Brother McLeod's proposal—and yours," he told Adam, "but my office requires that I address certain—difficulties that have yet to be overcome. Did you never consider becoming a Mason yourself?"

"I have considered it, yes," Adam said. "If you knew my

father and grandfather, then you also must know that either would have sponsored me gladly, had I asked.''

"And why did you not do so?''

"The demands of my profession, coupled with my other commitments, have always been such that I was reluctant to seek membership where I could not offer commensurate service,'' Adam said truthfully.

"A worthy enough reservation,'' the Master agreed. "How, though, if you were to find yourself in a position to render one unique service that would answer for a lifetime of lesser calling? But you must ask, Sir Adam, for I may not.''

Slowly Adam stood, McLeod rising as well, though the latter signalled Peregrine to remain seated.

"Worshipful Master,'' Adam said quietly, "of my own free will and volition, I ask that you do me the very great honor of admitting me to the Brotherhood of Freemasonry, of such level as will fit me to render you this service.''

As Peregrine swallowed hard, the Master gave Adam a faint, satisfied smile and nodded.

"Are you willing to take the obligations of our Brotherhood, according to law and custom?'' he asked.

It was not simple courtesies they exchanged, Peregrine suddenly realized. Adam's acceptance of Masonic membership was a key factor in rendering him suitable, in the Brethren's eyes, to head a joint command.

"Saving obligations already sworn before another Tribunal, I am willing,'' Adam said.

Standing, the Master gave a slight signal to Crawford and turned his attention to the wide-eyed Peregrine.

"I'm afraid I must ask you to leave us now, Mr. Lovat,'' he said in a tone of genial command. "Brother Crawford will escort you to the library. Your companions will fetch you back when we have concluded our business here.''

When Adam reinforced this injunction with a look, Peregrine had no option but to obey. Going reluctantly with Crawford, who left him alone in the library, he alternately paced and fretted for the better part of an hour. Eventually, however, he heard a light, firm tread approaching the door that he recognized as Adam's. A moment later, Peregrine's Masonic minder opened the door to admit McLeod and then Adam himself.

"Before you ask,'' the latter told Peregrine with a wry smile, "suffice it to say that I have been inducted into the Brotherhood of Freemasonry as a Master Mason and entrusted with the attendant signs, words, grips, and tokens. The Master—who is

Grand Master of all Scotland, by the way, and was a very good friend of my father's—the Master informs me that it's called making one a 'Mason at sight.' Apparently it isn't often done, but it does save a great deal of time.''

McLeod allowed himself a hearty chuckle at the look on Peregrine's face.

"As the Grand Master's just-appointed special deputy, it also now gives him full authority to direct the appropriate resources of the Masonic Fraternity, in addition to our own resources,'' he said.

"But, come on back down to the great hall now,'' Adam said, laughing. "I'm reliably informed that the butler who met us so imposingly at the front door has had his minions slaving this last hour and more to prepare us a hot supper before we settle down to serious planning. And just as well, too, because sandwiches are not sufficient for what we still have to do tonight. Now that we've got reinforcements at hand, the game truly is afoot!''

Meanwhile, amid the opposition in that game, Francis Raeburn was attempting to explain to his superior just what had gone wrong at Melrose. Just returned by helicopter, after winding up the loose ends left in the wake of Napier's execution, he was personally revitalized by the energy drunk from Napier's death throes—and determined not to accept any blame for Napier's ill judgement.

"Yet, it was you who had charge of the lightnings!'' the Head-Master rasped. "Why did you not hold back?''

The white-robed Raeburn, kneeling in token submission in the midst of the Head-Master's cowering circle of acolytes, did not flinch before his superior's wrath.

"The opportunity was already lost to accomplish what originally was intended,'' he said reasonably. "By the time Napier informed me of what he had done, it was too late to retrieve the medallion and position it in the abbey before the Masons moved out. Given the change of circumstances, it seemed most expedient to go with the plan as Napier had changed it. The strike on Sinclair's car was precise and powerful. I cannot explain how he managed to detect the danger in time to escape, but attacking him in this manner, without due preparation, was not my first choice.''

"Wasted, wasted . . .'' the Head-Master muttered, in senile petulance. "We could have given hundreds to Taranis—and then for Sinclair to elude us again. . . .''

"I fear it may come to a matter of *us* eluding *him*, Head-Master,'' Raeburn said uneasily. "He surfaced briefly this morning as I guessed he might—he and McLeod and Lovat. Unfortunately, the

Freemasons appear finally to have made a connection between those three and the misfortunes that have befallen so many of their brethren in recent weeks. All three were taken into police custody before I could take any action. I'd hoped it was an arrest, which at least would keep them out of commission for a while, but my agents were unable to confirm any official police action in the matter. Apparently they've not been charged with anything—which leads me to believe they are actually in Masonic custody rather than police. There was a limit to how far I dared pursue the matter.''

"Then it means the Freemasons are listening to what Sinclair has to say, and it's only a matter of time before he convinces them to become his allies,'' the Head-Master said. ''Ah, he's canny, this Master of the Hunt. One must wonder whether it was he and his who intruded on our perimeter defenses last week.''

"So we must assume,'' Raeburn replied. ''And if so, they'll be back, probably with reinforcements.''

"Aye, and in the next two days, if they hope to harness the momentum of the waxing moon,'' the Head-Master replied. ''We must make preparations to ensure that Taranis will be ready for them—an even more acceptable sacrifice to his glory!''

That night, Adam began briefing his new allies in further detail on the form he wished the Masonic support to take in the coming assault on the enemy. The Master had decided that the full details of the campaign should not go beyond those present and a few carefully selected additional participants yet to be determined, though he was set to order a general working for their support, once a form was determined. After the supper break, the great hall took on the aspect of a war room, with maps spread out at one end of the long table and rosters of possible recruits taking shape at the other. McLeod was in the thick of it, acting as Adam's lieutenant to interface with the Masons, many of whom he knew.

Peregrine, having no military background and little more formal esoteric experience, mainly stayed in the background at first, listening and watching, mostly feeling like a fifth wheel. Excusing himself at the first opportunity, he ensconced himself in one of the guest rooms and finally set himself to drawing what he had sensed at the site under the bridge, producing what McLeod assured him the next morning was a near-photographic likeness of Francis Raeburn—or Tudor-Jones—presiding over the grisly execution of Napier.

The stark horror of what he had drawn underlined, in a way mere words could not, what Adam had been trying to tell them about the callous brutality of their enemy. It set the mood for even more discussion as the day progressed. By mid-morning, Peregrine was beginning to feel himself a part of the operation at last, though he hardly knew whether to be more surprised at the situation, which was fast looking like it might require an actual military operation, or at himself for accepting it so readily.

"I sort of understand the esoteric aspect of all this," he told Adam after the morning briefing, as they drew mugs of tea from an urn set up at the far end of the hall. "At least I understand what has to be done—I think. But you're also talking about a physical assault on that castle. These men aren't qualified to do that. The ones that know enough are too old, and the ones young enough don't know enough. That's obvious, even to me."

Adam set down his tea mug beside a telephone and pulled out a chair to sit down.

"I've been considering that," he said with a thin smile, "and I think I know just the man who can give us a hand."

As Peregrine looked on in question, Adam picked up the phone and dialled. General Sir Gordon Scott-Brown was agreeably surprised to hear from him.

"Adam!" he exclaimed, "this is an unexpected pleasure. I was just getting ready to leave for church, but I've a few minutes to spare yet. What can I do for you?"

"I'd like to request a private meeting with you," Adam said. "*On the square.*"

A slight pause on the other end of the line suggested that the Masonic key phrase had registered.

"I see," Sir Gordon said in an altered tone of voice. "Yes, I believe that can be arranged. When did you have in mind?"

"As soon as possible," Adam said. "I realize it's short notice, but it's important—for the sake of the Widow's Son."

"Yes, I understand that. It's clear that you're speaking on the level. How about one o'clock at the castle?"

"I can't thank you enough, Gordon."

"My pleasure. Actually, it might expedite matters if I send a car to collect you," Sir Gordon went on. "Say, about noon?"

"Ah—I'm not at home, Gordon," Adam said, suddenly recalling that he still had no idea where he was—not that it had mattered for the last twelve hours.

"Well, tell me where you are and I'll send him *there*," Sir Gordon said.

Feeling just a bit foolish, Adam covered the receiver and craned his neck in the direction of the owner of the house, who was exuding clouds of pipe smoke as he bent over one of the maps.

"Sir Neville, where are we? I've gotten an appointment with Gordon Scott-Brown, and he wants to send a car for me."

"Gordon?" The old man grinned and came over to take the phone from Adam, continuing to puff on his pipe.

"Hello, Gordon. Neville Stephenson here. Yes, Sinclair's at my place. He'll tell you all about it when he sees you. Yes. Yes, he is."

He paused and nodded, continuing to puff away, grunting occasionally, then nodded again.

"Well, I can send him with a driver, Gordon, but if you'd rather . . . Hmmm, yes. Security. I understand. Yes. Well, if you want him at one, you'd better have your man leave right away. Yes. Yes, I'll tell him."

He handed back the receiver to Adam, but the line was already dead.

"Well, you heard that," Stephenson said. "I expect his driver will be here shortly before noon. Ask Cromarty to find you some clean clothes and a razor. You're a mite scruffy for calling on generals, especially on a Sunday."

Restraining his impatience, Adam set the phone back on its cradle.

"I'll do that," he said evenly, though he had no such intention. "You haven't answered my question, though."

"Hmmm?"

"Am I allowed to know where this place is, or do I wear a blindfold to and from the castle?"

Stephenson blinked at him, puffed a few times, then broke into a wide grin around his pipestem.

"Good heavens, didn't anyone tell you yet?"

"No. And frankly, I've been too busy to ask."

"Well, it's certainly no secret, now that you're one of us."

As Stephenson went on to detail their location, Adam had to smile. They were not that far from Strathmourne, if farther west. When he could extricate himself from the loquacious Stephenson, he did see about a razor and a shower; but when the general's own staff car whisked him away a little while later, he was still wearing his quasi-military attire of the day before, to underline the nature of his visit. Bracing a notepad against the back of the critical map, he scribbled additional notes as his military driver sped them southward in light traffic. It was starting to snow, with the promise of worse to come.

Just before one, they were slipping and sliding up the cobblestones of the Royal Mile and across the ice-slick esplanade of Edinburgh Castle, rumbling across the drawbridge past guards smartly turned out in trews of green Hunting Stewart tartan, who snapped to attention and gave salute as the car passed. An adjutant was waiting to escort him to Sir Gordon's regimental office. When they were alone, the general came forward to offer Adam a cordial handshake in the Masonic style, smiling broadly when Adam returned the grip.

"This is a most interesting development," Sir Gordon said, eyeing the younger man up and down. "Permit me to offer you my warmest congratulations. I'd ask for details on your decision to enter the Craft, but I gather from your rather uncharacteristic attire, as well as what you said on the phone, that other priorities are in order."

"The two are related," Adam replied, as they sat to either side of a table at one end of Sir Gordon's office. "That's precisely why I'm here."

He went on to explain the situation, spreading out his map, omitting nothing of what he had already related to the Grand Master and his council. Sir Gordon listened in grave silence as Adam outlined his most pressing needs. At the end of his recital, the general's sharp eyes were twinkling in martial appreciation for what the younger man proposed.

"Let's start with the aerial reconnaissance—which sounds like your most pressing need at the moment," he said, glancing at his watch. "We'll be out of daylight in another couple of hours—and it will take a little while to organize this, anyway—but barring drastic deterioration in the weather, I can have a couple of helicopters in the air at first light tomorrow. Between mountain rescue and military maneuvers, we have aircraft in that general area pretty much year-round." He cocked his head at Adam and grinned. "Some of those RAF chaps get rather spectacular aerial recon footage of the local wildlife. Might even spot a lynx or two."

Adam gave him an appreciative smile.

"Thanks, Gordon. I knew I could count on you."

"All part of the service. Now, about these other items on your list. It's true that I can't give you the army," he said with a tight smile. "Not officially, at any rate. Unofficially, though . . ."

He glanced aside, fiddling with a pen, then nodded.

"Yes, I have just the man for you. You won't have to worry about anyone asking awkward questions afterward. Just tell me when and where you want your support to show up."

"That's something else I wanted to ask you about," Adam said. "We'll need a staging area up in the Cairngorms, for my civilian contingent. Any suggestions?"

"I'm already one step ahead of you," Sir Gordon said. "I happen to have access to a shooting lodge up near Drumguish, perhaps twenty miles from the area you're talking about. It even has a helipad. Would that suit you?"

"Ideal," Adam said. "You're sure it won't cause you problems, though? Given the nature of the operation, it's essential that no word of this gets out.''

"That goes for my chaps as well," Sir Gordon assured him with an arch grin. "It's secure, though. Consider it my personal contribution to this whole enterprise. Now, when do you want them?"

"Would noon tomorrow be too soon?" Adam asked. "The moon's full tomorrow night—which is helpful on several levels."

"Understood," the general said. "It's cutting things a bit fine, but we'll contrive." He jotted a note on a pad and went on.

"All right. We'll cover tomorrow's recon as a mountain rescue exercise, and for the rest—well, with any luck, they'll be in and out before anyone's the wiser. Besides that, we've already got military exercises scheduled up in that general area starting next weekend—which will explain the requisition orders I'll have to slip in to cover this." He paused to flash Adam a sly grin.

"You know, with a full moon and it being New Year's Eve tomorrow night, that should also cover any fireworks you might stir up when you go into action. Noel will like that, since he's the one who'll probably end up trying to explain to the press, if anything does leak out."

Adam smiled. "I treasure your optimism, Gordon—and your help. If we manage to pull this off, you'll have earned a large share of the credit."

"Not at all, my boy," said Sir Gordon. "I only wish I could be there in person to help out. As it is, my wife and I are locked into attending a black-tie Hogmanay party tomorrow night—you know what people expect of generals. I'll be with you in spirit, though, never fear."


Adam made several telephone calls before leaving the general's office, also requesting Sir Gordon to make another call for him, after he had gone.

"Her name is Dr. Ximena Lockhart," he told him, handing over a slip of paper with the pertinent information. "I don't have telephone numbers to hand, but you'll be able to reach her either at the Royal Infirmary or this address. You needn't identify yourself; just say that I asked you to call, that I'm all right, and that I'll call her as soon as I can—hopefully to wish her a Happy New Year."

He had his driver swing through Kinross to collect Christopher then, also pausing at Strathmourne to pick up the items he had asked Philippa to have ready for him.

"I'll be relying on you to keep things tight on the astral," he told her, with a kiss before getting back into the car.

"You can count on me, dear. I've even managed to get through to Lindsay. Good hunting!"

"God bless," Adam murmured, as he settled in next to Christopher and the general's car headed back down the drive.

That night, with all preparations made for an early departure for Sir Gordon's shooting lodge the next morning, Adam assembled his Masonic team in the great hall and introduced Christopher, who would be directing their visualization from the staging area the following night.

"The very best image I can give you," Adam told them, "is that of a canopy or umbrella of brilliant white light surrounding and protecting the planet. That's what your work in Lodge supports, whether or not you've ever been aware of it, and that's especially what I want you to concentrate on projecting tomorrow night, when we make our assault on the opposition. Simultaneously, as you know, your Brethren all over Scotland will be working to reinforce that image in less specific terms, offering up peace and good will as the new year turns. Their work will help bolster what we'll be trying to do, but they, alone, can't do what needs to be done—so it's up to us."

They moved out next morning as planned, in an assortment of Land Rovers, jeeps, and other four-wheel-drive vehicles—nine in all, carrying nearly forty men. They tried to avoid the appearance of a convoy as they headed north by back roads to link up with the A9. They reached the lodge by Drumguish shortly before eleven and settled in to wait, munching sandwiches provided by Sir Neville's household staff and drinking tea from thermos flasks. Even at midday, the temperature was dropping and there was a bitter chill in the wind. As Adam paced on the lodge's front porch, he tried not to think about more snow, but he could not help wondering whether the opposition had the power to influence the weather.

Just after noon, two yellow Wessex helicopters with Air-Sea Rescue markings came chuffing down out of a pewter-colored sky. The lanky SAS major who jumped out of the second one and ducked under its slowing blades to jog toward them had a large manila envelope under one arm, and seemed to have been well-briefed.

"I'm to ask for Sir Adam Sinclair," he said, eyeing Adam in tentative recognition.

"I'm Sinclair."

The major grinned and stuck out a hand that also conveyed a Masonic grip with his handshake.

"General's compliments, Sir Adam. Ian Duart. I believe you

requested some recon photos—and some work to be done. If you'll tell me where you want us to set up, I'll get my men unloading our equipment.''

"Thank you, Major. Mr. Crawford and Mr. Lovat will direct your men," Adam said, taking the envelope the man offered. "Meanwhile, perhaps you and your Second would care to join me inside, and we'll have a look at these and brief one another.''

At Duart's signal, the helicopters disgorged another dozen SAS men, in addition to the pilots. As they set about unloading gear and a light snow began to fall, Duart and a captain named Kinsey spread out their maps and photos in the dining room for the perusal of Adam and McLeod. Their Masonic allies stuck to the drawing room or clustered outside to watch the SAS men's preparations.

"I was told to expect that the photos would blur, so I did some overlays last night from older aerial surveys," Duart said, smoothing a sheet of acetate over one of the maps. "This one was taken about a year ago. Whatever fogged today's photos wasn't there then. But you can see how the approach to the castle is protected by these cliffs." He traced the line with his finger. "If whoever's in charge of the place has got any sense, they'll have men posted all along that cliffline with as much conventional firepower as they can muster."

Adam nodded agreement, though he did not expect conventional firepower to be their main concern.

"I'd guess that what we're after is in this tower," he said, pointing it out. "The house itself is Victorian—which means that most of the rest of this was done for show, not real defense." He ran his finger along a line of mock machicolations. "But the tower is clearly older than the rest. I'd guess the walls are probably close to twenty feet thick.''

"Difficult, but not impossible," Duart agreed. "Are you worried about damage to the tower?''

"No, just getting to whoever's holed up there. I'd rather not knock the whole thing down around their ears until I've had a chance to see what's really going on, but I'm not choosy, if it comes to protecting our own people.''

"Understood." The major scanned the maps again, obviously solidifying his plans, then glanced appraisingly at Adam and McLeod.

"There's one more thing you should know," he said. "It didn't show up on the photos, and nobody else saw it, including me, but one of my chaps swears he saw a civilian-type helicopter on this apron out front. Neddy's a little fey—but I believe him.''

"So do I," Adam said, not batting an eye. "We'll keep that in mind."

"Right," Duart replied. "Let me talk to my men, and then we'll decide if the weather's going to make us do this the hard way."

By two, Duart's men were set, but by half past it was clear that the choppers would not be going airborne again today. Non-plussed, Duart shifted his focus to the fleet of civilian vehicles, from which one of his sergeants had already selected three Land Rovers and a jeep as backup transport. While the SAS shifted their gear into the vehicles, Kinsey directed one of his men to outfit Adam, McLeod, and Peregrine with winter camouflage gear. In their white coveralls, over-boots, and parkas, the three blended in immediately with the rest of the team, and thus attired, withdrew briefly to an upstairs bedroom with Christopher. There the priest gave them communion and his blessing before accompanying them back downstairs to see them off. It was shortly after three, on the last day of December, as the little convoy set off through worsening snow toward the distant heights of the Cairngorms.

The light was failing rapidly by the time the column turned between the fieldstone markers, snow falling steadily now. Peering eagerly forward through the windscreen as they labored along the rough roadbed, Adam and McLeod close to either side, Peregrine scarcely knew whether he felt frightened or elated at the prospect of the impending struggle. Either way, he was glad that Adam had seen fit to let him be a part of it.

They got all the way to the perimeter fence without apparent opposition. As the jeep ground to a halt at the iron gate and Duart and his sergeant got out to deal with it, Peregrine became aware at once of a harsh, subliminal crackling to the air that hadn't been there on their previous visit. Abruptly he sat forward, his hazel eyes narrowed to perceptive slits behind his spectacles.

"Adam, is that—"

"Yes, it is," Adam said. "He knows. But keep warning me if you see anything. I can't always second-guess."

Duart's sergeant was already at work on the fence. Within a matter of seconds, he had disarmed it, cut the rusty padlock securing the gate, and swung back the barrier of corrugated iron to let the convoy pass.

"You realize, don't you," McLeod muttered, as Duart and the sergeant came back to the jeep, "that this is about as good as ringing the front doorbell?"

"Can't be helped," Adam murmured. "From here on out, there's no looking back."

The vehicles rolled on through the gate and began slowly climbing the sticky, snow-clogged roadway, showing no headlights. They met with no physical resistance as they skirted the stream, but Adam was aware of a brooding, watchful tension in the air as thunder rumbled low on the horizon. The defenders of this place, he knew, were only biding their time.

Proceeding with due caution, they halted just short of the rise where the three had made their earlier reconnaissance. Duart bailed out to signal the others, and behind them, the other vehicles shut down their engines and men began to pile out. Adam and McLeod disembarked more cautiously, Peregrine following. McLeod had an H-K MP5 submachine gun around his neck, like the SAS men carried, and a Browning Hi-Power in a shoulder holster over his parka. Adam appeared to be unarmed, but Peregrine knew he wasn't. Peregrine himself didn't even have his sketchbox, though there were pencils and a pad in an inside pocket of his parka, and he wore his ring under his glove, as he knew the others did.

It was almost full dark now, a heavy inky twilight barely relieved by the growing glow of the moon beginning to rise beyond the mountains to the southeast. The snow had stopped, but Peregrine could see no stars. The SAS men broke into two forward patrols of four, with Duart and a third group of four to bring up their civilian partners. As the point patrols moved out, quickly invisible against the snow, Peregrine fell in to shadow Adam, slogging and stumbling along with him and McLeod as they headed on toward their objective. He could just see the dark silhouette of the castle as the moonlight grew brighter, a few lights showing at the windows— hardly looking worth all the trouble they were going to.

The group he and Adam were with had gotten within a few hundred yards of the last, relatively smooth approach to the castle's outer wall and its Victorian gateway when Peregrine suddenly felt himself almost overwhelmed by a sick, queasy pang of naked fear that almost set him retching. Simultaneously, a chatter of automatic weapons fire erupted briefly from the gloom farther ahead and across the little valley cut by the stream, nearer the castle's base, then was silent. As Duart and his men faded into cover, Adam drew Peregrine and McLeod back a few paces. The animal fear immediately receded. Peering ahead at the castle again, Peregrine suddenly tugged at Adam's sleeve.

"Adam, do you see that?" he whispered urgently.

"See what?"

"It's a—hard to describe it, actually." He squinted, trying to make the focus sharper. "I think we've got one of those—holes in the astral umbrella that you've been mentioning. Right over the castle.''

"A *hole*?" Adam asked. "An actual *hole*?"

"Well, yes. It's more dense than a hole, though—like it's covered or stuffed with black gauze, or—or tulle—almost cobwebby.''

As Adam digested this new bit of information, Duart scuttled back to join them, crouching down in the snow.

"They're pinned down, all ahead,'' he informed Adam. "In addition to the firepower, there's sort of a zone of darkness surrounding the place. When we tried to force our way through, it was like walking into a vat of glue. Can you do anything about it?''

"Aye, possibly,'' Adam replied. "Tell your men to stand by.''

As Duart withdrew to comply, Adam pulled off his right glove and stuffed it into a pocket. When the hand emerged, it was holding his familiar *skean dubh*, the stone in its pommel glowing softly, mate to the one in his ring. Signalling Peregrine and McLeod to give him space, he pulled the sheath from the *skean dubh* and pocketed it, then touched the flat of the blade to his lips in salute before bending to trace a large pentagram in the snow, one point aimed at the castle beyond. When he had completed the symbol, he knelt down in the midst of it and bowed his head, the blade pressed flat to his forehead.

*Author of Lights, give strength and guidance to those who seek to do Your will*, he prayed silently, centering his intent. *Ye ministers of grace, defend us, that the bulwarks of darkness may be breached and the Adversary be cast down before the Light of Lights.*

A profound silence seemed to settle just in that one small space, though desultory gunfire continued to punctuate the night. Looking up, Adam opened his arms to Peregrine and McLeod in unspoken summons. Without hesitation, Peregrine came to kneel at Adam's left while McLeod sank down to his right. As he bowed his head and closed his eyes in imitation of his mentor, he was spontaneously drawn out of himself to stand by Adam on the astral plane, along with McLeod.

Nor were they the only ones arrayed there. Present also, in the flowing sapphire robes of their calling, were other members of the Hunting Lodge: Philippa, Victoria, Lady Julian, and others whom Peregrine had encountered before only in the visions of his initiation—and Christopher, trailing the variegated skeins of fraternal harmony that were the offering of the Brethren he directed back at the staging site.

The whole shining company seemed to be gathered on the porch of a temple Peregrine had not seen before—all majestic greens and imperial shadows. Beyond *them*, Peregrine could sense the more general outpouring of other minds and hearts contributing to the offering of good will, a gentle glow of strength and harmony.

The temple's lofty doors were glossy black, like polished coal, shot through with mobile glints of iridescent green, like floating dust of emeralds. Standing tall before them, Adam reached up with his ring hand to trace the sigil on the door as Peregrine had seen him do on the night of his initiation. When he spoke the ringing Password, the doors shifted without a sound to disclose heavy draperies of deepest green. The wind that breathed between them carried a faint vital tang of newly-turned soil.

Adam led the way into the chamber beyond—a lofty hall whose great supporting pillars were like the trunks of living trees. The presiding Presence within the great hall was ebony-dark, yet green light seemed to flow from it like water from an underground spring.

Adam knelt, the rest of them kneeling beside and behind him, heads bowed.

*Lord of Earth*, Adam said, *as Master of the Hunt and servant of the Light of Lights, I come seeking aid on behalf of the Widow's Sons, followers in the footsteps of Solomon the Temple-Builder. Tonight we and they stand ready to do battle against the servants of Shadow, who would destroy the Temple which you yourself commissioned them to build in the name of Adonai—blessed be His Name.*

*But the Enemy shelters in earth, though the very stones cry out for justice*, Adam continued. *We pray you, breach their unholy sanctuary and rend the veil of darkness that obscures them, that the cleansing of the Light of the Lord of Hosts may be focused upon them.*

Adam bowed his head, hands upturned in supplication. As Peregrine waited, not daring to look up, the Being's living presence surged outward to envelop Adam in a shimmering aura. The aura continued to widen, reaching out beyond the confines of the temple. Caught in this upsurge of power, Peregrine was swept away in a rushing sensation of soul-flight that ended in a dizzy qualm of vertigo.

When he opened his eyes, he was back in his own physical body, shivering and dazed in the chill embrace of a winter's night. With his next intake of breath, he felt a sudden tremor through his knees that seemed to come from deep underground.

The tremor rose and swelled, sending rippling shock waves coursing along the ground. The attendant rumble of shifting rock built up to a crescendo. Even as Peregrine instinctively clapped his hands to his ears, a sonorous boom split the air, like a jet breaking the sound barrier, and the earth seemed momentarily to drop out from under him.

# CHAPTER THIRTY-EIGHT

PEREGRINE grounded with a jolt that was more psychic than physical. As he made a gasping effort to regain his equilibrium, the opaque canopy of darkness covering the castle was suddenly underlit with a shimmering green glow. Hair-fine filaments of emerald radiance broke the surface of the earth, uncurling like a carpet of new-blown seedlings. The tendrils thickened and branched, flowering upward like a whole spring unfolding in a moment. Charged with the strength of the earth itself, the blossoming vines overspread the darkness like ivy growing up a garden wall.

Everywhere the shining vine-growth spread, it put out rootlets, thrusting them deep into the fabric of the dark. As the net of verdant lights thickened and contracted, the murk began to crack like worn masonry, fragments of opaque blackness began to fall away like pieces of rotting eggshell.

Those who had fashioned such defenses fought to hold and repair them. Thrown off balance by a counterwave of hostile energy, Adam felt his own control slip and waver. The fog began to gather again, blotting out the night sky. Trembling with strain, Adam pointed his *skean dubh* at the castle and uttered a silent plea for support from the ranks of his Masonic brethren. He felt its support flowing into him, strong and comforting, but then, suddenly, a vast column of darkness fountained upward, superimposed on the castle tower, all but overwhelming what progress had been made.

Trembling with the effort, Adam launched himself upon the astral again, willing himself before his superior, who was Captain-General of all the Hosts of Heaven. His wordless plea did not go unheeded. In dizzying rebound, he found himself reeling on his knees between McLeod and Peregrine, catching himself on his hands as vertigo made him momentarily lose his equilibrium. And Peregrine's gasp drew his gaze heavenward, to look northward where McLeod also pointed—at the shifting curtain of Aurora Borealis parting to reveal a celestial host already at the charge.

Quicksilver swords raised round a noble banner, joyously singing as they came, the warriors thundered across the moonlit sky, armored in light, mounted on fiery battle chargers whose coats shone like molten gold and whose massive hooves struck sparks off the tips of the Cairngorms and made the earth tremble anew. As their column wheeled over the castle, the celestial knights began hacking great rips in the gauzy stuff that shrouded the tower and hid its inhabitants. Where their swords dealt cleansing fire, the shadows withered and shriveled. Adam could feel the shadow lifting, and tottered to his feet with his *skean dubh* directed at the castle once again, focusing all the power the Brethren had placed in his hands, hurling it through the focus of the *skean dubh*'s blade.

And inside the castle, in the high tower room, the Head-Master fell to his knees with a choked exclamation. The collapse of the castle's psychic bulwark rocked the tower to its very foundations. As two of the closest acolytes rushed to his aid, he thrust them away from him with palsied hands, his black eyes snapping with fury.

"No time for that!" he snarled. "We must prepare new defenses. Victory will still be ours!"

Without knocking, Raeburn burst into the room, his lean face smudged with dirt and the torc askew at this throat. His white robe was rent at one shoulder. Pale eyes still slightly glazed from what he had seen outside, he took in with a glance the vast bloodstain down the front of the Head-Master's robe, the crumpled body of Wemyss lying in a widening pool of blood not far from where the manuscript lay on its mat of black ram skin.

Wemyss' wrists were bound high behind him with a scarlet cord that also had bent his head back for the sacrificial blade that had opened both jugulars. The knife itself was lying nearer the manuscript—not the razor-sharp scalpel Wemyss had used on *his* victims but a black, ancient weapon, kin to the torc. Raeburn could taste the residual power of Wemyss' dying—heady stuff—but it had not been enough to hold the tower's defenses.

"The psychic quake has collapsed a section of the west wing," he reported neutrally, forcing his gaze away from Wemyss. "The house is now open to forced entry on that side. I've posted my men and the servants there with Uzis from the arsenal, and instructed them to hold their positions at all cost, but if we're physically attacked from that quarter in any strength, they won't be able to last indefinitely."

"Then you must assist them," the Head-Master said coldly. "Take four men from here to guard the base of the tower itself." He gestured toward the four nearest the door. "Go back to your men and remain there. Establish a redoubt among the ruins and set a medallion in place there. If our enemies do succeed in breaking through, call down the lightning and destroy them."

It represented a death sentence on friend and foe alike. Raeburn's pale eyes flickered.

"Head-Master," he said evenly, "you do realize, don't you, that what you're asking would be suicide?"

"Only if you fail to hold the west wing as ordered," the Head-Master retorted. "Let that be an incentive to you and your men. Now go! I have business of my own to attend to."

He gestured dismissal with a curt, slashing motion of the hand. Raeburn hesitated a moment, his mouth tight with unspoken arguments. Then abruptly he spun on his heel and departed the way he had come, his reinforcements silently following.

Muttering under his breath, the Head-Master ordered his acolytes back to their places. Having given Raeburn four, there were only eight left, but they were his elite; they would not fail him.

"Now," he said, as he spread his gnarled hands to them. "We are far from beaten—as our opponents will shortly discover. Let us see how the Huntsmen respond when their prey becomes an invisible predator. . . ."

With Peregrine's "black hole" now cleared and at least a fragile patch applied to the canopy of light where the rift had been— courtesy of Christopher's ongoing efforts with his Masonic backup team back at the staging area—Adam's SAS allies could now settle down to doing what *they* did best. The celestial raiding party had withdrawn behind the shimmering curtain of the Aurora Borealis, and the castle was plainly visible in the light of the full moon.

Moving with the brisk precision of the professionals they were, Duart and his men began to advance, Adam and McLeod cautiously easing after them with Peregrine. The west wing had taken considerable damage in the quake, and now presented a definite focus for a physical assault. The incline was less steep than they had feared, well-broken by boulders and outcroppings.

The exchange of gunfire continued on both sides of their forward position as Duart's two flanking parties of troopers began working their way systematically across the flat, taking advantage of every shadow and every piece of cover. The air was acrid with the stink of cordite. When they reached the shelter of the wall, which was only about four feet high, short bursts of enemy gunfire continued to spray the copestones, sending stinging chips of rubble showering over the men crouched in the shadows below.

"This is getting us nowhere fast," McLeod muttered, rearing up from cover to fire off a quick burst—three-and-three, in imitation of the troopers—in the direction of a gap in the west wing wall.

There was the thin whine of a ricochet, followed by a return burst of hostile fire. McLeod dropped back with a muttered imprecation and braced himself for the next opportunity to fire. This kind of almost continuous volleying lasted for nearly ten minutes, until suddenly the gunfire from the building ceased.

As the last sporadic echoes died away, an eerie stillness settled over the area. The sounds of continuing gunfire from elsewhere within the perimeter receded, suddenly distant and strangely muffled.

"Something's happening," McLeod muttered, turning his head to and fro as if to catch an errant sound. "Can you feel the change in the air?"

Adam nodded without speaking. As he cast around him psychically, he became all at once aware of a ghostly stir of movement behind a snowbank beyond the wall. He caught a fleeting impression of something fanged and bestial gathering itself to spring. Even as he called out a warning to the men to either side, there was a racing surge of motion and the creature overleapt the wall to land in their midst.

A man screamed and toppled backwards, braced hands outflung as if grappling with an invisible monster—as, indeed, he was. A bloody set of gashes appeared on his chest, like the marks of feline talons. As the men around him fell back in confusion, looking for an enemy, there was another flurry of unseen movement and two more members of the party went down screaming.

"Look out!" shouted McLeod. "Here comes another!"

Adam was already on his feet. Gripping his *skean dubh* in his right hand, he flung up both hands before him in a gesture of warding as a heavy, invisible weight crashed down on him from the top of the wall. Hot animal breath fanned his cheeks as unseen fangs snarled and snapped at him a hair's breadth short of his face. He wrestled it away with a thrust of his crossed forearms, and threw himself to one side as McLeod, cursing, pumped a triple round of bullets into the space where the creature's chest should be.

There was an ear-splitting feline yowl as the entity turned on McLeod. Adam seized the brief moment's respite to shift his full awareness to the astral. At once their attackers became visible in the likeness of enormous lynxes with burning eyes and tufted cheeks.

"Noel, to me!" he gasped. "Peregrine, use your soul-sight!"

Pressed half-stunned against the wall, Peregrine roused to the sound of his superior's voice. Turning a deaf ear to the momentary panic around him, he struggled upright and narrowed his gaze, focusing beyond the visible as his mentor had taught him.

"I see them!" he cried as the nature of their attackers manifested itself. "What should I do?"

Instead of answering, Adam raised his *skean dubh* above his head and cried out a Word of command that rang deep as a tolling alarm bell. There was an answering flash of unearthly light. Briefly blinded, Peregrine knuckled his eyes and discovered that his perceptions had shifted totally to the astral. Casting a look in Adam's direction, he caught his breath in astonishment, for his mentor's aspect had completely changed.

Gone were the winter camouflage fatigues and the close-fitting watch cap Adam had been wearing in common with every other man in their party. In their place, he wore now the guise of a medieval knight, with a sapphire-blue surcoat belted over chain mail that shone in the darkness like quicksilver. The *skean dubh* had been transformed into a gleaming longsword with a hilt and quillons of gold. The gauntleted hand that gripped the sword bore a ring that flickered and flashed like the evening star.

Nor was Adam the only one to have changed. As McLeod moved in at Adam's right, Peregrine saw that he, too, was armored in light. He glanced down at himself and saw that he was similarly arrayed, with a sheathed sword hanging at his side that called to his hand.

Before he could question the transformation, Adam raised his sword in a sweeping battle arc and hurled himself at the nearest of the lynxes. As the creatures turned to counter the attack, McLeod rushed in to close with two more of the beasts. In that split instant, Peregrine's bewilderment gave way to sudden blazing knowledge. No longer in fear or doubt, he swept his own blade free of its sheath and charged one of the beasts that was savaging another of Duart's men.

416

His first stroke creased the creature's flank. Snarling, it wheeled and crouched, swiping at him with claws that dripped poison. His surcoat came away in tatters, but his mail turned aside the slashing talons. He struck again, this time at the head, and scored a slash across the beast's gaping muzzle.

Instead of recoiling, it attacked, cannoning one shoulder into him with the fury of a charging boar. He struck the ground with a bruising force that jarred the breath from his lungs. Before he could struggle to his feet, the creature fell upon him with all its weight, pinning his blade against his chest as it sought to crush and smother him.

The blood roared in his ears. He croaked out a hoarse cry for help. The pressure on his chest increased until he was sure his ribs would crack. Hissing in anticipated triumph, the creature drew back one enormous forepaw to rake across his face, then abruptly arched and reared back, claws flailing the air as Adam's sword point took it squarely between the shoulder blades.

Yowling and thrashing, it made a writhing attempt to dislodge the blade. Face set like iron, Adam held fast with both hands, driving the point deeper. Still struggling, the great lynx gave a piercing banshee screech and collapsed on its side. An instant later it wavered and vanished.

Peregrine drew an aching breath and shut his eyes briefly. When he opened them, Adam was bending over him against the filmy background of the Scottish night sky, the aspect of warrior knight gone away.

"Well done," he whispered, giving Peregrine's shoulder a pat. "You fought well."

"Not well enough on my own account," Peregrine said weakly, as Adam moved on to check the SAS man Peregrine's efforts had saved.

"Is he all right?"

"He'll have to be, for now," Adam replied, moving quickly among the other injured.

As Peregrine struggled up onto his elbows, he looked around anxiously.

"Where are the lynxes? Are they gone?"

"As many as attacked us here, aye," said McLeod's voice from the shadows on his other side. "With any luck, it was enough to force a general retreat. Are you ready to move yet?"

Peregrine heaved a deep breath. His chest still ached, but he was relieved to find himself otherwise undamaged.

"I think so," he said. "But I wouldn't mind an assist getting up."

McLeod grinned and extended a hand. As he struggled to his feet, Peregrine looked around and saw that there were several men down, only one of them not moving. Ahead, Duart and a handful of his men had regrouped and again were stalking the approach to the west wing. Farther back, one of the other patrols was giving covering fire.

Peregrine flinched as the quiet burp of the submachine guns was suddenly punctuated by several shotgun blasts in quick succession. He glanced back at the heavy door just in time to see two troopers kick the door in and then fade to either side as a third tossed something inside. The dull *whump* of a stun grenade jarred them even outside, and then Duart and his men were through what remained of the door, firing in quick bursts, more men running up from farther back.

Raeburn was with Barclay and the four acolytes guarding the entrance to the tower when he heard the door to the west wing blow. The stun grenade was too far away to do more than set their ears ringing, but he knew what it was, and that it was only a matter of time before the attackers won through. His men would put up a good fight, and die before being taken, but they could not hold out against such as these.

"Sinclair's brought in the damned SAS!" Barclay said bitterly, caressing the Uzi slung around his neck. "I told you that was no mountain rescue operation this morning!"

"Yes, and I told *him*," Raeburn replied, nervously eyeing the far door that led from the west wing. "But I may still be able to salvage something. Go and do what we discussed."

With a curt nod, Barclay took off at a jog along a corridor that led away at a right angle from the west wing. The acolytes stirred uneasily, perhaps suspecting what he planned, but Raeburn knew they would not dare to defy him—not while he wore the torc and carried a charged medallion. Leaving them there with instructions to hold their positions, he himself mounted the spiral stair to the topmost room.

He found the tower chamber in a state of complete disarray. Five of the Head-Master's remaining eight acolytes lay sprawled on the floor, either dead or comatose. Those others who were still sitting upright looked pale and dazed, trembling with the strain of their recent exertions. The Head-Master himself was crouched over his precious manuscript, running a twisted finger down a yellowed page, muttering bitterly to himself. As soon as Raeburn appeared, however, he left off his murmurings and staggered to his feet, his eyes fiercely aglitter in his skull-like face.

"You!" he panted hoarsely. "What are you doing here? Why aren't you at your post?"

Raeburn declined to answer either question. Meeting his superior's gaze dispassionately, he said, "The west wing is in the process of being overrun. Sinclair and his men will be here shortly. I thought you should be informed."

The Head-Master was breathing hard, his face contorted in black rage.

"Why do you tell me things I already know?" he demanded. "What you have yet to answer is why you have seen fit to disobey my orders!"

"With respect, Head-Master," Raeburn said evenly, "I do not think the Patron of Shadows requires us to sacrifice ourselves in a pointless act of defiance, just because Huntsmen have run us to ground. The helicopter is standing by in the rear courtyard, thus far undamaged. I've sent Barclay to warm up the engines. We can take you to safety."

The Head-Master's face contorted. "What kind of counsel is this? The battle is not yet lost!"

"No, the battle *is* lost," Raeburn said. "But the war may yet be won—*if* we leave now."

"Craven!" the Head-Master rasped. "This is all your fault! You were ordered to call down the lightning rather than allow this fortress to be overrun. Why did you disobey?"

"Because it would have been a pointless waste of resources," Raeburn retorted, advancing a step or two in anger. "Can't you see? We serve no one but Sinclair if we allow ourselves to be driven into taking our own lives. Sacrifice is one thing; suicide is quite another."

The Head-Master's mouth was working furiously, his withered lips flecked with foam.

"Traitor!" he shrilled. "You are unworthy to be called the Son of Taranis! Give me back the torc!"

Raeburn's hand moved in reflex to his throat, where the torc lay cold against his flesh, potent with power. Standing straighter, he shook his head.

"If you will not come, give me the manuscript," he demanded, "and allow me to take it to safety."

The Head-Master's black eyes went wild.

"So *this* is what you've been intending all along!" he

screeched. "To wrest the Führer's manuscript from me by fair means or foul! Oh, you are so like your father! He thought *he* could do it, but he was wrong—and so are you!"

He lashed out with one hand. A bolt of black flame shot from his fingers, kindling the torc with such a surge of blinding pain that Raeburn cried out and flung it from him. It rolled to rest in the bloody pool by Wemyss' lifeless body, and as the Head-Master pounced to retrieve it, skidding in the blood, Raeburn produced the yet-unused medallion he had been carrying, flung it bitterly after the Head-Master, then swooped in to snatch up the sacrificial knife. He considered going for the manuscript as well, but the Head-Master shrieked as he turned and saw Raeburn's intent, one bloody hand already locked around the torc. The implied threat lent wings to Raeburn's feet as he turned on his heel and fled.

Nothing stirred in the west wing. As Duart and five of his men swept systematically through it toward the tower, their progress periodically punctuated by bursts of machinegun fire, Adam rounded a corner and came to a standstill.

"Listen!" he said. "What's that noise?"

McLeod cocked an ear. "Sounds like that helicopter nobody saw. Duart!" he called sharply. "Out the back! I think some of our birds are about to flee!"

As Duart's signal sent a four-man patrol off at a jog-trot, Adam said, "Go with them!" and McLeod trotted after. Duart, meanwhile, had won through to the ground floor of the tower, where three bloody, white-robed bodies lay sprawled in various attitudes of sudden and violent death—not the work of Duart and his accompanying trooper. A door stood open to the winding spiral of a dark stairwell, and Duart was already edging cautiously up the first steps as his partner made sure of the three men on the ground.

"This is it, isn't it?" Peregrine whispered, white against his snow-camouflage as he peered queasily past Adam at the carnage.

"Almost," Adam said, slipping past Peregrine to follow the two SAS men. "I'll go first."

The spiral of the stairwell was a second, smaller tower shaft set close along the side of the first, faintly lit by moonlight streaming through narrow lancet windows set at every turning. Only one landing opened off the tower stair before they reached the top—an empty bedchamber and a dark, shuttered chamber fitted out as a library. Adam and Peregrine waited on the stair until Duart and his man had pronounced it safe, then continued climbing behind them.

Gradually a glow of yellow light began to brighten from beyond the upward turning of the stair, and Adam hissed at Duart to slow. The very air of the stairwell was dark with hostile intent, but it was time for Adam's expertise to take over now.

Slipping past the SAS major, Adam led the way cautiously around the curve to halt just short of the final landing, where yellow gaslight spilled across the threshold of a chamber beyond. Something metallic lay glittering on the floor just inside the threshold—a not-unexpected Lynx medallion—and its placement warned him that at least one of those no doubt lurking in the room beyond had slipped beyond the bounds of reason.

He turned quietly to Peregrine and the two soldiers, retreating a step. As Huntsman, he well knew the danger of a cornered quarry; as Master of the Hunt, he was obligated to see that quarry taken, with as little injury as possible to his fellow Huntsmen and those under their protection. Duart thought he was protecting Adam and Peregrine, but in fact, it was Adam who must now protect all of them.

"I'll take it from here," he said to Duart. "You two go back to the base of the tower and wait with Mr. Lovat."

"Adam—" Peregrine began.

"Do it," Adam said in a tone that brooked no argument. "What happens from here on out is my responsibility."

They retreated with obvious reluctance, but not before Duart had pressed a Browning Hi-Power into Adam's left hand, pointedly thumbing the safety off, though he said not a word. The gun at his side, his *skean dubh* clutched firmly in his other hand, Adam squared his shoulders and silently commended himself and all those with him to the ongoing protection of the Light, then drew upon himself the mantle of authority that proclaimed him not only Master of the Hunt but Keeper of the Peace. Given what those in the tower chamber had already accomplished, Adam had no doubt they would be able to see the astral overlay of that authority as well as his physical form. He also knew the source and scope of their power now, and that he had the means to counter it.

Serenely, then, he mounted the last three steps, coming to a halt a pace outside the chamber.

His quarry sat crouched in the midst of a pile of scarlet cushions to one side of the room—a bald-headed, gnome-like figure in a flowing white robe, bloodstained down the front. Around him lay nearly a dozen bodies, one of them obviously the source of the blood. Several others lay merely dead, exuding the psychic signature of over-extension in the Overworld—probably those who had launched the lynx attack.

But the three nearest him, two of them women, had scarlet cords knotted around their throats, apparently but recently strangled. Adam could sense the power their slayer had absorbed by their willing sacrifice, their heads laid on the pillows around him, arms outflung in surrender, but his real concern was for what the old man held.

Claw-like hands clutched a yellowed sheaf of parchments to the bloody bosom. The thin neck was encircled by a heavy torc of meteoric iron, its blackness lifted by murky cairngorms and Pictish symbols traced in silver. Adam had glimpsed it before in visions, and recoiled now from the dark, elemental power radiating from it. Sensing the evil potency that linked it with what was inscribed within the manuscript, Adam bent to lay his pistol gently on the floor of the landing—useless here—then drew himself erect, never taking his eyes from his quarry.

"Are you Head-Master here?" he inquired sternly.

Fierce black eyes glared up at him balefully out of a wizened, ash-colored face.

"I am," the robed figure whispered.

"Then by the authority vested in me by the Council of Seven, as Master of the Hunt, I order you to resign that office and to surrender such artifacts and implements as are presently in your charge."

"How dare you?" The Head-Master's response was a whisper like grave cerements, rising on a note of hysteria as he lurched unsteadily to his feet. "How dare you make such a demand of me, and in my own house? Surrender my power to you? I think not! Not while I yet possess the means to determine my own fate! *Here* is the seat of my power!" He laughed maniacally and jerked a thumb curtly toward the torc about his throat. "And *there!*"

He stabbed a finger at the lynx head medallion lying on the floor between them, lips parted in a death's head grin, then took a backwards step and raised both arms in a theatrical gesture of summoning.

Just as swiftly Adam moved across the threshold. As the air in the room came alive with the hum of building energies, he set his foot deliberately across the medallion's chain on the floor. Locking eyes with the Head-Master, he pointed his *skean dubh* at the medallion and uttered a Word. Light flared blue from the blade, the stone in its pommel, and the ring on his third finger, and with a sullen whine, the dark aura of power in the air faltered and collapsed, like the sound of a dynamo shutting down.

Aghast, the Head-Master glared at Adam, the astral authority beyond mere physical presence finally registering.

"The game is ended, Head-Master," Adam said quietly. "That Which I serve will not allow me to come to harm at your hands. I know the source and measure of your power. Once again, I charge you to lay aside what you have stolen and misused, and submit to the lawful authority of the Light."

"You cannot judge *me*," the Head-Master rasped, clutching the manuscript more tightly to his bosom. "I have spent a lifetime mastering what lies here. The goal is within reach. Taranis calls me to be *his* scourge against such puny mortals as play like children with what they can never grasp or understand. Why seek the light when Darkness beckons with such sweet power? You cannot judge *me*."

"It is not my place to judge, but only to bring you before judgment," Adam said. "Put down the manuscript and the torc."

Trembling, the Head-Master shook his head, glancing wildly around the room for some escape.

"It's mine!" he whispered. "I will never give it up—*never*!"

"Neither you nor it will leave this room," Adam retorted sternly. "Put down the manuscript and the torc."

The Head-Master's shoulders slumped. It seemed for a moment that he was about to capitulate. He bent stiffly from the waist to set the manuscript reverently at his feet. Then, without warning, he reared back, twisted hands set to either side of the torc and thrusting his wild, searching glance toward the ceiling and beyond.

"Strike, Lord Taranis!" he shouted shrilly. "Strike, Thunderer! Receive your servant and the offering of the deaths of your enemies!"

Thunder rolled overhead and burst with a loud crack. It was the torc that drew the lightning now. Flinging up his hands in a warding gesture, Adam snatched the astral power at his command and shaped it round himself like a bell-jar, mirrored on the outside. With a ruinous crash and an explosion of blinding light, the roof disintegrated as a bolt of blue lightning clove straight and true as a lance to the torc about the Head-Master's neck.

Too quick to register save in after-image, Adam saw the rigid body engulfed in a blistering sheet of flame, the expression on the wizened face that of ecstasy and anguish both, as Taranis claimed his own. Adam was backing urgently into the landing even as he shielded his eyes from the flash. The gaslights exploded in a secondary roar and the entire floor of the chamber gave way.

The force of the concussion hurled Adam back into the

423

stairwell, where he flailed to catch his balance as another, even brighter flash rent the air, opening a yawning rift in the dimensional fabric of the sky above the tower. Even as he flinched back, celestial fire came scouring down out of the rift to purge the room with flame, sweeping away everything in its path. Within the fire, Adam thought he caught a glimpse of their astral allies of before, afoot now, laying about them with fiery swords, sweeping corruption before them where their blades passed, lifting them in a blaze of celestial glory as unlike the lightning of Taranis as the blaze of the sun is unlike the moon. The wake of their departure sucked the pages of the manuscript upward in a mad spiral of flaming leaves, like the fireworks arching over the heavens in other places as the new year turned.

Then, in one last burst of brilliance, the rift in the sky slammed shut with a resounding boom.

Out behind the castle, in the bleak silence after suspension of gunfire, McLeod and his SAS men watched impotently as the lights of a fleeing helicopter receded into the night. Kinsey, standing next to McLeod, jerked out the spent clip from his H-K MP5 and slammed another into the receiver.

"Damn!" he muttered under his breath.

"Ditto that," McLeod replied, gazing after the disappearing lights.

One of the sergeants was already on his walkie-talkie, calling back to base to get their own helicopters in the air, but it would not be in time to stop those now escaping. They were turning to head back inside when the roiling clouds overhead suddenly parted and a colossal crack of lightning arched arrow-straight to the tower roof. The concussion hurled them to the ground, frantically shielding their heads with upraised arms as debris began to rain down.

And at the base of the tower, as a heavy silence descended, Peregrine picked himself up and peered fearfully at the entrance to the stairwell. Behind him, Duart and his men were stirring, one of them in urgent voice communication with others of their number elsewhere in the area.

"Christ, what was that?" Duart muttered, his voice edged with a touch of awe. "Lovat, don't go up there! This place could come down around our ears at any second!"

But Peregrine was already scrambling past the threshold, charging up the stairwell, slipping and stumbling on debris that choked it increasingly as he climbed. He had gotten to the mid-landing, where minutes before he and Adam had waited for Duart and his man to clear a library and a bedchamber. Now the full shaft of the tower gaped open where the library had been, down as far as he could see and open to the sky far above. Sick with fear, Peregrine turned to gaze up at what remained of the stairwell—and cried out with relief as a tall, upright figure in soot-smudged winter camo emerged from the clearing dust and smoke.

"Adam!"

Still a little unsteady on his feet, Adam stumbled the few remaining steps to the landing and sank down on the last, one hand braced on Peregrine's shoulder.

"I'm all right," he said. "So is everything up above."

"But, what happened? There was this most colossal boom!"

Adam smiled thinly. "The Master of the tower called upon his dark lord to receive him—and he did. Not, I expect, in the manner he had hoped. One does not bargain with elementals. And once the fragile balance was disrupted, those appointed at a higher level to redress such imbalances swept in and did a general housecleaning."

"The ones we saw before?" Peregrine breathed.

"Another unit of the same force," Adam said with a chuckle. "Meanwhile, take a look up."

Overhead, as Peregrine also turned his sight heavenward, he could see what he had hoped to see before—the astral canopy contracting over the castle to close over the hole. Already, the bright skeins of light plaited by Christopher and by the Hunters back at Strathmourne were filling in the gap, weaving a new fabric of light over the hole, making it even stronger than before. Supporting their Work was the subtler glow of those others, all around the world, adding their strength to the canopy of light as the year turned—the good will of men and women everywhere, whether or not they were aware of the good work they did, seeking the Light in their myriad ways.

"At least I think the fireworks are over," Adam said, getting to his feet and giving Peregrine a hand up. "Meanwhile, we'd better go back down. I'm still a doctor, and I may be needed."

Downstairs, Duart was assembling his men outside the front door, medics among them tending the injured. Between gunshot wounds and lacerations there were few of them unscathed, but none were dead. The SAS major stood as Adam came out, snapping to attention to render brisk military salute with his H-K MP5, then coming forward to exchange with him a Masonic handshake, one Master Mason to another. McLeod was not far behind Adam and Peregrine, and raised his weapon in more casual salute as they turned to greet him.

"Raeburn?" Adam said quietly.

McLeod shook his head. "He got clean away. We'll get him next time, though."

In the distance, the chutter of helicopters was gradually coming into range, the bright searchlight beams of two Wessex helicopters quartering the darkness. Adam moved quickly among the wounded men, confirming that the first aid measures already rendered were adequate, then headed toward where the first of the helicopters was settling on the snowy lawn. The Grand Master was first out, and stared owl-eyed at Adam before his gaze danced back to the scene of obvious devastation.

"Mission accomplished, Grand Master," Adam said, offering the other a Masonic handshake. "The Brethren performed their part beautifully."

"But, what—"

Adam smiled. "Later, sir. I still have to sort out some of it myself. But the Brotherhood can rest easy now and carry on its Work. The canopy is restored."

"But, this is all . . ."

"I know," Adam said wearily. But as he spotted the pilot climbing down from the Wessex, he excused himself and headed in that direction.

"Lieutenant, I need a personal favor," he said, drawing the man back toward the aircraft's open door. "Can you patch me through to a land line on your radio?"

"Well, sure, but—"

"Then, let's get on it," Adam murmured, urging the man back into the helicopter, smiling wearily. After calls to Strathmourne and Edinburgh Castle, there was a very intriguing lady doctor back in Edinburgh who needed to be wished a Happy New Year.

426